Praise for *Legends of t*

"It's always fun to go back and see where an author started—the raw work, full of energy and with hints of the good things to come. Such is the case with Richard Knaak's *Legends of the Dragonrealm*. All of the ingredients—great world building, memorable characters—that have marked Richard's long and success-ful career are there, and in reading it, it's easy to see why Richard has enjoyed so much success."

—R. A. Salvatore, *New York Times* bestselling author of
*The Demon Wars Saga, Forgotten Realms*®, and more

"Richard's novels are well-written, adventure-filled, action-packed!"

—Margaret Weis, *New York Times* bestselling author of
*Dragonlance Chronicles, Legends,* and more

"Richard Knaak's fiction has the magic touch of making obviously fantastic characters and places come alive, seem real, and matter to the reader. That's the essential magic of all storytelling, and Richard does it deftly, making his stories always engaging and worth picking up and reading. And then re-reading."

—Ed Greenwood, creator of the *Forgotten Realms*®

"Endlessly inventive. Knaak's ideas just keep on coming!"

—Glen Cook, author of *Chronicles of the Black Company*

# LEGENDS
## OF THE
# DRAGONREALM
## VOLUME III

# RICHARD A. KNAAK

GALLERY BOOKS

*New York   London   Toronto   Sydney   New Delhi*

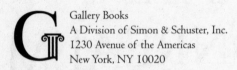

Gallery Books
A Division of Simon & Schuster, Inc.
1230 Avenue of the Americas
New York, NY 10020

*The Crystal Dragon* copyright © 1993 by Richard A. Knaak
*The Dragon Crown* copyright © 1994 by Richard A. Knaak
*Past Dance* copyright © 2002 by Richard A. Knaak
*Storm Lord* copyright © 2003 by Richard A. Knaak
*The Still Lands* copyright © 2003 by Richard A. Knaak

These titles were originally published individually by Warner Books, Inc.

First Gallery Books trade paperback edition November 2011

GALLERY BOOKS and colophon are trademarks of Simon & Schuster, Inc.

For information about special discounts for bulk purchases, please contact Simon & Schuster Special Sales at 1-866-506-1949 or business@simonandschuster.com.

The Simon & Schuster Speakers Bureau can bring authors to your live event. For more information or to book an event contact the Simon & Schuster Speakers Bureau at 1-866-248-3049 or visit our website at www.simonspeakers.com.

Manufactured in the United States of America

10  9  8  7  6  5  4  3  2  1

ISBN 978-1-4516-5138-6
ISBN 978-1-4516-5192-8 (ebook)

These titles were previously published individually.

# CONTENTS

N
W E
S

*Sea of Andramacus*

Land of the
Hill Dwarves

Gordag-Ai

*Elven*
*Settlements*

DAGORA
FOREST

**ESEDI**

**ZUU**

**LAND OF**
**QUEL**

*Legar*
*Peninsula*

**THE BARREN**

### The Dragon Kings and Their Domains

Ice Dragon - The Northern Wastes
Red - The Hell Plains
Blue - Irillian by the Sea
Storm - Wenslis
Black - Lochivar
Crystal - Legar Peninsula
Green - Dagora Forest
Gold - Tyber Mountains

Brown - The Barren Lands
Iron - Unnamed area in the Northwest
 that includes the Hill Dwarves
Bronze - Region that includes Gordag-Ai
Silver - Land that exists below the Tyber Mountains
Talak is bound to Gold's Domain and is just
 south of the Tybers
Penacles is ruled by the Gryphon

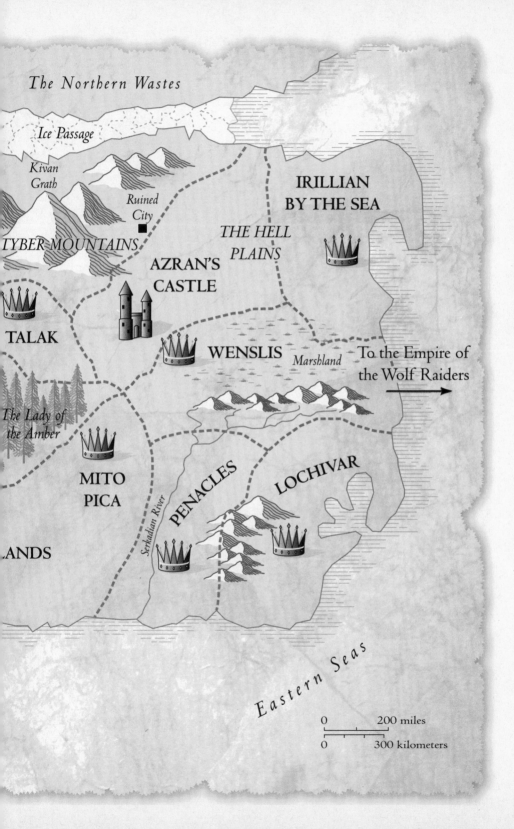

# A JOURNEY AROUND
# THE DRAGONREALM

THE DRAGONREALM is a place of myriad domains and fantastic creatures, and a careful traveler should know much of the land if he wishes to travel it safely. Here, then, are some of the places that you will come across. . . .

*The Legar Peninsula* thrusts out of the southwest edge of the continent. This is where the burrowing Quel—once masters of the Dragonrealm—live. This mountainous domain is inundated with gleaming crystal formations. Here is the domain of the most reclusive of the Dragon Kings, the Crystal Dragon.

*The Sea of Andramacus:* The violent waters west of the Dragonrealm. Little is known of them, but legend has it that they were named for a demon. . . .

*Land of the Hill Dwarves:* There is no true name for this region, but the hill dwarves are said to live in the eastern part of the region and the ambitious Iron Dragon rules without mercy.

*Esedi* lies southwest of the Iron Dragon's realm. This is where the Bronze Dragon holds sway and the human kingdom of Gordag-Ai is situated.

*The Kingdom of Zuu:* This other human kingdom is located southwest of Esedi and deep in a valley that is bound to the edge of the vast, magical Dagora Forest, situated in the center of the continent. The people of Zuu are famed for their horses. . . .

*The Dagora Forest:* This far-stretching forest is where most elves are said to live and where the more benevolent Green Dragon rules.

*Mito Pica:* A human kingdom lying east of the Dagora Forest and at the edge of the Hell Plains, Mito Pica holds a secret that will change the history of the Dragonrealm. . . .

*The Hell Plains:* To the northeast lies the volcanic Hell Plains, ruled by the Red Dragon. Here, it is rumored, also lies the castle of the foul sorcerer

Azran Bedlam. It is guarded by the Seekers, an avian race once masters, but now slaves.

*The Silver Dragon* rules the unnamed land to the north of the Dagora Forest. He serves also as confidant of the Dragon Emperor, but covets his position.

*The Tyber Mountains* are situated north of that and include the mountain citadel of the Gold Dragon, also known as the Dragon Emperor. The mountains are riddled with deep caverns.

*The Kingdom of Talak* lies at the base of the Tyber Mountains. Though somewhat independent, it is supposed to show fealty to the Gold Dragon. Its ruler is Rennek IV, but his son, Melicard, is already taking much of the reins.

*The Northern Wastes* may be found far north of the Tyber Mountains. They are home to many great burrowing creatures and are the domain of the Ice Dragon.

*The Barren Lands* lie south and southeast of the Dagora Forest. Once lush, they were destroyed in a magical upheaval during the Turning War. What remains is ruled by the bitter Brown Dragon.

*The Kingdom of Penacles*, east of the Barren Lands, is no longer ruled by a Dragon King. Instead, during the Turning War, it was liberated by forces led by the Gryphon, a unique creature who resembles the mythic beast. He now rules, but must constantly be on guard against the Dragon Kings. The Serkadian River runs north to south next to Penacles.

*The mist-enshrouded land of Lochivar*, east of Penacles, is ruled by the Black Dragon. It is said he has dealings with the Wolf Raiders, who come from a land across the eastern sea.

*Wenslis* is a rain-drenched kingdom under the rule of the Storm Dragon, whose domain is north of both Penacles and Lochivar. The most vain of the Dragon Kings, the Storm Dragon thinks himself a god.

*Irillian by the Sea*, ruled by the Blue Dragon, is northeast of the Storm Dragon's lands. An aquatic being, the Blue Dragon is not as benevolent as his counterpart in the Dagora Forest, but sees use in humans and has allowed them to be an almost-equal part of his kingdom. He has, of recent times, had dealings with the Gryphon, much to the frustration of many of his kind.

These are but some of the fantastic places a traveler will discover. The Dragonrealm is a place in flux, and new and ancient wonders are revealing themselves. . . .

# INTRODUCTION

I AM HAPPY to welcome you to this third collection of the Dragonrealm saga! It has been with great pleasure that I have watched the response to the reprinting of the novels and novellas written about such characters as the wizard Cabe Bedlam, his wife, Gwen—the enchantress known as the Lady of the Amber, the Gryphon—the part-avian, part-leonine ruler of Penacles, the great shadowy stallion called Darkhorse, and the enigmatic, accursed sorcerer, Shade. We have met the Dragon Kings, Cabe's mad father Azran, the Lords of the Dead, and other creatures and even delved into the secrets of the Dragonrealm's long and surprising history.

With this volume, we come back to the present. These stories are combined with some specific reason in mind and I think they read well together. There are long-arching plot lines brought to conclusion while new ones arise. Most important, we are going to learn something—but not *everything*—about one character in particular.

*The Crystal Dragon* brings Cabe to the forefront again, along with Darkhorse. It also features the return to the Dragonrealm of the Gryphon and his new family. However, the dread war across the sea has followed him to the Dragonrealm's shores and, to all places, the land of the most mysterious of the Dragon Kings. However, in the kingdom of the Crystal Dragon, there are things more deadly than even a force of renegade Wolf Raiders. . . .

Time does pass in the Dragonrealm and even children must grow . . . including the heir to the Dragon Emperor. With a possible peace at last between the two races, the choices of the young successor will be of the utmost importance. Will he be a champion of that peace or the one to crush all hope of it? That may all depend upon Duke Toma, back at last to claim the power and heritage of which the drake feels that he has been cheated, even if all the Dragonrealm must fall into chaos . . .

In "Past Dances," Valea Bedlam learns that the ghosts of the Manor are not necessarily merely memories of the past, but portents of the future . . . and that souls may be intertwined with one another for centuries, even if one of those souls happens to be that of the faceless sorcerer, Shade . . .

Love leads to foolhardy mistakes in "Storm Lord," as Aurim Bedlam, Cabe's son, learns when choosing as a place of rendezvous with the half-human daughter of the Green Dragon the edge of Wenslis—the realm of the Storm Dragon. Worse, it is also where the absolute proof that Shade still lives comes in a form putting a new twist on the multiple personality aspect of the hooded spellcaster's curse . . .

But Shade's return in "Storm Lord" only presages the catastrophic nature of his curse's new direction, a direction the necromancers known as the Lords of the Dead seek to use to not only control their wayward kin—Shade—but also draw the Bedlams into "The Still Lands." There, in a place between life and death, even the shadows of evil may kill . . .

I hope you enjoy this collection as much as the previous ones, the more so as it leads into the latest Dragonrealm novel, focusing on Shade and the clue that may either at last redeem him . . . or lay waste to the entire Dragonrealm.

Thanks for reading!

Richard A. Knaak

# THE CRYSTAL DRAGON

## I

HE WOKE TO find his world invaded. A shadowy plague in human form swarmed over the glittering, rocky landscape, tainting it by merely existing. He concentrated, allowing the crystalline chamber to show him more. A myriad collection of images related to his request filled the walls. He saw the three great ships, black as pitch, anchored off the shore and wondered how they could have come so far without him noting them. It was a troubling sign, an indication that he had slept deeper than he had desired.

Rather than contemplate it further, he studied the other reflections. One facet revealed a detailed image of some of the invaders and this he brought to the forefront. He hissed. They were familiar to him although the name by which they went did not come to him at first. In contrast to the sun-drenched region they now occupied, the figures wore armor the color of night, armor un-adorned save for the helm. Atop each, a crest fashioned into the snarling visage of a wolf's head leered down, a reflection in many ways of the men themselves. In the distance he could see the banners fluttering in the wind. The profile of the same wolf, surrounded by a field of deep crimson, watched over the army, for that was what it was.

The name came to him at last. As a people, they referred to themselves as the Aramites. Yet to those they had preyed upon for generation after generation, there was another, more apt title.

*The wolf raiders.*

Now they were here, in his domain. He released the image he had chosen and sought among the others. At first glance they seemed all the same, reflection upon reflection of dark-armored men infesting his kingdom. He hissed again, growing ever more frustrated. None of this aided him.

The desire to return to his slumber, to ignore the situation, grew stronger. He knew, though, that falling prey to such a tempting choice was to invite the downfall of all that was his. Despite the danger to his mind . . . to his very being . . . he had to stay awake. The wolf raiders were familiar enough to him that he knew they could not be left unattended.

"Aaaah . . ." There they were. The officers. The overall commander the Aramites termed Pack Leader was not there, but the rest of the jackals, his subordinates, were.

With the exception of the black and crimson cloaks they wore, there was little to mark them as anything other than common soldiers. In addition to the cloak, the Pack Leader would have a more elaborate helm and a single badge with the mark of the wolf upon it, but that was all. The Aramites cared little for insignias of rank otherwise. An officer was an officer, whatever his level, and that was all that mattered. Officers were meant to be obeyed in all things. Blind obedience was part of the wolf raider creed.

His first glance at them revealed nothing of significance and he was almost tempted to seek another reflection when the scene as a whole suddenly registered. The wolf raiders had a *prisoner.* He could not see who or what it was at first, for the ebony-garbed soldiers surrounded the hapless soul, as if fascinated by what they had captured. They poked at the unfortunate with short swords and talked among themselves.

There was one among them who did not laugh, but rather stood to the side, his round, young face a mask of boredom. He might have seemed entirely indifferent to the world around him if not for the hunger visible in his eyes. They darted back and forth, drinking in everything yet never resting on any object for more than a few moments. Interested despite himself, the watcher sought a reflection giving him a closer view of this one raider.

He was smaller of stature and unassuming at first glance, but there was that about him that made one wary. When the eyes of the young Aramite suddenly turned in his direction, the intensity with which they stared was so unsettling that the watcher almost thought he had been discovered. Then, the wolf raider returned his own attention to the captive, breaking the spell.

Chagrined, the master of the crystalline chamber followed the Aramite's gaze and, for the first time, beheld the wolf raiders' captive.

It was a Quel. Even bound and on his knees, he was nearly as tall as the humans. Gray netting enshrouded him from the top of his armored head to the ground, but enough was visible. The watcher marveled that any rope could hold the creature, especially a male as huge as this one. The Quel's long, tapering snout had also been bound, either to put an end to his hooting or to prevent him from snapping off the fingers of any raider foolish enough to reach too close. The raiders had also been clever enough to pull their prisoner's thick arms back so that the Quel could not make proper use of his lengthy claws. Designed to dig through the harsh soil of this land, the claws of the underground dweller would easily pass through the armor and flesh of an Aramite soldier without pause. Likely, the wolf raiders had already learned that fact the hard way, for it was doubtful that the capture had been an easy task. Even *he* respected the incredible strength behind those rending hooks.

*Why a Quel?* He pondered that. Had the Quel attacked the camp? Had they somehow simply caught this one unaware as he had surfaced? The latter seemed unlikely, considering how well the subterranean creatures knew this region, for they had been here longer than even he. It *was* possible that the raiders merely thought their prisoner a beast of some sort and not of a race older than their own. Humans could be presumptuous when it came to their place in the scheme of things.

He had no care himself for the fate of the Quel. The race stayed clear of his domain, despite the fact that it had meant abandoning what had once been a part of their mighty, subterranean city. To a Quel, nothing short of death would make one of them invade his realm. They feared not only him, but the power he controlled.

*The power he controlled* . . . For a moment the watcher forgot his own task and laughed silently at himself. If he controlled the power, then it controlled him just as much. Likely more. He could never be free of it, for to be free would be to lose himself forever.

His mind began to drift and the chamber, responding to his every thought, conscious or otherwise, allowed the multitude of images to fade, almost immediately to be replaced by one and one alone copied over and over in the facets of the crystalline walls. It was a single, rough-hewed face partly obscured by a helm and a beard, a face in many ways too akin to the visages of the wolf raiders. A warrior, a soldier obsessively obedient in character no matter what the cause.

It was too much. Roaring, he rose from his resting place and waved a huge, taloned hand at the array of faces. The images vanished as swiftly as they had materialized. In their place returned the encampment of the invaders. Slowly, the fear and anger dwindled, albeit not completely. Once more, the Quel and his captors took the stage. They were almost welcome now, for anything was better than lingering too much on a past so long dead it no longer seemed anything more than another dream.

When he gazed at the walls this time, however, he saw that all was *not* yet well. Something, in fact, was terribly wrong. The reflections wavered, twisted, making it seem as if the world beyond the chamber had become fluid. At first, he thought it was his own raging mind, but that was not the case. He had lived with the chamber for so long that he knew its ways, knew both its limitations and idiosyncrasies as well as he knew himself. Possibly better.

Whatever the cause, it came from without and he could not doubt that somehow its roots led back to those who had dared to think they could make his dominion into theirs.

Reaching out with his thoughts, he used the power of the chamber to seek out the source. The pictures wavered further and many of them altered as he narrowed his focus. The cause was near where the Quel was being held, but try as he might, it was impossible to focus exactly on the location he wanted. That, too, was peculiar; nothing ever long escaped the chamber's intrusive ability.

Briefly, the milky vision of a tent surfaced in several of the facets of the glittering walls. Peering closer, the watcher struggled to strengthen the images. He was rewarded with new visions, just as murky as the first, of an armored man seated in the tent. There was a glimpse of a beast of some sort wrapped around his shoulders and another picture that indicated a second figure standing behind the first. Of the second all that could be said was that he was as tall as the young raider guarding the Quel had been short and his skin appeared to be, of all things, a vivid blue.

*More! I must know more!* Few times had the chamber, his sanctum, failed him so. That it did now only made the need to discover the truth even more essential to him. If the wolf raiders were the cause of this, then they were truly a threat to the fragile balance he had maintained for so long.

His talons scraped at the floor, gouging the already ravaged surface. His breathing grew rapid. It was a strain to have to concentrate so, especially without sufficient rest. Now more than ever, there was danger that he might lose himself, become as the others before him had become . . .

Almost he had the image, a thing held in one hand of the seated Aramite, likely the Pack Leader he had sought earlier. In his eagerness to see it, however, he allowed his control to slip ever so slightly. The vision wavered again . . . then became a meaningless blur.

"Curssssse you, you malevolent mirror!" he roared, forgetting himself and the danger such rages represented to him.

Flame licked the multiple images of the wolf raider camp as his frustration became action. His tail lashed out and struck the opposing wall, where more than a dozen identical Quel gazed up into the dark eyes of more than a dozen identical young officers, each of whom had removed a foot-long rod from his belt. A second burst of flame momentarily scorched the reflections of a score of soldiers searching among the crystal-encrusted rock, their purpose in doing so a mystery that, for the time, held no interest to the maddened watcher.

As his eyes reddened in fury and he prepared to lash out again, the wolf raiders once more faded away. For a single breath, the chamber of crystal turned opaque. Then, the dull gray walls gave way to a new reflection. The flame within him died an abrupt death. He stared, paralyzed, at the legion of maddened, reptilian visages. They, in turn, stared back, a gleaming array of monstrous heads all bearing the same expression of disbelief and horror that he did. The toothy maws were open wide and from each a forked tongue flickered in and out. Eyes narrow and inhuman burned into his head. Gemlike skin rippled with each harsh, halting breath. Leathery wings unfurled and furled.

He recoiled from the condemning images, but there was no escaping the fact that each and every reflection was of him.

*Yessss . . . I am the massssster of the Legar Peninssssula, am I not? I am the monster men call the Crysssstal Dragon . . .* He faced the reflections again, this time in defiance. *But I am also myself and I shall always be!*

Despite his defiant stance, however, he knew he had come much too close to succumbing, closer than he had in centuries. The past few years were much to blame. Nearly two decades before, he had been forced to spend himself rescuing the Dragonrealm from his fatalistic counterpart to the north, the unlamented Ice Dragon. Reversing the spell of chilling death that the mad drake had unleashed had taken too much. The rage had almost overtaken him then. He had not come as close as now to being lost, but he had come close.

The wolf raiders would not leave of their own will. Like the parasites they were, they would remain until they had either been eradicated or had wrung from the land all that they could. If they did not know of the Quel's legacy yet, the Crystal Dragon had no doubt that they would before long . . . and that legacy would also lead them to him. The monarch of the Legar Peninsula understood all too well that even his presence would not deter men such as these. Their tenacity was almost reminiscent of another time, another people.

*And so, in the end, I must fight . . . even should it mean a victory in which all I desire to save is lost!* He tried to erase the repellent notion from his mind, but it had already embedded itself firmly within. There would be no escaping it. It would haunt him awake and asleep. Finally surrendering to that inevitable fact, the Dragon King settled down. Sleep, which he needed, was no longer really even an option for him. He could rest, but he could not afford the luxury of deep, enshrouding oblivion. The blight upon his realm had to be removed before it spread beyond his ability to control.

The Crystal Dragon shuddered at the thought of what he would be forced to do if that happened. There would be only *one* choice left to him then . . . and it might leave behind a legacy compared to which the devastation attempted by the Ice Dragon would seem a *blessing.*

Still, to *him* it would be worth the cost.

# II

THE MANOR HAD no other name, none that had stuck, anyway. Many called it the Green Manor, but that was more a description than a true title. To Cabe Bedlam, it was simply called the Manor. How long ago it had been built and by whom was a matter of conjecture. The style was like nothing the dark-haired warlock had ever seen before or since. Though much of the building had been cut from stone, the right side was actually formed by a massive tree as old as time. Depending where one stood in front of it, the Manor was either two or three stories tall. Marble columns jutted upward on each side of the doorway. Near the roof, the metallic effigy of one of the Seekers seemed ready to swoop down on any intruder.

Some assumed it had been built by the avian race, in part because much of the statuary and artwork seemed to revolve around the lives of the bird folk. That a tree formed part of the Manor strengthened that theory. Yet, it always seemed strange that creatures who normally lived in the heavens and made their rookeries in high mountain caves would build so earthbound a home. It seemed more likely to Cabe that the statues and such had actually been added later on, long after the departure of the original builders.

Actually, the history of the Manor meant far less to him than the fact that he was now its master. Here in the midst of the Dagora Forest, he and his wife, the enchantress Gwendolyn, ruled as lord and lady. Here, they raised the children . . . both human and drake.

From his position on the second-floor balcony of their private quarters, Cabe could survey much of the vast garden of the Manor. He watched as servants of both races went about their duties or spent their free time enjoying the day. *The first time I saw this place, I was running for my life.*

The Dragon Kings had discovered him, the unknown and unassuming grandson of Nathan Bedlam, a sorcerer who had nearly brought down the ruling drakes. The silver streak in his hair, the mark of sorcery, would have been enough to condemn him already, for the drakes despised human mages, but the discovery of his ancestry had sealed his fate. Some of the Dragon Kings had panicked and sought to kill him immediately, but instead one of their own had perished, in the process stirring the long-dormant magical powers of Cabe to life. He had fled here and found Gwen, the Lady of the Amber, frozen for more than a hundred years by the novice warlock's own father, Azran. Together, Cabe and the enchantress had survived Dragon Kings, armies, and mad sorcerers. After Azran's death and the scattering of Duke Toma's army, they had come back to the Manor and made it their own . . . if it was possible for anyone to actually lay claim to the ancient structure.

A giggle made him look down. Cabe stiffened as he saw his daughter, Valea, come charging into sight, a greenish yellow drake as large as a full-grown man behind her. Just coming into womanhood, she was the image of her mother down to the fiery red tresses. Clad in a riding outfit of emerald green, much more practical than the dresses Gwen tried to make her wear, she should have been able to outrun the beast.

She did nothing of the sort. Instead, Valea whirled about and reached for the running drake with open arms. Cabe raised a hand to defend her, then held back as the beast suddenly began to shimmer. Reptilian legs straightened and softened. Leathery wings shriveled to nothing, as did the tail. As the shifting creature stood on what had once been its hind legs, the draconian visage pulled inward, becoming more and more human with each passing breath. Hair of the same greenish yellow sprouted from the top of the head.

Where once had stood a monster, there now stood a beautiful maiden only a few years older than Valea. She was clad in an outfit identical to that of her companion save that it was of a pale rose, not emerald green.

Valea came up and hugged her tight. From where he stood, Cabe could hear both of them.

"That's the fastest you shifted yet, Ursa! I wish I could do that!"

"You think I'm doing better?" the older girl asked hopefully. Her narrow eyes contrasted sharply with Valea's almond-shaped ones. Like all female drakes when in their human forms, she was breathtaking and exotic. Her shape already vied with human women twice her age and her face was that of a siren, full-lipped and inviting. Only her childlike manner prevented her from already being a seductress. "Kyl keeps saying I'm so slow I should be with the *minors!*" She sniffed. "I don't, do I?"

Cabe grimaced. Minor drakes were beasts, pure and simple, and what he had mistaken the drake girl for a moment before. They were little more than giant lizards with wings and were generally used by their brethren as riding animals. In what was possibly the most peculiar aspect of the drake race, both minor drakes and the intelligent ones could be born in the same hatching. Even the drakes could not say why. To call Ursa a minor drake was the worst of all insults among her kind. He would have to speak to Kyl, something that was never easy.

The two girls were laughing now, Valea having evidently said something that Cabe had missed. The duo ran off. Cabe marveled at how easy it was for his daughter to accept a playmate who shifted from human to monster form, especially as the latter was the girl's birth form. He still felt uneasy around most of the drakes and was not reconciled by the fact that they, in turn, had a very healthy respect for his sorcerous abilities.

*Darkhorse would laugh if he knew . . .* He wondered where the elemental was. Still chasing the ghost of the warlock Shade? He hoped not. Shade was dead; the shadowy steed had seen it himself. Yet, Darkhorse had searched the Dragonrealm time and time again, never trusting what his own eyes had shown him. There was, admittedly, some justification. It had been Shade's curse to be reborn after each death, ever shifting from darkness to light to darkness again depending on which side his previous incarnation had followed. The last death had *sounded* final . . .

Cabe dropped the thought before he, too, began to see ghosts. There were other matters of importance. The news that King Melicard of Talak had passed on to them was disturbing, more so because one did not know what to believe and what not to believe. Oddly enough, it was not the more substantial rumors of a possible confederation made up of the survivors of decimated drake clans or the rise of a new generation of human warlocks that remained lodged in his mind, but rather the least likely one.

Someone had claimed to have sighted three great black ships on the northwestern seas of the Dragonrealm. Ships that had been sailing south.

It seemed unlikely, though, since the source of the rumor was said to be hill dwarfs, well known for creating tall tales. The Aramites hardly had the time and resources to start a new venture of the magnitude that the rumors indicated. Three such vessels meant hundreds of sorely needed soldiers taken from the defense of the wolf raiders' crumbling empire.

Yet . . . no news of the great revolt overseas had reached the Dragonrealm in about a year. At last word, one of the mightiest seaports left to the raiders had been ripe for falling. The forces of the Gryphon had been only days away.

He hoped the tide had not turned somehow.

"What are you thinking too much about now?"

The warlock turned to his wife, who had just entered the room. Gwendolyn Bedlam was a tall woman with fiery red hair that cascaded downward, falling nearly to her waist. A single wide stripe of silver ran back across her hair, marking her, as it did Queen Erini of Talak and Cabe, as a magic user. She had emerald eyes that sparkled when she was pleased and full lips that were presently curled into a smile. The forest green robe she wore was more free-flowing than his dark blue one, yet somehow it clung to her form, perfectly outlining her voluptuous body. He met her halfway across the room and took her in his arms. Their kiss was as long and as lingering as the first time they had ever kissed.

Cabe, with his slightly crooked nose and roundish face, had often wondered how someone of such ordinary features and mild build as himself had ever been so fortunate as to win her hand.

When he was at last able to separate himself from her, Cabe replied, "I was thinking of many things, but mostly about what we learned in Talak."

"The black ships?"

He nodded. "Maybe I'm just worried about the Gryphon. He did so much for me when I was confused and afraid all those years ago. He gave us refuge. Now, not a word in so much time . . . and then this sudden rumor."

"The trip across takes a long time, Cabe." Gwen took his arm and started to lead him out of the room. "Perhaps the last ship was delayed."

He nodded, but the nagging feeling would not disappear. "Maybe, but I can't help feeling that something has happened."

"Troia and Demion would not let anything happen to him. Demion sounds very protective of his father." Although they had never met the Gryphon's mate or his son, they knew them almost as well as if they had visited them every day.

"I suppose . . ."

*His father was a bear of a man, taller than he was and with so commanding a presence that he always felt compelled to kneel before him. Both of them were clad in the same green dragonscale armor, but whereas he merely felt hot and uncomfortable, his father truly was the warrior incarnate, a true standard by which the rest of the clan measured itself.*

*The bearded figure looked down at him. "I expect complete loyalty from all of my sons! You won't fail me like your brothers, will you?"*

*And it seemed that more than one voice answered, for it seemed there were others beside him, all kneeling before the man they called father. . . .*

"Cabe?"

"Father?" He blinked. "Gwen?"

She turned him so that they faced each other. There was deep concern in her eyes, concern bordering on fear for him. She stroked his cheek. "Are you all right? You froze there for a moment and your eyes turned upward. I thought you were about to pass out!"

"I . . ." What *had* happened? "I had . . . a flash of something."

The enchantress pushed aside several locks of crimson hair that had fallen over her face in the excitement. Her expression clouded. "You muttered 'father.' Was it . . . was it Azran?"

The name still sent chills running through him. "Azran's dead and I'd never call him father, anyway. He was only responsible for my birth. Hadeen, the half-elf my grandfather got to raise me . . . he was my father if anyone was. Besides, this was someone else's father . . . though I felt as if he and I were the same for that moment."

"What did you see?"

He described the scene to her, discovering then how murky everything had been. It was as if the vision were very old. Cabe mentioned as much to Gwen.

"A ghost of the far past . . ." she suggested, glancing around at their surroundings. "The Manor is very, very old. It could be you walked into one of its memories." In the time since they had made the Manor their home, they had discovered that it was haunted. Not by true ghosts and undead, but rather by living memories of the many who had either lived here or stayed for a time. Most of the visions were quick, foggy things. A glimpse of a tall, severe-looking woman in a gown of gold. A creature like a wolf, but more upright, possibly of a race now dead.

A few images were more distinct. Short-lived events like the one that Gwen had seen in the first days. It had been a wedding, but the image had lasted only long enough for her to hear the two participants give their agreement. There were other visions, darker ones, but they were rare and only those very gifted in sorcery even noticed the most ordinary memories. The Bedlams had learned to live with them, for there was nothing in those memories that could hurt anyone.

"This was stronger than usual," Cabe muttered. "But it did follow the pattern of the others. I'd just never seen this one before."

"There's probably a lot we haven't seen. When I was here the first time, in Nathan's time, I experienced a few that I have yet to see again." Her grip on him tightened. "Are you still suffering from it?"

He shook his head. Even the last vestiges of it were no more than memories of a memory in his head. "I'm fine."

She nodded, but he could see that she was still not satisfied. Cabe knew that she was thinking of another possibility.

"No, it wasn't a Seeker. I know how their mindspeak feels and this wasn't like that. This truly felt *ancient*. I could sense that. What I saw was something that had happened long ago, maybe even before the Dragon Kings, the Seekers, and the Quel had ever been, although I didn't think humans went back that far in the history of the Dragonrealm."

His reply seemed to relieve her. She kissed him lightly, then cupped his chin in one hand. "Very well, but if it happens again, I want to know."

"Agreed."

They walked slowly down the hallway, their conversation turning to the more mundane concerns of managing what was turning into a small village. Both Toos the Regent, ruler of Penacles, and the Green Dragon, who controlled the vast forest region surrounding their home, insisted on adding to their already vast number of servants. With some effort, the Bedlams had increased the area covered by the protective spell of the Manor. The humans and drakes in their service already needed to build new homes, for the smaller buildings that made up the Manor estate could no longer hold everyone. Once Cabe had joked about slowly becoming master of a tiny but growing kingdom. Now, he was beginning to think that the joke was becoming fact.

Their conversation came to an abrupt stop as something small dashed across the hall.

"What was that?" Gwen's brow furrowed in thought. "It almost looked like a . . . like a . . ."

A twin of the first creature raced past in the same direction. This time, the two had a better look.

"Were you going to say 'a stick man'?" Cabe asked in innocent tones.

Yet a third darted into the hall. This one paused and stared at the two huge figures despite having no eyes to speak of. Like the others, its head was merely an extension of the stick that made up its torso. Its arms and legs were twigs that someone had tied to the larger stick with string.

Its curiosity apparently assuaged, the ludicrous figure scurried off after its brethren.

"We have enough folk living here without adding these now," the enchantress decided. "It might be a good idea to see where they're going."

"Or where they came from," added Cabe. "Do you want to follow them or should I?"

"I'll follow them. You find out who's responsible, although I think we both know."

He did not reply. She was likely right. When tiny men made of twigs wandered the hallways of the Manor or bronze statues turned into large and lethal flying missiles, there could only be one person responsible.

The stick men had come from the stairway leading to the ground floor. Cabe descended as swiftly as was safe; there was no telling if he might trip over yet another tiny figure. He reached the bottom of the stairway easily enough, but perhaps a bit too much at ease because of that, the warlock almost did not notice the living wall coming from his right.

"Do pardon me, my Lord Bedlam. I must admit my eyes and my mind were elsewhere or I would have certainly made note of you."

Benjin Traske stood before Cabe, an imposing sight if ever there was one. Traske was more than six feet in height and had the girth to match. His face was full and round and on any other person would have seemed the jovial kind. On the scholar, however, it was more reminiscent of a judge about to pass sentence. He wore a cowled scholar's cloak, a gray, enveloping thing with gold trim at the collar, and the ebony robes of his profession. Traske also wore a blade, not part of the usual fare for a man of his occupation, but the warlock had learned the day of the tutor's arrival that he was a survivor of Mito Pica, a city razed to the ground by the armies of the Dragon Emperor in their search for one young Cabe Bedlam. Benjin Traske had seen his wife and child die because he had only had his bare hands with which to protect them. He himself had barely survived a wound to his stomach. The blade had remained with him since then, a symbol of his willingness to defend those under his care at the cost of his own life.

There had been some question as to whether he would be able to live among drakes, much less teach their young, but the Dragon King Green, who had discovered him, had assured the Bedlams that Benjin Traske saw cooperation between the two races as the only possible future.

Even when he was not tutoring, Traske sounded as if he were lecturing. Cabe found he could never listen to the man without feeling like one of his charges. "No apologies, Master Traske! I was hardly paying attention myself."

The tutor ran a hand through thin gray hair peppered slightly with silver. An expression of exasperation crossed his face. "You have seen your prodigy's latest effort, then. I feared as much. They have journeyed upstairs, I take it?"

Cabe nodded. "All three of them. The Lady Gwen is hunting them down now."

"Only three of them? There should be five."

Such knowledge in no way encouraged Cabe in the efforts of his son. "We saw only three."

Traske sighed. "Then, if you will excuse me, Lord Bedlam, I will hunt out the other two while your good bride deals with the three above. I feel at some fault, for when he lost control, my mind was elsewhere."

"You were teaching him magic?" While there was a hint of sorcery about the tutor, he had never struck Cabe as an adept.

His remark seemed to amuse the man. "Teach him magic? Only if young Master Aurim desires to know how to lift a feather for the space of three seconds. No, my lord, my skills will never be much more than wishful thought. If I were an adept, the fall of Mito Pica might have taken a different turn. I was merely his audience. I believe your son was trying to impress the teacher, so to speak. No, the magic of mathematics and history is the only magic I can teach."

"Well, I think I'd better teach him a little about concentration and patience . . . again. Where is he?"

"In the center of the garden." Benjin Traske performed a bow, a momentous achievement for one of his build. "If you will excuse me, my lord, I do not want my quarry getting too far afield and if the other two are not upstairs, then that means they must be headed in the direction of the kitchen."

"Mistress Belima will have a fit if she sees one." Belima was the peasant woman who ran the kitchens as her own kingdom. Considering the results she achieved, Cabe was more than willing to grant her that territory.

"Indeed." The hefty scholar departed, moving with a swiftness and grace that the warlock could only marvel at.

It took only minutes for Cabe to reach the location where Traske had said his son would be. Aurim was seated by himself on one of the many stone benches located here and there around the garden. His head was bowed and his face was buried in his hands. The silver streak across the middle of his head contrasted sharply to his shoulder-length, golden hair. He wore a robe similar to his father's, save that it was of dark red.

"You'll never find them like that."

Aurim looked up, his expression changing from one of frustration to embarrassment. Overall, he resembled his father, but fortunately, as far as Cabe was concerned, he had inherited from his mother's side a more noble chin and a straighter nose. Although only a few years older than Valea, he was generally able to pass for someone several years into adulthood . . . except when failure reared its ugly head.

"You know."

"I *saw* them. So did your mother."

The boy rose. He could already meet Cabe at eye level even if he could not meet Cabe's eyes themselves. "It was a *simple* thing! You and Scholar Traske are always telling me my problem is patience or concentration! I made the stick men to practice. There's ten different routines I can make them do, all to prove I'm being more careful and concentrating better!"

"And so?" He tried to be encouraging. Unlike Aurim, Cabe had come into his powers almost full-flung. The experience and patience that his grandfather, Nathan, had *literally* passed on to him had given him an advantage no other spellcaster had ever had. Even then, his own inexperience and uncertainty had made for a constant battle of wits with himself playing both sides. He still had much to learn. His son had no such advantage; everything he learned he learned from the beginning. Sorcery, while it looked simple to understand and utilize, was anything but.

"And so I lost control again! Halfway through the second set. They just ran off." A sullen look crossed the lad's countenance. "And now you can lecture me again."

"Aurim . . ."

His son clenched fists. "If that stupid vision hadn't—"

"*What* vision?" All thought of Aurim's recklessness vanished.

"Like the other ones. The memories of the Manor, you and Mother say.

Only this one was sharper. Men in scale armor. One big one talking to others. I think . . . I think they were all his sons."

"And you were one of them. He spoke to you about loyalty. How he demanded it from you."

The boy looked at him, wide-eyed. "You know it?"

"I had the *same* vision . . . probably the same time as you, in fact." Cabe grew uneasy. Nothing like that had ever occurred before. The visions generally only appeared to one person, usually Gwen or him. Only lately had Aurim started to sense them and he, knowing of them from his parents, had had little trouble accepting them. If the things were changing, becoming more intrusive into the world of the present, would it mean that some day they would have to abandon the Manor?

Aurim, who knew his father well, put aside his own troubles for the moment and asked seriously, "Does this mean something?"

"It might." He no longer had the memories of Nathan Bedlam to guide him, but Gwen knew far more about the whims of sorcery than anyone now alive save the Dragon Kings and possibly the Gryphon. She might be able to shed some light on this sudden turn.

*Gwen!* She was still hunting down the stick men! "We need to discuss this further, but first we have to take care of a little problem still running loose."

The tall boy's cheeks turned crimson. "I've been trying to think about what to do. Couldn't we just summon them with a spell?"

"Have you tried a summoning?"

"Yes." The defeat in Aurim's tone increased tenfold.

"I was afraid of that." In the heat of the moment, the idea had not even occurred to Cabe, but he knew that at some point Gwen would have thought of it. The warlock was doubtful it would have worked, anyway. Aurim's creations were never easy to deal with. It was a sign of his great potential. "Did you maintain your concentration?"

"I did! This time I *swear* it!"

"Then they probably won't listen to anyone . . . and we have to go hunting. You go after Master Traske; he'll need the help. I'll find your mother."

"Yes, Father." Aurim paused. "I still can't get the vision out of my mind. Are there others so vivid?"

"Only a few. We'll have to talk about how to shield yourself from them if they bother you so much."

"Oh, I don't mind them; any other time, they're interesting. Who do you suppose they were?"

Cabe knew that his son was stalling now, mostly because Aurim had little desire to face his tutor after such an abysmal display. Still, for once it was a question that the warlock wished he could answer. "I don't know. They remind me of something I've read, but nothing specific comes to mind now."

"What's the Legar Peninsula like?"

There were questions and there were questions and Cabe, who tried to be an understanding father even though he considered nearly two decades not near enough time to learn how to be one, had had enough. "I think Master Traske would *truly* appreciate your help soon, Aurim. Then, when you're done, *he* can give you a lecture on the geography of Legar or anywhere else."

Frustrated, Aurim grumbled, "I only wondered if it really glitters as much as it did in the vision . . ."

"What was that?" Stepping face-to-face to his son, Cabe repeated his question and added, "You saw Legar in the vision?"

Aurim swallowed, not knowing what he had done wrong now. He nodded slowly and gasped, "In the background. It was there sometimes. I . . . I thought it was. You've always talked about how much it sparkles and Master Traske said once it was covered with diamonds."

"Not diamonds. Not exactly," Cabe halfheartedly corrected him. "Crystals, yes." He looked away. "And it does glitter; enough to blind a person during midday if you look in the wrong direction." *And I didn't see it. Why?*

The visions of the Manor had never extended to regions so far away. They had always dealt with the ancient structure itself or the lands it occupied. If Aurim had seen Legar, and Cabe did not doubt him, then this was more than a simple time-lost memory.

He could not say why or how he knew, but somehow, standing there, Cabe Bedlam was certain that the answer to this mysterious vision had to do with three black ships.

THE BEAST WAS dead. It was not often that Orril D'Marr overestimated his prey, but the blasted creature had seemed so impervious to pain that he had pushed too hard. It was a pity. Lord D'Farany would be displeased, which was always a danger, but D'Marr was certain that what little he had gained out of the creature just before the end would more than make up for his error.

The young Aramite officer scratched his chin while he watched the soldiers drag the Quel's body away. That it had been more than a simple animal had surprised him at first, but he should have known that when the blue man said something was true it was most definitely true. D'Rance was a fountain of knowledge and had, fortunately for the expedition, studied the history of this abysmal land in great detail. It was a shame he had not been born a true Aramite rather than one of the untrustworthy, blue-skinned folk of the northern reaches of the empire. Everyone knew it was only a matter of time before one of his kind turned on you. D'Marr hoped he would be the one given the order to kill the northerner. It would be interesting to see how the blue man died.

The sun was going down rapidly. That was fine with D'Marr. The weather here was beastly, fit only for creatures like the overgrown armadillo he had just killed. The sun burned all day, making the black armor seem like a fire-hot kettle. What made it worse was that no one else seemed to notice it.

D'Marr turned and started for a ridge to the west of the camp. It was a long walk, but he knew that was where he would find the Pack Leader and possibly D'Rance, too, although the blue man was supposed to be leading the hunt for the cavern entrance now. One never knew about the northerner, though. What he did often went against what a wolf raider was supposed to do. No doubt only the fact that he achieved results kept Lord D'Farany from putting a rather permanent end to the blue man's antics.

Yes, it would be interesting to see him die.

He reached the ridge some ten minutes later. The sentries positioned near the bottom saluted him and immediately stepped out of his way. Most soldiers were quick-witted enough to know that one did not stand in Orril D'Marr's way for very long. As he walked between them, the young officer smiled lazily at the taller of the two. The man's eyes widened, then looked away. Once past, D'Marr dropped the smile and forgot them completely. They were nothing to him. Only one man among all those who had become part of this desperate venture had earned his respect and obedience . . . not to mention his fear.

As he neared the top, a snarling sound made him look up. A savage creature the size of a small dog but built more along the lines of a giant rat peered down at him. Its ugly face was flat, almost as if at birth someone had pushed it in, and when the jaws opened, there were jagged teeth everywhere. When D'Marr came almost within reach, it snapped at him. The mask of boredom slipped from his visage as the Aramite silently cursed the animal and swatted at it with one mailed hand. Still snarling, his furry adversary trotted back several steps. D'Marr hated verloks and would have gladly done away with this one save that it was his master's pet. Only Lord D'Farany would ever consider such a vicious creature for a plaything.

No longer with an advantage, the verlok trotted back to its master. D'Marr took a moment to both catch his breath and organize his thoughts. He stared at the backside of the Pack Leader, who stood at the opposite edge of the cliff gazing out at the sea. The evening wind whipped Lord D'Farany's cloak like some mad dervish, but otherwise the master raider was as still as stone.

The Aramite commander was alone, but as D'Marr strode toward him, he heard D'Farany's voice.

"Can you feel it? So very near yet so far. The land fairly glows with power . . ."

D'Marr came within arm's reach of his commander and knelt beside him. The verlok moved away, glaring. "My lord."

"You killed him, D'Marr."

He glanced around to see if somehow he had missed someone else, someone who could have informed Lord D'Farany about his mistake. There was no one. The anxious raider looked down at the ground. Time and time again he reminded himself that his master was no longer a *keeper*, no longer one of the Aramite sorcerers whose souls had been tied to the wolf raiders' savage and very real god, the *Ravager*. When their god had abandoned them just prior to the revolt, he had taken his gifts with him. That had meant madness and death to most of the keepers, for the power of the Ravager had used as much as it had been used. It had enslaved them to the will of the wolf god. Without it, the survivors had become as helpless as newborn pups . . . all of them save Ivon D'Farany.

D'Marr realized he had not yet responded. "Yes, my lord."

"You were overzealous."

"I was, my lord."

"Rise, Orril, and join me." The Aramite commander had still not shifted his gaze from the sea. D'Marr stood up and waited, knowing that his master would speak when he chose to.

More than a minute had passed before Lord D'Farany finally commented, "From here, they still resemble hunters, don't they Orril?"

It took D'Marr the space of a breath or two to understand what his master meant. Then his eyes fixed upon the three massive ships that had carried the wolf raiders this far. It was true; they still did resemble the hunters they had once been. Tall, black, and, despite their great size, as swift as any other vessel sailing the seas.

*And swift enough to carry us away from the revolt while our tails still hung between our legs . . .* "They've served us well, my lord."

"And suffered because of us."

"Yes, sir." Suffered, indeed. From a distance they might still resemble the terrors of the sea they had once been, but up close the ravages of the empire-wide revolt became all too evident. The sails had been patched so many times that there were now more patches than original sail. Scorch marks and cracked timber on the hull spoke of the accuracy of the enemy's weapons. On board, it was even worse. Most of the rails were either broken or completely missing. There were still gaping holes in the decks because there was no longer enough material with which to repair them. Aboard one vessel, the crew had barely managed to secure the main mast after one strike had nearly torn it free. It was a wonder the raiders had made it so far with only a few losses at sea.

The three ebony ships were hunters no longer. They were merely shadows now.

"Scuttle them. Tonight."

"*My lord?*"

The raider commander turned then. D'Marr swallowed. Lord D'Farany had not escaped the madness that had taken his fellow keepers and the vestiges of that madness remained forever a part of his countenance. His skin was pale, almost white, and there were scars, insufficiently hidden by a short, well-groomed beard, where he had tried to claw his own skin off during that period. Three days of screaming had left his lipless mouth forever curled upward at the ends, making it seem as if the former keeper found the world around him ever amusing. Worst of all, though, were the eyes, for they never seemed to focus, yet somehow they snared one's attention, forced one to look at them. To D'Marr, to whom the world was an enemy ever needing to be watched, being bound to stare into those eyes and those eyes alone was sheer horror.

"Scuttle them. Tonight. They deserve to rest." The eyes drifted to the direction of the sea but did not quite reach it.

"Y-yes, my lord." D'Marr found himself shaking as he broke contact. Then his fear faded as he contemplated what the Pack Leader's command truly implied. They would be trapped here, then. They would be forced to not only survive, but to strengthen themselves as swiftly as possible. They would have to make this realm theirs or perish.

It did not occur to D'Marr to protest, to refuse the order. One did not question the Pack Leader. It was not the Aramite way. "I will do it myself, my lord. There's something I wish to test and this will give me the chance."

"You should have been more careful, Orril," Lord D'Farany said, switching back to the previous subject as was often his habit. He snapped his fingers. The verlok came trotting over to him. Reaching down, the Pack Leader took the monstrosity in his arms. It growled quietly as he began to stroke it, the closest it could come to a purr. "This . . . this . . . *Quel* . . . was valuable."

Here was his chance to redeem himself. "Yes, my lord, he was. More so than we could've ever realized."

The hand stroking the backside of the verlok paused. Pale, gray eyes shifted to a spot just to the side of the officer's head. Not a word was said, but D'Marr still knew that he had just been commanded to speak.

"I know now where the surface entrance to the caverns lies, my lord," he began. "The entrance to the city of the underdwellers. To their power. All the searching in the world would not have uncovered it, Lord D'Farany. It's extremely well hidden."

"But you can find it."

"Yes, my lord. Easily."

Nodding his approval, the Pack Leader turned away. D'Marr, however, did not take that as a signal that he had been dismissed. He knew his master too well to assume such a thing.

"Tomorrow, then. You will lead the search."

"As you desire." Despite his hatred of the heat and the blinding sunlight he would be forced to suffer, the young raider was pleased. The glory would be his, not the blue man's.

"There is something else, is there not?"

*Something else?* D'Marr could not recall anything of significance other than what he had reported. The location of the monster's home had been his only trump card, the only one he had thought necessary.

"What of the dragon, Orril?"

*The dragon!* How could he have forgotten? The dragon who ruled here had been the only worrisome question, the only threat to the advancement of their plans.

"The Dragon King will be of little concern to us, my lord. This one hides in his citadel and never comes out. This I learned through the Quel. So long as we do not seek to enter, he and the handful that make up his clan will not bother with us. We may do as we please. All he seems to do is watch. Watch and do nothing." The last statement was pure conjecture on the Aramite's part, but it made sense to him. The Crystal Dragon apparently cared not who trespassed in the region that was supposedly his so long as he was left alone. "So we may proceed and the dragon may be left for later when we are more secure in our power."

Lord D'Farany did not immediately respond. Instead, he turned slowly back to his subordinate and, for the first time since D'Marr had joined him, fixed his eyes on the young officer. The verlok grew oddly still, as if as frightened as D'Marr. "You had best be correct in your assumption, Orril. The dragon cannot be taken lightly. He could not have lived so long surrounded by so much power and not been affected by it." The Pack Leader began stroking his pet again, but this time the animal was in no way soothed. "Should it come to a confrontation between the dragon and me, rest assured that I will bait a proper trap for the reptile . . . and you will be the *bait*." The eyes unfocused again and the Pack Leader began to turn away. "You are dismissed."

It took all of Orril D'Marr's willpower *not* to run as he departed the ridge. Someone in the camp would suffer tonight; someone would have to suffer to assuage his fears. It was the only way he could purge himself, the only way he could face the tasks tomorrow with the mask of indifference in place.

Better the dragon any day, he thought, than the wrath of his master.

CLEAVING ITS WAY through the turbulent waters of the Eastern Sea, the lone vessel neared the Dragonrealm. Where the ships that Cabe Bedlam pondered about had been deadly leviathans, giants designed for terror, this one was low and sleek, a tiny juggernaut built to carry a mere handful of passengers swiftly to their destination. There was, in fact, only one trait it shared with the three massive raider ships.

It was utterly black.

# III

"WE ARE VERY close now. I can hear its call. It was good of the Quel not to lie to us," Lord D'Farany commented as he watched his men advance across the gleaming land toward the place where the dying Quel had claimed the entrance to his city was hidden. Lord Ivon D'Farany did little to stem the madness in his voice. He knew the others could not sense what he sensed, for none of them had ever been trained as a keeper. They were to be both pitied and envied, he decided. Pitied because they had never known the seductive power of the Aramites' great god, the Ravager, and envied because they had not had to suffer the soul-wrenching horror of withdrawal when that power had been abruptly torn away just prior to the war. He was considered one of the fortunate ones, but then no one else could ever understand the emptiness that was now ever with him. His hand twitched as old reflex actions still sought the talisman he had once owned, the link to his god.

"But that will change . . ." he whispered. "So much will change, then." The ends of D'Farany's thin mouth rose ever so slightly, the closest he generally came to a smile. It was never a good idea to smile, for it upset the men so.

When the power of his god had been torn from his soul, he, like the rest, had fallen into madness. He had screamed and then laughed, a laugh that had chilled his watchers. In his mind, he had died, completely and utterly. When sanity at last returned, a different man occupied the body. The desperate commanders had sought the power of a keeper to aid them in the sudden and overwhelming revolt that had arisen, but they had found something else instead. Something that would not be manipulated but rather would manipulate in turn.

Recalling where he was, Lord D'Farany glanced about him. Despite the sun and heat, his men were still moving at a brisk pace. The common ranks did not know what they truly sought, only that their leaders had ordered them to watch for a cavern and be prepared for battle.

It might be that he was wrong, that this was not the place that he had dreamed of for the past few weeks. He had not, of course, told anyone else of the dreams. He never did. The ship captains had obeyed his command to steer toward this land rather than one of the more lush regions to the north, but it was clear that they considered the gleaming peninsula an interesting but hardly useful bit of dirt. Vegetation was sparse and older reports had warned that the interior was inhospitable, consisting mainly of endless hills of rock and crystal. There was nothing here of value to the average wolf raider; the crystals were fascinating, but they were, for the most part, common.

He knew otherwise. He had first felt the power emanating from the near-barren domain *days* before they had landed. Now, ashore, he more than felt it; he *lived* it. Here was a force that could fill the emptiness inside, make him complete at last.

All his men had to do was take it from the beasts below.

"This is a mistake, yes?" came a knowing voice to his left. While phrased as a question, as much of what his companion said was, the comment was actually a statement.

"Give Orril his opportunity, Kanaan. It is both his reward and his punishment."

"There is another way, my lord. A better way, I think."

D'Farany knew what his aide meant. He nodded slowly. "When it is needed. Patience, Kanaan."

The tall figure beside him grew silent, but the Aramite leader knew that Kanaan D'Rance was by no means mollified. Like most of his kind, he was impatient and ambitious, a combination of traits that would have had him executed on the first day by most commanders but suited Ivon D'Farany just right. The Pack Leader had a fondness for things mercurial and the blue man was certainly that. He was also a fount of information. D'Rance had made the Dragonrealm his obsession.

The gaunt northerner had been a rare find. His talents perfectly complemented Orril D'Marr's own considerable skills, yet the two were of such different minds that their constant competition also served D'Farany. The latter also assured that the two would never combine forces and cause him threat. He would have hated to see that happen. It would have meant the need to eliminate two valuable weapons. He did not dare do that until he was complete again.

Complete . . . the Pack Leader frowned. Even this would not make him truly complete. Nothing save his glorious god's return could do that. *Still, I will be close.*

It was then he felt the power around him shift and shape and though he *knew* what it meant, Ivon D'Farany merely stood there and drank in the sensation.

The world exploded in light . . . and the belated screams of men.

"I *warned*, did I not? I warned that this would happen, yes!"

D'Farany forced his eyes to focus. He did not see as normal men did, not anymore, but there were times when it became necessary to try. When the raider leader did at last see what the underdwellers had done, he could not help but smile, despite the horrific sight he knew he created. "Magnificent!"

Before him, his soldiers scattered in an attempt to make themselves less of an inviting target. The Pack Leader barely noticed their frantic efforts. His eyes only saw the wonderful result of so much power, power that was to be *his*.

There had been a small rise where the beasts had struck with their sorcery, a small rise populated by a few scraggly plants and, at the moment of the attack, likely a dozen or so soldiers. Now, the rise was a flat, iron-hot pool of *glass* and the plants and the men unfortunate enough to be there at the time . . . were nothing.

Yet still the raider force moved on, for they had been given a command and that was all they needed.

"Magnificent . . ." the Aramite commander whispered again. His hand twitched as he once more sought the talisman that would have let him manipulate such power.

The same sensation swept over him. A second flash burned away the world in a sea of light. D'Rance and the others were forced to fall back and shield their eyes, but Lord D'Farany barely noticed. He breathed in the holocaust air and felt a strength he had not felt in years.

With an almost wistful expression on his ravaged countenance, he slowly turned toward the blue man and quietly commanded, "Bring me the box now, Kanaan."

Still blinking, the bearded northerner reached into the depths of his cloak and pulled out a tiny, rectangular container. The Pack Leader nodded pleasantly, having known all the time that the blue man would have it on him despite orders to the contrary. He forgave D'Rance such things, because it pleased him to do so. There would come a time when he overstepped himself and when that happened D'Farany would either punish him properly or turn him over to D'Marr, who had never made it a secret that he wanted the blue man's skin.

The Aramite commander liked to think of himself as a fair man. He was also perfectly willing to give the younger officer to the northerner if circumstances warranted it.

He removed his gloves and, with great respect, took the tiny black box from D'Rance. The former keeper ran one finger over the lid, outlining the wolf's head engraved there. It had taken him much effort and time to gather the forces stored within and he treated them with the care they deserved.

A third burst of light raised anew the shouts and screams, but the sounds were merely insignificant irritations to him as he opened the top and admired his prize.

In the days of the keepers, it would have been called the *Ravager's Tooth*. A curved artifact shaped to resemble a hound's fang, it was small enough to fit in his palm. He had once had one like it, before the day of emptiness. With great eagerness, Lord D'Farany removed the talisman from the box and cupped it in his left hand. The terrible smile stretched tighter as he allowed himself to briefly become ensorcelled by the tooth.

*My master, why have you forsaken us?* In the talisman was the residue of the Ravager's unholy will. Long ago, a younger D'Farany had discovered that although their god had vanished and taken his power with him, there were traces in the talismans of the keepers . . . even traces in the keepers themselves. It had meant dark work, locating the artifacts and the bodies and drawing the lingering power from them, but he had prevailed. Yet the power this piece contained was limited; each use drained the talisman. It would soon be as empty as he was.

"But not for long . . ." The Pack Leader cradled the piece in his hand and returned the box to the blue man. He then turned back to where his men fought to survive and held out the talisman toward the gleaming landscape where he supposed the cavern entrance was.

Yet again the earth was shaken by a burst of deadly light. The Quel might no longer be masters of the realm, but they still wielded power. Their strikes were also systematic; each time the raiders shifted away from the previous blow, they were attacked anew from the opposite direction.

A silence seemed to surround the former keeper as he held the talisman up to the sky. The only one still daring to stand near him was D'Rance, who eyed his commander with both anticipation and envy.

D'Farany whispered, "Behold the legacy of my Lord Ravager. Behold his glory."

The carved tooth glowed bright.

Its effect was not something that was seen, not, at least, by the wolf raiders who were there. At most, a few who were sensitive, such as Orril D'Marr, felt a rippling in the fabric of the world itself. The rippling washed across the area like a tide coming into shore. It passed through rank after rank, moving swiftly toward the front and then beyond.

"Mustn't destroy," muttered the Pack Leader to himself. "Mustn't take the chance. Merely take the fight from them."

The silence around D'Farany spread as well. Even the screams and shouts seemed to fade away as the power unleashed by the talisman blanketed the land.

Those who did not have the touch of sorcery within them still could feel that something was different.

At last, the tooth ceased to glow. Lord D'Farany looked at it with great sadness. The spell had drained it of everything he had collected. Now, it was no more than a useless trinket. Nonetheless, the Pack Leader did not throw it away, but rather returned it to an overawed D'Rance, who gingerly placed it back in the box.

"They may advance again."

The command proved to be unnecessary. Already, soldiers were reorganizing and moving forward. D'Marr had understood what had happened. The Aramite leader nodded to himself. It was an example of why the young officer was one of his favorites.

Now the raiders moved unimpeded. Even Lord D'Farany did not know what he had unleashed, but he knew that the Quel would be helpless now. Their power had been negated for a time and that time would be enough to ensure total Aramite victory.

"Come, Kanaan. It's time to join them."

The blue man bowed. "Yes, my lord."

As they trailed slowly after the advancing troops, D'Farany contemplated what he would do with that power now that it was his. Building new ships was a possibility, but what sense was there in returning to rescue the fools who still fought back home? How much better to claim a portion of this realm and begin expanding here. How much more satisfying to take from the Gryphon's friends the same thing the birdman had taken from the Aramites.

D'MARR PEERED INTO the darkness of the cavern entrance. The walls gleamed faintly from the torch he had directed one of his men to throw inside. There was nothing to be seen, but that did not mean that there was no danger. D'Marr was not that naive.

He turned to the man nearest him. "Inside. Double file. Do watch the ground and the walls. . . . and the ceiling, for that matter. They could come from anywhere."

The raider blinked, then hurried to obey as D'Marr's free hand slowly shifted toward the rod hanging from his belt. The Aramite officer nodded and watched as two ranks quickly formed. He allowed the first three pairs to enter, then tightened his grip on his sword and entered with the next.

*Where are you, my little beasts?* Even with the intervention of Lord D'Farany, it could not be this easy. There had to be resistance. There had to be battle.

Farther and deeper they marched and yet still they did not encounter the creatures whose lair this was. A sense of unease spread throughout the lines, even infecting D'Marr. No enemy gave up so easy. Lord D'Farany's magical counterattack, while potent, should not have been able to eliminate *all* opposition.

He was almost pleased when the first man finally died.

He had commanded them to be wary of all directions, but no one save those who had been involved with the capture of the first Quel could have understood the speed at which they could burst through the earth and strike at their foes. Suddenly there was a huge, taloned hand erupting from the tunnel floor. It took hold of the ankle of the nearest soldier and withdrew as swiftly as it had come. That the hole that had been created was far too small for the human form did not matter. The helpless raider was pulled as far as the gap in the floor allowed and then pulled farther.

It was not a pleasant sight, but it gave D'Marr new respect for the strength of the overgrown armadillos.

"Leave it," he warned the two who started to reach for the remains in some vain hope that there was still a chance. "I want spears and torches ready." He had had some of the men bring light spears, weapons about a foot longer than a short sword and quite useful in tight areas. As light as they were, the spears were very, very sharp and highly resilient. "Right flank watch right wall and ceiling. Left flank watch left wall and floor. The man who misses the next one will not have to fear death at the beasts' claws. I shall be more than happy to oblige him myself."

Yet, even as he spoke, another arm burst through the wall across from him, seizing the nearest man by the throat and bringing his head hard against the rock face. The crack and snap echoed throughout the cavern, then was drowned out by the noises of belated action as the raiders closest tried to cut the hand of the creature off. One man managed to slice the back of the huge paw, but the digger quickly retreated into the earth.

*How do they move through it so quickly? It might as well be water the way they come and go!* There was only a small, collapsed hole to mark where the second attack had originated from.

He did not have time to consider the matter further, for the third attack was directed at *him.* D'Marr was turning when the talons came shooting from the wall next to him. With a swiftness he did not know he had, the officer ducked back. Even still, his reaction was nearly too slow. Huge claws slashed at his jaw, leaving a bloody trail. His sword was up in almost the same instant. The raider had the great satisfaction of watching the blade cut up through the arm just past the wrist of his attacker. A shower of blood drenched his breastplate.

The Quel's arm shook, its actions nearly twisting the sword free of D'Marr's grip. He took hold of it with both hands and held on for dear life. One of the soldiers raised his own weapon and brought it down on the still exposed limb. The armored hide of the Quel was thick, but not thick enough. The edge of the sword embedded itself in the arm, causing a new shower of blood.

The attacker tried to withdraw, but the swords prevented that. A soldier with a spear moved forward and thrust into the hole. D'Marr again wondered at the vast stamina and strength of the armored beast. Even as badly wounded as the Quel had to be, there was no sign of weakness.

The wall before him shattered, pelting men with bits of rock. The Quel, unable to retreat into the earth, had chosen to come to them instead.

The subterranean dweller filled the passage. D'Marr could not tell whether it was male, like the first, or female and did not really care. As an *it*, the Quel was terrible enough. With its good arm, it took the man with the spear and threw him into the soldiers behind him. The raider with the sword had wisely retreated already. D'Marr released his hold on his own weapon, having realized that he would be next if he insisted on maintaining his grip any longer. The young officer had no delusions that he could take on one of the beasts single-handed.

Still . . . he reached for the rod by his side even as the Quel pawed at the blade buried in its wrist. Both arm wounds still bled profusely but the monster moved as if nothing were wrong.

"Don't just gawk! Bring the spears in!"

There was a scream and then much commotion farther down the line. The Quel were no longer attacking one at a time. He had no time to concern himself with the others, however, for the one who had tried to kill him evidently was intent on completing its task. D'Marr suspected that the creatures had known all along that he was the leader of the invading force. The initial attacks might even have been made so that they could better locate him among the rest. He suspected that the Quel relied greatly on their sense of hearing or some similar trait when they moved through the ground.

With a loud, long hoot, the monster swung at him with one huge paw. D'Marr ducked away and pulled his staff free of his belt. He held the long rod before him. Several men with spears had now closed on the Quel. Two feinted from the left of the huge digger. When the Quel turned toward them, those on the right jabbed with their own spears. One caught the massive creature in the arm that had been wounded. This time, D'Marr's adversary unleashed a shrill, unmistakable cry of agony. While it was thus occupied, the other lancers also attacked. Three spears penetrated the armored hide of the Quel.

*So you do have a soft shell in places*, the Aramite officer noted with some satisfaction. Like the creature it resembled, the Quel had less protection near the stomach region. That was not to say it was not protected well there, for two of the spears had snapped in that initial thrust, but of necessity the subterranean monster could not have as thick and hard a shell as it wore on its back. D'Marr had suspected as much from his time with the prisoner, but knew better than to trust that all the creatures were built the same way.

The Quel was staggering now, even its great stamina unable to compensate for the many dripping wounds. It took one last swipe at him and then began to back into the wall from which it had emerged.

"You'll not be leaving us so soon," hissed D'Marr. He thrust at the retreating Quel with his rod.

The wounded creature's howl shook the tunnel and echoed on and on long after the huge figure had collapsed to its knees.

Orril D'Marr touched the tip of the rod to the armored head. He smiled with grim satisfaction as the Quel shivered, hooted mournfully, and finally slumped.

"Yesss . . . I thought all it needed was a little adjustment." He looked from his conquered foe to his favorite toy. With the prisoner, he had overcompensated with the rod, killing the Quel. The short staff was a magical tool that he had inherited from his late predecessor, who had, in turn, paid dearly to have a sorcerer not of the keeper caste create it. It had thirty-two levels of pain, many of which could kill. The captive Quel had died from level twenty-one. He had given this one level twenty. D'Marr was quite pleased. Lord D'Farany would want hostages to question. It would make up for his earlier overzealousness.

The raider leader turned to aid in the other attacks, only to find that there were no longer any. He summoned one of the lesser officers.

The wolf raider, a bearded veteran named D'Roch who, like most of the men, had to look down at D'Marr, saluted him and nervously explained, "They simply withdrew, my lord. Right after that beast you took down howled."

It seemed odd that they would abandon the attack simply because one of their number had fallen. Such cowardice went against the Aramite way. "How many were there?"

"Counting yours, sir, four."

"Four?" D'Marr frowned slightly. They had only dared expend *four* of their kind in defense of the tunnel against a force the size of his? There was a piece of the puzzle missing. "This place is too lightly defended."

It was clear that the other officer did not think so, but he was wise enough not to say anything.

A soldier returned D'Marr's sword, carefully cleansed of all blood, to him. The young raider inspected the weapon, then sheathed it. The rod would serve him better, it seemed. With the blade, he would be dead long before he finished hacking up one of the beasts. They now feared the rod and D'Marr enjoyed nothing more than wielding fear.

He glanced down at the Quel. It still lived, if only barely. "Bind that thing tight and put it somewhere safe. Lord D'Farany may desire to see it."

D'Roch saluted. "Yes, sir."

"Re-form ranks. I see no reason why we shouldn't continue on, do you?"

"No, sir. At once, sir."

He had them under way in little more than a minute. They continued on down the passage, ever wandering deeper and deeper into the bowels of the earth. Once more, the trek became quiet, uneventful. The wolf raiders remained wary, however, for they had fallen prey to that trap once already.

D'Marr tapped the side of the rod against his leg. *Where are you, you cowardly monsters? Come out and play with me!*

The men began to mutter among themselves. There were whispers of plots involving the collapse of the entire length of the tunnel. The notion had entered D'Marr's mind earlier, but he had felt no need to mention it. Lord D'Farany had given a command and it was their duty to obey. Now, destroying the passageway did not even seem a likely trick, for if they had wanted to do it, he was certain that the Quel would have been better off if they had collapsed the passage earlier. They had not done so, preferring to risk themselves in more personal assaults that, to him, indicated again that something was amiss.

It was at the end of the passage that he found the first clue to the truth. The cavern that suddenly materialized before them took everyone by surprise, so accustomed had the raiders become to the narrow tunnel by that point. D'Marr pushed his way past the foremost rank and stared, his eyes drinking in everything. The mask of indifference barely remained in place, for although he had had time to contemplate the world of the Quel, the Aramite had failed to fully imagine its scope.

In a cavern that was nearly a world of its own, the vast city of the subterranean race silently greeted its invaders.

Enough of it resembled a human city that they understood instantly what it was. There were buildings that rose several stories and paths that could only be roads of a sort. Everything had been carved from the very rock. The path on which D'Marr found himself standing circled around the edges of the expansive cave. At various points, new tunnels branched off into the earth.

There was one peculiarity that would forever forbid anyone from thinking that humans had built this place, for while with great effort it would have been possible for men to carve out part of the city in the cavern walls, no human would have been able to live in places turned at such haphazard angles as these. Hundreds of gaps and outcroppings had been turned into tunnels and quite obvious living quarters, but to utilize them, the inhabitants would have had to virtually hang by their feet and hands at all times at heights that would have meant instant death to even the hardiest. Only creatures with long claws that could dig into rock would be able to make use of so peculiar a design. Only something like a Quel could call this home.

That the invaders could see all of this was the result of yet another marvel. Even despite the fact that they were likely hundreds of feet below the surface, the vast cave glowed as if the sun itself shone above the city. Instead of a burning orb, however, a fantastic array of crystals somehow gave off enough light to fill the chamber with day. Gazing up at them, Orril D'Marr knew that they were somehow linked to the outside, that, in a sense, the sun *did* shine on this subterranean spectacle.

"It appears to be a little larger than we expected," D'Marr muttered to no one in particular. He was beginning to appreciate the Quel and what they had accomplished. He was also beginning to appreciate what he had been sent to face by Lord D'Farany.

Granting him command of the assault forces had not been so much a reward for the information he had recovered from the captive, but rather a punishment for killing the beast before all his knowledge could have been squeezed from him.

Somewhere, he was certain, the blue man was laughing.

As the wonder of the place faded, the reality of what he saw finally sank into D'Marr's mind. *Where are they? Where are the cursed little beasts?*

"D'Roch."

"Yes, sir?"

"Tell me what you see."

The other raider frowned, not certain whether he was the focus of some game his superior was playing. He studied the city for a moment, hesitated, and then replied, "I see a vast underground city, the home of those abominations. It seems to be empty, but that shouldn't be surprising since we've broken through their defenses."

All in all, it was not a bad summation; the only one that could be given. Yet, it did not wholly describe what D'Marr saw and felt when he stared at the city of the Quel. "Nothing more?"

"Nothing."

"And how long ago would you say that it had been abandoned? Minutes? An hour?"

D'Roch squinted as he studied the sight before him again. With great trepidation, the older raider answered, "It seems . . . it seems longer, sir. It seems . . . *much* longer."

Slowly Orril D'Marr walked along the edge of the path. He tapped the head of the scepter lightly against the rock wall. After he had surveyed all he had desired to, the Aramite commander turned his bland visage back to his men. His voice was nearly a whisper. "Much longer, indeed. Look carefully at the dust, at the wear and tear that even a place buried so deep in the earth cannot escape. Think in terms of years. Try, perhaps, even *centuries.*"

There was confusion among the ranks. Word began to filter back. D'Roch and the other officers looked at one another, then at D'Marr.

He laughed then. It was not a pleasant sound, even to his ears, but he could not resist. When D'Marr realized that the others did not understand, he pointed at the city. "You unmitigated oafs! Look at our enemy! There he is! A city of the dead where maybe a handful of survivors still play with the power of their race! We are an army fighting the skeleton of a race!"

They still did not understand, he saw. D'Marr shook his head. He suspected now that there were probably no more than a dozen or so of the Quel, maybe even less. It would explain why only four had attacked them in the cramped quarters of the tunnel when a dozen, a hundred, could possibly have even eradicated them. He thought he understood why they had not collapsed the tunnel; they did not have the strength.

It was possible his suppositions were off the mark, but he was certain he was close. There was only one way to find out. The wolf raider glanced at each of the branch tunnels breaking off from the path circling the city. Most of them were exceedingly ordinary, but one to the right was wider and higher and D'Marr almost thought he saw some light source within.

"Re-form line. Single file," he called back. Then, without waiting to see if they had obeyed his command, D'Marr started toward the other branch. "Follow me."

There *was* a light source at the other end of the tunnel. The passage itself was not a long one, not after the first one, and it was wide enough to let four men pass side by side without being cramped. He had the officers redivide the ranks to accommodate, then pressed on. The glow teased him, taunted him. He was near to the truth, of that he was certain.

As if to add credence to his belief, the Quel renewed their attack.

The ceiling collapsed in the center of the tunnel, crushing several men and battering a number of others. From the hole dropped three of the armored leviathans, long, wicked battle-axes in their paws. Even as their feet touched ground, the Quel were swinging their weapons, taking full advantage of the wider and higher dimensions of this passage.

D'Marr cursed as the nearest ranks were decimated by the horrendous on-slaught of the trio. With their tremendous reach and long weapons, the Quel had an advantage that not even the spears could overcome.

*There are only three*, he scolded himself. *Only three.*

Three they might be, but they were worth three times their number even without the advantages of their weapons. Two of the creatures were pushing back the men advancing into the tunnel while the third dealt with those, like D'Marr, who had been in front of the attempted cave-in.

Still, Orril D'Marr had planned for even worse than this. It was annoying that the creatures had already wreaked such havoc, but it had not been entirely unexpected. Having hunted one Quel, he had devised ways of dealing with them . . . if his men were still capable of following commands.

"D'Roch!" He searched for the other officer and found his battered corpse half buried under the rock from the collapse. D'Roch had probably not even seen his end coming. The loss was more of an annoyance than anything else; it meant that he would have to do the work himself.

Scepter in hand, he moved closer to the battle and shouted, "Keep the lines steady! Get the nets up front!"

A quick glance at the lancers showed that they had already spread out as best they could along the length of the tunnel. His own side was in a much worse position. He had only a few lancers and one of those died, his breastplate and chest sliced open like a piece of fruit, even as D'Marr looked on. His side also had none of the nets, for the men carrying those had perished with D'Roch in the tunnel collapse. There were, however, men with torches. Most of them were using the flames much the way D'Marr planned to, but with far less results than he hoped to have. The frustrated officer grabbed one of the men in the back and pulled him close.

"You'll die wasting your time and mine like that, you lackhead! There's a bet-ter way! Give me that!" He hooked the rod back onto his belt and stripped the blazing torch from the soldier's hand. With his other hand, he reached into one of the small pouches that most raiders wore on their belts. From it, D'Marr removed a tiny leather bag with a single, thin string attached to the top. It was something he had been toying with just prior to Lord D'Farany's decision to take the three ships and flee to the western edge of the Dragonrealm. He had experimented with three just like it only recently . . . and they had performed with perfection, enabling him to scuttle the vast raider ships virtually on his own.

As he adjusted the string, he calmly told the soldier, "Tell them to retreat three steps. Quickly if you please."

D'Marr gave the man the count of five to warn his fellows, then lit the string. It sizzled and began burning down, the flame edging closer and closer to the bag and its contents. When he was satisfied that the string had burned low enough, the Aramite let the small pouch fly.

His aim, of course, was flawless. The bag struck the Quel in the chest, then fell to the ground. D'Marr was pleased to note that the beast's reaction was what he would have expected from a human. The armored creature paused to glance down at the insignificant object, likely both puzzled and amused by the harmless assault.

The bag promptly *exploded.*

It was a much smaller amount than he had used on each of the ships, but it was still enough to tear the Quel to pieces. D'Marr brought his cloak up to avoid the majority of bits that he and his men were showered with. He smiled as he saw that he had been correct; the blast had not been strong enough to further weaken the ceiling. It would have been a bit embarrassing.

To his surprise, however, there was a second benefit to his attack of genius. The remaining Quel were on their knees, their weapons forgotten and their heads almost buried in the tunnel floor. They were hooting madly and rocking back and forth, clawing at the ground.

D'Marr was not one too slow to act when good fortune came his way. "Get the nets in fast while they're stunned. Do hurry."

The agonized creatures were still trouble despite their present state and for a short time he was tempted to take the scepter to each one in order to hurry things. Finally, when it became apparent that the injured Quel would indeed soon be nicely bound and out of the way, the wolf raider turned his attention to the haunting glow mere yards from him. Without hesitation, D'Marr started toward it, his sub-officers quickly following after, albeit with much more trepidation.

*We've stepped into the heart of a diamond,* was his first thought as he froze at the entrance to the chamber. Nothing else he had seen in the glittering realm of Legar, or anywhere else, for that matter, could have prepared him for this. *Is there no end to your surprises, Dragonrealm? First, a glittering land, then a city beneath the surface, and now . . . this.*

The walls were covered almost entirely in crystal, save where three other tunnels led off to other parts of the Quel domain. It was obvious that nature had not created this marvel. There were too many patterns, too many intricate designs, for it to be pure chance. The gemstones also came in a variety of colors that could never have formed together. Staring at it, D'Marr was reminded of the empty city and its light source. The crystals there had been arranged so that the subterranean dwellers could bring the sun to their world. Who was to say that this was not similar?

All this passed through the Aramite's mind in the space of a breath. It was during the second that he noticed the Quel.

The hulking creature leaned across a platform of sorts upon which had been placed a large gem that was in turn surrounded by an array of smaller crystals. The Quel, a male, D'Marr judged, was waving his clawed hands above the arrangement in what was most definitely a desperate manner. Inhuman eyes glared back at the intruders, specifically the young officer. The creature was saying something, his hooting rising and falling with a rhythm that made it impossible not to listen. D'Marr was struck by the nagging thought that the Quel was working to keep their attention.

"I'm afraid that won't work," he quietly informed the armored underdweller. He knew that the Quel understood him by the narrowing of his black orbs. "Your power has been smothered by my Lord D'Farany's might." The raider commander inclined his head toward the officers to his left side. "Take him. Kill him if need be."

As the wolf raiders rushed toward him, the Quel made one last pass over the crystal.

It glimmered. Only for a second, but it glimmered. The spell cast by Lord D'Farany still held, but D'Marr knew it must be weakening badly for something to happen this soon. It was fortunate, he thought, that they had not met any more resistance than they had. The power the beasts controlled was even greater than he had assumed.

The Quel hooted in satisfaction, then stepped away as he was surrounded. Unlike his fellows, he made no move to resist. At another time, Orril D'Marr would have been amused by the absurd sight of the creature calmly holding out his huge arms to be bound, but the Quel's note of triumph disturbed his sensibilities. He studied the chamber carefully, seeking what clue he could not say.

Then it came to him that there were only two other tunnel entrances besides his own. When he had scanned the chamber earlier, D'Marr had been certain that there had been *three*. He turned to the nearest man and asked, "How many ways out of here were there when you came in?"

Looking puzzled and nervous, the soldier glanced around and answered, "I see two, my lord. Besides the one we entered by."

"That's not what I asked." It was futile to explain, the young raider decided. Instead, he stalked over to the area where he recalled the missing entrance being and placed a hand against the wall. It was very solid. D'Marr ran his hand along the crystal, searching for anything that seemed not quite right. As far as he could discover, however, it was very, very real.

Taking the rod, he tapped lightly on the wall. A quiet but solid thud argued against there being a thin, false partition before him. This was a barrier of rock and crystal and a very thick one at that.

He was tempted to test its strength against one of his exploding bags, but knew that the Pack Leader would never forgive him if the chamber was damaged.

"You have my congratulations, Orril."

His round visage carefully banal, D'Marr turned and saluted his master. He nearly grimaced when he saw that the blue man was with the Pack Leader. "I thank you, Lord D'Farany."

The Aramite leader walked slowly into the room, his unnerving features fairly aglow with delight. "Yesss, this is it! This is what I felt!" He put a hand on the platform that the Quel had vacated. "A bit of study . . . and then we shall put it to use."

D'Marr glanced at the Quel as Lord D'Farany finished speaking. If it was possible for one of the monsters to look almost smug, then this creature was exactly that. *You have a secret, my little beast, and it's yours for now. Enjoy that time. When the opportunity arises, I'll take that secret of yours and everything else your mind holds.*

He would be more careful than with the last one. This time, D'Marr would not let death rescue his prisoner. This time, he would squeeze every bit of knowledge from the beast no matter how long it took and how much pain it meant.

As his eyes returned to the glittering wall, he met his own gaze. The multi-faceted crystals made the face behind the gaze a twisted, distorted thing, a creature almost as inhuman in appearance as the Quel . . . and far, far darker within.

# IV

TWO DAYS PASSED while Cabe sought news that might confirm his fears. There was, in that period, no reoccurrence of the vision and as evening of the second day came and aged, he began to have small doubts. Not about what both he and Aurim had seen, but how he had interpreted it.

That very night, those doubts were erased as he slept.

*He was among them again. One of them. Clad in the green dragon-scale armor, they mounted their flying drakes and took to the air. The wind was hot against his face. There was something horribly wrong with the heavens, for there was no blue, but rather a sickly green vying with a bloody red. Clouds swirled like whirlpools and wild, free magic was rampant.*

*The lead rider—his father—turned to him and, in a voice that demanded obedience, called, "Don't dawdle back there! We've far to go!"*

*Suddenly his father's face stretched beyond belief. His body hunched over and his arms and legs became twisted. Wings burst forth from his backside . . .*

*A dragon loomed over him. He tried to turn his drake, but now he lay sprawled on a rocky plain, the animal nowhere to be found. The dragon, huge and terrible, lowered his head and hissed, "You cannot essscape what isss inevitable . . . you cannot escape . . ."*

*Then he, Cabe, found himself in the Legar Peninsula. He had barely time to register it when a shadow covered the land. The warlock raised his head and saw a vast sailing ship, black as pitch, slowly sinking toward him from the very sky. He tried to move, but pain suddenly jolted him. His head was on fire. It felt as if he were being torn apart.*

*Cabe glanced down at his hands, which tingled, and saw with horror that they were stretching, becoming more beastlike than human. Frantic, the spellcaster tried to reverse the effect, but it was as if his magic were no more. He could not even perceive the lines of force from which he drew his power.*

*The looming shape of the black vessel grew larger and larger. The ground beneath his feet trembled. Cabe was certain that he saw movement around him, as if large creatures lurked just below the surface.*

*The ship was almost upon him now. Cabe raised his hands in hopeless defense, then could not help stare at them despite the oncoming leviathan.*

*His hands were reptilian, the clawed paws of a dragon, but that was not what held his gaze so. It was the skin, a dragon hide that fairly glittered even in the shadow of the ebony ship.*

*He had become the Crystal Dragon.*

Cabe woke sitting bolt upright, raw magical energy dancing and crackling at his fingertips. He shivered uncontrollably, not so much because of fear, but because the vision had looked and *felt* so very real.

Slim arms took hold of him in the dark and a concerned, caring voice whispered, "It's all right, Cabe. Nothing was real. Nothing in the dream. You are in the Manor. You're home."

The quivering slowed, then finally ceased. He looked down at his upturned fingers and watched with vague satisfaction and relief as the glow about them dwindled to nothing.

"Cabe?"

"Gwen?" Blinking, the warlock turned toward the voice. His eyes adjusted to the dark, allowing him to make out the dim image of his wife. He conjured a small light instead of using his abilities to adjust his eyesight further. Changing any part of one's form, even temporarily, was a task that required precise concentration for all but a few human mages. It was one area where the drakes would always be superior in the arts of sorcery. He was surprised that he was even able to create the light, considering how turbulent his mind presently was.

She pulled him close and kissed him, more from relief than anything else. They held each other tight for several moments, then Cabe finally broke the embrace. He looked into her eyes. "I had another vision."

"I suspected as much. It's not a memory of the Manor, is it?"

"Hardly." Wiping his hand across his face, he related to her the various images and events he had suffered through. Describing them, however, brought them back to life for him and by tale's end he was shaking again, albeit not near as much as the first time.

Gwen took his hands and held them until long after the shaking had ended. "Something has to be done."

"We both know what, Gwen."

The enchantress squeezed hard. The strength in her hands was amazing. "Don't even think of it, my love."

"What other way is there? This is too demanding. I am either wanted by someone or something or I'm suffering some sort of premonition . . . and it all points to the Legar Peninsula in the end. That means the Crystal Dragon."

She did not want to believe that, he saw. In truth, he really did not want to believe it, either. Of all the Dragon Kings, the Crystal Dragon was the most enigmatic, the most ominous. Even the late Ice Dragon or Storm, the drake lord who ruled Wensils, the marshy, rain-drenched land far to the northeast, were definable dangers. No one knew much about the Crystal Dragon, not even his fellow monarchs. He had stepped in during the last rage of his northern counterpart, Ice, and, with what seemed a simple gesture, had helped turn inevitable defeat into salvaged victory. In the years since then, he had been silent, ignoring the vast changes in the Dragonrealm that steered it closer and closer to being a human world.

"The lord of Legar tolerates intruders in his domain, Cabe, but not when their interest lies in him. His predecessors were all the same, it's said. Secretive and hermitic, yet more than willing to raise their power against those few who dared to disturb them. The Crystal Dragon, whether this one or any of his ancestors, has always been a creature to avoid at all costs. Look what arrogance cost the Ice Dragon."

"I've been to the peninsula before, Gwen, and not always by choice."

"But you never sought *him* out! That's the difference, Cabe! This time, you may end up confronting him! I don't like the thought of that happening!"

The warlock sighed. "I don't like it, either, but what else can I do?"

Gwen paused, then suggested, "Why not go to the Dagora Forest? Perhaps he can help."

"The Green Dragon?"

Her voice took on an urgent tone. "You know he will do for you what he can. At least hear his advice."

He considered her words. Green's borders, now extending into the realm once called the Barren Lands, were close to those of the Crystal Dragon. The Barren Lands had once been ruled by their counterpart, Brown, but after his death, which a young Cabe had unwittingly caused, the Master of the Dagora Forest had claimed them for his own. The Crystal Dragon, in typical fashion, had remained silent on the matter.

If anyone might be aware of something amiss in the peninsula, it would be the Dragon King Green.

"All right, I'll go to him. It's possible that he might be able to explain what's happening to me." Cabe stiffened. "Or to *Aurim!*"

"Aurim!" Gwen released his hands, recalling what her husband had told her about their son's sharing of the vision. The warlock was suddenly alone in bed. It took him a moment to realize what she had done. By that time, the enchantress had already returned.

"He's sleeping," she said, relief paramount in her voice. "Sleeping quietly. This time he must not have shared it with you."

Cabe rubbed his chin. "Why earlier and not now? It doesn't make sense." He frowned. "No, it does. This is no premonition. Someone does want me . . . me alone. It *must* be the Crystal Dragon!"

Gwen took his hands again. "Even if it is, talk to Lord Green first. *Please.*"

"Don't worry; I will." He took her in his arms and the two of them lay down again. "I promise you that."

It was near dawn when Cabe was at last able to relax enough to sleep.

ALTHOUGH HE HAD known the Green Dragon since his earliest days as a spellcaster, it made his audience with the monarch of the great forest land of Dagora no less imposing. He was, after all, facing one of the Dragon Kings, the legendary rulers of the continent. Until his own involvement with them, Cabe would have never believed that the drake lords were in the twilight of their reign. There were few things in the Dragonrealm he found as overwhelming as the draconian monarchs even after having watched their empire crumble to a few deeply divided kingdoms suspicious of each other and of the humans who were taking their place.

Green was different, though. He had accepted the decline of power as a natural course for his race, yet the drake had no intention of merely letting his people fade away. He wanted to see both races working together, for in that was his own future.

Cabe liked to consider the reptilian monarch his friend as well as his ally and he hoped that the Dragon King felt the same way.

"To what do I owe this visitation, Cabe Bedlam? It is not yet the time for a report on the progress of the emperor's hatchlings."

"They fare well enough, though," Cabe informed him. "The same problems still exist with Kyl."

"Of course. He is like his progenitor."

The lord of the Dagora Forest sat in an immense, human-style throne carved from rock and situated atop a marble dais in the back of the vast underground cavern complex that was the lair of his clans. Like so many of the drake race, he had a fondness for the humanoid shape, eschewing his original dragon form for it for months at a time. In Cabe's opinion, the dragon people were becoming more and more human with each generation.

There were those, however, who would argue that and would point out the Green Dragon as their example. Humanoid though he was, the Dragon King was most definitely not human. To the eye, the seated monarch resembled a tall, massive knight clad in dragon-scale armor of the finest detail. He would have been more than seven feet in height had he been standing. In truth, the drake lord resembled more what an elfin lord would have looked like were those folk inclined to such warriorlike garb and not the lighter woodland outfits they wore. The armor was a vibrant shade of green, a forest green that spoke of the strength and majesty of the vast wooded region. It covered the Dragon King from his feet to his neck, only giving way above, where the helm, with its intricate dragon's head crest, nearly covered all else.

It was impossible not to stare at the dragon head, for anyone who stood before one of the drake lords would certainly feel that the head was staring back. The crests of the wolf raiders were crude in comparison. With their long snouts, toothy maws curled back in what was almost a smile, and narrow, seeking eyes, the dragon heads looked almost alive . . . and very hungry. It was not so surprising. The crest was more than simple decoration; it was the true visage of the Dragon King. The face within the helm was a mere parody of humanity. The face *above* the helm was the reality. In fact, the entire image the drake presented was false. What seemed like armor was actually his very skin. The scale armor was dragonscale still attached to the original. His helm could not have been removed, for it *was* his head as much as what was within pretended to be. In attempting to make use of the human form, which they had found so practical for so many things, this had been as close as the male drakes could come. Their progress was slower than that of the female drakes, although no one could say why. Yet, if Kyl and Grath were any indication, the next generation of males had finally crossed the barrier . . . in terms of appearance. Like the Dragon King before him, they still had much to learn about humanity itself.

For that matter, so did many humans.

Cabe forced himself not to focus on the crest, which always tended to draw his eyes first. "I come on a matter of great urgency, my Lord Green, and I thank you for this swift audience. I realize I was very abrupt when I requested it."

The Dragon King lifted his head, and if there had been anyone in the chamber still thinking that the figure before Cabe could be human, now would have crushed any such foolish notion. From within the false helm, two bloodred eyes burned into those of the warlock. Although the helm obscured much, there were glimpses of a flat and scaly visage. There was no nose, only two slits. When the drake lord spoke, his lipless mouth revealed the sharp teeth of a predator. A parody it might be, but the humanoid visage that the Dragon King wore was in its own way almost as terrible because of that.

A narrow, forked tongue darted out on occasion when the Dragon King spoke, yet except for some slight sibilance every now and then, he spoke more clearly and precisely than many humans. "Sssso formal, friend warlock! It truly must be an urgent matter then, if you would speak to me so."

The chamber was empty of all save them, which had been as Cabe had requested. Torches lit the great chamber. Its rock walls were too smooth, which long ago had led Cabe to the conjecture that one of the Dragon King's ancestors had dug it all out. There were plants of all shapes and sizes in the cavern and skillfully woven tapestries, some incredibly ancient, decorated most of the walls. Some Dragon King long ago had worked hard to make his lair a thing of beauty and had succeeded, but the dark-haired mage was by no means calmed by the regal setting. It was never possible to forget that this was the nest of a dragon and had been so for countless generations.

Cabe had debated on a number of ways to begin, but none of them had seemed satisfactory. Being blunt still appeared to be the best route. "My lord, I seek information concerning events in the realm of your brother, the Crystal Dragon."

"Do you?" The Dragon King could not entirely mask his surprise. "And why do you desssire this?"

The warlock stepped closer, stopping only when he stood at the bottom of the dais. He kept his face devoid of all emotion. "I believe something is happening there. I believe it may involve the wolf raiders."

"Aaah?" Now he truly had the drake lord's attention. If there was a threat other than human magic that the Dragon Kings respected, it was the ever-hungry wolf packs of the Aramites. The black ships had been a scourge that even the most cunning of the Dragon Kings had been unable to put an end to. The revolt that had forced the Aramites to abandon their plundering had been a blessing. "Tell me more, friend Cabe."

Cabe told him of the visions, leaving out nothing. The Dragon King was silent throughout. The warlock knew that his host was already considering possible meanings to the visions and what those meanings might demand of him. By the time Cabe was finished, the drake lord had already formulated some thoughts of his own on the subject.

"I have heard rumors, but this . . . It should not surprissse me that the wolf raiders have come to the Dragonrealm. They are your kind at their most tenacious. If they have chosen the lands of my brother Crystal, then I cannot possibly predict what might occur. The lord of Legar is an enigma even to his brethren." The Dragon Kings all called one another brother, but the term referred to their supposedly equal status, not any blood relation. As far as the mage knew, none of the surviving kings were truly brothers.

"Have you no contact with him . . . in any way?"

"He is not one for conversation, human. Ever has his line kept to itself. He does not seek our company, and in truth, we have ever avoided his."

Cabe considered this. "You have *no* contact with him?"

The drake lord bared his teeth, but not because of any anger toward the mage. Rather, he appeared frustrated at himself. "I have no contact, friend warlock. No spies. Through no method have I ever succeeded in divining his purposes . . . if he has any. Do not think that I have not tried. Do not think that my brothers have not tried, too."

"What about the rest of Legar?"

A reptilian smile briefly crossed the shadowed countenance. The Green Dragon straightened, then rose from his throne. Cabe did not step back, as many would have done, but merely crooked his neck and looked up. He knew the Green Dragon well enough to know that the monarch respected more those who stood up to him. "Of the rest of Legar, there is generally nothing of interest, friend Cabe. The land glitters, but it is devoid of a soul. One might as well observe the snow-smothered Northern Wastes, for there is just as likely something happening there as there is in the hot, dry domain my brother rules." The smile died. The Dragon King stepped down from the dais so that he was more or less at eye level with his guest. "Yet, I trust your word and your judgment when you say that now that may have changed. You make me curious for the first time." He paused, then hissed. "If you will join me on a short walk, perhaps there is a way to answer your questions . . . and your fears."

"Where are we going?"

"I have been awaiting the opportunity to test a creation of mine. I see no reason why this should not be the perfect time. Come. It would be better to show it to you before I explain."

The drake lord led him into one of the branching tunnels and through the mazelike passages that were common among the lairs of his kind. Some of the passages were huge, perfect for a full-grown dragon, but others, newer, were designed strictly for creatures the size of a man or a drake in human form. Cabe knew that many Dragon Kings, especially the line that had ruled Dagora, often had human servants, but they did not generally dig their tunnels to accommodate those servants. The smaller pathways had come into existence about the time that the drakes had begun to favor the humanoid forms.

They came at last to a pair of plain bronze doors, something rare in the depths of a dragon lair. The bronze doors indicated how valuable the contents of the chamber behind them were to the woodland monarch. Four guards, all *human*, interestingly enough, were another good sign that any who trespassed here forfeited everything.

At a gesture from the drake lord, the guards stepped aside and the doors swung open. The reptilian ruler waved a taloned hand at the warlock, indicating he should enter first.

Cabe never knew what to expect when he was brought to the Green Dragon's inner sanctum. Each time, something was different. The lords of Dagora had always been scholars, their prime interests tending to run either to the vast history of the continent or the workings of magic as various races used it. There was no one save perhaps the Crystal Dragon who knew as much.

To a mage, the chamber was a collection worthy of envy. Seeker medallions hung next to tapestries by a race whose face and form not even the Dragon King knew. The tapestries were older than anything else and the images always revolved around landscapes that did not exist, at least now, anywhere in the realm. There were bottles filled with specimens of both animal and vegetable origin and row upon row of great tomes, many of which the drake lord had long ago admitted he had yet to decipher.

The Dragon King turned to the guards. "You may close the doors. No one is to enter, no matter what you might hear. That includes everyone."

"Yes, my lord," the men chorused. Two of them took hold of the handles and pulled the bronze doors shut. The Green Dragon's human servants were ever swift and thorough in their obedience, but unlike those who served many of the other drake lords, these obeyed out of pure loyalty. The Masters of the Dagora Forest had almost always cared for their humans as much as they did their own kind.

When they were alone, the reptilian knight turned back to his guest. "Have no concern, Massster Cabe. The warning was more for the sake of our privacy than to hint of any danger to our beings."

"I hoped as much." Despite the words of his host, however, Cabe was not completely at ease. Any venture that involved delving into the realm of the Crystal Dragon had to have at least a tiny element of danger inherent in it.

The Green Dragon stalked toward a small alcove in which a pedestal no higher than the warlock's waist stood. Carved into the flat top of the marble artifact was an array of symbols that looked vaguely familiar to him. The memory was so distant and hazy, however, that he wondered if perhaps it was not one of his own but rather something left over from when he had shared the memories of Nathan.

"This is what I wished to show you. It isss far superior to anything that my brothers have . . . save perhaps the one we seek to learn more of. I have only recently completed its creation; one would almost think that your request had been foreseen by the Dragonrealm itself."

The warlock did not like to think about that. Too often, it seemed that the Dragonrealm somehow controlled his life and the lives of those he cared for. "What does it do? How does it work?"

"An explanation now would pale against the actuality. It is best if you simply observe."

Cabe watched as the Dragon King first passed his hand over the symbols and then touched three of them. Again, a memory of the far past teased Cabe, but he forced it down. All that he knew was that the patterns carved into the pedestal were of a language of sorts, but not the common tongue spoken by humans and drakes. However, there had been many races that had preceded the Dragon Kings and at least some of them had spoken and written in other tongues. In the Dragonrealm, there were even those kingdoms where the written form of Common was undecipherable by any save those who had grown up learning it. When time permitted, he would ask the Dragon King about the markings, but now there were more important tasks at hand.

As he completed a second arrangement of symbols, the drake lord explained some of what he was doing. "The patterns are directly tied to specific forces in the Dragonrealm, almost the way a sorcerer's mind is when he reaches out to use power, but more precisely. There isss less chance for random failure due to a lack of concentration and a greater ability to focus on specific regions or even individualsss." The drake's sibilance grew as he became excited about the subject. "It alssso drains the mage usssing it less than mossst mechanisms becaussse it does not require the great amount of willpower that cryssstals often do."

The Green Dragon performed one more pass over the pedestal, then stepped back.

"What happens now?"

"Wait . . . and watch."

At first, it was only a small black spot. It hovered over the center of the artifact, slowly growing. When it was the size of his hand, its form shifted, making it look more like a dark cloud about to unleash a tempest. He almost expected to see lightning and torrential rains. Slowly, though, the cloud thinned until it was almost transparent. As it thinned it continued to grow. Only when the dark mass was the size of Cabe's chest did it stop. By this point, he could see the wall beyond through it, but other than that, there was nothing, not even the most vague of images. After several anxious breaths, he finally could wait no longer. "Is there something wrong?"

"No," was all the drake replied.

Even as the Dragon King spoke, the thin cloud convulsed. Cabe almost took a step back, but when he saw that the Dragon King was nodding his head, he realized that this was part of the spell. The cloud continued to convulse, but now the changes in its form became specific things. Leaning forward, Cabe held his breath as he realized what he was seeing. The things became true shapes and the shapes became distinct features. Tiny hills sprouted and ravines deepened. The upper half of the vision turned blue as the heavens divided from the earth. The now nearly formed landscape suddenly glistened as light from an unseen source blanketed it.

A miniature world had blossomed into being. No, not a world, Cabe corrected himself, but simply a portion of one. A very familiar one.

It was the rocky, glittering hills of Legar. They floated before the two, not as some flat image, but as a very real place. It was as if someone had stolen a part of the land, shrunken it down, and brought it before them. The warlock wanted to reach forward and see if he could touch it, but he knew that the sight before him was illusion, nothing more.

"What do you think, Master Bedlam?"

"It's . . . nothing's good enough, my lord. The detail is unbelievable!"

"We can focus on even smaller areas. Like so."

The image changed. This time, it had magnified so much that Cabe could now make out individual leaves on one of the few hardy bushes that dotted the viewed region. A small creature no bigger than his hand scuttled from under a rock to the bush.

"That wasss the easy part," his host commented. The Green Dragon's entire body spoke of sudden uncertainty. "What we see is on the very borders of the peninsula. Now, we mussst delve deeper into Legar . . . and that will most certainly invite the interest of my brother!"

"You don't intend to try to contact him?"

"It may be that we can learn what we need to know without resorting to that."

The dark-haired spellcaster glanced surreptitiously at his companion. *He's afraid of the Crystal Dragon!* Immediately after thinking that, Cabe felt ashamed. Not afraid. More wary than afraid. The Green Dragon knew and respected the power of his counterpart to the west. Cabe, having witnessed that power in the past, understood some of what the Master of Dagora must be thinking. No one, not even the most vicious of the Dragon Kings, wanted to invite the wrath of the Crystal Dragon down upon them.

Yet, if the lord of Legar was so great a power in the realm, what did Cabe's visions mean? What was there that might threaten the enigmatic drake lord and the rest of the Dragonrealm as well?

How were the wolf raiders involved? By themselves could they possibly be so great a danger? He wished that he knew more about the Crystal Dragon.

He wished that *someone* did.

The Green Dragon touched the markings again. The image wavered, then shifted as the Dragon King sought to journey deeper into the domain of his counterpart. They saw nothing unusual at first, simply the same crystal-encrusted hills and the occasional bit of plant life. Now and then, a bird flew overhead, likely on its way to more hospitable climes. The image of the first such avian amused Cabe, who almost expected it to go flying beyond the edge of the scene and on into the chamber where he stood.

After several minutes of this, however, the warlock grew impatient. He began to wonder whether the Green Dragon might be just a little hesitant about moving toward the western shores of the peninsula. Cabe very much respected the monarch of Legar, probably at least as much as the drake lord beside him, but Green had not suffered through the visions. Cabe wanted an answer and he wanted it soon. At the present rate of progression, it would be some time before they even reached the central lands, the region where the clan caverns of the Crystal Dragon were supposed to start.

"My lord." His determination slipped a bit as the drake turned his blazing eyes to him, but Cabe persevered. "My lord, can't we leap from where we are now and view the western tip of Legar? If, as I believe, the answer lies out there, then we may discover it and be done with this within a matter of minutes."

The Dragon King vacillated, then, with great reluctance, nodded agreement. "Asss you say, it might indeed speed the matter to an end. Very well, give me but a moment, warlock, and I will sssee what I can do."

Cabe wished he could help, if only to encourage the drake to greater swiftness, but the Dragon King did not ask for his assistance and there was no way that he could offer it without the reptilian monarch taking the offer as a slight to his courage. He satisfied himself with trying to ready his own courage in the face of whatever the magical window revealed to them, especially if what it revealed was the enraged visage of the Crystal Dragon.

"Odd. Very odd."

The warlock glanced up. "What?"

"There is . . . something . . . blocking our view. See for yourself, Cabe."

He looked. Over the pedestal, the image that had earlier been conjured wavered and twisted, becoming more of a distorted shadow of its former self. Superimposed on that vision, however, was another. In that one, a much less

distinct image than even the first had become, Cabe could make out the movement of several figures. Whether they were human or not was impossible to say,
but Cabe stiffened when he realized that all of them were dark, possibly black.

"Sssomething is *fighting* it!" snarled the Dragon King. His unease had vanished, replaced now by annoyance that something had dared wreak havoc with
his creation. He passed his taloned hands over a different arrangement of symbols. The images only became more tangled. Now it looked as if the ghostly
figures were trying to walk through the hills.

"By the Dragon of the Depths!" The furious drake lord tried another arrangement, evidently hoping that some combination of forces would overcome
the unknown obstacle. Both visions dwindled away, this time to be replaced by
a thick, grayish cloud that sparkled as it turned slowly within itself, almost as if
a legion of fireflies had gotten themselves trapped in the maelstrom. The Green
Dragon stepped away, clearly taken aback by this latest result. After a moment
of contemplation, though, he reached once more for the markings on the pedestal.

There was a flash. A sparkling field of light engulfed the unsuspecting drake.

As the flash died, a head filled the air above the artifact; it was the startled
countenance of none other than the Crystal Dragon. There was no mistaking
the other Dragon King. Only one drake had skin that gleamed like diamond.

His body quivering violently, the Green Dragon shrieked and then fell backward; the face vanished.

Cabe leapt to the side of his companion, the magical window all but forgotten in his concern. He knelt beside the drake, who still quivered, and checked
his breathing. It was ragged, but strong enough that the warlock was fairly
certain he would live. Taking the Dragon King's hands, Cabe saw that the drake
had been burned bad in each palm. He used a spell to ease the damage and was
relieved to note that it was successful. Injuries caused by high magic were sometimes impossible to repair.

As he lowered the Dragon King's hands, he became aware of the heavy silence that had befallen the chamber. It was the sort of silence, Cabe somehow
felt, that preceded utter catastrophe.

From where he knelt, the warlock turned.

An ebony hand vast enough to engulf both Cabe and the Dragon King
stretched forth from the pedestal.

Cabe knew that unleashing sheer power at the thing might result in devastation encompassing more than just the chamber, for the Seeker medallions on
the shelves alone likely held enough potent force in them to do that. If his wild
spell destroyed the talismans, that power would also be released. With all that
the Master of the Dagora Forest's collection held, it went without saying that

the medallions would surely not be the only magical artifacts to unleash their long-imprisoned forces.

With no time to consider a counterattack, Cabe chose instead to simply defend. Moving one hand in a swift arc, he surrounded the two of them with a transparent shield. It was basic but potent, one of the earliest spells that he had learned to use by instinct alone.

The fingers of the darksome hand struck the surface of the invisible shield and stopped. Cabe could almost sense the frustration. The guiding force behind the hand was not deterred, however. Readjusting so that its fingers completely gripped the outer limits of the barrier, the malevolent extremity *squeezed.*

Cabe Bedlam knew that the scene above him was merely the visible representation of two spells seeking to counter each other, but it was impossible not to believe that a real hand was slowly closing upon him. His own spell was buckling already, a sign that whoever or whatever fought him was not only adept at sorcery but was able to draw together forces that would have overwhelmed even Cabe, whose own ability was not slight.

Yet, in the end, the shield accomplished its task. Given a precious moment, he now struck back. There was no need to waste further seconds seeking some elaborate solution. Cabe summoned up a spell that was as much a part of him as it had once been a part of Nathan, his grandfather. A golden bow formed before him, a golden bow that had, in the past, killed a Dragon King. It was a legacy from Nathan. The few sorcerers who had been able to create and make use of it, for the binding of the necessary powers was a time-consuming and touchy matter, had been called such things as the Sunlancers, although Sun Archers would have been more appropriate. The spell took much out of those mages and they were often not able to re-create the bow for months after, but one shot was all that was ever needed. As much as it took out of the spellcaster, it took more out of the target.

A single, gleaming shaft, a streak of blinding brilliance, shot forth from the bow. The shaft flew unimpeded through the shield, since they shared both common origin and cause, and struck the menacing hand. Barely slowed, it continued through the palm and out the other end before Cabe could even blink.

As the sunlit arrow exited, the black hand released its grip and thrashed madly in the air above the warlock. Breathing heavily, Cabe strengthened his shield as best he could, but the act proved unneeded, for the hand was already fading, its magic disrupted and, hopefully, its caster painfully regretting his assault on the two. By the time Cabe drew another breath, the magical menace was no more. Had not the Green Dragon been lying unconscious and injured by his side, he almost would not have believed that the attack had ever happened, for nothing else in the room had been touched by it, not even the pedestal.

Secure, the warlock removed the defensive barrier and hurried to the bronze doors. He took hold of one and flung it open. The anxious but ready gazes of more than two dozen guards, both human and drake, met his own. Cabe pointed behind himself. "Get in here, quick! Your master may need aid! I can't promise that my spell of healing dealt with all the injuries he suffered!"

There was much visible apprehension. The Dragon King had never allowed more than a handful of his subjects, be they drake or men, into his sanctum. Fortunately, the health of their master outweighed their fear of disobedience. A half-dozen or so sentries darted around Cabe and seized the unconscious Dragon King by the arms and legs. With great care but also great speed, they carried their master out of the chamber. Cabe assured himself that all was now calm in the room, then followed.

He turned at the doorway and quickly commanded, "No one is to enter again without your lord's permission. There may yet be some danger in there. Is that understood?"

The remaining guards nodded. The spellcaster wasted no more time on them. He knew that the Green Dragon would receive the best of aid from his people and that there was no real need for him to attend, but guilt forced him on after the injured monarch and his attendants. It was his fault that the Dragon King had become involved in this, his fault that the drake had pushed further than had been safe.

Now more than ever, Cabe knew he had to journey to the inhospitable land of Legar. The images and the attack had only fueled his curiosity and resolve. It was not likely, based on what he had seen, that the Crystal Dragon had been at the heart of the attack. Moreover, that Dragon King had looked truly stunned by the intrusion into his kingdom. No, the attack had come from elsewhere, and although it was hardly evidence enough, the black hand that had nearly taken the two of them seemed to speak to Cabe of the wolf raiders. Worse, it spoke of wolf raiders with power, keepers such as the Gryphon had once spoken of. Cabe had thought that the Aramite sorcerer caste was no more; at least, the lionbird had hinted as much.

Whatever it was that threatened from the domain of the Crystal Dragon, he would have to face it, but he would have to face it alone. The Green Dragon was helpless. Gwen, the warlock knew, would desire to join him once she saw that he could not be turned from this, but they had long ago made a rule, one that even *she* would be forced to abide by, wherein one parent would remain with the children during such times. There had to be someone to watch over them. They could not risk both of them and possibly leave Aurim and Valea, not to mention the drakes under their care, without a ready protector. Aurim was too wild to leave in control yet and Kyl . . . Kyl was not ready, either.

There was no choice. Cabe would have to journey to the Legar Peninsula on his own.

*Unless* . . . he hesitated in the passageway, the servants and their burden momentarily pushed from his immediate concerns. There *was* one other he could turn to for help, *if* he could only find him. The trouble there was that Cabe might search the entire Dragonrealm without success, for the one he sought was not bound by this world nor any other. The warlock could not waste the time on such a prolonged search; whatever events were unfurling in the domain of the Crystal Dragon might at any moment come to a head. At most, Cabe could spare a day, maybe two.

Still, it would be worth it if he could find Darkhorse.

"D'RANCE! THERE YOU are. Rummaging through garbage again?"

The blue man, his cloak wrapped around his angular form almost like a shroud, turned to face his shorter counterpart. Unlike the others, his cloak also had a hood, which was presently pulled so far forward that it almost reached his eyes. His helm and gloves lay to the side on a makeshift table he was using for his work. One hand emerged from the obscuring cape and deposited a small, crystalline statuette onto the same table. The chamber that he had chosen for his work—and his privacy—had evidently once been the equivalent of a Quel library, but only a few loose fragments of scrollwork and crystal still remained. D'Rance was of the opinion that the rest had been spirited away by diggers that still remained at large, but he had so far not seen any reason to share his theory with his companions. "I have been here some time, Orril D'Marr, yes, and what I do is not rummaging. My lord has instructed me to inspect all questionable items of the diggers. There may be artifacts of power, talismans, yes, among what you so blindly label 'garbage.'"

The young officer responded with an indifferent shrug. The blue man silently cursed the Quel for being unable to rid his life of the insolent little martinet. He had a knack of stepping in at the wrong times, almost as if he had a sixth sense. Steeling himself, D'Rance grated, "I must assume, D'Marr, that you have some reason for disturbing me, yes? Or is it that you have come to love my company?"

"Something happened . . . some surge from the beastmen's thing, that magical device. *Our* Lord D'Farany requests your presence so that you might aid him in unraveling the mystery. He's been requesting your presence for several minutes now and he doesn't like being kept waiting. You and I both know that."

The blue man turned away from D'Marr and, using the same hand as before, picked up another of the artifacts the blindly obedient soldiers under his command had gathered for him. He pretended to study it, but in reality he had been forced to turn because at that moment it had come close to being impossible to hide the truth of what he was actually doing. The strain would have shown on his face. Unlike D'Marr, Kanaan D'Rance was a creature of emotions, more so than even many of his own kind. *But just this once and only in this matter, I would wish to wear a mask with the skills that you do, little man, yes!*

"I will be but a moment. You need not wait, yes."

"Lord D'Farany's waiting. I think he has something."

Forcing his hand not to shake, the blue man put down the second figurine. He looked over his shoulder. "As I said, I will be but a moment."

A thin smile played fleetingly across D'Marr's countenance. D'Rance knew that it was because one took a deadly chance when one did not leap to respond to a summons from the Pack Leader. It was something that D'Rance had never adjusted to and he knew that only his usefulness to his master had kept him from being punished for his continuous transgressions. D'Marr, he knew, was hoping that this latest might be the final straw. The blue man did not care. He needed a few more minutes before he could dare go before Lord D'Farany. Summons or not, he risked more by responding now rather than waiting until he was better able to compose himself. His secrets had to remain *his* secrets.

He noted how one of Orril D'Marr's hands touched the pommel of the Aramite's favorite toy, the magical rod he liked to use too often on others. The scepter would be the death of him if D'Rance did not kill him first.

"I'll inform our lord of your response."

"Do that, yes."

With obvious anticipation, a silent D'Marr departed. The blue man watched him disappear from sight, then exhaled sharply. He thought of how his counterpart would relate his response to the Pack Leader. There would be much embellishment. D'Rance would have to speak with a silver tongue, but he had always been good at that. It had gotten him across the vast sea to the land of his goals and it would keep him in the good graces of the Pack Leader until the blue man was ready to abandon the raiders to whatever fate was in store for them. *You have shown me much, yes, my Lord Ivon D'Farany, and I thank you, although you could not know just how much you truly taught me, no . . .*

Allowing the cloak to fall away, he stared at the hand he had hidden from D'Marr.

Visibly, there was no sign of a wound, not even the smallest mark. Yet the pain still coursed through him as if someone had thrust a knife into his palm. The hand was twisted into a shape more the parody of a bird's claw than a human extremity. Even the slightest movement caused the pain to increase a hundredfold, but he could wait no longer. He had to straighten it now.

Gritting his teeth, the blue man strained to bend his fingers back. Sweat poured down his forehead as he fought the pain. Slowly, the hand resumed a somewhat more normal appearance, although even achieving that resulted in yet more excruciating torture. In the end, D'Rance could not help moan under his breath. He would somehow find the one who had done this and make him regret it all.

It had been foolish, he knew, to test himself so soon, but the opportunity had presented itself like a gift and the blue man, unable to resist, had leapt in. His reward had been the agony.

*But it goes better,* he consoled himself. *I grow more skilled, yes . . .*

Forcing himself to use his injured hand, the better to begin living with the pain, D'Rance removed his hood. He began to pick up the helm, then thought better of it. Glancing around to make certain that he would not be interrupted, he pulled from one of the pouches on his belt a small looking glass. Raising it to eye level, the northerner held it so that he could see the left side of his head.

A tiny streak of silver in his hair, a streak that had only weeks ago not existed at all, greeted his gaze.

The blue man smiled. He was making definite progress, yes.

# V

"IF YOU THINK that I'll let you make this journey alone, Cabe, then you've not known the true me even after all these years!"

Had he been anyone else, the warlock would have been more than a little fearful at the sight his wife now presented. She was, for the moment, the woodland goddess, the Lady of the Amber, that many still thought her. Power radiated from her. Her brilliant scarlet tresses fluttered with a life of their own and she seemed to stand almost twice as tall as Cabe. Her emerald eyes sparkled bright, twin green flames that, at other times, had driven him to pleasant distraction. The expression on her face he had only seen once or twice in the past and both those times had been when her children had been threatened.

It hurt him to see her like this, for he knew that it was only her love and fear for him that had raised such a fury.

"You know what we agreed, Gwen. It's not for us; it's for the children. It isn't fair to risk both of us. Someone has to be there for them . . . just in case. You were the one who originally thought that up, remember."

"I know." She looked bitter. "But it would be easier if it was me who had to take the risk. Then I'd know that you were safe and watching the children. Whatever I faced, I would be able to face it better knowing that."

"And I wouldn't? Gwen, you know that you're my partner as well as my mate, but this time it has to be me and me alone. The visions came to me—"

"And Aurim."

He conceded her point. "But I think it might be because he and I are so much alike in many ways. The second time, only I saw the images. Besides, I can't take *him* with me. He's not ready . . . unless his control has greatly benefited from the other day."

Gwen managed a smile. "This morning I found one of the stick men wandering through the garden. Apparently, when Aurim tried to reverse his spell, he couldn't keep track of them all and this one escaped. No, even if I was willing to risk our son—which I am *not*—I agree that he is not ready."

"Good."

"But I will not let you go alone, either. At least wait for the Green Dragon to recover."

"It'll be too late. Physically, the attack did little, but magically, it's drained him. He'll be too weak for some time." The warlock strode the length of the bedroom to one of the windows overlooking the gardens. Below, the people whose lives he guided went about their daily activities, only vaguely aware that some important event now occupied the interests of their lord and lady. The two spellcasters had been at this since waking . . . actually, since the night before, when he had broached the subject. He had waited until he was certain of the Dragon King's condition, because he had hoped the same as her. The Master of the Dagora Forest had agreed that the situation was too great to ignore and had wanted to join him, but at the moment he was even less capable of aiding Cabe than the warlock's young daughter Valea was.

"Then I *have* to go with you." She joined him by the window, leaning against his back and putting her arms around him. "We will have to ask Toos to watch the children."

"I can just see that. I have another idea."

"What?" Her tone indicated that any idea would be welcome as long as it meant that he would be safe. Unfortunately, both of them knew that there could be no such idea as long as he planned to journey into the depths of Legar, especially if there were wolf raiders there.

"I'm going to try to find Darkhorse. I think I know where he might be and I think that he would be willing to help."

There had been a time, long ago, when the mere mention of the demonic creature would have brought nothing but a stone silence from the enchantress. Darkhorse was a thing of the Void, an empty place beyond the plane of men. Though he had long worn the form of a giant, shadowy steed, he was more a living hole. His ways were not always the ways of other living creatures, if *living* was a term that could be applied to what he was.

In truth, it was not only what he was that had made him a thing somewhat repulsive to the enchantress, but also the company he had kept. Darkhorse had been a companion to Shade, the warlock whose quest for immortality and power had made him a force swinging from light to darkness with each new incarnation. Only Darkhorse—and perhaps Cabe and Queen Erini, who had come to know the faceless warlock best toward the end—mourned Shade.

Gwen had finally reconciled with Darkhorse, in great part because of his friendship with Cabe. "If you could find him, I would feel much better about this, but that raises the point. How do you hope to find him quickly? He could be anywhere and you yourself said that you really only had this one day, a day we've already used part of. He could be anywhere, even beyond the Dragonrealm, you know."

The dark-haired warlock exhaled. "Other than us, there's only one person he ever truly visits."

"Erini."

"Erini. I'll visit her and ask if she's seen him or has news of him. I only wish I'd thought of it when we were there last."

The enchantress released him and came to his side. She joined him in watching some of the drake and human workers carry a pair of long benches into the depths of the garden. The Bedlams had encouraged their people to make use of the sculpted land, providing they were careful about maintaining it. The population of their tiny domain had grown, however, and so it had become necessary to make some additions and changes to the gardens.

"Melicard may not be too pleased to see you back so soon. I've often wondered whether he still blames us in part for his father."

"Blames me, you mean. Kyrg and Toma were hunting for me when Kyrg brought his army to the gates of Talak." Cabe frowned, recalling the young prince he had first met. At the time, he had shared much in common with Melicard. Both of them had been unseasoned, naive, when they had been thrust into the center of things. It had cost Melicard his father, but at the same time it had cost Cabe more. He had lost not only the elf who had raised him and had been more of a father to him than Azran ever could have, but also, albeit only in spirit, his grandfather. "I suppose it doesn't really matter what the truth is in this case. Melicard is Melicard. We have to live with that and I've got to put up with that when I arrive there."

"Then you had best depart now."

Cabe realized that he had been hesitating, that he could have left minutes before but had talked on. He leaned forward and kissed his wife. It was a kiss that spoke too much of the fact that while they would likely see each other again before he departed for Legar itself, it would only be for a very, very short time.

"Good-bye," he whispered . . . and disappeared.

UNDER NORMAL CIRCUMSTANCES, Cabe would have materialized in one of the greeting areas where dignitaries from other kingdoms awaited an audience with Melicard. Times were not normal, however, and so the warlock chose to instead appear in the most likely chamber where he might find the queen. He hoped to locate her and find out what information he could, then leave before Melicard discovered his presence. It would be easier that way.

Erini took her lessons and tested her magical skills in what had once been an auxiliary training room for the palace guard. Much to his misfortune, though, she was not there this day. Cabe had hoped she had been practicing. It was the right time of day, but he knew that Erini occasionally altered her schedule. Scratching his chin, he contemplated his next move. There were perhaps two or three other places he might find the queen alone, no more. Other than those locations, he stood a good chance of confronting the king, too.

She was not in the riding range nor was she in the next location he visited, the private rooms of Princess Lynnette, only child of the king and queen. Standing among the elegant but fanciful pictures of woodland creatures that decorated the princess's chambers, Cabe quietly swore; he did not have time to go running about searching for Queen Erini. Time was short enough. There was still the monumental task of locating Darkhorse.

He recalled then another place. There was a possibility that the king might also be there, but it was less likely than his remaining choices. He teleported.

She was sitting in a chair, a tiny globe of light shining above her head, when Cabe manifested not more than an arm's length before her. Queen Erini dropped the book she had been reading and gasped, but she was quick-witted enough to recognize the warlock and thereby stifle the scream that would have surely followed.

"Cabe! By Rheena! You know that you are always welcome in my presence, but certainly *this* is rather extreme!"

Queen Erini of Talak did not much resemble the image of a sorceress or a witch as most in the Dragonrealm thought of the type. She seemed, in fact, more the perfect storybook princess. Slim and delicate in appearance, with long tresses the color of summer accenting her oval face, Erini looked hardly out of her teens even though she was long past that time. Her pale features were without flaw. Unlike the day of her last lesson, she was now clad in a more sensible and less formal silver and red dress, one that a person could actually walk around and sit down in. It still had its share of jewels sewn into it and the typical puffed sleeves of royal garments, but otherwise it was actually rather plain. He suspected it was probably her favorite dress for that very reason. When last he had seen her, she had been wearing an elaborate gown of gold, an affectation of her former homeland, Gordag-Ai. It had completed the image of a young queen who should have been more at home doing embroidery in the company of her ladies-in-waiting than attempting to perform a magical spell of moderate complexity. Yet while it was true that Erini was fond of embroidery, she was also a woman who had let it be known long ago that she would be more than a showpiece for her husband, King Melicard I. She was a person who followed her own mind in all things, although she did respect the opinions and thoughts of others, especially her husband.

The king, to the surprise of many in those first years, had argued little. He loved his wife for what she was, not what she represented.

Cabe Bedlam quickly knelt before her. It was likely not necessary, for Erini considered both spellcasters her social equals, but it made Cabe feel better for the shock he had given her. "Forgive me, Queen Erini! I searched for you in the most obvious places and then recalled your fondness for the royal library." The bluerobed warlock glanced around at the impressive array of tomes that had been collected in the oak-paneled room. Other than Penacles, the City of Knowledge, Talak boasted one of the finest collections of writing in the Dragonrealm. The books were, for the most part, copies, however. Melicard had sent scribes throughout the continent on quests to obtain access to whatever bits of writing they could find. At Erini's urging, he was now also having some of the *copies* copied so that others could share in what his people had discovered. "I've come on urgent business so my arrival was a bit more abrupt than I would've wished. I hope that you will overlook my transgression."

"Only if you take a chair and cease to be so formal, *Master* Bedlam." She indicated one of the half-dozen elegant and padded chairs situated in the carpeted room. A slight smile played at her lips. "And you need not fear my husband's presence. He is engaged in some proper time with his daughter, someone he sees too little of considering the great love he bears for her."

"My thanks, Que—Erini." Although Cabe's body was tense with anxiety, he forced himself to sit across from the queen.

The warlock waited until she had picked up her book and put it on the tiny table beside her. The ball of light, which had bobbled about during her initial fright, remained situated above her head. Cabe nodded at the magical lamp. "I see you've been practicing. It's very steady."

"I only wish I'd practiced years ago. To think of the time I've wasted!"

He shook his head. "I wish you'd quit thinking that. Erini, if there's one thing I know, you've not wasted time. You have a husband and a beautiful young

daughter. You've made Melicard a king more accessible to the people's needs."
Cabe waved a hand at the rows of neatly arranged books. "You've encouraged
learning to read. The only access I ever had to reading was what Hadeen the
elf owned. In fact, the only reason I ever learned to read was because of him.
Now, you threaten to make Talak second only to Penacles in the education of
its subjects." He folded his arms. "I could give more examples, but that should
be sufficient."

"I threaten to make Talak second to none, actually," the slim monarch replied. The smile had not only returned, but it had spread. "You are correct,
Cabe, but I still cannot help feeling angry at myself for all those years I left my
power to languish."

"You'd seen too much death and destruction. It wasn't what you were raised
for."

"Neither were you."

Cabe shook his head. "I am Nathan Bedlam's grandson and the birth child
of Azran. If I wasn't raised to be in the midst of trouble, I don't know who
is. Somehow, trouble generally finds me . . . which brings me back to why I'm
here." The warlock leaned forward, his voice quiet. "I'd hoped to find Darkhorse
here. I can detect traces of his presence, but nothing strong enough to tell me if
he is near or where he might have gone. I need his aid, if he's willing to give it,
on a journey into the midst of the Legar Peninsula."

"You are talking about the Crystal Dragon's domain!"

"I am. This is no ordinary trek, either. If it were, I might be willing to travel
alone. Under normal circumstances, the Crystal Dragon would ignore me unless I tried to invade his caverns."

Erini's gaze was steady. "And now?"

"And now, there may be an army camped in the very midst of his kingdom.
An army under the banner of the wolf."

"The Aramites? The rumors are true?" She paled slightly. "I think that perhaps Melicard *should* be here. Commander Iston, too." Iston, a native of Erini's
homeland, had, for the past several years, been Talak's chief intelligence gatherer.

"Please!" Cabe almost jumped from his chair. "Not until I'm gone. Then
you can tell him everything. The important thing is that I need to discover just
exactly what *is* happening. That's why I was hoping to find Darkhorse."

"And if you don't find him?"

"Then I'll go there alone."

Her left hand tightened into a fist and her voice grew deathly quiet. "Gwendolyn would never accept that."

"She won't know until it's too late. I'll make certain of that if I have to,
Erini. I won't have her coming after me."

It was clear that she did not agree with him, but she finally nodded. "As you wish, Cabe. This means that I must help you find Darkhorse no matter what. I would never be able to face Gwen if something happened to you because I failed to locate him for you."

"She'd never hold you responsible."

"No, but *I* would." The queen rose, smoothed her dress with her hands, and stared off into space, her perfect features twisting into an expression of intense concentration. "He's not been here of late and I've not been expecting him. Therein lies our greatest problem. There are two places that we generally meet, though. One lies within the palace and the other far beyond Talak's high walls."

"Outside?" The notion that Melicard would allow Erini to wander beyond the safety of the city rather surprised the warlock.

"If you think that your relationship with my husband has its tentative moments, you should ask Darkhorse about his own experiences. The only thing that truly holds them together is me, Cabe. Melicard is grateful for what the shadow steed did for me when Mal Quorin, my husband's traitorous counselor, sought to take Talak for his master, the Silver Dragon. Darkhorse knows that I love Melicard. Both of them, however, remember the circumstances under which they met, when my husband-to-be had poor Drayfitt snare and imprison the eternal and even torture him in his quest to make Darkhorse his servant."

Cabe shivered. He recalled that. Darkhorse was not a forgiving sort, either, not that anyone could blame him.

"Sometimes, especially when I am around, they are very cordial, almost friendly, but their mutual past always returns. That's why there are times when it is better to visit Darkhorse in a place far from the eyes of my husband. I love my husband but I will not abandon my friends . . . as you know."

"I do." Rising, the blue-robed spellcaster readied himself for what was to come. "Where's the first location? The one in the palace."

"My private rooms." She took his hand. "Please. Allow me."

Even as the queen finished speaking, the scene around them shifted. They now stood in the midst of a vast, elegant suite of the like that made Cabe stare in open awe. Huge columns stood in each corner of the chamber, the white marble decorated with golden flowers so lifelike he at first thought them real. The floor was also marble, but of different colors arranged in a beautiful abstract pattern. Long, thick fur rugs ran from the massive wooden bed to each of the four doorways. Where there were no doors, gay tapestries decorated the walls. A row of closets spoke of the volumes of clothing royalty wore, as did the wide mirror to the side of the closets.

The bed and the rest of the wooden furniture in the suite had all been carved from the now-rare northern oak. The wood had not been so rare at the time of their creation, but the winter of the Ice Dragon had created enough damage that the oaks had still not yet recovered. Despite the magic that had been used to reverse the effects of the magical winter, the most northern places had still suffered much too much.

As impressive as his surroundings were, they paled in comparison to what the queen had just done. "You did that without flaw, Erini! I waited, thinking I'd probably have to help you along, but you brought us here as if you'd been practicing for years."

"No, for some reason I find that spell easier to perform. It only took me three or four attempts to master the proper concentration for it. Why is that, do you think?"

Cabe shrugged. "Gwen is the one who usually has the answers. With me, magic came almost full-blown. That saved my life in the beginning, but it means I never really had the incentive to learn *why* spells work the way they do. Gwen's taught me much since then, but that still doesn't mean I understand completely." He gave her a rueful smile. "Which is why for the fine points, my wife has been instructing you."

"You have both been excellent teachers."

"I muddle through." The warlock again glanced around at the sumptuous apartment. "A room definitely fit for a queen, Erini."

"It is exactly the way it was when I first arrived in Talak. Such a waste of a room," the queen commented dryly. "Since I do not sleep here, the only use it usually gets is when I must be dressed for yet another interminable ball for some ambassador and the necessary gown is not among those in my closets in our royal suite. Still, there are times when it's nice to be alone . . . and it gives Darkhorse and me a place to talk. The library is too cramped, too."

"Then why do you need the other location? This seems private enough."

"Darkhorse rarely talks below a roar, Cabe. You should know that." Erini strolled around the room, visibly recalling memories. Cabe knew that this was where she had first stayed after her arrival in Talak. This apartment had been her refuge in the days when she had first struggled to be accepted by the disfigured king, whose torn mind had been further turned to the dark by his malicious counselor. He did not doubt that she kept it as it was rather than alter it to some other use simply *because* of those precious memories.

As loath as he was to interrupt her reverie, he knew he had to. The day was advancing quickly. "Your Majesty . . . Erini . . ."

"Yes, he is not here, of course." Her memories put aside for now, the slim monarch pondered the matter at hand. "That only leaves the hills. I wish I could be more help to you. Can you not follow his trace?"

"Too old and too faint. It also crosses itself so many times, I couldn't tell which way he went last. If he teleported, that makes it even closer to impossible."

"And I thought magic made everything easy."

"Sometimes it makes things more convoluted and frustrating, not to mention life-threatening. There're times when I wish I was back in that tavern, still waiting on tables and getting threatened by half-drunk ogres. Dragon Kings, Seekers, Quel . . . I could do without all of them."

"But not without the Lady Gwendolyn, I imagine." The queen moved to the center of the room and reached out a hand to him.

"Makes everything else worthwhile." Cabe took her hand and steadied himself, more comfortable now that he knew that Erini was adept at this spell.

"I hope you tell her that on occasion," Erini responded even as their surroundings shifted from the planned elegance of civilization to the raw beauty of nature. She released his hand and stepped away from him in order to better survey the region. The hills were actually the beginning of the Tyber Mountains, but somewhere in the planning, they had been cheated of the great height of their brothers. While few folk ever cared to make the journey through the treacherous chain, the hills did garner some traffic of their own. There was good grazing land here, not to mention the only decent wood within a day's ride of the city. Talak, for all it had, was forced to go to its more outward lands to fill its wood needs.

There were dangers here, of course, but generally only the ordinary ones such as wolves and the rare wyvern or minor drake. Since the death of the Dragon Emperor, Melicard's vast forces had worked hard to clear every corner of the kingdom of the monsters and larger beasts that had once preyed on travelers. For the most part, they had been quite successful.

"I was afraid of this, Cabe. I doubted he would be here, but it was the only place left that I could bring you."

He nodded, his smile one of resignation rather than pleasure. "I didn't think it would be easy. I've got a few other ideas, but I was hoping that I'd find him with or near you."

Erini was downcast, but then her face brightened. "I can *help* you search for him! The teleportation spell is my best. I should have thought of that before. It will cut your searching by nearly half!"

"No."

"*No?*" Her tone became frost. "Do you think to command me, Cabe?"

"In this instance, yes, *Your Majesty.* You are too important to Melicard, Talak, and, because of both, the rest of the Dragonrealm. If anything happened to you, what would the king do? Think on that before you answer me."

She did. He watched as her face fell. Both of them were too familiar with

Melicard's moods. It was Erini who had changed him for the better, but those changes might slip away if she was injured or even . . .

Her eyes suddenly widened. "There's . . . I think there might be one more place to search, Cabe. It's a thin possibility, but it just might be . . ."

"Where?"

"I'll have to take you there; it's . . . it's the only way to make certain we arrive at the proper location."

The warlock caught the hesitation in her voice. "Where *is* it, Erini?"

"In the *Northern Wastes.*"

"I forbid you from coming! Tell me approximately where and I'll go there my—"

Erini stalked up to Cabe and gave him her most royal glare. He hesitated just long enough for her to interject, "You can forbid me nothing this time, Cabe Bedlam! As frustrating as it is to me personally, I concede to you that it would be better for us if I did not risk myself! I love Melicard, but I agree that if I were injured or even came close to harm he might, in his unreasoning anger, do something that we would all regret! I have a very good reason, however, for needing to lead you to this one last location. The Northern Wastes are nearly half the size of the rest of the continent and far more troublesome to search. You could pass within yards of the area and not see Darkhorse standing before you. I can lead you to the exact spot; like him, I will never forget it."

Her skin was pale and her body trembled. Queen Erini stared at Cabe in such a manner that he knew she would have actually preferred *not* to make this final trek. Only the importance of his mission compelled her to do so.

"What is this place, Erini?" he asked quietly. "And why would it have such a hold on both you and Darkhorse?"

"Because it is where the warlock *Shade* died."

HE HAD NEVER been able to convince himself that the blur-faced warlock was dead. At the same time, he had never been able to convince himself that Shade was still alive.

So Darkhorse had searched the world and beyond for nearly a decade, always wondering if the human who had been both his friend and enemy was merely one step ahead of him, watching and waiting for the proper time to emerge. One part of the shadow steed hoped and prayed that the weary sorcerer was at last at peace. The other missed the good incarnations of the man, for only Shade had ever come close to understanding Darkhorse's own emptiness.

Which was why, Erini told Cabe before they departed for the Wastes, he often stood for days at the site where the warlock had simply faded away after expending all his might in a last effort to make up for what he had become.

When they materialized in the midst of the freezing, windwracked tundra of the Northern Wastes, it was almost as if he had been waiting for them. The queen brought them to a point barely ten feet from where the huge ebony stallion was situated.

Darkhorse slowly turned his massive head toward them. His ice-blue eyes seemed to burn into the warlock's very soul. The eternal's voice was a thunderous rumble even despite the rather subdued tone. "Erini. Cabe. It's good to see both of you. This is not a place for your kind, however."

"We . . . we came in . . . in search of you, Darkhorse," the queen managed.

Studying her, Cabe Bedlam grew worried. Erini was a competent sorceress, but it was possible that she had overextended herself. He had provided himself with a heavy cloak to offset the cold, but she had not done the same even though the need should have been obvious. The warlock quickly remedied the situation.

Erini gave him a weak smile. "Thank you."

Darkhorse's hooves kicked away snow and ice as he moved closer. At his present height, he was half again the size of a normal steed. Size, however, was irrelevant to a creature who could manipulate his form in ways no other shapeshifter could. Had he chosen, the ebony eternal could have become as small as a rabbit, even smaller. He need not have resembled a horse, either. Somewhere in the far, forgotten past, Darkhorse had hit upon the form and found it to his liking. The black stallion rarely shifted anymore, although occasionally his body would resemble more the shadow of a horse than the real animal. Cabe had decided that this last was an almost unconscious action. There were things that were normal for a human to do; the same likely could be said even for as unique an entity as the black leviathan before them.

"You should not be out here in the cold, Queen Erini!" roared Darkhorse. It was almost necessary to roar; the wind had picked up. A storm was building. It was hard for the warlock to believe that anything could live in the Northern Wastes, but many creatures did. "We should return to Talak! It will be much more cozy there . . . at least for you two!" The demonic steed chuckled.

"I—" was as far as Erini got. Suddenly she was falling toward Cabe. He caught her at the last moment and stumbled back under her sudden weight. Darkhorse's eyes glittered. He trotted a few more steps toward them.

"What ails her?"

Cabe adjusted his grip. "She pushed herself too far! She insisted that she be the one to bring us here and like a fool I agreed!"

Darkhorse snorted. "I doubt you had much choice with her! Best take her back to her chambers quick!"

"The private ones where you two sometimes meet?"

"You know them? Good! Take her there! I shall follow! Perhaps, if we are fortunate, good Melicard will be out running down drakes or some such foolishness! Hurry now!"

Tightening his hold, the warlock teleported—

—and found himself face-to-face with *King Melicard*, who stood within the suite, one hand on the door handle. Another moment and it was likely they would have missed one another, for he was turned as if just planning to depart.

There were still those to whom the lord of Talak was an effrontery or even a thing of horror. Melicard no longer cared what those people thought. Erini and Princess Lynnette were the only two whose opinions mattered to him and they, of course, loved him dearly.

Despite the yoke of leadership he had worn for almost two decades, Melicard at first glance still looked very much like the handsome young prince that Cabe, with his own rather ordinary features, had always secretly envied. Tall and athletic with brownish hair just now turning a bit to gray, he had once been the desire of many a woman, both royal and common. If Erini was the storybook princess, then Melicard, with his strong, angular features and commanding presence, was the hero of the tale.

He was still handsome . . . but now more than half of his face was a magical reconstruction. The left side from above the eye down to the lower jaw was completely *silver* in color, for that was the natural shade of elfwood. Much of the nose was the same and there were even streaks of silver stretching across to the right side, almost like a pattern of roots seizing hold of what little good flesh remained of the king's visage.

Magic had stolen most of his face and because of that, the damage had proved impossible to repair. Only elfwood, carved into a reproduction of his very features, could give King Melicard the illusion of normalcy. The wondrous wood, blessed, so legend said, by the spirit of a dying forest elf, was capable of mimicking the movements of true flesh. The more the wearer believed in it, the better it pretended. It could never replace what had been lost, but for Melicard the choice had been the mask or the monster beneath. For the sake of his own sanity and the princess he was to marry, Melicard had chosen the former.

He was clad in a black riding outfit that covered him from neck to foot, including his hands. Melicard generally wore outfits with long sleeves and always used gloves, but not for reasons of fashion. The ravaging forces that had taken much of his face had also taken from him his left arm. Had he removed his gloves, Cabe knew that the king's hand would also be silver. The king could not so easily disguise his features, but he could at least hide his arm.

"Warlock! What are you—" His eyes, both real and not, focused on his beloved queen. "Erini!"

"She'll be all right, Your Majesty," Cabe quickly said. "Just help me carry her to the bed, if you please."

Melicard was already moving. The two of them helped Erini walk to the bed; the novice sorceress was not actually unconscious, but seemed lost to the world around her.

When they had her lying down comfortably, Melicard hastened to the door and flung it open. Cabe, glancing up, saw two very nervous guards come to attention.

"Get Magda!" the disfigured monarch roared. "Get Galea! Get someone for the queen! She's been hurt! Now!" He did not wait for them to respond, but rather turned immediately back to the bed, slamming the heavy door shut behind him as he did.

Cabe immediately stood up and faced him. He could not allow Melicard's anger any leverage. He had to meet the king man-to-man and make him listen.

It was at that time that Darkhorse made the unfortunate decision to materialize. Melicard fell back from the newcomer, but Darkhorse did not notice him at first. "Does she fare better? How—" The pupilless eyes froze when they fell upon the furious king, who stood against one side as if the shadow steed filled the entire room. "Melicard . . ."

"I should have known you would be involved, demon! You may be virtually indestructible, but my queen is not! My Erini—"

"Is to blame for her troubles, my love."

The three turned to the bed, where a still pale Erini was forcing herself up to a sitting position. She succeeded only as far as leaning on one elbow. Lines of strain marred her beauty.

"Erini!" Melicard, forgetting any pretense of dignity, ran to the side of the bed and hugged the queen.

"Gently, dear Melicard," she gasped. "I'm not yet fully recovered."

"Praise be!" Darkhorse bellowed. "You had us all fearful, dear Erini! You must take greater care in the future!"

"Greater care . . ." The king turned to face the warlock and the steed. "What did you make her do?"

"They . . . they did nothing, Melicard. I overextended myself. Cabe would have performed the spell, but I did not think he would find Darkhorse. I knew exactly where he would be if he was anywhere in . . . in that region."

"Where *were* you?" He touched her skin. "You're cold, Erini; I should have noticed that sooner . . . you've been to the *Wastes*, haven't you?"

It was clear it was a strain for her to keep speaking, but the queen was not one to let others take the blame when she considered herself at fault. Cabe felt guilty that he allowed her to continue, but if anyone could make the ruler of Talak see reason, it was Erini.

"Listen to me, my love. I have to tell you everything the first time. I do not have the strength to repeat myself. Do you understand?"

Much of Melicard's anger dwindled away as he realized what effect his fury was having on her. Still holding her, he sat down on the bed. "Very well; I'm listening, my queen."

They were interrupted by a knock on the door. An older, plump woman, one of Erini's two longtime companions from her former homeland, peered inside anxiously. "Your Majesties . . ."

Erini steadied herself. "Please wait without until I call for you, Galea. It will be but a moment."

It was not to the woman's liking, but she nodded and withdrew. The queen's ladies were very protective of their charge, especially Galea and Magda.

"Now," began the queen. "Let me tell you what happened, my beloved."

She told him everything, glancing at the warlock for understanding. Cabe nodded; he agreed that there was no longer any reason to keep the purpose of his mission a secret. Melicard deserved the explanation even if, to the warlock, it might complicate something already too complicated. The king's face was a mask in more ways than one now. Neither the real nor the elfwood side betrayed any emotion. Melicard was simply absorbing the facts. Afterward, when he had had a chance to consider what she had relayed to him, he might again become the living fury he had been a moment ago. The warlock hoped not, but there was no predicting Melicard. He would have to wait and see.

Erini was forced to pause several times in order to regain her strength, but at last she finished. More drained than before, the exhausted queen fell back onto the bed. Melicard rose to call her ladies in, but she reached up, put her hand on his, and said, "Not just yet, my lord. Let us finish here first. I'm only tired; nothing more. I promise you."

"You're certain, Erini?"

"I am."

"I would never let anything happen to her, Your Majesty," Cabe added. "My power stands ready to aid her if necessary. She's overtaxed herself like she said. It can happen . . . I know that too well . . . when a fairly new mage succeeds too quickly with some spell. I apologize, however, for letting her go as far as she did. That was *my* mistake."

"Erini has a stubbornness worthy of me!" commented Darkhorse. He was more his old self now. Cabe was thankful for that; if his old friend agreed to join him, he would need Darkhorse at his best. Distracted, he could become more of a danger, for Cabe would then himself be distracted from his course.

"When she chooses to do something, she does it! One might as well ask the Tybers to move aside for them rather than convince the queen to change her mind on certain subjects!"

"I am . . ." the king began, "very much aware of my wife's qualities. Foremost of those is a tendency to be open and straightforward with the truth. That and her beauty were what struck me that first day we met as adults." He turned to face the two. His expression was calm, but his tone was just slightly cold. "I take what she says now as the true and complete story . . . as she knows it. You have my apologies, Master Bedlam, for my accusing you of being responsible for her condition."

"There's no need to apologize, Your Majesty. Under the circumstances, you reacted as anyone might have."

"Indeed." King Melicard rose. "And now that you've found what you were searching for, Master Bedlam, I am sure that you must be on your way. This news of Legar and the wolf raiders I will pass on to Iston. I will respect your mission. We will do nothing for now except watch. When you've discovered what you can, I would appreciate being told."

They were being asked to leave and leave now. Melicard's words teetered on the edge of bluntness, but at the same time he was sounding civil. It was all that could have been expected from him at a time like this. Cabe was more than ready to depart. As the king had almost said, he had found *who* he had been searching for. *Thank the stars Darkhorse didn't take him to task for that slight!*

"I was glad . . . glad to be what help I could, Cabe," whispered Erini from the bed. She managed to lean up a bit. "Good luck."

"And where do we go from here, Cabe?" asked Darkhorse. There seemed no question in his mind that he would follow the sorcerer to the inhospitable peninsula. Darkhorse was very loyal to those he considered his friends.

"Thank you, Erini, and you, too, Darkhorse. First to the Manor, I suppose, to let Gwen know I've found you. Then, I think on to Zuu."

"Zuu?"

Much to Cabe's surprise, it was Melicard who answered the demon steed for him. "Zuu would be appropriate. There is no human city closer to the domain of the Crystal Dragon. They may have some word there that has not reached us yet." He hesitated, then added, "Good luck, Master Bedlam."

The warlock bowed. "Thank you, Your Majesty. It may be that this will be simple and swift. The danger may be limited. There *is* something going on there, though, and for reasons I don't understand, I seem to have been included."

"Have no fear now, Cabe!" Darkhorse roared. "With me at your side, it is our foes who must worry!"

The demon steed's brash confidence, while not enough to change Cabe's own dour opinion on the matter, still succeeded in bringing a smile to his face. It was hard not to be at least a bit more hopeful when he was with Darkhorse.

"Give Gwen my love," Erini added from the bed.

"I will." He looked at his unearthly companion. "Are you ready?"

"I was ready long ago, Cabe! I look forward to this adventure with great anticipation!"

The warlock concentrated. "I'm glad someone is."

Darkhorse was still laughing when they vanished.

AT THE SOUTHEASTERN edge of the land of Irillian, a longboat from the lone black ship slowly made its way toward shore. The black ship had waited until just the right time to come close enough to deposit its cargo. There were those who would have gladly sunk the vessel without so much as a question or a warning. Its mere presence, even in the distance, would have sealed its fate no matter who had been aboard.

There were three aboard the longboat, all of whom wore heavy cloaks designed not only to protect them from the spray and rain, but also, if need be, to protect their identities. Only one rowed; the other two sat and watched, wary.

They did not beach the longboat. Instead, when they were near enough, the two passengers climbed out into waist-deep water and waded their way toward shore. The third figure slowly began to turn the boat around so that he could return to the other vessel.

Both passengers moved swiftly through the sea. Their reactions were those of folk who little loved the water and suffered it now only because it was necessary. When they were at last on the beach, the duo shook themselves off, the wild wind and their cloaks making them look like the specters of dead seamen rising from the depths. They then turned and briefly watched their companion row back to the dark hunter. Satisfied that the ship would depart undetected, the two quietly conferred and then started inland, the taller one leading the way.

The journey ahead would be long and tiring, but they were undeterred by that thought. All that concerned them was the reason that had brought them to this shore in the first place. They were hunters, both of them, and they had come to the Dragonrealm because that was where their prey was. Whether it took ten days or ten years, they would complete their quest, for with them it had also become an obsession. Either they succeeded or they died. Living with failure did not occur to them; it was not their way. Either their prey was vanquished or they were killed in the attempt. Those were the only choices.

At the top of a rise overlooking the cloud-enshrouded, rolling landscape of southern Irillian, the lead figure stopped. He motioned to the other, then pointed to the far southwest in a direction that would take them on a route north of the distant city of Penacles. His companion nodded, but said nothing. They had discussed the route in advance. They knew their destination and how long it would likely take to reach it. All that mattered now was getting there without being discovered, a difficult task, but not an impossible one for two with their skills.

Confident and determined, they began both the climb down the other side of the rise . . . and the final leg of their journey to the Dagora Forest.

# VI

"I STILL DO not see why we cannot just teleport to where you want to search in Legar and then leap back!" Darkhorse grumbled. In order to converse with Cabe, who rode on his back, he had twisted his head around in a manner that would have broken the neck of any true steed. Fortunately, it was dark now and they were some distance from the actual city, having materialized so far away for safety's sake. Mages were still a rare and gossip-stirring sight. The warlock wanted no interference with his mission.

Cabe sighed and adjusted the hood of the traveler's cloak he wore. The hood was the only way he could properly hide the great stretch of silver in his hair. Dyes merely washed away before they even had time to set. It was said that a god had created the mark as a symbol of his respect for the legendary Lord Drazeree, who had borne a similar streak, but if so, Cabe thought that the least the unthinking deity could have done was allow for times when a spellcaster *had* to hide his nature. Mages were always forced to resort to hats, cloaks, helms, and rather touchy illusion spells to obscure the silver. There were times when that made their lives tricky.

"You weren't there when the Green Dragon was struck down, Darkhorse. I don't want to go blindly into Legar. We need to move with stealth. I also want to see if I can find out any information beforehand. It's possible that not all news has made it back to Talak yet."

"You should have asked Melicard to give you the names of his spies! We could ask them and be done with it!"

"I'm sure that would've pleased the king. Now, for the last time, you'd better start behaving like a real horse. I'd like to avoid too much notice; it's possible that the wolf raiders, if they are in Legar, might also have spies in Zuu."

The shadow steed snorted and turned his head to a more savory position. Cabe relaxed a little. For a creature who had lived for thousands of years, the eternal could be very impatient at times. Tonight, he was even more restless than was normal. The warlock was certain that Darkhorse's anxiety focused around

Shade. Darkhorse had done little in the past few years besides search for traces of the ageless sorcerer.

They would have to talk about this some time in the future. Whether Shade was truly dead or not, Darkhorse could not spend eternity thinking about it. He had to be made to see that there were other matters—and friends—waiting for him.

"There is the city," whispered Darkhorse. Unfortunately, his concept of whispering still resembled more of a shout.

"I see," Cabe responded quickly. "We'll have to be doubly careful. We may encounter other riders at any moment."

His ploy worked. The demon steed nodded and resumed his role of faithful horse.

To the eyes of another traveler, one who carried a good torch, that is, the two would resemble a weary rider and his large ebony stallion. Darkhorse had shrunk down to a more tolerable size, although he was still large for most breeds. Cabe, meanwhile, was clad in a simple gray outfit consisting of pants, cloth shirt, knee-high leather boots, and the aforementioned riding cloak. While his outfit was a bit old-fashioned, it was not an uncommon sight. The style was a throwback to his life near the now ruined city-state of Mito Pica, which had been destroyed by the Dragon Emperor's forces for having unknowingly secreted a young Cabe Bedlam. Many survivors had become wanderers since then, even almost two decades after the event. Hence, the warlock would look like one of the youngest ones finally grown up. Most people respected the privacy of such wanderers, especially the people of Zuu.

Cabe had never journeyed to the low, sprawling city of Zuu, possibly, he now admitted to himself, out of some small guilt. During the brief war that had been instigated by the Dragon Kings' search for him, the rather independent-minded folk of Zuu had sent a contingent of their famous horse soldiers to the aid of Penacles. The young warlock vividly recalled the band of huge blond warriors clad in leather and how they had wanted to come to his aid when airdrakes had flown down and attacked Cabe and Gwen. He especially remembered their leader, a scarred man named Blane, the second or third son of the king at that time.

Blane had died defending Penacles, but not before he had killed Duke Kyrg, the drake commander and brother to Toma. It was no surprise that Talak and Zuu were on excellent political terms with each other, not that such prevented each from having their share of spies.

Blane's brother, someone named Lanith XII, was now king, but Cabe had no intention of introducing himself to the man. If things went according to plan, he wanted to be out of the city before morning. That meant little or no sleep, but to a spellcaster of his ability, one night missed meant nothing. For the past several years, he had enjoyed a full night's slumber all but a handful of days. In truth, Cabe did not miss the sleep so much as the peace and quiet.

He gently prodded Darkhorse's sides, the signal for speed. There would be no peace and quiet tonight nor likely the next.

Zuu lay in a valley that was vaguely bowl-shaped. Around it were miles and miles of grassland. The nomadic founders of the city had chosen this location for the latter feature. Horses had been and still were the most valuable possession of any citizen of Zuu. Merchants from all over the continent came to this region to purchase the best animals.

Because of their obsession with their horses, it was not so surprising to Cabe that even in the dark Zuu resembled one endless array of stables. With few exceptions, no building generally topped more than two floors. Most of the structures had a boxy appearance that was evident even from where the warlock was. Adding to the effect was the one drawback to having business in the city: Zuu also *smelled* like one vast stable.

Cabe had wanted to avoid spells, for they had a way of drawing the attention of other mages, but he could already see that the odor was going to become more pungent with each successive step nearer. With a single thought, he adjusted his sense of smell. He did not go so far as to make the odor pleasant, but he made it less noticeable. That required less manipulation. Cabe disliked using sorcery to alter his form. It was there that a mage could cause himself irreparable harm; his concentration might waver just enough that his spell would go awry. There were legends of spellcasters who had died like that. Too often, the ease with which some learned magic made them too careless.

It was not long before they approached the city gates. Up close, Zuu was a well-lit city, a sign of its prosperity in the horse trade. Behind the walls, Cabe could make out some of the nearer structures. Zuu did not have high walls to protect it; the people relied on their own skills. There were few forces, either drake or human, who willingly went against the horsemen of Zuu. Not only were they expert riders, but they could fire arrows or throw spears with amazing accuracy even when their horses were at full gallop. More important, it was not just the men an enemy had to be wary of. Under Zuu law, every adult, male or female, was a fighter. There were many women in this city who could have stood among the finest warriors in the land. Even the children could be dangerous should a battle somehow reach behind the walls. The citizens of Zuu were of the opinion that it was never too early to teach a child how to defend his own.

It was something to consider, especially since six of those horsemen were now waiting for him at the gate.

They were typical of what Cabe had known. Tall, blond, and looking as if they had been riding since birth. Most of them were wearing leather pants and jerkins, the latter not entirely succeeding in covering their bronzed chests. They wore short helms with nose protectors, but otherwise no armor. Not all the inhabitants of Zuu resembled the nomadic image, but the city guards most certainly did. Many of them were likely the latest in a long family line of city guards. People here tended to follow in their parents' footsteps . . . or maybe horsetracks.

The evident leader, a somewhat heavier man with a blond and gray beard, urged his horse toward Cabe. He was followed a few steps behind by another rider who carried a torch. The other guards had their bows ready. The warlock wondered if he could teleport away fast enough if he somehow offended them. The archers of Zuu were not only accurate; they were swift.

"Welcome, stranger! What do you have to declare, eh?"

There had been the temptation to simply materialize in the midst of the city and forgo meeting the city guards, but despite its reputation for respecting the privacy of its visitors, Zuu paradoxically also liked to keep track of everyone. Had he given in to the temptation, Cabe soon might have found himself the object of several curious and suspicious soldiers. No, passing through the front gates like a normal traveler would much better aid him in the long run.

"Only myself and my steed. A few supplies for travel, but nothing else."

The guard leader was eyeing him up and down. "You've never been to Zuu, have you, man?"

Had he done something wrong? "No."

"Hilfa." At the summons, a sentry from the back of the group rode forward. A woman. She was perhaps a year or two younger than the warlock looked, tall, and just as capable-looking if not more so than some of her companions. Modesty, Cabe saw, was not a strong point of the folk here. Hilfa wore the same outfit as her companions, which made for some distraction above the waist. She seemed unconcerned about his slight embarrassment. How foreigners acted was only a concern if they broke the law.

When she was even with the guard captain, Hilfa waggled the bow in her hand, a salute of sorts to her superior.

"Give him a marker."

Reaching into a saddlebag, the woman quickly produced a small, U-shaped talisman on a chain. This she tossed to the waiting spellcaster without preamble. Cabe had to move with swiftness to catch the marker before it fell past him.

The leader pointed at the talisman. "That's your marker. Carry it with you at all times, either around your neck or in your pocket, but carry it, man. When you buy somethin' or talk to anyone from our city, produce it."

Cabe inspected it. There was a touch of magic to it, but so little it could not be meant to harm him. Unwilling to remove his hood, he thrust the marker into a belt pouch. Zuu evidently had one or more mages who worked for them. An interesting aspect he would remember for the future. How many more were there and what were *they* doing?

"Let him pass."

Hilfa backed her horse up, allowing the sorcerer access. As Cabe rode by, however, she reached out and put a hand on his. He looked at her. Up close, she had strong features, but not unattractive ones. Like many of the inhabitants, Hilfa looked like she was related to her companions. "That's a remarkable animal you have there. I've not seen one like that anywhere. What breed is it?"

"It's unique. A mix." Cabe had considered this problem. Folk as interested in horse breeding as these would not let a steed like Darkhorse pass through their city without some questions. Mixes were not considered as valuable as pure-breds, however, so he had hoped that by calling the eternal a mix, he would be able to dampen some of that interest.

That was not the case. In the end, a good horse was a good horse to some. "Would you consider selling it?"

"I don't think he'd let me. Sorry."

She removed her hand, somewhat puzzled by his response. The gates had opened while the two of them had talked, so Cabe quickly took advantage of her silence and urged Darkhorse forward.

This was the entrance through which most of the foreign visitors first passed and so Cabe found himself entering a bustling market still filled despite the night. Merchants from both Zuu and beyond had set up their tents along his path. Travelers from all the continent over, even far Irillian, wandered about admiring and often buying things they did not necessarily need. The two men from the seaport of Irillian, recognizable in their sailor-style shirts and wide, blue pants, were discussing the need for a pair of small daggers with silver handles. A merchant family wearing the bulky, elaborate garments of Gordag-Ai was sitting at a row of benches eating freshly purchased meat pies. Cabe wondered what sort of meat might be in it. He was discovering that he was now hungry enough to eat almost anything, even horse.

Soon he would eat. He had forced himself not to so that he might be able to order meals at more than one inn. From his early days, when he had been but a simple steward at the Wyvern's Head Tavern, the warlock knew that one of the best places to overhear the local rumors was a tavern or inn. Good company, food, and plenty of drink could loosen a man's tongue just as quickly as a mage's spell.

There were sure to be many such places and Cabe was prepared to visit most of them, but he wanted to find one frequented just as much by the citizenry as it was by strangers. It was more likely he would hear news from a home source than from a stranger, but he did not want to rule out the latter hope.

Finding a stable would be easier, he soon discovered. They were everywhere. Compared to even the royal stables of Penacles or Talak, these were also the cleanest. The dark-haired spellcaster finally chose one near an inn entitled Belfour's Champion. From the image painted on the sign, he gathered that the name had something to do with an actual horse once prominent with this quarter of the city.

At the stable he showed the marker to a groom, who led them to a private stall after an exchange of money. On the pretext that he desired to personally take care of his own mount, Cabe succeeded in being alone with Darkhorse.

"I like this place," the shadow steed rumbled. "They know how best to treat an animal. I should visit Zuu again in the near future!"

"They won't treat you so well if they find out it's you scaring all their other horses."

What Cabe had said was true. Around them, the other mounts were stirring, the voice of Darkhorse unnerving them. The shadowy stallion tried to speak quieter. "I wish I could enter with you, friend Cabe."

"That would certainly raise a few eyebrows and shut more than a few mouths. I don't think even the locals treat their horses *that* well anymore. You'd best stay here for the time being. It won't be a loss, either. This close, you should be able to pick up a number of the voices outside. You'll also have people coming and going here, too."

Darkhorse scraped the floor of his stall, gouging out a valley in the rock-hard dirt. He was not pleased with his end of the mission, but he understood that there was no way he could blend among people. Given time—more than they had now—the eternal might be able to copy the basic structure of a human, but he would *not* be able to copy their ways. A human-looking Darkhorse would still garner too much attention; despite the centuries among men, the demon steed had a rather unique thought pattern and personality. He did not and could not act like a mortal. Neither, for that matter, would he have been able to pass for an elf or any of the other races.

There was and there would always be only one Darkhorse.

The inn was surprisingly clean compared to many that Cabe had experienced. His sense of smell, despite having been dulled, was still able enough to pick up the delicious odors coming from the back. The warlock's stomach grumbled, hoping to remind him that while he had a mission here, so did it.

The interior of Belfour's Champion had much in common with many inns, of course, save that here there was no escaping the symbol of the place, the horse for which it had been named. There were small statuettes, trophies won by the selfsame steed, lining one wall. Tapestries revealing the various feats of a chestnut goliath covered most of the others. If even half of them were true, the animal had been a wonder.

Perhaps the most unusual bit of decor was the clean, polished skull that hung above the rock fireplace across from him. From the small wreath below it, he gathered that this had once belonged to the famous horse. It was, to the warlock, a peculiar way to honor even a most favored companion, but this *was* Zuu, after all, and it was Cabe who was the foreigner here.

Cabe found an empty bench off to one side of the eating area and sat down. Almost the second he was comfortable, a sun-haired serving girl was at his table. Unlike the guards, she was dressed in a more conventional outfit. Yet while the skirt and bodice were of a style that might have been found in any tavern across the Dragonrealm, the form barely hidden within was not. Cabe was of the opinion that there must be much to be said for the Zuu way of life; both the men and the women seemed remarkably fit.

"What can I get *you?*" she asked after he had revealed the marker. She had slightly elfin features, but with what could only be described as a saucy touch to them. The warlock was uncomfortably reminded of a serving girl named Deidra who had been all but able to wrap him around her finger when they had worked together in the Wyvern's Head.

"What's best? Food, I mean."

"That'd be the stew."

Cabe's stomach rumbled again. "That's fine. Stew and cider."

She vanished in a swirl of skirts, leaving Cabe to recover. He loved Gwen, but a man had to be blind not to notice some women, just as he was certain it worked the other way.

There were a number of other travelers in the place, not to mention three good-sized parties of native Zuuans or Zuuites or whatever they called themselves. A few scattered individuals here and there verified that Cabe would not stick out. He picked out the loudest conversation, that of a trio of horse merchants, and started to listen.

His meal and drink came a couple of minutes later, by which time he was more than ready to abandon his first attempt. The serving girl dropped a heaping bowl of delicious-smelling stew in front of him along with a chunk of brown bread. As she reached over and put down the mug of cider, she hesitated long enough for him to admire the view if he desired. Cabe, who was familiar with the ways of some taverns and inns, gave her a noncommittal thank you and enough coins to satisfy both the bill and her. Once she had disappeared back into the crowd, he started in on the stew while at the same time choosing his next target.

The stew was superb, which made concentrating a bit harder at first, but he soon picked up on one of the other conversations. This one, between a pair of the locals, at first sounded like yet another talk about horseflesh, but then switched.

The first man, a thin elder, was muttering, ". . . dwarfs keep insisting. Even said they saw the place glow once."

"Ain't nothing happens in that godforsaken place. I don't even think there's no Dragon King there. Never hear anythin'." His companion, about half his age and with as thick a beard as any the warlock had ever seen, picked up his mug and drank long from it.

"So? We ever hear anything from our drake? You see a few in the city near the king's place, but old Green never shows up or demands anything. Could be the same with this one."

The younger man put down the mug. "But still . . ."

Their conversation shifted again, talking about Dragon Kings and kings in general. Cabe held back a grimace. The glow and the dwarfs interested him, but he could hardly walk over to the men and ask them. He wished that he could be like Shade had been. The master warlock had not only been able to hide his presence in a full inn, but he would blatantly summon people, ask them questions, and send them away without them recalling or anyone else taking the slightest notice. Cabe could have done the same, but he felt wrong about doing so.

He focused on two other discussions, found nothing, then discovered that even with his concentration, he could not make out any of the others clearly enough. The stew lost some of its flavor as he realized that he would have to re-sort to sorcery and modify his hearing. Again, it was a simple spell, but he still did not care for any transformation, however minor.

It took him but a moment to do it. Now, he was not only able to hear con-versations on the far side of the room, but he could pick them out of all the others and hear those speaking as if no one else were making a sound.

Much to his regret, however, it turned out that no one had anything con-crete to add to what he knew. Cabe had expected it, but had hoped for more. He would have to search elsewhere. Rising, he left the nearly empty bowl and mostly untouched cider and departed before the serving girl returned.

There was no dearth of inns in this quarter. Not all of them were up to the standards of Belfour's Champion, but all of them were surprisingly neat. Com-pared to the worst, Wyvern's Head had been a stable.

*No, not a stable,* Cabe thought as he entered the next one. *You can literally eat off the floor in these stables.*

At the next two places, the warlock picked up a smattering of information. An intruder killed in the west, his identity unknown. He had been carrying a pouchful of foreign gold and a few valuable gemstones. Two guards had died in taking him . . . and the patrol had originally only wanted to ask him the same simple questions they asked every visitor. Another body found, this one stripped of all his possessions. Oddly, the two did not seem directly connected.

There was mention of the glow again, a brief brightness that had lit up part of the western sky the *very* night that Cabe had had the second vision. Only a few had actually seen it; most of those he listened to knew of it only second-hand. Evidently Zuu did actually keep a few hours aside for rest.

After the fifth inn, Cabe came to the conclusion that he had heard all he would hear this evening. While he had not garnered much more than he had begun with, he was not unsatisfied. Slightly fatigued, the warlock started back to the stable where Darkhorse was no doubt impatiently waiting for him. The eternal would probably be disappointed in his findings, but that did not matter.

He was just passing Belfour's Champion when he sensed something amiss, although what it was he could not say.

"Well, it's our visitor who eats and runs without saying farewell to a girl."

It was the serving woman from the inn. In the flickering light of the torches, she almost reminded him of a drake woman, so magical did her beauty seem. She had a shawl over her shoulders that could not have served to keep her warm and certainly had not been chosen to protect her modesty.

"Is that a custom I missed?"

The woman, who appeared to have been walking quietly along the avenue, smiled and shook her head. "Only an opportunity." Slowly she pulled away the shawl. "But there are always other opportunities, other chances, for the right man."

He stood his ground even though a part of him urged swift retreat. Before Gwen, he had never been better than inept with women. Cabe was still not certain how he had been so fortunate as to marry her. "I'm flattered, but I'll have to decline."

She hesitated for a brief moment, almost as if she was confused by his response. Then she advanced toward him again, growing somehow even more desirable than she had before.

Again, Cabe sensed that something was amiss. He blinked, then stared carefully at the girl. She mistook his expression for a positive response to her advances and reached out to him. The warlock took her proffered hand . . . then reached out with his power and froze her where she was. He allowed her only to speak.

"Let me go! What are you doing?"

"There are certain things an enchantress should be careful about doing and one of those is picking the wrong victim to use your spells on." Cabe led her by the hand to the side of the stable, where they would not so readily be seen. The would be seductress followed, walking in jerky movements. He now controlled her actions; she could do nothing but breathe, see, and hear. Even her ability to talk hinged on Cabe's desire. He disliked having to do this, but he could not take chances with so wild a sorceress. There was no telling what other tricks she might know.

When they were safely ensconced, he whispered, "You will speak softly. I won't hurt you if you don't try anything and if you answer me honestly. Understand?"

"Yes."

"Good." Even with her spell of seduction removed, it was difficult for him to stand so close to her. If he backed away, however, he knew she would notice. That would throw some of the advantage back to her, which was not what he wanted. "Who are you? Why did you seek me out?" He studied her hair. His eyes had not been augmented for the dark, but up close, he should still have been able to see it.

"You may call me Tori, warlock, and what I wanted—and still want—is simply you." Her smile was dazzling. Understanding his confusion, she added, "The streak is on the left, buried beneath another layer of hair. All it takes is some artful combing."

That would not serve her forever, the warlock knew. Soon, the mark would make itself so evident that nothing short of false hair or a hood like his would be sufficient. However, that was not so important now as what she was doing here. "Why? Why do you want me?"

"Are you serious? What sort of life have—"

He waved her to silence. "You know that's not what I meant. There were certainly better choices in there than me."

She cocked her head to one side. Cabe had not realized that he had allowed her more mobility. That was a bad sign; it meant that she was either stronger than he had supposed or her influence on him was. Either way, it spelled trouble. "True, there were men who were *prettier*, master warlock, but pretty is not all I want. I want someone who thinks as well, someone with ambition and ability . . ."

He understood now. "And someone with skill in the art of sorcery."

"Yes. Very much so. Not just for the sake of that power, though that certainly sweetens things, but because I want someone who understands what it's like to be so . . . superior and different. I want someone of the same world as I. When I saw you, I sensed somehow that you were like me, that you were the one I was searching for. All my patience and sweat have been for something after all. I was beginning to believe that I would be working in taverns for the rest of my life, searching for someone else like me. Someone like you."

Although it seemed that each week brought rumors of new mages, they were still few and far apart. Cabe understood Tori. Here she was, with skills she had not been tutored in the proper use of, trapped in a place where there was no one else like her. Or was there?

"There must be at least one other spellcaster here, Tori. These markers are magical."

"There are a few, master warlock, but they are hardly the company I would keep. Besides, they work solely for Zuu and I will have my own life. You would be wise to watch that marker. It lets them know if a mage is in the city. That's how the king recruits."

"Recruits?" All thought of Tori's attempted seduction faded.

"King Lanith wants magic users. He hasn't decided what he wants to do with them, but he wants them." She put a cool hand to his chin. "You know, there may have been some prettier ones, but I like the character and strength in your face more. You could teach me how to use sorcery properly and I could—"

"That'll be enough of that. There's a certain enchantress, the mother of my children, who might take offense. She and I are very protective of each other. If you want training, then something can be arranged."

"With you?" With the swiftness of a feline pouncing on her prey, she was against him. Cabe started to push her away, but then both of them stopped and turned their attention to a sound coming from beyond the street. Tori glanced up into his face. "You had best be leaving, my love. I carry a false marker, so I'm safe, but you must have been using much magic tonight. Those little toys aren't usually so efficient."

"What is it? What's coming?"

"Lanith's hired mages and the city guard." Even under the circumstances, she took the time to run a finger slowly over his chest. "They are not much to look at and separately they're inept, but the three of them together with the guards could give you trouble . . . and I wouldn't want that. We *will* meet again some day, my warlock."

She leaned up, gave him a swift but powerful kiss, and vanished before he could ask her his next question. Tori had the potential to be a very adept mage, it seemed, if her skills were honed so well already.

Disconcerted, Cabe stood there for several seconds. He had come to Zuu for information, not in order to be involved in some enchantress's wild notions or another king's murky ambitions. Legar was beginning to look more and more inviting with each passing moment.

There was a clatter in the street, a clatter with a very definite military sound to it. Cabe felt the presence of other mages. Unlike Tori, they made no attempt to mask themselves. He sensed them draw upon the natural forces of the world, but draw upon them in such haphazard manner that it was a wonder they did not accidentally unleash some wild spell on themselves.

"He's around, he is," came a gruff female voice.

"Well, it's your task to find him, mage. Do so."

"Do not proceed to tell us our duties." This voice, male, was more cultured than that of either of the previous two.

The warlock pressed himself against the wall, a frown on his lips. His best choice was to teleport to Darkhorse and for the two of them to leave instantly.

Thought was action. Cabe materialized a few stalls down from where he had left Darkhorse. The warlock purposely chose a spot near the stable wall, the better to avoid being seen by some boy or groom. Other than the horses, though, he saw no one. Cautiously he stepped away from the wall and started toward the shadowy steed.

"Dark—" The warlock bit off the rest of the name as he found himself staring at a tall figure clad in a long, flowing robe of white. The man stood like one of the storybook wizards Cabe had grown up hearing about, the ones that only existed in tales. He even had the long white beard.

The man stared at him. After a breath or two had passed, Cabe came to the realization that the man was not staring at him, but rather at the spot where he stood. He did not see the warlock at all. Becoming daring, the bemused warlock waved a hand in front of his counterpart's countenance. The bearded mage might have been a statue for all he noticed.

"He came barging in all important," mocked a voice from behind the still figure. The gate to Darkhorse's stall opened of its own accord and the demon steed trotted out. "I think he must have been looking for you but sensed me instead. Then, just as he had decided to give up, you came along. His powers are not that great, not by far, but he *is* very sensitive to the presence of magic. I did the only thing I could do under the circumstances. Who was the hungry female?"

The question caught Cabe off-balance for a second, but he quickly replied, "Another spellcaster."

"They seem to be breeding like mice these days. There are two others nearby."

"I know; that's why I'm here. We have to leave."

"We would not think of letting you leave without first hearing the offer our most benevolent lord has commanded us to present to you."

It was the male spellcaster Cabe had heard moments earlier. In contrast to his companion, he was clad like a minister of state from one of the northern kingdoms, like Erini's own Gordag-Ai. In one hand, he carried a cane whose top was two silver-and-crystal horse heads. The mage himself was tall and narrow of face with a long mustache and thin, oiled hair. Beady eyes glanced at the petrified figure behind Cabe. The thin mouth curled up into a slight smile.

"I'm sorry, but I'm not interested." The warlock was feeling too popular of late. Unknown forces were summoning him to Legar, enchantresses were seeking him for . . . for many things . . . and now kings wanted his services. He only wanted to go home and spend the next couple of hundred years with his family and friends.

"You have not heard the offer yet." The other spellcaster tapped the end of his two-headed cane on the stable floor. "And you shall not leave until you do."

Cabe could feel a sudden change, as if a blanket had been thrown over the stable. There was a dull ache in his head. His counterpart was trying to cut him off from any use of power. While that likely worked against an untrained or novice sorcerer, Cabe Bedlam was neither. With a simple, forceful thought, he cut through the magical barrier and restored to full intensity his link to the Dragonrealm.

The other mage's cane promptly exploded.

"What? What?" The white-robed figure was mobile again. He glanced this way and that, trying desperately to figure out what was going on. Distracted by the surprising explosion, Darkhorse had lost control of the spell holding him in place.

Blinded briefly by the burst of sorcerous energy unleashed, Cabe could only now see what had happened to the elegant mage. The dull ache in his head had now become a raging headache, likely a backlash from the chaos of the cane's destruction. The blast had thrown the other spellcaster back into one of the stable doors, where he lay unconscious. He wondered what sort of idiotic matrix the man had incorporated into the staff that would make it backfire like that when the spell was disrupted. Having never faced someone of true power, the other must have been unaware of the dangers. The cane was an interesting device, but when one chose to tie an item to a particular spell in order to save one's concentration and strength for other things, one should make certain that the matrix, which stored or drew the power depending on the spell, was fortified in all dimensions. Obviously, there had been a weak link somewhere. Cabe was furious; it was not his intention to harm anyone. He did not wish to do anything that might strain relations between Zuu and himself. So far, no one knew who he was, but that might not be the case in the future. If King Lanith discovered it was Cabe Bedlam who had caused the chaos, there would likely be repercussions.

"What have you done? Hold there, young man!" The white-robed spellcaster reached for Cabe.

"Oh, do be still!" bellowed Darkhorse. Once more the figure froze. "Are we leaving now? This grows most tiresome!"

"Yes, we are! I—" His head still pounded. "I'd better ride you and let you teleport! That way we're guaranteed to be together! My head—"

"Feels much the way I do! My entire body feels twisted inside out! I should give that mage a sound kicking! Next time, I will! Where to? Legar?"

"No, not yet! Somewhere near what used to be the edge of the Barren Lands, where the Brown Dragon once ruled! I need time to clear my head!" Cabe scrambled aboard the darksome steed and clutched at the reins. Before now, they had been merely for show since Darkhorse obviously did not need to be led. Now, though, they were the warlock's lifeline. He swayed in the saddle as the pounding continued. His entire body felt sluggish. If this was what came of leaving new spellcasters to train themselves, then it was important that they start the new schools as soon as possible. Sorcerers left unchecked might someday gain the potential to ruin the world. It was a wonder it had never happened before.

He looked around. They were still in the stable and the sounds of soldiers outside warned that time was rapidly melting away. Cabe did not want to cause an incident. No one had recognized him so far, but he could not take the chance. "What's wrong? Why are we still here?"

"That infernal explosion has addled me! I cannot summon the concentration to depart! Me! Darkhorse! I *should* kick that prestidigitating popinjay all the way back to his master!"

The warlock put a hand to his head. It did not stop the pain, but it eased the pressure a little bit. "We'll have to ride through the city! Can you do that?"

"They shall have but a trail of dust to mark our time here!"

*Mark?* That made Cabe think of something else. He did not want anyone following them. Reaching for the U-shaped talisman, he took the item and threw it as far from him as possible. Did the Green Dragon know what was going on in his own kingdom? He was certain the draconian ruler would find all of this interesting. All Cabe had to do was find the time to tell him.

"I'm ready, then!" He heard pounding on the stable doors. Where the stableboy was, he did not know, but he thanked the stars that no one was there to immediately open the way for the guards. "We'll have to ride through the doors when they open!"

"Why wait?" Darkhorse laughed, reared, and went charging toward the thick wooden barriers.

The anxious warlock bent down low and prayed he had concentration enough to shield himself when the doors shattered.

As luck would have it or not, depending on the point of view, the guards managed to open the doors then. They were greeted by the sight of a huge stallion with gleaming blue eyes like the chill of winter coming at them at a speed that allowed no hesitation in choice. Most of the guards made the correct choice and dove to the side. A couple stood their ground, not experienced enough to understand why the veterans were scattering. After all, it was only a horse.

Darkhorse charged through the first one, then *leapt* over the head of the other.

The demon steed roared with laughter as he raced away from the stables. Cabe, still clutching tight, was thankful that none of the men could see that it was the mount and not the rider who was mocking them. Darkhorse was known well enough throughout the Dragonrealm, even if half of those who knew of him thought him legend. If word reached King Lanith that the shadow steed had been in Zuu and that a warlock of considerable skill had been seen with him, it would be reasonable for the monarch to assume that it was the warlock most known for his friendship with Darkhorse. What Lanith would or would not do was a question that Cabe did not want to have to consider.

Through the streets of Zuu the two raced. A few people here and there scattered as the great black beast fairly flew past them. One man actually stood his ground and raised a hand in encouragement as they went by. The last thing they heard from him was, "Aaryn's Spur! I'll give a hundred gold for the next colt he sires! What do you . . ."

They were just out of earshot when Darkhorse turned down a side avenue. Cabe looked up, noticing that they were now heading away from the gates of the city. "Where're you going? This is the quickest way out!"

"But not the best!" The eternal's voice was a subdued roar. It was still doubtful that in the dark anyone could tell that it was him talking. "Look before you!"

He did . . . and saw only the wall circling Zuu before them. There was no gate, only solid stone. "Are you—"

"Since I cannot teleport . . . yes!"

These streets were deserted, the only good thing to happen to them this night as far as the warlock was concerned. Cabe tried to concentrate again, but the headache only grew worse and his body tingled so much that he had to squirm despite his precarious balance. He would have to trust Darkhorse. Darkhorse had not and would not fail him. He would not.

The black stallion leapt into the air and over the wall. The harried mage took one look down at the shrinking world and decided that closing his eyes might be best after all.

They began to plummet earthward.


THE PANDEMONIUM AT the stable had drawn both natives and visitors and even several minutes after the escape by the unknown rider, many of the spectators were still milling around trying to piece together the story.

The mages, looking disgruntled, perplexed, and dismayed, quickly departed the scene, none of them uttering so much as a single word. Some of the guards, however, were more vocal, the common folk of Zuu liking to tell or hear a good story whenever possible. Soon, a very distorted version of what had happened spread among the populace. There had been a score of riders. A band of spell-casters had been using the stable for their rituals. The king's mages had been practicing, but something had gone wrong and they had summoned a demon out of the ether.

None of the stories was correct, but a careful listener who wandered about could piece together much from what was said, almost enough to re-create the true event.

To a spy clad in the stolen clothing of a murdered merchant, such a thing was child's play.

# VII

THEY HAD LOST two men in the tunnels during the night. Two men suspiciously close to the chamber where Lord D'Farany and the blue devil worked to decipher the monsters' secrets. Two men too many as far as Orril D'Marr was concerned. There was something special about the chamber, something other than the obvious, and he was the only one who suspected the truth. D'Marr was certain that the deaths had to do with a passage that was not there . . . at least not now.

It did not help that he was certain the beasts he held prisoner were laughing at him. Even when he questioned them, put them to the scepter, they seemed to be laughing. There was some great riddle that only they knew the answer to and they were not talking. He had come close to killing one, but for some reason the almost eager look in the beast's eyes had made him draw back.

Lord D'Farany would not hear his suspicions and the damned blue man merely gave him a smug smile each time. If there was a problem, Lord D'Farany had said, then it was up to D'Marr to deal with it. That was his function, after all.

*I will deal with it, oh, yes* . . . Each time his master descended into the tunnel, the Quel seemed to grow expectant. Each time he returned, they grew morose. The young officer had first thought that they were expecting an attack on the leader of their enemies, but then he saw that his assumption was wrong. The armored beasts *wanted* him to go to the chamber . . . but why?

To discover that reason, he had decided to drag one of the overgrown armadillos to the chamber and try a few tests.

Neither Lord D'Farany nor the northerner was in the chamber. That was as he had planned it. The only ones that D'Marr wanted here were the few men he needed to keep the Quel under control. This was *his* moment.

"Bring him forward so that he can see what I do."

The soldiers dragged the wary beast toward the center of the room. D'Marr removed the scepter from his belt and walked slowly over to his captive. Some of the wariness in those inhuman eyes faded. The Quel had almost become used to the magical rod. It was an enemy that the prisoners understood.

The young officer touched the tip of the scepter against the underside of the Quel's snout. As he had expected, the creature flinched. D'Marr smiled ever so briefly at the puzzlement he could read in the other's eyes. There had been no pain. D'Marr had not activated his toy.

"I know you can understand me, so listen well. There are two things you should note, my ugly beastie." He kept the tip of the scepter no more than a few inches from the Quel's eyes, now and then swinging it back and forth so as to keep the prisoner off-guard. "The first is that you should never think of me as predictable." He tapped the rod against the Quel's snout, this time giving him but the least of the pain levels.

He had the creature's attention now. D'Marr backed up and began to walk about the chamber. He continued to talk as he played at studying its interior. "The second item you should be aware of is that I have not bothered with the speech stone this time. Your answers would only be repetitive. Also, what I need to know from you now does not require words or images."

Out of the corner of his eye, he could see the look of cautious curiosity that had spread across that monstrous visage. D'Marr put a hand on the crystalline device. He sensed the Quel flinch almost as much as when he had put the scepter to the subterranean's head.

The Aramite officer brought the weapon dangerously close to the crystals aligned on the top of the alien creation. Then, as if unaware of both what he had nearly done and the Quel's reaction, D'Marr stepped away. He walked to the far end of the chamber and started pacing the outer edge, occasionally tapping the wall with his staff as he went. The Quel's eyes never left him.

"There are things you are hiding from us, beast." *Tap.* "I have been trying to be reasonable about this." *Tap.* "You must understand, my lord's becoming impatient." *Tap.* "And now your fellow monsters have taken two of our men." Orril D'Marr stopped and turned to face the captive. "Two men very near to this place. Two men, who might have seen . . . what?"

Still facing the Quel, he snapped his arm back and struck the wall beside him soundly with the top of the scepter.

The armored leviathan gave a muffled hoot and tried to leap forward despite being bound. His guards dragged him back, although it took some effort to do so. D'Marr allowed himself a rare full, satisfied smile as he watched the Quel's unsuccessful struggle. Noticing his tormentor's own reaction, a look that might have been equivalent to human consternation crossed the inhuman features.

"Thank you." The wolf raider glanced at the mace. Despite its somewhat fragile appearance, it was very sturdy. The head was not at all chipped. When his predecessor had had it created, he had wanted a weapon that could be used in combat as well. D'Marr was thankful for his forethought. It would take much to even scar the scepter.

He turned to inspect the area that he had struck. It was the same region where, on the first day, he had thought that he had seen another chamber or tunnel. That day, D'Marr had inspected the area and found only solid wall, but he had been nagged ever since by doubt. He was not one to imagine such things. Now, thanks to the Quel's violent and unthinking response, D'Marr was certain that there was indeed a chamber or passage hidden behind the glittering facade.

Even had the Quel not responded as he had expected, there would have been proof of a sort to back his suspicions. Each time he had brought the baton against the glittering wall, he had left a tiny trail of cracked crystal and rock behind him. Yet, despite utilizing the full strength of his arm, his last strike had not left so much as a single scratch in the surface of this section of the wall. It might be that he had happened to strike an area of exceptionally resilient crystal, but D'Marr doubted that. No, there was something special about this particular bit of wall.

The raider officer turned away from the others and ran his hand over the suspect area, as he had done the first day. There was no sign of a break. There was nothing that might betray the falseness of the wall. "Nonetheless," he whispered, "I shall have to tear you down. Stone by stone, if necessary."

"To do that, Orril, would be a most distressing thing to me."

He spun around. "My *lord?*"

As the officer fell to his knees, the Pack Leader slowly entered the chamber. He was accompanied by the blue man and his personal guard. Standing in the tunnel, just beyond the entrance, was what appeared to be a full squadron. Lord D'Farany looked about the chamber, his expression that of a man who is home at last. "You know nothing of the work of sorcery, Orril. Of the intricate matrices that must sometimes be arranged. Of the nuances of concentration, so simple in theory but perplexing in practice." D'Farany stroked the side edge of the Quel artifact. His eyes fixed on a location above D'Marr's head. "Of the *care* one must take. . . . If you understood such things, you would certainly realize what permanently damaging the integrity of this room might do to my prize."

The young officer had *not* considered that. He recalled the minute but very real damage he had already caused the wall. Would that be sufficient to upset the balance of the magical array? If so, then he had handed his own head to the blue man.

"Forgive me, my lord. I had our interests at heart. I'm certain that there's a hidden chamber behind the portion of the wall I was inspecting. The beasts know it; I've watched them. I tricked this one into betraying himself. There may be something, some threat to us, hidden there."

"And so trusting of the Quel, who would seek to trick, you would destroy all this, yes?" interjected D'Rance. The two men locked gazes. The northerner was enjoying this.

"There will be . . . none of that." The Pack Leader actually shuddered, as if the mere thought of any damage to this place physically pained him. He pointed in the direction of D'Marr. "The wall, Kanaan . . ."

"My lord." Bowing, the blue man stalked across the chamber. As he neared his rival, he smirked. D'Marr's grip on his scepter tightened. Given the least of excuses, he would have been willing to strike down the blue devil right there and then.

D'Rance ran both hands over the questionable section. His eyes were half-closed in concentration; he almost seemed in a trance. At last, he turned back to his master and said, "This wall feels like the others, my lord, yes, but I am only a simple soldier." After a moment's hesitation, he slyly added, "He does not seem to have damaged it yet, either."

"There will be no breaking down of walls." To Lord D'Farany, that was evidently the final word on the subject. He turned his attention to the Quel device. D'Marr exhaled quietly. He would find other ways to pursue the matter . . . and take the blue man to task while he was at it.

D'Rance was not finished with *him*, however. The northerner stepped past the Aramite and studied the floor. D'Marr grew still. After a brief inspection, the blue man looked up. "My lord, I fear that there may be damage to the chamber after all. There are several places where the crystal face has been chipped, perhaps by a blunt weapon, yes."

*Perhaps I should chip your face with this blunt weapon* . . . He readied himself for punishment. There would surely be no escaping it this time.

Lord D'Farany leaned over the crystalline device. He was silent for nearly a minute. Then, "We shall see what will happen, Kanaan. I do not like to execute a man for no reason."

Familiar with his master's ways, D'Marr was not at all comforted by the comment.

"Now come, Kanaan. I can wait no longer."

That there were not only more than a dozen soldiers present but also a Quel as well did not appear to disturb the Pack Leader in the slightest. He only had eyes for the crystalline magic of the chamber. His gauntlets put aside, he carefully inspected each and every major facet of the peculiar artifact.

The blue man, on the other hand, was not at all pleased with the crowd. As he joined the Aramite commander, he asked, "My lord, would it not be better if those unnecessary would depart, yes? They could cause distraction and perhaps also unknown harm. It would be best, yes, if they retreated back to the previous passage even."

"Do what you will," D'Farany responded rather distractedly, his response accompanied by a curt wave of his hand.

Kanaan D'Rance dismissed everyone, including even the guards that D'Marr had brought with him. The sentries urged the Quel to his feet, but as they were dragging him toward the tunnel leading to the surface, the Pack Leader turned his ambiguous gaze in their direction. "Leave it. Orril, the thing is your responsibility."

"Yes, my lord," responded the short raider. He rose quickly to his feet and took control of the prisoner. At his command, the Quel knelt again. Two guards remained long enough to bind the beastman's legs together, then, saluting, they hurried after their comrades.

"Would it not be wiser to—"

"It shall watch, Kanaan. I want it to watch."

There was no argument. One did not argue with the Pack Leader . . . at least not *often* if one wanted to keep one's head.

The raider leader touched several crystals. D'Marr felt a tingle, but it passed away. The Quel was leaning forward, his dark eyes narrowed. *You don't like what you see, do you, beastie? Did you underestimate my lord simply because his world is not always ours? What were you expecting, I wonder.* He observed with care the way the captive followed each and every gesture made by Lord D'Farany. There was growing apprehension in the monster's ugly countenance. This was more than what the Quel had expected, he thought. *He uses your toy like an adept, doesn't he? You expected less of him, didn't you?*

It was then that the chamber . . . *twinkled.* That was the only word that D'Marr thought appropriate. Even though they were well into the depths of the earth, stars now shone bright above them. A thousand points of light sparkled, almost a dizzying effect. Colors from one end of the spectrum to the other danced about like fairies wild and gay. There was a low, almost inaudible hum that seemed to course through the mind. The young Aramite gritted his teeth. The others were either unaware of it or affected in a different manner. D'Marr only knew that it set him on edge, made him want to flee the area. He could not, of course, do any such thing.

"Kanaan . . . I will take the box now." Perhaps it was some trick of his addled perceptions, but D'Marr thought it seemed as if it were a different Lord D'Farany who stood there. This one was almost sane in speech and manner. The eyes were nearly focused on what he was doing. His words did not come out in sometimes random phrases, but rather as complete and, for the most part, coherent statements.

Somehow, it only made him that much more frightening.

The blue man removed a small black box and turned it quickly over to the Pack Leader. Orril D'Marr squinted. He knew what was in the box, but could not fathom what purpose the Pack Leader had in mind for the contents. The thing within was dead, powerless. The Pack Leader had drained it during the initial assault against the Quel. It was nothing more than a memento of the past now . . . wasn't it?

Lord D'Farany opened the box and removed from it the Aramite talisman that he had used to silence the Quel's power.

A muffled hoot made D'Marr glance down at the captive. The Quel had evidently fathomed the raider leader's intentions. He squirmed anew, trying to free himself from bonds designed to hold creatures much stronger than he. D'Marr increased the intensity of his scepter and jolted the Quel back into submission. He would have liked to have asked the beastman what concerned him so, but he had neither the time nor the means to do so. *We will know soon enough . . .*

The former keeper inspected the curved artifact. "There can be no flaw," he explained to no one in particular. "All of my calculations of the past days demand that. Any flaw would mean disaster."

It was no comfort at all to the young raider that D'Rance was just as dismayed by the comment as he was. The blue man took an involuntary step backward and, if anything, was a much paler blue than he had been seconds before.

D'Farany looked up from his work. He gazed at the Quel as if seeing him for the first time. "This device is recent, isn't it? I thought as much. It lacks the care and design of so much else here, yet it holds so much more potential. Why did you build it?"

The Quel, of course, could not and would not answer. This was apparently unimportant to Lord D'Farany. He shrugged and returned his concern to the Aramite talisman and the peculiar creation of the armored underdwellers.

"It is incomplete. I shall complete it for y—for *me.*"

With his free hand he rearranged the central pattern, plucking gemstones from their chosen locations and replacing them with others from the array. The Quel started to shake and twist, but still to no avail. D'Marr gave his captive another touch of the rod, but even then the massive figure continued to shift.

Satisfied with his alterations, the Pack Leader added the talisman to the arrangement.

The room crackled . . . and from each point of light a bolt of blue darted toward the Quel creation.

D'Marr covered his eyes and ducked down. The blue man pressed himself against the wall nearest to the entrance to the chamber and simply stared. Beside D'Marr, the underdweller rocked back and forth as if expecting the end of everything.

The wolf raider was almost inclined to agree with him.

Tenuous, frantic strands of light, the blue bolts struck the crystalline device, bathing it in brilliant color. D'Marr felt his hair stand of its own accord and saw that the others suffered the same effect. Only Lord D'Farany, standing within the bright cobalt glow, was untouched . . . at least on the surface.

He was smiling. Smiling as a lover might while in the tender embrace of his desire. It was perhaps a very apt description, the officer realized, for to the former keeper the power that bathed him *was* both his love and desire. The loss of it had killed most of his kind and sent him into madness.

Orril D'Marr was too young to really recall the keepers when they had been at the apex of their glory. He only knew the stories and the few survivors he had seen. He knew that without the will of the Ravager and the work of his most trusted servants, the keepers, the empire had begun to crumble. Part of him had always wondered at the speed of that decay. Why had the great armies so depended on a tiny minority in their ranks?

Seeing D'Farany, he thought he understood. A keeper at the peak of his power was an army unto himself.

The Pack Leader still smiled. His eyes stared upward at the spiderweb of energy pouring into the crystalline artifact. Blue sparks drifted from his fingers whenever he moved his hands. His *eyes* gleamed blue.

With each passing second, the glow surrounding both the Pack Leader and his newfound toy became less bearable. D'Marr turned away, but found himself facing the blinding glow in a thousand reflections. He turned farther, seeking some respite, something that did not reflect the light.

What the raider found instead was the very passage he had been searching for.

A gaping mouth, it was so blatant a sight he could not understand how it had taken him even this long to notice it. He took a step toward it, but then something caught him by the foot, nearly sending him crashing to the harsh floor. The Aramite regained his balance and glanced over his shoulder. He saw the desperate Quel, the inhuman eyes wide, struggling to roll over to him and somehow stop the raider's advance. D'Marr smiled briefly at the pathetic sight, but a sudden change in the Quel's eyes, a change from fear to burgeoning hope, shattered the smile and sent the raider's attention flying back to the secret entranceway.

It was already fading. The same crystal-encrusted wall was slowly re-forming, growing more solid with each passing breath. The Quel suddenly forgotten, D'Marr raced toward the vanishing passage. The wall was still transparent, but that was rapidly changing. Reaching out in desperation, he slammed a hand against it, but his efforts only rewarded him with pain. It was too late to cross through. The split-second delay caused by his gloating had lost him his opportunity.

Still, he had a moment, but only a short one, in which to glimpse what secret lay behind the cursed wall. It was a harried glimpse, made the worse by the lessening transparency of the stone and crystal. Nonetheless, he was able to make out shapes, hundreds of shapes, in a cavern that must have been nearly as immense as the one in which the city lay.

D'Marr saw no more than that. The wall became completely opaque, the stone and crystal completely innocent in appearance.

He slowly turned back to the others and was not at all surprised to find that Lord D'Farany had *just* completed his work. The tentacles of energy had withdrawn; if not for the blue glow about the top of the Quel device, the chamber would have looked exactly as it had before they had entered.

"Not the same . . ." the Pack Leader was muttering. Despite his words, however, a smile had crept across his scarred visage. "Not the same, but so *very* close . . . I will just have to accept that."

His eyes were *still* focused.

"My lord, I shall remove the tooth, yes?" D'Rance looked exceptionally eager. D'Marr momentarily put his discovery aside and started to mouth a protest. He knew, through careful observance, that the northerner had some trace of power. Was it possible that he had more? Did he have the will and ability to control the keeper talisman? That would take more skill than the Aramite had suspected him of having.

His words of protest never left his lips, for Lord D'Farany was quicker to respond. His eyes bore down on the blue man and D'Marr had the distinct pleasure of watching his rival cringe under the intensity of those suddenly alive orbs. "Your readiness to assist me in all is commendable, Kanaan, but you may leave it where it is. There is no more secure place for it now than where it presently stands."

D'Rance assumed a more servile position. "Yes, my lord. I meant nothing by it, my lord."

The Pack Leader had already dismissed him from his attention. Now those eyes focused on the peculiar scene of the Quel lying on his side far from where he had been earlier positioned and Orril D'Marr standing near the wall, *much too far* away from the prisoner that he had been charged with guarding. "And you, Orril?"

The raider wondered how he was to convince Lord D'Farany of what he had seen. An entire cavern lay hidden from the invasion force, yet only he believed—*knew*, rather—that it was there. The Pack Leader and the blue devil had been so engrossed in the spectacle above them that they had missed the unveiling of the Quel's secret.

"Forgive me also, Lord D'Farany. Sorcery is not my realm. I admit to having been somewhat . . . overwhelmed . . . by the results. I've seen things I'd never expected to see."

"*Wonderful* things . . . and there will be so much more . . ." The Pack Leader gazed down at the Quel creation, his eyes filled with great fondness. "We shall do so much together, the two of us . . ."

The eyes were losing focus.

With a last gentle touch, the Pack Leader separated himself from his prized possession and, to neither subordinate's surprise, departed without a word. Kanaan D'Rance remained behind only long enough to look from the device to his rival before he disappeared into the tunnel after the Aramite commander.

D'Marr stared thoughtfully at the wall that had, so far, beaten his efforts to unmask it for what it was. He would have to find another way in than this place, that was all. Perhaps there was another chamber that also shared a wall with the hidden cavern. It would be a simple matter of exploration, of hunting. He excelled in hunting, no matter what the prey. Then, with the aid of his explosive toys, he would create for himself a new and *permanent* way inside. There would be no magic to stop him then.

From the mouth of the tunnel, a wave of black armor flowed into the room. It was the guard contingent Lord D'Farany had brought with him. The ranks split as each man entered, one line moving to the left side of the chamber and the other to the right. D'Marr signaled two of the soldiers to take custody of the Quel. The captive departed without protest, but inhuman eyes watched the young officer until the depths of the tunnel swallowed the creature. The other guards shifted their ranks to make up for the slight loss to their number.

*I will have to make measurements,* D'Marr thought, returning with anticipation to the project ahead. Too much powder and the explosive would bring down not only the wall but the rest of the cavern as well. *Best to find the proper spot first. Then I can judge how much will be needed.*

There were already men mapping the complex system of caverns and tunnels that made up the Quel domain. While far from complete, he was certain that their charts already revealed enough for his present concerns. With so much importance placed on this particular section of the underground world, it had only been logical to map it first.

He had much work ahead of him, but Orril D'Marr was pleased. He was on the verge of shattering the last hope of the beastmen and discovering what great secret lay in that cavern behind the wall.

The guards came to even greater attention as he passed them on his way out of the chamber, but the raider officer paid their fear of him no mind this time. His only thought was on the coming success of his project and the look on the blue man's face when D'Marr revealed to Lord D'Farany the most closely guarded of the underdwellers' mysteries . . . whatever it was.

THEY DID NOT know how close they had come.

The Crystal Dragon stirred himself from the self-imposed stupor. Trust the wolf raiders to be both predictable and unpredictable. He had been certain that they would somehow seize control of the Quel's domain. He had been fairly certain that they would have *some* success with the subterraneans' mechanisms. What he had not been prepared for was the *level* of that success. The invaders already had a grasp of the abilities of Quel might. Given just a little more time, they would grow adept. A little more . . . and they would dare to confront him.

He should strike before they grew too strong. He should risk himself, for delaying the inevitable only made the later consequences worse.

*How? How do I sssstrike? It mussst be effective but taking the least effort and concentration possible! There cannot be too much risssk. That might lead to . . .* If only there had been time to rest. That would have changed everything. They would have been insects to crush beneath his huge paws.

The glittering leviathan twisted his neck around and sought among the treasures he had accumulated over time. Some were there because of simple value, some because of purpose. Carefully he scoured the vast pile. There were times when he had thought of organizing it again, storing it anew in the lower cavern chambers, but that would mean leaving the protection of his sanctum and doing so might prove the final, fatal blow.

*Sssomething . . .*

Then, to one side of the pile, almost separate from it, the Dragon King sighted the answer to his plea. It was not what he had wanted, not in the least, but the longer he stared at it the more the dread monarch knew it was his only choice. Massive, daggerlike talons gently picked up a small crystalline sphere in which it seemed a tiny, reddish green cloud floated. There was something unhealthy about the cloud, for the colors did not speak of life, but long and lingering decay. The sphere was no larger than a human head, which made it tiny indeed for one such as he, but he had learned care in using this gargantuan form, for even shifting to the manlike image his counterparts preferred was dangerous now. Each transformation distracted him, made him more vulnerable to . . . to the danger of losing himself. Now especially he dared not transform. It might be just enough, combined with his lack of rest, to defeat his long efforts.

He was careful for another reason. What the cloud represented could not be accidentally released full-fledged upon the world, not even for as short as a single blink of an eye.

*But what of a tiny fragment of its evil? Might that do?*

With the tenderness of a parent holding a newborn babe, the Dragon King brought the sphere to near eye level. A distorted image of his monstrous face glared back at him, but he forced himself to ignore it as he always did.

"Yessss, you could aid me. You could act where I cannot. You could blind them; lead them assstray. Perhaps you could even remove this blight on my kingdom." The Dragon King laughed bitterly. "A blight to plague a blight. So very apt."

He continued to contemplate the sphere. The cloud swirled, briefly revealing a hellish landscape. The crystal artifact was not a thing designed to contain but was rather a door of sorts . . . a door to a nightmare that the drake lord had lived with since almost the beginning.

"Nooo . . ." whispered the crystalline-skinned dragon. "Not yet. I mussst consssider thisss firssst . . . yet . . ." He twisted his head to one side and looked at the deadly cloud from another angle. "If only the decision were not mine anymore."

Lowering his paw, the Dragon King summoned up the images of the raider camp. He stared long and hard at the army and its leaders, memories of another time and another invasion slowly seizing hold of him.

"Ssso very much alike they are," he hissed. "Asss if the world hasss gone full circle."

The malevolent cloud in his paw shifted violently, almost as if it were reacting to the words of the drake. The Crystal Dragon did not notice the change, caught up as he was in both the sights before him and the phantoms stirring anew in his mind. The scenes reflected in the multiple facets blended in with those phantoms, creating a myriad collection of twisted and misremembered pictures.

"Full circle," the Crystal Dragon muttered again. "Asss if a door to the passst had opened up . . ." The gleaming eyes narrowed to little more than slits as the drake lord became further enmeshed in the visions. "A door open . . ."

In the sphere, a storm began to rage.

# VIII

IT WAS NOT until well into the day that Cabe and Darkhorse were finally able to shake off the effects of the mishap with the magical staff. They had dared not enter Legar in such condition and so the two of them had been forced to simply wait. Cabe used the time to first compose a carefully worded message to be sent by magic back to Gwen and the children and then to rest; Darkhorse chose to make use of the wait by constantly grousing about time ever wasted. It was not that the wait was not necessary. Even the demon steed knew better; he could simply not stop himself from complaining over and over again. The warlock knew deep down that what drove his companion to such impatience and bickering was the ebony stallion's own knowledge that with nothing else to occupy his thoughts, the haunting memories of Shade would return. Darkhorse was seriously trying to free himself of his obsession, but it was a monumental task even for him.

Thinking of memories, Cabe could still not recall the night before without shuddering a little. Darkhorse often forgot that as mighty as his friend was, the warlock was still guided by human instincts and preconceptions. Plummeting earthward from such a height had nearly been too catastrophic an event for the mage's heart. With his own skills in question, he had been forced to rely solely on the eternal. Even as good friends as they were, Cabe could not completely put himself into the care of a being who could never truly understand death as men did.

Fortunately, this time Darkhorse *had* known what he was doing. The shadow steed had landed hooves first on the ground, but the warlock had felt only the slightest of jolts. Such a landing would have shattered the legs of a real horse and killed both animal and rider instantly. Yet Darkhorse had ridden off into the nearby hills the moment he was certain that his passenger was secure and safe.

They now waited in the foothills of southern Esedi, the great western region that had once encompassed the domain of the Bronze Dragon. The kingdom of Gordag-Ai, Queen Erini's birthplace, was actually a part of the northernmost reaches of Esedi. That was not why Cabe had chosen it for sanctuary, though. Rather, he had chosen the location because from where they were they could look down into the northeastern borderlands of Legar.

"It is late, Cabe! How much longer need we wait?"

"How do you feel now?" the spellcaster asked. He presently sat on one of the many rocky outcroppings dominating this hill. This part of Esedi was actually related to the hills of Legar although it lacked the heavy growth of crystal unique to the peninsula.

The dark-haired sorcerer had cause to question his companion's condition. For him, it had been more than an hour since the last lingering effects had finally faded away. The eternal, however, had continued to suffer to some degree, enough to make Cabe hesitate to leave. Darkhorse, being, in essence, magical himself, had been affected much more severely.

In response, the dark stallion suddenly reared and struck out at one of the nearest formations with his hooves.

Fragments rained down upon them as the single blow pulverized the rock and sent it scattering.

"I am ready," concluded the massive steed.

"Then let's leave." He rose and swiftly mounted. In truth, Cabe, too, was anxious to begin the final leg of the journey. He had not wanted to mention anything to Darkhorse, but during his rest he had been visited by yet *another* vision. It had not been as strong as the others, perhaps coming only as a reminder. Still, it had been vivid enough to make him fear that his delays, both accidental and *intentional*, had cost them precious time.

Unlike the others, this vision had consisted of only one scene and a short one at that. Cabe had stood in the middle of the rocky landscape of Legar, but not with Darkhorse. Instead, he had found himself facing an armored figure, a bearded man clad in the same dragonscale of the previous visions. The man was an adversary, but he was also an ally, for even as the warlock had settled into the vision, a black shadow had spread across the land. Both of them had known at the same time that it was coming for them. His companion had pulled out a sword, but it was no ordinary weapon, for the blade was fire-drenched crystal. He had swung the blade again and again at the shadow, cutting it into fragments, but the pieces simply merged and sought them out anew.

The warlock had tried to help, but not even the least of spells had obeyed his will.

Before him, the armored figure had thrown down his sword and raised his hands in what was obviously the beginning of a spell of his own. There had been a look in his eyes, a fatalistic look, that Cabe had discovered he feared more than any threat from the black shadow. It reminded him too much of the eyes of the Ice Dragon. Somehow, he had been certain that the spell would destroy them as effectively as the shadow. It had also been clear that his companion had not cared in the least.

He had run toward the man, shouting "No!"

Cabe had been too late.

It was at this point that he had stirred. The vision had lingered a second more, but all that the half-asleep spellcaster could recall was a shuddering sensation of nothingness worse than even what one felt in the empty dimension called the Void. Cabe Bedlam knew that what he had experienced had been a taste of utter *death.*

He had no intention of relating the experience to Darkhorse. The shadow steed might think to leave him behind, something that Cabe could not permit. As much as the latest vision unnerved him, it only made him more determined . . . and more curious.

Cabe had barely settled onto Darkhorse's back when he felt the massive figure stiffen. The eternal was staring out at the western horizon, ice-blue eyes focused on something that his human rider could evidently not see. The shadow steed sniffed the air around them. "What is it, Darkhorse? Something wrong?"

"It may be nothing, but . . . there is a fog or mist spreading across this region of Legar. Can you not see?"

Squinting, he tried to make out what Darkhorse claimed to have seen. The hills near the horizon had a vague, indistinct quality about them, but nothing that would normally make him worry. Then, as he continued to study it, the landscape just a bit closer also grew murky. A minute more and he could no longer even *see* the hills at the horizon. There *was* something there, he finally had to admit, and at the pace it was spreading eastward, there could be no doubt that it was nothing natural.

"It will have engulfed much of Legar already, Cabe."

"We'll have to travel by land, not teleportation. Will the fog cause you difficulty?"

Darkhorse snorted. "I will only know that when we are in the midst of it. What do you say?"

"I don't have a choice, but you—"

"That is all I need to know!" The ebony stallion started down the hillside at a pace and angle that made his rider cringe even though his abilities were now strong enough to protect him from any fall he might have.

Cabe's original intention had been to teleport to a region of Legar that he vaguely recalled from an undesired trek long ago. When he realized just how vague those memories were, however, he had then decided that a better plan would be to use short hops involving line-of-sight teleportation. After all, it was a rare day that did not find the sun-drenched peninsula a clear sight all the way to the horizon. A rare day like today, apparently.

They dared not materialize in the midst of so thick a fog, not when there might be raiders nearby. It was impossible to know exactly how great an infestation there was and it had been risky enough to consider teleporting when the two of them could *see* their surroundings. All of Legar might be under the watch of the Aramites. They were nothing if not efficient in that category.

Regrettably, they were only a short distance into the harsh land when the first tendrils of mist surrounded them. Before they could even react, the fog had already overwhelmed the sky above them. Legar no longer glittered; it was now merely a dull, rocky domain where life struggled. Darkhorse was almost immediately forced to slow to a crawl as the mist continued to thicken at an alarming rate. Cabe Bedlam shivered as they entered the enshrouded realm. The peculiar green and red coloring of the mist did not strike him as healthy for some reason.

"I'd almost swear that the fog surged directly toward us," whispered Cabe. He did not have to whisper, but something about the dank mist made him want to do so.

"That may be. It certainly shifted in our direction with superb accuracy . . . and as far as I can ascertain, the wind does not blow hard enough to have done it."

"Do you sense anything out of the ordinary?"

The towering steed unleashed a short, mocking laugh. "I sense mostly that we will be journeying through this muck for some time to come. The fog seems to flow both around me and within. I cannot say that I expected less." He sniffed the air. "There is something obscenely familiar about this muck."

Cabe Bedlam did not understand the last, but he most certainly agreed with the rest of what the ebony stallion had said. With much effort, it was possible to sense his nearby surroundings, but trying to reach out and study the path far ahead was nearly impossible. At best, he had vague impressions of the landscape and the possible knowledge that there were a few life-forms, none of very significant size, lurking about in the strange fog.

Worse, he, too, felt it within, as if it sought to possess him, make him a part of it.

"I have come to the conclusion," mocked Darkhorse, "that the Dragonrealm likes nothing more than to see the creatures who inhabit it existing in constant frustration and despair! Yes, it makes perfect sense to me!" He pawed at the ground, strewing age-old rock behind him as easily as if it had been loose sand. "It will be slow going I am afraid. I might be more willing to risk myself and travel at a quicker pace, but your kind is not as durable. Should something happen, I would never forgive myself."

The warlock tightened his grip and adjusted his seating. "I want to get moving, too. Do what you can; I'm more durable than you think, Darkhorse."

This brought a short but honest chuckle from his fearsome companion. "You may be right! Very well, hold tight to the reins; you will need them *this* time!"

Darkhorse began to trot, but it was a trot no other horse could have matched. The massive stallion's pace quickly ate up ground. Even despite the swift pace, however, both were careful to keep themselves at their most wary. By this time, Cabe had become fairly certain that the wolf raider camp did exist. It was likely they were still too far away from it to be noticed, but there was still the danger of scouts. The raiders were not the only threat, either. What the Quel might be up to while all this was going on, he could not say, but the warlock was certain that they had to be involved somehow. It would have been impossible for the invaders not to have discovered some trace of them. Likewise, it was improbable that the Quel would share the Crystal Dragon's apparent unconcern about the overrunning of their domain. It was just not the Quel way. Cabe was too familiar with the underdwellers not to understand that.

The fog continued to thicken until it almost seemed they were traveling through a wall of rotting cotton rather than mist. Even after he had given in to the inevitable and had enhanced his vision, the frustrated spellcaster could still see no farther than two, maybe three yards in any one direction.

"It might as well be night!" grumbled Darkhorse.

"At least we'd be able to see at night," returned Cabe. He wondered what things would be like when the sun did set. Could it be any worse than *this*? "Are we at least heading in the correct direction? I can't tell."

"More or less yes is the best response I can give you, Cabe. This is a malevolent mist; it seeks to turn me in circles, I think." Again, he sniffed the air. "There *is* a foulness here that I know from long ago. I cannot believe that it might be what I think it is, but what *else*? We would have been better off coming here half-dazed and stumbling in the darkness!"

"What can we do now?"

Darkhorse had no answer for that. A depressing silence lingered over the two for some time after. Cabe was certain that it was induced by the sinister haze. It was just too cloying a feeling. No matter how hard he sought to fling it off, it stuck to him.

They journeyed for what was at least three hours by Cabe's admittedly questionable reckoning, but forced to slow down because of the lack of visibility and their inability to sense much farther than they could see, the pair had hardly made any headway in that time. He hoped that anyone else they might encounter would at least be at the same disadvantage. His one fear was that this was a trick of the raiders, yet it would have been extremely complicated to create a spell that would blind one's adversaries but allow one's own army to see. Such a spell would require more than a simple thought. It would require such mental manipulation of the natural forces of the world that it would take days to even prepare for it.

The raiders also suffered from a lack of competent mages, if he recalled one of the Gryphon's earliest messages describing the beginning days of the war overseas. Admittedly, years had passed since that message and it was possible new sorcerers had risen since then, but nothing of that sort had ever been mentioned by the lionbird in any of his later dispatches. The Gryphon would not have excluded such news.

*But we've heard nothing from him of late* . . . Although that thought would continue to nag him, Cabe was still fairly certain that the fog was not the work of the Aramites. It was not their sort of weapon.

It was only minutes later that they heard the clattering of rock.

Darkhorse halted and swung his head toward the direction of the noise. He said nothing, but twisted enough so that he could meet his companion's eyes. Cabe nodded. One hand went to the short blade at his side. Magic was his foremost weapon, but he had learned to keep other options available.

They remained still. For a time, the only sound was the warlock's quiet breathing. Then they heard the shifting of more rock, closer and more to their right.

The black stallion abruptly raised his head. "I smell—"

A gray-brown form the size of a large dog leapt at Cabe.

The thing was almost upon him before he struck back with a crude but handy force spell. Cabe smelled breath so rancid his stomach nearly turned. The creature howled as it was thrust back from its prey. He had not used enough power to kill it, but the thing was stunned. There was no doubt of that.

Darkhorse did not wait to see what it was that had assaulted them. He reared and came down on the beast's head with both hooves. The skull might have been made from the most delicate crystal, so completely did it shatter under the tremendous strength of the shadow steed's legs.

The warlock turned away in disgust. The massive stallion peered down at the horrendous carnage he had caused, then finally muttered, "Only a minor drake! A *small* one at that!"

"It was large enough for me, thank you. Strange, I didn't even sense it with my sorcery."

"Nor I! It was my sense of smell that did it in and that only when it was near enough to spring!"

Cabe finally forced himself to look down at the mangled corpse of the creature. It was not large by the standards of its kind, but, as he had commented, definitely large enough. Its presence puzzled him, however. "It should've never attacked us."

"Yes, that was its undoing to be sure!"

"That's not what I meant." Cabe pointed at the still form. "A minor drake that small rarely attacks something our size. Maybe if it had been part of a pack, but it seems to be alone."

"That *is* true," Darkhorse conceded. "Perhaps it was confused by this infernal fog."

"Confused and frightened. Maybe more."

"Meaning?"

The human sighed. "Meaning that we had best be even more cautious. I think this fog's as much a danger to our minds and our bodies as it is to our eyes."

Darkhorse shook his mane and laughed. "We are far superior to this hapless beast! We know what this mist can do; therefore we are prepared!"

"I hope so."

They left the corpse and moved on. More time passed, but how much more, Cabe could no longer even estimate. When the twinkle of light caught his eye, the warlock was not certain whether it was a torch or perhaps a star. For all he knew, night had already come upon them. The longer one was trapped in the smothering mist, the duller the senses seemed to become. Still, Cabe was fairly certain that what he had seen was real, not imagined. He pulled on the reins.

"A simple 'stop' will suffice, you know. I am *not* trained for the reins."

"Sorry." The warlock's voice was low, almost a whisper. "I saw something to"—if they were traveling west . . . *if*—"to the south. A light. It twinkled."

"Perhaps this blasted blanket is finally being thrown back, hmmm?" The eternal looked in the direction his rider had specified. "I see nothing nor do I sense anything out of the ordinary . . . not that there is much ordinary left."

"I was certain . . ." He saw the twinkle again. "There!"

Hesitation, then, "I see it. What would you have me do, Cabe? Shall we investigate it?"

"There doesn't seem to be any other choice. Have you noticed anything else that has had the ability to pierce this thick soup? I'd like to know what that is."

"Then it is settled. Good!"

Darkhorse picked his way carefully toward the glimmer. Cabe noticed for the first time that the shadow steed's hooves made no sound as he crossed the uneven, rock-strewn ground. They had probably not made a sound since the eternal had entered Legar. It was often hard for even Cabe to remember that his companion's external appearance in no way represented what Darkhorse truly was. The eternal simply admired the form. That did not mean that he obeyed every physical law demanded by such a shape. Darkhorse did what Darkhorse *chose* to do.

Below him, the shadow steed snorted in what was clearly anxiety. That bothered Cabe, for Darkhorse was not a being who often grew even the slightest bit nervous.

"I *know* this foulness . . ." he whispered. "I know this stench; I do!"

The light winked out again. The shadow steed halted. The two studied the area before them, but everywhere they looked, they only spotted the same murkiness.

"Where did it go? Do you see it, Cabe?"

"No . . . *there!*" His words were barely audible. Even sound seemed deadened by the murky fog.

Darkhorse followed his outstretched hand toward the light's new location. It was now to their right, which was west, the direction they had been originally headed. The ebony stallion snorted. "How did it come to be *there* now?"

"Magic."

The eternal slowed. "I will not go about this dismal land chasing phantom lights!"

"I don't blame—" The dark-haired spellcaster broke off as he noticed the twinkling light begin to move. "You won't have to! It's coming for *us!*"

Even Darkhorse could not have moved fast enough to avoid it. Cabe raised his arms over his face and summoned a shielding spell that he hoped would halt at least a substantial part of the oncoming juggernaut's power.

The light struck them . . . and scattered into a thousand tinier sparks that quickly faded away, leaving no trace of their fleeting existence.

"Someone wants to play *games* with us?" Darkhorse snorted and looked around for someone or something on which to vent his anger. "I will be more than happy to show them a new game!" He tore at the ground with one hoof, scattering rock.

"Quiet!" Cabe whirled around in the saddle.

"What is it?"

"I thought I heard . . ." Something clinked. It was the familiar and ominous sound of metal upon metal, a sound that from Cabe's vast experience spoke of men in armor. Men in armor who must be *very* near.

He heard it again, but this time it was in front of them. Below him, the shadow steed pricked up his ears, an equine habit learned during those long ago first days when the eternal had first experimented with the form.

A tall black figure coalesced before them.

Of the three of them, the wolf raider was the most surprised by the encounter, but that in no way meant that he was the slowest to react. His blade already out, he moved in on Cabe. There was no question, no demand for surrender, simply a strange, high cry and then an attack.

Darkhorse easily kept himself between the Aramite and the warlock. The raider slashed at him with the sword and Darkhorse, chuckling in an evil manner, allowed the edge to strike him in the neck. It was as if the attacker had tried to cut through solid stone. The blade snapped and the entire weapon fell from the startled raider's hand.

His confused hesitation was all the time the deadly stallion needed. Rising just a bit, Darkhorse kicked the Aramite in the chest. The force of the blow was enough to send the armored man flying back into the mist. Cabe winced as a heavy thud finally put an end note to the raider's haphazard flight.

Where there is one wolf raider, however, there must be others. The Gryphon had often written comments like that in his missives. The Aramites were, for the most part, pack creatures like the animal that was their namesake. Cabe, already cautious, sensed them before he heard them. They were coming from all sides in numbers enough to startle him.

"We've run into a patrol!" he whispered to his companion.

"Excellent! Rather would I fight something real than wander much longer in this thick morass!"

"That's not—" He had not time enough to finish, for the first shapes materialized then.

They moved in with fair but not exceptional precision. It was clear that the wolf raiders were put off by the rank fog, but they had been trained to suffer most any environment in the pursuit of their tasks and so they were adapting as best possible. Listening, Cabe now understood the purpose of the initial cry by the first raider. The Aramites were using it to keep in contact with one another, evidently deciding that stealth was not worth the cost of possibly losing every man to the mist.

"Well?" Darkhorse was suddenly shouting to the oncoming shadows. "Come, come! I have not all day! There are still other tasks I must deal with after I have finished with all of you!"

"*Darkhorse* . . ." This was not what the warlock had wanted. He had hoped to avoid danger as much as possible, which was one reason he had sought out the shadow steed. Darkhorse, while always willing to face an enemy, generally also respected the safety of his companions. Now, however, he was taking chances that Cabe felt were more than a little risky. The eternal was begging for a fight and it could only be because of Shade again. Wandering through the fog, seeing nothing, the shadow steed's thoughts must have returned to the subject that had become so much a part of his recent life.

It was too late to do anything about it now. The Aramites were coming at them from all directions and it would have been sheer folly to attempt to teleport away. Something within warned Cabe Bedlam that a teleport threatened his life more than this attack.

Two other swordsmen tried to cut Darkhorse's forelegs, but met with the same results as their predecessor. The demon steed kicked one of them back into the fog, but the other managed to avoid the blow. He pulled a curled dagger from his belt and threw it, but at Cabe, the rider, rather than Darkhorse. It still had not registered in the minds of the raiders that the horse was the greater of the threats to them. They assumed that with the rider under control or dead, the battle would be won.

The warlock saw the dagger coming and although he had shielded himself against ordinary weapons, he deflected it, deciding that it was not wise to risk himself because of overconfidence. Then he turned as both his magical senses and his ears warned him of several raiders coming from the rear. A lance came within a yard of him, but with a spell he lifted both the weapon and the man and used them to clear four other soldiers nearby. The spell suddenly went awry, however, and the lancer dropped to the ground like a rock. The raider scrambled to his feet and back into the fog.

"Careless," a voice said.

Cabe looked at Darkhorse, but the stallion was busy dealing with both the raider who had evaded his first assault and two others who had joined the survivor. One was trying to rope the eternal, a foolish maneuver if ever there was one. Darkhorse caught the rope in his teeth and, while the Aramite was still holding it, pulled with such might that he sent the soldier flying into his companion. Both collided with a harsh clang and crumpled to the ground. The soldier who had survived the earlier attack backed away, almost immediately disappearing into the fog. The shadow steed laughed.

Forgetting the voice, Cabe returned to his own dire situation. Where the eternal had no qualms about the destruction of his adversaries, Cabe still felt pain every time he was forced to kill, even though most often it was in self-defense. He held back as much as he could, trying instead to dissuade or knock senseless the attackers. With his abilities suddenly once again in doubt, the warlock felt justified in resorting to flying rocks and tiny windstorms to beat back his opponents.

This did not mean that he was not forced to kill. Some of the Aramites could not be stopped any other way. They brought their own deaths by charging wildly into the storm of rocks. One reached close enough to almost pull Cabe from the saddle. Try as he might, the sorcerer could not free himself and he discovered then that some Aramite weapons would hurt him regardless of his protective spells. The dagger that caught him slightly on the leg was bejeweled and also likely bewitched for just such a battle. Over their long history of war, it made sense that they would learn to deal with spellcasters. In the end, he had struck back out of sheer reflex . . . and had sent a jolt of energy so great in intensity that he had literally burned the man to death in less than a breath.

Still they kept coming. It was almost as if the entire raider force had found them.

"Unngh!" The blow against his head shook Cabe so hard he had to struggle to keep in the saddle. His first thought was that someone with a sling had caught him unaware, but his spell should have protected him regardless. When he heard *Darkhorse* grunt in pain, though, the warlock knew that it was no mundane weapon that had hurt him.

Where was it? None of the raiders he had sensed carried any such weapon. In truth, the greatest danger he and Darkhorse faced was likely not the Aramites, who only had sheer numbers on their side, but rather the malevolent fog, which continued to sap his will and play havoc with his magical abilities.

He kicked out at a swordsman who had somehow gotten past Darkhorse, then shocked the man before he could close the gap again. The Aramites were giving him little time to think. Even as the soldier fell twitching to the earth, Cabe himself was stung. Every bone in his body seemed to quiver. This time, the addled warlock slipped almost halfway off of his companion. It was only quick shifting on the demon steed's part that kept Cabe from falling.

"Cabe! You must hold tight! I cannot fight and maintain your balance!"

"I . . . can't." It was painful just to straighten. He was almost flung off again when Darkhorse spun about to defend his right flank.

"Very well . . ." The ebony stallion almost sounded disappointed with the turn of events. "Hold on as well as you can, Cabe! I will take us to safety!"

The warlock gripped the saddle tight and forced himself to look up. Darkhorse had abandoned the fight and was now clearing a path through the attackers. Several went down, but there always seemed to be more. Arrows struck both warlock and eternal, but Cabe's spell still held and Darkhorse was Darkhorse.

In the midst of the fog and chaos, the weakened spellcaster caught sight of a truly peculiar figure squatting atop a rock formation. The Aramites, who streamed past his very location, took no note of him. The mist partly obscured the figure, but Cabe made out long, spindly legs and arms and an obscenely round torso. The head was mostly covered by a long, wide-rimmed hat that fell down over the face . . . if indeed the odd parody had one.

*A spider*, was his first impression. *A human spider.*

The entire scene wavered then, but not because of Cabe's condition. Rather, a wave flowed over the area, shaking rider and mount and throwing the pursuing raiders into new turmoil.

Cabe recognized it although he had rarely experienced the sensation before and certainly not of the magnitude of this ripple. *Wild magic.* The term was not quite correct, but it was as close as any description could come to explaining what was happening.

One of the rock formations nearest to them melted. Flat ground began to rise. The warlock heard a scream and located the source just in time to see one of the raiders *fold* into himself and disappear. Several of the Aramites were struggling to free themselves from ground that had become liquefied. An empty suit of armor, half corroded, indicated that something else had happened, but Cabe was not in a hurry to discover exactly what that was.

"What . . . what . . . what . . ." Darkhorse was shivering. The demon steed appeared caught in some sort of fit. He was changing, too, becoming stretched out like a true shadow. Cabe felt the saddle move. He looked down and saw that it was sinking into his companion.

The spellcaster threw himself off. The saddle disappeared within Darkhorse as if it had never existed. *Wild magic.* Once in existence, it could create earth-quakes, fires, anything. The very fabric of reality would be turned about for the time it existed. Literally anything that magic was capable of doing might happen depending on the intensity of the wave. It could also concentrate in one area, become a well of sorts where anyone who entered became subject to its insanity.

Sometimes it was caused by an irregularity in the natural forces of the world. Most often, it was because some mage had been too careless. Reckless spellcast-ing could pull and bend those forces beyond safe limits. Sometimes the world repaired itself, but other times it tried to adjust to the new patterns of force and then would come the ripples or waves of pure energy. Pure, unfocused energy.

There was nothing that could be done. Cabe only hoped that the wave would play itself out and leave them alone.

"You! Keeper!"

He realized the voice was directed at him. The warlock twisted around. A gruff, bearded Aramite wearing the cloak of an officer was moving toward him, battle-ax in his huge hands. Cabe felt a buzzing in his head, then saw the small crystal hanging around the soldier's neck. A Quel talisman and one evidently designed to deflect sorcery.

"Stop what you're doing to my men, keeper, or I'll save the inquisitors the trouble of questioning you!"

The title by which the raider called him puzzled Cabe Bedlam until he re-called that to the Aramites the only mages were all of the keeper caste. "This isn't my doing!"

"You lie!" He swung the ax, coming within arm's length of the anxious warlock's chest. "Your last chance! Do it! Don't think you'll be able to take me, either! Your spells won't even touch me! I'm protected!"

"*Are* you now?" came a singsong voice. Cabe recognized it as the one he had heard only moments earlier. "Or *aren't* you?"

To Cabe, the voice cut through all else, demanding his complete attention. Not so for the Aramite, who still waited for the warlock to obey. Then, both of them looked at the crystal, which had, without warning, begun to glow with an internal fire.

The officer snarled. "What did you do?" He reached for the crystal with one hand. "You *can't* have—"

The Quel talisman melted through his breastplate before he could even finish the statement. He dropped his ax and tried to take hold of the crystal, but it was already too deep for him to reach that way. The raider's eyes widened. He scrambled to tear the chain from his neck but his fumbling, gauntleted hands were too slow.

Cabe tried to help him even before the screaming began, but the man would not hold still and the warlock's spells would still not affect him. There was the smell of burning flesh.

It was over relatively swiftly. The crystal burned through his chest with rapid, unchecked success. When the end came, the Aramite literally had only time to stiffen and gasp before collapsing in a limp heap on the inhospitable ground.

"Not very strong it was. Strong it definitely wasn't."

"Who are you?" Cabe searched for the owner of the singsong voice, fairly certain that it was a strange creature with a round form and long, spidery appendages.

"Cabe . . ." At first he thought that the voice was mocking him, but it was not the same one. Turned about by the sudden series of events, it took him several seconds to recognize the demon steed.

Darkhorse still stood where he had been, but now he was able to move his head a bit. Cabe rushed over to him and would have taken hold of his companion, but Darkhorse vehemently shook his head. "No, do not touch me! I am not yet stable. You might be pulled in. I could never forgive myself for that!"

"Are you all right?"

"Not by far, Cabe! Now I recognize this madness! I thought it impossible. I thought the last traces had perished with Shade, but this is too real. This has the taste of Vraad about it . . . the taste of a cursed realm called *Nimth*."

They both knew of Nimth, the place from which, countless millennia ago, a race of sorcerers called the Vraad had fled into the Dragonrealm. Humans today were the descendants of the Vraad, although from what he had unearthed of them, Cabe would not have cared to call the dark race ancestor. They had flourished briefly in this new world, but had disappeared as a culture, if arrogance and indifference could be considered a culture, before the first generation finally died off.

Yet it was said their world still lived despite the damage they had done to it with their careless, godlike attitudes toward sorcery. Shade had hinted that and he, it had turned out, had been one of them. Darkhorse had even known them, although he refused to speak of that time and could not or would not remember much of it. Some Vraad, it appeared, had had a penchant for torture.

The ground rose under them again, but not much. There were fewer shouts now. Most of the wolf raiders had either vanished back into the mists or were dead. Only a few, either stubborn or trapped by the ever-shifting reality, still remained. At the moment none of them was very concerned with the horse and rider. They were either trying to help fallen comrades or simply trying to survive. "It can't be Nimth, Darkhorse! Nimth is lost, sealed off from everything!"

"Not so sealed. Shade always had a link with it. I tell you it is Nimth . . . or a taste of it at the very least."

"But how?"

"That, I cannot—"

A thing like a nightmare hodgepodge of plant, animal, and mineral formed from empty space. Without preamble, it charged the warlock before it was even fully solid. It had hundreds of vinelike tendrils for legs, reptilian forearms that ended in claws much like those of a crab, and an oval body that resembled a simple hunk of granite. Carved into the center of that was what at first glance appeared to be a crude image of a human face, but the jade eyes that stared with hunger at the warlock and the huge maw that opened and closed, constantly revealing row upon row of sharp teeth, looked real enough. It moved at an incredible speed, considering that each tendril had to push forward to give it momentum. It spattered a greenish slime about as it traveled. Cabe noticed with dismay that the trail it left behind it burned into the hard ground beneath as the monster passed. There was no doubt that it was a magical construct; no creature could have been born so.

"Stand away, Cabe!" Darkhorse demanded, putting himself between the monster and his friend. "I will deal with this abomination!"

The warlock stepped aside, but not to protect himself. There was no way that he could prevent Darkhorse from trying to defend him, but he was also not the kind of man who would let others do battle while he stood by watching.

The magical abomination slowed as it neared Darkhorse. It shifted to one side, as if trying to get around to the eternal's flank. Darkhorse kept the monster before him, which resulted in Cabe ending up behind the shadowy stallion.

The warlock started toward the left, but then the abomination moved again and Cabe once more found himself standing to the rear of his companion.

The two leviathans continued to square off. Darkhorse, Cabe knew, was try-ing to evaluate the thing's abilities. Where anything associated with Nimth was concerned, the demon horse was unusually careful. He had a long and bitter memory of things spawned from that sorry realm.

The warlock once more tried to join Darkhorse and once more the madcap abomination shifted also, again leaving Cabe where he had started. Things were going from bad to worse, for in addition to the beast, the fog was thickening further. Already, both Darkhorse and his adversary were half-hidden from his view and that with the warlock only standing two or three yards from the ebony stallion's backside. If they had to battle this thing blind, there was no telling what the outcome would be. Darkhorse was *not* invulnerable and Cabe thought even less of his own chances.

Despite his wishes, the foul mist continued to thicken . . . no, at this point, *solidify* almost seemed a more fitting word. The magic-wrought beast was already little more than a shape. Not wanting to suddenly find himself alone against a threat that might be able to see when he could not, Cabe decided to risk the danger and come up on Darkhorse from behind. If he could not be at the shadow steed's side, he would at least remain close enough so as not to lose him.

As he took a step forward, however, the abomination backed away an equiva-lent distance. Darkhorse, needless to say, followed his monstrous adversary. Like Cabe, he had no intention of losing sight. Unfortunately, each step he took seemed to make him fade a little more.

"Darkhorse . . . Darkhorse! Don't follow it! Wait for me!"

Either Darkhorse chose to ignore him, which was not likely, or he could not hear the warlock, for the eternal not only did not reply, but also trotted even farther ahead. Now, not only could Cabe not even make out the vague shape of the magical monstrosity, he could barely even see the outline of the massive stallion.

Dignity aside, the anxious warlock shouted more frantically, "Darkhorse! It's a ploy! We're being separated! Come back!"

He tried running, but for every step he took, his companion took four. Little by little, Darkhorse became a thin shadow in the dank mist. Cabe's shouts went unheeded. Even when he tried to send a burst of sorcerous energy in the shadow steed's direction, the magical fireball only made it halfway before fading to nothing in midflight.

Something tangled in his legs and sent him falling. He rolled around for several seconds, trying to untangle himself from whatever had snared him. Whatever it was, though, it disappeared as quickly as it had appeared. Swearing to Lord Drazeree, the spellcaster rolled back onto his feet and turned his gaze quickly in the direction he had last seen Darkhorse.

Neither the demon steed nor his adversary was in sight. In fact, Cabe could see nothing at all, not even the ground just beyond his feet.

"Darkhorse!" He did not think that the other would hear him and so when there was no reply, it did not surprise him in the least. He was, for all practical purposes, entombed as good as if he had been buried miles beneath Legar's surface.

As dangerous as it might be to teleport in such a magical mire, Cabe knew he had to risk it. He would return to the hills of Esedi and hope that Darkhorse followed suit once he discovered that the human was missing. Then they could decide what to do about Legar.

He was careful and deliberate as he teleported in order to ensure that there was no mistake. A spell that normally would have taken him only a swift thought became an elaborate series of mental exercises, each designed to create success. Although all of that only took him the blink of an eye to complete, to the mage it was an eternity.

What made matters worse was finding himself still lost in the deadly reddish green mist when all was said and done.

"*Tsk,*" came the singsong voice from behind him. "Not one of my better. One of my better it certainly was not."

He spun around, seeking the source. "Who are you? Where are you?"

"Good enough, though. Enough to be good."

Cabe squinted. Was the visibility just a bit better? He saw that it was, for now he could at least make out a few patches of ground beyond arm's reach. The fog continued to thin even as he watched. It was becoming too obvious that whoever had spoken must certainly be the reason behind his separation from Darkhorse. The warlock clenched both fists and carefully turned in a circle, seeking with his eyes, ears, and magical senses some evidence of where the culprit was located. This could not be the work of the Crystal Dragon, at least he thought not, and it did not seem the kind of weapon the wolf raiders appreciated.

That only left . . .

Then he saw the rock, a vague, miniature hill just off to his left. Atop the rock, spindly arms and legs bent, squatted the same outlandish form he had noticed earlier, the form he was certain had been responsible for the raider officer's gruesome death.

The fog parted slowly but certainly from the rock and its lone inhabitant. Cabe saw that the figure was more or less human, but as oddly shaped as anything he had ever seen. The bizarre figure was clad in a strangely patterned courtier's suit of purple and black that would have looked clownish on any other person but somehow was perfect for its present wearer and not just because of its shape. The hat's flap still covered most of the face. All he could see was a chin that ended in an almost extreme point.

The head lifted a little, allowing him then to see the curved line that was all there was to the mouth. "I am Plool the Great," the spidery figure abruptly said. Other than raising his head, he did not move, not even to remove his hat. "The Great Plool I am."

Cabe Bedlam shivered as he became aware of what it was he was facing here. Plool was at home in the foul mist. He manipulated it to his own desires in the manner of someone long accustomed to the practice. Yet Darkhorse had called the fog a thing of twisted, decaying Nimth, the hellish place from which the mage's own ancestors had fled.

He had never thought to wonder if perhaps some had *not* fled Nimth. He had never wondered what they or their descendants might have become, living as they did in a world where the natural laws had all been torn asunder and wild magic flowed forever unchecked.

Plool could only be a *Vraad* . . . and now he was loose on the Dragonrealm.

THE MISSIVE FROM Cabe in no way calmed Gwen. She paced the floor of their bedroom, cursing the fact that she could not be with him. It *had* been her own idea to have one parent remain behind. Her own parents, long, oh, so long dead, had instilled in her the need for someone to be there for the children. Cabe was of the same mind, although the enchantress did not doubt for one moment that he would have also raised a protest if it had been her task and not his.

None of which made the waiting any easier. The magical message that she had received had given her a brief rundown of Cabe's time in Zuu, but knowledgeable as she was where her husband was concerned, the Lady Gwen knew there was more to the story than what he had written. His tale of King Lanith's rather heavy-handed recruiting of mages reminded her too much of the days when Melicard had sought out spellcasters, talismans, and even demons in his quest to eradicate the drake race. Lanith's ambitions would have to be looked into and not just by her. Toos and Melicard probably knew all about this already, which somewhat infuriated her since they had not seen fit to pass on that bit of knowledge. One was never certain just how much information was being held back at the "councils" she and Cabe attended with the two monarchs.

It was not the gathering of mages that bothered her, though. It was the thought that more had happened in Zuu. She could not help feeling that perhaps Cabe and Darkhorse had not simply entered Zuu, stayed there for a time, and departed. Because of that feeling, she wondered what else her husband might have left unsaid and what dangers he might still have to face.

*Worry doesn't help him*, she angrily reminded herself. It made her feel no better. Gwen sighed. There were other things that needed to be taken care of. Perhaps, she hoped, they would be enough to keep her from dwelling too much on what might be happening to the man she loved.

As she departed the bedroom, she almost walked into a figure just beyond the doorway. The other caught her in his arms and held her just a second too long for her tastes. She freed herself and backed a step away before realizing that doing so only added to the newcomer's amusement.

He was tall and lean, with arrogant but striking features that had many females, human and drake, eyeing him with speculation that he often encouraged. His eyes were narrow, burning orbs that could snare a person and almost make one kneel. He wore a tight-fitting, emerald and gold suit reminiscent of those of the royal court of Gordag-Ai. Gwen knew that he had chosen this particular one in part because it appealed to her tastes. Kyl and the younger drakes wore real human clothes, not magical constructs formed from their own skin, which was what the elder drakes often did. It was not quite the same color combination as his skin, which was a more elegant mixing of the green and gold, but it was still eye-catching. Still, Kyl could have probably created a perfect duplicate if he had wanted to do so. His skills were much more advanced than those of his older counterparts. Sometimes, the Lady of the Amber thought that they were *too* advanced.

"What are you doing up here, Kyl?"

He gave her a sly smile that long practice had made overwhelming against many a maiden, but Gwen simply had to look at the slightly edged teeth to remind herself that this was indeed a drake, not a man. "Your pardon, Lady Gwendolyn. I should not walk with ssssuch hasste. I hope that you were not disturbed in any way."

She held back the smile that she wanted so badly to display to him. Kyl, for all his perfection, still slipped back into drake sibilance more often than either his brother or his sister. He especially had difficulty when he was in her presence. "And what brings you here in such haste?"

"I come to tell you, gracious lady, that the Manor has visitorsss."

"A servant could have told me that." Try as she might, the enchantress could never warm to Kyl. He was always trying to be near her or, more to her dismay, near Valea. The young heir to the Dragon Emperor throne was always good with her daughter, but his constant "accidents," which always somehow involved touching Gwen, made her worry about the future. It would not be long before

Valea was old enough to truly gain the attention of males. In that respect, she was already too pretty now. "You need not have troubled yourself so."

"These are special visitors, my lady. Ssspecial visitors demand special treatment."

"Who are they?" She could recall no one whom she was expecting.

"They are clothed so as not to be recognized, but one hasss shown an insignia given to him by the Blue Dragon himself!"

The Lady Gwen ignored the way Kyl's eyes lit up whenever he mentioned another Dragon King. *Emissaries from Irillian? But why disguised, then?* "Lead me to them."

Kyl led her through the Manor and out the front. Any other time, the sorceress would have enjoyed a walk through the grounds. Kyl's close presence and the mystery of the two visitors, not to mention Cabe's situation, made that all but impossible.

The two visitors indeed resembled monks more than emissaries. Nothing but cloth was visible, but she thought that the taller of the two had to be the male that the drake had mentioned. The unknown duo stood just beyond the invisible barrier that protected the Manor grounds from unwanted guests and marauding beasts, which sometimes turned out to be the same thing.

"I am Lady Gwendolyn Bedlam. Before you say anything, let me see the ring that you revealed to the boy here." She heard Kyl hiss quietly. Perhaps he would stop trying to play her now that she had dropped him down a few levels. It was good to remind him on occasion that while he was the heir to a throne, he was also under *their* guardianship.

It looked as if the one she had directed her demand to was about to say something else, but then he shrugged and raised a hand toward her. The sleeve fell back. The enchantress glanced down to study the ring.

When she saw the hand that wore the ring, however, all interest in the Blue Dragon's gift vanished.

The hand was covered with *fur*, which by itself was unusual enough, but then Gwen noted a trace of *feathers* toward the wrist. Astounded, she looked up. With his free hand, the visitor was pulling back his hood. A dignified but weary avian face had been hidden under that hood. Toward the back and sides, the feathers gave way to fur. It was as if someone had crossed a lion, a bird of prey, and a man together.

"It's good to see you, my lady," the Gryphon politely whispered.

She could only gape. After so *long* . . .

"You have not changed, Lady Gwen," the Gryphon added when no comment was forthcoming from the enchantress. "Still as beautiful as ever."

"You . . . You're here!"

"That we are." There was something sad in the way the monarch of Penacles said that, but Gwen was still too shocked to really take note of it.

Her head jerked toward the other traveler. "Then, this must be——"

The smaller figure pulled back the hood. Again, the sorceress was taken aback. She had never met the Gryphon's bride, only corresponded with her. Seeing Troia now proved to Gwen that imagination had hardly readied herself for the truth. She was, as the Gryphon had first related, a cat woman.

*More woman than cat*, Gwen could not help noticing. Even the cloak could not completely hide the lithe body underneath. Every movement, no matter how small, was fluid. Her features were exotic. Her dark, arresting eyes, so truly cat-like, were half-veiled. She had a tiny, well-formed nose that twitched now and then and long, full lips ever so inviting when she smiled. The hair on her head was cut short and went from pitch-black to dark brown. A closer glance revealed that the tawny, striped coloring was not her skin, but rather a short layer of fur that, if the enchantress recalled correctly, covered her entire body.

Seeing her for the first time, Gwen could not help but feel a little relieved that Troia had come here as the mate of the Gryphon and not a single female. Aurim was already too susceptible to the charms of women.

Only one thing marred Troia's appearance and that was the row of scars on the right side of her face. They did not succeed in detracting much from her beauty, but they made one curious. The Gryphon should have been able to remove them with ease. His sorcery was easily on a par with that of the Bedlams.

She realized she had never finished greeting the cat woman. "I have waited so long to actually see you, Troia!"

"And I you, Lady Gwen." Again there was the hint of sadness that the enchantress had first noticed in the Gryphon. What was wrong?

"May we enter?" asked the lionbird. "I was not certain if the barrier would still admit me and I knew that it would not admit Troia. Also, politeness dictated that we ask *permission* to enter." He glanced at his bride as if this had been a minor point of contention between them. From their letters, Gwen had been given to understand that there were times when Troia could make her look like a shrinking violet in comparison.

"Where are my manners? Of course, you can enter here!"

The duo stepped forward with caution. The barrier had various ways of dealing with outsiders, many of them seemingly of its own design. Having been given permission by the lady of the land, though, neither the Gryphon nor his mate was hindered in any way.

Gwen turned to Kyl. "Kyl, if you would be so kind as to alert someone that we have special guests, I would like some food and drink ready by the time we reach the garden terrace. Would you please do that for me?"

The drake lordling bowed gracefully to both his guardian and the two newcomers. "I should be happy to, my lady. If you will excusse me, Your Majessstiesss?"

The Gryphon tried to hold back a hint of amusement that had dared to rise against the sadness. "By all means."

With a surreptitious glance at both Gwen and Troia, the young heir departed. The three watched until he had disappeared from sight, then returned to their conversation.

The Gryphon shook his head, whether amused or annoyed by Kyl's ways, Gwen could not say. "I had not thought about how near to adulthood the hatchlings truly were. Aurim must be almost a man, too."

"Very much so, although there are lapses. One expects those, however, at his age." Something had been nagging at the redheaded sorceress's memory and now she knew what it was. "And where—"

Troia's eyes widened and the Gryphon raised his other hand in a request for silence. Gwen noticed with horror that two fingers, the lower two, were *missing*.

"*Gryphon!*"

He sighed. "I see there is no purpose in holding back."

"Tell her, Gryph," the cat woman hissed. "Tell her why we've braved pirates and raging sea storms to come to her."

The lionbird took hold of his wife, who shook as if every fiber of her being wanted to cry out at the world. Gwen's face went grim; she suspected that she already knew the answer to the question that the Gryphon had prevented her from finishing. *Rheena, please let it not be true! Let me be wrong!*

"You were going to ask about our son, Demion, were you not?"

"Yes, but—"

The Gryphon, his eyes chilling, would not let her continue. "Demion is in Sirvak Dragoth, Lady Bedlam, his home forever more now." His voice was toneless. "He died at the hands of the wolf raiders."

# IX

FOR TWENTY MINUTES they had sat together in the privacy of the garden terrace and for twenty minutes Gwen had been unable to come any closer to the story behind the terrible words the Gryphon had spoken concerning his son. In truth, only she and Troia sat; the lionbird stood staring off into the main garden, his claws sheathing and unsheathing, his mane stiff. Neither he nor his bride had spoken more than a handful of words since their arrival.

Troia stared at her husband as if nothing else around her existed. *That may very well be the case to her,* the enchantress pondered. *With Demion . . . dead . . . they can only turn to each other.*

Still, there were limits to her respect for their turbulent emotions. It was clear that they had been dwelling on their loss since before their voyage, certainly a long time. Gwen did not believe that they should simply forget the loss of their sole offspring, but she was one who believed that life should go on, if only in the very name of the one who had been taken from them.

"Gryphon . . . Troia . . . I share your grief, you certainly must know that, but I need to know what happened; I need to know and I think you need to tell me."

"You are correct, of course, my Lady of the Amber. I have been remiss." He turned back to the two women. A table stood between them, a table with food and wine. Neither had been touched even by the enchantress, but now the Gryphon took the decanter and poured some of the glistening plum wine into one of the gold and silver chalices. Quite suddenly, the avian features transformed into those of a handsome, silver-haired man with patrician features. That image, though, lasted only long enough for the lionbird to swallow the wine in one swift gulp.

The Gryphon returned the goblet to the table, then glanced at his wife. "I will make this short . . . for all our sakes."

She nodded, but said nothing more. A look had come into her eyes, but one directed toward neither her mate nor the enchantress. It was a look that could have only been directed toward the unknown wolf raiders who had stolen a precious life from her.

"How did it happen?" Gwen encouraged. "Is the war—"

He seemed to dismiss the war as something inconsequential to the topic. "The war goes well. Morgis and the Master Guardians of hidden Sirvak Dragoth have helped lead many of the former slave states of the empire to freedom. We have also done our small part."

*Small part, indeed!* thought the flame-tressed sorceress. She knew, through missives sent by the drake Morgis, of the many things that the Gryphon had accomplished. He, more than any other individual, had been the driving force behind the continent-wide revolt against the sons of the wolf. It was odd that she and Cabe had learned much of what they knew from one of the get of the Blue Dragon. It was odder still that a drake could become so loyal a friend and companion to the Gryphon. From respectful adversaries to comrades-in-arms.

"The war goes well," he repeated, "but because of it, the Aramites grew— have grown—more desperate and treacherous in their actions. When we overthrew Luperion, they began to gather their forces in and around their original homeland, especially in Canisargos, the seat of their power." The Gryphon paused and gazed forlornly at his hostess. "Lady Bedlam, Gwendolyn, you have to understand that we are not like your kind. I was created a hunter and Troia's people are born that way."

"I made my first raider kill at the age of eight summers," whispered the cat woman. Her eyes were narrow slits. "Three of my brothers made theirs at seven. It's the way we are."

The lionbird nodded in agreement. "What I try to say is that Demion was not unfamiliar with the war. He had fought and made his first kill only months before . . . and that far, far later than he could have. We had barely been able to keep him in check for these past four years and believe me, we *tried*."

Gwen nodded, understanding. She understood quite well what it meant to grow up in wartime.

"Chaenylon, it was." The monarch of Penacles unsheathed both sets of claws again. "Chaenylon, which will forever mean despair to us."

They had only taken the Aramite port city some three months before, but in that short time it had quickly become a valuable part of their western campaign. Chaenylon gave them a new location to ship supplies to the forces ever inching closer to the heart of the empire, Canisargos. After all these years, the empire's great citadel was within striking distance. The Aramites had always been more willing to give up their slave states rather than leave Canisargos anything but much overdefended. Now, not even that would save them. The confederation of free kingdoms, with the help of the Gryphon and Duke Morgis, had put together a combination of armies that would soon launch an attack in the direction of the Aramite city. It was possible that the wolf raider empire would cease to exist within the next three years.

That did not mean that the raiders would be defeated. There would be pockets of resistance for years and more than a few ships had slipped away into the open sea.

Gwen flinched when she heard the last. She had still not told her guests of the wolf raider rumors, in part because she feared that they would leave the moment they knew, but also because she herself *needed* to know what had happened overseas.

"Either they knew about the impending attack or it was pure bad fortune, but whatever the case, one morning Chaenylon itself came under assault. *Six* warships simply sailed in. The harbor was madness. They utilized special catapults to bombard the city. There were gryph—gryphon riders everywhere. Worse, from every ship there came an armed force. We turned back the first wave, but there was no way of keeping the second from landing." The lionbird's eyes lost their focus. He was once again in the midst of battle. "Western

Chaenylon was in flames. The Aramites seized control of the docks, then spread through the city."

Lady Bedlam recalled the siege of Penacles long ago. She and Cabe, fleeing the Dragon Kings who had sought the grandson of Nathan Bedlam, had been given refuge by the Gryphon. The drakes had not taken kindly to that. For days, they had tried to take Penacles. While the battle had never quite escalated to the sort of fighting that the defenders of Chaenylon must have gone through, it had been terrible enough. She could only imagine what her two guests had suffered through.

"We can never be certain of what happened."

"We know *enough!*" hissed Troia. "We know that it was *D'Farany* again or at least one of his puppets!"

"Yesss, we know *that*. We know it was D'Farany's curs, Troia, or else why would we be here in the first place?" Gwen would have spoken then, but the Gryphon, not noting her reaction to this latest revelation, continued with his horrific tale. "It happened during the fighting. We thought he would be safe where we had placed him. Understand, Lady Bedlam, that we valued Demion above *all* else. He was our pride. Despite his desires, we kept him away as much as we could, but no one could count on wolf raider tenacity."

They had moved Demion and several others to what was considered the safest quarter of the city. Well behind the haphazard line of fighting. Not only was there a line of defense to protect him, but there was also little in that quarter that should have interested the raiders. Chaenylon had been one of the empire's centers for cartographical study and thus great archives housing much of the sum of their seafaring knowledge had been built there. Maps dating back thousands of years were stored in the archives as were the most current. Whether drawn up by the Aramites themselves or stolen from some captured vessel, the maps were all carefully stored for future use. Much of the region where Demion had been placed was simply an outgrowth of those archives. There were only small stores of weapons and food there. Anything of true value to the invading force should have been near the fighting.

Yet, someone among the raiders had evidently found some need for those maps. Enough need to send a small but efficient force to hunt down the archives. They had somehow slipped past the lines, a trail of dead sentries marking their way. Their target they reached with minimal resistance, for everyone's attention was on the main struggle. Once inside the buildings, they had proceeded to ransack the archives.

There it was that they had also evidently come across Demion, who had left the safety of the building he had originally been housed in by his parents.

Here again the Gryphon straightened. His mane bristled and his voice was both proud and bitter as he added, "We know that he and a few soldiers evidently with him gave of themselves the best they could. Nine raiders met their end there, three of them definite kills by our son." He clenched his fists together. "But there were more than nine."

"And the coward that *cut* him down did so from behind!" roared the furious and frustrated cat woman. She was on her feet in an instant, her own claws flashing in and out as she no doubt pictured the scene in her mind.

Despite barely being able to keep her own composure, Gwen responded in soothing tones. "But he did not let them take him without paying for it, Troia, Gryphon! He did not let himself be taken without payment. He fought honorably to the end. I grieve for your loss, but it is the good memories of him you must keep in mind from here on. The memories of what he was to you and how he will *always* be with you no matter where you are." She was aware how different the thinking processes of the two were compared to that of either herself or Cabe. Both the Gryphon and his mate were civilized, but they were also predators, more than even humans were. She could only hope that her quick words carried some meaning to them. "Demion would want you to be looking forward, not dwelling in a maelstrom of hurt and anger."

"We look forward, Lady of the Amber. We look forward to the final hunt, the snaring, and the running down of the curs responsible for his death." The Gryphon's part-avian, part-human eyes glared at the empty sky. Both he and his bride calmed a bit, if only on the outside. "Curs who have run to the Dragonrealm, if what we discovered is true."

"The Dragonrealm?" It was a verification of everything she had feared, but Gwen did not reveal that fear to the duo.

Unwilling to sit down again, Troia began to pace gracefully back and forth. "In the end, we repulsed the damned dogs' attack. They lost two ships there, but Chaenylon was in ruins. It took us the better part of the day to discover . . . his body. Whether the raider who killed him returned to the ships with the other survivors or died in the city before he could flee, we'll probably never know, my lady. I wish we would . . . I'd follow him personally to the ends of the world . . . What we do know is that they seemed most interested in charts concerning the Dragonrealm."

"And we discovered then that three of the ships never returned to the empire," interjected the Gryphon. "Three ships, including the one carrying Lord D'Farany."

"You mentioned him twice now . . . who is he?"

"He is a keeper, Lady Bedlam. An Aramite sorcerer."

His words struck her with the force of a well-shot bolt. Having kept abreast of the distant war since its inception, the enchantress was aware of most of the major events. There was one in particular she recalled about the sinister keepers. "But they all died! Almost twenty years ago!"

"Died or gone *mad*, you mean? Lord Ivon D'Farany did not die; as to whether he went mad, that is another question."

"Even still, he should be powerless!" Was Cabe heading toward a confrontation with a sorcerer of the darkest arts? "You said that they—"

"Had lost their link with their god, the unlamented Ravager, yes. You recall correctly. That loss, that withdrawal, was enough to kill most of them and leave the others mindless." He squawked. "Somehow, a young keeper named D'Farany survived and although it cannot be vouchsafed that he had no power of his own, he has time and time again brought forth sorcerous talismans and artifacts that were thought lost and used them to the raiders' advantage." The lionbird held up his maimed hand. "This is the work of Lord D'Farany; even my skill is insufficient to heal it proper. Troia, too, bears the mark of one of the keeper's discoveries." She turned so that Gwen could better see the scars across her face. For the first time, the enchantress noticed that they *glowed* ever so slightly. Glowed bloodred. "He, more than anything else, has slowed the course of the war by at least three, perhaps four years."

"And he does all this even though the dogs themselves mutter about his sanity!" Troia snorted, still pacing about.

Her quick, constant movements were disrupting Gwen's attempts to remain calm. "You think he's here."

"He *has* to be," the lionbird returned, almost pleading again. "There is no other place for him to hide so great a force. He cannot stay anywhere near the empire or the free lands. D'Farany, by abandoning the war, has in a sense made himself enemy of both. That is why he must be here."

"What about the war? What will happen with you gone?"

He looked closely at her. "The war now moves well even without us and especially without D'Farany to aid them. We have given more than a decade of our own lives in addition to the life of our one child. There was no one who did not think we were entitled to depart. I did not abandon them. In fact, Sirvak Dragoth would only be too happy to see an end made of the curs. D'Farany and his men, as long as they live to fight again, will forever be a fear covering the freed lands and the surrounding waters."

"We'll find him, my lady," hissed the cat woman. "He killed Demion as good as if he were the one who struck the blow. His death alone will pay for our son's."

The anxious sorceress could not help but blurt, "Do you truly think so?"

Neither of them could look at her then, but Troia slowly replied, "Nothing else will balance that scale, not even . . ." She held her tongue at the last moment, apparently unwilling to share some further revelation with her host. "Nothing."

"The voyage across did nothing but stir the embers to new life," the Gryphon added. It seemed whenever one faltered, the other was there to continue the tale. To Gwen, it revealed just how close the duo were to each other and in turn how close they had been to their son. "When we arrived on the shore of southeastern Irillian, I was barely able to control my desire to use sorcery to speed our journey to here along. Out of respect of the Blue Dragon, I held off until we reached the borders between his domain and that of the Storm Dragon. Then I found I could not wait any longer. Daring the lord of Wenslis's ire, I teleported us from his lands to the ruins of Mito Pica, just beyond your forest. We would have even materialized at the very border of your domain, but the Green Dragon has ever been a good neighbor to Penacles and I would not wish to cause my former home any ill will."

"We've told you our story, Lady Bedlam." Troia stalked up to the enchantress, then nearly went down on one knee just before her. "Gryph said that if anyone could help us, if anyone had some word, it would be the Bedlams."

The Gryphon stood beside his mate, the maimed hand on her shoulder. "Even if you have no word of the raiders, I ask that you might grant us the boon of letting us stay but one night so that we might be refreshed for the hunt ahead of us. You have my word that I will make amends for the trouble."

She looked at them, at their eyes that both pleaded and hoped, and wanted to say that she had heard nothing. Like Darkhorse with Shade, they were obsessed. Gwen could not find it in herself to lie to them, though, possibly because she knew that under the circumstances she would have acted the same way.

"We think the wolf raiders are in Legar."

They stood motionless before her, not at first comprehending her blunt statement.

"Cabe is there . . . and Darkhorse, too."

The Gryphon did not question her reasons for not volunteering the information earlier. Perhaps he understood that she had wanted to hear his tale first. Instead, he asked, "How long ago? Where exactly?"

Troia stood up and clutched his arm. Her claws dug into it, but the Gryphon did not seem to notice.

"We do not know. Cabe—and Aurim—had a vision. Then, Cabe had another. They were peculiar, but both pointed to Legar. Both pointed to the Crystal Dragon . . . and wolf raiders."

"The Crystal Dragon."

Familiar with the Dragonrealm only through the stories told by her husband, Troia did not note the significance. "Can we speak with this Dragon King? Will he aid us?"

Again, the lionbird's mane bristled. "The Crystal Dragon is not like Blue or Green, both of whom we might appeal to under certain circumstances. He is like none of his counterparts, Troia. He and his predecessors have ever been reclusive. He will tolerate those who, for one reason or another, find themselves traversing the peninsula, but woe betide anyone who seeks to disturb his peace. It was he who helped turn the tide against one of his own, the Ice Dragon. Without his aid, the Dragonrealm might now be a dead land under an eternal sheet of ice and snow." The Gryphon grew contemplative. "Tell me about Cabe and his journey. Tell me everything."

Gwen did, describing the visions, the Bedlams' decisions, and the attack on the person of the Dragon King Green. The Gryphon tilted his head to one side during the telling of that incident and also the mention of the black ship in the vision. Cabe's missive from Zuu particularly attracted his attention. New life had come into his eyes, but it was still a life dedicated to one cause, finding the ones responsible for his son's death.

"Zuu. I remember Blane. His horsemen."

"And Lanith?" asked the enchantress.

"He is unknown to me and hardly a factor in this."

She did not think so herself, but telling the Gryphon that was not so easy. "You're planning to go there."

"Yes."

"We should leave before the sun sets," urged Troia to her mate.

He gave her an odd look, even for his avian visage. Then, with some hesitation, he said, "You are not going with me. Not to Legar. Any other place, even the Northern Wastes, I would take you, but not *Legar.*"

"What do you *mean?*" The fine fur along the back of Troia's head stood on end. "I will not be left behind! Not now!"

"Legar is the one place where the risk is too great for the two of you."

Gwen glanced from one to the other. *The two of you?*

"Any other time, any other *place*, I would welcome you at my side, Troia, but I will not lead you into Legar."

"I'm far from helpless, Gryph! My stomach is not yet rounded!"

She was pregnant. The enchantress cursed her own words. If she had only known, she would have spoken to the Gryphon in private. Like Queen Erini, Gwen was not the kind to sit demurely to one side while others did the fighting, but one thing she found very precious was the creation of new life. Chasing after wolf raiders was terrible enough, but to do so now and in the domain of the unpredictable and possibly malevolent Crystal Dragon was sheer folly for an expectant mother, especially after having lost her only other child.

It was clear that they had discussed this issue several times in the past and it was clear that Troia had always won. That there should be someone capable of matching the Gryphon in stubborn determination would have been amusing under more pleasant circumstances. Now, however, it only threatened to muddle the situation further.

"Troia, you are with child?"

The cat woman spun on her, then recalled herself and settled down. She seemed more worn out than she had been before her burst of anger at her husband. "For these past eight weeks. I thought at first it was sickness from the trip; we're not fond of the sea, either of us. It stayed with me, though, and I soon recognized the symptoms from—from Demion's time."

"You have grown tired quicker these past few days, too," the lionbird reminded her. "In truth, I was beginning to worry even before we landed." His voice was more understanding, more concerned. Both he and his mate were mercurial creatures.

*The years have changed you, Gryphon, or perhaps merely opened you up more.* The sorceress studied Troia. Despite the litheness of her body, there were hints here and there of aging that had nothing to do with the years of war. How long did the cat people live? Troia had little or no sorcerous ability, which meant she, like King Melicard, would age faster than the one she loved. For that matter, it had never been clear just how long the Gryphon would live if permitted to die of old age. He was not like Cabe or Gwen; his life span might be as long as that of a Dragon King or maybe even *longer.* Likely he had thought about that, which meant his time with his wife was all the more precious to him. To know that her life span was limited in comparison to his . . . it only added to the importance of seeing that this new child was allowed to enter the world happy and whole.

*And she has had only one child in all this time,* the enchantress pondered, still studying the anxious cat woman. *This may very well be her last chance.* There was no doubt, either, that Troia very much wanted this child. From what little Gwen knew of her kind, they generally had many children. Troia, however, had only had the one and among her people children were precious and well cared for. She could not afford to lose this one.

"We made a pact that we would follow this through together, Gryph!"

The Gryphon flexed his claws again, but the action was not directed at his bride. "You will be with me, Troia, I promise you that. I also promise that I will return with D'Farany's head if need be to show you that Demion has been avenged, but I see now I must do it alone."

"You will not be alone, Gryphon," Gwen quickly pointed out. "My husband and Darkhorse are there ahead of you. Find them. Their quest is tied to yours." *And see to it that Cabe comes back to me!* she silently added.

"There is that." He took his wife in his arms. She was stiff at first, but then she took hold of him in a grip that vied with his own for pure intensity. "I know the Dragonrealm, Troia. Believe me when I say that this is one place I will not risk your health and that of our offspring. You know why Lady Bedlam remains behind; do you consider her any less than her husband because of that?"

The cat woman locked gazes with Gwen. "No. Never. I've known her too long in letters to believe foolishness like that. If only I could come, though! I left Demion in that place!"

"*We* left Demion in that place. There was no way either of us could have foreseen what happened." He squawked, the equivalent of a sigh. The Gryphon had a habit of switching between his human traits and his animalistic traits without thought. "We came to hunt and we will hunt, but this time I must make the kill alone. I will, too."

The tall sorceress shivered. Again, she was reminded that her guests were not to be completely judged by human standards, but that was not all there was to it. The war and Demion's death had indeed changed the Gryphon the way the Turning War never had. *It's become much too personal. Would that I could keep him from going, too.* Yet she welcomed his coming, for it meant more hope for Cabe.

"You will need food and rest, Gryphon. I will not allow you to leave until you have had a bit of both."

He nodded his thanks, then looked back down at his wife. "If the Lady Bedlam permits it, I would prefer you stay here. There is no better place for you than with her."

"There's one place," Troia corrected him. "That's with you."

"After Legar."

"She is welcome to stay as long as she needs, Gryphon. You know that."

"Then tonight I will leave for Zuu, to see if I can pick up Cabe's trail."

"You'll teleport?" Troia sounded suddenly disturbed again.

The Gryphon did not appear to notice it. "I am familiar with the region and it will save days of travel. From there, I will teleport as carefully as I can into the midst of Legar."

"Is that not dangerous?" Gwen asked. "You might materialize before a patrol of wolf raiders."

He gave her a look almost devoid of emotion. "No one knows them as well as I do. Trust in me, my lady."

Troia bared her sharp teeth. "I still don't care for it. I should be with you, Gryph."

"And you will be." The Gryphon put one hand on his heart. "You will always be here."

Gwen allowed them their peace while she thought of Cabe. She, like Troia, was still upset about being left behind even though both of them knew it was not because their husbands saw them as lessers. Even had the Gryphon offered to take her place and watch the children, she was aware that she would have turned the offer down. There had to be someone here for the children, especially with the Dragonrealm so volatile in other ways, and this *had* been Cabe's mission from the very beginning. He was the one who had been contacted. It was not the choice every parent would have made, but it was her choice and she would live by it.

She consoled herself with the fact that the Gryphon's presence would make Cabe's safety that much more possible. Between the lionbird, her husband, and the irrepressible Darkhorse, neither the wolf raiders nor the Crystal Dragon were tasks insurmountable. It was possible that the situation was not even as terrible as they had assumed. There was even the chance that Cabe might very well return before his old friend was able to depart.

That was assuming that nothing had happened to him already.

THE BLUE MAN stumbled through the godforsaken fog, cursing its magic-spawned ability to creep even into the most obscure passages below the earth. It was hard enough to see even with the torches lit let alone with such a thick morass enshrouding everything around him.

Yet, there was something else, something inviting about the fog. He could taste power, raw, wild forces, coursing through the mist. D'Rance had seen the proof of that, too. He had watched floors twist and turn, a man sucked into the walls as if he had never been, and fantastical figures prancing about in the fog. Mere tips of the proverbial iceberg, the northerner knew. Above, those on the surface would be facing much more. The Quel city seemed to dampen the effects of the wild power. Whether that was intentional or simply chance, he did not know. That subject could wait until later, after he had reached the surface and explored farther. As much as he disliked the fog, it offered him possibilities that even Lord D'Farany could not match. He had to find out where it had originated from.

He was nearly to the mouth of the tunnel when a dog-sized form skittered over his feet, causing him to fall against one side of the passage. From near his left, he heard it growl.

Verlok. From his time in Canisargos he knew the sound well. There was only one verlok on this side of the world.

"Kanaan. How good of you to be where I wanted you."

"Lord D'Farany?" He could see nothing save the dim image of the verlok . . . and this with the light of day supposedly trying to cut through the murky fog.

"We were on our way down. It was not necessary to meet us."

"Yes, my lord." The blue man clenched both hands tight. "I must apologize, yes, for not noticing you sooner. This thrice-cursed mist wreaks havoc on the eyes, yes?"

A shape took form before him. The Pack Leader. "I suppose that could be troublesome, but it's hardly a concern compared to other things. Fascinating, wouldn't you say? As if entering another world."

*A world gone mad, yes!* Kanaan D'Rance wanted to study the magical forces involved, but he by no means cared for any other aspect of it. If he could find a way to manipulate it, that was all he desired. "It is unique, yes."

"But of course something must be done about it; it disturbs the men, you see. Disturbs my work."

*And that is all it is doing?* The blue man was often fascinated by the Pack Leader's peculiar pattern of thought.

"It's magical, as you've no doubt guessed. Not like anything else. Not at all like *his* power. A shame, truly." D'Farany reached down and picked up his vile pet. "It repels rather than attracts. I think I *must* remove it from this place and send it to wherever he unleashed it from."

"He?"

"The Crystal Dragon, of course." Lord D'Farany walked past him, the verlok taking the opportunity to snarl at the blue man. D'Rance quickly followed, knowing how easy it might be to lose someone in this mire.

The floor of the tunnel was shifting beneath their feet, but where the blue man struggled to keep his balance, the Pack Master simply stepped here and there, moving along as if nothing were the matter. A misshapen tentacle of rock darted out from beside them, but somehow missed D'Farany. The northerner, on the other hand, was forced to duck, not an easy act when the ground beneath his feet continued to move.

*He acts as if this is the way of the normal world! Could this be what* he *sees, yes?* If so, it explained much about Ivon D'Farany.

Although nothing major impeded their blind trek, it was still with relief that the blue man entered the chamber some minutes later. Relief and curiosity, for he immediately saw that the crystalline room was not touched as the others were. There was no fog even though the tunnel just beyond was dank and impossible to navigate by sight alone. For once, the sentries posted here must have felt themselves fortunate, he thought.

The Pack Leader, oblivious to all else, leaned over the Quel device and visibly sighed. Removing his gloves, he tenderly touched the various crystals in the arrangement, finishing with his own addition.

"Where is Orril?"

"I regret, my lord, that I do not know where he is." *He is hopefully lost forever.* D'Rance knew he could not be so fortunate. D'Marr would likely show his blank little face at the worst possible time.

"No matter." The former keeper began to activate the magical creation.

Interest was overcoming uncertainty. He had watched closely as Lord D'Farany had become quickly adept at the use of the diggers' tool. Watching the raider leader had been a learning experience, although soon he would not need to watch. Still, if Lord D'Farany had a plan to disperse the dank and decay-filled mist, then there were still things the blue man could learn from him. "If I may, my lord, you have a plan, yes? What will you do, please?"

He did not catch the fascinated smile on the Pack Leader's crystal-illuminated countenance but the tone and the words were enough. "I have no plan, Kanaan. I'm simply going to *play.*"

D'Rance suddenly found himself envying the men on the surface. They only had the fog to fear.

# X

IN A PLACE where darkness was unchallenged by light, a sleeper long undis-turbed stirred briefly to sluggish life . . .

*THEY WERE ABLE to move mountains, create castles from nothing. A world had been theirs to play with and they had played ever so hard, tearing that world asunder and making it into a reflection of their own, uncaring souls.*

Plool gazed down on Cabe in what appeared to be expectation. At least, Cabe thought so; the wide-brimmed hat still obscured the upper part of his in-credibly narrow face. Everything about the odd figure was a parody of human-ity, but the warlock found no humor in the other's physical appearance. Plool was a creature—an *inhabitant*—of dreaded Nimth. Worse, he had to be *Vraad,* one of the terrible race of sorcerers that had created the madness of Nimth in the first place.

"You are a curious creature," the macabre figure pronounced. "In a curious world. How curious."

He still spoke in the peculiar, singsong tone he had used earlier, but he changed his pattern of speech now and then, almost as if it were a game with him. Plool seemed of a whimsical nature in many ways, which did not necessar-ily mean that Cabe could relax. Whimsy had its dark side, especially where the Vraad were concerned. From his notes he had gathered that the race of sorcer-ers had had a dark sense of humor.

"Tell me, curious creature, your name?"

"Cabe. Cabe Bedlam."

"Bedlam. I like that. I am Plool."

The warlock nodded a cautious greeting, deciding that it would be better not to mention to Plool that he had already introduced himself. So far, the Vraad was acting quite civilized with him, but he was not about to forget that Plool had slowly and quite casually burned a hole through the Aramite officer's chest using a medallion that should have been resistant to most sorcery. The nightmarish mage was of a highly capricious nature and anything Cabe said might be enough to set him off. As long as the foul mist of Nimth surrounded him, it behooved the warlock to stay on the madcap figure's good side.

If that was possible.

"Where is Darkhorse?"

"The black beast? Following my imagination, the black beast is. Following my imagination the better so that we may speak. He, I understand. A thing of chaos, a thing that is not what he seems. You . . . you are different."

Different? "I'm simply who I am, Great Plool."

"And *that* is why you are so different! You are so much what you seem, so . . . constant. Constant you are, never changing. Yet, how long will you last, Bedlam?" Plool's head shifted under the vast hat. He appeared to be observing the shrouded landscape around him for the first time. "This is a new place; I've not seen its like formed before. Not ever, ever not. Will it stay long?"

Cabe had no idea what the other was referring to and so kept silent.

"All so . . . still. Quite a different little variation, with all you ephemerals running around and the land so *unchanging*. Like you . . . a novel thing."

Unchanging? The wary spellcaster tried to recall what else he had gleaned from his research on the Vraad and the ancestral world of Nimth. There was very little, but one other thing that had been hinted at was that in the violent, magic-tossed realm, everything, *including* the creatures who lived there, faced dismal and horrific existences in which they were twisted and reshaped almost continuously. Nimth was supposed to be a world ever decaying, ever collapsing. Yet, it still existed even now.

The ground beneath his feet suddenly burst upward.

Cabe barely had time to stumble and readjust his balance before he found himself on a column of earth nearly the height of Plool's rocky seat. The column then began to twist and turn, drawing the warlock closer and closer to the madcap creature. Girding himself, Cabe did nothing to prevent or even slow his journey. If Plool had wanted to cause him harm, he would have done so. It was more likely that he simply wanted to better study the young warlock.

The column came to a halt just before the Vraad. Cabe noted that Plool had worked it so that even at full height the warlock would be a head shorter than the seated Nimthian.

"You *are* a most peculiar-looking piece of work," Plool commented. How he saw anything from under that hat was a miracle. "Everything's so *orderly*. Would you like me to change that? It must be awful for you. Awful it must be."

"Thank you, but I'm happy with the way I am." The words flew from Cabe's lips. The dark-haired sorcerer tried to hide his anxiety. He did not even want to imagine what the Vraad might have in mind. A form like *his*? *Never!*

"Are you certain?" As he spoke, Plool at last lifted his head enough for the warlock to view the rest of his narrow face.

Cabe almost gasped aloud. It was only with the best of efforts that he prevented himself from stepping back in shock and possibly falling from his perch.

Only in Nimth could Plool have become possible. The lower half of his countenance, while peculiar, was not overly unusual. Even the nose, long, narrow, and pointed now, was within the realm of reason.

But the *eyes* . . .

Both were set on the left side of his face.

They were positioned one right atop the other, like some madman's portrait. On the right side of the face, there was a blank area of skin where the one eye should have been. Had he been born that way or was it a later legacy of Nimth?

The eyes blinked. Once over the sight of the lids closing and opening in unison, Cabe discovered another peculiarity about them. Around the pupil, they looked almost crystalline, so crystalline, in fact, that they probably glittered in sunlight.

The disconcerting eyes were fixated on him. "You and yours are a strange sight; a strange sight you are. So much is strange this day. When I saw the hole, I could not be but curious, yes, curious I could not help but be. Where did it lead? Where had it come from? There are so many things of wonder in my world, but this . . . I think this is not Nimth."

Cabe remained silent.

The eyes blinked again. "The hole. It pulled me in and I found myself here. Then it was gone. Why is that, do you think?"

The warlock shook his head. He had ideas, all involving wolf raiders and Dragon Kings, but he was not about to relay any of them to Plool. The less the bizarre mage knew, the better.

Plool rose, at the same time extending the height of the earthen column so that Cabe was still a head shorter. The odd-looking figure stood atop the formation and once more gazed around at the mist-covered land. It was still impossible to see beyond a few yards, yet the Vraad studied his surroundings as if the fog did not even exist.

"And so where am I, Bedlam? Where has the great Plool, Plool the Great, found himself? What do you call this little place?"

"This is Legar." The answer was safe enough. It told Cabe's companion nothing, which was all he wanted Plool to ever know. Somehow, there had to be a way to return him to Nimth.

"Legarrrrr . . ." The spiderlike figure mulled over the word. His crystalline eyes closed for a time. When he opened them again, they were even brighter and livelier than before. "An amusing name."

"Great Plool, if I may ask you a question?"

He almost preened himself. "You may do so."

"Where was this hole you came through?"

Plool looked sly. "Trying to rid yourself of my presence?"

Cabe actually was, but he was not going to admit that to the Vraad. "I share your curiosity about things, about *your* world."

The answer satisfied Plool. He nodded, thankfully obscuring his unnerving eyes, and responded, "I like you, Bedlam. Would you like to see the hole?"

"If it is safe."

The Vraad shrugged, chuckling all the while. "What *is* safe, Bedlam?"

Cabe blinked. They now stood atop the peak of one of Legar's taller hills. The warlock looked down and saw nothing but the dire mist; he was on the edge of a precipice. Cabe quickly backed away, only to bump into Plool, who floated, legs crossed in a sitting position, just high enough to gaze down at the young mage.

"Sweet, sweet Nimth," the spiderlike Vraad nearly sang. "Your loveliness envelops all . . . and chokes it to death."

*He doesn't sound very eager to return. I hope there's no trouble. Somehow I have to convince him to leave.* "I don't see the hole, Great Plool. Where was it?"

"The hole is closed, but the door remains."

"And the door?"

"Below us."

Cabe turned his gaze downward once more and saw only murk. He could not even see the rest of the hill, merely a few feet of earth below them. Fog obscured the rest. "Down there?"

"Yes, here."

Every muscle in the warlock's body grew painfully taut as he once again found himself transported to another location. Plool had a habit of teleporting others from one spot to another without warning, something that Shade had often done and even Darkhorse still did without thinking. Cabe had never liked being pulled along in the past and he certainly did not like it now.

They were down in the murky soup he had just been observing from above.

From where he stood now, Cabe could not see the top of the hill. How high did the fog go? All the way to the sun?

He reminded himself that it was not the fog that mattered. For now, he needed to concentrate on the magical doorway that had allowed all of this, including his erstwhile Vraad companion, to enter unchecked.

The object of his desire lay between them. A sphere. At first, Cabe studied it with some confusion. He had expected a portal or a tear in reality. Certainly not a glass ball. It looked more like a container than a doorway.

"Can I touch it?"

"If you like."

He did. A mild shock made him pluck his hand back. Plool chuckled. Cabe steeled himself and reached out again. The same mild shock coursed through him, but it was only momentary. Slowly he ran his hands over the artifact. It was not glass after all, but crystal. There was also still something inside. The mage could not be certain, but it appeared to be more fog.

"This is how you came to be here?"

There was a hint of annoyance in the Vraad's voice. "This is how I came to be here; I came to be here because of this. Do you want to ask again, Bedlam?"

"I'm sorry," he quickly responded, "it just amazes me."

Plool squatted. His legs seemed to be built for that. He now resembled the spider again or perhaps a spider and a frog combined. The round torso was so great in girth that it was a wonder the spindly legs could maintain such a balance, yet they did. "Came I through this little sphere, Bedlam, but the opening was much more vast. When I saw what had been the cause and it tried to fly away, I brought it down to this spot and with my might forced it to the ground. It stays there now until I deign to release it to its master."

*To its master* . . . There was only one being that Cabe could think of who might have been responsible. Certainly not the wolf raiders. Now he was certain that it could only have been the Crystal Dragon.

But why? This seemed a strange defense for a leviathan who had turned the might of the Ice Dragon back. It was, for all its strength, a rather halfhearted and in most ways foolish sort of attack. Cabe was certain that he, in the Dragon King's position, could have devised more than a score of countermeasures much more efficient and less haphazard than the unleashing of Nimthian decay. What happened if the deadly mist became permanent? Might it not also spread?

He sighed. Why was nothing ever simple? It was terrible enough that he had been forced to come here and seek out both the lord of Legar and the Aramites, but now he had the fog and a Vraad to deal with.

*The Dragonrealm does like to play with us, doesn't it?*

Thinking of that, he suddenly had a wary thought. Plool would not know the lay of the land, but he might know enough about this region in general to answer a few questions. "Great Plool, are we far from where we first met?"

"Nothing is far away . . . but Nimth now."

So perhaps the answers would not be forthcoming for now. Trust Plool to speak in riddles and poetry. Standing, Cabe studied what little he could see of the hill formation. The one thing he was certain of was that he was high in the sky. These hills were the closest Legar had to true mountains and only some arbitrary decision by ancient mapmakers had prevented them from falling into the other category. He could recall only one area in all the peninsula where such high hills were located. If his estimates were correct, and it was still quite possible they were not thanks to the concealing fog, then he was in a region very near the underground city of the Quel and the caverns where he suspected the Crystal Dragon's clans made their home. That would also put him near enough to the shoreline of the peninsula, which meant that the wolf raiders, too, might be his neighbors.

*This is not what I had in mind when I began this journey.* He looked at Plool. Could he convince him to leave Legar? The hills of Esedi would be the most likely place to reunite with Darkhorse, although what the demon steed and the Vraad would do when faced with each other worried him. Darkhorse he was certain he could calm, but the madcap figure beside him was more unpredictable. He had clearly been responsible for separating the two.

Cabe saw no other choice. His best chances for putting a finish to all these matters lay in combining his skills with those of Darkhorse and Plool, the latter because of his ability to work and exist in the Nimthian mist. Cabe also wanted Darkhorse with him in order to keep a better eye on the Vraad. True, the ebony stallion was weakened by the very fog that Plool thrived in, but between the two of them they should be able to keep him in check. The warlock hoped it would not come to that, however. Plool was not evil, not exactly; his was simply a different world. He might be willing to help if only because he found the situation entertaining.

"Great Plool, there is another place we should go, a place where there is someone I hope to meet. I think you'll find it a fascinating place, so alive with stability and so unchanging." *I begin to sound like him.*

"The black beast. You hope to meet him."

He had been careful not to mention Darkhorse, but Plool had made the connection regardless. "His name is Darkhorse. He means no harm to you." *I hope!* "He is my friend and companion on this journey."

Indignation. "I am Plool! I do not fear anything! I can create castles in the air! I can make monsters from mud!"

"I didn't mean—"

The indignation vanished, to be replaced by curiosity. "But so much . . . unchanging . . . not even Nimth has created such!" The eyes blinked. "I will enjoy this world . . . *yesss* . . . I will come with you and see this place, talk to the hole, too. The hole I will talk to, this Darkhorse!"

"Good," Cabe returned once he had pieced his way through the Vraad's quick and confusing words. The warlock had no idea what he would do if Darkhorse was not there. Return to Legar with Plool, he supposed. Not to this location, however. Better to choose one of those he was vaguely familiar with from long ago. Plool appeared willing to listen to him, although who knew why, and with the Vraad to aid him he should be able to find a better place to materialize than here.

First, however, he had to find a way to get Plool to teleport the two of them to Esedi. The Vraad had been quite agreeable so far to teleporting them from one place to another. Maybe he would do so again. Cabe did not want to risk his own sorcery if he could avoid it, not here in this malevolent mist. "Master Plool, if you could be so kind—"

The eerie figure executed a bow, an act that, considering his shape, bordered on the absurd. "I am ever benevolent to those in need; to those in need benevolent I ever am."

"My gratitude. First let me—"

Plool was already acting.

Cabe started toward him, hand out. "Wait!"

The familiar hilly and, thankfully, clear terrain of western Esedi manifested before him. Despite his not having described it to the Vraad, Plool had known where to go. He could have only done so by seizing the image from Cabe's *mind.*

His relief at escaping the fog made the invasion of his thoughts almost secondary, at least for the time being. Cabe exhaled in relief and started to look for the other mage.

He heard a gasp of pain from a voice that could only be Plool's, then the world around him began to spin. He struggled to maintain balance, but the force tugging at him was too strong.

Cabe was torn from the earth. Everything around him shimmered in an all too familiar way. There was a brief instant when he was surrounded by nothing. *Pure* nothing. The nothing was followed by a body-rending shock as the startled warlock was flattened against a rocky surface.

It was not enough to severely injure him, but it did leave him stunned and aching for several minutes. Eventually, he tried to see where he was, but his surroundings seemed but a blur no matter how many times he blinked.

No. Not a blur. As his head cleared, Cabe saw that it was not his vision that was at fault.

He was back in Legar. Back on the hill near where the sorcerer from Nimth had shown him the crystalline sphere.

What had happened to Plool? Cabe recalled the brief, agonized sound. He scanned the region, but his search was limited to a few yards at most in any one direction.

"Gngh!" A terrible force dragged him upward. His frantic thought was that the teleportation spell was still in effect, but then he ceased moving. Cabe simply hung where he was, his arms and legs mysteriously bereft of movement. There was an uncomfortable pressure around his chest that made it difficult to draw a breath.

"Bedlam, I do not like pain! Betray my faith, my goodwill! I have punished for less; much less have I punished for, *Bedlam!*"

"Ploo-ool?" Cabe managed to choke out.

The Vraad floated before him on a throne formed from the very mist. His round torso was tipped back so far that Plool had to practically peer over it. He was breathing hard and one hand shook. The maddening eyes were narrow in dark thought.

"Wh-what have I *done?*"

"*The pain!*" Plool roared. "The pain, the pain, and the pain! My very body twisted and boiled! Were I not Plool the Great, I would be dead, torn apart!" Somehow, Plool managed to lean forward. "As you shall be for my sport and vengeance!"

"I did nothing!"

"Lies and lies and lies and lies!"

It was growing nearly impossible to breathe, much less speak in his own defense. "You've freely invaded my mind, haven't you? Do it again, but this time seek out the truth about me! Try to prove that I betrayed you!"

He hoped his plan, born of the second, would succeed. Otherwise, Plool would use him as he desired. A Vraad's desire. The very notion turned his stomach. He knew the legends.

Plool's long, hodgepodge face leaned even closer. Was it Cabe's imagination or was the upper eye slightly more to the other side? That was preposterous, of course, the product of his predicament. It was a moot point, anyway. What mattered was what the furious Vraad drew from his mind.

One breath.

Two breaths.

Three and four, all harsh.

The pressure on his chest eased. Slowly, both he and Plool sank toward the ground. Plool ceased descending when he was roughly a man's length from the rocky surface of the hill. He still used the chair of mist to support his massive form. Cabe, on the other hand, was unceremoniously dumped. The gasping warlock managed to keep his balance.

From the Vraad there was no apology, but a careful study of Plool's insane countenance revealed to Cabe enough to satisfy him. Plool had read his mind and found what the desperate mage had wanted him to find.

Nothing more. Cabe was certain of it now. There were things his mind held, thoughts concerning the Dragonrealm and his fears of Plool, that the searching Vraad would have surely noticed and acted upon. That he had not noticed meant that like Darkhorse, Plool had limits as to how deep he could plunder another's mind. It was good to know. Cabe had feared that he would not have the power to direct his menacing companion's mental search toward specific thoughts only. His mind was his after all.

"I was in great and terrible pain, Bedlam," the floating spellcaster hissed. His tone bespoke his condition; Cabe grew more and more interested in what had happened to him. "Terrible and great pain."

"I feel your pain," Cabe returned, all politeness. "But I am not the one responsible, as you now know."

"Then *who? Who*, then, Bedlam, hmmm?"

The Crystal Dragon? It was unlikely. Not at all like the Dragon King, if the warlock's opinion was correct. The lord of Legar was generally satisfied with his enemies fleeing from his kingdom. He would have been more likely to take both of them and fling them farther from the peninsula, say all the way to the Dagora Forest. Still, nothing was predictable anymore. It might very well be the Crystal Dragon.

The Aramites certainly would not have left Cabe alone, so it could not be them. He also doubted it could have been some trick of Lanith's mages. They were not that organized.

Could it have simply been something about Esedi itself? Or Plool even?

Plool . . . yes, it was a possibility. He tried not to change his expression as he covertly studied the misshapen body of the Vraad. What had he thought earlier? Only in Nimth could someone like Plool be possible?

Only in Nimth and not *beyond* the borders of its foul mists.

"I don't know," the warlock finally responded. He despised lying, but in this case he was not certain the truth was any better. Plool might choose to believe him or he might not. Besides, there might still come a time when Cabe would need that bit of knowledge to save himself; the Vraad had already proven his instability.

His reverie was interrupted by a look of sudden inspiration on the horrid visage. Plool's eyes widened, then narrowed. "But I think I know who it must be . . ."

*Gods, no! If he blames Darkhorse, then the two of them could come to blows without any chance of explanation!*

It was not Darkhorse. "They will boil in their suits of black armor. Their heads I shall use for a stairway in a citadel built from their bones; from their bones a citadel will be built. Even then, I shall not let them die, death being too good for them for having caused me such pain . . ."

*Black armor.* Plool had chosen the wolf raiders as his scapegoats.

The maddened Vraad was looking directly at him again. "And you, Bedlam, will aid me; aid me you will, Bedlam."

It had been Cabe's early hope that if the Aramites had truly landed on the shores of Legar, as he now knew they had, he would find some means, some allies, that would force the raiders from the Dragonrealm forever. What he had *not* been searching for was someone like *Plool.* Definitely not like Plool. To join the Vraad on his campaign of vengeance would be folly of the greatest kind.

The Vraad was quiet for a time, but his anger by no means diminished. He was thinking, contemplating. Cabe used the time to try to clear his own thoughts. How could he steer Plool from the direction the other sorcerer was heading to one in which the Vraad chose to return to Nimth?

The sphere! The doorway! In some ways, Plool was like a child. Cabe suspected that once turned toward the puzzle of how to open the doorway again, Plool would forget his insane vengeance on the wolf raiders. At the very least, it was worth the attempt. Plool was likely to cause more chaos than good by attacking the Aramite encampment.

Where *was* the sphere? The warlock looked around. It should have been in sight. Plool had embedded it in the rock, but from Cabe's angle it still should have been visible.

"What do you search for?"

"The sphere. Your doorway home. It's vanished."

Plool hardly seemed put out by that fact. "Then, I will be staying."

"You don't understand . . ." Neither, in fact, did Cabe. He did, however, have a very bad feeling that his assumptions had gone astray, that he had left out something.

He was even more certain when his feet began to sink into the hillside.

The spell that he cast in an attempt to free himself did nothing. Cabe was not even certain that it had completed, for there was no sign of any reaction, no twinge in the magical forces that held the Dragonrealm together. The warlock looked down; the earth had already swallowed him up to his shins and it was evident that the rate of sinking was increasing.

"Plool!" What was the Vraad doing? Watching him? Did he find this all entertaining?

When he looked up, Cabe saw that the truth was anything but. Plool was not standing over him, merrily watching his predicament. Plool might possibly not even be standing there, although it was hard to say, for in his place there was now a vast, opaque sphere, a glimmering monstrosity taller than a man. In some ways, it resembled the sphere that Cabe had investigated, but whereas that had been a doorway, a gate, this one was more likely a prison. A prison for a dangerous and unpredictable sorcerer like Plool.

The sphere, too, began to sink, but the struggling mage hardly cared now. He was more concerned with his own freedom, for without that he could hardly help the Vraad. His legs were now completely enveloped. At the rate he was being dragged under, he had only a minute, maybe two, to act.

Somewhere, Cabe found the strength. Tensing, he threw himself into the spell, stretched out a hand, and pointed at an outcropping. A single magical tendril shot forth and pierced the rock. The warlock attached it to himself, creating a lifeline.

His rate of sinking slowed, but that was not enough. Pleased with his success at casting a spell despite the malevolent mist, Cabe anchored himself in a similar manner to another outcropping. Now, his downward progress was nearly negligible. The strain on his body, however, was growing stronger by the moment. It felt as if a giant had taken him by the feet and head and was trying to tear him slowly apart like a piece of fruit. If he delayed too long, whoever sought to capture him might finally do so, but they would have to settle for half his body.

The third tendril was easier to create and cast than the previous two and while he wondered about that, there was no time to consider the reasons. This third he bonded to a formation before him, but not in the same manner as the ones on each side of it. This one Cabe kept bonded to his hands, so that it seemed as if he were holding on to a magical rope.

His concentration fixed upon the stream of power running from his hands to the rock, the warlock caused it to shorten ever so slightly. It did and to his joy he found that he rose a little. The strain was still incredible, but it was no worse than before. Still, he wished he could trust his abilities enough to do something else. He wished he had the *time* to think of something else. Yet Cabe was also aware that more complicated or stronger spells might not function as well here. More subtle spells, because they did not stir the forces as much as the greater ones, were less likely to go awry under present circumstances. His own attempt at teleportation was a fine example.

Becoming more daring, he shortened the strand by nearly half a foot. The warlock rose by a similar height. He allowed himself a quick smile, which promptly faded as his concentration slipped and he started to sink again.

Another attempt brought him back up, but the effort was beginning to take its toll. His sides ached terribly and his breath was becoming a little ragged. Cabe dared not turn his attention to Plool's dilemma, assuming that Plool was indeed a prisoner of the sphere. He did not even know if the sphere was still visible or whether it had already sunk unchecked into the hill.

His next attempt faltered and instead of the foot that he hoped to rise, he barely gained more than an inch. Still, Cabe persevered. As long as he continued to rise, he would eventually triumph, he told himself.

On his next attempt, however, he felt a new force combating him. It was not magical, but physical.

Something had clamped on to his ankles and was pulling him under with renewed vigor.

One of the two lines linked to his body simply faded. Cabe sank to his waist almost instantly. He tried to strengthen the other one, but between his need to monitor the magical bond pulling him free and the strain on both his mind and body, the tiring spellcaster could add little. Cabe watched in frustration as whatever force had eliminated the first also caused the second to dissipate.

The ground was already creeping up to his chest. Cabe put his entire will into the one bond that remained to him. His sinking slowed, then stopped again. He even succeeded in winning back an inch or two of freedom.

Then, the ground behind him shook, something shot by the left side of his head . . . and Cabe Bedlam had a momentary glimpse of a massive, taloned paw just before it covered his face and, with the aid of others like it, finally pulled him underground.

# XI

*THERE IS SOMETHING different about this place.*

Sometimes, it was hard to recall that more than twenty years had passed since his last visit to Zuu. It had been before the crisis centering around Cabe Bedlam and his emergence from hiding.

*I live too long a life*, the Gryphon thought not for the first time. Even the sorcerers he knew gradually aged and, if allowed, died peacefully. He, on the other hand, went on and on, fighting wars and trying to find his place in the world. Even when he had learned his own origins, learned that once his body had been that of one of the Faceless Ones of the other continent, he had not felt as if he knew who he was. There had only been two places where he had ever felt comfortable with himself. Safe. One was Penacles, which had embraced him as its leader despite his monstrous appearance.

The other place was wherever his family happened to be. With Troia and De-mion, he had known *true* peace of mind, even during the worst years of the war.

Now Demion was dead and Troia, still chafing about being left behind, would someday also die.

When would he?

The Faceless Ones were virtually immortal; he was not so certain that he wanted to be. Yet neither was he the suicidal type.

Reshaped to pass for human, the Gryphon walked among the inhabitants of Zuu. Things *were* different. There was more order, more attention. Lanith, who he recalled vaguely as a young, obstinate child, must be more ambitious than his father. The Gryphon hoped that that ambition in no way mirrored that of King Melicard. The Dragonrealm looked to be in enough chaos without two human monarchs seeking to take on the mantle of conquest the Dragon Kings had given up.

He fingered the medallion given to him by the guards at the gate. More familiar with its like than Cabe was, the lionbird understood its true purpose. The talisman was crude, however, and so it had only taken a simple spell to adjust it so that anyone attuned to it would not notice the sudden presence of a master mage.

Two hours of wandering Zuu's market area had already told him most of what he wanted to know. Again, as with the talisman, he was more familiar with how the rumor and gossip system of cities worked. Cabe, for all his skills, had not lived in the lower reaches of civilization for as long as the Gryphon had. True, the human had grown up around the taverns, but there were other levels of information. He had not had to survive as the lionbird had had to do in the early days. Few, if anyone, had the sum total experience that the Gryphon had.

*And how I envy you that, Cabe.*

He saw no purpose in remaining any longer. The sun was already down and each minute he delayed added to the off-chance that one of the king's new spellcasters might, just might, detect him. The Gryphon, like Cabe, did not want to cause an incident. He already knew of the mysterious goings-on in the city and suspected that the warlock and the demon steed had nearly been discovered. While it was possible the Gryphon would be able to call upon his role as monarch of Penacles to protect himself, it would be embarrassing to his former kingdom and good Toos to try to explain why he was skulking about in another's domain.

One item he had learned interested him most of all. There was some news about Legar. A dank fog had risen and those who had dared traverse the regions near the border had told of a mist so thick it was impossible to see anything. Curiously, this mist ended almost exactly at the inner edge of the peninsula, less than a few yards from where Esedi began. No one doubted it was magic, but having lived near the domain of the Crystal Dragon for so many generations, the people of Zuu were inclined to believe it was simply a step by the lord of Legar to further isolate himself from the world. After all, the fog *did* end before Esedi, not after. Not even the least tendril extended into those lands claimed by Lanith's kingdom.

*It is amazing, the peace of mind some can have.* The Gryphon was not so confident. To him the foul haze meant that the wolf raiders *must* be there, as the Bedlams had feared. That meant that Cabe might be in more danger than he was prepared for, even with the aid of Darkhorse. From experience, the lionbird knew of some of the Aramites' deadly tricks. He knew them better than anyone and knew also that D'Farany would be plotting others.

Abandoning his listening position at one of the danker establishments, which he still found of higher quality than many he had visited during his long life, the Gryphon sought out one of the more secluded alleys. It was time to begin following Cabe's trail and for that he needed to perform a little magic. It would be subtle enough to escape the attention of the third-rate sorcerers who had created the talismans, but still powerful enough to accomplish its mission.

In the darkness of the narrow street, he removed a single object from the folds of his weathered cloak. The object had been carefully wrapped in a piece of cloth so as to be affected as little as possible by his own presence. Both the cloth and what it enshrouded had come from the personal effects of Cabe Bedlam.

He quickly unfolded the cloth and removed his prize. It was a short blade of the type used for shaving. One of the warlock's foibles concerned shaving without the use of sorcery. Cabe's detestation of any sort of magical alteration to his physical being amused the Gryphon at times, but in this instance it had come in handy. Metal objects were always best for this sort of spell. They had a better affinity for their user, especially mages. There were reasons why this was so, but they were of no concern to the lionbird at the moment. Finding Cabe's trail was.

For one of his vast experience, the spell was nothing to perform. He felt the tingle as the blade became attuned. It would lead him along the path Cabe and Darkhorse had followed. The lionbird never considered following the magical trail left by the demon steed. As unique as that trail was, enough time had passed that following it would be more troublesome than what he was doing now. A physical object was always better, even in this case.

His hand and the blade once more buried in the voluminous folds of his cloak, he set out. The vague trail that most every spellcaster left led the Gryphon toward one of the countless stables he knew dotted the city. Likely

Darkhorse had been stabled there. The trail grew confusing, however, which meant that not only had Cabe spent much time here, but he had moved around quite a bit in the nearby vicinity.

Some might have questioned the need to search at all, considering that the dark-haired spellcaster's last message had mentioned the hills of Esedi, but the Gryphon was concerned with more than just his human friend. The Lady Gwen had not been entirely forthcoming, but he was certain that she was very concerned too with what had happened in Zuu. Cabe's note was deceptively matter-of-fact. So much so, in fact, that the lionbird had agreed with the enchantress's assumption that Zuu had not been a simple pause in the warlock's journey.

Gwendolyn's concern was for the health and well-being of her mate. The Gryphon's concern included Cabe, but also the potential danger Zuu might now represent. Not merely Zuu, either. For all he knew there were already Aramite spies in the city. Again, the raiders were nothing if not efficient.

Much had happened at the stable, of that he was certain. That along with what he had heard verified much. He would have to relay his knowledge to Toos once this was over, assuming that the lanky former mercenary did not already know. This kingdom would bear watching.

It was impossible to avoid other folk, but this was hardly the first time the Gryphon had performed such covert activity. His every step was carefully planned despite how casual his actions might appear to an onlooker. At the stables he toyed with one of his boots, acting as if something had slipped inside and was now causing him annoyance. Dressed as an outsider and already having been in more than one tavern, it was hardly surprising that he also staggered to and fro a bit as he walked. Since he was clearly a visitor it was also no surprise that he would be glancing around at everything.

The trail left the stables simple enough, but near one of the local establishments, a strong pull made him turn. He stared at the well-lit entrance to a place called Belfour's Champion. There was another trail leading off into the far streets, but this one was stronger, almost as if it were so recent it had not had time to dissipate.

*Now what do we have here?* There was no reason for Cabe's return to Zuu. Knowing the human as he did, if Cabe had finished his mission, he would have returned home to the Manor the instant it was possible for him to do so. Yet, the blade tingled as if the warlock himself sat inside.

*Only one way to discover the truth.*

He entered the inn, all but ignoring the enticing smells. Belfour's Champion was a bustling place and it was everything he could do just to scan the crowd while not looking suspicious. The blade hidden in his hand gave him focus.

He carefully stumbled in the direction, noting with satisfaction that there were a few empty spots on some of the benches ahead of him. Should it become necessary, he could take one and pretend to wait for a serving girl while he continued to search.

The Gryphon passed around the shapely backside of a particularly fetching girl, then immediately dodged by two very overstuffed patrons on their way out. He paused to get his bearings and could not help but frown. The direction had now changed. Not only had he passed the location, but it was *receding* from him even as he stood there.

The Gryphon eyed the path he had taken. He saw no one that resembled the warlock. It was possible that Cabe was disguised and that although the lionbird wore a human face nearly identical to the one Cabe had known him by long ago, he would not know to look for one of his old companions in this faraway city. Still, something was wrong. Could his spell have caused him to follow a coin that the warlock had spent? Unlikely. The trail was too strong. Even if the coin or coins had just left his hands, Bedlam would have had to handle them for quite some time. It also would have required more than a few coins to create such a pull. They passed through too many hands too quickly to generally have much attachment to any one person.

Pretending to have sighted someone who *might* be an old chum, the Gryphon started back. His eyes carefully inspected each person. He sidestepped several more patrons entering, the same serving girl, and—

And the trail altered again. Out of the corner of his eye, the Gryphon glanced at the woman he had twice now passed.

The more he studied her, which was something no one there would have found unusual anyway, the more he was of the opinion that she had some secret. What?

*I am becoming senile!* He knew what it was now. Only sorcerers of some ability would even recognize it, which still gave him no excuse for not having noted it before. Now that he knew, the woman's secret fairly screamed to him.

*A sorceress! One of some mean skill, too, I would think!*

What was her connection to Cabe? Why did his spell draw him to her?

She happened to turn in his direction then. Although his actions were still innocent enough, the look that passed briefly across her beautiful countenance told him that she knew he was not what he seemed. In fact, he was certain that she knew what *he* was, too.

It had to be the case. Suddenly the golden-haired woman found things to do that took her to the back of the inn. The Gryphon did not wonder whether she would return, only how many exits there might be back there. He doubted she would use her skills while still inside. A sorceress who worked in taverns and inns generally did so because she was hiding what she was. That meant he still had an opportunity to catch her.

The lionbird had not been idle while he had thought all this out. Already he was at the front doorway. If he could find her before she slipped away, it would simplify things for him. If the unknown enchantress *did* teleport away, he still had one trick up his sleeve. The same object that had first drawn him to her would allow him to find her again.

Despite the hour, or perhaps because of it, there were a number of folk wandering about. That encouraged him, for while it slowed his progress, she could hardly use her sorcery in front of people who might recognize her as working at the inn. The blade also informed him that she was still nearby, although it was possible that the sorceress had removed the item from her person. Since she could hardly know why he was after her, he did not think she would know to do that. If he was wrong . . .

The tug he had felt suddenly ceased.

*Teleported!* Cursing quietly, the Gryphon turned round. Nothing was ever too easy. Still, if she ran true to predictability, she was probably not too far away. Just far enough to consider herself safe.

Sure enough, he felt the same tug. Not for a moment did he think it was anything other than her. He had performed this spell too often, too.

Without hesitation, the Gryphon teleported after her.

She was facing his direction as he materialized, but caught off-guard, her reflexes were too slow. Moving with the inhuman swiftness that had allowed him to survive for so long, the lionbird reached forward and caught her with his good hand. Only after that was done did he become aware of where exactly they were. She was bolder than he had thought, for from their location, he could just make out the inn far to his left. The woman had been watching for him rather than simply escaping, an obvious sign that no matter how skilled she was, she was still a novice in many things.

"If you even think about escape, *don't.*"

It was very clear that the serving woman understood. He could sense the tension coursing through her body. On the other hand, he could also sense the excitement she felt. The Gryphon was familiar with her type, having met more than his share. *Very fortunate that neither Gwen nor Troia came with me!* This was not the sort of woman either wife would care to see around their mates.

In the few seconds since his sudden arrival, she had already become bold enough to ask him questions. "Do we visit the king now?"

"Should we?" He decided to play along.

One thing she was, was quick. The toying smile that had started to spread across her exquisite face faltered. "You're not with the king's herd of pet mages."

The rumored spellcasters of King Lanith. Now he understood her earlier panic. She *was* hiding, hiding from her own monarch.

"I should have known." The smile had started spreading again. "You are much too talented for one of that bunch. Not to mention much more pleasant to look at."

He kept her from reaching up and stroking his cheek. Had Troia been here, the scene would have become very unpleasant by now. In her own way, the woman before him was just as much a predator as his bride.

"Thank you, but I am spoken for."

"From the way you followed me, I wouldn't have believed that." She leaned forward ever so slightly.

He leaned forward, too, but not because of the grand and glorious sight before him. "Do not play your games with me. I might surprise you."

His tone was menacing enough that she quickly withdrew. Even subdued for the moment, however, the young enchantress was still imposing. She would be much more trouble in the years to come.

"What do you want of me? If you're not from the king, then who are you?"

"My name is unimportant, but I believe you and I share an acquaintance. One from whom you have a token of remembrance."

Her smile twisted into a grimace and one hand flinched. The lionbird reached toward a small belt pouch hanging against her thigh. He tore the pouch off. Releasing her but still keeping his eyes focused in her direction, the Gryphon opened the pouch.

There were several small items in the pouch, but only one that could belong to Cabe. The Gryphon's high sensitivity to magical auras allowed him to pick it out. A small dagger that many people carried when traveling. It was more useful for mundane tasks than cutting thieves, but then Cabe Bedlam hardly had to worry about thieves . . . excepting this one, of course. "You planned to follow him at some point? Was not one rejection enough for you?"

"You're *his* friend?"

"We go back a long way. How did you come by this?"

One look at his eyes warned her about lying. Unleashing her dazzling smile, she replied, "He came into the inn. I could see that he was different, one of us."

"And so you tried to seduce him . . . for what?" He thought carefully. "Training and more, I imagine. The road to power for a mage."

He had come close to the truth. The Gryphon understood the present situation concerning spellcasters. Hunted for years by the Dragon Kings, they were only now reappearing in any number. Other than Cabe and Gwen, he had only known a handful of mages of any ability who had survived the constant purges. Toos, once his second-in-command during his mercenary days, was one.

"What is your name?"

"Tori. Tori Winddancer."

Winddancer, just the sort of name one found in this region. The appellation no doubt revolved around the swiftness of horses. She was a native of the kingdom of Zuu, then. There would be even less chance for her to find someone like her in this region. Although the Green Dragon was an ally to humans now and his particular line had always treated people fairly well, the days after the Turning War had seen the beginning of the strongest of the mage purges. That cleansing had been under the control of the Dragon Emperor, and knowing his counterpart in the Dagora Forest, it was said that extra care had been taken to make the purge in and around Dagora very thorough.

"What happened to my friend while he was here?"

"You heard about what happened near the stables?" At his nod, she continued. "That was him. That was some horse he had, too. I heard some people claim it could fly, but they probably didn't know your friend was a warlock."

*And you do not know about Darkhorse, evidently.* So much the better. "Were the king's men after him?"

"The guards and the mages . . . or bumblers, after the way they handled him. He made fools out of them I hear."

"You hear?"

She smiled again. "I left the moment I knew they were coming. Your friend didn't understand about the medallion . . . but you do, I guess."

"I've been around longer." So now he had verification. Cabe and Darkhorse had run afoul of King Lanith's tame spellcasters. He could not blame the warlock for leaving the incident out of his message to the Lady Bedlam; she had more than enough to worry about without adding this. It was over and done.

"Are you through with me or would you like to talk of other things now?" From the way she looked at him, it was clear what she meant.

"There are those who will aid in your training without you having to resort to seduction."

"I'm looking for more than training as you know, silver hair." She tried to touch the hair, but he blocked her hand. "I'm looking for *much* more than that."

"My wife would claw you into little pieces if she knew you had even been this familiar with me. Literally claw you."

"What is she, a cat?"

"Yes."

She looked at him carefully, expecting some sign of amusement, then saw that he was deadly earnest. "Some people will marry into the strangest families. A human and a cat?"

"Did I say I was human?"

Tori had no response to that, but he noted that she leaned back a little, as if seeing him in a new and unnerving light. "I asked you a question. Are you finished with me?"

"Nearly. Are you familiar—" He paused as a drunken trader dressed in the clothes of Gordag-Ai stumbled in their direction. He heard other voices nearby. The Gryphon took Tori's arm. She did not resist but neither did she try her charms on him again. His comments concerning himself and his mate had her wondering. "Let us walk back to the inn. Be friendly."

The enchantress nodded. Ahead of them, the trader was trying to decide which side of the narrow street he wanted to give up to them. The Gryphon pointed to his left and the man steered that way. Turning his attention back to Tori, he started to ask his question again.

The footsteps of the drunken man stilled.

A normal man would have been too slow and that fact was perhaps all that saved the Gryphon, for it probably made his attacker just overconfident enough. He threw the woman to one side as the trader fell upon him, knife in one hand. The lionbird heard Tori gasp, but then his attention became completely focused on the battle situation. His adversary weighed far more than he should have, which made the Gryphon certain that beneath the outfit one would find armor. Black armor.

He had grown careless, spending too much of his time on some things and forgetting his own thought that there might be spies here. He had also grown careless in another way, for the face he wore now was the one he often preferred. Cabe would not be the only one capable of recognizing it. After so many years of facing him, it was not surprising that many of the raiders, especially the spies, would recognize that striking countenance on sight. The Gryphon knew he had not only become careless, but also vain. Had he chosen faces of less distinction, he might have avoided this. His maimed hand might still have given him away, but not nearly as quickly as his vanity had.

They struggled on the ground, the wolf raider maintaining his advantage above through sheer weight and the Gryphon's inability to get a strong enough grip with his damaged hand. The raider's own features were nondescript, as was most common with those in his profession, but the quiet determination he radiated told the Gryphon that his adversary was a veteran of many a campaign. There would be no room for mistakes against this man.

If physical strength was not enough to rid him of his assailant, then the lionbird was more than willing to resort to his magical skills. When the situation called for it, one took the advantages one was given and sense of honor be damned, that was his belief. Survival first and foremost.

The Aramite must have known what he was attempting, for suddenly he abandoned the knife attack and, disregarding injury to himself, swung his head down, catching the Gryphon square in the forehead.

It was all the Gryphon could do to keep from blacking out. Worse, the force was enough to make the back of his head strike the ground. The world around him began to spin. His grip weakened, allowing the wolf raider to press his advantage.

"My life for yours!" the dark figure hissed. "A small price for the empire's triumph!"

*So now it ends,* he managed to think. *Cut down at night in a street far from anything I might call home.*

He heard a small, startled grunt from the raider. The weight on his body shifted to one side. Instinct took over. The Gryphon followed the shifting of the weight and pushed his attacker off in that direction. He heard a clatter and realized that the knife had fallen from the Aramite's hand. Now, even with his head still ringing, the advantage was becoming his.

The raider was by no means defeated, however. Once more he tried to butt heads. The lionbird was ready for him, however, and tipped his own head out of the way. Then he did the only thing he could think of doing that would end the flight in swift fashion.

He transformed. For most shapeshifters, such an act would have left them helpless for a few precious seconds. For the Gryphon, long practiced at shaping at a moment's notice, it was not so. Two decades of war had kept that ability well honed.

The spy let out a yelp that the Gryphon's taloned hand all but muffled. Taken back by the astonishing sight of his adversary shifting form, the Aramite was too slow to block the attack that came next. With grim satisfaction, the Gryphon twisted his adversary's head to one side, snapping his neck.

Verifying that the man was dead, he slowly rose and whispered, "Your life for that of my son . . . hardly a balance but certainly a beginning."

It was only then that he recalled Tori. He transformed back into a human even as he turned to where he had last left her. It was not surprising to find her gone. Still, something had caused the Aramite to grunt in pain and shift his weight. It could only have been an attack of some sort by the enchantress. A kick in the head, he suspected. Why bring attention to herself as a spellcaster when a simple physical assault worked as effectively?

The area had grown conspicuously devoid of people and the Gryphon knew that such emptiness usually preceded an appearance by the local guard. He regretted that he had allowed his anger to seize mastery; the spy might have given him some further information, including how many of his ilk had already spread through Zuu. The city guard would have to be satisfied with the corpse.

Certainly any other spies in the city would go into hiding now that one of their number was dead and they had no way of knowing who was responsible. This one had acted on his own; if there had been more, they would have entered the struggle, for he was not flattering himself when he thought they considered him a target of prime importance.

The brief respite, however much it might have put him in danger of being sighted by the city guard, had served its purpose. His head still throbbed, but his concentration was sufficient for spellcasting. It was time to leave Zuu and follow Cabe's trail.

Trail. The Gryphon searched for the knife that the woman Tori had stolen from Cabe, but found nothing. It might have been thrown into the darkness during the struggle, but he suspected it was once more in the hands of the enchantress. She would gain small success with it now, however. In the short time he had held it, he had made a few magical alterations. If she sought out the warlock after this, she would simply reappear in the same location she had started from. Let her search for Cabe Bedlam if she chose, but she would have to do it on her own.

*One of the first lessons in magic is to never assume it will always work the way you desire.*

It was a lesson he tried to remind himself of each and every day. It was a lesson he was certain he would need to recall when he entered the desolate domain of the Crystal Dragon.

The city guard was near. With one last bitter glance at the raider's sprawled body, the Gryphon regripped the guiding blade and teleported away . . .

. . . to the hills of Esedi.

The trail was stronger here, as he had expected. The blade had probably brought him to within a few yards of where Cabe himself had materialized. He allowed himself a brief human smile, for teleportation was always a chancy thing when one was not familiar with the location, then let his human guise melt away since it was no longer needed.

Cabe and Darkhorse had done fairly well in their choice of locations. Under normal conditions, they would have enjoyed an excellent view of the eastern portion of the peninsula. Not all of it, of course, but enough to enable them to plan the journey's beginning. Legar was not as massive a region as Esedi or even the immense Dagora Forest, but it was filled with hills, crevices, and a system of underground caverns that rivaled those in the Tyber Mountains. Add to the treacherous, uneven landscape possible encounters with the Quel and now the wolf raiders, and you had very good reasons to move slowly and carefully through Legar.

*And now this mist* . . . He was familiar with the Grey Mists, the dank, mind-sapping haze that covered Lochivar. Lochivar, on the southeastern edge of the

Dragonrealm, was the kingdom of the Black Dragon, who was the source of that magical fog. Knowing what the Grey Mists could do, the Gryphon was glad he had not simply decided to teleport into this murk. Even from here he could sense its evil. There was something wild about it, but it was the wildness of a thing in its death throes, for there was also a feeling of decay about it.

*If this is how it seems under the dimness of the moons, then how is it in the daytime? Worse? How will it be when I actually enter it?* He would find out soon enough. There was no real reason to remain here for even a fraction of the time he had spent in the city. Cabe and Darkhorse would have waited here only long enough to prepare themselves for Legar and the Gryphon was as prepared as he would ever be. He would learn nothing new from these silent hills, nothing that would aid his mission and his vengeance.

*Nothing?* He paused, noticing something for the first time. Why was it so deathly quiet here? Was the poison covering Legar so great that the wildlife could not stand to be even this close to it? That could not be. In the distance, the lionbird could barely make out a few of the normal sounds of night, nocturnal birds and animals. It was only this one region where the creatures had either grown silent or fled. Only the region in which he stood.

The Gryphon's sword was out and ready before his next breath.

"Well, I must admit I was not expecting *you!*"

From the darkness emerged a huge shape blacker than the night. Ice-blue eyes glittered without the aid of the moons' poor illumination.

"Darkhorse!"

The shadow steed dipped his head. "You are far from your war, Lord Gryphon, but then your war seems to have strayed as well!"

"You've seen them then. The raiders."

"Seen them and fought them!"

"Fought them . . . and where is Cabe, then, demon steed?" Was he too late for the warlock? Had D'Farany added to his list of victims already?

The leviathan's response did not encourage him. "I . . . lost him."

"He—"

"No!" Darkhorse grew vehement. "He is *not* dead! He cannot be! We were merely separated in the foul mist! He said nothing and I thought he must be behind me, keeping clear!"

The Gryphon cut him off with a curt gesture. His general uneasiness around the pitch-black creature had given way to his concern for Cabe Bedlam and the need to know what sort of things he might face in shrouded Legar. "Tell me from the beginning. Speak carefully, tell me all, but do so fairly quickly."

Darkhorse's easy acquiescence surprised him at first until he reminded himself that Cabe Bedlam was one of the eternal's few true friends. The telling of the tale was short and swift. When it was over, it was clear that Darkhorse was dismayed by what he considered his terrible carelessness. There was something more to what had happened than what the shadow steed had related to him, however. Whatever it was, its roots went deep. Some distraction in the eternal's mind that had caused Darkhorse not to notice that he and the warlock were being purposely separated.

Oddly, knowing that the creature from the Void could become so distraught lessened some of the Gryphon's wariness of him. He felt he understood the workings of Darkhorse's mind better than he ever had in the past.

"The monstrosity you fought was an illusion, you say?"

"Yes, and when I turned to comment so to Cabe, he was also gone! I never heard him call out!"

"He might have, but you still might not have heard him. In that place, I would not be surprised." The Gryphon stared at the mist, so unsettling, so hungry, even in the calm of night. "You couldn't find his trail, either."

"I detected nothing! I, Darkhorse, could not sense him!"

"Yes . . ." The lionbird contemplated the situation. The knowledge that the wolf raiders were active throughout Legar made his mane bristle and his claws unsheathe. He wanted to hunt down each and every one of the marauders like the animals they were and savor their deaths; yet the Gryphon knew that not only would it still not fill the hole inside, but he could not abandon a friend. In that he and the shadow steed were one. Cabe Bedlam was missing and if he had been captured by the Aramites, then there would be opportunity enough for the Gryphon to try to satiate his need for vengeance. If Cabe's fate was otherwise, then the raiders would have to wait. He had no doubt that they would still be there. Once the Aramites gained a foothold, the only way to remove them was to kill them.

He was willing to try, but not now.

"Do you think you can find the last place you left him?"

Darkhorse gazed out at the ominous mass blanketing Legar. "I might be able to take us that far, but what use will it be?"

"It may be of some use, believe me." The Gryphon revealed the small blade he had utilized to follow the warlock's trail this far. "You had nothing of his to aid you in your search."

"Even if I had, I do not think it would have worked. The mist has the taint of Nimth upon it, Lord Gryphon! You are one of the few with sufficient knowledge to understand what that means! You *also* knew Shade!" The shadow steed paused. "Nothing works as it should down there! The laws of magic—the laws of *nature*—cannot be trusted in Legar so long as that foulness remains!"

"We can only try." The lionbird gazed at the blade. "This may be Cabe's best, possibly only hope. Our combined skills might prove to be enough to overwhelm it."

"Overwhelm *Nimth*? You must surely jest! I knew the Vraad! I knew Shade!"

The black stallion's tone each time he spoke of the blur-faced warlock revealed volumes to the Gryphon. Shade was somehow tied to Darkhorse's troubles. What had the Bedlams' messages said? Darkhorse continued to search for Shade as if he might somehow have survived. Was he that afraid of the tortured warlock?

*No, not afraid. If there was anyone who might understand Darkhorse and what he is, it would have been Shade.*

He had no time to ponder further. Darkhorse's inner struggles would have to wait until there was peace, assuming that ever happened. Now it was time for Legar.

"This is not Nimth and neither the Crystal Dragon nor the wolf raiders are Vraad. What exists down there can only be a *reflection* of Nimth's chaos. I think that if we try the spell from as near as possible to the place where you two became separated, then we stand a chance. If it fails . . . we still have to enter. You know that Cabe would have returned here by now if he could have. He would know to do that."

Darkhorse kicked at the ground. "I know that, Lord Gryphon! Ha! I have been thinking about it since I materialized back here! I thought he might have accidentally teleported elsewhere, but there is no place here that I have not searched and if he in some way eluded my search he would, indeed, still have returned to this location by now!"

"Then we should not hesitate any longer."

"Very well." Darkhorse trotted closer. "You shall have to ride me as he did, Your Majesty! We did not trust that we would arrive at the same destination, this being the Crystal Dragon's realm. The foul fog makes the danger of that worse."

"I agree." As he mounted, the lionbird thought of what his companion had just said. "And do you also find it odd that the Dragon King has been so quiet even though he has in the past always dealt swiftly with those who would disturb his existence?"

A snort. "I still think that this was his doing! I, for one, would not call this doing nothing!"

"Nothing it certainly isn't, demon steed, but it's an unfocused, dangerous method by which to rid himself of the Aramites. If this was the Crystal Dragon's doing, I would like to know why he chose such madness as a tool. It is as much a risk, perhaps more, as the wolf raiders are."

"Be that as it may, we *still* have to journey through it!" The leviathan swung his head around so that he faced dark Legar. "Give me but a moment and I will be ready." Darkhorse's head tilted to one side. "Curious!"

The Gryphon leaned forward and tried to see what interested his mount so. "What is it? I don't see anything."

Darkhorse shook his head, sending his mane flying. "I suspect wishful thinking is all it is! When I stare at the fog, it looks not quite so dense as it was earlier! Truly, it must be the moonlight!"

Squinting, the Gryphon could see nothing. If there had been a change in the density of the fog, he could not tell. From the shadow horse's words, it would have happened before he had even teleported to here. Whether or not it *had* happened, the lionbird could still not make out even the slightest detail beneath the upper surface of the shroud of fog.

Darkhorse finally stirred. "Well! It matters not! We must find Cabe! That is all that matters!"

*That, a legion of wolf raiders, and a Dragon King who does not act as one would expect,* the Gryphon silently corrected as he held tight. *Other than those few things, we have nothing to worry about.*

# XII

CABE WOKE TO the jarring sight of a Quel face looming over him. The long snout was mere inches from his own countenance. The warlock's nose wrinkled; the Quel's breath was putrid.

His head was suddenly filled to bursting with overlapping images. Cabe gasped, put his hands on his head, and tried to shut the sensations out. He saw himself, the wolf raiders, the Quel, a vague image that must be the Crystal Dragon, a beach . . . there was just too much!

"Stop! I can't take it all in!"

Mercifully, the Quel presence in his head withdrew. As he regained control of his senses, the weary spellcaster sat up and surveyed his surroundings. They were in a small cavern with only one exit, an exit guarded by yet another of the underdwellers. Cabe counted three Quel in all, but then he realized that the third, off to the far side of the chamber, was slumped over. A single image touched his mind, confirmation from the one near him that their companion was dead and had been so for some time.

He wondered how long he had been unconscious. Cabe had faint memories of being pulled under, of watching the earth fill in above him. He recalled little else after that, for something had caused him to pass out.

The Quel inquisitor reached out and pointed by the warlock's right hand.

Cabe looked down and saw a gem. He vaguely recalled it having been in his hand when the images had first struck him. He nodded understanding to the armored leviathan and picked it up.

*Injury . . . urgent need . . . question?*

The combination of images, sensations, and emotions was as close as the Quel could come to speaking in the human tongue. Cabe was aware of the communication crystal and found it a fascinating tool, but it took careful thinking to sometimes decipher what was meant. It was possible for the Quel to communicate to him without it, but then the images would have been less detailed and many of the projected sensations would have failed to even reach his mind.

*They want to know if I'm injured in any way.* He shook his head. Considering that any injury would have been the Quel's doing, Cabe was not entirely impressed by the subterraneans' concern. Still, it was unusual that they should place any importance in his well-being, unless they wanted something from him.

Something involving the wolf raiders?

The images projected by the one Quel, a female, if the warlock was correct, shifted almost the instant he formulated the question. Although the question had merely been for his own contemplation, the Quel answered as best she could.

*Black shells . . . defenders . . . the hungry magic . . . defeat . . . the city lost . . . statement.*

*Statement.* The manner by which the creatures communicated made the reply sound almost matter-of-fact until one stared into the dark, inhuman eyes of the Quel and saw the loss there. Her city, the Quel city, was in the hands of the Aramites, who had used some sort of magic spell to nullify the defenses. She and a few like her had escaped capture, he imagined. There were only a few Quel at any time and so they had not had the resources to completely combat a foe as determined as the wolf raiders. If they had, he suspected that the raiders would have found themselves in the midst of one of the worst hand-to-hand struggles they had ever come across. One Quel was worth more than a few human soldiers any day, no matter how well trained the latter were.

*Black shells . . . hunt . . . too few . . . statement.*

He saw them hunting down a lone guard every now and then, but such attacks were not enough. One by one, the secrets of their cities fell into the hands of the invaders.

Cabe stiffened. "What about—"

The response was swift. *Sacrifice . . . hidden . . . suspicious but unable to find . . . safe . . . for now . . . danger in thought . . . statement.*

Their greatest secret was safe, but the Aramites were thorough. They might at any time find it. The Quel did not even wish to think about that, for fear that doing so might somehow bring the discovery to pass. Cabe received a swift, curt look from the female who told him there would be no more questions on that matter.

He had no delusions that the underdwellers saw him as anything more than a means to an end. Their concern was for their own kind; they saw in him only someone who shared an obvious interest in seeing the black shells, as they called the raiders, gone from the Dragonrealm.

"You don't make cooperation very enticing," he bluntly informed his captor. "What difference would it make for me to help you?"

A single image of a tall, opaque sphere flashed into his mind.

For the first time, Cabe recalled Plool. The Quel still had the Vraad hidden away and were attempting to use him as a bargaining chip. It almost made the warlock want to laugh. In one respect, there was a temptation to leave the Vraad where he was, for it would be the best way to ensure that he caused no further chaos with his Nimth-spawned magic.

Cabe knew he could do no such thing, though. Even Plool deserved a chance. Also, the Aramites *were* a deadlier threat to the continent, at least now. The Dragonrealm had survived centuries of Quel, confined as they were to only a few wandering above and below the surface of Legar. The raiders would never settle for that. They would seek to rebuild their power base. He was certain that other ships sailed the sea, other ships seeking a new port. The longer the wolf raiders had, the deeper they would be entrenched.

He would work with the Quel for as long as it was safe, but he knew better than to trust them. "What about the one who was with me? What about your prisoner?"

The answer was short, succinct, and proof that this was meant to be no partnership but rather a situation demanding his complete obedience to their cause. Cabe lost whatever little sympathy he might have ever had for his captors. Memories of his past experiences with the Quel returned to him. They were vivid and sometimes painful memories.

The warlock wished it were possible for him to just forget Plool, but he was not that sort of person . . . and the underdwellers certainly had to be aware of that.

His inquisitor rose and indicated he should follow suit. Rising stiffly, the wary mage followed the Quel to the tunnel mouth. The other creature, taller and definitely a male, waited until the two had passed before joining. The male moved with some stiffness, as if working with muscles long unused. The Quel were careful to keep him sandwiched in between, he noted. A brief touch with his mind also indicated that they were doing what they could to stifle his magical abilities, but their strength was not enough to completely disable him. His mind already shielded so that the gemstone he still had to carry would not betray him, Cabe pondered his possible options. Down here, his sorcery appeared to work, but what would happen if he tried to teleport to the surface? Could he do it safely? More to the point, did he have the concentration and strength to even perform the spell? He doubted it. Still, he was fairly certain he would be able to defend himself when it came time for the Quel to turn upon him.

The warlock wondered what he would do about Plool when that happened.

As they walked, Cabe, with growing curiosity, carefully studied the tunnel. It was a claustrophobic thing, not at all like the larger passages he recalled from his earlier encounters. There was barely room enough for one of the diggers to pass. More important, after the first few steps, the only sources of illumination became the occasional crystal embedded in the walls. They were of the same type as those in the vast tunnels, but so scattered and so few, it was as if they had been added only recently and with great haste.

*This is a new tunnel. Very new.* "Where are we going?"

He received no response from his companions. The more he thought about it, the more they seemed to be growing increasingly anxious. The warlock did not find that comforting. Anything that worried the Quel surely had to be fearsome.

There was only one thing he could think of that would put such uneasiness into the minds of his captors. One creature.

Only the Crystal Dragon.

*They wouldn't! That would be suicidal!*

Unfortunately, he could think of no other explanation. Cabe had intended on seeking out the lord of Legar, but now that he was possibly on his way to do just that, the idea had turned sour. Who was to say that the Crystal Dragon might not find his intrusion just as irritating as that of the wolf raiders? What had he been thinking? One could not just walk up and ask to see the Dragon King!

But that was what the Quel intended *him* to do. He knew that the moment they came to the end of the tunnel. Before him was a vast cavern that glittered so great that he had to shield his eyes for several seconds before they finally became accustomed to the brilliance. Gemlike stalactites and stalagmites, looking much like the jagged teeth of some great beast, dotted the cavern. The faceted walls reflected themselves again and again and again, an infinity of cold, gleaming beauty. Cabe began to sweat heavily, but not because of fear. The heat in the cavern was ghastly and when he stared at the floor, which was also of crystal, he knew why. Some subterranean source of heat buried deep beneath was what turned the chamber into an oven. It even gave the floor a reddish tinge. It was not enough to make travel across impossible, but the warlock did not intend to stand on any one spot too long.

What he saw beyond the chamber made him forget the heat. Carved into the far wall was a temple that, in many ways, resembled the Manor, a place that Cabe wished he had never left. Columns rose high, at least two stories. There were three doorways. Symbols that the warlock did not recognize formed an arc over each of them. Cabe knew that the work was very, very old, but it was still in immaculate condition. A sense of ancient power radiated from the temple.

He was on the threshold of the Dragon King's inner sanctum.

The Quel in front of him shifted to the side. *Journey . . . the crystal lord . . . (fear) . . . seeking an audience . . . statement!*

So this *was* to be his role. They wanted him to do what they could not, namely face the Dragon King and seek his aid. The warlock found himself amused. He was expected to go where they refused to tread and seek aid on their behalf. It almost made him laugh aloud. Their capture of him must have been a lucky but desperate venture. It said something for their ability to plot under dire circumstances but little for their bravery.

The male took hold of his shoulders and shook him. New images danced in Cabe Bedlam's head. *Audience . . . the crystal lord in his sanctum . . . dispersing the floating death . . . driving the black shells back into the sea . . . statement!/question?*

It took him time to decipher the last. The message was evidently a list of requests the Quel had for the Crystal Dragon, requests that they wanted Cabe to make. From the way the male gripped him, he knew that even the very thought of asking the drake lord for such aid unnerved the subterraneans. They *deeply* feared the might of the Crystal Dragon . . . and Cabe could hardly blame them for that.

He was prodded from behind. The Quel would not join him on this last part of the trek. They would trust that their captive would make the warlock do what they wanted. It had probably never occurred to them that Cabe might have gone even without a threat.

Slowly he entered the gleaming chamber. What wonders the underground recesses of Legar held. It was amazing that the surface of the place did not collapse, considering how extensive the world beneath was. Of course, more than a little of it had been carved by intelligent hands, not the forces of nature. Those hands had made quite certain that their efforts would not end up buried in rubble.

Cabe still found it amazing, nonetheless.

The temperature was steady, which was fortunate. He still found he had to loosen the top of his robe. It was bad if not worse than being on the surface during noontime.

The walk across passed without incident, although at one point the Quel hooted something. He turned, but even holding the gem, he could not understand what they wanted. They did not appear to want him to return, so Cabe finally turned back to the glistening temple and continued on.

It was not until he stood before the carved structure that he discovered a problem. While there were indentations representing windows and doorways, none of them were real entrances. As far as he could see, the temple was nothing more than a vast relief.

*There must be something!* He stared at his reflection, distorted by the multifaceted surface, and thought. The Quel would not have sent him to this place if they had not believed it to be a way to the Crystal Dragon. Yet if they were too frightened to come this far, then perhaps none of their kind had ever journeyed close enough to see that this was no more than some sculptor's masterpiece. It hardly seemed possible, but . . .

"Who seeks passage?"

The voice, piercing, echoed all around him. Cabe stepped back from the temple and as he did an astonishing thing happened, for his distorted reflection, instead of copying his movements, stepped *forward.* Not only did it step forward, but it left the confines of the wall and continued toward him.

"Who seeks passage?" This time, it was definitely his macabre reflection that spoke.

"I do," Cabe responded, finally able to find his own voice.

Although the crystal golem—the warlock could find no better term for what faced him—looked his way, the eyes did not exactly fix on him. Rather, they appeared focused behind him, perhaps on the Quel. "You alone seek passage?"

"I alone seek passage, yes. I would speak with the Crystal Dragon."

The guardian was silent. It was eerie to stare at himself, especially a self who was twisted and jagged. Cabe reached up to rub his chin in thought, a habit he had long had, and watched bemused as the reflection followed the same course. Cabe wondered what the creature would do if he started to dance.

An eternity passed before the golem finally said, "You may pass through."

Cabe glanced beyond the golem. He saw no doorway. "Where do I go?"

The guardian looked at him with vacant eyes. "Follow."

He began walking backward.

After a moment's hesitation, the warlock obeyed. The crystal creature had no trouble walking backward, but the sight made Cabe stumble twice. He kept waiting for a passage to open in the temple wall, but nothing changed. As the guardian reached the wall, Cabe braced himself for the collision.

The golem melted into the crystal.

The warlock froze, uncertain as to what to do now. He stared at his reflection. Almost it seemed to be waiting for him.

Its mouth opened. "Follow."

"Follow?"

"Follow yourself if you would enter," was the only explanation he received.

He thought he understood, but that made it no easier. Nodding, Cabe focused on his reflection, tensed, and walked forward.

He closed his eyes just before he would have hit the wall and so he was never exactly sure what happened next. Instead of a harsh, very solid wall, the anxious mage walked into a substance that reminded him of syrup. Gritting his teeth, he continued through it. The voice of the guardian urged him on now and then. Despite being surrounded by the odd substance, the warlock had no difficulty breathing. That in no way meant that the crossing was easy on him. He was reminded of Gwen, who had been trapped in an amber prison by his father, Azran, and left there for nearly two hundred years. The thought of being so imprisoned sent a chill down his spine.

When his hand broke through to empty space, Cabe sighed in relief.

Only when he was free did he dare open his eyes. He did not look around but rather spun back and faced the wall through which he had passed. The warlock stared at it. To the eye, it was as it should have been, a crystal-encrusted barrier of rock. There was no passage and when he touched it, he felt only what one would expect to feel. Rock.

"If you are finished, huuuman . . ."

A drake warrior stood waiting for him in the new chamber, a drake warrior like none he had ever seen. Thin, glittering, his skin armor was an array of multifaceted jewels, not all of them the same color. There were deep greens, sunlit golds, ocean blues, and so much more. When the drake moved, it was a graceful movement, almost as if the creature were a dancer, not a fighter.

"Your Majesty?"

The flat, half-seen reptilian visage broke into a thin-lipped smile. "I will take you to him."

Cabe reddened slightly. He should not have assumed. It might be a mark against him now. The Dragon King might take umbrage at being mistaken for one of his mere subjects.

His new guide led him along a well-worn path that, like all else here, spoke of incredible age. Most everything down here had been built long before the Dragon Kings; Cabe was certain of that. He wondered if the Quel had built it. Possibly. Then again, they, too, might have come across it and decided to simply move in. Some additions looked more recent than others. Differences in style could be seen here and there. Everything gleamed, but fortunately not with too great an intensity.

They passed only two other drakes, both warriors like the first. He wondered how small the clan was. Some drake clans were larger than others. The Ice Dragon had sacrificed the last of his people for his master spell and several other clans had been more or less decimated over the past couple decades by their struggles with each other and the humans, but some, like Green and Blue, were actually increasing in number for the first time in generations. Cabe doubted that this particular clan was large. Legar could not support so many. Their principal source of food would have to come from the sea, for life was not abundant enough here. True, there were things that grew well under the surface, but these *were* dragons he was speaking of, which meant they needed meat of some sort.

Their journey ended before the mouth of another tunnel. Two warriors flanked each side of the mouth. Within, Cabe could make out only darkness.

His guide turned to him. "He awaits within, Cabe Bedlam."

"You know who I am."

"*He* knew. I simply obey." With that, the drake abruptly turned from him and walked away.

One of the guards used a lance to indicate that he should enter. Putting on a mask of resolve, the warlock stalked past the sentries and stepped into the darkness before hesitation got the better of him. It was not, he was grateful to see, like crossing through the wall. Instead, the moment he was through the entranceway, the darkness was burned away by a brilliant illumination. Cabe blinked, found himself blinded again.

"There isss an object in front of you, Cabe Bedlam. Pick it up. Itsss purpossssse will become apparent to you."

The blinded warlock reached down, then recalled that he was still holding the Quel device. He started to pocket it, but a warning hiss made him halt.

"You have no more need of that. Drop it."

Cabe did . . . and a second later heard a crackling sound, as if something were melting. He did not dare try to look, but rather searched for the vague shape of the object the voice had mentioned. His hands came upon a curved item that upon very close inspection proved to be a visor of sorts. It was designed to be worn over the ears like a pair of the glasses that were now fairly common among humans. Gingerly he put it on, blinked a few times, and let his eyes complete the task of adjusting.

Even with the visor on, the chamber still gleamed. Now, at least, he could see it . . . and also its lone inhabitant.

"Welcome to my domain, Massster Bedlam."

He knew of the Crystal Dragon, knew what he looked like from the visions, but still Cabe was not completely prepared for the leviathan.

The lord of Legar was possibly the largest of the Dragon Kings he had ever seen. Like his counterpart Blue, however, the Crystal Dragon was sleeker than some of the others. Yet it was not size that so overwhelmed the warlock. Neither was it the image of a dragon who seemed carved from the very crystal he took his title from. The drake warriors had dazzled Cabe's eyes enough, but their monarch positively blinded. In fact, it was the Crystal Dragon who so made the room blinding.

What overwhelmed him was the age. There was no particular thing that indicated it, but staring at his host, Cabe knew that here was the oldest of the present Dragon Kings. Even older than Ice, who had claimed the mantle of age often. It was said that the drake lords tended to live a thousand years at best, mostly because of the violent world of their kind. The warlock doubted that any of the other Dragon Kings were more than seven hundred years old. They might have the potential for long lives, but the drakes always found conflicts to kill themselves in . . . much the way humans did. Unfortunately for the drakes, their kind did not multiply as quickly as Cabe's race did.

Sharp diamond wings spread. The huge head dipped down so as to better observe the tiny human. "You have ssssought me, Cabe Bedlam, and I have given you an audience. Do you now intend to ssssimply sssstare for that time?"

It did not help that no matter where he looked, all he saw was either the reflected image of the Dragon King's unique countenance or that of his own, uncertain visage. Each face was distorted. He felt as if they all watched him, awaiting his response.

"Your pardon, Your Majesty. This is, I hope you'll understand, much to take in."

"Isss it?" An unreadable look crossed the draconian features.

Try as he might, Cabe could not completely calm himself down. This chamber was by far the most daunting. It served some distinct purpose, a purpose that he could not help but think that the Dragon King was trying to hide from him. All this blazing brilliance, brought forth by the drake lord himself, was meant to distract. The warlock was not certain how he had come to that conclusion, just that it made some sense when he viewed the chamber and its lord as a whole.

"It is," he finally answered. Clearing his suddenly dry throat, Cabe continued. "You must know, my lord, that even though it was the Quel who led me here, I would have come to request an audience with you regardless."

"Then you are here about the black plague ssssswarming over *my* realm." The Dragon King shifted. Although he pretended control, his movements looked forced to his human guest, as if the crystalline monarch was trying too hard to appear confident. The drake lord's entire body spoke of a creature at war within. Even his disinterested tone was too perfect.

*What goes on here?* This was not what Cabe had expected. "I am, yes. You should know. It is your summons that brought me here in the first place."

*"My what?"* The reptilian eyes widened. Almost it seemed that fear was the dominant emotion, but Cabe could not believe that was possible. What could frighten the Crystal Dragon?

"Your . . . summons. The vision and the dream."

"Visions . . . dreams?" Lifting his head high, the glittering leviathan turned his gaze toward the walls. The Dragon King had an apparent fascination for his reflections, but not because of any vanity. The mage watched him closely. Although he had only been in the Dragon King's presence for a minute or two, Cabe was already beginning to worry about the drake lord's sanity.

"You didn't send them?" Cabe asked after a long silence had passed.

Instead of answering his question, the Crystal Dragon quietly ordered, "Tell me of the visions."

Having few options, the worried spellcaster did that. He described his first experience and how he had shrugged it off. Then Cabe described the dream and how Aurim had also been affected. At that the reptilian monarch glanced his way, but the images soon snared him again. Cabe concluded with the vision he had suffered while recuperating in the hills of Esedi. When his tale was complete, the warlock waited for some comment.

Another long silence ensued, but at last the Crystal Dragon gazed down at him. The look in those great, inhuman orbs was enough to make Cabe Bedlam stiffen. There was sanity in them, but not much.

"I did not ssssummon you, warlock . . . or perhapssss I did."

"I don't understand." Why did it feel like he was always saying that? The frustrated sorcerer wondered if *anyone* understood what happened in the Dragonrealm. Sometimes it was as if life was but a game. A macabre game.

The great dragon unfurled and furled his wings over and over again. The talons of his forepaws gouged deep into the floor. Cabe looked around and realized that the chamber had grown darker.

"No . . . you wouldn't. No one would, warlock. That issss my bane, the ssssword that hangssss over my head. *No one* understands what I live with." The cold tones only added to the image of a creature slowly going mad. "I thought of ssssummoning you, Master Bedlam, thought of it but did not." He looked away from the tiny human and studied the chamber from wall to ceiling. "To thissss place, though, ssssuch a thought wassss good enough." The Crystal Dragon hissed. "Away with you!"

Cabe's first inclination was that his audience had come to an abrupt end, but it was not he to whom the drake lord roared the command. Fascinated, the warlock watched as the images all around him faded away. The crystalline walls dulled. They no longer reflected. The illumination also faded, albeit not completely.

"I ssssometimes think it hassss a mind of its own," the dragon murmured. He continued to stare at the now blank walls. "I ssssometimes think that the chamber controlsss me and not the other way." The Crystal Dragon laughed in self-mockery. "Ironic if true, would you not say?"

The warlock kept quiet. Noticing the lack of response, the behemoth tilted his head so that he could see his human guest out of the corner of his eye. "It takesss my thoughtsss, Cabe Bedlam, and makessss them reality. I can ssssee anything, any place, any perssssson in the Dragonrealm with the aid of thissss chamber. It showsss me the world ssso that I do not have to risssk myself and venture out.

"But there isss another sssside to it. Another side. It isss not ssssatisfied with my direct commandsss, no! It mussst have my deeper thoughtssss, my ssssleeping thoughtsss!"

The massive drake stirred. Cabe wanted to step back, but something within told him it would behoove him to stay where he was. He had to maintain a strong front. "So you thought of summoning me but did not."

The Dragon King quieted at the sound of his voice. Cabe's calm provided him with an anchor for his sanity. "I thought of you more than once, recalling your part in the sssstruggle with the dragon lord Ice."

*Which might explain why there had been more than one vision.* Perhaps each time the drake had thought of him, a vision had been sent. So he had journeyed here under a misconception. The dragon had not called him, but rather only *thought* about doing so. If he understood his host, then the chamber had taken his desire for Cabe's aid and acted upon it even after the Dragon King had chosen otherwise.

"I understood some of what I saw, but some of the images made no sense. The men in dragon-scale armor; what does it have to do with the wolf raiders?"

*"Nothing!"* snapped the Dragon King. Then, realizing how he had reacted, he withdrew into himself. "Nothing. A twisssting of random thoughtssss and dreamsss. Nothing to concern *you.*"

*Perhaps or perhaps not,* Cabe thought. Whether or not it concerned him, it appeared he would receive no clarification from his host and the warlock had no intention of pressing the subject. He had no way of predicting what the Dragon King's reaction would be then.

"Then you don't require my aid?"

A pause. "I am the Crystal Dragon."

He knew what the drake lord's response was supposed to imply, but the hesitant manner in which it was spoken belied that implication. The Crystal Dragon was trying to hide something and failing miserably. Yet Cabe dared not make mention of that fact. It would be far too easy for his host to take out whatever frustrations and fears he had on the warlock.

"Your Majesty—"

"I have the ssssituation in hand, mage! That issss your anssssswer; be sssatisfied with it!"

"I only had a question, Your Majesty." When the Dragon King said nothing, Cabe dared push on. "*Was* it you who unleashed this deadly fog upon your own kingdom?"

His first thought was that he had indeed stepped over the line, for the Dragon King rose to his full height and hissed loudly. The chamber grew stifling. The leviathan spread his wings wide; his talons sliced at the air before him. He thrust his head toward the human, stopping only a yard from Cabe. The warlock struggled to maintain his composure even though every fiber screamed for him to run. Cabe did not consider himself a brave soul in the heroic sense of the word. He remained where he was basically because he knew that to run would be futile. Better to face a threat than turn one's back on it.

"I releasssed it, Cabe Bedlam! I releasssed the foulness upon my own domain and it isss my resssponsssibility!"

"But to even call upon a shadow of Nimth's dec—"

"*Nimth?*" The Crystal Dragon recoiled as if Cabe had just informed him that he carried plague or some other dire disease.

*Could he have not known?* It was not a simple task to read those draconian features. There was fear there, but of what only the Crystal Dragon knew. "Yes, Nimth, Your Majesty. A world lost in time, ever dying. There was a race of sorcerers there, a race called the *Vraad.* They—"

"I *know* what they were! I know better than you!" The glittering behemoth shifted yet closer. "I know all there issss to know about their foul ways! Did you think I wanted to do this?" Again, the Dragon King looked away. His stentorian voice grew softer. "I knew what it wasss I would unleash. I have alwayssss lived with that. But it isss only a shadow, assss you mentioned. A shadow! No ssssubstance!" He quieted yet again. "But I fear it will not ssssstop them. They will be sssslowed, but not defeated. You are correct to be fearful of it. I dared let it go no further than I did, lessst ssssomething else come through. Things of Nimth wreak only deadly havoc in this world."

Cabe took a deep breath. He had to tell the Crystal Dragon. Only the lord of Legar could possibly send Plool back. It would not solve the problem of the wolf raiders, but it would prevent the Vraad from possibly causing further chaos. That, they did not need. If Plool could have been trusted, Cabe might have held his tongue, but Plool could *not* be and the warlock knew that.

"You . . . did let something through, Your Majesty. Someone, I should say."

The dragon's eyes narrowed. There was the slightest tremor in his voice, a tremor that shocked the mage despite all he had already noted about his terrible host. *"What . . . did . . . you . . . say?"*

"A creature . . . a man . . . of Nimth came through when you opened the way. A . . ." Would the Dragon King know enough about the history of Nimth? So far, it sounded as if he might know even more than the warlock did. "A Vraad sorcerer."

"You *lie!* The Vraad are dead and forgotten! I know! I—" The gleaming titan's denial ended in a roar that echoed again and again throughout the chamber. Cabe was forced to cover his ears. This time, he was certain that the Dragon King had lost permanent control. This time, there would be no escaping the obvious madness of the drake lord.

Yet . . . yet, the Crystal Dragon *did* calm. It was as if a different creature were abruptly there before Cabe, a creature more cold, fatalistic.

*Like the Ice Dragon?* He hoped it was not so. One of the few reasons that the Dragonrealm was not a dead, frozen waste was the leviathan before him. If the Crystal Dragon was now mad in the same manner as his counterpart to the far north had been, then the wolf raiders might become the least of the continent's worries.

"Wheeeerrre? Where issss it?" A scarlet, forked tongue flickered forth. "Where isss the Vraad?"

Cabe was regretting his idea now. He did not want to hand even someone like Plool over to the dragon; yet he had committed himself. "The Quel have him. If you could send him back . . ."

"Ssssend it back? Sssend the monstrosity back?" The Dragon King's maw snapped shut. He closed his eyes for a brief time. When he finally opened them, the Dragon King nodded and said, "You are correct, of coursssse, Cabe Bedlam. That would be for the best. Requiring little in effort, yesss."

"Can you take him from the Quel?" The warlock was startled to find himself asking such a question. He had grown up always believing that if any one of the present Dragon Kings was omnipotent, it was the Crystal Dragon. A few Quel should have required the least of his power.

Here the titan recovered his aplomb a bit. "I do not have to take him. They will *give* him to me."

The chamber gleamed. The crystalline walls were alive with not only the Dragon King's reflection but the mage's as well. The drake lord stared at one of the walls and suddenly the reflections melted away, becoming other images. They were images of another cavern, a place where a single Quel toyed with a device. The vision of the Quel was repeated from a thousand different angles and distances, but mixed in with those images was a more important one that Cabe focused on. The sphere that held Plool.

He frowned. It had a reddish tinge to it. It was the same sort of reddish tinge he associated with heat. Were they trying to *burn* the Vraad alive?

The shimmering leviathan leaned toward that particular vision. "He isss mine."

A host of identical Quel jumped as if bitten. A legion of startled, identical countenances looked around in panic. Cabe took some small satisfaction. He had no more sympathy for the Quel plight.

The Crystal Dragon spoke again. "You will give him to me."

The images faded away. Cabe blinked as he watched his own face multiply over and over across the chamber walls. No matter where he looked, he saw only his own uncomprehending visage.

"Hold out your handsssss, mage."

Cabe obeyed.

"You hold the doorway to damnation."

In the warlock's hands was the very sphere that Plool had led him to atop the hill. It had not been taken by the Quel, the Crystal Dragon had summoned it back to him. He tensed, fearful that his grip might slip and send the fragile-looking artifact to the hard floor. If the door was broken, *all* of Nimth would flow into the Dragonrealm.

The dragon saw his dismay. "Ssssimple clumsiness will not bring about the end of our world, Cabe Bedlam. It would take tremendousssss power to even sssscratch the surface of thissss toy. It would take more power than even that of a Vraad . . . or a hundred Vraad, if sssssuch cooperation wassss posssible."

It was unnerving to know what he held in his hands, unnerving to know that what he saw within was an entire other world. It was a world that his ancestors had twisted beyond repair and then abandoned . . . most of them. Yet Nimth had struggled and had survived, if what Plool had become could be called an example of survival. He wanted to throw the horrific sphere away, yet at the same time he wanted to hold it tight so that nothing, no matter how remote, would threaten it.

"It issss time."

With those words, the Vraad's deadly prison formed between them. The reddish tinge that Cabe had noticed before was still there, but it looked older, like a mark left over from something that had already happened. Were they too late? Had the Quel acted as the Crystal Dragon had been tempted to do?

Cabe was no longer certain he wanted to see the contents of the tall sphere.

"Hold the artifact before you. Be prepared."

*For what? How? Why do those who say that never really explain?*

The Dragon King eyed the spherical prison. He started to reach toward it, then hesitated. The reptilian nose wrinkled. Again, the Dragon King reached toward the sphere and again he paused. His expression went from wary expectation to puzzlement to growing fury.

"Thissss shell holdsss nothing! It issss *barren!*"

The warlock lowered the artifact in his arms. "Barren?"

"Empty." Long, narrow eyes burned into the warlock's own. "The Vraaaaad hasss essscaped!"

Cabe stared at the prison. He had misinterpreted the scorch traces. The marks were not the work of the Quel, but rather Plool himself working from within the trap. Both the warlock and his armored captors had underestimated the skills and tenacity of the eccentric Vraad.

"A Vraaaad loossse . . ." The Dragon King was talking to himself. "But I dare not . . . do I? I *musssst* . . . unlesssss . . ." He blinked and seemed to study Cabe anew. "Yessss . . ."

A taloned hand reached forth. The malevolent sphere tore free of the sorcerer's grip and flew to its master. It came to a halt only a foot or two from the dragon's snout and hovered there, waiting.

Cabe relaxed a little, realizing now that it was the device that had interested the Dragon King, not him. "What will you do?"

"What musssst be done. I musssst withdraw what I have unleashed. It will not sssstop . . . *stop* . . . the wolf raiders, but it will deal with that *thing* from Nimth!" Now that he had decided on a course of action, the Crystal Dragon sounded almost human in his speech patterns. There seemed no predicting how he would act from one moment to the next. Cabe hoped that this new attitude would remain for a time. "I must risk it. I will not allow that curse to reenter the world. When all that is Nimth is thrust back through the doorway, he will be weakened. He will be so weakened that the threat will become negligible!"

*Weakened . . . with all traces of Nimth gone . . .* What was it that bothered Cabe about that? Something about Plool and teleporting. Something . . . Of course! "Your Majesty, if you could hear me out. Instead of what you do, let me try to find Plool first. He can be made to see reason. If you do what you plan—"

"It will be done." The finality in the drake lord's voice left no room for compromise. In his eyes, a single Vraad was more a threat than a legion of Aramites. It almost appeared to be a personal vendetta, as if the Dragon King had dealt with Plool's kind before. Could that be?

What was it that hid behind the mask that was the Crystal Dragon?

The glittering titan closed his eyes. Before him, the dark contents within the sphere shifted and turned. It was a trick of the eyes, of course. The artifact was only a doorway. Perhaps what the Crystal Dragon did disturbed some small area of Nimth, but he certainly could not control the entire world. That much was evident from his fear of anything Nimthian, especially a lone Vraad.

Cabe was torn. On the one hand, he wanted the madcap entity called Plool removed from his world because of what chaos the Vraad *might* be able to cause even restricted to this one region. On the other hand, the warlock despised what he considered murder. Plool was deadly, but Cabe would have preferred to try to turn the bizarre mage first. Plool was Plool only because of where he had been born.

He had to try again. If his words failed to convince the Dragon King, would he be tempted to action? Was everything else worth risking for a creature he barely knew? "Your Majesty?"

The Crystal Dragon did not hear him.

"Your—" Cabe Bedlam's mouth clamped shut. Suddenly the walls surrounding them had come alive with faces, but not all the same. There were copies of his own, some of them older, some of them younger. He saw the face of the Gryphon and wondered at that. There were others, though, and with a start, Cabe eyed the face of what could only be one of the raider leaders. A tall man with a short beard, much like the wolf raider D'Shay, whom the Gryphon had killed years ago. His face was ghastly, a drawn, scarred thing. Yet, what bothered him most upon sighting that face was the expression, for in many ways it resembled a human variation of the present expression on the Dragon King's reptilian countenance.

Then, among all the other faces, he saw one that made him forget even that of the wolf raider leader. It was a face he had seen only in a vision, but one that had remained with him. A bear of a man, a leader, who wore armor of dragonscale. It was the face of a conquerer, one who brooked no defeat. There was something so compelling about the figure, something that reminded him of Shade. It was the man he had thought of as his father when the vision had controlled him. It was . . . *whose* father?

Cabe stared at the entranced drake lord. The thought was ludicrous. It was.

*Dragon Kings do not live that long . . . and he is a Dragon King at that.*

The Crystal Dragon hissed and his eyes flew open. His gaze shifted from the sphere to the wall . . . and to the image of the gaunt, scarred figure that Cabe had taken for the Aramite commander. Their eyes seemed to lock.

The sphere exploded.

# XIII

**A SHIVER RAN** through the sleepers. They did not wake, but something in the spell that had kept them under for so long had changed. What it was would have been hard to explain in any terms save perhaps to say that now they did not sleep so deep.

Not deep at all.

*WHAT ARE THEY doing down there with that blasted toy?* Orril D'Marr stalked across the dark, fog-enshrouded camp trying to keep the men organized. Those who were supposed to be getting some precious sleep were still awake for the most part, the mist and rumors keeping many of them too wary to even lie down. The soldiers on night duty, meanwhile, were turning and slashing at shadows and ghosts in the fog. Sentries kept reporting sightings of creatures that did not, *could* not, exist.

All of this was taking him from his more important tasks. D'Marr had stolen a few precious hours of slumber for himself so that he would be alert for the project he had planned for this night. Tonight he had been planning to open the way to the hidden chamber and finally find out what it was that was so precious to the beasts that they were willing to suffer at his tender hands for it. The explosives were ready and he had chosen the blast points. There would be little damage to the areas nearby and none at all to his master's precious chamber.

That was if he ever had the opportunity to set the explosives. With both his lordship and the blue devil down below, still working after all these hours, Orril D'Marr was the senior officer available. That meant that he had to maintain control, which amounted to running around and beating the other officers until they began acting as their ranks demanded. The officers were his duty and the men beneath them were *their* responsibility. He did not have time to go running from soldier to soldier.

*Something is happening.* The fog swirled about, a violent storm of shadow and light. Sometimes, the area was lit for several minutes, as if the sun had risen and finally managed to slice through the mist. At least it had thinned a bit, he thought. Even when it was properly dark it was possible to make out shapes several yards away. Whether that change was due to some success on Lord

D'Farany's part or was simply a natural occurrence, the young officer did not care. He was only glad it was happening.

D'Marr hated this place, but the damned heat and sunlight was preferable to this mess. So far this night, two men had simply disappeared and a third . . . well, there were some things that made even him queasy.

*And that patrol scattered, more than a dozen men lost there, too.* Oddly, that both irritated and excited him. The reports spoke of a huge dark stallion with a rider, the latter having a dozen different descriptions. The survivors all seemed to have been obsessed with the monstrous steed . . . no surprise, if it was what he thought it was. One of the spies from that kingdom, Zou or some such nonsense it was called, had reported trouble involving a mage on a large black horse.

The Gryphon had an ally in this realm who matched such a description, a demon called Darkhorse. D'Rance, of course, had been able to supply that tidbit of information.

Two sentries stumbled across his path and swiftly backed away. They saluted, but the young officer just waved them aside. He had no time for men doing their duties. It was the ones who were not who would feel his wrath if they were so unfortunate as to cross him. D'Marr wanted to be done with this task. Once he had the officers under control and they in turn the men, he could return to the tunnels.

His mind drifted back to the patrol's encounter with the monster known as Darkhorse. The demon could not possibly have come across them by chance; he had to have specifically come here searching for the wolf raiders. Any notion that contradicted that was not acceptable to either Orril D'Marr or his lord. Even the blue man agreed with him on this matter.

The Gryphon had to be here. It fit. The black steed's appearance had come too quickly after their landing. He had a rider with him. If the rider had not been the damned birdman, then it had to be one of his friends. Either way, they could only have known of the raiders' presence through the Gryphon. It made sense to him.

Admittedly, there was some logic missing in the argument, but one other reason superseded all others in this matter. D'Marr recalled the attack on the port city. Lord D'Farany had hoped to accomplish two things there. One had been to steal a series of charts that would aid them in this venture and the other had been the hope that they would catch their greatest adversary off-guard.

They had been unable to kill the Gryphon that day, but his brat had paid for the deaths and defeats the empire had suffered. Not satisfactory, but it would do until the Gryphon's head decorated a lance tip.

*And that time is coming soon.* True to form, the bird had followed them across the seas. D'Marr had predicted he would and for once he had outdone the blue devil in that respect. *You're coming to me, Gryphon, coming to join your brat!*

His hand touched the pommel of the scepter. When he had finished the Gryphon, there would remain only the cat woman. She would follow after her mate, being as predictable in her way as he was when it came to revenge. *Then I will have taken all three.*

No one would deny his greatness then.

His course took him around the camp until he returned to the mouth of the tunnel leading to the Quel city. The camp was at last in order. The officers were now in line and they, in turn, had the men under rein. D'Marr had done as best as was possible. Now it was time to—

A tall figure emerged from the tunnel. From his walk and his manner, D'Marr had no trouble identifying the northerner. The man looked bedraggled, exhausted. The young officer smiled briefly, then once more fixed his expression into one of detachment.

D'Rance saw him and did not bother to hide his own distaste. He tried to walk past his shorter counterpart, but D'Marr was having none of that. To know that the northerner had been put through the paces made his own tedious day more palatable. "Tired already?"

"You will play no games with me, Orril D'Marr. Our lord has struggled long and I was forced to help maintain him, yes?"

"And what could you do for him, blue? Wipe his brow when he sweated?"

D'Rance sneered. "The knowledge of a scholar is a greater weapon at times than the sword of a simple soldier, yes? You would have pounded on the crystal device with that toy on your belt, I think, as you did to the walls. Such effort, but so little result."

"You're a scholar of magic?"

The blue man suddenly lost interest in the battle of words. "I have given my all for our effort, little man, yes, and our Lord D'Farany knows this. I have been given leave to rest and rest I shall."

The exhausted northerner turned and stalked into the fog. D'Marr watched him disappear, then glanced at the tunnel mouth. All the blue devil's efforts would amount to little before this night had ended. Whatever favor he had curried with Lord D'Farany would fade when D'Marr revealed the secret cavern.

He started down the tunnel, finalizing his plans. He would need four or five men, just to be on the safe side. They could plant the explosives in the proper locations and light the fuses. There would be rubble to clear away, too, which meant that five or six men would work better. The most important task D'Marr would save for himself, however. It was he who would be the first to enter the unknown, he, the discoverer. *And whatever secret, whatever treasure lies behind there, I will be the first to know it.*

"Sir!"

Although his expression remained bland when he turned back toward the mouth of the tunnel, inside, Orril D'Marr was seething. *What do they want now?* "Yes?"

An understandably nervous officer even younger than he stood at attention at the edge of the entrance. No doubt he had been volunteered by his superiors for this mission. That way, if D'Marr chose to take out his wrath on someone, it would not be them. "Sir, I have been ordered to report that there is some confusion in the eastern flank. Several men have reported a roving light. Two went out to investigate and have not returned. Another man reports . . ."

He waited, but the other officer did not go on. "Reports what?"

"Someone laughing . . . from above him."

The corners of D'Marr's mouth edged downward. His work was *already* falling apart. If this was an example of the situation being under Lord D'Farany's control, then it was no improvement. Success was supposed to mean that the fog would either vanish or obey the commands of his master. It had, so far, done neither as far as D'Marr could see. If anything, this latest report indicated things had turned worse.

He returned to the surface and looked around. How he was supposed to keep this rabble organized was beyond him, but it was his function. That meant chasing down those incompetent officers and uncovering the truth about things that went bump in the fog. He was growing tired of this. There would have to be some changes made in the ranks.

"What's your name?"

"Squad Leader, Base Level, R'Jerek, sir."

The man's superiors had picked the lowest officer they could find. He still bore the R' caste designation. Anything above him would have the D' like D'Marr's name bore. His estimation of the value of R'Jerek's superiors dropped further. "Your immediate officer?"

"Captain D'Lee, sir."

"Lead me to him, D'Jerek."

"Yes, sir . . ." The younger officer paused. "It's R'Jerek, sir."

"Not after I'm through with your superior, *Captain*."

His guide said nothing more after that.

Orril D'Marr gave the tunnel one last glance. *Tomorrow,* he swore to himself. *It'll hold until tomorrow.*

*SO MUCH POWER!* Kanaan D'Rance stumbled toward his tent, which was, not by chance, away from the rest. As much as he would have been happier to sleep among the fascinating Quel artifacts, that was not allowed. Still, he had smuggled a few of the items into his tent, where he tried to understand and make use of them. His skills were growing; he had even managed to heal his hand without anyone ever discovering the truth. The streak in his hair was becoming a problem, however. He was certain that the Aramite leader suspected.

The secrets the trinkets held paled in comparison to the struggle that had gone on tonight, a struggle in which Lord D'Farany had all but triumphed. The mysterious adversary was vanquished; now, the Aramite commander only had to bind the magical fog to his control. Lord D'Farany was already talking of making use of the deadly mist, an idea contrary to his first inclination. Despite the wrongness of the sorcery tied into the fog, or perhaps because of it, the keeper now saw great potential in it as a weapon *for* the raiders.

Kanaan D'Rance agreed for the most part, but he differed with his master in one respect. He wanted control of the mist for himself. *There is a power there, yes? A different, alien magic!* It had repelled him at first, but now it attracted. The blue man felt he could accomplish great things with it once he learned how it had come to be. He needed time, though, time alone in that chamber. Time alone to study.

Thrusting aside the flap of his tent, the tall figure darted inside. It was not until the flap had closed behind him that he noticed something was amiss. Something that only his burgeoning magical senses could note.

With no effort at all, he created a small ball of light brilliant enough to illuminate most of the interior.

*Lord D'Farany's work?* Was he now toying with the blue man? He did not like the thought of ending up as one of the martinet's playthings. Orril D'Marr excelled at slow death, yes.

It was then he noticed that his carefully hidden collection of Quel artifacts had been taken out and scattered over his worktable.

*Who would dare?* This was not the way of Lord D'Farany. D'Marr, then? One of his spies? It made no sense; they could learn nothing from his collection save that he had palmed some pieces. The little martinet would know that such efforts would be a waste of everyone's time.

Somehow, he knew that this could not be the work of the Aramites . . . yet, who did that leave?

One of the figurines on the table, a small crystal bear, leapt up from the table and past his shoulder.

Stunned, he spun around, trying to keep track of it. The Quel talisman stood on the ground behind him, as motionless as it had been before its extraordinary leap into momentary life. With great caution, Kanaan D'Rance reached down for it.

The tiny bear sprang away from him, flying into the dark shadows in the corner of his tent. The blue man snarled and started for the spot. Although he could not see the artifact, he knew that it could go no farther. The tent would impede its progress. Now it was a simple matter of searching those shadows. The scholar in him took over. Once he found the peculiar little piece, he intended to study it thoroughly until he discovered the reason for its sudden animation.

A laugh from within the shadows made him pull back his questing hand.

A grotesque, round figure who could have not been hiding all this time squatted in the shadows. He could see nothing of the face except the long, narrow chin and the slash of mouth. The creature raised a spindly arm to the huge, broad-rimmed hat he wore and lifted it just enough to reveal the rest of the unholy visage. It was all D'Rance could do to keep from shouting. He stood there, petrified.

"A fascinating struggle; a struggle fascinating to me," said the intruder. "*Especially* to me."

"Who . . . ?"

The mouth shaped into a mischievous grin. A bony hand formed a fist, then opened again. In the palm of the hand was the elusive figurine. "Plool I am; I am Plool . . ." The grin grew wider. The eyes, the ungodly, crystalline eyes, glittered merrily. "A *friend*."

"**SOMETHING HAS DEFINITELY** changed, Lord Gryphon, and not necessarily for the better!"

The Gryphon noticed it, too. There was indeed a change in the air, or rather the fog. He shivered and was not exactly certain why. The change might have been for the better; they had no way of knowing otherwise.

*Pessimism?* More likely experience and common sense. The lionbird had been in too many dire situations not to expect the worst. Usually, through no effort of his own, he was proven correct in that assumption.

"What do you make of it, Darkhorse?"

The shadow steed snorted. "Nothing! I make absolutely nothing out of it. It is from Nimth and as far as I am concerned, that which is Nimthïan is a threat to all!"

"Like Shade?" he could not help asking the eternal.

Darkhorse was prevented from answering by what sounded like a crack of thunder. He stumbled. The entire area was suddenly aglow even though it was still night. The Gryphon heard a rumbling, glanced down, and, with the aid of the mysterious light, saw the earth opening up before them. He started to point it out to his companion, but the stallion was already backing away. The chasm began to widen and from it poured forth a grayish substance much like clay.

"Can you leap over it?" He had seen Darkhorse clear gaps far wider than this one.

"I will do so once I am certain that it is *safe* to do so! Do not trust appearances in this place; there is usually more to come!"

That was when the molten clay turned toward them.

From the center of the bubbling mass burst forth a crude, thick tentacle. At the same time, the Gryphon felt his *own* body twist. He stared in horror as his arms began to lengthen and his torso started to turn sideways.

"Darkhorse!" The Gryphon struggled to maintain control of his fingers, which were trying to bend backward of their own accord.

"Hold . . . hold on to . . . me!"

He did. As best as his distorted form would allow, he held on to the dark stallion. His fingers still struggled for independence, but his will was stronger.

The lionbird felt a surge of movement from the eternal, then the rush of air, foul air, as Darkhorse leapt.

It took forever to land, at least in the Gryphon's mind, and when they did, Darkhorse did not stop. He continued to run. Over hill and flat earth, the terrain did not matter. All the while, the light remained with them. They raced on for what had to be several miles before the Gryphon recovered enough to demand that his companion come to a halt. Darkhorse did not acknowledge his words, but he nonetheless came to a reluctant halt some few moments later.

The Gryphon looked himself over, wary of what he might find but determined to see what terrible changes might have been wrought on him. To his astonishment and relief, he saw that he was just as he had always been. Leaving the vicinity of the chasm had restored him to normal.

"Grrryppphhonnn?"

"Darkhorse?" In his relief at finding he had survived intact, the lionbird had nearly forgotten the one who had saved him. It had not occurred to him that the eternal might also have suffered some monstrous alteration. "Darkhorse! What is it?"

There was no response from the shadow steed, but he was shivering noticeably. The Gryphon glanced at the rocky ground beneath them, saw nothing out of the ordinary, and gingerly dismounted. Darkhorse continued to shiver. He did not even look back at his rider, simply stared ahead.

"Darkhorse?"

"I . . . cannot . . . fight it this time!" The shivering grew worse yet. The shadow steed stumbled back a step.

"Fight what?" How could he help the eternal?

"Fight . . . what almost took . . . control . . . when I was . . . with Cabe!"

The last word ended in a scream.

Darkhorse *melted.*

He was quicksilver, flowing in all directions. A black pool with vague equine touches to him. The lionbird danced away from him, aghast. "Darkhorse! What do I do? What can I do?"

"Urra . . ." From the horrific mass rose a figure the color of ink. Cold, blue orbs stared out from a face that was and was not a copy of the Gryphon's own. Every detail of the Gryphon's own form was copied, yet it was a flawed reproduction. He raised one clawed hand toward what his companion had become.

The shape melted, but re-formed almost instantly. A thing of many arms and eyes, the latter all blue, sprouted before the Gryphon. He did not back away, although experience should have demanded otherwise.

As quickly as it had formed, this shape, too, melted. A new one, another humanoid figure, coalesced.

This one the Gryphon also recognized. "Shade!"

Shade, but with the definite outline of a face. Quick as the lionbird was in attempting to see those blackened features, he was not quick enough. Shade, the shape of Shade, rather, poured to the earth before the Gryphon could make out the details of his visage. The Gryphon watched the melting with some disappointment despite the circumstances. For all the years that he had known the warlock, he had never discerned the true features of the man. Not even Shade had been able to recall what he had once looked like.

Yet a new form grew, but this one, it turned out, was to be Darkhorse again. It was a slower shaping than the others, possibly because it looked as though the eternal was forcibly willing himself back into existence much the way the Gryphon had struggled with control of his fingers.

When at last he was fully formed, the ebony stallion shook his head and eyed his companion. "I had thought I had beaten the urge when last I was here, but the fog, Nimth, is stronger still."

"What happened to you?"

Darkhorse took an unsteady step. His form rippled. "Still not completely safe! You will have to give me a little time. What happened to me? I am even more susceptible to the wild powers of Nimth than you are! Ha! I am worse than wet clay in the hands of those powers! When I was here with Cabe, it almost happened. I fought back and succeeded then, but not this time! I failed! I was twisted into whatever shape it could derive from my memories. *Any* memory."

"Including Shade?"

The eternal steadied himself. "He will haunt me forever! I had forgotten that I had ever known his true visage. It was in the last days . . . or . . . was it long, long ago?"

That was all that his companion wanted to say on the subject, so the Gryphon turned to studying their surroundings. The odd light—*where is its source?*—enabled him to see maybe five yards away from them in any direction. He had no idea where they were save that they had gone farther west. Darkhorse had not thought about his course. If not for the Gryphon, they might still be racing through the fog. He was glad he had managed to speak out or else they might have kept on racing until they ended up in the middle of the Aramite camp itself. The lionbird did not want to confront his adversaries until he knew the advantage would be his.

He wondered how close they were. Close enough that his claws unsheathed in anticipation. The peninsula was very, very long, but Darkhorse moved swifter than the wind. What would take a true steed days to reach could take him only hours. The Gryphon was aware that his mount had paid no attention to his speed, so there was no satisfactory method of calculating where they were.

The mysterious illumination at last began to dim. Nothing remained constant here. From what the shadow steed had related to him about this foul mist, the lionbird was surprised the light had lasted this long. He was not sorry to see it go. Despite the temporary increase in visibility it had created, it made the Gryphon more anxious. Night was supposed to be dark. He was more comfortable with that. In the night, his reflexes and senses were an advantage over most foes. Hunting the wolf raiders was best done at night.

The Gryphon stared into the darkening fog. He could imagine the scene. Lone soldiers wandering in the night, unable to see much save with torches that marked them for him. If the warlock was their prisoner, they would lead the Gryphon to him. If Cabe was not at their mercy, then that would simplify matters for the lionbird. He would not have to hold back.

The images became so real that the Gryphon could almost see the shadowy forms and hear the clink of metal upon metal. His good hand clutched the grip of his sword.

He was jolted by a strange, whistling sound . . . then it became impossible to *breathe* as something thin and tight wrapped itself snugly around his throat.

"Gryphon! Beware!"

Ignoring the belated warning, the Gryphon reached down and drew his sword. He knew that it was a whip that encircled his throat and knew very well who was at the other end. What he counted on was the other underestimating his strength. The lionbird was stronger than most humans, even despite his three-fingered grip. He took hold of the whip and pulled, at the same time bringing his sword into play. His attacker had no chance to react; the Gryphon's blade ran him through in the neck.

Pulling his sword free before the soldier could even fall, the Gryphon whirled about. No figment of his imagination were these men. He *had* seen shapes and heard sounds, but like a senile fool, he had paid them no mind. Perhaps it was time for *him* to die. When one grew old and careless, that was what was supposed to happen.

*No, for your sake, Troia, and for the memory of our Demion, I will not!*

They swarmed toward him. Darkhorse had described in detail his first encounter with the patrol and so the Gryphon knew that this second patrol was much larger and better prepared than its predecessor had been. Someone understood too well what they might be hunting and had supplied the soldiers with tools designed just for the likes of Darkhorse and him.

Even as he took down a swordsman, the Gryphon knew that he alone would not be able to escape the Aramites. *They must have heard us; they must have heard Darkhorse as he struggled.* There would be little aid from Darkhorse. The shadow steed was situated but a few yards to his left and already struggling against more than half a dozen attackers. Darkhorse and his opponents seemed at an impasse; they could not reach him, but he was still too weakened from his inner battle to do them any harm.

Already three swordsmen fought him from different angles. He was able to keep them more or less in front of him long enough to disable one in the leg, but others were already gathering. Four men with a net worked toward his back. A lancer and yet another swordsman joined his attackers. A pattern developed, a lance thrust followed by one or more sword attacks, generally together. The Gryphon fought them off, but he was forced to back up each time.

When the net came down on him, the lionbird knew that he had allowed himself to be played like a puppet. That there had been no other choice in no way assuaged his anger at himself.

His sword was yanked from his grip, but he had the satisfaction of severely clawing one of his captors before they wrapped the net tight around him. When they were done, he was trussed up like a piece of game . . . and to the wolf raiders he probably was. The Gryphon heard one of the Aramites call out to Darkhorse.

"Hold, demon, or we will fillet your friend here and now!"

He would have urged the shadow steed to ignore the threat, but someone rapped him on the side of the head, dazing him for several seconds. By the time his head cleared, Darkhorse had already surrendered.

"Watch him!" ordered the same voice, likely the patrol leader. "Commander D'Marr will want him in good shape for questioning!"

The Gryphon could not see his captors' eyes, but he noted that a couple of the men who were handling him stiffened at the mention of the name. *D'Farany's torturer.*

"Bind his mouth."

Someone shifted him around so that another guard could wrap thick cloth around his beak. In the darkness of reborn night, the lionbird could make out the outline of the demon steed. Darkhorse had lowered his head. Two Aramites were looping something around the eternal's neck. It could not be a rope noose. Something as simple as that would never hold Darkhorse. No, it had to be a magical bond of some sort, a bond whose power they trusted to work despite the tricks of the fog. The Gryphon was not certain he would trust any sorcery or sorcerous artifact while lost in this mist. He hoped their faith would come back to haunt the wolf raiders before this was all over. If not and their toys worked as they should . . . then it was all over already.

Unless Cabe was not a prisoner . . .

If not, where was he?

A pair of boots crossed his limited field of vision. They paused before him. "Make him docile for the trip. That'll keep the demon in line."

The Gryphon knew what was coming and braced himself for it. The blow to the back of his head was a good one, he was just barely able to note, for alone it was enough to send him spinning into unconsciousness. He would have only one fist-sized lump when he woke.

Provided the Gryphon woke at all.

WAKE HE DID, but it was no relief to do so, for the Gryphon saw that they had reached the Aramite encampment. It was still night, he supposed, but there were many awake. He sensed a certain tension that permeated the area. The raiders were not at ease in this place. There was not much satisfaction in knowing that. His captors would be that much more anxious, that much more ready to kill him. Although he knew he faced potential agony at the hands of the Aramite inquisitor, the lionbird was determined to survive. He had given up part of his hand already and he was willing to give up much more if he was granted the deaths of Lord D'Farany and his men.

His eyes little more than slits, the captive continued to survey his surroundings. One item of vast importance was missing. He could neither see nor hear Darkhorse. What had happened to the eternal? Surely he was aware that the raiders would kill the Gryphon no matter what? They would be searching for methods of binding the ebony stallion to their will. The Gryphon was fairly certain that the wolf raiders would find some adequate device. This batch had probably stolen whatever they could before they abandoned their fellows back in the empire. *So much for the loyalty of the pack!*

He was dragged on and on, so long, in fact, that he almost believed they intended to drag him to death. It was not a very imaginative death, if that was the case. From D'Farany the Gryphon expected more. Something slow and agonizing.

This was *not* how he had planned it.

All at once, the Gryphon was dumped to the harsh earth. He suppressed a grunt and remained as still as possible.

"What is it now?" The voice was indifferent, almost bored.

"Sir, a prize most wonderful! It's—"

"Don't bother to tell me; show me."

"Y-yes, Commander D'Marr!"

Ungentle hands rolled him onto his back.

"Forget rolling him free. I have other things demanding my time, Captain. Cut him out of there."

Evidently in the darkness it was troublesome to make out anything more than his shape. A possible advantage? The Gryphon heard the sound of a dagger being drawn from its sheath. A blade flashed by his visage, but he did not flinch. With little care for his well-being, the soldier began to cut him loose. He tensed. If there was ever an opportunity for escape, it was when he was nearly free of the net. He was swift, far swifter than most of them would think. It was a slim hope, but if they bound him after this, his odds would shrivel to next to nothing.

A heavy boot landed atop his throat. The Gryphon gasped. He felt the tip of a mace against his forehead. Around him was nothing but silence.

"What are you gaping at, you fool? Finish releasing our friend here." Was there just a tinge of excitement in the officer's otherwise monotone voice? "He won't be trying any tricks *now.*"

When the last of the netting had been cut away, the Gryphon was seized by both his arms and his legs. Only when he was certain that his prisoner would not be able to free himself from the guards' grips did D'Marr take his foot off of the lionbird's throat. "You might as well open your eyes all the way, birdman."

The Gryphon did. Peering down at him was a round, clean-shaven countenance. At first glance, he almost wondered if the Aramites had been reduced to promoting children to the officers' ranks. Then, as they tugged him to his feet, he was better able to glimpse the eyes. Young, D'Marr might be, but he was by no means a child. There was more death in his eyes than most men the Gryphon had ever faced.

*And is my son one of those deaths?*

The Aramite commander stepped closer. The Gryphon cocked his head in sudden amusement as he saw that D'Marr came up only to his chin.

The head of the mace went deep into his stomach.

His guards would not let him fall forward or clutch his stomach in pain. As he gasped, he heard the young commander say, "You've made an otherwise long and annoying night worthwhile, birdman. You have no idea how much I've waited for this confrontation."

"Shall I alert his lordship, sir?"

D'Marr looked at his prisoner, then at the guards, and then at last at the man who had spoken. He never seemed to look at any one thing for very long, the Gryphon noted, not even the face of an adversary whose image had become synonymous with Aramite defeats. "No. Now would not be the best time. Lord D'Farany has only just retired and his victory over the fog has cost him." The men looked confused over the last part of the statement, but D'Marr ignored them. He smiled ever so briefly at the lionbird. "I'm certain that we can find accommodations for our special guest until then. We need time to prepare the best welcome for him. We need time to properly plan his death. For that Lord D'Farany will want to be fully alert and able to *enjoy* his pain."

"I hope I will be a disappointment," the Gryphon managed to respond. He was still in pain, but it had subsided enough so that he could pretend it had vanished.

"You speak." D'Marr raised the tip of the mace to the underside of the Gryphon's beak. The lionbird could sense a spell of some sort, a strong, complicated spell, locked into the weapon. Judging from its owner, he was certain that the mace was a treacherous little device. "How entertaining. I'd begun to think you incapable. Don't worry yourself, Your Majesty . . . you are supposed to be a king or some such dribble, aren't you . . . my lord will hardly be disappointed. If you think that I'm eager for your company, you'll be amazed at his enthusiasm. You are the cause of all his suffering. Years of suffering."

"Good."

A shock coursed through his body. He would have fallen if not for the guards. D'Marr waited for him to recover, then held the head of the mace close enough so that the Gryphon could see how it had been designed. "That was one of the low levels. You'll be tasting the others—as many as you can take— when you're brought before our master."

"I am always eager to meet the men I want to kill. It has been a pleasure meeting you, in fact."

D'Marr started to smile again, but then he stared at the avian visage before him and the smile faded. "The only one you'll have the pleasure of meeting will be that brat of yours. The one who died much too quickly."

*Demion* . . . It was as if his heart had suddenly been wrenched from his chest. Blood madness took him. The Gryphon's world shrank. It was a world large enough to contain only two. One was himself and the other . . . the other was the *beast* who had killed his son.

No, two was still too many. He would not be satisfied until there was only one.

"Demion . . ." Nothing would keep him from the beast. He felt some sort of resistance holding him in place, but with a twist of his arms he freed himself. The monster backed away from him, eyes wary and prepared for struggle. Good, it would make his death that much better.

The Gryphon felt something pull at his arms again and this time he lashed out, striking flesh and bone. Not once did he look to see what the source of that interference was; his eyes could only see the black figure before him. The jackal.

He leapt, but the beast struck him with the scepter, sending him through a new crescendo of agony. Still the enraged Gryphon would not accept defeat. The pain gave way to his anger, his bitterness. He slashed at his adversary, but his claws caught only the hard metal of the beast's armor.

The net came down on him before he could strike again. Still fighting, the maddened lionbird was pulled to the ground. A blow to his head finally succeeded in lessening some of the blood lust.

"Don't kill him. Keep him bound." The beast stood where he knew the Gryphon could not help but look. His placid face broke into that brief smile again. "You are a feisty one, aren't you?"

"I will have you, D'Marr," the prisoner replied in much calmer tones. He was furious at himself for allowing his base instincts to take over like that. He had not served the memory of his son nor the love of his mate in any way by becoming the animal. There was a line between animal and humanity that the Gryphon had always walked. Now, he had allowed himself to fall prey to the unthinking side. It was never right to allow one side or the other complete control. Only with both sides in balance could he triumph. "I will have you and your master."

D'Marr squatted and pointed the tip of the mace at him. The top just barely flicked against the side of the Gryphon's face, who flinched before realizing that there was no pain this time. "No, that's for later, birdman. That and so much more." The Aramite officer rose. "Bind him properly this time and take him to the other beasts. They can stare at each other until he's needed for the festivities. Is the demon under control?"

"We've bound it as you've instructed," responded the patrol leader. "It doesn't seem to be able to free itself."

"Watch it. Make certain of that." The youthful raider yawned in the Gryphon's direction. "Now that we have things settled, you'll excuse me if I retire. I have so much to do tomorr—excuse me, later today." He pointed at the guards with his scepter. "These men will see to your discomfort. If you have need of anything, please ask."

"Just your head."

D'Marr tapped the side of the weapon against his palm. He stared thoughtfully at the captive, then politely asked, "And how long do you think before we might be graced with the presence of your cat? I'm looking forward to completing the set."

This time, the Gryphon did not respond. D'Marr was working hard to keep his mind in turmoil and he was achieving that goal all too well. As desperate as his situation was, the only hope that the Gryphon had was in retaining his calm.

"Well, I suspect she'll be here soon enough. I will be certain to greet her with open, loving arms." His countenance once more a bland mask, the young officer gave the tangled lionbird a mock salute and departed.

Watching him walk off, the Gryphon knew that he had to somehow free himself despite the odds. If he did not, then Troia *would* follow, as D'Marr had predicted. The thought of her in the hands of someone like the sadistic Aramite made him shiver.

*I'm looking forward to completing the set,* D'Marr had mocked. If the Gryphon did not find *some* way to escape his fate, without the aid of Darkhorse, apparently, it was all too possible that the deadly raider would do just *that.*

# XIV

"RISE, CABE BEDLAM."

The voice sounded familiar, yet it also did not. Cabe, his body responding as if it had long ago given way to rigor mortis, managed to rise to a sitting position. He found himself staring at the blurred images of one countenance, a countenance that every facet of every reflective crystal repeated. It was the face of a man much like the one the warlock had seen in the visions, but despite the blurriness, he could see that this one was a younger, varied copy. A son, perhaps. Until the detail became much more focused, he could guess no more.

"You are resilient, warlock."

He turned to the source of the voice and only then discovered that it was not the images that were blurred, but rather his own vision. Not really a shock, considering what had happened.

*Dragon Kings will be the death of me yet . . . even when they are not purposely trying to achieve that result.*

"Your—Your Majesty?" He blinked several times, but to no discernible effect.

"Wait a moment. Your vision should clear. You were not, fortunately for you, struck in the eyes. I did what I could for you otherwise."

What did that mean? Cabe started to reach up with his left hand and was wracked by dagger strikes of pain. He quickly lowered the arm and clutched it with his other hand, which thankfully did not hurt. "What—what happened?"

"You deflected most of the fragments, but a few stronger ones broke through your shields. Only a few pierced you; it was the force of the explosion, which I fought to contain, that left you unconscious."

"The fragments. The sphere. One of the pieces struck me in the arm?"

He knew it was the Crystal Dragon who spoke to him, but still the voice sounded so different from *anything* he had heard before. What new change had the explosion wrought upon the Dragon King's personality? "It did not strike your arm. It *pierced it*, warlock. The wound goes completely through your upper arm. I did what I could, but it will not heal for me. It may never heal, you understand, not completely."

*Never heal.* Much the way King Melicard's face and arm had never healed after the burst of magic that had maimed him. Cabe was aware that his own wound did not even approach the severity of Melicard's, but he could not help but be more upset by it.

"There are also small scars on your neck. You were very fortunate, warlock. Your skills are impressive."

*Skills? More like pure luck!* Cabe pulled his robe askew so that he could study the wound. A jagged, green scar surrounded by red, swollen skin marked the fragment's passage. With great trepidation, he touched it. The soft touch was still enough to make him grunt in intense pain. Bracing himself, the wounded mage touched the back of the same arm. Again, the pain struck him.

*Never heal?*

He was still staring at the wound when the Crystal Dragon spoke again. "We are both fortunate, Cabe Bedlam. When the sphere was shattered, the doorway to Nimth was closed, not opened. That was how the device was designed, but there was no true way of testing it except by an occurrence much like this explosion."

Cabe looked up. His vision had cleared enough so that he could now clearly see the Crystal Dragon. The drake lord looked unmarred, but that did not mean he had not been wounded. More important now was his state of mind. He seemed sane enough . . .

"What happened?"

"I underestimated the wolf raider leader. I underestimated so much. He has wrested control of the mist from me. Before long, he will understand something of how to utilize it. Things go from bad to worse." The glittering leviathan closed his eyes.

The warlock's gaze darted back and forth between the massive dragon and the face that stared at him from all directions, but his attention remained on the subject at hand. "What will you do now?"

"Nothing."

"Nothing?"

"I *must* do nothing!" The Dragon King's long, narrowed eyes opened again . . . and was this the first time that Cabe had noticed how crystalline they appeared? They were almost like the insane orbs of Plool. "I dare not! I will not lose myself!"

Cabe's gaze again drifted to the multiplied countenance covering the walls. This time, however, he studied them closer. *Not lose myself,* the leviathan had just said. Did that mean what Cabe thought it did?

"Who are you?"

The Crystal Dragon settled back. He seemed almost to welcome the strange question. The huge head turned and indicated the faces. "Once . . . I was *him.*"

Him. The faces in the visions. The eyes of Plool. The obsession with the foulness of Nimth. It all began to make sense to the warlock.

"You're a *Vraad.*" He found he was really not that astonished by the revelation. So much had pointed to it. Yet, if the knowledge that the Crystal Dragon had once worn a human form was not shocking, then the fact that he still lived was. How long had it been since the coming of the Dragon Kings?

"How did it happen? *When?*"

The dragon's laugh was harsh and humorless. "By the banner, I no longer even know, warlock! Centuries, yes. Millennia, yes. How many it has been I have forgotten! I have watched generations come and go, live and die! I have seen the rise of the Dragon Kings and I have watched their pitiful decline! The others passed on, but I lived! Ha! *Lived?* I am fortunate that I have not gone insane!"

The last word echoed throughout the chamber. Cabe stood, careful to avoid stress to his arm. He had to hear. "Tell me."

"Tell you?" The Crystal Dragon contemplated that. His expression was weary. "Tell you of Logan of the Tezerenee? The dutiful son, one of many sons, to Lord Barakas Tezerenee, he was. Not like Gerrod or Rendel or Lochivan, he was. Logan obeyed blindly as was proper. When the Vraad fled Nimth, he was there to aid his father. When Barakas claimed this land under the dragon banner, Logan was there to enforce that claim."

Cabe Bedlam listened transfixed as the history of the first Dragon Kings began to unfold before him. The wound was all but forgotten as the time-worn leviathan spoke of the fatal error that had led to his present existence.

"It was the bodies, the bodies his father and Master Zeree and his brothers Gerrod and Rendel had created, created from the stuff of *dragons!* They were people-shaped, but they were dragons in heart. The spirits, the ka, of the Tezerenee crossed the path of worlds to this one and claimed those bodies. Claimed their own eventual destruction."

The sorcery-shaped bodies had worked well for the Tezerenee. Most of the other Vraad had crossed over physically, but that door had not been open at the time of the Tezerenees' crossing. So the folk of the dragon banner truly became dragon men, which served to increase their power and presence among the other refugees.

It was not until a few years later that people, not merely the Tezerenee, began to notice some changes. Their skill in sorcery faded, but even that was not so insurmountable a situation to the Tezerenee, who had always espoused the physical even while they made use of the magical. For a time, it served to make the Vraad more reliant upon the clan. Not enough to accept the rule of Lord Barakas, however. When he sought to take his rightful place, there was resistance. Strong resistance. It was that in the end that forced Lord Barakas to seek a new kingdom overseas.

"They claimed that land." The Dragon King did not seem to consider how the Tezerenee had made the long crossing from one continent to the other without ships and sorcery important enough to discuss. Recalling what little he had gleaned from Darkhorse over the years, the warlock wondered if this was where the eternal had fallen prey to the Vraad. It might explain the shadow steed's bitterness and, yes, fear where things relating to Nimth and the Vraad were concerned.

Lord Barakas had evidently expected to fight the Seekers, but the avians' civilization had collapsed in some war and only a few bands were strong enough to give them trouble. Flushed with success, they conquered the mountain stronghold of the bird folk and took its ancient secrets for their own.

*Kivan Grath.* Cabe recognized the place from the Dragon King's description. Kivan Grath, the mountain whose caverns would become the citadel of the Dragon Emperor. *Odd how he recalls so much but not how much time has passed. Then again, he may want to recall his humanity, but not how long it has been since he lost it.*

As he spoke, the Crystal Dragon seemed to shrink a little. More and more he became a man seeing a horror ahead than a great leviathan who ruled and was feared. With great unease, the warlock noted how the multitude of faces copied the drake lord's emotions. It was like being surrounded by a thousand tormented ghosts.

"It may be that the land was fearful of them and although it could not destroy the Tezerenee, it made them into its own. Or perhaps the bodies themselves, formed from that which was dragon, at last sought to revert to what they had been meant to be. In the end, all that matters was the changing. First one, then another. No one understood then. No one saw it was happening to all, not merely a few."

He shuddered, blinked, then looked directly at his human guest with something approaching desperate envy. "I remember the pain that day. I remember screaming as my arms and legs stretched and bent at angles no human appendages had been meant to bend. Do you know what it feels like to sense burgeoning wings squirming beneath the flesh of your back and then having them burst fully formed through your *skin*? To feel and see your skull reshape itself and then realize that your eyes, too, are shifting, changing? To scream and scream again as the transformation tears through armor and sends you crashing to all *fours* . . .

". . . and then to know oblivion."

Cabe, thinking of his own fear of even the minutest shifting of form, swallowed.

The reptilian monarch looked down at the floor. "I recall vague images, the thoughts of a beast struggling to think. How long, I do not know. I only recall that one day I began to think as a man, but I was not *myself*. I was a *creature*. I was . . . a dragon. This land was supposed to be my kingdom. Years it would be before I remembered that it had been chosen for me by my father, that all of us had, despite becoming beasts, claimed our particular kingdoms." His laugh had more than a tinge of bitterness. "I have never known whether he gave me this peninsula because he knew what wonders were here or simply because I was one of the least important of his many sons."

It was child's play to seize these caverns. The Quel civilization had been in worse condition than that of the Seekers, disorganized and much too busy trying to devise a method to save their kind to note the danger until it was too late. The self-proclaimed Dragon King explored his new domain and in doing so found a place that the Quel had obviously shunned. There were no signs of recent activity. Nothing but a dark passage before him, a dark passage leading to the mouth of an even darker cavern. His arrogance and curiosity got the better of him. The passage was wide enough to allow him through and so with no reason to retreat, the dragon entered.

"There was no flash of memory, no flood of recollections. I entered the chamber and stalked to the center, fascinated by the glitter. I was not yet what you see before you, although my form had already adapted to my kingdom. Turning about, I studied this place from floor to ceiling and from wall to wall. When I was finished, it came to me that this would make a most proper citadel for such a magnificent leviathan as myself. This chamber, I decided, would be my sanctum.

"And *then* it was the truth overwhelmed me. Then I recalled who it was I had *been*."

Cabe waited, but the Crystal Dragon lowered his head to his breast, as if that distant moment was still too terrible to speak of even now. The warlock suspected he knew what had happened. The images surrounding a startled dragon, images of what he had been. Memories rising from the buried portion of his mind. It would be like awakening from a long, deep slumber, but a slumber whose peace had been shattered at last by a nightmare of untold horror. Only this was a horror that would turn out to be all too real.

"I can only say, warlock," the Dragon King began again, lifting his head just enough to eye his guest. "I can only say that it was as terrifying as the transformation, which was my last recollection. Now I saw what had become of me. I roared in anger and madness and it would not be exaggerating to say that on that day I put the fear of the Crystal Dragon into all that lived in Legar." He scratched at the floor with his talons. "Not that I cared. My own fear was all that mattered. I tried to destroy this place, but you can see how well I did. Although it resembles other cavern chambers in this underground world, I think it lives, in a manner of speaking, lives and plots and does what it can to give it purpose. If the Dragonrealm is not a living thing, then it may be that this chamber is what guides the course of our land. Perhapssss it even viessss with the Dragonrealm for powerrrr."

Cabe tensed, noting the change in the Crystal Dragon's voice. The human quality in it had given way to the more reptilian sibilance that he was accustomed to from the other Dragon Kings.

Looking more and more exhausted, the drake lord slumped back. The hissing became more pronounced with each breath. "I wasss a man who wasss a beassst, but I knew who I wasss now and so I believed there wasss hope for my humanity. The others mussst have become like me. I decided to summon the other dragons, the onesss I was certain were of the Tezerenee, and bring them into the chamber one at a time. Surely, with all of usss once more knowing who we were, we could work to transform oursssselves back to what we had been."

It was not to be. He who had once been the Vraad called Logan summoned drake after drake into the chamber, only to find that none of them recalled even the vaguest of memories. One after another disappointment. When the last had been dismissed, he again attempted to tear the place asunder and was again defeated by the power that held the chamber together. He and he alone was evidently the recipient of the crystalline chamber's great sorcery. He had been *chosen*; that was the only answer that he could surmise. It would be useless to summon his brothers even assuming he could find them. They would be no different than the poor fools who were now his clan.

Humanity briefly crept back into the Dragon King's voice. It was as if there were a constant struggle going on between the two sides of his mind. "And so through the millennia, I have remained alone, my mind a man's and my form a monster's. The chamber gives much: the ability to view the land all over, power that reaches beyond the borders of my domain, and, most devilish of all, *life eternal*." He allowed Cabe time to think of the ramifications of that gift, then resumed, "But it does not give me the power to become the man I once was. Nothing has. If I try to transform, I risk losing control over my very thoughts. All that is left to me is my mind. After so long, *that* is little consolation, but I will not give it up. I have watched the others give way to generation after generation of heirs, each more of a monster than the lassst. I have watched the rise of humanity, who thinks that it, in turn, inherits from beasts and not from its own ancestors. I have watched . . . and watched . . . and watched."

A lengthy silence followed. It was a silence that the warlock knew meant the tale was at an end, or at least as much of it as the drake was willing to tell him. There were many questions that Cabe wanted to ask, including whether Shade was one of the Tezerenee and how the Crystal Dragon had kept his immortality secret from his counterparts, even barring his hermitic existence. Perhaps someday he would be told the answers to his questions, but not this day. What he *had* learned was stunning enough. The Dragonrealm was ever a cornucopia of surprises.

The silence continued without foreseeable end. At last able to stand it no longer, Cabe dared speak. "Your Majesty?"

There was no response from the massive form.

"Your Majesty?" The warlock paused, then shouted, "Logan Tezerenee!"

The Crystal Dragon's head shot skyward. Blazing, reptilian eyes fixed on the small, defiant figure standing before him. The monarch of Legar hissed. "You have my attention. Make it worth the danger."

Cabe Bedlam had had enough, however. He took a step closer and retorted, "I don't fear the danger. If you were anything of a threat, you would be acting against the true problem, the wolf raiders. Instead, you remain here, dwelling on a past that is lost. If you care so little about your existence, then you should have ended it long ago."

"Beware of how you ssspeak, human!"

"Listen to yourself! Is that a man speaking?"

The glittering behemoth rose to his full height. Even then, the warlock would not back down. He dared not.

"You are purposely trying to annoy me! Why?"

Pointing at the walls, Cabe responded. "You've seen what's out there. *You* unleashed the fog. Now, instead of bringing down the Aramites, it may become a weapon they can use. You *have* to do something."

"The fog will eventually dissipate! It must! It cannot hold itself together, not even if he commands it. The raiders will wipe themselves out trying to conquer this land and that will settle the situation." He hesitated. "Now leave me . . ." The Dragon King started to turn away. "I must rest."

Cabe could not recall ever becoming so infuriated with a Dragon King before. The very notion surprised him even now, but he knew that he was nonetheless fast approaching the point where he would lose his temper . . . and then probably his life. There were too many people relying on him, however, for the incensed sorcerer to give up.

"You've been hidden away here too long, content with observing through this device rather than seeing the world through your own eyes! You've become afraid of the outside, afraid of becoming part of the Dragonrealm!"

"*You* understand *nothing!*" roared the Crystal Dragon. "You understand nothing! I *cannot* leave this chamber! If I do so I lose *everything!* I will become as the others did, as I once was! I will be a creature, a monster, in form *and* in mind! I will lose myself! And this time it will be forever, I feel it!" The enraged dragon tried to calm himself down. "The sssame it isss if I exert my power too often, asss I nearly did when Ice sssought to end all things with his foul spell! I have rested much since then, but it is still not near enough!

"It almost happened once, when I decided to seek out some of the others and see if they, too, with the aid of this chamber could recall their past. As I started to leave, though, my head began to swim and my thoughts grew beast-like. I only barely made it back here. It was *three* days before my mind was calm enough to think my bitter experience through. I came to realize that only here was I myself. Only *here* could I survive intact."

*Intact?* Cabe found that debatable. His shoulders slumped in resignation. There would be no alliance with the lord of Legar. Now, Cabe was truly alone unless somehow he could find Darkhorse.

"Then there's no need for me to remain here," the warlock stated. He readied himself for the worst. "Am I free to depart or have you told me this fantastic story with the intention of keeping me here?"

The Crystal Dragon no longer seemed even interested in him. He curled up in what was obviously a prelude to slumber. It dismayed Cabe to see what the Dragon King had become. "You were free to go the moment you woke. You are free to go now."

*What are you waiting for?* the sorcerer demanded of himself. To his surprise, he tried once more to convince the Dragon King to see his way. "If you would only consider—"

Glittering, inhuman eyes that had been nearly closed widened. A hiss escaped. "I ssssaid *leave!*"

With those words, the warlock began to spin. Cabe gasped and tried to stop, but was helpless. He spun faster and faster, a frantic, living top. The cavern became first a bright blur and then a murky nothing. Cabe tried to concentrate, but the constant twirling threatened to make him black out. It was all he could do to keep conscious.

All at once, he simply stopped.

With a grunt, the stunned mage fell to the floor, but a floor that was hard and, strangely enough, very uneven. Cabe shook his head, then regretted the action as vertigo set in again. He settled with putting his head in his hands and waiting for the world to come to a halt on its own. Only when it finally did was he willing to look up.

Cabe first saw nothing. Wherever he had landed, it was pitch-black. Cabe summoned a dim sphere of blue light, then grimaced at what the illumination revealed. He was in another tunnel, but unlike the ones leading to the drake lord's lair, the malignant fog held sway here. That meant that Cabe must be closer to the surface. Closer to the surface and, he suspected, almost beneath the Aramite encampment.

With the Crystal Dragon's aid no longer a hope, the warlock was on his own. The surface was where he now needed to go, but which was better, he wondered, journeying in the direction he was already facing or turning around and seeing where the other end of the tunnel led? Did he *really* want to continue to the surface or would it benefit him to descend farther into the earth? At this point, it was impossible to tell which path led to the surface and which did not. One thing was certain: no matter which direction he chose, the mage would have to walk. As long as the tendrils of Nimth had hold of Legar above and below ground, the warlock dared not try teleporting save as a last desperate venture. There was too much chance of something going wrong with the spell.

Grumbling, Cabe at last chose the direction he was facing and started walking. What he hoped to accomplish without the aid of the Crystal Dragon, he could not say. Yet, even without the Dragon King's might behind him, the warlock knew he had to attempt *something.*

By the time he did reach the surface, Cabe hoped he would know exactly *what* that something was supposed to be.

*ONE HOUR 'TIL dawn, yes?* thought the blue man. It was hard to be certain in this godforsaken place, but that seemed a good estimate. Kanaan D'Rance estimated he had two hours at most to accomplish his task before Lord D'Farany rose. If all went as his grotesque visitor said, that would perhaps be an hour more than he needed.

D'Rance did not at all trust the macabre creature who had visited his tent, but Plool did indeed know things about sorcery that the northerner had never come across before. What especially interested him, however, was the stranger's knowledge of the magic that was the fog. With that to add to his own growing skills, the blue man would have need of no one. He could leave the mongrels to their own end.

The blue man entered the tunnel mouth and hurried down the deep, descending path. The guards in the passages would think nothing of him returning since his other work was down here, but those who kept watch in and around the chamber would be suspicious if he entered without Lord D'Farany. None of the Aramites trusted him that far. His skills were still not sufficient enough to deal with so many, otherwise he might have been able to do this without Plool's aid.

One thing he pondered about was why his bizarre ally could not work the Quel device himself. Plool refused to enter the chamber, not because he did not want to, no, but because he could *not* do so without endangering himself somehow. That, at least, was Kanaan D'Rance's humble opinion, yes. The creature needed D'Rance for that reason alone and that reason alone was why the blue man knew that the advantage was his. He was familiar enough with the magical device to know some of the things he could do with it, enough that he would be prepared when his ally turned on him.

Plool was still an enigma to him in most other ways and D'Rance was willing to admit that he had perhaps been a bit too hasty in joining forces with the ghastly, deformed mage. Yet, when Plool had spoken of the power to be obtained by working together, it had been too enticing. More than enough power, horrid Plool had hinted, to make the dangers negligible.

He was a part of the mist, that much the blue man had gathered despite his ally's confusing manner of speech. Plool had come from *somewhere*, drawn to this place at the same time as the fog had been. Plool had originally wanted to go home, but he could not. To open that doorway would require more effort than both he and D'Rance combined could summon. Searching for such power had brought the sorcerer to the camp and the caverns, where he had observed enough to know that somewhere below the surface there was a thing of great potential. Yet, it was a creation of a foreign sorcery. Plool did not understand that sorcery and so had sought out someone who might. Someone who also would have an interest in aiding him. In return, he could show that someone how to manipulate the magic of *his* world. Then, his part of the bargain kept, he would return to that other place—*Nimth*, was it?—and leave the spoils to his temporary ally.

The skill and knowledge to control two very different types of magic. The blue man had taken the bait . . . but was careful only to hold the hook, not bite it. From studying the efforts of Lord D'Farany and devising a few secret theories of his own, he was certain that he knew more than enough to ensure that this partnership would end in his favor. D'Rance even suspected he knew almost all he needed to know about Plool's magic. In his own grand opinion, he certainly knew enough about the Quel's creation to guarantee that whatever else happened Plool would not be able to betray him.

Still none of the scattered sentries questioned his presence in the passages. Likewise, he crossed the abandoned city of the diggers without any trouble, save that the damnable mist, which somehow remained strong even down here, made walking a matter of stumbling every few yards. At least it was thin enough here that he could see the men just ahead of him. It would not do to walk into one of the guards. Some of them might be tempted to attack first and question afterward.

Each time, the sentries straightened as he passed, strictly because of his position as aide to their leader, D'Rance understood, and did nothing to slow him. He nodded to each man. With luck, this would be the last time he saw their ugly, pink faces.

Then, almost before he realized it, the blue man was at his destination. The entrance to the chamber stood before him. He saw two guards standing there, seemingly oblivious to him. That, D'Rance was certain, would change with a few more steps. He was puzzled, though, that nothing looked different. *Where are you, my misshapen friend? Something should have happened by now, yes?*

"Enter you may, whenever you like," a familiar voice whispered from his right. "You may enter whenever you like."

Although it took all his will, D'Rance neither jumped at the sudden sound nor did he turn in the direction it had originated from. The northerner already knew that there was no one to see. If Plool had been visible, the sentries would have been able to see him from this distance, if only as a strange shadow demanding investigation.

"The sentries are dealt with, yes?"

"Will be bothering you not; you will not be bothered."

The blue man grimaced. If the Aramites thought *his* manner of speech was strange, they should listen to this clownish figure.

Standing straighter, Kanaan D'Rance walked toward the two silent guards. Even with the mist, his identity should have become apparent to them, yet they did not move to bar his way. At the very least, they should have been calling out, asking what business he had here alone.

It was only when he stood face-to-face with one of them that he saw that the man looked somehow different. His eyes had a glassy, blank look and his skin was smooth and bright pink, almost as if it had been carved from wood and painted over.

The *mouth* . . . was it actually cut like—

The sentry suddenly bent over in a comic bow, one arm flopping loosely, and said in a familiar singsong voice, "Enter, O seeker of knowledge!"

D'Rance nearly choked. He stepped back from the horrific monstrosity. The guard straightened again. D'Rance could almost imagine strings holding the dead figure up and making it move.

The lower jaw of the macabre puppet slid down and Plool's chuckle filled the tunnel.

*He cannot enter the chamber! Remember that, yes!* A bit more shaken than he would have cared to admit, the would-be sorcerer walked toward the entrance. To the opposite side, the second guard slowly turned his head so that he was staring at the newcomer. D'Rance shivered as the man's head continued to turn beyond normal limitations. The sentry's countenance was a monstrous copy of the first man.

What of the guards inside? Had they heard nothing? Had Plool somehow dealt with them, too? How?

There was only one way to find out, of course. He stepped into the chamber.

*Gods!* What sort of creature had he aligned himself with? The blue man surveyed the carnage with growing horror. He had braced himself for the worst once he had seen what had become of the two guards outside, but it was Plool's playfulness that daunted him. The two sentries had been twisted into marionettes, puppets. Here, where the madcap monster could not physically go, Plool had chosen a different but still effective manner of mayhem.

As with the sentries outside, each soldier appeared to be standing ready. They would stand ready forever, or until someone had the nerve to remove them, for from head to toe they had been *pierced* by long, thin needlelike projectiles of metal. So great had been the velocity of the deadly needles that the guards must have barely had time to realize what was happening, for several still held their weapons. Glazed eyes stared ahead, eyes that might have barely acknowledged the flying death before it struck. Strangely enough, there was hardly any blood, which only served to make the scene that much more frightening for it gave the tableau an unreal quality. Recalling what little damage Orril D'Marr's scepter had done to this place, D'Rance swore under his breath. Plool's lances had penetrated armor and rock with little effort.

Plool himself might not be able to enter, but his power reached easily enough. D'Rance steadied his nerves. He would have to be on guard.

"Admiration later," whispered the peculiar voice from behind him. The blue man could feel those terrible, lopsided eyes on his backside.

"You should not have done this, yes? By damaging the walls, you may have ruined everything!"

"It will function; function it will. To your task."

Avoiding the accusing eyes around him, the blue man made his way to the Quel's great toy. Here was where he had the malformed spellcaster at a disadvantage, the blue man reminded himself again. Plool might be able to kill a dozen or so men with a single strike, but he dared not use his sorcery on the magical construct. Without the understanding of how it worked, Plool was more likely to destroy it. This was a thing requiring careful, physical manipulation of the patterns and crystals.

Thinking of crystals, D'Rance glanced quickly around the array. The Aramite talisman was still there, ready to be used as his key to unlocking the secrets of sorcery. He had been mildly worried that the Pack Leader might have decided to take it with him when he retired, but D'Farany had apparently assumed it was secure here. Kanaan D'Rance smiled at such egotistical naiveté.

As he bent over the platform, the blue man shifted so as to obscure one side of the array from his companion's sight. There were some adjustments to be made that he did not want Plool to know of. They would be of value when the time of betrayal came.

It took several minutes to organize the crystals to the pattern he wanted. So far, he had not had to summon much power to aid him in the binding of the new array, only enough to make the pattern stable. Still, even as little as he called made the chamber take on a reddish gleam. The blue man could feel the forces stirring above and around him, growing stronger with each passing second. Soon, he would have to move to the next stage . . . which meant including Plool in the spell.

How much of a fool had he been to go along with this insane scheme? A truly great fool, but it was often the fools, he knew, that became the masters.

D'Rance straightened. "I am ready, yes?"

"Do it, then," came the voice from the corridor. "All was explained to you."

The fog itself would be the key. Lord D'Farany had bound the deadly fog to the Quel creation. He did not know the specifics of how the Aramite commander had done that fantastic deed, but that did not matter. All he needed was to seize control of the magical cloud, spread its might to this chamber, which had somehow been neglected by the fog, and use it to open the way. He would have his power and the monster would have his path home.

The would-be mage touched the shimmering keeper talisman. In the process of combining the two sorceries, he would also make certain that Plool would not steal all that power from him. The blue man had seen D'Farany use the talisman enough to know that redirecting all those forces away from where his mishapen companion expected them to go would be simplicity itself. D'Rance smiled, his uncertainty giving way to confidence as he saw how everything was under *his* direction.

His fingers gently played across the array of crystals. Every movement that Lord D'Farany had performed was etched into his mind. Now, all that careful observation was going to profit him.

*I will be the greatest mage to ever live, yes!* What other mage had ever held in his figurative grasp two distinct and deadly variations of sorcery? What other spell-caster could lay claim to such power?

He traced the last pattern.

A bluish glow surrounded the Quel artifact, burning away the reddish light and bathing the entire room in its own magnificent color. *Yes, very appropriate!*

"Mind yourself!" Plool called. "You should mind!"

The blue man ignored the warning. He *knew* what he was doing! As the glow strengthened, he glanced up at the macabre legion surrounding him. The eyes of the dead guards watched him, he thought. *The greatest moment and all there is to see my victory are a score of blue-tinted ghosts and a monstrous jester from beyond!*

Kanaan D'Rance reached down to again touch the Aramite talisman. It would be the receptacle of all that combined might. A receptacle that only he would wield.

A second later he snarled and pulled back *blackened* fingers. There was blood where the skin had cracked the worst.

"This should not be hot," the northerner muttered, fighting back the pain. Lord D'Farany had touched the talisman time and time again during his experiments and never had there been any visible sign of such terrible heat. The keeper was no god; his fingers should burn as easily as D'Rance's had. What was wrong?

He spat on his injured fingertips and carefully wiped away the blood. He would cure the wound when the power was bound to him. The pain was not so much that he could not make use of those fingers. A slight adjustment of the Aramite artifact was all that was needed. A simple mistake was all it was.

Kanaan D'Rance reached for the talisman again.

This time, the blue man shrieked.

The hand he pulled free was burnt, torn, and twisted. Still screaming, Kanaan D'Rance fell forward. His arm was a wave that knocked aside crystal after crystal from the delicate arrangement. Blue light darted forth from the device to the walls and back again. The northerner stumbled away from the wreckage, only partially aware of what he had done.

"Plool!" he managed to croak. Through blurred eyes, the blue man sought out the ungodly form of his ally in this venture. Waves of agony coursed through his body. His lower arm was not only burnt, it was also cut to ribbons. The blue man did not wonder how the second had occurred; sorcery was just that way. All he knew was that he needed help quickly and there was only one who could provide that help.

No response. It was as if Plool had fled . . .

There was a sound like a crack of thunder, thunder that was in this very chamber. Even maimed and in agony as he was, D'Rance turned in curiosity.

A *hole* had formed above the battered array of crystals. Within that hole he could see another world, a dark, violent, misty world smelling of decay.

"I have d-done it, yes!" he hissed, the pain fading for a time. "Yesss!"

It was beautiful in its own way. Beautiful and seductive. Kanaan D'Rance stumbled back to the battered crystals, a trail of blood forming behind him, and looked up. A smile spread across his sweat-soaked face. "Y-yesss!"

The smile remained on his face even as he collapsed backward to the floor.

# XV

BOUND AND TOSSED among the captive Quel, the Gryphon felt the terrible change in the air. The fog began to move with more violence, at times becoming a veritable maelstrom. A chill ran down his spine. He stared at his fellow captives who, as one, looked up and then at each other.

The lionbird studied the other prisoners closely. They almost seemed to be anticipating something. The Quel were excited, almost . . . hopeful?

He renewed his efforts to free himself. The collar he wore around his throat prevented him from conceiving any spells, but that did not mean he did not try. Whatever was happening, the Gryphon did not want to be bound and gagged when it reached its climax. What could possibly make them so—

The Gryphon let loose a muffled squawk. There could be only one thing that so interested his fellow prisoners, but . . . could it be true? Was there a chance that the spell had been broken?

Had the wolf raiders, in their arrogant ignorance, woken the *sleepers?*

He struggled even harder. Dawn was fast approaching and the Gryphon had a suspicion that this was to be a day of reckoning.

For everyone.

**THEY WOKE.**

There was no preamble, no slow stirring. Eyes simply opened and took in the dark. Stiffened forms slowly shifted, trying to make muscles work after thousands of years of ensorcelled sleep.

None of the sleepers were aware of how much time had passed. They only knew that they were all awake. They only knew that being awake meant it was time to reclaim what had once been theirs.

It was time to reclaim their world.

**IN THE TUNNELS,** a weary Cabe came to a halt as the first sensations of change washed over him. The warlock gasped at both the intensity and the source of those emanations. By now, he recognized the touch of Nimth too well. Something had caused a resurgence in the fog, a terrible growth. It was as if Nimth were trying to intrude farther upon the Dragonrealm.

*The wolf raiders!* It had to be them. They had control of the sorcerous mist. The Crystal Dragon would not have dared try opening a new doorway to foul Nimth. The Aramites, experimenting, must have done so themselves. Perhaps they had tried to discover the source or perhaps they had hoped to strengthen the fog's power.

What the reason was did not truly matter. What did was that everyone— every*thing*—might be in danger. This felt almost uncontrolled. The Aramites, even if they had a sorcerer of their own, might not understand what it was they played with.

Cabe could sense in what direction the magical ripples originated from, but he was still hesitant to try to teleport. It was because of that hesitation that he had spent so much valuable time wandering in what he hoped was the right direction. Teleportation had not worked the first time he had tried it in the fog and even if it succeeded now, he might find himself far from his intended destination. Yet there was no way of telling whether it would be possible to trace a path through the tunnels. For all he knew, they might lead him away from the danger.

The last was a tempting thought, but the dour mage knew he could not avoid the threat any more than he had avoided the rest of his mission. The magic was growing wilder by the moment. It could not possibly be under the guidance of anyone with the skill and knowledge needed. Cabe was not certain that even *he* had such knowledge, but there was no one else. The Crystal Dragon had made it emphatically clear that he wanted nothing more to do with the outside world.

"I've got to try," Cabe finally muttered. There seemed to be times between the ripples of newly released power when things almost became normal. If he attempted a spell, then . . .

He cringed as the next wave of sorcerous energy washed over him. So far, nothing had changed. No hands grew out of the walls. No creatures materialized from the ether. It appeared that Nimth did not immediately affect its surroundings, but that bit of good fortune could not last much longer.

The wave passed and an area of calm surrounded him.

Cabe teleported . . .

. . . and found himself staring into the dead eyes of a soldier who had been pinned to the wall like some gruesome decoration. Cabe bit back a yell and turned his gaze away, only to confront a similar grisly sight. He surveyed the walls in morbid fascination. There was no doubt in his mind who was responsible for this. Even the wolf raiders would not tolerate such insanity from their commanders. The Quel would not have killed in such a way; the damage to the chamber was extensive.

Plool had left his mark here. Only the Vraad would kill in such a manner.

Belatedly, the warlock saw the hole.

A black, oval space surrounded by a halo of wild light, the hole floated high in the center of the chamber. It was a small thing, but its simple presence here was danger enough. Cabe could sense the same malevolent power that permeated the fog, the power of ancient Nimth. As the hole pulsated, that power seeped into the Dragonrealm, adding to the foulness already admitted by the Crystal Dragon. There was a faint hint of mist in the chamber, but nothing approaching conditions on the surface.

He did not have to ask how it had come to be here. Cabe recognized the thing in the center as a creation of the Quel. It was a new creation, for he could not recall it being here during a previous encounter with the subterranean race. What its original purpose had been was impossible to say, although the warlock had some suspicions. The wolf raiders had usurped it for their own desires, obviously recognizing the potential power but not respecting the likely danger of trying to use the device.

By its side lay another body, but this one was different from the rest.

Cabe had never seen a blue man, although they had been mentioned briefly in one or two of the Gryphon's dispatches. Moving to the corpse's side, he inspected the body. The hood of the man's outfit had fallen away, revealing the silver mark of the warlock in his hair. His one hand was a burnt and ravaged horror that made Cabe greatly desire to look elsewhere. Shock and blood loss had likely killed him. Judging by the trail he saw, the foreign sorcerer had walked toward one of the tunnel mouths and then back again, as if he had not even noticed his life ebbing from him. Evidently, his dead counterpart had overestimated his skill in manipulating the power and had paid with his life . . . or perhaps Plool had overestimated it. Glancing up at the hole again, he began to have some idea of what the Vraad might have wanted and what the blue man might have been offered.

Where *was* the Vraad? Cabe could not sense him nearby, but with Plool that did not mean much. Plool was like nothing he had ever come across before; it might be that the Nimthian sorcerer was invisible to his senses most of the time.

Rising, he studied the damage to the device. Crystal sorcery was not Cabe Bedlam's forte, but he understood the basics. Much to his regret, however, what he knew in no way aided him in deciphering the scattered array before him. In his death throes the blue sorcerer had pushed almost everything aside. Cabe had no idea how to even begin re-creating the original design.

Yet, as he touched some of the crystals, certain images played in his mind. He picked up one piece, wincing briefly in pain when he raised his arm too high, and positioned it. Once that was done, the warlock chose another piece and placed that in a position on an angle from the first. Around him, blue lightning crackled to life, but as it was high above him, he paid it little mind. After assuring himself that the piece was in its proper place, Cabe searched the pile again. It almost seemed logical that the next two crystals that he chose went where they did. So did the two after them.

Before his eyes, he watched the arrangement take place. Everything he picked up had its niche. There were some crystals that interested him not at all, no matter how many times Cabe tried to find a spot for them. He felt as if his hands were being guided, but not by any source without. Rather, the sorcerer felt he was being guided by some force within.

Had his grandfather, Nathan, known crystal sorcery? Was that what guided the warlock's hands? The thought that he might be drawing upon Nathan's past did not at all surprise Cabe. Nathan Bedlam had known something about everything and had tried to pass on as much of himself to his grandson as was magically possible. There seemed no end to the skills the elder Bedlam had possessed. If he lived to be three hundred, the warlock wondered if he would ever feel he had lived up to his grandfather's legacy.

As Cabe re-created the pattern, he noticed that the hole's pulsations decreased. The lightning, which had played about the chamber throughout his work, now ceased. Encouraged, Cabe worked faster, trying to align everything. He soon depleted his supply of usable crystals, but still the array was not complete. Searching the floor, the warlock located several pieces around the body of the blue man. He reached down to gather them up, then paused. Just noticeable under the body and arm of the corpse was something that was not a crystal but still cried out to him to be used. Cabe gingerly moved the body to one side.

It was a carved object. A talisman. Whoever had carved it had fashioned it into the shape of a jagged tooth reminiscent of a hound's or a . . . a *wolf's.*

An Aramite talisman. To be more precise, a *keeper's* talisman. The thing radiated such power that he almost pulled his hand away. Yet, a feeling inside insisted that the warlock add it to his collection. The pattern would not be complete without it.

Cabe reached forward and started to wrap his fingers around the carving.

It flew backward from his grasp, heading in the direction of one of the cavern mouths behind him. Cabe turned, intending to give chase.

A hand caught the talisman. An elegant figure clad in the black armor of the wolf raider empire stepped forward. Despite his aristocratic features, there was a definite hint of insanity in his eyes. Sometimes the eyes focused, more times they did not. It almost seemed as if the newcomer were uncertain about which direction in life he preferred. Cold sanity or even colder madness. Cabe recognized the scarred visage from glimpses in the Crystal Dragon's sanctum during the battle of wills. Here was the victor of that battle.

"My precious . . . prize! My treasure! What . . . have . . . you done . . . to my . . . prize?"

He pointed the talisman at Cabe.

With but a thought, the warlock shielded himself. Tendrils sought to snare his arms and legs in a viselike grip, but his own spell held. The tendrils could find no grip on his person and slipped off. They tried again with the same result, then faded away.

The Aramite sorcerer did not even pause before striking with a quick, swordlike slash. Cabe parried a long, gleaming blade that formed from nothing with a magical blade of his own. The two traded blows for several seconds before the wolf raider withdrew. Cabe, his head and heart pounding and his arm in agony, did not try to seize the advantage. There was too knowing a look on the raider's marred face. He *wanted* Cabe to come to him.

The Aramite caressed the carving. "Who are you, warlock? I felt the tooth call to me, for we are bound together as two halves of a soul. Did you think that I would not notice? Kanaan should have known better, but I see that does not matter any longer. A pity for him."

He did not bother to answer the wolf raider. Cabe debated his chances of teleporting safely while continuing to fend off the attacks of the Aramite. From their brief exchange of spells, he could already see that his opponent was quick and a master of power. Cabe doubted his chances of simultaneously escaping and defending himself against the sorcerer. That meant it was to his benefit to take the offensive.

A shower of rock struck the Aramite sorcerer from behind. As he moved to defend himself, Cabe unleashed the second half of his assault. It materialized above his adversary's head, a leathery thing as large as a shield and resembling nothing more than a sheet. The wolf raider, engaged in repelling the rock storm, did not notice the danger above him until his head was suddenly covered. He reached up to pull the sheet off, but the covering would not be removed. It wrapped itself tight around the face and helmet of the raider, cutting off his air supply.

Then it dissolved.

Cabe stepped back. The eerie eyes turned his way again. In the Aramite's grasp, the talisman fairly glowed. "I ask again, warlock. Who are you? I think you must know the Gryphon, our friend. I think that is why you are here. That would make you one mage in particular. What was the name? Yes . . . *Cabe Bedlam.*"

From behind the raider came the sound of many armored men running. The first of the soldiers reached the entrance, but when he sought to enter, the Aramite sorcerer waved him back. From the soldier's quick obedience, it was obvious who was in command of the invaders.

"Your chance to yield has forever passed, Cabe Bedlam."

The talisman flared.

Cabe tensed, but there was no attack against him. He glanced back and forth around the chamber, never letting his eyes completely shift from the raiders. Still he saw and sensed nothing.

Then, from all around him, there came horrible, wrenching noises. He could not place the sounds save that they reminded him of metal scraping against rock. The warlock took a step back and tilted his head enough so that he could see more of the right side of the room while still keeping an eye on his foe.

What he saw turned his stomach and almost made him forget the threat before him.

They struggled from the wall, freeing themselves slowly but surely with a strength far in excess of that of any living man. With eyes as blank as the sorcerer who controlled their strings, the dead sentries, the lances still piercing their torsos and limbs, shambled toward Cabe. Some had their weapons ready, but others merely reached for him. Caked blood splattered the floors and walls.

The warlock fought against the unreasoning panic rising within him. Necromancy was the darkest use of sorcery. Cabe's first introduction to it had been when Azran had sent the rotting apparitions of two of Nathan Bedlam's old companions, the sorcerers Tyr and Basil, to kidnap the young Bedlam and bring him to the mad mage's keep. That horrific meeting had forever left its mark on him, although he had never admitted such to Gwen. Cabe Bedlam disliked shapeshifting, but he *feared* necromancy.

Fear, however, did not equate panic. Not quite. He stepped around so that the Quel device stood between him and the Aramite. The wolf raider stirred, but, as Cabe had prayed, his adversary still held some hope of making use of the artifact and therefore hesitated to cast any spell that Cabe might deflect to it. That hesitation gave the warlock the extra breath he needed to combat the more immediate threat. Even if the barriers he had raised held, the unliving army was too great a distraction. If Cabe let them surround and harass him, he would eventually fall to his true opponent.

It was the metallic lances that skewered each of the undead that finally inspired him. Cabe lunged forward and reached among the crystals he had arranged earlier. Drawing upon the same knowledge that had let him create the pattern before him, he transposed three of the pieces.

A storm broke above his head. A lightning storm that raced so swift from one end of the room to the other that it created a web of ever-shifting design. The warlock ducked back as the bolts struck the array as well, creating a bluish glow about the artifact. From the other side of the Quel device, he heard the keeper shout in frustrated realization.

From his studies, Cabe was familiar with the attraction of lightning to metal rods. So, too, it was evident, was the wolf raider.

The chamber shook as the bolts struck. There was no escape for the undead, pincushioned as they were by so many lances. Some were struck several times in a single moment while others were touched but once. One or a hundred times, however, the effect was still the same. The raw power behind those bolts was more than enough to incinerate the stumbling corpses. Some few burst into flames while others simply dropped, their forms charred black. More than one literally burst, sending gobbets flying.

Cabe crouched on the floor, his cloak protecting him from the awful rain. From where he was, he could see that the other spellcaster had backed all the way into the tunnel. The raider's spells might protect him, but armored as he was, he evidently thought himself too tempting a target for the magic lightning.

The last of the unliving legion fell. Cabe felt some small pity for the unfortunate men, but reminded himself of what they had been. Whatever decency had once existed in them when they had lived, the Aramite war wolf had worried it to death. The Gryphon had spoken of many gallant folk among the raiders' race, but the soldiers of the empire were, with very few exceptions, not among them.

Risking the storm that still crackled above, the exhausted mage stood. Much to his dismay, the keeper chose that same moment to dare to reenter. Cabe would never be able to sufficiently describe the expression on that ravaged countenance, but he knew that the next duel between them would be the last.

The duel was never to be, though, for as the raider commander raised the talisman, the chamber shook anew with a frenzy that nearly sent both men to the floor. Someone cried out about earthquakes, but this was no natural tremor. The walls, floor, and ceiling were being buffeted from within, almost as if a ghostly fist was trying to battle its way out of the cavern. Only the shield that Cabe had raised against the Aramite mage was preventing him from being tossed and battered like a piece of soft fruit. As it was, each passing moment left him weaker and weaker, for the pounding was growing stronger with each wave.

Across from him, the wolf raider was also struggling against the tremor. In his one hand he clutched tight the talisman. Beyond the sorcerer, Cabe could make out the faces and forms of several of the soldiers. To his surprise, they moved as if barely hindered by the quake. The greatest force was confined to the chamber itself, at least for now. Once the crystalline walls began to crumble, who was to say how far it would spread.

The cause, of course, was the hole between Nimth and the Dragonrealm. Feeling much like a fool, Cabe realized that the struggle between the two sorcerers had upset the balance he had created. It not only had recommenced pulsating, but with greater intensity than previously. Worse, although the tremor made it impossible to focus long on the terrible hole, the thing's dimensions appeared to be *expanding*.

Damaged as they were from the deadly rain of spears, the walls were not long in commencing to crumble. Large chunks of rock crystal broke free and tumbled to the floor. Long, wicked cracks spread from one side of the chamber to the other. Damaged already and now with its support weakening, the ceiling, too, cracked and shook.

The entire place was about to collapse.

Having succeeded in righting himself, the Aramite sorcerer retreated once more to the cavern mouth. Although they did not exactly focus upon the warlock, not once did the raider's eyes leave the vicinity where Cabe stood. The talisman remained poised.

*He means to trap me!* Caught between the danger of the collapsing ceiling and the threat of the keeper's sorcery, Cabe initially did nothing but stand where he was. His adversary continued to back away until he was well out of the chamber. Then the Aramite stopped and waited. The warlock cursed his counterpart. The keeper was trying to make certain that Cabe's quandary became a fatal delay.

The warlock knew he could not hope to escape through one of the other exits, not with the keeper waiting to strike. Yet, that left only teleportation and while the spell had served Cabe well enough to bring him to this place, he knew that under present circumstances he now stood a greater chance of materializing a hundred feet above the surface than he did in actually arriving at his hoped-for destination. That was if the warlock did not teleport into solid rock instead of thin air.

It was the ceiling that made his decision for him. No longer able to withstand the battering, the entire thing collapsed.

Cabe never knew if the Aramite mage tried to prevent him from escaping. He was only aware of his own sudden desire to be elsewhere and that, combined with his skill and natural affinity for sorcery, was enough to make the spell happen. Even as the ceiling came down, the warlock vanished.

He did not reappear in solid rock nor did the harried mage materialize high above the surface of Legar. Rather, Cabe came to an undignified stop against a small rocky outcropping. He yelped in pain as his arm briefly rolled against the harsh surface, then grunted as he continued to roll downward.

The outcropping was a low one and so his descent was short, if bruising. Fighting back a moan, Cabe Bedlam looked up.

The warlock had *not* materialized a hundred feet in the air, but he *had* materialized three or four yards from the feet of one very eager soldier.

Mages popping into existence must have been a familiar sight to this veteran. Even as Cabe noted his presence, the raider was already charging him, likely aware that the only chance he had against a spellcaster was to catch him while his wits were still addled. Cabe caught a glimpse of a well-honed blade rising. He reacted instinctively, raising his own arm to block the blow. From anyone other than a sorcerer, this would have been but a feeble, fatal attempt. From Cabe Bedlam, however, the action was what saved his life. The soldier's blade came down . . . and stopped two feet from the warlock's forearm.

Cabe did not wait for the soldier to recover from his surprise. He made a cutting motion with his arm.

The wolf raider's head snapped back. The soldier grunted, then fell backward. He sprawled on the ground, his neck broken as easily as if the warlock had stepped on a dry twig.

*I'll never get used to killing.* That might be true, Cabe supposed, but it no longer prevented him from doing the deed. This journey was becoming too much for him. Where he had tried to avoid killing his adversaries unless pressed, he now considered it the only expedient route in this case. The wolf raiders were without pity; they would kill him outright or save him for a slow death. Worse, they were more than willing to let his friends and family share that slow death.

The sons of the wolf had to be pushed back into the sea. Even one was one too many.

*I'm beginning to sound like the Gryphon,* he thought. Why not? He had lived through the war through the lionbird's messages, hearing of the battles and deaths. While the war had from the start been in the rebellion's favor, the immense size of the empire had meant years and years of struggle to free the continent. Years and years of folk giving their lives to overthrow the night-clad soldiers and their masters.

The brief, contemplative respite allowed him to recover enough so that he could go on. That he was in Legar was obvious. That the mist seemed a bit lighter and the land a bit more visible made him suspect that dawn was coming fast. Cabe had wondered exactly how long he had been unconscious after the Crystal Dragon's sphere had exploded. Longer than he had imagined.

Where was he in relation to the Aramite encampment? That was the true question. Was the dead raider a lone soldier who had gotten separated from his patrol or was he a scout?

Cabe rose and took a step toward the direction the raider had come from. Despite the rocky soil, he could make out a partial track here or there, at least enough to give him a place to start. He continued on for several paces, then recalled one last thing. Turning, Cabe eyed his attacker. The corpse might not be noticed for quite some time, but he could not risk it.

The spell was simple, as had been the one that had so handily killed the soldier in the first place, and thus there was less chance of it going awry. The Nimthian fog was almost dormant for the moment, but that was not likely to last. The present calm was probably like the quiet before the storm. Cabe had not forgotten the destruction raging somewhere below him, destruction that would affect the surface before long. That was another problem that needed quick solving, but the warlock knew no way to close the portal without the now buried Quel device. Besides, he had enough on his hands at the moment as it was. All he could do was hope that some solution would present itself before all of Nimth poured through.

The spell began with a tiny whirlwind whose width was just enough to include the remains of the soldier. As the whirlwind spun, dust and dirt flew up and around the body. The compact tornado whirled faster and faster, dredging up more dirt and rock. Before long, it was impossible to see anything within. Cabe let the whirlwind spin for another two or three breaths, then made it stop.

When the dust had settled, there was no sign of the body. In its place was a small mound not much different from many other mounds formed by the uneven land. A close examination would reveal the truth, but Cabe was trusting the fog to work with him. Unless one of the other warriors tripped over it, no one was likely to find the remains for quite a while. By that time, the warlock would either be finished here or *dead.*

He grimaced. He *was* sounding too much like the Gryphon.

The trail twisted and turned, but Cabe somehow managed to keep sight of it. Before long, he came across more tracks, also from Aramite soldiers. The boot shapes were more or less identical and Cabe doubted that there could be too many other armies wandering around Legar. Most of the trails led from one general direction. At first, he was surprised at the ease with which he was able to follow the tracks, but as he came across more, it occurred to him that the wolf raiders were not being very careful about covering their trails. It seemed unlikely that they would be so careless unless he was—

In the distance, he heard the familiar clink of metal upon metal.

Cabe located a nearby rise and hid behind it. He peered over the top, ready to duck if someone looked his way.

The clink of metal was joined by the stomping of booted feet. In the mist, the warlock was just barely able to see the outlines of four figures wearing helms and carrying swords or lances. They were wolf raiders; they had to be. As Cabe had thought, the Aramites would not have been so careless about covering their tracks unless those tracks were in an area very, very close to the encampment.

*A little more distance and I might have landed in the center of their army!* He considered it fortunate that he had been forced to deal with only one soldier. This close, he might have found himself confronting yet another patrol . . . a better *prepared* patrol, this time.

Cabe allowed the foursome to pass. Once they had, the wary mage continued on. He was not exactly certain of what he hoped to accomplish, but the closer he journeyed the more something new began to drive him toward the camp. It was almost as if someone was calling to him. Not anyone malevolent; his senses were acute enough for him to know that. No, someone who needed his help. That was what it felt like to him. Even if he was wrong and the feeling of need was only a figment of his imagination, Cabe would have still been willing to invade the Aramites' camp. He had to know how many men there were and how well supplied the army was. Most important of all, he had to know what their plans were. Where might they strike other than Zuu? Without the Crystal Dragon's magical sanctum, which saw everything and everyone, skulking through the encampment was the only way by which he could hope to gather the information he needed.

So far, his last few spells had worked the way they were supposed to work. Cabe wondered if he dared one more. He was taking a risk with this one, for it required a much longer duration. There was a good chance that the spell would deteriorate unexpectedly in the sorcerous mist.

The sounds of camp life reached his ears. Even throughout the night there would be those who were on duty and those who simply did not sleep. Sleep had probably not been quick in coming for the Aramites, not in this magic-wracked fog.

He would have to risk the spell. If it worked, it would give him a free hand. If it did not, the Aramite keeper might yet have his life.

He cast the spell about him. Unfortunately, there was no way to tell whether he had succeeded until he confronted someone. Under normal circumstances, Cabe would have been certain of his success, but so long as Legar was blanketed, nothing was certain.

With great care, the warlock walked toward the camp. It was not far, he discovered. The first of the sentries came into sight only a few minutes later. A trio of wolf raiders conversed with one another. It was time for the changing of the guard. With the two sentries was an officer, marked so by the cloak he wore. What they were saying, Cabe could not hear, for their voices were too quiet. He braced himself and walked toward them.

One of the guards glanced his way. The warlock stiffened, ready to do what he had to do in order to protect his anonymity. His patience was rewarded, however, for after a brief moment, the raider turned his attention once more to his superior.

The spell worked. Unless Cabe drew added attention to himself, he would be able to walk unnoticed through the entire army. He was not actually invisible, but like Shade had done so many times in the past, he now blended into his surroundings. It was an easier spell and one that did not require as much will and power to maintain. It was also a bit more of a danger.

He was careful to give the trio a wide enough berth. Once past them, Cabe did not look back. There was too much ahead of him that needed his attention.

Cabe had seen armed camps before, but the organization and efficiency of this one dismayed him. He had assumed that the wolf raiders would be a more haphazard bunch after their flight from the war, but while the men and equipment did have that weary and battle-worn look to them, this was not an army of refugees. These soldiers were here to fight. They would grumble and their officers would beat some of them, but this was most definitely a force to fear.

Walking among an army that would have slain him in an instant if his spell failed, Cabe could not help but feel ill at ease. Nonetheless, he moved through the camp with little hesitation, noting the number of tents and men he saw and

estimating how many more there might be. The warlock listened to fragments
of conversations about the war in the empire and the decisions of the expedition's leaders. He heard the name "D'Farany" used more than once and always
in fearful respect. From what he discerned, Cabe was certain that the Aramite
sorcerer was the very same man. His worry increased a hundredfold. Under a
leader like the keeper, the wolf raiders became an even greater threat. D'Farany
was the sort of commander who would drive his men beyond normal limits, if
only out of fear of him.

Several times soldiers on sentry duty crossed his path and during one such
incident one paused before him, squinting. The guard tightened his grip on his
sword, but after staring for several seconds, he blinked and continued on. Cabe's
heart did not start beating again until the guard was far away.

The warlock was in what he guessed was the center of the encampment when,
to his shock, he sensed an all too familiar presence. It could only have been
because of the fog that he had not noticed it sooner. In fact, Cabe was certain
that the sense of need he had felt earlier could only have come from this source.

"*Darkhorse . . .*" he muttered. *They have Darkhorse!*

Like a beacon, the shadow steed's presence drew him along. Cabe was forced
to walk around several tents and avoid numerous sentries, but at last he saw a
huge, looming shape in the distance. The ensorcelled mage glanced around. The
light had not changed much for the past several minutes; this was evidently as
bright as the day was to become. Cabe was relieved. It would be difficult enough
to rescue Darkhorse, out in the open as he was, without more illumination further increasing visibility. For once, the fog worked to his benefit.

The distance that remained he covered in swift enough fashion, but the last
few yards were still the hardest he had crossed yet. Not because of any encounter with sentries, but rather because he was at last able to see what had become
of his old friend.

The ebony leviathan stood silent in an open patch away from the main encampment. Two sentries stood watch from a more than healthy distance, but
they were there more for decoration and were not even looking at the captive.
What truly held the shadow steed prisoner was a peculiar, metallic harness
device that hung around his neck. From the harness stretched four thin lines
whose other ends were looped around his legs just above the hooves. Cabe
could detect the power ravaging Darkhorse even from far away. The baleful
Aramite device was designed not only to hold its captive in place, but to slowly
drain him of any will or strength to escape. Judging by the way the eternal's
head dropped and how dim the once-blazing eyes were, the foul creation of the
wolf raiders was doing its work and doing it well.

The guards did not notice him, but when the warlock was only a few yards from Darkhorse, the shadow steed raised his weary head. He did not look at the spellcaster, but Cabe felt a weak touch in his mind. Cabe shuddered at the feebleness of that touch. How had the eternal come to this?

He continued on past the guards, who looked too caught up in their misery at having had to stand night duty to ever notice a specter crossing their paths. The silent warlock walked until he was next to the prisoner, then turned around so that he could keep watch on the sentries while he and Darkhorse conversed.

"Can you speak?" Cabe whispered.

"That . . . power is still mine. I had . . . given up hope . . . for you, Cabe. My heart lightens."

The shadow steed's tone did anything but lighten his. This close, he could better feel the wicked work of the harness. Each moment further drained his companion of his might. Darkhorse, however, was almost all magic; if the harness was allowed to continue its work unheeded, it would eventually drain the eternal's very essence away.

"You can't shift?"

"No, the harness prevents that."

Cabe studied the diabolical creation while he talked. "How did you come to be here? Did the patrol capture you after we were separated?"

A little of Darkhorse's bluster returned. The harness might be sapping his strength, but the return of the warlock was a revitalizing force. "That rabble? They scattered in every direction and never came back."

One of the guards turned, a look of curiosity spread across his war-ravaged face. His comrade also turned, but seemed more curious about what the other sentry was doing. The first man took two steps toward the eternal and stared at him. With a casual turn of his head, the black stallion stared back. The guard swallowed and stumbled back, much to the amusement of his companion. Both men swapped glares at each other, then returned to their duties.

"Talk quieter!" hissed Cabe. "At the level I do."

"I have become . . . careless . . . but it is so good to see you, Cabe! I thought my obsession had cost you your life. In dwelling on the loss of one friend, one enemy, I did not pay heed when another friend needed me."

"You were trying to protect me," the human protested, still attempting to find some way of removing the harness. He had to be wary; there were alarm spells woven into the arrangement. They were old, however, likely implemented when the harness had first been created. If he was careful, Cabe was certain that he would have no trouble bypassing them. Actually releasing Darkhorse from his magical chains was a more troublesome predicament. The sorcery involved in the evil work of the device was bound also to the captive. In trying to free his friend, Cabe might kill him instead.

"Do you have any notion as to how this may be removed?"

"I do not." Darkhorse sounded much stronger, if not any more confident. "Forget me, Cabe. There are other matters you would be better off attending to."

The warlock thought about the wild Nimthian sorcery loose below, but said nothing concerning it to Darkhorse. He could not leave the shadow steed here. Besides, with the stallion's aid, perhaps a solution to that situation could be discovered. "I'm not leaving you."

Both sentries turned. Cabe moved as close as he could to his companion. Darkhorse eyed the two raiders, and as had happened before, the soldiers quickly turned away. The dark leviathan's ice-blue orbs brightened in amusement.

He tilted his head toward Cabe. "Then hear this thought. You asked how I had come to these dire straits. When I discovered that we had become separated, I searched for you. Unable to find any sign, I returned to Esedi, hoping that you would also return there. Much to my dismay, I did not materialize where I had intended. Thinking that the same . . . the same had become of you, I searched the hills carefully. Upon my return to our original point of departure, I was greeted with a surprise."

As desperate as he was to hear the point of the story, Cabe did not try to hurry Darkhorse. The eternal would explain in his own manner and at his own pace.

Fortunately, this was not to be a long tale. "Awaiting me in the hills was none other than the Lord Gryphon."

"*The Gryphon!*" It was all the stunned mage could do to keep from shouting the name. The one thing he had not expected was the lionbird's return from the war.

"The Gryphon, yes. He it was who joined me when I entered Legar this second time. He it was who was with me when a second and better-equipped patrol found us." The leviathan lowered his head, the gleam fading a little from his unsettling eyes. "He it is who is now, too, a prisoner of these jackals."

Which was why the shadow steed had surrendered, no doubt. Cabe forgot the harness. Turning to gaze out at the mist, he asked, "Where? Do you know?"

"There is a large, flat-looking tent to . . . to your present right. It is some distance from here. When I was being led here, I saw them put him in there."

"After I free you, we'll rescue him." His face was grim. The warlock had wished for aid in his mission and he had received it in the form of two prisoners, one weakened near to the point of collapse and the other . . . Cabe tried not to think about what the wolf raiders might do to their most hated enemy.

"You miss my . . . my point, Cabe. Rescue the Gryphon now for two reasons.

The first is that he might have the knowledge to free me from this vile contraption. He knows the curs better than either of us. The second reason is of the most import; this morning he is to be presented to the leader by some despicable little monster calling himself D'Marr. I heard that much. If you do not rescue him very, very soon, I fear we will lose our only chance. This D'Marr sounds ready to treat the Gryphon to the tender mercies of the empire at this morning's confrontation. I do not think our friend is supposed to survive the event."

Cabe hesitated but a moment. As dire as the shadow steed's situation was, there was no argument that the Gryphon faced the most immediate threat. For years, Aramite spies and assassins had tried to put an end to what they considered the empire's chief foe. Now, that foe was in their clutches. It would be an inspiration to D'Farany's forces and no doubt a way of wreaking vengeance for his own personal losses if the keeper was able to present the Gryphon's battered and torn body to his followers.

"Show me again the direction," he finally whispered.

Darkhorse dipped his head toward the unseen tent. "The camp is starting to stir. They have not slept well this last night. Go swiftly but go very cautiously."

Cabe faced his old friend. "I *will* be back for you."

"I have faith. Your being here gives me new strength with which to battle this thing of torture. Now go!"

Slipping past the two sentries, the warlock again moved nigh invisible through the camp. He was pleased his spell still held true, but was aware that each moment made the chances of mishap greater. Cabe had to find the Gryphon, release him, and return to Darkhorse. With the Gryphon to aid him, they would surely be able to find some way to free the eternal. Darkhorse was also large enough to carry both of them, which would be a necessity once either escape was noticed.

He had just sighted the tent when a minor tremor shook the area. It was short and mild, but its appearance raised a muttering among the soldiers nearby, including those who had been sleeping before the quake had begun. Cabe gritted his teeth as he pondered what could be done. Had D'Farany tried to halt the destruction and failed or had he simply abandoned the underworld under the mistaken impression that the violence would not affect the surface?

Guessing was futile. Cabe set his mind on his present task. First the Gryphon, then Darkhorse, and finally escape. Once they were secure, then they could discuss their next move.

Although he was positive that he had found the correct tent, the warlock nonetheless decided to risk reaching out with his mind to discover who or what was inside. It might be that the lionbird had been moved to another location. It also might be that Cabe had chosen the wrong tent. Surely there had to be more than one tent so designed. Moving over to another, much nearer tent . . . just to be on the safe side . . . the warlock probed.

*Gryphon?* He sensed more than one being in the tent. There were several, in fact, and Cabe's impression was that they were all prisoners of the wolf raiders. Cabe investigated one of the other minds, then immediately withdrew in disgust. *Quel!* They had put the Gryphon in with a band of Quel.

*At least I know that he's in there, too.* His probe had been able to verify that fact even though Cabe had not actually linked with his former comrade. Still, it would be a wise move to alert the Gryphon to his coming so that the lionbird would be ready when the time for escape arrived.

Then, before he could act, a new presence invaded his senses. Cabe flung himself against the tent and tried to shield his own existence from the other. He prayed it was not too late. If he was discovered now, it was the end for all of them.

Out of the mist came the tall, familiar figure of Lord D'Farany. The keeper strode across the camp accompanied by several men, including a much slighter but foreboding officer who carried on his belt a crystal-tipped scepter that radiated sorcery. The shorter raider was fitting his helm on his head and looked to have been only recently asleep. He was muttering something to Lord D'Farany, who nodded once but did not otherwise reply.

The keeper suddenly came to a halt. As all but the slight officer looked at one another in confusion, the Aramite commander shifted his gaze toward the tent where Cabe hid. The talisman in his hand glowed, but no discernible spell was cast. At his side, the sinister aide also studied the spot where the warlock stood.

Despite the years it seemed, only a handful of seconds passed before the raider commander turned away. The other Aramite continued to watch a moment longer, but when his master resumed his walk, the officer had to follow.

It was not until the danger to his own person was past that Cabe noticed where the party was heading. His fists clenched in frustration and he silently swore in the name of his Vraadish ancestors.

He was too late. The wolf raiders had come for the Gryphon.

# XVI

AS THE DAY began, soldiers all around the encampment noticed changes from the previous days. The fog moved with renewed violence and this time with a virile wind behind it. There were tremors now and then, each a little stronger than the last. Some also left in their wake peculiar humps of earth almost resembling the upturned dirt left by the underground passage of a mole or go-pher, only larger. That started muttering about the need for fresh meat, which was quickly quelled by officers, who secretly agreed.

No one paid too much attention to the changes. There was nothing that the army could do about them and rumor had it that the expedition was at last going to be moving on to better climes. That sort of rumor was more welcome and soon became the only topic of importance.

Meanwhile, the tremors increased and the mounds, sometimes appearing even when there *was* no quake, soon crisscrossed the entire camp.

THE GRYPHON CEASED struggling with his bonds the moment he became aware of the sounds of armored men approaching the tent. Much to his dis-may, the Gryphon had made very little headway in his attempt to free himself. D'Marr's men had performed a practiced effort upon him; try as he might the bonds had not loosened one bit. That he had less than a full complement of fingers on one hand did not help matters.

Both he and the Quel looked up as a soldier pulled the tent flap aside. A col-umn of six men entered the tent, the last two being D'Marr and a tall, scarred figure who could only be Lord Ivon D'Farany.

One of the guards removed the gag around the Gryphon's beak. The lionbird opened and closed his mouth a few times to see if it still worked.

"You have not changed much after all these years, Gryphon," the Aramite commander commented in quite polite tones. He reminded the captive of D'Rak, the senior keeper at the time of his arrival on the other continent. The same tone was there, although in this case, it was tinged with borderline mad-ness. The Gryphon did not have to look into D'Farany's unholy eyes to recog-nize the sickness.

"So, we have met before," he replied.

The keeper toyed with his talisman, one of the largest of the so-called Ravager's Teeth that the prisoner could ever recall seeing. "Under the streets of Canisargos, in the days when the true Pack Master still ruled, the Lord God Ravager smiled down upon his children, and I was chosen to be my Lord D'Rak's successor."

"Under the streets?" The Gryphon recalled battles and flight as he and the drake Morgis, the latter in humanoid form, were pursued by the minions of the empire. The keepers in particular had been avid hunters. That hunt had ended in chaos and destruction, however, when the spell that had prevented Morgis from transforming into a dragon had been broken. Bursting upward through the very streets of the massive city, the dragon, with the lionbird on his back, had flown off, leaving behind him ruin.

A lipless smile crossed the drawn countenance of the raider leader. "I led that patrol that fought you. When the dragon brought the city down upon the catacombs beneath, I was nearly crushed. I *did* survive though . . . only to suffer *much* greater later on, when our Lord Ravager's gift was withdrawn."

The Gryphon could still not recall D'Farany's features, but that had been almost twenty years ago and humans tended to change more with time. Sorcerers, even keepers, lived longer, but the Aramite commander had also suffered withdrawal from the addictive power of his dark master. That had probably done more to twist his features than the entire war.

Glancing about, D'Marr dared interrupt his commander. "Lord D'Farany, you said that we must have the camp ready to move as soon as possible. While the order has just gone out, we don't have much time."

"I am aware of what I said, Orril. I am. A pity, though." The eyes suddenly focused. "It is a pity, Gryphon, that we cannot make a grand ceremony of your death. I, for one, would have found it inspiring. I was thinking of first giving my verlok a few moments of your time and then allowing Orril to show us his prowess in the art of lingering pain."

"Death by vermin. My apologies for the disappointment." There was no great visible reaction from D'Marr, although his eyes might have flashed in anger for an instant. The lionbird tried to judge the distance between himself and Lord D'Farany. Even bound as he was, he was almost certain that a good push would send him rolling into D'Farany. It was a desperate venture, but if he was meant to die now he at least wanted one last chance at one of his foes. After what the Gryphon had learned from D'Marr about his son's death, he would have preferred the young officer's throat, but D'Marr was too far away to even consider.

"I will live with it . . ." Lord D'Farany gingerly shifted his grip on the glimmering talisman. "I made the brief acquaintance of a friend of yours, by the way. A dark-haired warlock . . . Cabe Bedlam was his name."

The Gryphon tensed.

"It would have been so cozy to bring such old friends back together, but he didn't want to come . . . so I left him buried beneath the rubble from a collapsed cavern."

Cocking his head to one side, the lionbird carefully studied his captor. The drawn face, the constantly moving hands, and the stiff body told him more than the keeper's words. Cabe might be dead, but that death had been costly for the Aramite commander. He began to ponder the sudden decision to break camp when it was obvious that the Quel city could hardly be stripped of all its prizes. Cabe or Cabe's death had instigated something that bothered Lord D'Farany enough to make him uproot his entire force without warning.

D'Farany took his silence the wrong way. "I thought you cared about your friends more. You are little more than an animal, birdman. It would be best if we just put you out of your misery."

By the side, Orril D'Marr removed the scepter from his belt.

A hand stayed the raider officer. "He does not die this morning. Have him readied for the journey. His death will entertain us on the morrow."

Looking somewhat disappointed, D'Marr nodded. He glanced at the Quel, who stared back with unreadable expressions. The Gryphon thought that they looked a bit too calm considering their situation. "What about these little beasts?"

Lord D'Farany did not even give them a glance. "Kill them before we leave, Orril." To his prisoner, the Aramite softly added, "I want to spend a little time with you before your death, birdman. I want you to know the pain and suffering you caused me all those years ago . . . and I know it was you. It had to be. I have never been whole since the day the gifts of the keepership were stripped from my soul." He stroked the talisman and again smiled that lipless smile. "But here I have come close."

With that, the keeper turned and departed the tent. His aides, with the exception of Orril D'Marr, hurried after. Only the young officer and the guards remained. The former studied the bound captives and scratched his chin in contemplation.

"I should do this all myself, but I've not the time. Too bad; it would've been fun." He swung the tip of the scepter around until it was pointed at the lionbird. "At least I'll have the pleasure of dealing with you later. Let's see if you can scream as long as your son did."

Holding back the rage that boiled up within him, the Gryphon calmly and quietly responded, "My son did not scream."

It was not merely his belief. He *knew* Demion had not screamed. Demion would never have screamed. The Gryphon was also aware that his son had died quickly and in the heat of battle. D'Marr had never had time to torture him.

That in no way released the wolf raider from the lionbird's vengeance. Somehow, he would take the little man down.

Seeing that his attempt to ruffle the feathers of his adversary had failed, Orril D'Marr replaced the mace on his belt and summoned the two guards. "Bind his mouth and kill those obnoxious beasts. Do you think the two of you are capable of executing those orders? I mean, they *are* bound hand and foot."

The soldiers nodded. D'Marr turned to go, then stopped to stare at the Quel again. He reached into a pouch and removed something too small for the Gryphon to make out. Crouching, the Aramite spoke to one of the Quel males. "I have decided to give you one final chance to save your miserable lives. What's in that cavern? What were you hiding? Speak to me!"

The Gryphon guessed that the unseen object in D'Marr's tightly clenched fist had to be a magical creation similar to the crystals that the subterranean race used to communicate with those not of their kind. Talk of a hidden cavern interested him, especially the cold silence it brought forth from the Quel that D'Marr had questioned.

"It's buried forever! There's no use keeping it a secret any longer! I want to know!"

It was interesting to see the bland mask of the young officer slip away. He had obviously become obsessed with this cavern.

"Bah!" The Aramite rose, then turned toward the lionbird. "Stupid beasts won't talk even to save their useless lives."

*Likely because they know what your promise is worth. At least they can die knowing they've frustrated you in this.* Aloud, he wryly remarked, "You seem a bit put out. What won't they tell you?"

D'Marr's face returned to its more common banality. "You. You might know about it." He leaned over the prisoner. "Far beneath the surface, past the Quel city, there was a chamber with some sort of great magical device."

"Fascinating."

The Aramite looked ready to strike him, but held back. "It's what lies beyond, what I *alone* of the camp knows lies beyond, that interests me more. The beasties used sorcery—I witnessed the very end of that spell—to change the entrance to solid wall. There is something so valuable in there that they willingly die to preserve the secret. I was planning to set some explosives against one of the outer walls, but circumstances worked against me. Something *always* worked against me. Now Lord D'Farany says the passage is gone and we must leave here, but I still need to know what was in there." While he had been talking, Orril D'Marr had put away the tiny talisman and once more removed the scepter from his belt. He began poking the head into the lionbird's chest, but, fortunately for the Gryphon, did not make use of the weapon's more devilish aspect. "Do *you* know what secret they hide from me?"

Certain as he was of the cavern's contents, the Gryphon had no intention of passing that information on to the wolf raider. D'Marr could offer him nothing. The Gryphon had no love for the Quel and they certainly cared little for him, but here, for the moment, was a common foe. Let D'Marr's curiosity eat at him. It was a small, petty bit of revenge, but at least it was something.

"I have never been to the domain of the Quel."

It was an honest statement, as far as it went. The raider officer looked ready to strike him, but their discourse was shattered by another tremor, this one more violent than its predecessors. D'Marr almost fell on the Gryphon, who would have gladly snapped off the Aramite's throat with his powerful beak if given the opportunity. One of the Quel did seek to roll into a guard, but the soldier backed out of the way and, without ceremony, thrust a good length of his blade into the creature's unprotected throat. The armored beastman gave a muffled squeal and died. His companions rocked madly back and forth, but there was little they could do.

The tremor took long to settle. Now, the Gryphon had a better understanding of why the wolf raiders were beginning to break camp. This portion of Legar was no longer stable. That should not have been so, unless . . . *The fools must have played too much with things they did not understand!*

Collecting himself, D'Marr stepped back to the tent opening. He looked from his adversary to the sentries, his frustration revealed only in his eyes. "Finish the rest of those beasts and make him ready for travel. I want this tent struck immediately after. We march in one half hour. Anything or anyone not ready by then will be left behind."

With one last glance at the Gryphon, D'Marr vanished through the tent flaps. The two soldiers matched gazes, consulted among themselves for about half a minute as to how best to dispose of the bodies, then turned with grim purpose toward the captured Quel.

The Gryphon felt the ground beneath him rise and braced himself for another tremor. When that did not immediately happen, he looked down and saw that he now sat on one end of a spreading rise of dirt much like a mole's trail. The width of the rise spread as it neared the soldiers and their victims, in the end becoming twice as wide as either man.

Throwing himself to one side, the lionbird braced himself.

His sudden and peculiar action caught the attention of the two raiders just as they were about to dispatch a pair of the Quel. One of the guards sheathed his sword and started after the Gryphon.

The Aramite was thrown screaming into the ceiling of the tent as the ground before him burst skyward and several hundred pounds of armored destruction erupted from the depths of the earth.

The Quel was huge, even by the standards of the race. In one massive paw he carried a wicked, double-bladed ax that somehow he had managed to drag with him even while tunneling. The first soldier had still not recovered, but the second was already attacking. Much to the raider's misfortune, though, he thrust his blade too low and it shattered off of the rocklike shell of the newcomer. The Quel, completely silent throughout all, brought the ax around and proceeded to nearly cleave the armored soldier in two. Blood and much too much more decorated the interior of the tent, but only the Gryphon seemed to care.

Turning, the armed creature stalked toward the remaining raider and buried one edge of his deadly weapon in the chest of the still dazed man, who managed another short scream before he died.

The Quel threw down his weapon and began freeing the other prisoners. Dragging himself along like a snake, the Gryphon tried to move as far from the sight of the Quel as was possible. So far, they were all ignoring him, but one of them might decide to leave no witness to the escape.

A soldier stepped through the flap. "What goes—?"

Reaching for his ax, the rescuer rose to face the stunned newcomer. Two Quel whose hands had been freed hurried to undo the bonds around their legs. The Aramite was not so caught off-guard that he was not able to defend himself. His blade was out and biting before his hulking adversary was able to bring his own weapon into play. This time, the Quel was not as lucky. The wolf raider caught him in a fairly unprotected area near the neck and managed to slice off a good piece of flesh. The Quel fought back a hoot of pain and swung. His ax passed through where the human's chest should have been, but the wary raider had fallen to a crouch. The soldier started to shout at the top of his lungs.

Meanwhile, the lionbird, who had continued to move away from the battle, found himself against the side of the tent. He rolled over so his face was toward the material. Seizing the heavy cloth in his beak, the Gryphon tried to either tear a hole in it or pull it free from the ground. There was no other way out.

A true tremor struck. He lost hold of the material but quickly regained control. Unfortunately, the tremor continued to grow in intensity. It was all he could do just to hang on.

Then, someone tugged on the tent from outside. The Gryphon was so surprised that he lost his grip again. A figure in a robe peered inside.

"Gryphon?" asked a not-so-silent voice. The quake rumbled on, making it hard to hear anything below a shout.

He looked up into the worn but ready countenance of the warlock Cabe Bedlam.

"It would be nice to occasionally meet under more pleasant circumstances," the imprisoned lionbird managed.

That brought the shadow of a smile to the visage of his old friend. Cabe started to crawl in, but the Gryphon shook his head. "Pull me out! There's Quel in there!"

Cabe glanced past him and nodded, likely having known already. The Gryphon was glad the tremor and the anxious work of the wolf raiders was keeping most others from noticing the battle yet, but was certain that that would change in the next few seconds. The warlock seized him and dragged the lionbird out. Then he pointed at the ropes around the Gryphon's arms and legs. The bonds loosened and fell to the ground. Rubbing his wrists, the former mercenary tried to remove the collar from around his throat. A sharp, immediate pain on each side of his neck made him cease his efforts.

"Let me." The warlock reached forward and touched the sides of the collar with his index fingers. There was a brief, reddish glow. Cabe took hold of the Aramite creation and pulled it apart.

"My gratitude." The Gryphon rubbed his sore neck. He noticed Cabe glancing at his maimed hand. "A gift of the war. A gift I blame on men such as Ivon D'Farany and Orril D'Marr."

"I've met the first. Is the second a shorter, younger officer?"

"The same. There's a blue man from the north of the empire that completes the set."

Cabe shook his head. "That one's dead. Would-be sorcerer. Killed himself with overconfidence, I think. These tremors are the result of that."

The Gryphon straightened, the news bringing him some little pleasure. Still, there was no time to savor the death. "Tremors aside, we cannot remain here. The battle will draw others."

"I have a spell. One that makes others ignore me unless I confront them. Let me include you under its shield."

Tired as he was, he only nodded in reply to the warlock's suggestion. Cabe blinked and, a moment later, smiled in satisfaction. Then, his face clouded again. "Now we have to return to Darkhorse and rescue him."

"Darkhorse?" The Gryphon was too ashamed to admit that he had been thinking of searching out D'Marr and his master. It seemed that the eternal was not the only one with an obsession.

"He's not far. Over there," the warlock continued, pointing. "I came across him first, but the trouble is I can't release him as easily as I did you. The harness device they have on him is linked to his very being. I've not seen its like before."

"I have. They call it a dragon harness in the empire. It saps the power and will of the minor drakes and makes them docile. The wolf raiders also use it on other, more intelligent creatures. I was fortunate that they thought the collar was sufficient. Evidently they wanted me hale and hearty for my prolonged execution."

"Can you release him?"

"I think so. I think I know how."

As he started in the direction that the mage had indicated, Cabe grabbed his arm. "Wait! There's something you should know about these tremors . . ."

"Tell me. Quick."

Condensing the story to only the most basic details, the tired spellcaster told of his meeting with the Crystal Dragon, the battle of wills between the Dragon

King and the keeper, Cabe's ouster from the drake lord's realm, and, lastly, his discovery and duel in the cavern.

"And as the hole grows more unstable, this region of Legar grows more unstable as well," the Gryphon commented. The quake had begun to subside, but both knew that the next would not be long in coming . . . and it would probably be the next one that they would have to fear the most. There was a point of no return that had to be fast approaching. "Is that everything you know?"

"All that's necessary." Cabe Bedlam was hiding something, something that concerned the Crystal Dragon, but the lionbird assumed that whatever it was, the warlock felt it was not important to their immediate danger. He knew Cabe well enough to trust that decision. Later, they would talk.

"We'll worry about—Dragon of the Depths!"

The ground exploded, tossing the two in opposite directions. Even as the Gryphon landed hard on his back, he knew what was happening. This was no tremor, but a much more localized threat.

Another Quel had burst through the rocky soil. The Gryphon continued to back away . . . only to find the earth behind him sprouting into a new mound. He rolled aside just as a second Quel tore his way through to the surface.

All around the Aramite encampment, the same thing was happening. Mounds formed, became craters. Bursting forth from each of those craters was a Quel. Wherever there was a trail of dirt coursing through the wolf raiders' camp, there sprouted the armored, hooting figure of one of the subterraneans. One by one and then a dozen by a dozen, they burrowed from the deep to the day. Many carried large war axes, but others were satisfied to use their claws. It mattered not where they rose, be it open ground or beneath a stack of weapons, the Quel came on and on and on. The Gryphon knew that there would be hundreds of them, hundreds of tawny, hulking behemoths whose sole intention was to rid themselves of the surface dwellers. Like an army of the unliving released by the Lords of the Undead, they kept coming.

The *sleepers* were not only awake; they were angry.

Few folk alive knew the full story, although the legend had spread across the Dragonrealm. Once, before the Dragon Kings and before the Seekers, the land had been ruled by the Quel. Their race had prospered for a time, but like so many others preceding them, the armadillolike creatures had watched their empire decay. The avian Seekers became dominant.

The Seekers and their immediate predecessors shared one common trait. They could not accept a rival for power. The bird folk sought to eliminate the last bastion of Quel domination, the peninsula. What the Seekers did instead, however, was unleash a spell so terrible that not only did it nearly succeed in driving the Quel to extinction but also the avians. The bird folk retired to what few rookeries remained to them and tried to rebuild their depleted population. They would never succeed in raising the numbers, for many of their females would die.

As for the Quel, they sought a different solution to the disaster. Their already inhospitable land ravaged and the neighboring regions little better, the survivors devised a plan by which the race, through high sorcery, would slumber until the day would come when they could reclaim their realm. The notion had been suggested even before all the destruction, but the Seekers' monstrous spell made its casting a necessity.

So the Quel race, excluding the sorcerers who had devised the spell, gathered into one of the largest of the underground chambers. The sorcerers and their apprentices would remain awake long enough to complete the grand spell and train successors, for there had to always be a handful to monitor events, keep the sleepers safe, and know how to awaken them when the glorious day came.

Something went terribly wrong, however, and those who knew how the spell worked perished in the process of casting it. It did put the race to sleep, but the secret of awakening them was lost. One other part did succeed; for each Quel who died, a successor was brought back to waking. There would be guardians, watchers, but none who understood what had happened. Over the centuries, the Gryphon knew, the Quel tried an endless variety of methods to bring their race back to life. They had never found success.

Until today.

*Trust Nimth and the wolf raiders to wake something as unsavory as the Quel race!* he thought. What would happen to the Dragonrealm with the Quel awake, the lionbird could not say. In his opinion, it could only be ill. He doubted that their long slumber had taught the overgrown armadillos the concept of sharing their world.

Around the Gryphon's vicinity alone more than a dozen Quel had already risen. He looked for Cabe but did not see the warlock. That was not too surprising. The Gryphon had been thrown back several yards. It was a credit to the lionbird's astonishing constitution that he was able to rise relatively unharmed, albeit more than a little dazed, by his flight and landing. Much to his dismay, though, the same Quel who had knocked him aside desired to change his good fortune. Heavy, taloned paws reached out for him.

He ducked and called out Cabe's name, fearful that his companion was unconscious or worse. There was no response. The rising din made it impossible to hear any one voice unless the speaker was within a few feet. He gave up just as the monster attacked again, this time slashing down with his fearsome claws. Again, the Gryphon evaded him, but barely.

There were more sounds of battle. The wolf raiders had recovered in swift fashion. Years of war had no doubt made the wolf raiders well practiced in everything. *They should thank me.*

He dodged yet another swipe from the leviathan's paws, all the while searching for something with which to combat the Quel. His reach was nothing near that of his adversary, so hand-to-hand was an option that the Gryphon wanted to reserve for last.

The lionbird found his weapon in the form of a pole tangled in the remains of a tent someone had been dismantling. He gazed at the deadly top of the staff with grim satisfaction. *Only the Aramites would make tent poles with pointed tips at the end.* Better still, the makeshift lance was made of good hardwood. Metal would have been best, but the Gryphon was not about to argue. He freed the pole, swung it around, and immediately jabbed at the Quel. This time, it was the beastman who backed away.

Taking advantage, he pressed the attack. The Quel hooted and took a defensive swipe at the wooden shaft.

It snapped in half.

Seizing the initiative, the massive creature stalked toward the Gryphon, all confidence now. Glancing around, the lionbird saw that there was no other object that he might use in place of the shattered pole. It was the lance or nothing.

In his long, bloody history, he had killed with much less.

The lionbird lunged. Surprised by the short figure's temerity, the Quel left himself open. The Gryphon, well aware of the weaknesses of the race, aimed for the not-so-armored neck.

Backed by his momentum, the jagged end of the pole went into the tender throat and up into the back of the head. The Quel squealed mournfully and struggled with the staff, but the wound was mortal. Wheezing and with blood flowing down over his torso, the digger finally slumped forward. The Gryphon barely had time to leap out of the way before several hundred pounds of dead behemoth crashed to the ground.

The behemoth's fall put an end to any other use of the pole, for the weight of the monster was enough to crush the staff into several small, meaningless pieces.

Only when his own battle was over did the Gryphon truly notice the growing intensity of the war around him. Men screamed or shouted or did both. The pain-wracked hoot of a Quel now and then pierced through the other noise. There was the constant clash of arms and orders cried out by the wolf raiders' officers. Above, he heard the roll of thunder, which would have made him believe it was going to rain, save that the rumbling never ended, just went on and on and on. Now and then, there was green lightning.

The earth began to shake again. From the severity of the new tremor, the lionbird knew that the end was very near. *The Quel's world must already be a maelstrom of destruction!*

*Which is _why_ they have come to the surface fighting,* replied a chilling, vaguely familiar voice in his head.

*I know you!* The Gryphon's eyes widened. His mouth went dry. He still recalled the details of the battle against the Ice Dragon.

*Then you know that I may be an ally.*

*Cabe said—*

The voice became defensive. *I have changed my mind. I will aid your efforts.*

"Because the Crystal Dragon's own domain is *also* at risk?" the Gryphon could not help asking out loud.

The lord of Legar did not reply to the question. Instead, he acted as if all were settled. *You may rest easy where Cabe Bedlam is concerned. The warlock will know his part to play in this. If all goes well, all will be ssssettled before long!*

The Gryphon did not miss the sibilance toward the end. He recalled Cabe mentioning the Dragon King's struggle with sanity, but was careful to shield the thought from the drake lord. At the moment he was willing to accept almost any help, even that from a mad creature like the Dragon King.

*What do you want of me?*

*You must free the demon steed. I will show you how the dogs' toy can be removed.*

*That's all? What about all this?*

The Dragon King's voice began to fade away. *We will ssspeak again when you have reached the ssstallion . . .*

"Come back here!" the lionbird squawked. It was no use; the link the Crystal Dragon had created was no more.

The drake lord had spoken of Cabe playing a part. He feared for the human, knowing from the past how Dragon Kings toyed with their "lessers." Still, the Crystal Dragon *had* helped save the land from his bone-numbing counterpart.

Whatever the case, the Gryphon had lost Cabe and pandemonium now reigned supreme over the wolf raider encampment. Freeing Darkhorse was the only path left to him. Cabe might even be there, despite the Crystal Dragon's hints.

He knew that he would have chosen to rescue the eternal, regardless of what else happened. Not only did he owe the shadow steed much, but, astonishing as it was to sometimes believe, Darkhorse was a friend. A loyal friend. The Gryphon could not have left him behind any more than he would have left behind Cabe or his own wife.

The Gryphon began wending his way toward the area where Darkhorse was supposedly being held. In each hand he carried a blade retrieved from the corpses of mangled Aramites. The path was not an easy one. Not only was the spell cast by the warlock no longer protecting him, but a pitched battle had spread across the entire camp. The Aramites were fighting back against the Quel with lances and arrows. There were even explosions on occasion. Oddest of all the things that he heard was a series of high-pitched notes being blown on battle horns. He did not understand what purpose that served until he spotted soldiers with battle horns working in conjunction with a row of lancers. The lancers would try to pen in two or three Quel. All the while, the hornmen would take turns playing as sharp and long a note as they could. To the Gryphon's shock, Quel within a certain range nearly fell to their knees as they tried to block the noise out. Weaponless and in aural agony, the subterraneans were easy prey for the lancers.

*You see all possible things in war.* The Aramites were holding their own, but it was a bloody fight. The lionbird felt no sympathy for either side as he wended his way through torn tents and twisted corpses of both human and Quel persuasion. He wondered if Lord D'Farany or the treacherous little D'Marr was among the dead. Likely not. *Evil like those two seems to live on until the very last.* If they escaped, he would have to hunt them down even if it meant scouring the Dragonrealm for them. Such men had a way of attracting new followers to replace those they lost. Even without an army, the keeper and his aide were dangerous to everyone.

The fighting, it soon turned out, worked in his favor. The wolf raiders and the Quel were too occupied with each other and the growing quake to pay him much mind. He *was* forced to do battle more than once, but none of his adversaries was equal to his skill, not even the second Quel he confronted. The latter he caught while the underdweller was still rising from the earth. It cost him one of his swords, the tip of the blade having become lodged between the natural plates in the creature's armor, but he left the dead Quel on his back, half of the immense body still below the surface.

Then at last he came upon Darkhorse.

The black stallion struggled weakly against the harness that kept him in check, but his efforts were next to nothing. The Gryphon studied the area and saw no guards, which was as he had hoped it would be. Why, after all, guard something that was helpless while monsters from the depths of the earth were invading the camp? Nonetheless, he kept a wary eye on his surroundings as he completed the last bit of the trek. One could not be too careful.

Darkhorse looked up. "Lord . . . Gryphon. Good . . . to see you about. Where is Cabe?"

"He is safe." What could he tell the shadow steed? That the warlock was supposedly a pawn of the Crystal Dragon? *Speaking of the same, where are you, Dragon King?* The lionbird would definitely need assistance with the harness. He could sense that its spell was far more complex than the ones he had seen before.

There was still no response from the Crystal Dragon. The Gryphon tried again, but still without success. All the while he tried also to follow the pattern of the spell that worked the harness.

"Can you not free me?"

"I should be able to, but it is going to take longer than I had hoped. I was *supposed* to have help."

Darkhorse did not pretend to comprehend the last statement, but he dipped his head in understanding to the first part. "I will do what I can, Lord Gryphon, from within. Perhaps with the two of us striking at it . . . at it, we shall have an easier time."

"I hope so." The Gryphon stumbled. It was becoming more and more troublesome to maintain his footing.

The shadow steed's eyes closed and his head slumped. Had not Darkhorse given him some warning, the lionbird would have been dismayed. Darkhorse had entered what was the equivalent of a light trance in the hope that he might be able to assist in his own release. Working with renewed confidence, the inhuman mage began retracing the lines of the spell. Somewhere he had missed the beginning thread. Somewhere . . .

He had it! The Gryphon used his magical senses to follow the thread. He saw how it wound around the collar of the harness and split off, but the new threads did not go to the bonds around Darkhorse's legs. Rather, they returned to the beginning. He probed a bit further and found where they reconnected. The secret of the spell started to unravel before his eyes.

Then, a thousand needles turned his nerves to jelly.

The pain was almost enough to make him black out, but the Gryphon had fought against pain in the past. He fell to his knees, then would allow himself to fall no farther.

From behind him, the lionbird finally heard the sound of boots on rock. This time, he was able to roll away before the weapon could strike him in the back. The roll became a crouch, albeit an unsteady one. Only then did the Gryphon realize that his sword was not with him. It now lay at the feet of his attacker, who he had not heard because of his intense study of the harness.

*I am getting old,* he thought. *But it looks as if I may not be getting much older!*

"I *knew* I'd find you around here. Even in the midst of all this chaos and danger, you'd come to aid a *friend*. How sweet."

Orril D'Marr drew circles in the air with his magical scepter, circles or perhaps bull's-eyes, for the design centered around the Gryphon's chest.

"You *can't* leave now. Time to finish things, birdman. Time to die. After all, your son is *waiting* for you."

# XVII

CABE RECALLED BEING thrown aside when the Quel had burst from the ground. What he could not recall were the several seconds after that. Cabe only knew that he opened his eyes to the sight of a squalid whiteness. It took him several seconds more to discover that he had become entangled in a tent. The befuddled mage fought his way out of the canvas, then hurriedly looked all around him to see if he was in immediate danger.

He was not. The battle had been carried away from where he was. The Quel who had surprised the duo was nowhere in sight.

Neither was the Gryphon.

Cabe began to suspect that he had been unconscious for more than a minute. He reached back behind his head, which proved to be a painful mistake, for the warlock made use of his injured arm. That led to another few seconds while he struggled to fight the new agony.

*I can do nothing about the arm, but I have dealt with your head injury.*

"Wha—?" Cabe started, then clamped his mouth shut. *Why did you do it?*

There were actually two questions in that one. The voice, the Crystal Dragon, answered both. *You struck your head on a piece of wood in the tent. The wound was severe enough that it demanded immediate treatment. I need you as whole as possible for what we musssst do.*

The Dragon King had chosen to aid him after all. It was not too surprising to the spellcaster, not when the Crystal Dragon's own kingdom must certainly be threatened. Cabe was careful to avoid any comment or thought about the Crystal Dragon's earlier reluctance. The warlock needed a solution and it appeared that only the lord of Legar had one.

At least, he *hoped* that the Crystal Dragon had a solution.

"But the Gryphon—"

*Isss on his way to free the demon steed. He knowsss what your tassssk is to be.*

*My task?* the warlock asked in silence.

*There issss only one force capable of driving the evil of Nimth back to where it belongsss! That isss the evil itsssself! With the sphere and the Quel platform no more, there isss only one object with ties ssstrong enough to the cursssed sorcery of Nimth to be of usssse! We must have it!*

Only one object. Cabe could think of only one, but surely not *that*. "You don't mean Lord D'Farany's talisman?"

The silence that greeted his question told him that the keeper talisman was exactly what the Crystal Dragon meant. The warlock shook his head. There had to be something else.

*There is nothing else! It mussst be the tooth!*

Cabe stood his ground. *Even if I can find him in all of this, he'll never willingly give me that thing!*

*I shall do what I can to aid you. I promissse you, Cabe Bedlam, that if there were another way, I would take it! Thisss will either sssave all . . . or it will put an end to usss asss well!*

Not a statement evoking confidence, the spellcaster thought wryly. However, his link with the Dragon King was strong enough that he knew the other was not lying. The talisman was the only chance they had.

First, though, Cabe had to find the tooth and take it from a sorcerer more than capable of killing him with it.

*He isss to your right at the far end of the camp. I will guide you, but you mussst hurry!*

Hurry he did, but not before he first recast the spell making him unnoticeable to those around him. It might or might not work in the midst of all this anarchy, but Cabe felt safer. An invisible shield would have protected him better, but he wanted to save himself for the confrontation with the Aramite commander. The peculiarities of sorcery demanded that while the power was drawn from without, the will and strength of the mage was often paramount to maintaining many of the spells. He did not pretend to understand it; Cabe only knew that those were the rules.

Did a keeper have to abide by the same rules?

His path was surprisingly clear of violence, despite all he heard and saw around him. There was still no way of knowing whether either force had gained the upper hand. A Quel died with three bolts in her neck; the Aramites were quick to learn the weaknesses of their much larger foes. However, the Quel were learning, too. Those that did not have weapons tore from the earth massive hunks of rock, which they threw with uncanny accuracy at their smaller, quicker opponents. Cabe came across one body whose face and upper torso were crushed beneath a rock probably as heavy as the warlock was. He had always been aware of the astonishing strength of the diggers, but this new reminder struck home.

In some places, the threat was not from either side, but from the land itself. Crevices had opened up throughout the area and more were opening every minute. Cabe saw one man plummet to his death as the surface under him abruptly caved in. The warlock himself had to leap across growing ravines more than once. Only the Dragon King's guidance kept him on his course.

Then, amid the fighting armies and the trembling earth, Cabe saw Lord D'Farany. The keeper and three other raiders, all officers, were attempting to seize control of a number of horses penned up nearby, but were having limited success. Two animals were nearly saddled, but the other horses were too over-wrought and fought the wolf raiders.

D'Farany was mounting one of the two animals readied for flight.

Cabe started to run. He wanted to be as close as possible before he at-tempted a spell in this chaos, but his time was limited. The Aramite com-mander looked more than ready to leave his men behind if they did not hurry. Evidently Lord D'Farany had decided that the Quel attack was too long of a delay to risk. Even if his men defeated the underdwellers, which was not a cer-tainty, the time lost would be too great. This entire region was heading for total collapse.

In his anxiousness to cut the distance between the keeper and himself, the warlock did not watch his path closely enough.

He tripped over something large and moving, falling face first into the inhos-pitable soil with a jarring crash.

Groaning, Cabe looked up, fearful that the Aramite commander had already fled. What he saw was not the wolf raider, but rather a mouthful of jagged, yellowed teeth. The teeth were in the wide-open jaws of a monstrosity the size of a small dog, but more rodentlike in appearance. It had positively the ugliest countenance that the bruised mage had ever seen, and that included such crea-tures as the Quel or ogres. It looked hungry. Very, very hungry.

He tried to roll aside as it leapt, but the horror twisted in the air, and as Cabe turned onto his back, it fell upon his chest. Cabe gasped as all the air went out of him. The warlock was barely able to get his hands up in time to keep the beast from his throat. It snapped at him and the foul breath was almost enough to kill him, teeth or no.

His arm was in agony and a second snap by the thing added to the pain in the form of a shallow wound. He was able to push it back just enough so that the strong jaws could not keep hold. The viciousness of the beast was so aston-ishing that Cabe hardly had time to concentrate. Twice he failed and both times the monstrosity's horrid maw moved a little closer to his throat.

With a last desperate push, Cabe finally managed to put the ratlike beast at arm's length. Ignoring the throbbing pain, the warlock glared at his catch.

It squealed. Squealed in fear. He allowed himself a slight smile. It was nice to have something afraid of *him* for once. Despite its mournful squeal, however, he did not stay his course. The punishment had been chosen. The beast twisted and turned in his grip and as it did, it shrank. It shrank to the size of a rabbit, then a robbin redbreast, and then the rat it so resembled. Even that was not good enough. Cabe did not stop until his attacker was no larger than an acorn. At that point, he closed a fist around it and, stretching back his good arm, *threw* the vermin as far away as he could manage. The tiny beast vanished into the fog.

Cabe turned back, fearful that he was too late, but he found that Lord D'Farany had *not* yet departed. In fact, the keeper was looking in his direction and not smiling in the least.

The warlock searched his mind for the presence of the Crystal Dragon but could not reestablish the link. The Dragon King had seemingly abandoned him at the worst possible instant.

D'Farany spurred his steed and guided the animal slowly toward his enemy. He made no attempt at a spell but the warlock sensed the power flowing about the wolf raider, power whose source lay in a pouch at the hip of the Aramite. Behind him came the three officers, one astride and two on foot. *They*, unlike their master, were armed and ready to kill.

"You should be dead. Like I once was. But I came back to life and so have you. I think you must be, in your own way, as tenacious a foe as the Gryphon," D'Farany remarked, the lipless smile just barely coming into play.

"In some ways, more so. Is this raider loyalty I see before me? You weren't long in abandoning your men, were you?"

The officers took his slight as the final insult and moved to cut him down. Lord D'Farany raised a hand, halting them in midstride. "I do not abandon my men. I abandon wars that are lost and I have, in the past, abandoned sanity, but I do not abandon my men. I have the power to save them right here." He patted the pouch. "And as long as I have it near, I can do *anything.*"

The earth tried to swallow Cabe up. Literally. The ravine that opened had boulders for teeth and a sinuous, seeking column of clay that acted as a hunting tongue. Cabe had wondered if the keeper could control his power even when the talisman was not in his hands. Now he knew, although the coming of that new knowledge had almost been a second too late.

Yet, the warlock had been expecting the worst and so he was ready. Cabe rose above the gaping mouth and beyond the searching tongue. He felt D'Farany work his power. The tongue, like an earthen snake, followed after him, growing to match whatever height the dark-haired mage dared.

A violent wind turned Cabe's flight into a spinning terror. He first thought it was the Aramite's work until a chance glimpse showed that D'Farany, too, was having trouble controlling his sorcery. While the warlock was finding it nigh impossible to direct his flight, the wolf raiders were now having to do combat with the animated creation of their master. The column of clay darted in and out, first matching blows with the two officers on foot, then trying to seize either rider.

Nimth was overwhelming all of them.

*Dragon King, where are you?*

*I . . . sssspell . . . it will . . .* The message in his mind was meaningless garbage. Cabe struggled to force his will upon the spell he had started. In a sense, he finally succeeded, for suddenly the startled mage was plummeting earthward.

Cabe was unable to keep himself aloft, but in the last second, his will was strong enough to create a cushion of air, making his landing only a bit harsh. Lord D'Farany's creation did not seize him when he touched ground, which he assumed meant that it still fought with the Aramites. That proved true enough. In fact, the serpentlike appendage had wrapped itself around one of the horses, throwing the officer riding the steed to the ground, and was even now dragging the poor creature kicking into its maw.

Two soldiers pursued the trapped animal, but Lord D'Farany barked an order, causing them to backstep. Shrieking, the steed was pulled into the magical jaws. As the hapless mount disappeared from view, the mouth simply vanished. There was no sign of the ravine and no sign of the unfortunate beast.

Seemingly satisfied, D'Farany then pointed at the third man, the one who had been thrown off the horse, and said something unintelligible that the warlock assumed was an order to see to the condition of the injured officer. The two remaining officers obeyed without hesitation.

The keeper glanced in his direction. One hand went into the pouch where the talisman was kept. Lord D'Farany wanted a more direct control over his spells. The talisman was useful as a focus, but Cabe knew it was also a crutch of sorts to a sorcerer's imagination. Those who relied on talismans concentrated too much sometimes on what was in front of them, for that was where their toys were focused. That meant that on occasion they left their other defenses weak.

So he hoped.

The warlock did not wait for his counterpart to retrieve the tooth. Quite suddenly, there were ten Cabes all about the area. Each one moved with purpose, but not the same purpose as his twins. Some stood where they were while others moved toward the keeper and his men.

Among the latter was the true Cabe Bedlam, who now stood far to the right of his previous position. It was a risky spell, as all were in this place, but it had worked like perfection. The false Cabes moved their hands about in mystical passes that actually had no meaning. Creation and control of the illusions were actually not a great strain for him. They required much less power than true conjuration. Now he only had to hope that his adversary fell prey to it.

D'Farany did pause, losing a precious second or two while he studied his multiplied opponent. Then he pulled free the talisman and pointed it at one of the farther images. Out of the corner of his eyes, Cabe watched the duplicate ripple, then fade away. He hurried his pace. Just a little closer . . .

Swinging his arm around, the keeper brought the talisman to play on one image after another. His steed, made jittery by the madness around him, struggled with the Aramite, slowing D'Farany's work another critical few seconds. The warlock edged closer, glancing now and then at the other raiders. The two officers were still bent over the third, who would not be rising soon, if at all, from the looks of him. Cabe did not fear the two remaining. Only their master was a danger.

Then it was that Lord D'Farany's deadly talisman was pointed directly at him . . . only to continue on until the keeper had fixed it on the illusionary Cabe to the warlock's right.

The Aramite had assumed that one of the ten must be his adversary. He was wrong. Cabe walked among his duplicates, but to all eyes but his own, he was not there. Not unless they looked close. Cabe had relied on the tremors and his duplicates to draw attention from himself. Meanwhile, the same spell that had allowed him to enter the wolf raider encampment now allowed him to move toward the keeper. As long as D'Farany had other things to occupy his sight, he would not see the warlock. Of course, there were limitations. The nearer Cabe moved, the more chance there was that the Aramite sorcerer's will would overcome the spell. Had he tried to actually reach Lord D'Farany and pull him from the saddle, it was likely that Cabe would have been attacked long before he was close enough to do anything. Fortunately, he had no intention of getting *that* close.

At least, not at first.

He reached his destination just before D'Farany, still battling his anxious steed, focused the talisman on the last of Cabe's duplicates. The keeper was having trouble maintaining aim, which was what the warlock had hoped for. It gave him just enough time to prepare and then to unleash his own assault.

The ground before the nervous stallion exploded in one bright, raucous burst after another. The bursts of light appeared all about the steed, growing noisier with each consecutive explosion. Already flighty, the stallion could take no more of the happenings around it. It bucked and reared, trying to escape the explosions.

Lord D'Farany fought in vain to remain in the saddle. He first slid back, then fell forward as he tried to grab hold of the saddle with the hand not clutching the carved tooth. In the process of grasping, the keeper lost his hold on the reins.

Not daring to pause, the warlock turned on the remaining pair of wolf raiders, who even now rose to aid their master. Cabe dealt with them in the simplest of manners, using a tiny portion of his skill to raise two heavy stones and fling them toward the duo. Neither man had a chance to deflect the oncoming projectiles. Helms or not, the stones struck with enough force to knock both officers senseless.

Unable to collect his thoughts enough to control his beast, Lord D'Farany was finally thrown off his horse. The fall was not as harsh a one as Cabe had originally hoped, but the bucking stallion did manage to toss the keeper almost exactly where Cabe had wanted.

*Now* he leapt.

The determined spellcaster fell on top of his counterpart. D'Farany, still dazed by the fall, was unable to prevent Cabe from getting a grip on his wrists. Only when he realized that his precious talisman was no longer in his hand did the keeper truly begin to struggle. He did not even attempt a spell, although perhaps his kind needed their tokens on their person. The only magic that the warlock could recall D'Farany using on his own was when he had summoned the talisman to him and that might very well be only possible because of his link to the thing in the first place. There was too much that Cabe did not know about Aramite sorcerers.

Cabe, searching while he fought, saw the object of both their quests only a yard or so away. To his dismay, it was inching its way toward the two. Recalling how the tooth had flown to the hands of the Aramite sorcerer, he realized that as long as the keeper could think, D'Farany could summon the talisman to him. Only the fact that he battled with Cabe kept him from already retrieving his cursed trinket. A minute or two and he *would* control it again.

That time the warlock would not allow him. This close to each other, he, at least, knew how risky it was to cast any sort of potent spell. However, there *was* one more illusion he planned on trying. He only hoped that his imagination and the Gryphon's descriptions in a long-ago letter would be enough.

Cabe's visage melted, becoming the dark, murky outline of a great and terrible lupine creature with burning eyes and a toothy maw capable of taking in whole a man's head.

Lord D'Farany's face grew blank, then twisted into a horrific mask of reverence for the beast he saw above him.

Releasing one of the keeper's wrists, Cabe formed a fist and punched D'Farany in the jaw with as much force as he could muster. His hand ached for a time after, but the results were well worth the pain.

"Sometimes the direct way is the best way," he muttered to the unconscious keeper. Only against a man such as D'Farany would an illusion like the one Cabe had cast succeed. The Gryphon had described his meeting with the Aramites' rabid deity, the lupine Ravager, spending some length on the ghostly image of the monster and the devotion the keepership displayed for their dark-some god. D'Farany had reacted exactly as the warlock had calculated. A good thing, too; he would have been at a loss as to what to do next if his trick had failed.

*The talisman!* said a sudden, familiar voice in his head. *There is little time left to undo the damage!*

"If I'd had a little more help with this," the warlock snarled, climbing over D'Farany, "I would've been done earlier."

*I mussst conssserve my sssstrength!*

"What about mine?"

*The talisman!* the inner voice roared.

*I have it!* he sent back, more than a little bitter. Out loud, Cabe asked, "What now?"

*Now,* came the oddly hesitant but unusually controlled voice of the Dragon King. *Now you must hold it together at all costs. You must not allow it to shatter, lest all we manage to do is unleash further decay and chaos from the realm of my past!*

That sounded like nothing Cabe desired to be a part of, but he nonetheless held the talisman tight. "What are you going to do?"

*The keeper's toy is the only thing still with a link to Nimth and the dark power of that wretched world. It is not one I would trust long to survive the effort, but it is all we have. I will take the power of Nimth and use it as only one born of the Vraad could. I will take that power and bring peace to my realm . . . peace or death.*

"But—" Cabe's protest died on his lips as he felt the first surge of power flow into and then out of the talisman. Almost immediately he understood what the Dragon King had meant about holding the talisman together. There was so much energy, so much of the *wrong* magic being forced through it that the tooth was being stretched beyond its abilities. The Crystal Dragon was using it as more than just a receptacle or a focus or even both together and the strain was tearing it apart.

The Crystal Dragon's voice grew indifferent, distant. *Let the power of Nimth at last do something worthy. Let Legar hear its power . . . and then let Nimth be silent forever!*

From all around, there came a sound, a piercing sound that suddenly simply *was.* It was powered from the great forces pouring through the hole between worlds, but it was transmitted from all around. The storms, the wind, and the wild, drifting magic gave way to a trembling. It was not a quake. Cabe could only think of it as the entire land *vibrating* and the faster the frequency of that vibration, the greater the intensity of the sound.

*Keep your mind on the talisman! Let the ssssound drift away! I shall—*

The deafening noise sent the warlock to his knees, but he did not lose his control. It was not because of the knowledge that the spell would fade unfinished, but because he knew that to do so would mean his death. He only hoped the spell's success would not mean the same.

Then, coherent thought was no longer possible. There was only the sound. The damning sound.

AS CABE FOUGHT against the verlok, the Gryphon's own battle commenced. It began with circling, as the two wary opponents sized up each other. The lion-bird did so in silence; Orril D'Marr was the opposite.

"When I found the tent in ruins and the bodies of the beasts and guards lying there—but not yours—I was furious. To have caught you at last and then have you slip away . . . it was just too much. I've waited too long!"

The Gryphon glanced over D'Marr's back at Darkhorse, who remained motionless. There would be no help there, not that he wanted any. D'Marr was his and his alone. As much as the young officer wanted him, the Gryphon wanted the wolf raider more. Even though practicality was screaming that escape was the only option for either of them, neither would have stepped back now.

D'Marr's scepter glistened as Legar once had. The Aramite made two jabs with it, always withdrawing before the Gryphon had a chance to grab the deadly little tool by its handle. He was aware of how useless his power was against the wolf raider while D'Marr carried the mace. That was not a great disappointment to the Gryphon. Demion's death demanded a more personal struggle. Orril D'Marr had to be made to know what it meant to kill one of the Gryphon's own. Besides, he did not want to trust to sorcery too much in this place. A thing like the scepter might work here, but spells cast might kill the caster instead.

Around them, the earth shook and crevices opened. Green lightning still played with the plain. Neither fighter cared in the least. They had come almost to the point where interference by anyone, be it Quel, wolf raider, or one of the Gryphon's allies, would result in a bizarre alliance between the duelists against those interlopers. Only the rampages of the realm itself stood any chance at all of coming between them.

"Would you like your sword, birdman? Perhaps asking for it politely will gain you something." The Aramite's visage was still damningly indifferent. His eyes were not.

The Gryphon displayed his talons. "I have these. They are all I need for you."

"Well have the sword, anyway," D'Marr remarked, kicking it toward his foe.

Puzzled and wary, but knowing the sword *would* cancel out the advantage of length the wolf raider presently had, the former mercenary retrieved the blade. There was no lunge from D'Marr, merely that shadow of a smile. The lionbird had met few men who could unbalance him the way that this one did. Nothing about the Aramite could be trusted, not even the way he breathed. Still, now the Gryphon had a weapon he could make use of without coming dangerously close to the scepter.

"Whenever you are ready, D'Marr."

The wolf raider laughed . . . and brought his mace into play while the Gryphon was still marveling over the peculiar reaction from the normally diffident officer. He only discovered the reason for that laugh when his blade came up to parry the attack. As the two weapons struck each other, Orril D'Marr pulled his back, bringing the head of the scepter into contact with the metal blade.

The Gryphon was unable to stifle his scream.

He dropped the sword and stumbled away as quickly as he could, all the while keeping blurred eyes on the position of the Aramite. D'Marr was not pursuing him, however. He was simply smiling at the Gryphon's misfortune and at the success of his trick.

Compared to this present attack, the blow he had taken while engrossed in the effort of freeing Darkhorse had been only a bee sting. The lionbird could not stop shaking. His head pounded and his legs threatened to fold.

"That's a setting somewhere in the middle, birdman," smirked the raider officer. The true Orril D'Marr was coming to the surface at last. "Didn't you know that all I have to do is touch something you're touching? Could be metal. Could be cloth. If you wear it or carry it, you'll feel the mace's bite. My predecessor was wonderful with detail like that."

"What—what happened to him?"

"He was slow to realize my potential, but then the accident took care of that oversight." Even if the raider's words had not been clear enough in their meaning, the Gryphon would have understood what D'Marr was saying. The path to promotion in the Aramite empire was littered with the bodies of those not quick enough to know which of their brethren wanted their throats. It was encouraged; after all, it was the law of the Pack. The better officers would weed out the lessers.

Before him stood a prime example of the former. The tradition of blind obedience was for the lower ranks, the line soldiers, and those you feared enough to serve.

D'Marr gave his scepter a lazy swing. "Shall we have another go at it?"

The Aramite thrust with the mace, a maneuver that would have been foolish if not for the horrific ability of the head. Dodging aside, the Gryphon utilized his exceptional reflexes and slashed out at his adversary's weapon arm. Talons tore at ebony armor to no avail. The officer's armor was of a grade much higher than that of a common guard. Nonetheless, D'Marr backed away, aware that he was growing just a bit too careless.

Still, under the oncoming pressure of the scepter, the Gryphon was pushed farther and farther back. Each step was a precarious venture in itself, for not only was the ground increasingly uneven, but the intensity of the tremor had become so great that even on the flattest surface it would have been a challenge to maintain his footing. Even Orril D'Marr, working with a vast advantage over the lionbird, was finding it difficult to keep steady.

"Why don't you come to me, bird? Are you part chicken? Is that what all those feathers mean?" The Aramite officer pretended to lunge. "Are you going to prove as much a coward as that stripling of yours?"

If he hoped to goad the Gryphon into a frenzy as he had nearly succeeded in doing the last time he had mentioned Demion, the wolf raider was mistaken. For the memory of his son, the lionbird was trying his best to keep his instincts in check. They would have their uses when the moment came, but they could not be allowed control.

At that moment, his foot came down upon a small crack in the earth, a crack just wide enough to catch the heel. The Gryphon weaved back and forth, trying to regain his balance. Orril D'Marr charged at him, the scepter ablaze in hideous glory.

It was not the Gryphon who ended up falling. By dropping to a crouch, he managed to just barely stabilize himself. The eager raider, on the other hand, stepped on a portion of ground that that tremor had loosened but not broken up. D'Marr's heavy boot was more than enough impetus; a good piece of earth gave way, scattering about, and the Aramite went sliding down on his back.

It was all the feathered fury needed. He turned his crouch into a leap at the throat of the murderer of his son. Gasping, D'Marr twisted away, but not quite enough to escape untouched. The Gryphon went crashing into the harsh soil, but the claws of his maimed hand caught the side of the raider's neck. D'Marr shouted out in agony. The smell of blood reached the Gryphon and he felt the wetness spread down his fingers.

There was no time to savor the strike, for the Aramite was far from dead. Orril D'Marr continued to roll until he was facing his adversary again. Despite the fall, he had kept hold of the scepter, which he immediately swung at the sprawled figure beside him. The Gryphon blocked it with his arm, careful to meet the scepter at the handle. He tried to twist his hand around and grab hold, but D'Marr was having none of that. The wolf raider scrambled back, then rose to his feet. Blood was seeping from twin scars running along the side of his throat. The smile had been replaced by growing fury and perhaps a hint of fear.

Standing, the lionbird showed the raider officer his bloodsoaked fingers.

"The first taste, D'Marr. The first taste of my revenge. I will not stop until the skin on your face has been peeled away the same way one would peel away the hide off of a dead wolf. I doubt if there will be as much call for your hide, but I know two, counting myself, who will prize the experience."

"I'll see your head mounted on a wall first, birdman!" The wolf raider came at him again.

The Gryphon ducked the initial swing, then slashed at D'Marr as the raider's arm went by. Again, his talons caught on the armor, but he pulled away before the Aramite could swing the scepter back. D'Marr managed to kick him in the leg. The Aramite underestimated the lionbird's strength, however, and instead of sending his foe to the ground, he almost lost his own balance.

The Gryphon leapt once more. Orril D'Marr was not able to bring the mace down in time. The two collided and fell, locked in mortal combat. D'Marr would not release the scepter and the Gryphon had to put all his effort into maintaining a three-fingered grip on that arm. They rolled on for several yards with first the lionbird on top, then D'Marr, and so on.

It was the sound that almost put an end to the battle for both of them. A high, agonizing sound that cut through the ear and the mind. The duo separated, each seeking only to cover their ears and save their sanity. The Gryphon barely noticed that the earth no longer shook, but rather vibrated, a somewhat different and puzzling movement.

Orril D'Marr had thrown off his helmet and was rummaging in his belt pouches for something. He had dropped the mace, but the Gryphon was at first unable to act. It was all he could do to stand. A part of his mind pushed him on, though, reminding him that if he died Troia would come next. She would face Orril D'Marr on her own. For her and the sake of the child yet unborn, he could not allow that.

He took a step forward . . . and almost lost his life. Cracked and broken by the tremors, the cavern-riddled earth of Legar could little stand up to the constant vibration now occurring. Whole areas of the surface began to collapse into the underground system the Quel had established over the centuries. The ground before him gave way just as his foot came down. Only his reflexes saved him. As it was, the Gryphon lost his balance and slipped. His legs dangled over the new ravine for a time, but with effort he was able to pull himself back up.

A hard boot struck him in the side.

Orril D'Marr stood above him, a peculiar set of coverings over his ears. The Gryphon recalled the wolf raider speaking of working with explosive powders; D'Marr must have designed the coverings for his projects. It was clear that they did not completely filter out the sound, but they worked well enough for the Aramite to move about without having to hold his ears.

Unable to concentrate enough to shapeshift, the lionbird could do nothing about his own predicament. It was a wonder he was not deaf by now. Part of his magical makeup, no doubt. Still, deafness was the least of his worries. The greatest was that D'Marr once more had his foul toy in hand and this time he looked ready to try its strongest touch.

Knowing he could not be heard over the horrible sound, the wolf raider leaned over his shaking adversary and mouthed out an arrogant farewell. That proved to be his fatal mistake. Despite his knowledge of the Gryphon, Orril D'Marr was evidently unaware of the stamina and resilience of the lionbird. He thought the Gryphon too overwhelmed to have any fight left in him.

That was just the way the Gryphon wanted it.

His spinning roll caught the wolf raider's legs. The Aramite officer went down under him, but did not lose the magical mace. The Gryphon easily caught the awkward strike that D'Marr tried, then began to bend the raider's arm back, bringing the scepter toward its master's face. Although he felt he must soon black out, the former mercenary pushed with all his might. It was time for Orril D'Marr to understand what his victims had gone through.

The ground shifted, sinking lower on one side of the duelists.

Cursing, the weakening lionbird tried one last effort. Throwing his full weight into it, he forced the scepter into the wolf raider's snarling visage. D'Marr, however, twisted aside and the jeweled head went past his face. The snarl became a smile.

The tip of the scepter grazed the raider's shoulder.

Lying as he was half on his adversary, a prick of pain coursed through the lionbird, but it was little compared to what D'Marr must have felt. So very close, the Gryphon could not help but hear the scream. The Aramite had said that armor would be of no help and he had been all too correct.

Fueled by his agony, the wolf raider managed to throw the Gryphon off of him. He also succeeded in dropping the scepter as well. The ground tipped even more, but Orril D'Marr hardly noticed. He was still hunched together, trying to recover.

The lionbird had given his all, but now he realized it was time to get away. The area was collapsing and it would do no good to die here if he could ensure otherwise. Half stumbling and half crawling, he abandoned the Aramite to his fate. If they both survived, the Gryphon would be more than happy to renew the struggle. Staying here was simple foolishness.

BEHIND HIM, D'MARR recovered enough to realize his danger. He searched for the mace, found it, and hobbled after his enemy. When he had seen that the tip was coming toward him, he had tried to lower the weapon's intensity. It was all that had saved him. Now, though, D'Marr let the full power of the scepter rise again. One way or another, he would kill the birdman. He would.

ABOUT TO PASS out, the Gryphon rolled over and saw the wolf raider stumbling toward him. He also saw the ground just beyond his own feet begin to crack. The lionbird dragged himself back a bit more and watched in fascination at the tableau that unfolded before him.

Orril D'Marr obviously felt the earth collapsing, for he started to run toward his foe. Still suffering from the effects of his own toy, the Aramite stumbled and fell to his knees. He dropped the mace again and as he fumbled with the handle, trying to get a grip, the ground he knelt upon finally broke completely loose.

The last glimpse the Gryphon had of Orril D'Marr was the image of the wolf raider, his face composed one final time into that bland mask, raising the scepter to throw at his cursed enemy.

Then . . . there was only a cloud of thick dust as tons of rocky earth crumbled into the vast crater.

*Demion* . . . he managed to think. *Demion . . . he is no more, my son. The monster is dead.*

He settled back, willing to let oblivion take him, when a darkness covered him from head to foot. There was blissful silence and none of the oppressive heat of Legar. Too weak to wonder, the Gryphon merely accepted everything.

A stentorian voice broke the silence. "I . . . will protect you as . . . well as I can, Lord Gryphon! I cannot . . . promise you . . . but we may survive this yet!"

At the moment he did not care. All he wanted to do was sleep. Sleep for the first time in almost two days . . . and sleep *well* for the first time since his son's death.

# XVIII

NO PART OF Legar was left untouched by the sound, yet just beyond the interior edge of the peninsula, the region of Esedi and the kingdom of Zuu in particular heard nothing. Those who might have been curious enough about the fog to attempt an excursion into Legar would find themselves turning away in great unease. Even the agents of Lord D'Farany who attempted to return to the camp could not find their courage. Instead, they scattered northward, suddenly certain that it would be wise *never* to return to the inhospitable land of Legar.

Within Legar, the spell of the Crystal Dragon did its work. The Quel, whose hearing was far more sensitive than that of most other creatures, including humans, fell to the ground hooting in dire agony. The wolf raiders were unable to take advantage of their misery, for they, too, suffered from the terrible, piercing noise. Several Aramites simply stumbled off of the edge of newly formed cliffs and plummeted into ravines and craters. A few of the Quel did the same, but the pain was so great most of the tawny behemoths simply crouched on the ground and tried to block out the sound. Tunneling into the earth was no escape, for the vibrations collapsed passages with the ease that a foot could crush an ant. The shells of the Quel were strong, but not *that* strong, and even if they survived, they could only hold their breath for so long. In truth, there *was* no escape.

Cabe, almost oblivious to the world, still struggled to hold the Aramite talisman together. *Sssssoon . . . the Crystal Dragon had promised. Sssssooon it will be at an end.*

There was something strange and frightening happening to the mind linked to his, but Cabe had little opportunity to pursue the matter. All that was important was to keep the tooth from being destroyed . . . and keep *himself* from being destroyed while he was at it.

Around the camp, the Quel began to die. The sound shook their very being, destroying them through their ears. Enhanced by sorcery, it was an inescapable hunter, for there was nothing on the surface of Legar sufficient to dampen its intensity.

On and on and on it went. The fates of the Gryphon and Darkhorse concerned Cabe, but by this point he knew that nothing could be done if it had not been done already. The Crystal Dragon had not warned him of the enormity of what he was doing and for that Cabe was angry. Recriminations would have to come later, however.

That was providing that *later* actually came.

*The first . . . ssstep isss complete! Now, the time hasss . . . come to . . . clossse forever the . . . portal!*

"Ungh!" Cabe Bedlam's entire body shook as the flow of power suddenly reversed itself. He had thought that the strain had been great before, but so awesome was it now that he almost lost control. For a single second, the talisman was beyond his ability to suppress. Then, just before it would have shattered, the warlock succeeded in regaining control. Sweat soaked his body. The pain in his arm was laughable in comparison to what wracked his system now. He was certain that he was going to die, yet somehow the weary mage held on.

Slowly, ever so slowly, the vibrations lessened. The sense of wrongness in the air, the sense of Nimth's intrusion, weakened.

*Almost . . .* Cabe thought, trying to encourage himself. *Almost!*

A long, spindly hand *tore* the tooth from his grasp.

Jerked back into full consciousness, Cabe's first reaction was to scream as pure sound invaded his mind. He clamped his hands over his ears, which did little to lessen the agony, and turned to see what had happened.

Plool, looking not at all affected by the spell, scampered merrily beyond Cabe's reach. The macabre figure held the tooth high. His broad-rimmed hat was pushed back, revealing a V-shaped smile and bright, crystalline eyes that flashed in triumph. Whether he had simply stolen the talisman for the sake of his own survival or had thought that he could use it to turn the Dragonrealm into another Nimth, only the Vraad knew. Plool finally stopped, folded his legs underneath him, and, floating, tossed the tooth from one hand to the other.

Cabe knew he shouted, but not even he could hear his warning.

The Vraad lowered the talisman and his unsettling orbs narrowed in intense concentration. Tendrils of fog stretched toward him like children seeking their father. An aura formed around Plool. The thing in his hand glowed so bright it blinded.

The tooth exploded.

No longer held in check by either Cabe or the Dragon King, the power filling the talisman had at last stretched the boundaries of D'Farany's toy beyond its limits. Possibly the Vraad had not completely understood the dangers of the spell when he had stolen the talisman from Cabe. The sorcery of Nimth did not always follow the same rules as the sorcery of the Dragonrealm; the warlock's sparse knowledge of the other world included that bit of information at least. Unfortunately, such knowledge was too late to save the eager Plool.

Raw energy flowed over the Vraad and for a short instant, Plool resembled a deflating sack. So horrified was the warlock that he almost forgot the pain shaking him apart. Plool did not scream; he did not even appear to have time to notice his destruction. The madcap figure simply collapsed into an ungodly heap that, thankfully, dissipated immediately after. The spell that the Crystal Dragon had begun had been designed to absorb and make use of Nimthian magic. Perhaps Plool had literally been too much a creature of that foul sorcery.

With the Vraad gone, the realization of what Plool had done occurred to the pain-stricken mage. The talisman was gone and there was no way of completing the spell. There might not even be a way of dousing the horrendous noise.

*WARLOCK!* the voice burst through the noise. *YOURRRR POWERRR I MUSSSST HAVVVE! WE ARRRE ALMOSSST THERE!*

He did not argue. To tell the truth, Cabe did not have the strength to argue. At that moment, the Crystal Dragon could have had anything he wanted from him. Cabe only wanted the screaming to stop.

It did. Just like that. The fog burned away before his very eyes, returning the rule of day to the blazing sun. The ground ceased vibrating. It just *stopped*. All was as it had been before the coming of the wolf raiders . . . save that now there were new ravines and valleys all over the peninsula and bodies decorated the new landscape wherever one looked.

Cabe Bedlam crumpled to the ground, suddenly very much drained. He recalled the shouted plea for his power, his strength. The Dragon King had borrowed power through him to finish what they had begun, but he had almost used Cabe too much. To draw so much sorcerous energy into the warlock and through him use it had nearly burned Cabe out in the process. He was thrilled that they had finished the grand spell, but he truly wished that there had been another way.

Still, whatever the human spellcaster had suffered, the Crystal Dragon must have suffered more. He had guided the spell throughout. It was his will more than Cabe's that had been pressed. Knowing how fine a line the drake lord's mind had treaded before this, the warlock wondered if there was anything much left.

*Your Majesty?*

Silence. It might be that the Dragon King had simply broken the link, but Cabe knew somehow that his hermitic ally had truly suffered. How serious the damage was, there was no way of knowing unless Cabe returned to the sanctum. For all he knew, that chamber, too, was now a memory crushed under tons of rocky earth.

All but a few residue traces of Nimth's evil had vanished. Even without being there, Cabe knew that the hole had been sealed and that the power to seal it had been the magic inherent in the fog. Nimth's own might had been used to force it from the Dragonrealm. The Dragon King had used Cabe's added strength to force the alien magic to do his bidding, something only he, who alone understood both powers, could have done. All of this the warlock understood even though no explanation had been given to him. He simply knew because he had been a part of it.

*Gryphon! Darkhorse!* The images of his two friends formed in his mind. How could he have forgotten them? Thanks in part to him, they might even be dead, for the Crystal Dragon had never revealed to the warlock whether he had actually protected the two from the killing sound as he had Cabe. Cabe did not trust the Dragon King enough to have faith in their well-being. He turned, intending to head back to where the shadow steed had been held.

Lord D'Farany stood before him. Yet another thing that Cabe had forgotten. He silently swore and prepared to do battle even though he doubted that he had enough will to raise a feather an inch from the ground much less fight to the death with the keeper.

D'Farany, however, merely stood there, his blank eyes staring in the direction of Cabe but not at him. The spellcaster took a tentative step toward the raider and noticed that his mouth was moving. Lord D'Farany was muttering, but only when Cabe stepped even closer did he understand anything of what the Aramite commander was saying.

"Gone . . . tooth . . . empty . . . so . . . empty . . . cannot . . . cannot . . ."

The keeper had survived one loss of power, but only after madness had claimed him for a time. Cabe, staring at the shell that had once been a man to be feared, was fairly certain that this time madness had staked a permanent claim. The warlock looked around. The other raiders were gone; a sinkhole larger than the Manor and its grounds combined revealed the fate of both the officers and the horses their spies had bought or stolen for the never-to-be-released invasion of Zuu or whatever it was the Aramites had planned. Of the two groups, Cabe felt much more sorrow for the horses than for the raiders.

He turned back to the keeper and reached out a hand. As much as he despised the man, Cabe could not leave him out here, not in this condition. "Come with—"

Slapping his hand away, D'Farany, the pale, marred visage twisted into a look of suffering and loss, cried, "*Empty!* It can never be filled! I can never be *whole!* I can never be . . . be . . ."

The raider commander slumped into Cabe's arms. Under his weight, the warlock fell to one knee. After a short struggle, he managed to lay the still form on the ground. Cabe looked into D'Farany's ravaged countenance, then felt his neck. He uncovered the Aramite's wrist and checked there, too.

Ivon D'Farany, whose name had meant terror for almost a decade to those fighting against the wounded empire, was dead. He just could not stand the loss a second time, Cabe concluded. No man so in thrall to his power could have. *The Gryphon will be pleased, at least.*

That returned him once more to the fate of his companions. Leaving the corpse where it was, the warlock worked his way back to the camp. Compared to now, his first crossing had been the simplest of tasks. Legar was now a ruin and parts of it were still in the process of collapse. He came across no life in the areas he first wandered; most of this part had sunken into the underground kingdom of the Quel, taking all with it. A few bodies, both human and other-wise, still littered the place. A little beyond, though, Cabe could see hundreds of silent, unmoving forms. On a rare occasion, he spotted a few human figures, wolf raiders, but there was no fight left in them. They either ran if they saw him or simply walked on, ignoring him as they ignored all else. He doubted whether the latter had much left in the way of sanity. Not everyone had died because of the piercing noise, but looking at the survivors, he was not so certain that the ones who walked were the more fortunate.

Of living Quel, Cabe saw only signs. Burrow holes dotted the ravaged encampment; at least several score, probably more, of the diggers had made it back to the safety of the underworld. Several hundred more, both above and below, would never threaten Legar or the Dragonrealm. The survivors would certainly not, either, at least in his lifetime. He crossed his fingers on that score, but judging by what he had felt earlier and seen now, it would take the Quel several generations just to repair the damage. It would take them several more to rebuild their population, if that was at all possible. True, as long as one existed, they *would* be dangerous, but not nearly as much as they would have been if nothing had stopped their return.

*So no one will ever truly understand the threats that so briefly rose here.* It was ironic. The Quel sleepers had been a legend to many and a true danger to a few who knew. The Aramites, in as great a force as they had brought, could have brought the western part of the Dragonrealm to ruin even if they were finally defeated. The hole that had been opened, the hole that had allowed so much of poor, decaying Nimth in, spreading its sickness . . .

He did not want to even think about what would have happened if that had been left unchecked.

To his great relief, Cabe suddenly detected a familiar presence not too far off.

*Darkhorse?* he sent out.

For a moment there was no response. Then there came a slow, hesitant touch, followed by an equally hesitant response. *Cabe? Do you really live?*

*I do! Where are you?*

*Follow . . . follow the link. Cabe, Lord Gryphon is injured.*

The eternal sounded none too good himself. Summoning what will he had left, the warlock immediately teleported.

The devastation that greeted him was even worse than what he had already seen. The carnage brought on by the battle alone was sickening. For all their ferocity, the Quel had met a foe equally matched. Their size and armored bodies had not given the subterraneans the great advantage it should have. At the same time, the swiftness and well-honed battle skills of the wolf raiders had not saved them, either. It was a wonder that there had been any left to perish in the collapse of the surface.

Yet, it was Darkhorse who stunned Cabe even more than the horrible sight around them. Instead of the valiant black stallion the dark-haired mage was familiar with, a grotesque thing with primitive appendages and a vague, animal-like shape flowed before him. Only the ice-blue eyes were still there, but they were so pale they now seemed almost white.

"Darkhorse?"

"What is left of . . . of me, friend Cabe." Even the voice was subdued. "With . . . aid from . . . Lord Gryphon, I was just . . . just able to free myself . . . but it was almost too much . . ."

Cabe could not think of anything to do for the eternal, but he was willing to try. "What can I do? Is there anything?"

"I am beyond your help, Cabe. It will be up to . . . to me to recover . . . that will take . . . time. Best that you see . . . see what you can . . . do for the Lord Gryphon . . ."

"The Gryphon? Where is he?"

"Within me . . ." The murky, shifting form flowed to one side and as it did, the outline of the lionbird's form appeared. Cabe swallowed hard when he saw how still his companion was. "Is it too late?"

"He lives . . . but like me . . . he has been drained . . . drained of nearly every . . . thing. I protected him from the . . . the sound, which did not . . . harm me as it . . . did him." The eternal grew silent.

The warlock knelt beside the Gryphon and felt for a pulse. It was there, slow but steady. Then it jumped a bit. The Gryphon suddenly opened his eyes.

"Cabe?"

"It would be nice to meet under better circumstances once in a while," returned the warlock, smiling.

The Gryphon tried to rise. "The Aramites!"

Cabe eased him back down. "Dead or scattered. The same holds true for the Quel. Most are dead, I think."

"My son . . . his murderer . . ."

*"Demion?"* Neither Darkhorse nor the Gryphon had made mention of this terrible news before. "When? Who did it?" Fury rose within the spellcaster. If the lionbird was beyond avenging his only son, Cabe would try to find the strength to do it.

However, the lionbird shook his head. "No, Cabe. Demion's murderer . . . Orril . . . D'Marr . . ." The look of disgust on that avian visage spoke volumes concerning the wolf raider. "He lies in that crater there . . . buried under several tons . . . of earth." The Gryphon pointed at the gaping hole with his maimed hand. "D'Marr never did find out . . . the great Quel secret . . . was the Quel themselves. I would have liked . . . to see if *that* would have cracked that . . . mask of his." He laughed very briefly, then sobered. "My son can rest. *I* can rest . . . but only for a time. Lord D'Farany—"

"Your son, you, and Troia can *all* rest, Gryphon. The keeper is dead. I know. He died right before my eyes." In response to his companion's questioning stare, the warlock explained the Crystal Dragon's spell and the use of D'Farany's talisman. He also spoke of Plool and the Vraad's swift and foolish death. The very end of his tale he reserved for Ivon D'Farany's inability to suffer so great a loss twice in one lifetime. Addicted to his power, he could not survive a second withdrawal. "He collapsed in my arms and when I studied him close, I saw that he was dead."

"A—a fitting way for him. I thank you, Cabe."

The warlock shook his head. "I was only a part of it. The one who guided me through much of this, albeit not always with my approval, wa—"

"Cabe!" Darkhorse suddenly called, sounding more like his old self. He was still a shifting, near-formless thing, but the eyes seemed a bit brighter . . . and now very concerned, too. "I think I see . . . see soldiers approaching!"

With the Gryphon too weak to be of use, Cabe tried his best to make out the shapes in the distance. It was not noon in Legar, a fortunate thing, but the sun was bright enough already to force him to squint. He would have to create copies of the Dragon King's eye protectors when he had the opportunity. That is, *if* he had the opportunity. The figures did resemble soldiers and their high helms, at least from this distance, were shaped akin to the wolf's head helms of the Aramites.

"Some surviving officer must have . . . have reorganized survivors," the lion-bird added, becoming exhausted by the continual task of trying to talk coherently. "We'll have to fight . . . them."

Glancing at his friends, Cabe was not particularly hopeful. He might be able to get off a spell, but he was not certain as to its potency. If the wolf raiders had any sort of magical protection, then the three of them had little chance. Their greatest hope, Darkhorse, did not even have the strength to reshape himself.

The figures were still too distant. "Could they be soldiers from Zuu?"

"Are they leading horses?" asked the Gryphon in return.

"No, they're on foot."

"Then, they are . . . not from Zuu. A soldier of . . . Zuu always has . . . his mount with him. And they . . . do not . . . wear armor at all resembling . . . resembling . . . that of the raiders."

That was true, but Cabe had hoped. He continued to watch, thinking that maybe the soldiers would not see them, when he noticed a newcomer. It was a rider on some beast not a horse. Cabe's brow wrinkled. Then, the rider turned a little in the saddle and abruptly became a blinding, glittering beacon. The other soldiers, turning, also seemed to suddenly blaze with the glory of the sun.

"They're not wolf raiders," he informed the others. "They're allies." *I hope,* he added to himself.

THE GLEAMING WARRIOR astride the riding drake might have been the same one that Cabe had mistaken for the Crystal Dragon, but the warlock could not be certain until the warrior spoke.

"Master Bedlam. I am Gemmon, my lord's first duke. Pleased I am to have found you and yours alive in all this ruin."

"You were looking for us?" The perfection with which the drake spoke did not really startle Cabe any more than the interesting fact that the dragon men were not using the forms they had been born with, which would have made searching Legar swifter and easier. The Dragon King's human tastes had no doubt spread to his subjects.

"For you and survivors of both abominations. My lord leaves nothing to chance, although the humans will have scattered eastward and the cursssed Quel will burrow very deep. We lack the strength to hunt them down, but there are those lying among the dead who must still be dispatched and others wandering about that must be rounded up and dealt with in some manner."

Cabe was not certain whether the drakes were putting the badly wounded to death out of pity or their need for further satisfaction. The warlock knew that he did not have the strength to fight for those lives and, in truth, he was hard-pressed to find a reason to spare either the Aramites or the Quel. Still, it did bother him . . .

"I have been instructed," the drake continued, "to assist you and yours across the border into Esedi. Servants of the Green One will be there to help you return to your loved ones." He eyed Darkhorse with some confusion. "Although as to what—"

"I will make do," retorted the eternal. He sounded even stronger, but Cabe was not certain whether that might just be a front before the minions of the Dragon King.

"You have our gratitude," the warlock interjected, not desiring a confrontation. "But there is one thing I must ask."

"What is that?"

"I'd like to speak to your master. I insist upon it."

The warrior looked uncomfortable. "He . . . hasss secluded himself from all for the time being. The sssspell was taxing, even for him."

Cabe noted the nervousness, but would not be put off by the drake's fear. "Tell him I will make my visit short."

"I can tell him nothing. He will not even ssssspeak to me, human."

Glancing at the Gryphon and Darkhorse, Cabe said, "Then see to my friends. Help them on their way to the border. I'll join you all when I can."

The Gryphon stirred. "Cabe, surely you do not . . . intend to simply . . . simply materialize before a Dragon King . . . especially *this* Dragon King."

The warlock was already rising. "I do. Call it concern."

"Concern? For the Crystal Dragon?" Even the drake warrior found this a bit incredulous.

Shrugging, Cabe replied, "If not for him, then maybe a little concern for a man who once called himself Logan."

He vanished while the others were still puzzling over that last statement.

# XIX

*"WHAAAT DO YOOOU want, sssssorcerer?"*

Cabe, who had just materialized, was taken aback by the horrific change in the Crystal Dragon's voice. His voice was now more reminiscent of a true Dragon King.

Undaunted, the warlock replied, "I came to see how you were. I think I know something of what you went through, wouldn't you say?"

The Crystal Dragon was a hill of gemstones pressed tight against the far end of the chamber. There was little light and the walls were dull, opaque things. Cabe could not even see the drake lord's countenance.

"I . . . sssurvived. You need know nothing morrre."

It would do no good to press the point, Cabe decided. He was disappointed, but knew that there was nothing he could do. Instead, he asked, "What will you do about your kingdom? Legar is in ruins. If my help would be of any value to—"

From the darkness rose the head of the lord of Legar. An inhuman rage controlled his draconian visage. Narrowed eyes with only a hint of crystal in them glared at the presumptuous little figure. "Caaan you not undersssstand? I want nothing from you, huuuman! I want only ressst! Privacy and ressst! Why did you persssissst in coming here?"

"Because of Logan Tezerenee."

His words doused, for a time, the flames of anger. The Crystal Dragon recoiled into himself, looking much, much smaller. "I know the name . . . myyyy name . . . it isss me . . ."

"Logan," the warlock dared use the name. "Your kingdom is in chaos and you risked yourself in the end. By no means will I forget that it was all in your own self-interest, but what you did affected the rest of the Dragonrealm, too. Your subjects will need help in rebuilding Legar. There are prisoners and wounded from the wolf raiders who might be best turned over to other humans. Perhaps my friends and allies will be willing to aid you. Instead of the wreckage you now rule, there might even be a chance of turning the peninsula into a land of life. They could meet with you and perhaps—"

*"No!"* It was not anger this time, but rather fear that drove the Dragon King. His eyes widened and he hissed madly. "No. If I allow them so close, they will discover the truth and then I would be in danger! They will be furious that I have tricked them all! I might be forced to leave this place and I cannot! I cannot! I have exhaussted myssself more than I ever dared! The outside world in any form isss now a danger to me! Only here and alone am I ssssafe!"

Cabe could not believe what he was hearing: "You're wrong! Listen to yourself—"

With but a terrible glance, the glittering leviathan silenced him. "Your aid wassss mosssst appreciated, Massster Bedlam, but you will leave now! My ssssubjectssss will ssssee to your needsss all the way to Esssedi! Now go! I musssst ssssleep!"

"Logan—"

*"I am the Crystal Dragon!"* the behemoth roared. Draconian jaws opened wide . . .

Cabe teleported away before the Dragon King did something either of them would regret.

HE FOUND THE Gryphon and Darkhorse waiting for him, the latter, to the warlock's surprise, once more in his favorite form. A short distance from them, their reptilian escort waited in growing anxiety.

"What happened?" asked the Gryphon, lying atop the shadow steed. Darkhorse, the warlock would discover later, had not trusted the drakes. His obsession with Shade was at an end; now his greatest concern was for his living friends, including the Gryphon. Drawing upon his incredible will, he had not only succeeded in re-forming, but then had shaped himself so that the lionbird could rest comfortably on his backside. It was a peculiar sight, but one so welcome because of that peculiarity. Almost the mage was able to forget his meeting with the Crystal Dragon.

"We should leave. We may have just outstayed our welcome."

"What happened?"

Cabe shook his head. "I can't be sure . . . not yet."

The others did not understand, but that was probably for the best because even Cabe was not certain that he understood. He only understood that more than ever the line between Logan Tezerenee and the Crystal Dragon had become blurred. Which way, if either, the lord of Legar would eventually turn was anyone's guess. The only thing of certainty was the fact that be he drake or man, the lone inhabitant of that darkened sanctum would not leave that place no matter what happened. It went beyond the precious safeguarding of one man's mind; the Crystal Dragon had been in seclusion for so long that he could not bear either the thought of leaving his chamber or allowing the world inside.

One of the warriors offered him a beast. Cabe took the proffered riding drake and mounted, hardly paying any attention to what he did. The warlock continued to stare at ruined Legar, picturing in his mind the Dragon King dreaming of the face he had once worn in a world that was forever barred to him . . . by himself.

The drake duke signaled for the party to commence eastward. Cabe allowed everyone to precede him, even Darkhorse and the Gryphon. Only with reluctance did he finally urge the dragon beneath him forward. Legar still haunted him. If not for the Crystal Dragon, even what little remained intact would no longer have existed. Alone, the warlock doubted that he could have succeeded.

*So much power and so long a life*, he thought, finally having to turn his eyes to the path before him. *Yet, despite that, he's forever a prisoner of himself, fearful of losing a humanity that he might have already lost long, long ago.*

The notion was enough to make him ride in brooding silence for the rest of the journey to Esedi . . . and for some time after.

# THE DRAGON CROWN

## I

**THE RIDERS BEGAN** to collect at the outskirts of the great Tyber Mountains. They had not gathered for such a meeting in nearly two decades, and as they joined one another at the narrow pass leading into the midst of the Tybers, it was clear that none would have come even now if necessity had not demanded it.

Clad in immense, flowing traveler's cloaks that hid both face and form, the riders were a coven of gray specters astride mounts whose glittering eyes warned that they, too, hid secrets. There were no words of acknowledgment or, for that matter, even the simple nod of a head. Some of the band might, at times, have called one another brother, but the appellation was simply a matter of ceremony; there was little love lost among the riders.

When at last they were all gathered, there were those who would have set off for their destination, the sooner to end this unwelcome confrontation. One, however, chose that moment to begin pulling back the hood of his cloak. That led to a hiss from another and a low, painful, rasping reprimand.

"Not herrrre! Never herrrre!"

The one who had erred did not question his elder counterpart. He lowered his hand and nodded.

One of the other riders grunted, then urged his mount toward the path. The rest followed his example. Showing no sign of fatigue, the beasts snorted puffs of smoke and carried their masters swiftly among the mountains. Neither twisting and turning passages nor treacherous ravines slowed the group. Savage winds and slippery trails were obstacles also ignored. Though denizens not of man's world hid and watched, the riders were in no way hindered. The creatures of the mountains knew who and what the intruders were, and so remained at a respectful distance, many shivering in fear. Some simply fled in open terror as the riders approached.

None of the ghostly riders took notice of the onlookers. Their concern lay only in the vast presence looming above them, a mountain so massive that those surrounding it looked like vassals paying homage to their lord. Those of the band who had never been this close were hard-pressed not to be overwhelmed by the peak's grandeur and the power they could sense radiating from within it.

Kivan Grath. The name was old and without reliable origin, but all here were aware it meant "Seeker of Gods." No one knew the reason for the title, yet somehow it fit. The riders turned their steeds toward the peak. At this point, there was at last some hesitation from their beasts, but, unforgiving, their hooded masters prodded them on, silencing whatever protests the mounts made. The sooner the band reached its destination and completed the task before it, the sooner the riders could go their separate ways.

At the base of the vast mountain, they came at last upon that which they sought. As one, the band reined their animals to a halt, then dismounted. Their steeds secured, the hooded figures stared at the sight before them until at last one of the lead riders, known to the others for his tempestuous ways, snarled something unintelligible and stalked toward the dark cavern in the mountainside.

Buried in the side of Kivan Grath was a great gate of bronze that might have been as old as the peak itself, so ancient was its appearance. Once it had towered over onlookers, but no more. Now the gate hung awkwardly, a mortally wounded guardian frozen in midfall. Only one blackened hinge held it in place. The entire gate was a burnt memory of what once had been. Those who had been here before could recall how its surface had been decorated with a curious array of designs, but now the designs were gone, melted away by the terrible forces unleashed upon it by one mad power.

The one who had stalked forward suddenly faltered. The others did not move, as if waiting for something to happen. The tableau did not change for several anxious moments.

"Well?" questioned one whose tone was reminiscent of lapping waves. It had finally occurred to him how ridiculous he and his companions looked. "It isss not asss if we need to knock, now isss it?"

Abashed, the lead figure looked at the others, then turned once more to the gate and the pitch-dark abyss behind it. He then turned back to the one who had mocked them all. "A torch would be nice, eel!"

"Why not create our own light?" scoffed one of the younger ones, the same one who had thought to remove his hood during the ride. He held out a gloved hand. A glow formed in his palm.

"Not out here, you hatchling!" the young traveler's partner snapped. He had to struggle to make himself be heard, for, as before, his voice was barely a rasping whisper. It proved sufficient for the task, however, for the glow instantly faded away.

"There are sssome . . . *some* things that should be observed," added the one with the voice that spoke like the sea. He was visibly working to calm himself, an effort that the other riders immediately copied with greater or lesser results. "Some things that must be respected."

"There should ssstill be a torch on the inssside," gasped the whisperer. "Just beyond the gate."

Steeling himself, the foremost walked up and reached inside, his gauntleted hand running along the wall. His fingers struck something not made of stone. "I have it."

"Then light it and let us be done with this."

"You would be wise not to strain your voice," the young, impetuous one advised his compatriot, a hint of mockery flavoring his words.

Before his companion could form a retort, the others had the torch lit. The bickering figures quieted. Despite their distaste for one another, the band drew close together as they entered the battered passage. There were some fears—although none here would have admitted to such failings—that were stronger than hatred.

They walked for a short time through a tunnel that, while natural in origin, had also been improved upon by other means during the passage of time. Small shadow creatures fluttered away in vocal dismay at the intrusion of light, but the group ignored them. All other things paled in comparison to the place they had invaded.

The riders entered the main cavern.

Even in its ruined state, the cavern citadel left them in speechless awe. The interior resembled a temple, but one tossed asunder by a great upheaval. Effigies both human and otherwise lay strewn about, many shattered beyond recognition. Some still stood, frightful mourners at the funeral of their companions. Beyond them, at the focus of the chamber, was a cracked and half-buried throne atop a crumbling dais. Just before the massive stone seat, but buried by rubble from the collapsed roof of the cavern, was a wide open area where a full-grown dragon could have and *had* rested his massive form time and time again. The elder riders could recall the face and form of that reptilian behemoth. He had been a golden leviathan, the last of a line of scaled masters ruling the land called the Dragonrealm. The Dragon Emperor Gold.

A generation of men had grown since his death.

The one with the torch placed it in a location that would give them the necessary illumination for their undesired deed. Then the riders, forming a ragged half circle, knelt in homage: if not to the late tyrant, then to what he had represented.

A moment of silence passed before one rider, calmer than the rest, stepped forward and took the place where the Dragon Emperor, king of kings, would have stood. The others shuffled uneasily, but they knew that their companion sought only to speak, not to claim any right above them.

"Let the council convene." His words were softly spoken, but in the huge, still cavern they were thunder.

The forms of the riders suddenly became twisted, grotesque. They grew, and as they did their bodies became quicksilver. All semblance to humanity quickly faded. From their backs burst wings—long, webbed wings—and below those, serpentine tails sprouted. Arms and legs became clawed, leathery appendages. Already each figure was many times larger than it had been, yet the growth did not slow.

The cloaks had all been thrown aside at the moment of transformation, briefly revealing to the shadows a band of tall, dread warriors, dragonhelmed knights clad in scale armor. That image quickly gave way, however, as helms and near-hidden features melded together into monstrous, reptilian visages with long, horrid snouts and toothy maws. The scaled armor became scaled hides of colors that varied from figure to figure. There were blue, red, black, green, and at least a pair more gray than anything else. Other differences were obvious, but none more than the colors.

Where but moments before the riders had been, now the Dragon Kings stood.

The dragons stretched their vast wings and eyed one another with deep-rooted suspicion. They remained in pairs as they had since the beginning of this trek, one beast in each duo obviously dominant over the other. The lesser drakes backed up a few paces, acknowledging their lower status. One or two did this with great reluctance.

From the ranks of the dominant leviathans, a dragon of the darkest black, a sly creature with a savage scar across his throat, sneered at his emerald-green counterpart, who stood in the center. When the black dragon spoke, his voice was barely a whisper. Each word seemed a torture for the ebony creature.

"I am sssurprised that you even asked us to join together, Brother Grrreeeen! It isss not asss if you could not do asss you pleased in thisss matter!"

"We are inclined to similar notions," added a gray, preening drake, whose very tone made it clear that the "we" of his statement concerned him alone and not his companion. He plucked fastidiously at his hide, as if seeking something. In the past decade, as his interests had turned ever inward, the Dragon King Storm had begun to take on the airs of a would-be demigod. Among his brethren was a growing suspicion that he was going mad, a not uncommon affliction of drake lords. Yet, any who might have thought him a foolish sight need only listen for the iron in his voice to know that this was not a creature to be crossed. The Storm Dragon might be mad, but he was also one of the most deadly of those drake lords who remained.

The Green Dragon, master of the vast lands of the Dagora Forest, eyed them both. "*I* have always abided by the traditions."

"Enough of this bickering!" snapped their blue counterpart. His breath smelled heavily of fish, which made the black one wrinkle his snout in disgust. "We have matters to discuss which have been delayed all too long!"

Reminded of their duty, the others quieted. Green nodded his gratitude to the Blue Dragon, lord of Irrilian by the Sea, and, with a withering glance at his ebony counterpart, returned to his self-chosen role of speaker. "As Brother Blue so succinctly put it, we *have* delayed much too long in discussing this particular matter . . . *years* too long." He surveyed the group, its prominent members strikingly fewer than when last they had convened. "I refer, of courssse, to the *ascension* to the throne of the next Dragon Emperor."

Among his fellows there was some shuffling and discomfort. None of them had looked forward to this day, if only because they were uncertain as to what it meant to their kind. To some, it was an opportunity to reclaim past glory; to others, it was a final turning point. In the back of all their minds was the fear that it was all for nothing: a mere joke.

Once, it would have not been so. Once, the lands known both separately and collectively as the Dragonrealm had trembled under the iron rule of the drake race. Thirteen kingdoms and thirteen kings, with the line of Gold serving as emperor over all. So it had been for centuries, with new Dragon Kings replacing their progenitors either through the process of age or, more often, through subterfuge and deceit. A drake who became king relinquished his own name and became known by the symbol his clans had chosen so long ago in the lost past. Most were colors, said to represent the various shades of the magical spectrum. A few had gone by the strongest or most regal of the metals, such as iron or silver. One clan had even chosen the violence of nature's storms as its symbol.

The shape-shifting drakes were only the latest in a long procession of rulers who had risen to supremacy . . . and then had fallen. A few scattered remnants of some of their predecessors still existed, but most of the land's previous tyrants had faded with the lengthy passage of history. It now appeared as if the dragon folk themselves were headed into oblivion . . . and all here knew the reason why.

Mankind. Weak, clawless creatures, their race yet prospered. The Dragon Kings knew that they themselves were to blame for much of that progress and expansion. Humans had proven so useful in many ways, more than making up for the drakes' own lack of numbers. In time, their inventiveness and drive had made them indispensable to most of the Dragon Kings. Human cities had sprouted up and grown, their inhabitants loyal at first to their respective masters. But it was inevitable that as their own power grew, the new kingdoms chafed at the rule of monsters. Rebellions rose and were suppressed. Human kingdoms then grew subservient for a time, but when a new generation came into power, the cycle would often repeat itself.

Then came the sorcerers.

The *Dragon Masters.*

Human mages had always existed, and many had found their way into the services of the Dragon Kings. A few had desired to cause havoc, but ever the drake lords had kept a wary eye out for the strongest, the ones with the most potential for destruction. These were either recruited or destroyed. Some sorcerers, however, succeeded in remaining hidden from the drakes. They gathered others to them and bided their time, their only attacks being to undermine the foundation of drake rule. The Dragon Kings began to suffer a number of mishaps, small by themselves, but cumulative in effect. Despite the many mishaps, however, they did not realize what was happening. Only after many generations, when the mages decided the time was ripe for revolution and at last revealed themselves for what they were, did the draconian rulers realize the instability of their reign.

Thus began the Turning War. For nearly five years the battle was fought. For nearly five years the Dragon Kings lived in fear that they were at last to fall.

The Dragon Masters, though, had also underestimated a number of things, first and foremost the treachery of one of their number. Serving his own purpose, the traitor had killed several of the most prominent mages in the ranks, then fled before their leader, his father, could deal with him. Weakened, the sorcerers were finally defeated; but the victory was bittersweet, for in one of the final struggles, the drake lords had lost one of their own. Lord Purple, who had guided them in the actual fighting, died with the Dragon Master Nathan Bedlam. Both Purple's kingdom and the secrets of his great sorcery fell into the claws of the Gryphon, ally to the Dragon Masters. Weakened as they were, the other Dragon Kings could not oust him.

Those gathered now had long ago come to realize that the victory they had garnered in the war had been only a temporary reprieve. They had won themselves two centuries of anxiety and suspicion. When all was said and done, the empire had still crumbled. Infighting and misjudgment had done what the Dragon Masters could not.

For some time, the remaining Dragon Kings eyed one another. Then, at last, the ruined voice of the Black Dragon, he who controlled the domain of the Gray Mists, broke the uneasy silence. "Of what need have we of an emperor . . . essspecially one raised by humanssss?"

"More to the point," interjected a dusky green drake with touches of brown along his underside, "a Dragon Emperor raisssed by the grandsssson of Nathan Bedlam!"

The dragon's name was Sssaleese. Some of the others looked at the new speaker, open disdain on their reptilian countenances. In their eyes, this one was not a true Dragon King but a usurper, a pretender using the devastation of the drake race to his benefit. No birth markings had decorated his egg, of that they were certain. Yet, because he spoke for a loose confederation of clan survivors who had lost their own lords, it had been decided by the majority that his presence was required if this was to succeed.

Black had not been a part of that majority. The ebony drake sneered at the other and started to speak, but Green, recognizing the potential danger of those words, quickly replied, "Worthy comments both, but it would be well for *all* to remember that it wasss our rivalriesss and divisionsss which brought us to our present sssorry state."

That drew the attention away from Sssaleese, but kindled a new disruption. Storm, the gray, looked mildly amused. "As we recall, the dissension was a part of life *before* the death of Gold."

"Gold wasss Gold. Kyl, his heir, will be Gold in title only. He will ssstill be Kyl." Green's gaze swept across the cavern. "In that there isss all the difference! If we but give him our allegiance, our cooperation, then will we have what we desssire!"

"I ask again," Black hissed. "What need have we of an emperor?"

Green shook his massive head. To the side, he heard Blue hiss in frustration. Blue understood what some of the others did not. The drake race was on the brink. If they did not come together soon, they faced extinction. The humans outbred them and now had clawholds everywhere. Green firmly believed that the tiny mammals now had the strength to annihilate his kind, and there were more than a few of the creatures who desired just that. Melicard I of Talak, whose father had been driven mad by the drake Kyrg, had already tried genocide. Worse, it appeared that the king of Zuu, Lanith, was massing an army and gathering what human mages of skill he could find. No one knew *what* he planned, but Zuu was a particularly disturbing point since it lay in the boundaries of the emerald giant's domain. Lanith still gave his respects to Green, but grew ever more lax in responding to questions concerning Zuu's increase in military strength.

"We need an emperor to give our kind focusss," Blue returned, speaking in a manner one might use more for a child. "We need an emperor to show the humans that we are *one*, not many!"

"Yet you would give usss an emperor raisssed by humansss," reminded Sssaleese, eyes darting to Black, who remained silent. "How could we trussst one raisssed by a Bedlam?"

"Raised by human *and* drake." Green shook his head. "You sssee the disadvantages but not the advantagesss!"

"Could we not . . . ssspeak with him firssst?" an almost tentative voice asked.

The assembled drakes turned as one to the blood-red figure on the edge of the inner group. Although a Dragon King, Red was fairly new into his reign, a mere two decades or so. He had achieved his place upon the death of his progenitor on the sword of yet another Bedlam, Nathan's mad son Azran. Unprepared, he had never found his proper place among his fellows. Even Sssaleese, who had clawed his way to his position, was more comfortable in the role of ruler.

"Ssspeak to him?" repeated the Green Dragon.

"Yesss . . ." Storm nodded. "We have only your word asss to his worth." The gray behemoth met Green's eyes. "We would be happier in thisss instance if we knew that the emperor-to-be isss worthy of the august title."

"A notable suggestion," agreed Blue.

Sssaleese added, "I would be interesssted alssso in the opportunity to make a judgment."

Black merely nodded curtly. Red basked in the afterglow of his success and thus missed the look the Green Dragon briefly sent his way.

"Very well," the emerald beast muttered. "I shall sssee to arranging sssuch a talk."

"The Bedlamsss will never agree to it!" gasped the Black Dragon.

"Wait and sssee! I shall do what I can." A pause, then, "And if the heir meetsss your questionsss? Then will you acknowledge his rightful place?"

The others acquiesced one by one with Black, of course, last.

"Ssso, then. The matter is settled. That leavesss but the details. . . ."

A SHORT TIME later, the Dragon Kings departed through the broken bronze gate. In silence the band took charge of their steeds, mounted, and quickly left behind what had once been and might yet again be the Dragon Emperor's stronghold. They rode together through the mountains, but when the Tybers gave way to more open land, the band quickly split into pairs. Some headed in an easterly direction, others more south. Only one pair headed directly west. Sssaleese and his second.

The would-be Dragon King and his companion rode hard for more than a quarter hour, never looking back once. They rode hard until they came upon a small range of hills, in truth a stunted outreach of the Tyber Mountains.

Slowing their mounts, the two drakes entered the hills by one of the narrow paths that wound through the range.

When they were well within the protection of the hills, Sssaleese turned and glanced at his companion. The other drake, as nondescript a warrior as one of his kind could be, nodded. Both reined in their steeds. Only one moon was out this night, so Sssaleese could make out little more than the outline of the other, but he was certain that his companion was pleased. The confederation lord was not so certain that he shared that pleasure.

"You are sssatisssfied with what you have learned?"

"I am. They have not changed! They blunder around, each trying to take what he can without giving up anything! My sssire never trusted them! It wasss their fighting, their *betrayal*, that destroyed him! Now they ssseek to make the new emperor a puppet who will dance to *their* tune!"

Sssaleese did not respond at first. His situation was precarious, to say the least. He needed to be on fair terms with the Dragon Kings, yet there was much potential in taking a different course, especially if it meant the favor of the one who soon would sit upon the dragon throne.

*Or stand behind it,* he added. If the offer his companion had made him some months back held any truth, then the true lord of the drakes now sat in front of Sssaleese. "What will you do?"

The other considered. "The meeting will be a formality. They will find my brother a sssuitable candidate. All things may proceed as I planned." The drake leaned toward Sssaleese. "Or do you have any misssgivingsss?"

The brown and green grew indignant. "We have made an agreement!"

"Yesss . . . one which allows both of usss much room for plotting our essscapes." Sssaleese's companion chuckled. "They did not recognize me! They *never* recognize me!"

"For which I am thankful! If they had known it wasss you, my life as well would have been forfeit."

"Bah! You place too much confidence in their ssstrength. They are blussster!"

Sssaleese did not desire to pursue the conversation further. He had been subjected to his companion's tirades before. What counted to him were results, not words. So far, there had been little of the former. Yet, before he dared depart, he once more had to ask one particular question. "How do you propose to make the young heir yours?"

Once more he received the same cursed answer. "He will be."

There was no reply to that. Sssaleese shrugged. "I mussst return to my people. When shall we next meet?"

"I will contact you."

Being at the beck and call of this one irked the new monarch, who felt that he should be given some respect for the position he had worked so hard to attain. Yet he was not about to push. This was one drake he did not care to cross. "Very well."

Sssaleese turned his mount, intending to depart, when the other said, "We are kindred sssouls, friend. It isss usss against them! Their day is waning. We are the future, a place where the lack of *proper* birth markingsss does not mean one isss not fit to rule. . . ."

Sssaleese twisted around. "Let usss hope so, Duke Toma."

Toma laughed, a harsh sound that echoed in the quiet night, and confidently replied, "*Hope* has nothing to do with it, dear Sssaleese! *I* should know!"

# II

"THEY MUST BE mad!"

"I assure you, Cabe Bedlam, that they are very ssserious about thisss! They may not accept him otherwissse."

Cabe Bedlam stalked to the rail of the balcony and gazed down at the massive sculpted garden below. The Green Dragon, wearing the form of a tall, emerald knight in scale armor, remained where he was, red, inhuman eyes watching the master sorcerer from within the confines of a helm. The dragon crest—part of the drake's *true* visage—seemed also to watch. The drake lord kept a respectful distance at all times. Despite the human's young, unassuming face, Cabe Bedlam was a mage of remarkable power. The broad streak of silver cutting across his otherwise black hair was proof of that. All human sorcerers bore some sort of mark in the hair, either a stripe of silver or a peppering over the entire head.

Cabe turned slowly, obviously considering his response to the Dragon King's words. He looked but midway through his third decade despite being well into his fifth. That was common among those gifted with the power, but in Cabe Bedlam's case it was due to some spell his grandfather Nathan had cast long, long ago. In fact, with his jaw set and his bright eyes narrowed in contemplation, he greatly resembled his grandfather. Even the slightly turned nose was similar. The lord of the Dagora Forest had never told Cabe exactly how well he had known Nathan Bedlam, leader of the Dragon Masters. He did know that grandfather and grandson would have been as proud of one another as they both had been ashamed by Azran. The Bedlam family had ever been a fount of magical ability, whether for good or ill.

"I won't let them enter the Manor grounds," the human announced, a wave of his hand indicating both building and land. The Manor, as it was called by most, had existed for countless centuries. Green was of the opinion that the Seekers, the avian race that had preceded his own as masters of the realm, had built it, yet the bird folk did not normally devise structures so ground-based. Still, the Manor was not only carved marble; one entire portion of it was living tree. That and the many statues commemorating the Seekers were all the verification the Dragon King needed. Cabe had different notions concerning his home, and the two often argued amiably about the matter.

Whatever its origins, it could not be denied that the Manor had seen many, many masters over the centuries. Ghost images of scenes, some accompanied by sound as well, burst into momentary life, so Cabe had told him. Sometimes those images would also come in dreams. Only those with some magical tendencies were generally bothered by such. The drake knew he would not have liked living in the Manor, yet Cabe and his beautiful wife, the scarlet-tressed witch Gwendolyn, enjoyed their life here, as did the children, both the spellcasters' own and the drake young they had raised. Even the humans and drakes who acted as their servants somehow found life in the Manor enjoyable for the most part.

Although he had never said such to Cabe, the Green Dragon was unnerved by the Manor. Being what he was, he did not, of course, show any sign of that anxiety.

"I won't let them enter the Manor grounds," the warlock repeated. "They must take me for a fool." Without the Bedlams' permission, it was impossible to enter their sanctum. The Manor and the garden and woods that surrounded it all were protected by a strong magical barrier invisible to the eye. Only a select few could enter without having to request permission. The spell was ancient, a fading remnant from some previous lord; the witch and warlock had not only revitalized it but improved it as well.

"I thought, perhapsss, somewhere more neutral."

Cabe frowned and crossed his arms, wrinkling the dark blue sorcerer's robe he wore. "I don't care for the thought of surrounding myself or any of my family with Dragon Kings, present company excepted."

The Green Dragon's laugh was accented by a mild hiss. "I have never cared much for that myssself!"

Somewhere a harp began to play. Cabe's brow furrowed. He did not care for harp music, but his daughter Valea did. So, unfortunately, did the heir to the drake throne. Dragging his thoughts back to the present predicament, he tried to devise some sort of compromise. "Somewhere neutral might work, but . . . but I still have trouble with being surrounded by Dragon Kings." His face lit up. "What if the others chose a representative among themselves, someone you and they both trust? I could agree to something like that. We could meet in the Dagora Forest, if that's acceptable to you."

"If that isss your offer, Cabe Bedlam, then I shall relay it to them. I have no qualms about it. They might agree to a represssentative, but the meeting ground may be more questionable. I will try to convince them that thisss is reasonable."

"Who would you choose among them—if I may ask that, my lord?"

"There is no question," the drake lord hissed. "Black is trusted by no one, perhaps not even himself. Red is young; his opinion is still shaky. Storm . . . we fear for his sanity. None of us desire another Ice Dragon."

The name sent shivers through the mage. The Ice Dragon had been one of the eldest, most traditional of the present Dragon Kings. After the fall of the emperor, he had come to the conclusion that only a sheet of death-giving ice blanketing the entire continent would rid the realm of the human situation. Of course, it would also rid the land of the drakes as well, but the fatalistic monarch of the Northern Wastes had considered that worth the victory.

If the Storm Dragon was following the Ice Dragon down the path of madness . . . Cabe knew of at least one other Dragon King who fell into that category already, but at least the Crystal Dragon kept his insanity to himself.

"No one will trust this Sssaleese enough," continued Green, running down the list. "He was not born with the proper birth markings. That leaves but one real choice for any of us . . ."

"Blue." Cabe leaned against a chair. "He maintains a peace of sorts with Penacles even though the Gryphon doesn't actually rule there any more." The Gryphon, whose appearance resembled that of the winged beast, had ruled Penacles until his need to discover his own past had sent him overseas to the dark empire of the Aramites. For many years he had worked to bring down the wolf raiders, as the Aramites were better known. While he was away, his second, General Toos, had ruled in his place. Now many, including the Gryphon, called the general *king*, but the tall, elderly soldier insisted he was only regent. In the eyes of loyal Toos, the Gryphon would ever be his commander.

"His ssson, Morgisss, is also a good friend of the lionbird."

"Will the other drakes accept his opinion?"

"I think that I will be able to convince them of that."

The harp music had ceased. Cabe flinched when he realized that, but then silently reprimanded himself for thinking the worst of his daughter. She was intelligent, whatever her infatuation with the exotic and unquestionably handsome heir. "Then . . . then I will agree to such terms, my lord. It'll have to take place after the visits to Talak and Penacles, however. I wish there was a way to avoid those meetings, but as you pointed out, if we get acknowledgment from two of the major human kingdoms in the east, it will make the path to the throne that much easier. I hope. Gwendolyn is in Talak now, helping to prepare things." *And with Queen Erini's aid, perhaps keep King Melicard from changing his mind about the whole visit!* "The journeys to Zuu and Gordag-Ai are still planned for immediately after the ascension, so we have no trouble there."

The Dragon King nodded. Within the false helm, the thin, lipless mouth stretched into a toothy smile. "Understand that my fellows truly have no choice; the idea of a new emperor is repellent to some after two decades of complete independence, but they also recognize the need. My race isss faltering; *you* know that. If we are to survive in the world of men, a world the Dragonrealm hasss already become, then we must unite dessspite our differences!"

Cabe smoothed his robe, trying to think of a delicate way to say what needed to be said. He could find no way but the simple truth. "There are many who think that a reunited drake race is the last thing we need. There are some who say that now that humans have the strength, it's time to deal with your kind once and for all."

"I am certain that Melicard of Talak isss one of them."

"One but hardly the worst. The Dragon Kings, again your company excepted, my lord, have rarely endeared themselves to mankind. A new emperor is to some simply a resurrecting of old evils."

For a time there was only silence, as both drake lord and sorcerer considered what they were attempting. Then, the Green Dragon said, "I never expected it to be simple, but I know it must be done. So do you, Cabe Bedlam."

"I—" The warlock's agreement was cut short by the sight of a figure lurking just within the room beyond the balcony. Cabe abandoned his position and stalked over to the entrance. The Dragon King watched but did not question.

"What is it, Grath?"

Out onto the balcony emerged a drake, but one different in so many ways from the forest lord. Whereas the Green Dragon wore the form of a hellish knight of emerald hue, this one more resembled a human. Shorter than Cabe by two or three inches, Grath had sharp, almost elfin features on a human face. His hair was short and dark green, his skin gold with touches of emerald. The young drake smiled nervously, revealing teeth slightly more pointed than that of a human. Like his elder brother, Kyl, Grath caught the eye of many women, both drake and human, but unlike the heir to the drake throne, the younger offspring of the unlamented Dragon Emperor seemed not to notice. Grath spent most of his time in the libraries. If . . . *when* Kyl became emperor, it was intended that Grath serve as advisor and minister.

Cabe had always considered it a blessing that Grath had turned out the way he had. With him to counsel his elder brother, the possibility of Kyl doing something rash was greatly lessened. Not eliminated, but at least lessened.

The drake looked nervously at his guardian, then glanced at the Dragon King. "I . . . heard . . . that my lord Green was here! I just wanted to . . ."

Cabe rescued the faltering Grath. "You want to ask him some more questions, of course." The young drake nodded in silent gratitude. For the most part, Grath shadowed his brother, but given an opportunity to talk with the Green Dragon about drake history, he suddenly became a personality. Cabe could never have believed that a drake could be shy, but that appeared to be the case. "Something strikes me, though. Shouldn't you be taking lessons with Master Traske?"

Grath almost looked guilty. "Master Traske cancelled classes but a few minutes ago, Lord Bedlam. I swear that by the Dragon of the Depths!"

"I hope he's not ill." This was not the first time of late that Benjin Traske had abruptly cancelled a session. Granted the human tutor's duties were now limited since most of his charges were nearly of adult age, but the cancellations were coming with much regularity these days. Traske was a huge man in both girth and height, and almost twice as old as Cabe appeared. The scholar had a touch of magic around him, but evidently not enough to slow the aging process. If he was not well . . .

Grath quickly smothered his guardian's concerns for Benjin Traske's health by replying, "No, sssir. He seemed healthy . . ."

Cabe dismissed the matter, deciding that he would speak with the man when he had the opportunity to do so. "If His Majesty has time when we are finished—"

"I would be pleasssed to ssspeak with you, my lord Grath," interrupted the Dragon King. He treated the other drake with deference, almost as if it were Grath, not Kyl, who was about to ascend the throne. Cabe and Gwen, while they, too, respected the younger drake's royal lineage, tried to treat Grath as a young man, not a symbol. Both mages felt it was important to give the dragon heirs some notion of normal behavior. It had been too often the case in the past that kings had been raised with no concept of themselves as real individuals. They were trained to be a power, a living incarnation. While that was necessary to a point, it also meant that they tended to lack the ability to understand the lives of those they ruled.

Whether humans had ever raised drakes before the Green Dragon's suggestion roughly two decades earlier, the warlock could not say. Cabe had no idea whether he and his wife had been correct in their decision to accept the Dragon King's challenge; they could only hope that some good would come of the years the drake children had spent growing up here.

Grath brightened at the drake lord's response.

"But first I must speak with your brother."

That brought a brief darkness to Grath's visage, but he almost immediately recovered. Bowing, he asked, "Shall I go seek him out for you, Uncle?"

The term was strictly one of respect, as was the Dragon King habit of calling one another "brother." Since the various clans rarely mixed, the Green Dragon was no more Grath's uncle than he was Cabe's. However, in the eyes of the dragon prince, it was obvious that he thought of the visiting monarch as approaching as close to the blood tie as was possible. The lord of the Dagora Forest represented everything that Grath had grown up believing in, yet, because of his secondary position, would never be unless something happened to Kyl.

All knew that the younger drake would sacrifice his own life before he would allow *anything* to happen to his older sibling.

"That would not be proper," returned the Dragon King. "As he will be my lord, it is fitting that I go to him."

Which would only serve to further inflate Kyl's ego, the mage thought. Unfortunately, Kyl had begun to develop his personality long before he had been placed in the care of the Bedlams. While Cabe and Gwen had triumphed in reshaping some edges of that personality, as a whole the heir to the dragon throne was little changed from the day he had first come to them. Still, even the few changes wrought would make Kyl a more trustworthy emperor than his sire had been toward the end.

"Do you know where Kyl is, Grath?"

"Yes, Master Bedlam."

When he saw that the drake would not elaborate, the dark-haired mage grew suspicious. "Where *is* he, Grath?"

"With Aurim."

"Aurim?" It was not the answer Cabe Bedlam had expected. He wondered why Kyl's brother seemed worried. Aurim and Kyl did on occasion spend time together, mostly because there were few others living at the Manor who were of a similar age. Aurim was also likely the only one the emperor-designate considered near his own station. Fortunately, despite the time he spent with Kyl, Cabe's eldest had not fallen into imitating the drake's royal manner. "Very well, show us the way, if you please."

They could probably have transported themselves there by sorcery, but several reasons prevented them from doing so. One was that the Green Dragon considered it a matter of disrespect to materialize suddenly before his future emperor. Another was that Cabe felt such use of the power was frivolous and wasteful; the Manor grounds were not that huge, and it was certainly no emergency.

Last, but by no means least, was the simple fear that Aurim might be attempting to use his own magic. While born with the potential to be even greater than either of his parents, he still had trouble keeping his abilities under control. Spells went wild for no reason that anyone could discover. It was sometimes a wonder that the Manor had survived his childhood. Once in a while, the young warlock would make some progress in maintaining his control, but not often enough that the residents of the area could breathe easy.

As they followed Grath through the halls of the Manor, the Dragon King said, "I apologize again for the sssuddenness of this visssit. I felt that it was important that I relay the request asss soon as wasss possible."

"You need never apologize, Your Majesty! I'm only sorry that my wife will have missed you." The Lady Bedlam had been a protégée of sorts of the Green Dragon, and that bond had remained strong despite the years. Cabe, on the other hand, while he considered the drake a friend, was always aware of the reptilian monarch's inhuman side. Whether that was the result of his own prejudices, he could not say.

Marble corridor gave way on one side to living tree. The Dragon King paused momentarily to admire the skill with which the unknown craftsmen had melded rock and plant together. As they resumed their walk, the drake lord commented, "The Manor will ever be a sssource of amazement to me no matter how much I visssit it!"

"You should try living here."

"I would rather not, thank you. Still, it is a shame we know so little of itsss hissstory. For many centuries, it lay hidden even from many of my predecesssssors. To think that such a marvelousss artifact could exissst so clossse!"

Cabe hid his surprise. He had not been aware that some of the previous Dragon Kings of this region might not have known about the Manor. The warlock did not press for an explanation, but it gave him something to consider when he had the opportunity. One of his pet projects was trying to understand the ancient structure he called home, but so far his results could have all been written on the palm of his hand. The Manor had proved miserly when it came to giving up its secrets.

Eventually they left the confines of the tall structure and entered the immense garden regions behind it. The gardens were the center of life for those living in and around the Manor. Both the human and draconian servants often found reason to spend their free time here. Some even now looked up from their work to respectfully acknowledge the trio. More than a few of the Bedlams' people had made the sculptured lands their personal project, many times contributing to its upkeep even after finishing with their personal chores. There was something soothing about the gardens. The more one gave to the gardens, the more the gardens seemed to give to the person.

It had not always been so. When Cabe had first arrived at the Manor, fleeing the Dragon Kings, three drake females had tried to make a meal out of him. Then, in the garden, he had discovered Gwen, frozen in amber for more than a century thanks to Azran. Freeing her had almost killed *him*, he recalled with a smile.

The landscape was an artistic delight. Topiary animals, both fanciful and real, dotted the gardens. The sculpted animals seemed to need very little pruning. They had, in fact, looked nearly new when the warlock had first arrived. Beyond them, and the most likely place to find Aurim and Kyl, was a huge maze. The shrubbery walls of the maze rose to almost twice the height of a man. The initial part of the maze was simple, and many folk came there simply to rest. As one delved deeper, however, the puzzle became more complex, with turns growing wild and confusing. Having grown up with the maze, most of the children found it entertaining fun. Most of the adults, Cabe included, found it perplexing and confounding. If not for his sorcery, the master warlock would have become hopelessly lost on several occasions.

With Grath to guide them, they maneuvered through the dense bushes. Both Cabe and the Dragon King were silent as they followed. Each time he was forced to enter the deeper labyrinth, Cabe sought to memorize the path, there always being the slight fear that something would cause him to have to find his way out without magic. From the look of concentration he noticed when he happened to glance at his companion, the Dragon King was doing much the same.

Then, without warning, they came upon the children.

Children was an outdated term. Both the draconian heirs and the mage's own offspring were nearly all of adult age. The growth process slowed in drakes as they reached their teens, which made someone of Grath or Kyl's age resemble someone of Aurim's, who was a few years younger. Valea, a bit younger than her brother, was the only one who could even remotely still be thought of as a child, but only when she was angry. Young as she was, she was capable of turning heads and garnering admiring glances.

Which was why the tableau before him almost made the sorcerer want to reach for his daughter and drag her back to the security of the Manor.

Aurim, clad in a robe of deep, rich red, stood in the center of the small open area, hands raised. His name implied gold and, as a child, he had chosen to take that literally, forever causing his hair to shimmer like the valuable metal, save the silver streak marking him as a spellcaster. Even later attempts to change it back had failed. Cabe's son wore an expression of intense concentration on his handsome face, and the reason for that concentration was obviously the colorful display floating before him. Miniature comets of red, yellow, blue, green, and purple swirled about in a mad yet coordinated dance. At the same time, a constantly shifting array of tendrils worked to keep the comets in check. The spell was a test. Aurim controlled each and every facet of it. If he lost control of any one segment, the entire display would collapse. Outwardly, such a task might look minor to some, but only powerful and skilled mages were able to do it for very long. This one was the latest and most difficult in a series that the young spellcaster had begun two or three years back.

Had it been under other circumstances, Cabe would have taken time to admire his son's work. Unfortunately, his eyes could not help but be drawn to Aurim's audience. An audience of two, who were much too close together for his tastes.

He now saw what had bothered Grath. Kyl was with Aurim, true, but his attention was on the red-haired young woman sitting beside him on one of the maze's stone benches. Valea, a near copy of her mother, watched her brother practice. She wore a forest green gown that accented both her face and form. That was not a good sign; Valea generally preferred hunting clothes, more practical for a young woman often on the move, and only wore dresses when forced to do so . . . or when she thought she would be spending time near the drake.

If Grath and Aurim were considered handsome, Kyl was almost beautiful. He moved with a grace his brother lacked and wore richly styled clothing. In every respect he looked like an exotic, elfin lord. His shading was slightly different from Grath's, with a bit more gold in it. As the day approached for his crowning, Kyl seemed more and more to assume the royal colors of the dragon emperor. Next to him, even Aurim's blinding locks paled.

A shared joke here. A brief touch there. Everything he did was for Valea, and Cabe could see that she noticed all of it.

He was trying to control his fatherly temper when Grath suddenly called out, "Kyl! Lord Green has come to see you!"

The announcement shattered Aurim's concentration. A tiny maelstrom arose as the different segments of his spell collided with one another or went fluttering off. At the same time, Valea and Kyl straightened, both trying to pretend nothing had occurred.

As the last of Aurim's spell dissipated, Kyl rose. He was now an inch or two taller than Cabe but so lean that the difference seemed greater. There was a touch of arrogance in his smile. His eyes were burning orbs that snared a person if one was not careful. The elegant courtier outfit the heir wore was real, not a magical shaping like the scale armor of the Dragon Kings. His teeth were slightly edged. In dim light, it was possible some would not have recognized him for what he was. That illusion, however, failed each time Kyl spoke.

"Your majesssssty! How good of you to come! Forgive me for not greeting you sssssooner!"

Whereas both Grath and Ursa, the female of the trio of royal hatchlings, fell prey to sibilance only when excited, Kyl constantly suffered from it. It was a point of great annoyance to the emperor-to-be, who prided himself on perfection.

The Dragon King bowed. "It isss I who must apologize to you, my lord. Had this visit not been sssudden, I would have brought more than my own presence. I hope that you will forgive me."

"You have been my mossst ardent sssupporter, Lord Green! That will ever be gift enough in itsssself!"

"I hope, then, that I am not disturbing you?"

Kyl casually waved off the drake lord's question. "By no meansss! We were sssimply enjoying the day, were we not?"

It was questionable as to which of his companions the young drake was speaking to, but Valea was the one who quickly answered. "That's what we were doing, yes."

Cabe wondered if it was his own imagination that made him think that Kyl's mouth curled slightly higher when Valea responded.

"I . . . I solved the latest one, Father," Aurim added. "I told Kyl and Valea—"

"And I insssisssted that we be allowed to sssee." Kyl's tone was all innocence.

"A most impressive display it wasss, too," remarked the Green Dragon. "Now, though, if Your Majesty hasss time, there are details concerning your future which we mussst discuss."

"You mean the excursion to Talak?" Kyl's mood changed, becoming tinged with distaste.

"That and more, my emperor."

"If you think the mattersss worthy of our time, then I will trussst you, my Lord Green." Turning from Cabe and the Dragon King, Kyl nodded politely to Aurim. "You will have to show me that trick again when we have more time, Aurim." Focusing his attention on Valea, Kyl reached out and dared to take her hand. As Cabe tensed and his daughter's cheeks reddened, the dragon heir leaned forward and gently kissed the hand. "My lady . . ."

Kyl released her hand after what Cabe considered much too long a hesitation. Turning back to the newcomers, the young drake eyed his human guardian and asked, "Will you be joining usss, Massster Bedlam? Your advice isss alwaysss welcome."

Refusing to be the first to break, Cabe Bedlam continued to match gazes with Kyl. "I would be happy to give what advice I can, Kyl."

"Then shall we talk here or adjourn to the Manor?"

It was Aurim who decided for them. "There's no need for you to leave! Valea and I can return to the Manor. This place is as private as anywhere else, probably more." He looked at his sister. "Mistress Belima said she'd be baking today. Perhaps it might be in order to visit her now?"

Fully recovered now from Kyl's daring kiss, Valea eagerly took up Aurim's suggestion. She turned a dazzling smile on the Dragon King. "If you will forgive us, my lord?"

"By all meansss. I have tasted the human female's meat pies. Had I known her talentsss before I offered your parents her services, she would be baking for me."

Laughing lightly, Cabe's daughter curtsied. Aurim followed suit with a nervous bow. Having grown up around royalty, the Bedlams' offspring were used to excusing themselves when the time came for important discussions. It was not as if Cabe and his wife did not believe in the abilities of the two; Valea and Aurim were usually informed as to the results of such discussions. However, where the coming coronation was concerned, it was easier for all if only those truly necessary were involved. There were times when even the master warlock and his bride did not join in, leaving the conversation strictly between the Green Dragon, Kyl, and Grath, who Kyl always insisted be present.

The two younger Bedlams departed, Valea in more haste than was necessary. The moment they were out of sight, Kyl returned to the bench and seated himself. He looked up at the drake lord in expectation.

After a slight hesitation, the Dragon King said, "There isss a new matter we must discuss."

"You may proceed."

Cabe was amazed at the calm with which his companion accepted the royal tones of the heir. Nodding, the drake launched into the tale he had told the warlock, describing in detail the gathering of the other reptilian monarchs and their request. Oddly, despite the almost arrogant demand of the drake lords, the manner in which the Green Dragon presented it almost made it sound like lowly subjects requesting a most grand gesture on the part of their sovereign. The warlock surreptitiously glanced at the armored figure beside him. Never had he seen the Dragon King adopt so . . . so *servile* . . . a tone.

The emperor-to-be accepted it without question, although Grath, who had taken up a position behind and a little to one side of his brother, barely hid a frown. Kyl listened in silence to everything, then spent a moment or two thinking the matter over. At last, he glanced up at Grath. Something unspoken passed between them.

Nodding to himself, the dragon heir looked up at the mage and forest lord and said, "A meeting with the othersss isss not only acceptable but necesssary, asss you yoursssself pointed out, my lord." Once again, his unsettling eyes focused on Cabe. "However, Massster Bedlam makesss a wonderful sssuggestion! I like the idea of meeting with only one, the Lord Blue, asss you proposssed. It will show them that I am willing to hear them, yet will *not* bow to their demandssss!"

"I am certain that they did not mean it ssso, my liege. You mussst understand that they are only concerned for you."

Kyl's gaze leapt to the Dragon King. "I understand *their* concernssss very well." He nodded to himself again.

The Green Dragon did not pursue the matter. Kyl's nod was a signal both Cabe and the drake lord had come to recognize. It would be futile to continue, for the young emperor-to-be would pay no more attention from here on. He had come to his own conclusions, whatever they might be, and that, in his mind, was all that mattered.

"Have you chosssen a time for thisss audience with Lord Blue?"

"After the visits to Talak and Penacles," Cabe informed his royal charge. "Too many preparations have already been made; it would not look good if we were to cancel either one this late."

A dangerous gleam appeared in Kyl's eyes, but the drake merely nodded. "You are correct, Massster Bedlam . . . asss usual. Speaking of Talak, what thought hasss been given to our entrance?"

This had been a touchy matter where both Melicard and Kyl had been concerned. The king of Talak had expected Kyl to arrive at the southern gate of the city, accompanied by an entourage, in the fashion of most human monarchs. However, the dragon heir, fully aware that he had sorcery at his command, wanted to materialize in regal but dramatic manner in the very center of Melicard's throne room. *That* had not gone over well with the lord of the mountain kingdom. Talak had lived under the shadow of the Dragon Emperor for centuries, and now that it was free and a power in its own right, the present monarch had no intention of appearing subservient to *any* drake, especially one planning to ascend to the role of emperor. Part of the task the Lady Bedlam performed even now was to find some middle ground. Cabe did not envy his wife.

"That is still being discussed," the warlock commented in very neutral tones.

"If I may make a suggestion?" The lord of Dagora waited for acknowledgment from Kyl before continuing. "It might be good to be magnanimousss for your first two visits. I shall prepare a caravan consisting of both humans and drakesss to accompany you, a large enough caravan to indicate your great status but small enough to keep the folk of Talak from running in fear." The Green Dragon paused long enough to share a smile with Kyl. "This way, you will enter as he desires, but you will enter in glory! Thisss is not a sssimple matter; I wish I had a better suggestion, my lord, but I do not. Remember this, though. Talak will be opening itsss gates to *you* no matter how you arrive. It will be the first time they have done ssso *willingly*, and that in itself is a coup for you!"

Perhaps it was the *way* the Dragon King said it, as opposed to his actual words, for Cabe was both pleased and surprised to see Kyl accept the suggestion.

"Very well. Asssss long assss it isss undersssstood who it is who will be *emperor.*"

Lord Green bowed. "You may rest assured on that matter."

Kyl shook his head and smiled, revealing his sharp teeth. "What would I do without the two of you? My Lord Green. Massster Bedlam. You two have been the father I lossst!"

Cabe forced back a grimace, recalling his part in the downfall of the former emperor.

Evidently he did not completely succeed, for Kyl glanced at him. "You did what you had to do and I have come to understsssand that, Massster Bedlam! The battle wasss forced upon you, after all! I bear you no animosssity. I am not my father; I am *Kyl.*"

Not trusting himself to find the correct words, Cabe nodded what he hoped would appear a thankful acknowledgment. He had heard such remarks from Kyl over the years and yet still could not bring himself to believe them. There was always that hint of something in the dragon heir's tone . . .

. . . or maybe it was just his own distrust.

Grath, who had remained a silent shadow for most of the time, leaned over and whispered something to his brother. Kyl's piercing eyes widened, then narrowed. His lips curled slightly, never a good sign as far as Cabe was concerned. That smile usually preceded some sort of mischief.

"Thank you, Grath, for reminding me." The emperor-to-be returned his attention to his two visitors. "A notion occurred to me but a short time ago, a notion I meant to disssscusssss with you when next the sssubject of thessse royal visssitsss arossse."

"What might that be, Your Majesty?" the Green Dragon asked, a slight edge to his voice. No one but the warlock seemed to notice it, though.

"We would like the eternal, the demon ssssteed, to join usss for thisss journey."

"Y—" The Dragon King could go no farther. Both Cabe and he stared at the dragon heir as if all sense had left him.

Kyl leaned back. "Explain, Grath."

Nervous, the other young drake said, "My brother . . . my brother feels that the presence of Darkhorssse is esssential. It deals with many situations. First and foremost is that both Queen Erini of Talak and Toos the regent of Penaclesss are familiar with the shadow steed. Not only familiar, but on good terms with him. His appearance at the meetings with Melicard and Toos should assuage any misgivings they might have over the arrival of so many drakes. No one caresss to cross the eternal's path."

"Really, Your Majesssty—"

"We are not finished yet, my Lord Green," Kyl said quietly.

Grath hissed in anxiety as he resumed. "There is also one personal but highly important reassson for the presence of Darkhorse. My brother feelsss that, in this time of forging a new peace in the Dragonrealm, peace must also be made with the eternal himself."

"It isss time for *all* animosssitiesss to die," Kyl interjected. "Even *I* mussst admit to sssome failure when it comes to the great ebony ssstallion! Now, I would offer a peace between usss! Now, I would like to be able to call Dark-horsssse *friend*!"

"Your Majesssty is aware, I hope, that King Melicard bears little love for the shadow steed. It isss his bride, the queen, who isss so fond of Darkhorse."

"All the better, then, Lord Green." Kyl's long, tapering fingers formed a steeple. "It will give the human an opportunity to make hisss own peace with the black one! Talak would certainly benefit and Melicard would earn the per-sssonal gratitude of hisss lovely queen, who I know hasss alwaysss regretted the tension between her husband and her loyal friend!"

The Dragon King looked at Cabe, sending the warlock a silent appeal for help in this matter. Cabe was at a loss, though. He could see some reason behind the suggestion. Darkhorse had ever been a most deadly enemy of the drake race. At present, an uneasy truce existed, in great part due to Darkhorse's respect for the warlock's own position as guardian of the late Dragon Emperor's young. Only when attacked did Darkhorse now unleash his might upon the drakes.

Kyl had never before suggested such an overture, making Cabe suspect that perhaps Grath was responsible. Of course, the younger drake had always gotten along much better with Darkhorse than the emperor-to-be had.

"Darkhorse might not desire to come," he finally pointed out. Beside him, Green exhaled slightly. Evidently the Dragon King had decided that things were complex enough without throwing the shadow steed into the situation. Dark-horse was a matter that could wait as far as he was concerned.

Kyl did not think so. "If anyone can persssuade him, it isss *you*, Massster Bedlam! Give him my reasssons for requesssting thisss. Tell him that I know that we have not dealt well with one another before thisss and that I think it isss very much time that we made the effort."

Again there was the nod of the head, the sign that Kyl would not be swayed in this matter. He knew also that he could trust Cabe to make the request of Darkhorse. The warlock sometimes wished that the half-elf who had raised him had not been so brutally honest. Cabe *would* make the request, no matter how uncertain he was as to the wisdom of it.

He could only hope that Darkhorse laughed at it. Adding the eternal to the meeting between the two monarchs threatened to replace the carefully organized affair with a haphazard, tense confrontation.

Was *that* what Kyl wanted?

"I'll see what I can do for you, Kyl. Darkhorse can be anywhere; you know that as well as I do. It may prove impossible to locate him in time, much less pass on your request to him."

"I have faith in you, Massster Bedlam." The drake rose, each movement graceful and swift, like a cat. "My Lord Green, if there isss nothing elssse requiring my immediate attention, it isss time for my riding lesssons. Masssters Ssarekai and Ironshoe have been teaching me some of the more sssubtle differencesss between handling a drake and riding a horssse." He scratched his chin. "I have been thinking of riding one of the latter when I enter Talak. Much more graceful and regal than a riding drake, albeit not nearly ssso deadly looking. I have not made up my mind which would be preferable."

The master of the Dagora Forest shook his helmed head. "No, my liege. I have said what I came to sssay. I thank you for your time and trouble."

"Not at all." To his brother, Kyl added, "Grath, I will need to sssee you later."

Both drakes bowed to their future emperor. Cabe settled for a respectful appearance. He could not bring himself to bow, no matter how agitated he sensed the Green Dragon had become upon noticing the human's action. The dragon heir did not even seem to notice. He simply turned away and vanished into the labyrinth.

After a pause, the Dragon King straightened. He looked down at the warlock. "You should bow when he leaves, friend Cabe." When his companion would not answer him, the dragon turned toward Grath. "Well, my prince. Do you still desssire to speak with me? I have a little time to spare before I must depart for my kingdom."

"If I would not be disturbing you, Lord Green."

"Of courssse not."

Cabe, not desiring any animosity to remain between himself and the one Dragon King he trusted, suggested, "My children made mention of Mistress Belima before, my lord. I can assure you that she's found time to make some of the meat pies you find so fascinating. That may be because they're also Grath's favorites, I believe." A look from the young drake indicated complete agreement. "Perhaps you would care for a light meal. I'm certain that Grath would be interested."

That lightened the mood. They all knew of the young drake's near obsession with the pies. It was considered something of a miracle that Grath remained so fit.

The Green Dragon willingly took the peace offering. "That would be quite sssatisssfactory. Perhaps I can alssso use the opportunity to convince the woman to return to my servicesss."

"You'll face the full population of the Manor if you try that, including some very adamant youngsters!"

"Then, I shall sssimply have to visit more often."

"Shall I lead us back now, Master Bedlam?" At mention of the meal, Grath had become animated again. Yet again, Cabe marveled at the transformation the younger drake went through each time he and his brother separated. It was as if there were two Graths.

He almost wished there *were*. If Kyl were only more like Grath, Cabe knew that he would feel better about the upcoming visits. Yet, it was more likely the drakes would accept someone like Kyl. Grath might just be too human for them. In truth, the warlock knew that despite his misgivings concerning the dragon heir, Kyl was more likely to be able to control the Dragon Kings than his younger sibling.

*Now if only someone could control Kyl*, the warlock thought, then instantly regretted even considering the notion. That was one of the dangers both he and the Green Dragon feared. Once upon the throne, *would* Kyl prove to be the emperor that was needed, or would he fall victim to the twisted advice of one or more of the deadlier Dragon Kings?

Cabe belatedly realized Grath was still waiting for an answer to *his* question. The blue-robed sorcerer waved a hand at his charge, forced on a smile, and said, "Lead on! I'm beginning to feel a bit hungry myself!"

"This way, then, Lord Green. Master Bedlam."

As they followed the drake, Cabe's eyes strayed to the empty bench. Gone instantly were considerations concerning dangers to the ascension; instead, the warlock recalled two young folk sitting much too close to one another. The image reminded him that he had a personal reason for seeing Kyl safely through the visitations and the coronation. Kyl in his role as Gold, Dragon Emperor, would be far away, so far, in fact, that he might as well be on one of the moons. Cabe knew that what he wanted was selfish and likely prejudiced, but it was more than what Kyl was that made the master sorcerer desire him far from Valea. It was also *who* the dragon heir was, meaning the mind behind the exotic countenance. Perhaps it was simply the fear of a concerned parent, but he did not trust whatever intentions the handsome drake might have for his daughter. Telling Valea that, however, would avail him naught. She was just old enough to understand and just young enough not to listen. There *were* tales, some of them with much credence to back them up, of drakes and humans marrying and raising young. It *was* possible, according to what Cabe knew. Possible but unthinkable.

*Maybe I'm just imagining things. Maybe my own fears are making me see something that isn't there.* Yet, Gwendolyn, too, had expressed such worries. Could they *both* be imagining it?

This was not the time for personal matters, he told himself. As dear as his family was to him, the fate of the entire realm waited on the outcome of this venture with Kyl and the throne. Whatever was or was not happening between his daughter and the drake *had* to be secondary.

Cabe hoped he would be able to remember that in the weeks to come.

# III

"WELL, IT TOOK some pressure from both Erini and his daughter, but Melicard has finally agreed to the suggestions made by Kyl."

Cabe, seated, nodded absently as his wife talked. Normally, Lady Bedlam garnered his full attention, if only because he adored her so. Gwendolyn Bedlam was to him a forest goddess, a fire-tressed creature of the wild. She stood across from him now, a vision in green, her hair with its silver streak rippling nearly to her waist. The emerald riding outfit she wore perfectly accented a stunning figure. Her glittering eyes matched the color of her clothes.

Seeing that she was being all but ignored, the statuesque enchantress walked gracefully toward her husband, finally stationing herself directly before the warlock in an attempt to break him free from whatever spell held his mind.

Cabe looked up. "What is it?"

"Have you tired of me after all these years?"

His brow furrowed.

She knelt by his chair, one hand touching him softly on the arm. "You're starting to find other things that interest you more than I do."

He took hold of her hand and squeezed it. "Don't be silly. Nothing means more to me than you and the children." Cabe took the hand and kissed it. "Young or old, beautiful or not, you know I'll always love you." A smile briefly touched his face. "I just hope that you'll always feel the same way."

"You shouldn't have to ask." Her own smile faded a little as she recalled what they had been discussing. "You heard what I said?"

"Melicard's agreed. It took some doing?"

"For most of it, no. He actually found the suggestion concerning Kyl's entrance to be reasonable. Where that was concerned, it was simply a matter of discussing it with his advisors. *That's* what took three days . . . that, and the more delicate problem of Darkhorse."

"Darkhorse?"

She nodded. The sunlight that touched her face accented what Cabe considered perfectly sculpted features, a sharp contrast to his own plain face. He was thankful that both children had taken after her. Valea especially would resemble her mother.

"Melicard has grown more reasonable in the past few years where Erini's relationship with Darkhorse is concerned, but he doesn't like the notion of the eternal being a part of a state affair. Tensions will be high enough without his unnerving presence, so the king said more times than I care to count."

"It's understandable." Cabe tried to picture Darkhorse among the splendidly dressed courtiers. Both humans and drakes feared the eternal's power. To most, Darkhorse was part legend, a thing of shadows. It was one reason why the warlock had not been pleased by Kyl's suggestion. Darkhorse could cause the audience between the two monarchs to collapse simply by *being* there. "So has he agreed to the presence of Darkhorse or not?"

"He did. Finally. Erini and Lynnette had much to do with that. It's hard for Melicard to refuse them anything."

The warlock chuckled. "I think I understand *that!*"

She rose enough to give him a kiss, then stood. "You'd *better* understand that!"

He returned her playful smile, but other thoughts turned his expression sober. "I'm glad that's settled. Now comes the interesting part."

"You've still heard nothing?"

Cabe rose. He looked up at the ceiling, then back at his wife. "Nothing. It's been three days since I sent out a magical summons to him. Three days and still he hasn't come."

"How very odd." She put a hand to her chin. "Darkhorse is usually very prompt."

"Unless he's occupied with something. . . ."

Her expression said it all. *"Shade?"*

"I'd like to think not. I thought him over that obsession, but . . . I don't know."

Shade had been a warlock, possibly in his own way the most powerful that had ever lived. No one knew exactly how old the cloaked and hooded figure had been, but Cabe was certain that Shade could trace his origins back to the Vraad, the ancestral race of men. Shade, he was certain, had *been* Vraad.

The spell that had made the blur-faced sorcerer nigh immortal had also brought him to the edge of madness. Shade had been cursed to ever be reborn the opposite of what he had been in his previous life. Cabe had first known him as friend, but after the warlock's death during battle, Shade had returned as the horrific Madrac, one of the many splinter personalities that formed with each new incarnation. It had taken the full might of Darkhorse, who knew the ancient warlock best, to defeat Madrac.

Shade had returned again much later, but this time entirely confused, his personalities shifting back and forth without warning. Darkhorse, ever both friend and foe, had taken it upon himself to end the travesty, if only for the warlock's own sake.

Queen Erini, who had become for a time Shade's pawn, had been there at the end. Shade and Darkhorse had made their peace, and the warlock had given up his own life to prevent a disaster that he himself had been in great part responsible for creating. There and then, it should have been ended.

Darkhorse, however, had not been able to accept such a death. Shade had meant more to him than any of his mortal companions could have known. The gray mage was the only one who, in his own way, could understand the shadow steed, could comprehend the emptiness the leviathan kept buried within. There was no one else in the Dragonrealm like the black stallion, no one who could understand his longings, his fears. Immortal himself, save if killed, it was only natural that he be drawn to Shade.

Because of that, the shadow steed had spent the next several years utilizing much of his time searching for any trace of the vanished warlock. Part of Darkhorse wanted to make certain that Shade was dead, for if he was not, then the Dragonrealm risked great danger. Yet another part of the ebony stallion—and this only a handful knew—hoped that the warlock was alive, that the one creature who understood the loneliness he suffered was still there for him.

The obsession had almost cost Cabe his life. Ashamed, Darkhorse had all but abandoned his futile search . . . yet, there were times when the shadow steed would vanish to places unknown for long periods of time. No one was certain what Darkhorse did during these episodes, but the Bedlams feared that the obsession was growing again.

"What happens if we can't find him? The audience in Talak is drawing very near. Now that it's settled that Darkhorse is permitted there, it would seem a bit foolish if he was not at least *asked*."

The warlock sighed. "Kyl and Melicard will simply have to be annoyed. No one rules Darkhorse. I told Kyl I would do what I could, but I didn't promise a miracle. Even if I find Darkhorse, he might choose not to come." He shook his head. "I don't know why Kyl felt it so necessary that he be there. I don't know why Kyl does *anything* he does. . . ."

His wife came and put her arms around him. They held each other close.

"This isn't just about Darkhorse," she whispered. "This is about the same thing we always talk of."

"We tried to raise him as best we could, Gwen. Look at Grath. Look at our own children. I'm fairly confident about them, although Aurim's recklessness with magic is probably going to be the end of me soon. What *happened* to Kyl?"

"He was older, Cabe. He had already begun developing his own personality. We did what we could. Considering who he is, we've not done too badly."

"Did we? Of late, I've noticed myself thinking thoughts I'd have found reprehensible in others."

"Kyl is in great part responsible for that." The sorceress released him and stepped back. "Believe that. There are drakes here who would admit to it. As a ruler, Kyl may do great things, but as a person, his attitude lacks a certain responsibility."

They both knew that they were in part thinking of their own daughter, but neither desired to say any more on that subject for now. The two were certain . . . almost . . . that Valea was simply infatuated with Kyl's exotic appearance. She was too intelligent to think that there could be anything between them . . . they hoped.

Cabe made a cutting motion with his hand. "None of this solves the present problem. I'm going to see if I can find Darkhorse myself. The more I think about it, even if he doesn't appear in Talak, I want him to know what's going on. If anyone is planning to disrupt the event or, worse, strike out at the emperor-to-be, it wouldn't hurt to have Darkhorse nearby."

She cocked her head to one side and smiled a bit. "You know, I think this is all a *ploy*! I think you just planned this sudden little excursion so that you can escape the preparations for the journey!"

They both laughed at her joke, all the while aware that it was simply an attempt to lighten Cabe's ever-darkening mood. "Now why would I want to escape arranging and rearranging Kyl's caravan? I couldn't think of anything more entertaining!"

"Then I will go in your place, husband dear!"

"Not likely!" He took her once more into his arms. "If you leave it to me to organize this, we will be ready to depart by some time late next *year*!"

"Too true. . . ." The sorceress grew quiet, then said, "If you must go searching, you can avoid the region around Talak. I made mention to Erini that she should let us know if Darkhorse appears there."

"Then that's one place less. I have some other notions of where he might have run off to. I'm certain there's nothing to worry about." He kissed her. "This won't take long. If Darkhorse is at none of the places I have in mind, I'll leave him a sign that he won't fail to recognize. Then it will simply have to be up to him as to whether he answers or not."

"All this running around sometimes seems so futile, doesn't it? I shall be glad when Kyl is crowned so that we can at last breathe again."

Cabe forced his smile to remain where it was. "That's *all* I've ever asked."

He kissed his wife once more . . . then was gone.

As the warlock vanished, Lady Bedlam heard a knock on the door. She turned toward it and bid the newcomer to enter.

It was Benjin Traske. The huge, bearded scholar was clad in the colors and garments of his special calling—a gray, cowled cloak with gold trim on the collar and ebony robes beneath. The cowl was presently pushed back, revealing gray hair with a very slight peppering of silver. Like Cabe, Gwen sometimes thought that the tutor resembled more a condemning judge than the scholar he was. She noted also that he still wore a blade on his belt, despite such armament going against his calling. Traske had lost his family in the fall of the city of Mito Pica some years back and had always regretted that he had not had even a knife with which to protect them.

Something about his expression disturbed her. It was nothing that she could put her finger on. He seemed almost pensive, but that was not quite it.

"My pardon, lady. I thought Master Bedlam also here."

"He has left."

"I see." For a breath or two, it seemed the massive figure did not know what to say.

"I *am* Lady Bedlam, scholar. You can trust me with whatever it is you wished to speak to my husband about."

His expression became somewhat rueful. "My apologies. I did not mean to infer such . . ."

"What is it you want, Scholar Traske?"

He took a deep breath. "I realize that you have much on your mind and that I would only be further adding to your troubles, but I wish to speak to you about the excursion to Talak. . . ."

*THIS IS GETTING to be a habit!*

The wind howled around him. Everything was white, but it was the whiteness of death, the eternal winter. Snow and ice were everywhere. A few misshapen hills, possibly only large snowbanks, dotted the otherwise flat landscape. In the distance, the warlock could see some taller mounds, but he knew it would be a waste of time to go and investigate them. If Darkhorse was not here at the very spot on which Cabe now stood, then he was not in any part of the Northern Wastes.

Snow fluttered around the silent spellcaster but did not alight on him. The same spell that shielded him from the cold also shielded him from the other gifts the inhospitable wasteland offered. Snow that sought perch on him simply faded away.

He had come here because this, of all the places that the eternal frequented, was the most likely spot that Darkhorse would have chosen to return to had his obsession taken root once again. Here, in the emptiness of the Wastes, Shade had perished . . . or so Queen Erini said. She had witnessed it all. Years later, during a quest much like the one he was on now, Cabe had been brought here by the novice sorceress, who had explained to him the relevance of this chilling place. Although he was never certain exactly why he had done so, Cabe Bedlam had imprinted the location on his mind. Perhaps at the time it had simply been because Shade had been a friend to him as well and all he had wanted to do was remember.

Now, however, it was time to move on. Darkhorse was obviously not here, and the magical signature his passing always left behind was very old, perhaps more than a month. The ebony stallion had not been to the Wastes for some time.

Where next? There were any number of locations that Darkhorse, a wanderer, frequented to some extent, but only a few he returned to again and again. Talak was one of the latter, but Gwen had seen to that situation. The Northern Wastes had been . . . a waste. Cabe had no intention of searching too many locations. First of all, chasing after Darkhorse was like chasing after a phantasm. The eternal could be anywhere he chose to be at almost any time. Darkhorse also did not tire as rapidly as a human did. Trying to chase down Darkhorse was pure folly. It was also possible that Darkhorse might journey to the Manor even while Cabe searched the countryside for his old companion. That had happened to the warlock more than once during the first few years of their friendship. He had strived hard ever since the last time to make certain that it never happened again.

There were six locations he thought worthy of searching. After that, the warlock intended to return to his home. If Darkhorse had still not answered his summons by the next day, Cabe would try a few more. If even *that* search failed . . . he was not certain *what* he would do then. Cabe only knew that he never abandoned a friend.

With ease, the blue-robed sorcerer transported himself to the next destination on his mental list. His new location gave him a panoramic view of a bowl-shaped valley in the distance, for Cabe presently stood atop a tall jagged hill. Cabe knew the valley, having been to it with Darkhorse in the past. The city of Zuu, from where the horsemen ruled the land of the same name, lay near the center. In the daytime, the city was impossible to see, but night would reveal a sea of light, for Zuu never slept.

The shadow steed was not here, but the traces Cabe sensed were much more recent than those at the previous site. It had been only days since Darkhorse had passed through here; that much Cabe could ascertain. He tried to trace the path the eternal had taken, but was able to determine only that it went east, which, from Zuu's southwesterly location, meant most of the Dragonrealm. Still, it *was* something to go on. Two of his remaining choices were directly east. He would try them first, then head north where two of the others were. After that . . .

Again, it took only the simplest of thoughts to send him to his next destination. There had been a time when Cabe would have laughed if someone had told him he would find sorcery so comfortable a piece of his life. The young boy who had worked serving food and drink at inns would have been horrified even to think of wielding such might.

He found himself in a wooded region in the southern stretches of the central Dagora Forest. In truth, he was not at all that far from the Manor; a two-day journey by horse would see him at the boundaries of his tiny domain. However, Darkhorse did not visit this site as often as he did the first two, hence Cabe's decision to leave this one until now.

Again there was no visible sign of the shadow steed, but it was clear to the warlock that his friend had been here not too long ago. Cabe judged it to be no more than four days since Darkhorse's departure. Once again, though, it was impossible to judge exactly where the eternal had journeyed next. Darkhorse traveled either by magic or by running, and either method allowed him to move across the Dragonrealm in little time. Teleporting, however, was much harder to trace. It was one skill where Cabe was and probably always would be deficient.

He was ready to depart for the next location on his list when a peculiar sensation touched the edge of his mind. There had been magic cast here, but of a haunting sort. It reminded him of something old, yet something he should have been familiar with. . . .

It was gone. So slight had it been that Cabe was almost willing to believe that he had imagined it. Darkhorse followed a different magic—and, in fact, *was* that magic—but this was not some random trace left by the eternal. Frowning, the master warlock sought it again, but whatever he had felt was no more. Realizing how futile it would be to hunt for something that might have been the product of his own imagination, Cabe returned to the business at hand. He was tempted to depart for the Manor, but decided that it would not take that long to inspect the remaining places. It was possible that he might even find the shadow steed. Each jump seemed to put him closer.

With that thought to encourage him, he leapt to the next site.

A chill ran through him as he appeared among grass-covered ruins. It had been years since Cabe had come to this place, and over those years he had thought he had recovered from the destruction. Now, though, the sight of the broken, weather-worn rubble brought it all crashing back.

The ghosts of Mito Pica, the ghosts of his memory and conscience, danced around him.

He had been raised here. Under a spell cast by his grandfather, Cabe had remained a child for a century, maybe more. The warlock could not recall his early life, and so over the years he had come to wonder if Nathan had actually put him to sleep for most of that time. Still, whatever its elements, it had been a desperate spell, one that had been meant to save a dying baby. Its success had meant Nathan Bedlam's own death, for he had weakened himself enough so that when he challenged the Dragon King Purple, he had not had the strength to defeat the drake lord. In the end, both sorcerer and Dragon King had perished.

All thought of Darkhorse faded for a time as Cabe Bedlam drank in the macabre vision before him. Some parts of the wall that had surrounded Mito Pica still stood whole, as did several buildings. The city *could* have been rebuilt, but for some reason no one had suggested it. Yet, Cabe did not doubt for a moment that there were people living among the ruins. Scavengers for the most part, with some bandits thrown in for good measure. Possibly even a few half-mad survivors of the destruction itself. They would be old by now and probably very few in number.

After the Dragon Emperor's death, Melicard of Talak had sent his men to sweep through Mito Pica and bring any refugees they found back to the safety of his kingdom. There had actually been three or four such sweeps, so Cabe was fairly certain that all those who had desired aid had received it. Anyone living in the ghost kingdom now *wanted* to be there.

"Hadeen . . ." he whispered. Mito Pica had died because of him, and with it had perished the half-elf who had been his adoptive father. It was the other reason why Cabe had always found reasons to stay away from the ruined city. Hadeen had dedicated his life to caring for the grandson of Nathan Bedlam and his reward had been death at the claws of . . . of . . .

*Toma . . .*

He shivered. The voice had sounded almost like Hadeen's, yet it could not have been.

*Toma . . . Cabe . . . Toma teaches . . .*

Gasping, the wary spellcaster turned toward the wooded lands nearest to him. In that direction had been the home that Hadeen had built for the two of them. Almost it seemed . . . but that was *impossible.*

*Toma . . . masks upon masks . . .*

*My son . . .*

"Hadeen?" He could almost swear that the woods were *talking* to him.

Then the strong pull of another power snared his attention. The warlock cried out as he felt the force in the woods recede. He took a step toward the trees, but the second force, terribly familiar, beckoned to him, enticed him. Cabe stood transfixed, eyes darting from the trees to the darkness of Mito Pica, from where the new force seemed to radiate.

"*Hadeen,*" he whispered. A rare tear ran down his cheek. There was no reply, not even a gentle acknowledgment. Whatever had called to him from the woods had grown quiet again. It was said that when elves died, their spirits became one with their surroundings, especially trees. Did that also apply to half-elves?

The shivering warlock was not allowed time to pursue the matter, for once more he was pulled toward the ghost-ridden ruins of the city. With a start, Cabe recognized what now called to him. It was not only the same as the trace he had sensed at his last destination, but also identical to something far in his past. Only rarely had the sorcerer encountered such magic, for it was a thing *not* of this world, a thing that had briefly flourished long, long ago, when godlike mages had journeyed from their dying world to this one in an attempt to escape a doom they themselves had caused.

There was Vraad sorcery here, but Vraad sorcery with a peculiar taste to it. Cabe shook his head, unwilling to believe this. First Hadeen and now yet another terrible spirit from his past. He tried to reject the notion. The touch was unmistakable, however. Only one spellcaster had wielded such strange magic.

Shade.

Cabe followed the siren trail. He could do nothing else. It was almost a compulsion, but one that he knew was his own doing. He *had* to know. Hadeen, if it had *been* Hadeen, was lost to him again, but the trail he now followed was as strong as ever.

If it *was* the blur-faced warlock, somehow alive, would he be friend or foe? Did another sinister Madrac await Cabe, or would there instead be someone like the kindly but enigmatic Simon? Toward the end, the original personality of Shade had surfaced, or so Darkhorse had said. Would it be that one? What was *that* Shade like? He *had* been Vraad . . .

At the battered wall, Cabe paused. Part of him screamed that he should turn around, flee. Shade was more powerful than he. Yet, despite that plea, the warlock finally stepped through the broken wall. He had no choice. It would forever haunt him if he failed to discover the truth.

The first sight that met his eyes was disappointing. Weeds and more rubble. Dragon-torched skeletons of once tall buildings. Two decades of weather that had left some structures virtually unrecognizable. A skull, marking either the last resting place of one of the citizenry or a traveler who had made the mistake of thinking the ruins a safe place to rest.

There was no Shade.

The sensation had not faded. Cabe was close. He eyed the various ruined buildings, seeking the direction from which the Vraad sorcery emanated. His eyes alighted on what looked to have been an inn or tavern. He could not help smiling despite the seriousness of the situation. The first time Cabe had encountered the shadowy warlock had been where the young Bedlam had been serving ales. Shade had sat undetected at one of the far tables, watching the grandson of Nathan. He had spoken in a rather enigmatic fashion about Cabe's life, then had vanished before the serving boy could ask for clarification.

The path to the ruined tavern was filled with shattered stone and rotting wood, but Cabe chose to dare it rather than risk materializing inside. He kept his magical senses alert, but it was difficult to notice anything else in the presence of so strong a Vraadish force. The warlock could almost picture Shade sitting among the ghosts of Mito Pica, quietly sipping an ale he had summoned from the shadows.

He was nearly at the cracked and open doorway when the earth beneath his feet burst upward.

The speed with which the long black tentacles moved left him too stunned to act. They rose on all sides of him, never touching the spellcaster but instead coming together a foot or two above his head. As they touched, a green shimmer swept over the cage within which Cabe suddenly found himself trapped. The spell was one of the swiftest the baffled warlock had ever been unfortunate enough to experience. Freedom had become imprisonment in less time than it took to blink the proverbial eye.

Recovering, the warlock immediately probed his cell. What he discovered both unnerved and confused him. Other than capturing him, the magical prison meant Cabe no harm. It was simply designed to hold him where he was. He had expected some sort of death trap, but such was not the case.

As relieved as he was by the lack of any imminent threat, Cabe did not relax his efforts. Harmless the cage might be, but in the fulfilling of its basic function it excelled. Cabe searched every strand of the spell and could find no flaw. This was a cage designed to hold a spellcaster of astonishing power. The one who had designed it had worked long and hard. As he studied it again, Cabe had the sinking feeling that escape would be anything but simple. In fact, he had some doubts as to whether he could escape at all.

The warlock had to try, of course. He had no intention of idly passing the time while he waited the coming of the mage who had set the trap.

The trap's design still perplexed him. Why use traces of Vraadish magic as a lure? Few knew of the Vraad, much less their tainted power. For that matter, the trace had been a specific one, specifically that of Shade. Yet, Cabe doubted that Shade had had anything to do with this. The warlock was dead . . . as far as he knew. Somebody had simply decided to use the memory of him to bait the snare.

Which strongly hinted that the trap had been set for a particular being. . . .

Even as he contemplated that, the tenacious warlock was already at work seeking a way of escape. The tentacles themselves were not likely to break, but the place where they joined together above him might be a weak link. With intense concentration, Cabe sent a tendril of power up to the point of convergence. The tendril was thin, barely a whisper, but behind it he built up an incredible reservoir of energy. All Cabe had to do was find a slight gap in the point of connection, and then he would be able to funnel the stored power through. That, the warlock was fairly certain, would give him the opening he needed to destroy his cell.

The fault in his plan proved to be the simple fact that no such gap existed. Try as he might, Cabe could not locate a break. The tendrils had bonded together so perfectly that it was almost possible to believe that the cage had been created whole. Frustrated, the imprisoned mage continued to poke futilely about the top with his sorcery, trying to create his own gap. But even after he had exhausted every bit of sorcerous energy he had gathered for his escape, the spell controlling the magical prison remained unchallenged and unweakened.

This was the work of someone who had planned long and hard for this time. Yet how could they know that he would come here? Why such an elaborate ploy for him?

"No . . . *not* me . . ." Cabe muttered. The cold chill of reality danced down his spine. They could not have known so quickly where *he* would be, but whoever had devised this cunning trap *might* have been familiar with the ways of Darkhorse. Cabe doubted that he and Gwen were the only ones who knew that the shadow steed haunted this miserable place. Someone else must have noticed him.

There were many, not all of them drakes, who wanted the eternal for one reason or another. Most, though, would have been satisfied with destroying him . . . if such was within their power. Yet, this spell did nothing but keep one prisoner. Someone wanted Darkhorse, but for a purpose. In that, Cabe considered himself fortunate. A death trap created with the shadow steed in mind would have stood a better than average chance of killing the warlock. *He* was only human, whereas Darkhorse was . . . *Darkhorse.*

Cabe tried physical action, first pushing against the side of his prison, then attempting to tear through it. Success still mocked him. After several minutes of useless maneuvering, the weary mage finally sat down and stared at his surroundings. It appeared the creator of the sinister spell had planned for all contingencies.

Momentarily putting aside his escape plans, Cabe wondered where his captors were. Considering their effort, he would have expected them to appear the moment the trap had been sprung. Yet, as the minutes passed, no one came to claim him. It occurred to him that perhaps this might be an old spell left over from the destruction of the city, but the use of the false trail, the scent of Shade's sorcery, seemed to indicate otherwise. No one would have bothered setting such an elaborate trap in the midst of Mito Pica's downfall. Besides, Darkhorse had been to the ruins too many times for the shadow steed not to have noticed this spell before. At the very least, the eternal would have seen to it that the trap was harmlessly sprung rather than leave it for some unsuspecting fool . . . like Cabe Bedlam.

As he grimaced at his own ignorance, something that two decades of magical training *should* have had some effect on by now, Cabe suddenly became aware of the faint presence of another person.

No, he almost immediately amended, *two.* Repositioning himself, he tried to use his magic to seek out the newcomers. The cage, however, evidently muted his skills, for the two faint figures remained just that. With his magic unable to help him, Cabe resorted to simply scanning his surroundings, but a quick examination of the devastated region revealed nothing new. Everything was exactly as it had been the moment before he had been snared . . . yet somewhere out there were two nearing figures. Try as he might, the warlock was unable to discover any more.

Then, just as suddenly as they had come, the two vanished. Cabe could not feel their presence anywhere. The imprisoned mage had no time to wonder what had happened, for only a breath or two after the first pair disappeared, a third presence, more evident to his senses, popped into existence somewhere very near the warlock. Cabe glanced around the area again, but still the scene through the cage remained as it had. The new presence was nearly overwhelming in comparison to the first two, but where the others had been unfamiliar to him, this one he felt he should know.

The cell shook then, tossing Cabe around in the process. Stunned, it took the warlock time to realize that his magical prison was being probed . . . and by someone with seemingly no interest in his safety.

Had his captor come for him at last? That did not seem likely. The new-comer was inspecting the cage as if having never come across its like before. The sorcerous probes were tinged with a sense of curiosity, that much Cabe could note. He wondered, *Could it be . . . ?*

As the warlock had done before, the newcomer began to focus his efforts on the top, where the tentacles had come together. For the first time, Cabe's prison shimmered in a way he did not think was normal for it. Whatever the one on the outside was doing, it was having more effect on the magical cage than Cabe's own efforts. Yet the spell withstood the new attack. The hapless mage frowned as he felt the probes of the outsider finally withdraw. It was beginning to dawn on Cabe that he might be trapped within until he starved to death.

He moved as close as he could to the side of his prison. The scene around him remained static, yet the warlock was able to sense that his counterpart on the outside had not left.

Putting his face as close as he could to the wall of shimmering energy that ran between the tentacles, the desperate mage called out, "Hello? If you can hear me, please come closer! I mean no harm!"

According to what his magical senses told him, the other should be practi-cally in front of him, yet Cabe could see no one. Was his would-be rescuer invisible?

He called out again, but still received no response.

With no warning, the probes of the top of his cage began anew. This time, though, there was more purpose to them. Whoever it was, he understood better now what he faced. It was clear even from within the cell that the new series of probes had one purpose in mind and that was finding a weak link. Cabe grew disheartened at that; he had already tried and failed.

The walls of his prison suddenly crackled. Tiny mites of sorcerous energy darted about the interior, forcing the warlock to briefly cover his face.

Stealing a glance upward, Cabe initially saw no change in the cell's condition. However, when he adjusted his sight so as to see the world through the eyes of sorcery, Cabe was stunned to discover that his mysterious benefactor *had* man-aged to wreak some minor havoc on the spell that held the sphere together. To his great regret, though, the mage also noted that the spell began almost im-mediately to compensate for what had happened to it. The crackling ceased and the weakened bonds strengthened again. Once more the invisible probes of the unseen mage retreated.

"No . . ." Cabe groaned. An idea blossomed even as the other abandoned his efforts. The warlock was certain that he had a way out of the cage, but he needed the newcomer's aid. If it was left up to Cabe alone, the warlock had little chance for success.

Gathering his strength, the sorcerer concentrated as best he could on the mind of the other. *Try again!* he demanded. *Try again! You must!*

Cabe continued to repeat the message over and over, but after the first few times, it was difficult not to lose heart. The trap was designed too well. Despite the power the warlock wielded, he could barely sense what was happening outside. All that Cabe knew, all that he could base his hopes on, was the fact that the other had not yet departed. Yet, if his messages did not reach the other mage, how long before that other *would* abandon the effort, leaving Cabe to whatever fate the creator of the cage had planned for his intended victim?

Above him, he suddenly sensed new effort on the part of the other mage's probes. In his joy, Cabe almost forgot what he himself intended to do, but then the thought that this might be his last opportunity to free himself urged the exhausted spellcaster to organize his mind and renew his own attack.

It was impossible to say with any certainty whether his pleas had reached the other, but Cabe did note that the mysterious sorcerer now probed with even more force than in his previous attempts. That was all that the warlock could hope for. He needed his counterpart to make at least as much progress as he had in the last attack. Cabe was not at all certain as to the intensity of his own assault from within. If his own power was not enough . . .

The cage began to crackle once more with wild energy. The warlock quickly pulled away from the wall nearest to him, realizing that the unstable spell might do him harm in ways even the creator had not planned. Cabe held off from attacking, hoping for just a bit more success on the part of his benefactor. He had to do this at the exact moment . . .

He sensed rather than saw the straining of the spell. The weak links were suddenly visible. The warlock still hesitated, searching for the moment of best opportunity.

He found it.

Cabe struck out, unleashing with pinpoint precision the full extent of his remaining power. He sensed the spell caging him weaken further and also noted the increased assault by the outsider. Encouraged, Cabe somehow succeeded in drawing further from his very being. Augmented by the physical sacrifice, his own attack grew unstoppable. The tentacles shivered and the shimmering between them dimmed. The point of connection above his head was pulled to its most taut. The black tentacles sought to keep hold of one another, but the spell had its limits, and against the combined onslaught from both without and within, it could not stand.

The tentacles tore free with a blinding flash. They wiggled madly about, wild snakes in their death throes. Cabe was awash in darkness, and for a moment he feared that he had been permanently blinded by the magical burst. Then, as his eyes adjusted, he saw that it was not the sundering of the spell that had caused him to see such darkness.

Day had become night. Somehow, although snared but a few minutes, Cabe Bedlam had missed the rest of the day.

With a last feeble effort, the tentacles tried to reform. Their power, their very existence, was already too much on the wane, however, and so they merely succeeded in flopping about once more before beginning to shrivel. Cabe eyed them carefully, lest some last trick be played out, but the tentacles continued to shrivel, becoming dried out, emaciated things that finally crumbled. The master warlock watched as even the ash faded. In the end, the only sign that the magical cage had existed at all was a series of small holes around the sorcerer.

He straightened and for the first time saw the one who had helped save his life.

"Are you all right, Cabe?" roared a familiar voice. "By the Void, the one who sought your life will find his *own* forfeit!"

A shape blacker than the night looked down upon him with glittering, pupilless eyes of ice-blue. Most would have feared what they saw in those eyes, but the warlock knew them well enough that they did not frighten him . . . *much*, that is.

The eyes belonged to a huge stallion who, despite the rocky ground, moved with silent steps toward the weary mage.

"I don't . . . don't think that they were after me! I . . . I think that they . . . they were after *you*, Darkhorse. . . ."

A devious chuckle escaped the shadow steed, echoing through the night-enshrouded ruins. "And instead they caught themselves a sorcerer!"

"I was looking . . . looking for *you*! I came here because I know you visit the ruins of Mito Pica on occasion."

"It is to remind me of the drakes." The words were said with such loathing that even Darkhorse was startled by the tone. He paused, then in a quieter rumble, added, "It is to remind me that all things pass beyond me. I saw this city built, Cabe."

It was easy to forget just how old the demon steed was. Darkhorse had even known the Vraad, although he refused to say much about them. Difficult the shadow steed might be to kill, but Darkhorse was very familiar with pain. Much of his knowledge of it had come from being a prisoner of some of the ancient sorcerers.

For lack of anything else reasonable to say, Cabe repeated his earlier words. "I was looking for you."

Darkhorse appeared to recover his spirits with the change in topic. "Ha! I know all too well! I have spent the last few hours searching for *you*, my good friend! I arrived at the Manor some hours ago, only to find the Lady Gwen rather anxious as to your own whereabouts. It seems you were due back long before."

What he saw was *true*, then. Staring up into the night sky, Cabe shook his head. "As far as I know, it's only been a few minutes since I was trapped. It wasn't until I was freed from the cage that day suddenly became night!"

"A pretty ploy! I think you were not supposed to realize how long you had been held a prisoner. I have heard of such spells, cunning things, really!"

"But what purpose would it serve?"

"What purpose?" The shadow steed chuckled. "I've no knowledge of that, save that perhaps someone did not wish you to realize that time was slipping away from you."

*Time slipping away.* . . . Could someone have wanted Cabe to miss the audience with King Melicard? Why—"No . . . not me. I should have remembered."

"Remembered what?"

"When I was first trapped, I wondered how anyone could have known I was here. I'd already ruled out the idea that this was an old spell left over from the destruction of the city."

"Of course," Darkhorse rumbled. "I would have noticed it before this, coming here as often as I do! In fact—*wait!*" He sniffed the air, for the moment acting much like the animal whose form the eternal had long, long ago taken a fancy to. "I smell something *familiar*. . . ." Ice-blue orbs flared. "*Shade!* I smell Shade!"

"Or something like him," Cabe cut in. "Something Vraadish."

"No, this is Shade . . . but the trace is so very old." The shadow steed dug one hoof into the ground, gouging out miniature valleys. "I am reminded of another snare, different in practice but similar in bait. One that I almost stepped into but a day or so ago. . . ."

"A day or so?" The warlock recalled one of his previous destinations. Without preamble, he launched into his experience at that site, specifically the brief trace of magic that had reminded him also of the late, lamented Shade.

When he had concluded, Darkhorse dipped his head in an equine version of a nod. "That was the very same site! That trap was not nearly so well-planned!"

"So someone *is* trying to capture you."

"And, as I have already said, trapped you instead! I little like those who presume to complicate my existence, but when they also endanger my *friends* . . ." The ebony stallion pawed at the ground. His eyes gleamed. The magical forces that were Darkhorse pulsated. "Woe betide them, Cabe! They will find that I am *not* a very forgiving soul!"

The warlock was thankful that he was not the one responsible. The enemies of Darkhorse took on the role at their own risk. Darkhorse did not forget those who thought to play havoc with him or those he counted his companions. Thinking out loud, Cabe muttered, "I wonder who it could be?"

It was the wrong thing to say.

"Who, *indeed*?" The shadow steed's laugh was mirthless. "I could think of several. Certain drakes, for instance, or even once the monarch of a particular mountain kingdom. As I said, I do not forget!"

*And Kyl wants him at the audience in Talak*. . . . Had Gwen told the eternal of the dragon heir's request? If yes, did Darkhorse intend to be there? If no, how was Cabe to make the request now, with Darkhorse's suspicions roused? The shadow steed might view *both* sides at the audience as possible foes; it was clear from past conversations with Darkhorse that he did not trust the emperor-to-be. Kyl was offering an olive branch, but would the shadow steed see it instead as a blade?

"We should return to the Manor," he finally said, deciding that the change in scenery would only benefit him when he asked the question. Perhaps, with Gwendolyn there to aid him, Cabe could convince his old companion to make the journey to Talak.

"Yes, the Lady Bedlam will be doubly worried if we *both* do not return." Darkhorse shook his head, sending his mane flying wildly about. "No, I would not miss it for the world!"

"Miss what?"

The eternal chuckled darkly. "Why *Talak*, of course! Was that not what you sought me out for? To ask me if I would agree to Prince Kyl's little plot and appear at the audience between Melicard and himself?"

The startled mage grimaced. "I was afraid to ask if Gwen had said anything. I didn't know what you might say."

"Well, you may rest assured, friend Cabe, that I will not miss this little party. Not at all!" That said, the demon steed straightened. "Now, let us be off before the Lady of the Amber decides to go searching for you on her own!"

The image was enough to shake Cabe Bedlam at least momentarily from his ruminations. If there were *other* traps awaiting Darkhorse, then Gwen might be in danger if they delayed any longer. Then again, something would have to be done to assure that no one else fell prey to whatever traps, if any, remained.

As Darkhorse summoned up the power to transport the two of them back to the Manor, Cabe's thoughts returned to the shadow steed's earlier words. Darkhorse looked forward to the meeting between Kyl and Melicard, but not because of any hope for peace in the Dragonrealm. Old suspicions were rising to the forefront, suspicions regrettably based in fact. As well as he had gotten on with the king of Talak for the past few years, neither could forget their initial encounter. Did Darkhorse suspect Melicard of plotting anew? The disfigured ruler of the mountain kingdom could have many reasons for wishing to capture the eternal, including a strike against the new Dragon Emperor.

That he even thought of the possibility of subterfuge on the part of Melicard suddenly dismayed Cabe. It occurred to the warlock then that his companion was not the only one plagued by suspicions. Even *he* had begun to wonder.

The world faded away as the shadow steed's spell took hold. As emptiness briefly swirled around him, the sorcerer found himself wishing that his problems would disappear as easily.

# IV

DESPITE ALL, THE day at last came when it was time for the journey to Talak to commence. Putting together the caravan had proved a monumental task, but under the capable direction of Gwendolyn Bedlam, it was at last accomplished. There were more than a dozen wagons, all with the long-unseen banner of the Dragon Emperor fluttering above them, servants of both human and drake origin, and an honor guard large enough to fight a war.

The last had been most worrisome. Cabe understood that the drakes did not wish to arrive at the gates of the mountain kingdom without some show of their might, but the number of drake warriors accompanying the caravan was astounding. Most of them were soldiers of Lord Green, who journeyed with his future emperor, but a few were the grown hatchlings of drakes who had served Kyl's sire. There were two in particular who stayed close to the heir, a pair of golden warriors who had been brought to the Manor at the same time as the young princess. From the first they had seemed to understand their role as bodyguards, never assuming that they were playmates. It had been amusing at first, watching adolescent warriors doing their best to protect their cousin, but watching them now, Cabe found them only imposing. He had never gotten to know Faras and Ssgayn despite attempts to do so; they did not feel their place was among royalty, which evidently included powerful mages. When with Kyl, who seemed to find them amusing, they were even more silent than Grath. Faras and Ssgayn resembled the elder drakes, but in the dark could have passed for human. Anyone who had seen them fight, however, would not be able to make that mistake. The two fought as only drakes could, with both sword and fang.

Gazing at the army he was to join, Cabe Bedlam began to wish it had been possible after all for Kyl to simply materialize before Melicard and Erini. The caravan was as unwieldy a thing as he had ever ridden with. By themselves the heir's honor guard would have ridden in orderly enough fashion, but mixed with the wagons and servants, they only added to the tension and confusion. The humans in the caravan were on edge because of their lack of numbers, the drakes because they knew they headed for the domain of a ruler who had openly hunted their kind. The horses distrusted the roving eyes of their draconian counterparts, all flesh eaters, while the riding drakes had to strive to keep up with the better-trained, more intelligent steeds.

"Such a madhouse!"

The warlock gazed down at his wife, who had come up to the side of his own mount. "I hope we can reach Talak by the appointed time. This caravan is about ten times larger than I wanted."

"But as small as I could manage to make it, what with all of the 'requirements' I was given. I hope you're not angry about my staying behind, Cabe."

"With the Green Dragon and Darkhorse to accompany us, I doubt that there will be too much trouble. You'll meet us in Talak, anyway. I wish *I* had a reason for foregoing this trip."

"Yes . . ." The emerald-clad witch glanced surreptitiously back at the Manor. Cabe, following her lead, caught sight of Valea, clad in her finest, gazing at the throng below from one of the upper windows. There was no doubt as to who it was she was searching for among the gathered drakes and humans. The warlock had to fight down fatherly fury.

"She's watched everything from every window," Gwendolyn continued, as much ill at ease with the situation as her husband. "I'm fairly certain that Kyl has seen her, but whether he has acknowledged her at all, I could not say."

"I don't know which would be worse," Cabe muttered. "I don't like him playing games with my daughter!"

"Well, this will be the longest that Kyl's been away from here. I could not let an opportunity like this pass by. Now would be the best time to talk to Valea and see if I can rid her of this nonsense."

Cabe's horse began to shift back and forth in growing impatience. The mage regained control over his animal. "I take back what I said. I don't envy you your task. I think I prefer trying to keep a caravan of anxious drakes and humans together. There are few creatures in the Dragonrealm as stubborn as our Valea! And such an intelligent girl, too."

"Yes, and unfortunately we both know where she gets it from, do we not?"

Expression innocent, the warlock asked, "*Where?*"

He was saved from Gwen's retort by the sudden appearance of Aurim. Their son was being left in charge of much of the Manor, which both pleased and frightened him. Cabe could read these emotions in the way Aurim acted. The younger Bedlam reminded Cabe of what he had been like at that age, not that that was difficult. Physically, there had not been much change in the elder

Bedlam. Cabe looked only a few years older than he had been when first thrust into sorcery.

"Is there anything amiss, Aurim?" the young warlock's mother asked.

"Nothing, Mother. Just came to wish Father well."

"Don't forget that your mother will be departing in a few days." Cabe studied his son carefully. "Try to familiarize yourself with everything before that so that if you have any questions, she can answer them."

"I've only lived here my *entire* life, Father!"

"It's different when you have to manage this place," Gwen reminded her eldest. "We have an entire community here."

Aurim nodded, still a bit put out by what he thought was a lack of faith on his parents' part. Noting that, Cabe did his best to reconcile things. "I'm sure you'll do fine. We wouldn't leave you in charge if we didn't believe that."

Neither Cabe nor Gwen added that they were also leaving Benjin Traske behind to keep a watchful eye on the young mage. That had proven to be a much more difficult decision than they had expected, for the scholar had apparently assumed that he would be riding with the caravan. While Cabe had been searching for Darkhorse, the huge man had even confronted the Lady Bedlam about it. It was, so Gwendolyn had said, the first time she had seen Benjin Traske come close to anger. Only when he had heard her out did he suddenly calm. The Bedlams had always understood the protective attitude Traske had toward his charges, but they had never realized its extent until then. Knowing that Darkhorse and the Green Dragon were to accompany the heir to Talak had evidently helped much to ease the tutor's mind.

*What would we have done without Benjin Traske all these years?* Cabe pondered. It was chiefly because of the tutor that the first elements of the school of magic, located in Penacles, were finally coming together. The man was an exceptional organizer, and although he was not himself a mage of any strength, Traske understood the underlying theories about magic, especially after so many years with the Bedlams. His aid continued to prove invaluable. Cabe supposed that it was because teaching was teaching, no matter what the subject. A good scholar could turn his skills to almost any topic.

Gwen suddenly glanced past her husband. "Lord Green approaches. I think the caravan may be ready to leave."

"At last?" the warlock quipped. Aurim grinned. Cabe looked down at his golden-haired son. "We know you'll do fine, Aurim, but don't be afraid to ask your mother questions before she departs."

The younger sorcerer nodded.

Cabe Bedlam leaned down and kissed his wife for a long moment, which made Aurim grimace in embarrassment. Cabe chuckled.

"I regret ssseparating a family," came the voice of the drake lord. "But we are ready to depart asss soon as you desire."

"Now is as good a time as any." The warlock sighed. "Where is His Majesty?"

"Hisss mount is being readied even as we ssspeak. The horses would not remain ssstill for him and so he has decided on a riding drake."

Cabe could not blame the horses for not wanting Kyl to ride them. When mounted, the dragon heir's heritage often rose to the forefront; Kyl put his animals through paces that wore even the hardy riding drakes ragged. Horses, although swifter and with more stamina, did not have the thick hides and dull stubbornness of the reptilian mounts.

"Have a safe journey," Aurim said.

Looking up, Cabe saw that his daughter had vanished from the window, yet there was no sign of her among those who had gathered to see the caravan off. He disliked leaving without saying goodbye to Valea, but if that was the way she was going to act, then so be it. The warlock hoped his wife would be able to talk some sense into their daughter, but Cabe doubted it. Valea was in the throes of first passion, something that common sense and parental guidance had little sway over. He could only hope for the best.

"Friend Cabe, we had bessst be going."

He nodded, his eyes still lingering on the empty window. "The sooner the better."

"What about Darkhorse?" asked Aurim. "He's supposed to be going with you, isn't he?"

"It wasss agreed that the demon steed would meet usss en route," the Green Dragon hissed. There was a note of anxiety in his voice. "He hasss matters with which he must deal first."

Those matters concerned the traps the shadow steed's mysterious foe had set. Darkhorse had wanted to make certain that none still existed. He had also wanted an opportunity to search for any clue that might reveal the identity of his enemy. The eternal had agreed to meet the caravan the second night out. Swift as Darkhorse was, it did not matter where the others would be on that evening; he would find them. Kyl had acquiesced with no argument. It seemed that he was more concerned that Darkhorse be with the caravan when they reached Talak, not before.

With some reluctance, the warlock had allowed Darkhorse to go alone. He knew that a Darkhorse forewarned was proof against most threats, but there was still the fear that one of the snares might prove too much even for the eternal. If the shadow steed did *not* appear on the decided evening, Cabe was going to search for him, dragon heir or no dragon heir.

Once more he bid farewell to Gwendolyn and Aurim. Valea had still not made an appearance and he doubted now that she would. *I hope Gwen can do something about her. . . .*

He rode alongside the Dragon King as they returned to the waiting caravan. Caught up in his own thoughts, a habit he seemed destined never to break, the warlock was surprised by a comment from his companion.

"The world isss never an easy place, friend Cabe," the drake hissed quietly. "Asss much as we would like it to be so, it isss more probable that it will continue to plunge usss into one situation after another. We can only do what we feel isss bessst for all."

"Whatever that may be," Cabe agreed, amazed that the Dragon King should be so concerned and understanding. The master of the Dagora Forest was so very much unlike his counterparts, being almost human at times. Not for the first time was the weary spellcaster pleased to have the reptilian monarch for both ally and . . . yes . . . *friend.*

He glanced ahead and saw both Kyl and Grath mounted and waiting. Grath eyed them with curiosity. The emperor-to-be, on the other hand, wore an expression of regal indifference. Cabe, looking past the mask the dragon heir wore, could read the impatience in Kyl's eyes. Yes, both the journey and the audience held the promise of being . . . *interesting.*

Thoughts of the meeting in Talak mingled with worry for Darkhorse, concern for Valea, and a thousand lesser problems.

*The world is never an easy place,* the Dragon King had said.

*That,* the warlock amended, was an *understatement.*


VALEA LEANED AGAINST a pillar, trying to keep herself from watching the caravan as it slowly began to depart the Manor grounds. She belatedly realized that she had forgotten to say farewell to her father, but the mistake seemed minimal compared to her other loss.

*He will come back from this journey, but soon he will be leaving for the final time!* the young witch thought, a lump growing in her throat. Soon, Kyl would be sitting on the throne of the Dragon Emperor and Valea would be a fading memory to him. On the one hand, she knew that what she dreamed was foolish, but it was impossible not to imagine what life would be like if circumstances would only permit her to be Kyl's queen. She knew her own feelings for the young drake and was certain that his were of a similar vein. Did he not make excuses to touch her hand or arm whenever possible? Did Kyl not also show her special attention whenever they were together, no matter who else was there?

Out in the yard below, the caravan continued to move. By this time, she knew that it was already too late to see Kyl one last time. Determined to prove himself, he had chosen to ride at the head of the column. It was a brave thing to do. There were men, even drakes, who wanted his life simply because of what he was.

"You are missing the departure, Lady Bedlam."

Valea gasped. Benjin Traske was standing only a few feet behind her, yet she had heard nothing.

"I apologize if I startled you, my dear."

"I was just . . . just thinking."

Traske's brow rose. "It must have been important for you to miss saying farewell to your father. The proper thing to have done would have been to see him off."

From anyone else, even her mother, the young sorceress might not have taken the reprimand. Valea felt she was old enough to do what *she* desired, even if she knew that it might be wrong. Yet the scholar had a way of speaking to her that made her feel once more like a first-year pupil. Bowing her head, the redheaded sorceress returned, "He will not be gone long. Only a few days."

"Do you speak of your father, or the young drake?"

Her head snapped back up and she started to protest.

Traske raised a massive hand. "Do not seek to convince me otherwise, Lady Valea. I have watched you grow up. I have learned everything about you. About *everyone* here. I know for how long this . . . *yearning* . . . of yours has been going on."

The young woman colored.

Oblivious to her embarrassment, the scholar went on. "I was brought here by the lord of Dagora to act as teacher to both the heirs to the Dragon Emperor and to you and your brother. I have made that my life for the past many years, Lady Valea, and so you must believe me when I say that I could not perform this task for so long without becoming aware of each of your needs and dreams." He sighed. "In truth, you are all family to me, even your somewhat arrogant paramour."

"He's not—"

"He will *need* that arrogance, my lady, so I do not fault him for it, believe me. Kyl has become what he has become because of the great mission before him. There are certain things that he in his role must be able to do. I like to think that I have prepared him for many of those things." Traske's expression abruptly softened. "Although even I would have to admit that I was not thinking he might be so drawn to one not of his own kind."

His last statement drew Valea away from the pillar. Her eyes filled with hope. "Do you mean—I mean—does he—?"

"Very much so, I would say."

Without warning, she reached out and hugged the elder man. Benjin Traske stood motionless, evidently stunned by her outburst. Only when Valea finally released him did he react, and that was simply to blink.

"Did he actually say anything?" Valea asked breathlessly.

"He . . . he has said nothing outright." Traske visibly collected himself. "But what he has . . . inferred has been plain enough for me to understand."

Still reeling with joy, Valea whirled about and rushed to the window. She leaned outside and peered at the caravan. More than half of it had already vanished beyond her field of vision. The young sorceress leaned out even further, trying to get a better view of the vanguard.

Sturdy hands pulled her back inside. "*My lady!* It would be a tragedy indeed if you fell to your death!"

She smoothed her dress, shaken both by his attempt to rescue her and by the fact that he was correct about the danger. Her control of her skills was not as sure as that of her parents. If her mother's teachings were to be believed, it would not be the first time a mage had died through simple, physical carelessness. With power came the need for caution.

"Thank you, Master Traske," she finally muttered.

"I see that I have underestimated the extent of your . . . love."

*Love?* It was the first time that the word had entered the situation. Even Valea had never actually thought it. Love. It must be true, she realized. Master Traske was no blind man; if he saw love, it could only be because it was there for him to see.

"*I'm in love with him. . . .*" she whispered, noticing it as truth for the first time. Why had she never thought it before? It was so obvious! What other explanation was there for the way she felt?

Then the young witch thought of her parents and how they would react if she said as much to them. "No . . . I *can't* be!"

"You are." Traske put a hand on her shoulder. The touch was gentle, reassuring. "Denying facts is a futile waste of time. My classes should have taught you that by now, Lady Valea."

"What can I do?" She could not go to her mother for such advice. Benjin Traske was the only one whose counsel she could trust. He understood the world in a way that Valea had still to learn . . . might *never* learn, for that matter. Her parents were *so* protective.

"You must wait." The scholar's voice was low, confiding. He glanced around. "If there is one thing I know, it is that one must wait for the proper moment. It is how I've led my life, Valea. You must wait. I am certain that Kyl will make known the truth before it is too late. If he does not . . ." Traske shrugged sadly. "Then, it was meant to be that way."

298 Richard A. Knaak

"But you said he *loved* me!"

"One must consider all possibilities . . . you have not been paying attention during your classes, I see." He smiled, shattering the image of inquisitor. "I doubt, however, that matters will end that way. Just listen—"

At the sudden pause, Valea looked around. She did not notice anything at first, but then the sound of footsteps echoed throughout the area.

"We will speak later, my lady. Remember what I have said. If you want something, you must often wait. It may be a long time before you—Aurim! Do you look for us?"

Valea's brother stopped where he was. She noted that he looked slightly annoyed, which meant that he had not likely heard any of what she and the tutor had been discussing. The novice sorceress silently thanked Master Traske for his discretion.

"N-not you, teacher. Mother wishes to speak with Valea, though."

The girl frowned. She knew what her mother wanted to talk to her about.

"Best that you go, then, my lady." The huge man casually squeezed his charge's shoulder as he guided her toward her brother. "If there is one authority we must always be on the best of terms with, it is your mother."

Aurim attempted a smile, evidently thinking that the scholar was making a joke. While they were rare, Benjin Traske did occasionally make the wry comment . . . most of them concerning the diligence of his students.

Unenthusiastic about the prospect of facing her mother but lacking any escape, Valea joined her golden-haired brother. Aurim made to go, but the young sorceress took the time to bid farewell to Master Traske. "If you will excuse me, teacher." She curtsied. "My thanks for your time."

He bowed in turn, always an extraordinary feat considering the scholar's girth. "I merely do my duty."

"No more stalling," her brother whispered to her. "Mother's waiting!"

Valea knew that she had been fortunate that it was Aurim who had come for her and not their mother. The elder Lady Bedlam had a way of often divining the truth that at times unnerved her children. Fortunately, Aurim was not so observant.

Steeling herself, the young witch followed her brother. She did not look forward to the talk, knowing it would revolve around both her behavior today and her feelings in general for princely Kyl. Still, she was not completely disheartened. The unexpected support of Master Benjin Traske gave her strength. More and more his words made sense. She would listen to her mother and try her best to pretend compliance. The time would come. Master Traske had said as much, and she had rarely known him to be wrong.

She imagined herself as Kyl's bride, his empress, and . . . the mother of his offspring. Valea knew the stories; she knew that drakes and her kind had married before. There *had* been children. It *was* all possible.

If he loved her, Valea was confident that somehow Kyl would overcome all the obstacles to their love. Somehow, despite drakes and parents, they would be together.

# V

**THE FIRST DAY** of the journey passed with so little difficulty that Cabe could only marvel. Kyl was actually gracious and willing to follow the suggestions of the others. It took the warlock some time to realize that the change in attitude stemmed from the heir's hidden anxiety. Kyl *knew* that he had to make the proper impression on both the humans and his own people or else he would never sit upon the throne of his sire. Now, en route to the first of a series of very crucial confrontations, the pressure was finally affecting the dragon heir.

For once, Cabe found himself sympathizing with the young drake.

The caravan came to a halt in a lightly wooded region, the northernmost traces of the immense Dagora Forest. Under the guidance of the Green Dragon himself, camp was set up. The Dragon King was doing his best to see to it that his emperor-to-be's journey was a quiet, smooth one. The warlock, however, could not help but frown as he watched the master of Dagora go out of his way to see to it that every comfort was afforded the heir. A drake lord as old and as commanding as the Green Dragon should not have had to belittle himself so. It amazed Cabe to watch. What it was in Kyl that brought out such a manner from the otherwise regal Dragon King confounded him.

Protocol demanded that he eat with the Dragon King, Kyl, and Grath. A wide tent of human manufacture had been set up for the would-be emperor, and it was here that Kyl chose to eat, the better for privacy. The young drake had eschewed bringing along chairs, instead adopting a custom from one of the western kingdoms. Seated on pillows before a low table, Cabe was uncomfortable, but as none of his reptilian companions appeared to be having any difficulty, he remained quiet.

Fortunately, the meal was short and the conversation centered mostly on the kingdom of Talak itself, including such things as trade goods, history, and people. Kyl seemed to drink in every drop of information. Grath, too, asked questions, generally picking subjects his brother had not yet mentioned. A few times, the warlock either hesitated or admitted outright that he, in all fairness to King Melicard, could not provide the drakes with an answer. The dragon heir accepted this, although Grath appeared disappointed.

At meal's end, Kyl took a last sip from his goblet, then said, "The food hasss been excellent and the conversssation very informative. I think, though, I would like to take sssome time to digessst both further. I thank both you, my Lord Green, and you, Massster Bedlam, once again for your invaluable ssservice."

Warlock and Dragon King rose. Cabe winced as he stretched his legs at last. Next to him, the drake lord executed a perfect bow. "Should Your Majesty have need of my humble self again before retiring, pleassse do not hesitate to call for me."

Cabe simply nodded in respect. Kyl nodded back, again not at all perturbed by his guardian's attitude. Grath rose to guide the two to the tent opening. He bowed respectfully to both departing guests. "My gratitude also goes out to the two of you."

Outside, Kyl's two guards straightened. The Green Dragon and Cabe walked past the watchful pair in silence, each mulling over the dinner conversation. It was not until they were well away from Kyl's tent that the Dragon King spoke.

"I am encouraged, friend Cabe. Much encouraged. Hisss Majesty asks pointed and intelligent questionsss."

*Many of which seemed to originate from Grath*, Cabe wanted to add. He was thankful that Kyl's younger brother was along. Where the heir faltered, surely Grath would save the situation. "You think the audience with Melicard will be successful, then, my lord?"

"It *mussst* be! There is no room for failure! You and I both know that!"

Once more, they continued on in silence. It was not until they were among the other members of the caravan that the silence was broken . . . or perhaps *altered* was the better word.

The camp looked no different, yet Cabe suddenly felt as if someone had invaded it. He paused and looked around.

"Is something amisss?" the Dragon King asked quietly.

"I don't . . . maybe . . ."

*They were in the trees around the camp.*

"Seekers. . . ." he whispered to his scaled companion.

"What? Impossi—" The drake lord broke off as he, too, suddenly sensed the presence of many avian minds. One hand clenched tight.

"No!" Cabe hissed, fearing that the Dragon King would try to unleash a spell. He did not know what the birdlike Seekers wanted, but if it was to attack, they would have done so by now. Either that, or they would have fled, which would have made more sense based on the numbers that the warlock perceived. There were several of the humanoid birdfolk, but not nearly enough to endanger the caravan.

"What do they want?"

"I don't know. . . ."

Around them, several of the human and drake workers stared at the two powerful figures, most, no doubt, wondering just why it was their lords stood frozen in place. Cabe was thankful that none of them had been close enough to hear his discovery of the avian observers.

It was too dark to see the arrogant forms hidden among the treetops, but now and then the patient sorcerer heard the quiet rustle of wings. The Seekers seemed satisfied with observing. Cabe could feel no desire to attack.

"I think . . . they simply want to know a little about the future emperor."

"I shall have them shot from the treesss," snarled the Green Dragon. From his tone, he had still not come to grips with the realization that the Seekers had settled around the camp without his notice.

"Don't!" admonished Cabe. "I . . . I think we won't have any trouble from them if we simply let them be."

"*Seekers?*" The very idea of allowing the caravan and, especially, Kyl to remain surrounded by the bird folk went against the draconian monarch's notions of safety.

Cabe could hardly blame him. Still, he had no desire to start a conflict with the ancient race. Although only a vestige of their former might, the Seekers, once rulers of the land, were still a cunning and deadly foe when stirred. For now, it was simple curiosity that drove them.

Then, as silently as they had come, the Seekers departed.

Only the warlock and the drake lord noticed their withdrawal. The reptilian knight glanced down at his human companion. "Why did they leave?"

*Why, indeed?* "They must have discovered what they wanted to know."

"Peaceful intentionsss or not, I am putting the guardsss on alert, friend Cabe! If even *one* of the bird people returns, I will have it destroyed!"

With that said, the Dragon King whirled about and stalked away.

The mage watched him vanish into the night, silently hoping that there would be no further incident. Then, ignoring the still curious glances of the servants nearby, Cabe turned and headed toward his own tent. It would be wise, he concluded, to make a few additions to the spells he and the drake lord had cast. Stronger yet more subtle ones. There would be no repeat of the surprise visit. Next time—though in truth he hoped there would be no next time—he would be alerted to the avians' presence long before they became a threat.

Even still, Cabe knew he would sleep lightly this night. Very lightly.

TO THE WEARY mage's relief, the night passed with no return of the bird folk. Cabe had not slept well, not trusting that his newly cast defensive spells would be sufficient for the cunning avians. The nagging lack of confidence was something he had often fallen victim to in the past, and the warlock was quite aware that Aurim had inherited the tendency to doubt himself from his father. That, more than anything else, was why his son's spells went awry. Cabe hoped that one day Aurim, at least, would overcome the doubts. It was looking more and more as if *he* never would.

The caravan was ready to move on in an astonishingly short time, no doubt thanks in great part to the Green Dragon's threatening encouragement. He did not see the silent night as any sign the Seekers had meant no harm. To him, it meant that the avians intended something more monstrous later in the journey. The drake lord wanted to make as much progress as possible before that happened.

Cabe did not argue with him, deciding they were all best served by taking no chances. If circumstances called for him to step between the bird folk and the Dragon King, then so be it. He hoped it would not come to that.

The weather stayed clear, allowing them to cover much ground. There was little trouble, save an argument between a human rider and one of the drake warriors the Green Dragon had brought with him. It was the opinion of the human that his counterpart's reptilian steed was eying the horse with too much eagerness. Separating the two succeeded for a time in ending the matter, but when the accused riding drake started fighting for control with his master, his definite intention being to accost one of the other horses, the Dragon King had the drake warrior ride off and feed his mount. He was also warned that if the beast still hungered when the two returned, it would be its own master it was fed.

That this was the only incident of friction between the human and drake folk was encouraging. Even though the humans for the most part had originally come from settlements located in the lands of the Green Dragon, they had never mingled much with the drake race. Cabe's tiny kingdom had brought the two races closer together than in any part of the Dragonrealm with the possible exception of Irillian by the Sea. There, however, humans were second to their reptilian counterparts. They were treated well, but the divisions still remained. Such was not the case at the Manor. The warlock hoped that he would one day see the rest of the Dragonrealm follow their example. Even he had been amazed that the two races could work so well together.

Evening came none too soon for the mage, who wondered whether he had grown a little soft over the past few years. For the most part, he had traveled by means of either his own sorcery or the swiftness of Darkhorse. Cabe could not recall the last time he had gone on an extended journey with only true horse for transportation. He had forgotten how uncomfortable a saddle could be after two days of riding.

Thinking of Darkhorse, the saddle-worn mage wondered where the eternal was. The shadow steed was not yet late, but Cabe still feared that some other hidden trap had caught Darkhorse unprepared.

He was carefully dismounting when Grath joined him. "Master Bedlam. Can I be of any assistance?"

"Thank you, no. I'm fine."

Someone came to take the reins of his horse. Cabe gladly gave them up. Beside him, the young drake continued to wait.

"Might I speak to you for just a moment, Master Bedlam?"

The Green Dragon and Kyl had already started walking away. Cabe, seeing that he was not needed at the moment, nodded to his companion. "What do you want?"

Grath looked almost embarrassed. "The closer we come to Talak, the more uneasy *I* become. I do not mean that I fear danger, not with you, Lord Green, and soon Darkhorse to protect the caravan, but rather . . . rather I am fearful of the coming confrontation with His Majesty, King Melicard."

"Kyl's been well-rehearsed. He'll do fine." *At least*, Cabe added to himself, *I hope so.*

"It is not Kyl I am worried about. He has been trained from birth for such things. No, I fear my own lack of experience will tell. If I commit an error, it will reflect upon Kyl . . . upon *all* drakesss . . ."

Worried as he had been about the dragon heir's performance, Cabe had not really considered the pressures on Grath. He had always been of the assumption that Grath was capable of doing what had to be done. When was the last time he and the others had considered the situation from the younger drake's point of view?

"Grath," he finally said, trying to choose his words for best result, "you'll do fine. I've watched you. Gwendolyn and Lord Green have watched you. We probably haven't told you lately how proud we are of your efforts. You complement Kyl perfectly. He couldn't have a finer counselor."

"If my clutch had been first," Grath said, referring to his hatching, "I would have been the heir. Yet, although I am not, I am still to fulfill a role of great importance. That is why I have always strived to know all that there is to know. If I give wrong advice to Kyl, it could cause catastrophe." The drake looked down. "To be worthy of giving counsel to the Dragon Emperor, I have striven for knowledge as if I am the heir himself, but . . . but I ssstill . . ."

Cabe put a hand on Grath's arm. "You would be as good an emperor as Kyl, Grath! When the meeting between your brother and Melicard commences, you'll do just fine. Kyl would have no other beside him. He's said so many times, remember?"

"Yesss . . ."

"We're all weary from the day's ride, so—"

A familiar presence touched the warlock's thoughts. Grath, noticing his expression, tensed and glanced around.

"Ho there, Cabe! Hello, young Grath!"

Standing where nothing but the creeping darkness of the coming night had been before, was the irrepressible shadow steed. Darkhorse dipped his head in further greeting, then trotted silently toward the duo.

"You made it!" Cabe fairly shouted. Then, collecting himself, he said more quietly, "It's good to see you safe."

"So I noticed! Ha!"

"Welcome back, Darkhorse," Grath added.

"Thank you, one and all." The huge stallion's ice-blue eyes glittered. "It was an entertaining excursion to say the least!"

The warlock's relief faded. "You found *more* spell traps?"

"Two too many, my friend! Someone was trying to ensure most readily that I was snared!" Darkhorse's voice lowered to a quiet boom. "I did not admit to you the trouble the first trap caused me. It came very close to capturing me as the other captured you, Cabe!"

*Then what would I have done?* the sorcerer could not help thinking.

"Of the other two snares I found, I can only tell you that they were traps of great cunning! Had I encountered one of them first, it might be that both you and I would have struggled in both ignorance and futility while day after day passed without our knowing it!"

"How did you deal with the spells?"

The eternal chuckled. "They were designed to trap, not cope with *being* trapped! Once I understood their nature, I simply *swallowed* them."

"Swallowed?" Cabe tried to picture the sight, but failed utterly.

"They were quite tasty in their own way!"

Cabe was still deciding whether or not he should ask Darkhorse to expand on his remark when Kyl appeared, trailed by Lord Green and the two guards. The emperor-to-be was still clad in his riding clothes.

"Yesss, I *did* hear your voice after all, Lord Darkhorsssse! I give thanksss to the Dragon of the Depthsss that you have come back to usss whole!"

"Did you think it would be otherwise?" returned the shadow steed, an astonished tone in his voice.

Kyl frowned, as if wondering if he had offended the eternal somehow. Darkhorse was famous for his almost childlike self-confidence. "Of course not! I trussst your journey wasss little fraught with danger?"

"A little excitement! Nothing more!" Before the heir to the dragon throne, Darkhorse would want to show no weakness whatsoever.

"Good! I know that you do not eat asss we do, Lord Eternal, but I would be remisss if I did not invite you to sssup with usss thisss evening."

"I have already eaten," replied the shadow steed with a quick glance to Cabe. "If you do not mind, I would prefer to begin a search of this region. One never knows what one will come across."

"Yesss. Lassst night it was Ssseekers."

"Oh?"

The Dragon King had informed his future emperor of the previous night's incident. Cabe had wanted to make little of the incident, knowing it would only sow more anxiety, but had agreed that Kyl certainly had a right to know. To Darkhorse the warlock said, "I'll tell you everything that happened the first opportunity I have tonight."

"I would be pleased to hear!" Darkhorse gouged the earth with one massive hoof. "The knowledge of the birds' intrusion makes me all the more determined to survey the surrounding region. Your Majesty, I thank you for your kind offer! Rest assured, one way or another, we *will* speak before this excursion ends."

Kyl executed a bow. "I look forward to it, Lord Darkhorsssse!"

A sardonic laugh escaped the shadow steed. "Not, 'lord,' my lord! Never is Darkhorse lord of anything, save perhaps the nothing from whence I came. I am to my friends simply known by my name; to my enemies, I am *Death!*"

The dramatic announcement was followed by another chuckle. Possibly out of habit, the drakes clustered together. Even the guards were well aware of what Darkhorse was capable of, although to their credit they remained at the forefront.

"I shall return shortly, Cabe!" roared the eternal. Before anyone could even acknowledge his departure, the shadow steed had vanished.

"We are all together," commented the emperor-to-be. "It would require a grand fool to plot mischief now!" Kyl turned to his human guardian. "Will you be joining usss at sssupper, Massster Bedlam, or will you await the demon sssteed's return?"

Knowing that Darkhorse was safe and now watched over the camp eased the warlock's tensions a bit. Some food and drink could only help at this point. "I believe I'll be joining you, Kyl."

Even as he walked with the drakes in the direction of the heir's tent, Cabe was aware that the respite was only temporary. Before long, they would reach Talak . . . and there the times would truly become interesting.

For now, though, he would enjoy the evening. After all, a respite *was* still a respite.

AURIM WOKE TO the realization that there was someone in the room with him. He tried to be as still as possible. Through slitted eyes, the young warlock tried to spy whoever it was he had sensed.

There was no one within his range of vision. Aurim shifted in bed, pretending restlessness in his sleep. As he turned, his gaze swept the room.

Scowling, Aurim opened his eyes wide at the sight to the right of his bed.

A tall, thin man dressed in archaic robes was speaking to the air. Not a sound, however, escaped his lips. Had not Aurim known better, he might have thought he had gone deaf. He watched the man mouth words for several seconds before slipping out of bed to stand beside the silent intruder.

Up close, his suspicions were confirmed. He could see *through* the man to the window beyond.

The Manor held memories, centuries of memories, and some had a life of their own. This one was new to the younger Bedlam, but it looked similar to one his father had described. Cabe Bedlam had notebooks in which he chronicled each and every vision that appeared. Most of them remained mysteries. Over the centuries, many folk, some not human, had dwelled or passed through the Manor. Why their traces remained behind, neither the elder Bedlams nor Aurim knew. There seemed no reason for the particular time and place the visions were seen, nor the manner in which they appeared to the onlooker. Some included sound, others, like this one, were silent. The only link seemed to be that they materialized only before a mage. It mattered not whether the chosen one had any true power; as long as the person carried even a trace of sorcery within, he or she was liable to be confronted by the ghostly memories.

Aurim's spectral orator began to fade. The warlock circled the dwindling figure, curious as to why it had shattered his slumber so. He had grown up around the visions and was so used to them that, unless they burst into existence before his very eyes, he was hard-pressed to notice them. Unlike his father, the younger warlock was no longer very interested in these particular mysteries.

Until now.

What was so special about this one? It was hardly even a true shape anymore. More a wisp of smoke. Yet, it had disturbed him.

The last vestiges of his ghostly companion evaporated.

The feeling that someone else had been in the room did not.

One spell that Aurim had little problem with was changing one set of garments to another. For the most part, it was a frivolous, minor ability that had served him only when he woke up too late for his lessons. Now, however, he was thankful, for it was only the matter of a single thought to change what he wore in bed to his mage's robes. Likely it would not have mattered had he decided to forego the change, but Aurim preferred it this way. He did not want to accidentally run into one of the female servants, especially the ones near his own age, while clad in night clothes.

It was difficult to pinpoint where the trace had originated, but Aurim at last decided that the balcony was the most likely place. The trace was just a tiny bit stronger there.

Had someone been climbing into his room? Somehow, it felt more likely that, if there *had* been someone lurking beyond, that someone had remained on the balcony. Perhaps his room had simply been a stop on the way to another location.

As he walked toward the balcony, a tingle coursed through him. There was no explanation, but for a moment the golden-haired warlock faltered. Then, refusing to be cowed, Aurim pushed on. He reached the opening and carefully peered out. The warlock saw no sign of an intruder, but the hint of something lingered. Now, however, it felt a little farther away, almost as if it was coming from . . .

*Below.*

There *was* someone below him, someone on the path leading into the gardens. Although he could not see who that someone was, Aurim felt he should know the identity. He moved to the edge of the balcony and tried to probe with his power. Sorcery shielded the other, but Aurim did not give in. He knew that the potential lay within him to be more powerful and skilled than either of his parents, but this was the first time the young warlock had ever truly pushed that power to its limits. The Manor was his responsibility as much as it was the rest of his family's.

Carefully, he sent out invisible tendrils toward the hidden figure. It might only be his sister, once more pining for the drake, but if it was not . . .

His mind touched that of the intruder.

Aurim gasped. There was a familiar mind there, but underneath it, like a second layer of skin, was *another* mind. An evil mind and one that he belatedly realized he knew from stories. Acting instinctively, the anxious mage tried to withdraw before he was noticed. He had to warn the others! All these years, a monster had been masquerading as one of their own. Tears ran down his face. *How long?* How long had the charade gone on?

It was then Aurim found that he could *not* break the link.

*It isss not polite to intrude upon othersss, boy!* came the vile voice in his head.

He could barely move. A pressure built up against his mind, a pressure that seemed to be trying to crush all thought. In desperation, the young warlock tried to call out, hoping that someone might at least hear the truth. The devil that his father had often told him about was *here* after all these years. Here, during this most *crucial* of times.

"*Tom . . . Toma!*" Aurim croaked.

It was not enough. His voice was barely a whisper.

Aurim was overwhelmed.

HE STIRRED IN his sleep. Blinking, Aurim raised a heavy head and looked around his bedchamber. For some reason, he found himself expecting to see a ghost. While that happened now and then, for the most part the memories of the Manor did not disturb him. They were interesting to experience, but unlike his father, the younger Bedlam had never made a hobby of them.

Turning over, the warlock tried to go back to sleep. Yet, for some reason he felt a little uneasy, almost as if something had or was about to happen. Aurim sent out a weak probe, found the nothing he expected, and gave up. Probably a nightmare brought on by his new responsibilities. He had not told anyone, not even his parents, just how nervous he was about overseeing the Manor, even if only for a few days. Many people, human and drake, would be looking to him for answers.

Sleep began to take hold of him. His troubles turned to mist. Even the reason he had woke seemed irrelevant. If there *had* been something involved other than a nightmare, he not only would have noticed it, he would have dealt with it. Inexperienced he might be, but he had the power.

*Besides,* Aurim thought as he drifted into slumber, *what could possibly happen here?*

# VI

THE GREETING THE caravan received at the gates of Talak could best be described as grandly cautious.

The gates opened while they were still some distance from them, which Cabe read as a subtle hint from Melicard that he did not fear his guests. Knowing the king as he did, the warlock was certain that was true.

Banners hung from everywhere and the sight gave pause to more than one drake in the caravan. The flag of Talak, as designed by Melicard himself, consisted of a long, sharp sword crossing the stylized head of a dragon. The crippled king had designed it during his first years of power, when he had begun his vendetta against the race that had plagued his house so long. The vendetta was at an end—so Talak's monarch had promised—but the flag remained as a constant reminder of the king's hatred.

"Talak hasss very high wallsss," Kyl commented to no one in particular. In truth, there were few kingdoms with walls as impressive as those surrounding the mountain state. They would have been even more impressive if Cabe had not been aware that they had failed to stop the drake armies.

There were other defenses now, defenses that made up for the failure of the walls. Should there be a new conflict between the drakes and Talak, the dragon warriors would find the high walls the least of the city's shields.

Trumpets began to blare. From seemingly nowhere, people from the outer villages materialized on the sides of the road leading into Talak. There was some cheering, but overall the mood remained one of caution. More than a few of the villagers eyed the members of the caravan with suspicion. Most knew little about the heir to the dragon throne, but more than a few readily identified the Dragon King who rode beside him. Responses were mixed, albeit never approaching the point of anger. That Green had generally been a friend to humanity did not matter so much as that he was recognizable as a Dragon King.

Cabe's appearance also initiated some response, most of it simple puzzlement. His robes and the slash of silver in his hair marked him as a sorcerer of some distinction and any who followed the doings of the king and queen surely had had opportunity to learn his name. Cabe even heard "Bedlam" whispered by several people. *They probably wonder why I ride with devils. . . .*

Despite the size of the caravan, the presence of so many drakes, including a Dragon King and a future emperor, and the appearance of a master mage, it was Darkhorse who elicited the most response. Trotting alongside the caravan, yet far enough away so that no one might think he was some servant of the drakes, the massive, ebony stallion could not help but draw the attention of those who, for the most part, had considered him little more than legend. A few probably had seen him before, Cabe knew. The shadow steed had visited Queen Erini too many times not to have been sighted now and then. Still, it was one thing to catch a swift glimpse of the huge, equine form and another to watch Darkhorse trot casually toward the city gates with no one attempting to stop him. A wall of silence preceded the eternal with onlookers staring open-mouthed as he passed, then babbling to one another as Darkhorse moved on. Nothing, not even the future emperor of the drakes, could outshine the shadow steed.

Which was perhaps, the watchful sorcerer concluded, one of the other reasons that Kyl had wanted him along. With so many overawed by Darkhorse, the presence of the young heir would be slightly less fear-inspiring. They would remember Kyl, of course, but perhaps not in the same light as the elder folk would recall his unlamented father.

*He succeeded in using Darkhorse after all!* Cabe shook his head. He hoped the eternal would not realize that.

As the caravan neared the city walls, there erupted from the open gateway a troop of mounted soldiers. In rapid succession, they lined up on each side of the road, armor glinting, lances raised in ceremonial greeting. Melicard's royal guard. There were at least fifty, by Cabe's count, all veterans.

"An honor guard," said the dragon heir. "How consssiderate of Melicard."

Cabe listened for even the slightest hint of sarcasm in Kyl's voice, but found none. The warlock's gaze again rested on the soldiers from Talak. Despite the decorative, eggshell-shaped armor they wore, these men were warriors. Strong, tenacious warriors. Contrary to the ways of many other kingdoms, Melicard's royal guard was not just for show. The guard was made up of his finest soldiers, all willing to give their lives for him.

The Green Dragon raised a mailed fist, the signal to slow but not halt the caravan. While this was being accomplished, two well-decorated commanders broke from the ranks and rode toward the royal party. They looked to be a few years older than their men but no less fit. One wore a short, black-and-gray beard that covered part of a round, wrinkled visage, while the second, clean-shaven, sported two ragged scars on the right side of his face. As the newcomers' weapons were still sheathed, the Green Dragon allowed them to ride closer.

After questioning glances aimed toward the distant figure of Darkhorse, both men acknowledged Kyl. In rather patrician tones, the clean-shaven one said, "Our Majesty's fondest greetings to you, my lord! I am Baron Vergoth and my companion is General Yan Operion. We are to be your escort to the palace, where King Melicard and Queen Erini await you. Unless you have any objections, we can lead you there immediately."

"Have preparations been made for His Majesty's retainers?" asked the Dragon King.

"Places have been set aside for everyone. We do not think that you will be disappointed."

Green looked at Kyl. The emperor-to-be inclined his head, but otherwise did not respond. The Dragon King, however, seemed to understand what the younger drake was trying to convey, for he turned back to the two soldiers and, with a nod of his own head, replied, "Then, you may lead us now."

"Yes, my lord."

Cabe marveled at the politeness of the soldiers. Not a trace of their enmity toward the drakes showed through. Kyl might have been the king of Gordag-Ai, Queen Erini's father, so well were the men of Talak behaving. *Melicard must've talked to them after Erini talked to him!*

The baron glanced at the general, who turned his steed around and immediately returned to his place at the head of one of the two columns. Vergoth signaled an officer in the other column. The soldier saluted and barked out a command. With impressive precision, the column turned to face the gateway and began rearranging itself, becoming a spearhead of sorts with the officer in the lead.

When the baron saw that his men were ready, he turned his attention back to the drakes. "If Your Majesty and Your Majesty's people will follow me . . ."

Kyl signaled for Vergoth to proceed. The Talakian soldier saluted him and turned to face the gates. As Vergoth called out the command to move, the Green Dragon raised his fist and motioned for the caravan to follow suit. Urging their animals forward, the drakes and the wizard trailed after their escort, with Darkhorse continuing to stay far to one side of everyone.

Only the column belonging to the baron moved. Cabe studied the second column, especially its commander. The general eyed the moving caravan dispassionately. He briefly met the gaze of the warlock, but then continued on with his inspection of the visiting delegation. Cabe Bedlam had met both the baron and the general prior to this occasion, but usually on state business and only for brief periods of time. Neither man actually led the royal guard, but for this visit, Erini had no doubt deemed it proper that Kyl be escorted by men of proper rank. Melicard would have chosen these two because of his trust in their ability to turn the situation around should the drakes be determined to cause trouble.

The second column had still not moved even after Cabe and his companions had reached the last man. The caravan, then, was to have an escort riding *behind* it as well as ahead. Melicard's faith in the drakes was very definitely limited.

They entered Talak.

Each time he visited the mountain kingdom, the blue-robed mage could not help but admire the peculiar architecture. Talak was a city of ziggurats, stepped pyramids often looming high in the sky. The largest, of course, would be the palace, the tip of which he could already make out. The rest of the city was only a little less impressive, however. Every gate seemed to include first a visit to a marketplace. The caravan's path took it through a people-filled, bustling combination of tents, stalls, and permanent buildings. Even the arrival of the drakes' emperor-to-be did not stop most merchants from continuing to try to hawk their wares to the onlookers and even, in a few daring cases, members of the caravan. Cabe laughed and shook his head as one woman tried to convince him to purchase a roll of gaily-colored cloth. She followed along until he was at last able to convince her he had no interest, at which point she allowed him to move on while she attempted to assault one of the human servants farther back in the column.

Risking a study of the dragon heir, the warlock was interested to note the struggle going on in the handsome visage of the young drake. Kyl was fighting to keep his fascination with the city from becoming visible. His eyes, however, kept darting back and forth to admire one strange sight after another. The drake had made a few short visits to Penacles, which was closer, but had never been to the mountain kingdom. Cabe was aware that Kyl had believed Talak to be a rougher, less attractive abode. The dragon heir had expected a wind-blown, murky kingdom populated by sinister figures bent on the destruction of his kind. It was evidently becoming something of a shock to discover that these folk worshipped life and the enjoyment of it. There *had* been a period, from the years shortly after Melicard had assumed the throne to the time of his marriage to Erini, when Talak had come close to being the dark abode Kyl had expected. It was chiefly due to the queen that Melicard had not become the twisted monster his father's insanity and his own mutilation had nearly created.

They passed more and more permanent buildings, tiny duplicates of the taller ziggurats. People clad in the bright, loose-fitting clothing that was most common in Talak contrasted sharply with the armored soldiers keeping order. The crowds grew more excited as the drakes entered deeper into the city, but no one tried to create a disturbance. The warlock was pleased about that, although he knew it was all Melicard's doing. The king might be a good man, but he ruled with the proverbial iron fist.

The markets gave way to more permanent businesses, then to stately homes. The nearer they drew to the palace, the more elegant the travelers' surroundings became. This did not mean that the crowds became any thinner. On the contrary. Here were the folk who controlled much of the kingdom's commerce and politics. To them, the coming of the drakes, especially Kyl, was at least if not *more* relevant than their queen's initial arrival. Cabe recalled Erini describing her journey through Talak and smiled grimly at the notion that the aristocracy and wealthy merchant class considered the newcomers of so much more import. Of course, years ago, when the young princess had arrived, most of the powerful had expected her to take one sharp look at the disfigured king and then flee in disgust and horror. Erini had certainly surprised them.

Cabe dismissed the thoughts as the palace of the king and queen of Talak at last loomed before them.

The gates surrounding the palace grounds were open. A contingent of the royal guard, half stationed on each side of the gate, came to attention. Two heralds raised horns to their lips and announced the arrival of the visitors.

Kyl gripped his reins tightly. Cabe would have sought to encourage him, but the Green Dragon was swifter. He leaned close to the heir and pointed at the palace, as if explaining some fact about it. Cabe was not close enough to really hear, but it was clear to him at least that the Dragon King's words had nothing to do with architecture. Kyl at last nodded and relaxed his grip. Lord Green straightened again and pretended as if nothing had been amiss.

The warlock turned his attention briefly to Grath. Kyl's brother was taking in all of the splendor with much less difficulty than his elder sibling. Cabe was impressed. Grath was no more traveled than Kyl. Perhaps it helped to know that most eyes were not on him.

On the uppermost step of the palace entrance, looking calm and unconcerned, were King Melicard and Queen Erini. With them were members of the king's staff, looking not at all as unconcerned as their monarchs. There was no sign of the young princess, Lynnette, but it was not necessary for her to be here.

Melicard I of Talak was a tall and striking man. His hair had begun to turn to gray and there were lines etched into his angular features, but no one doubted his strength. He had a commanding presence; Cabe knew of few men who were not warlocks who were as overwhelming as the king. None of those few, however, could match Melicard's unique appearance.

Both the monarch's left arm and much of his face on that same side were *silver.*

In the early years of his reign, Melicard had begun his vendetta against the drakes. Two of his specific targets had been both Kyl and Grath. In order to combat sorcery that might be used to defend the hatchlings, Melicard had gone to the Seekers for aid. The avians had given him power of his own, in the form of magical medallions. Melicard had put them to good use at first. Then, during one attack, a medallion in his possession had shattered . . . discharging the stored power.

He had almost died. The injuries could be healed to a point, but the face was permanently scarred and nothing could save the arm. Seeking a semblance of normalcy, Melicard had sought out the rare, magical elfwood, a type of wood that could be trained to mimic whatever it was carved to resemble. A partial mask of the silver substance now covered every scar, even replacing most of the mangled nose. More astonishing, the elfwood arm moved with almost as much fluid grace as the original had.

The elfwood had been the beginning of the king's recovery, but his marriage to Princess Erini of Gordag-Ai had truly saved him.

The queen still looked as young as on the day she had first ridden into Talak to be the betrothed of the dark and mysterious king who ruled there. She was the fairy-tale princess come to life, with perfect features highlighting a pale, oval visage. Sun-drenched tresses almost comparable to the gold of Aurim's own head flowed behind her like a second cape. She was slim and somewhat petite, which caused more than one unknowing person to assume that the queen was a delicate, fragile person who relied upon the towering strength of her husband.

Such fools did not last long in the royal court of Talak. Erini complemented Melicard. It was Erini's love more than anything else that had made the king what he was. The queen was also not one to sit quietly and let others make decisions concerning her kingdom. Melicard and his bride ruled on an equal basis, although he would not have denied that she could sway his opinion to her thinking with but a smile.

Her ability to rule both her kingdom and her husband aside, Queen Erini possessed one more ability that made her a force to be reckoned with. Outwardly, the only evidence of that ability lay in the fact that she did not look much more than eighteen despite being more than a decade older than that. Melicard looked to be almost three times her age.

The queen of Talak was a sorceress. She had not wanted to be, but the power would not be denied. It had manifested shortly before her arrival in the mountain kingdom and had, Cabe knew, been instrumental in saving both her and the king from the machinations of Mal Quorin, counselor to Melicard and secret servant to the late, unlamented Silver Dragon. Like all other mages, she wore silver in her hair. At present, however, her crown and some subtle styling served to all but hide the telltale streak.

The king and queen waited in regal silence as Baron Vergoth led the column to a position before the steps of the royal palace. Cabe took the opportunity to once more admire the building and grounds. Melicard's palace, the largest structure in sight, was a sprawling ziggurat surrounded by a beautifully landscaped park. In the high season, flowers of all colors and scents blossomed everywhere. There were small groves of fruit-bearing trees and even a stream whose source was underground.

Despite the splendor of the grounds, the palace was by no means designed simply as a feast for the eyes. The ziggurat was well-defended, with arrow-slits as the only visible evidence. Many of the defenses were magical in nature or simply hidden. Talak itself was also protected by spells, but it was rumored that conquering the entire city would be simple in comparison to attacking the palace. Cabe could sense great power surrounding him, but he knew better than to probe. That was a good method by which to set off any of a countless number of spells. Even the warlock, who knew the king and queen well, was not privy to all of their secrets.

The caravan and its escort came to a halt. Cabe and the others dismounted. At the same time, Melicard and Erini, accompanied by their people, began to descend the steps of the palace.

Baron Vergoth led the warlock and his companions forward, save for Darkhorse, who chose to stay back for reasons no one dared ask. The two parties met at the bottom of the steps. The baron saluted his monarchs. "Your Majesties!"

It was as if the caravan and the rest of the population of Talak had disappeared. Now the world consisted only of the two small groups.

Melicard looked over the group before him, his eyes alighting briefly on first Cabe and then Kyl. "Welcome, honored guests, to our home! Welcome to Talak!"

Cabe had almost expected the Green Dragon to speak for his group, but Kyl surprised him by stepping forward. He bowed to both king and queen, adding a smile for the latter, and said, "You do usss great honor, Your Majesssty! We thank you for your hossspitality and hope that thisss meeting between usss will be the firssst major ssstep toward permanent peace between our two racesss."

"That we wish also," the queen returned. "But come! You've journeyed some distance to be here, and I do not doubt that many of your people could do with food and rest. If you do not object, I will have someone show your retinue to their quarters. We have set aside part of a wing just for them."

"That would be mosssst kind of you."

"As for yourselves, special accommodations have been arranged for all." Erini smiled at Cabe. "Master Bedlam will be familiar with the rooms we have given to him and I think he will be able to vouch for their comfort."

"They've been nothing less than perfection, Your Highness."

Her smile blossomed. "I am happy to hear that! Lord Kyl, if you like, I will be happy to escort you and your companions to those rooms. Then, after you have had a chance to refresh yourselves, perhaps you will join my husband and me for a light supper. The others, are, of course, also invited."

Becoming daring, the young drake suddenly reached for the queen's hand. Melicard and his men tensed, which made the drakes with Cabe also stiffen, but Kyl simply took Erini's hand, turned it palm down, and kissed the back lightly. He matched her smile with a brilliant one of his own—the type that the warlock had most recently noticed directed toward his own daughter. "You are both a graciousss hossstess and a mossst beautiful lady. I would be honored to have you essscort us. Your other sssuggestionsss I alssso find most agreeable. But name the hour for the sssupper and we shall be there."

For the first time, Cabe noted traces of suppressed emotion play across the face of Melicard. The flesh and elfwood countenance of the king briefly twitched in disgust and anger, but Melicard quickly and quietly subdued the escaping emotions. In a calm voice, he turned to the warlock and said, "While my wife escorts His Majesty to his rooms, I would like to take the opportunity to discuss a few minor details with you, Master Bedlam. If you have the time, that is."

*And it would be best if I did have the time, wouldn't it?* the mage thought wryly. He hoped that the king's temper would remain in check. Now was not the time for Melicard's hatred and jealousy to rise to the forefront.

"I'm at your service, Your Majesty."

"Fine." The monarch turned to Kyl. "My lord, I hope you find your rooms satisfactory. If there is any need we can fulfill, please do not hesitate to ask. I look forward to the supper and hope that it will be but the first step toward the peaceful relationship both of us desire."

Erini frowned to herself, then suddenly glanced past Kyl and the others. "But we are being remiss! There is one more who should be there!"

From behind Cabe came the stentorian voice of Darkhorse. "I do not eat nor do I require a place to sleep, gracious queen! Yet, if my presence is desired, I will come to your supper!"

*He's offering them the chance to forego his company.* Whether the eternal's reasons for making the offer were selfish or because he thought the two sides would be better able to negotiate without his presence to disturb them, Cabe Bedlam could only guess. Still, the very idea of offering the choice went against what the shadow steed had said to the warlock among the ruins of Mito Pica. Cabe wondered what the stallion had in mind.

Before the king and queen could say anything, Kyl spoke up. He looked at Darkhorse as if offended. "By all meansss, you mussst join usss! In fact, I will go ssso far asss to insissst."

"Yes," added a more reluctant Melicard, "it would be remiss not to include you."

His wife was pleased. "There! That's settled, then. Baron Vergoth, would you see to it that someone helps those with the caravan to settle in to their chambers? Also, something must be done about separating the riding drakes from the horses."

"As you desire, my queen." Vergoth saluted his lord and lady, then Kyl. "If you will excuse me. . . ."

Queen Erini separated herself from the king and made her way to Kyl's side, where she took the heir's arm. "Now, then, Your Highness, if you and your companions will follow me, I will take you to your own rooms."

Kyl was all courtesy. "You are too kind, my lady."

The two of them started up the steps, with Lord Green, Grath, and the two guards trailing close behind. Four royal guardsmen followed the party. Melicard watched them go, then turned back to the warlock. "Shall we adjourn to my private quarters, Master Bedlam?"

Cabe did not answer him at first, instead turning to where Darkhorse had been standing. "What about you—"

The shadow steed was gone. Scanning the area, Cabe could not find the eternal among the soldiers and servants.

"He vanished at some point between the moment it was decided that he would join us at supper and just now, when I turned my gaze back to you." Melicard's tone was cautious. "I will never understand that creature. Do not even you have any control over him?"

"Darkhorse does what Darkhorse chooses to do."

A half-silver frown crossed the king's unique visage. "I had noticed that. I still hoped."

The caravan and its escort had begun moving again. Cabe watched for a moment, then reminded the king, "You wanted to talk to me, Your Majesty?"

"Yes." The king of Talak looked around at his staff. "The rest of you may return to your duties."

The departure of the dignitaries left the two alone save for a second set of guards whose task it was to protect the king at all times. Melicard acted as if they did not exist. The heir to the throne of the mountain kingdom since his birth, he was very much used to the near-constant presence of bodyguards.

"This way, if you please."

Following the tall, regal figure up the steps of the palace, Cabe asked, "Has my wife arrived yet, Your Majesty?"

"I commanded those responsible to notify me the moment she does. Likely you will know before anyone else does."

That was probably true, but the warlock liked to ask, just to be certain. Gwendolyn had said she would arrive early in the evening of this very day, but exactly when had been debatable. Cabe hoped that she would appear before supper. He wanted her there if it was at all possible.

As they reached the top, Melicard casually asked, "What are your personal observations concerning this supposed emperor?"

The intrigued sorcerer arched an eyebrow. "Is that one of the minor details you wanted to discuss with me?"

A pause. "One of them, yes." The king fixed his true eye on his companion. Even after so long, it was sometimes hard to believe that the other one was not real, despite its silver shape, for the elfwood so well mimicked Melicard's original face that the false eye followed the direction of its counterpart with perfect precision. The disfigured monarch had never said otherwise, but Cabe occasionally wondered if he saw better than he pretended.

Mulling over the king's request, the warlock finally replied, "I'd be happy to give you my observations concerning Kyl."

Melicard actually appeared a bit startled. "I thank you."

The mage shrugged. "I would do the same for him in regard to you. Likely, I will whether he asks or not."

"That would be . . . fair."

Although he was able to hide it from the king, Cabe was vastly relieved by Melicard's lack of protest. Had the gray-haired ruler commanded him not to speak to Kyl, it would have created a precarious situation. Despite his position as one of Kyl's guardians, the warlock was desperately attempting to be neutral when it came to the talks between the two rulers. If either side felt that he leaned toward the other, it could only make the situation more perplexing . . . not to mention dangerous. It was even more difficult since, despite Melicard's constant formality, Cabe considered both king and queen good friends.

*The question is,* the sorcerer thought as he followed Melicard into the palace, *how long before I do* take sides*? Or have I done so already?*

He hoped that Gwen would make it in time for supper.

KYL WAS PLEASED with himself.

"I did very well, would you not sssay ssso, Grath?"

The dragon heir stood in the midst of the sumptuous suite that had been turned over to him by the very charming queen, who had just left his company not a moment before in order to make the final arrangements for the informal supper. Had his interests not been focused elsewhere, Kyl would have utilized his full charms on Queen Erini. It was clear that she controlled her husband, so whoever controlled her could have whatever he desired. Concessions, perhaps.

"You did well," Grath admitted. Unlike his brother, he maintained a quiet, almost reclusive air. Seated in a plush, gold-and-purple chair on one side of the vast room, Grath watched his sibling continue to preen. For the first time in days they were alone, Kyl's guards having taken up residence outside the entrance to the suite.

"I wasss grace and charm. I treated our two-faced hossst with the ressspect and care that he could hardly have expected from . . . how wasss it he put it long ago? . . . from 'a blood-thirsssty lizard that sssometimes walked on two legsss'?"

"He was, I believe, talking about Toma," Grath corrected.

"He wasss talking about *all* drakesss, regardlessss of which of usss he ssspoke of at the time!" The emperor-to-be stalked toward his brother and leaned over the chair. He smiled slightly as Grath shrank back. The other drake was not frightened, merely cautious. Both of them knew how valuable Grath was to him. When Kyl had a question, his younger sibling was generally there with the answer. The arrangement pleased the dragon heir. He had the best, most loyal of all advisors, one who had no designs on the throne himself. *He would rather bury hisss head in hisss precious booksss than rule a race!*

Yes, a perfect arrangement.

"We should prepare for the supper," Grath suggested quietly. "You have to press your advantage."

Kyl's handsome face momentarily revealed anxiety. The confidence that his performance at the steps of the palace had built evaporated somewhat. It would not be long before supper. He had the advantage now, having confused King Melicard's assumptions about the new Dragon Emperor. Queen Erini was especially pleased with the elegant young visitor, of that he was confident. What, then, was the best way to further capitalize on his success? With the mountain kingdom on the very doorstep of his own domain, he needed the good will of the king and queen . . . at least until the clans of Gold were once more a power to be reckoned with. That, however, would take a few years.

Kyl studied his brother's eyes. "You have sssome possible sssuggestion. I know that look."

"I think . . . I think you should make some sort of grand gesture, Kyl."

The emperor-to-be straightened. "A grand gesssture? I thought I *had* sssimply by coming here!"

Grath steepled his hands. "I mean a *perssssonal* gesture to King Melicard himself, Kyl."

A personal gesture. The elder drake could see the potential in that. Done properly, it would completely undermine the last vestiges of the human monarch's misgivings. "Tell me what you think might be a *worthy* gesssture. Tell me what you would do. . . ."

"It came to me while I was reading about Talak and King Melicard in general." Grath looked down, as if uncertain as to whether his suggestion would be worthy of his brother's time.

Kyl had no such doubts. His brother had not failed him yet. Giving his advisor a reassuring smile, the heir to the dragon throne urged Grath to continue.

The encouragement appeared to be all the younger drake needed to spur him

on. Looking more excited, Grath said, "It concerns His Majesssty's father, Ren-
neck IV, and our distant brother, the late Duke Kyrg . . ."

"Rennek and Kyrg?" Kyl could not see the connection.

The other drake leaned forward. "Thisss is what I think you should do,
Kyl. . . ."

# VII

**THE MANOR WAS** now *his.*

Pride and worry wrestled for control. Aurim's mother had left for Talak the
night before, leaving him in charge. He knew, of course, that Benjin Traske was
supposed to keep an eye on him, but even still, the Manor was now most definitely *his* responsibility.

As he walked through the garden, Aurim grew more confident. The Manor
virtually ran itself. Despite all those who had accompanied his father and the
others to Talak, there were more than enough people left who understood the
day-to-day running of the miniature kingdom. The young warlock was there
more as the symbol of authority, the final arbiter, he decided.

He felt confident enough in himself that he was willing to try a spell. Not
a grand, dangerous one, but a small yet complex incantation. Aurim glanced
around. There was no one nearby. The closest structures were the stables, and
there Ssarekai the drake and Derek Ironshoe, his human counterpart, would
have their apprentices and workers busy. With most of the animals gone, the
stable masters were hoping to give the buildings a thorough cleaning out—no
small feat.

The younger Bedlam held his hands before him, palms up. With his mind,
he sought the forces of the world, forces he thought of as part of the natural
makeup of the land but what most folk simply called "magic." The link was
made and drawn upon with but a single thought; to an outsider, the action
would have seemed instantaneous. Aurim knew that compared to his parents he
was still a bit slow, but the potential—and to his disgust it sometimes seemed it
would *forever* be only potential—was within him to be the greatest mage to walk
the realm since his great-grandfather, Nathan.

The expectations people had of him were ofttimes daunting, which was perhaps why Aurim still had trouble with his control. Now, however, no such fears
haunted him. In the comfort of his newfound role as temporary master of the
house, he was able to use his new confidence to strengthen his will.

A bouquet of flowers formed in his open hands. The bouquet was a good
foot high and as wide as his body. Bright colors running the full span of the

spectrum decorated the arrangement. Flower after flower blossomed, only to give way to their successors, which in turn gave way, and so on. . . .

To someone standing some distance away, the warlock's bouquet would have hardly seemed an amazing feat, considering the sort of things even a slightly competent mage was supposed to be capable of creating. It was only upon closer inspection that the complexity of Aurim's spell became evident.

The flowers were not flowers in the literal sense. Up close, it was possible to see the multitude of tiny, glittering figures constantly rearranging themselves to create new patterns. Each figure was a round, almost spherical, clown no larger than a fly. They crawled, climbed, jumped, and even flew. Aurim did not directly control each movement—no mage he had ever heard of in his mother's stories had had *that* much skill—but the young warlock did direct them in the manner in which they created the flowers. Their other actions were based on smaller subspells he had prepared in advance. The main spell, like so many others designed to hone one's concentration, had no apparent value other than visual delight, but the practice itself prepared a novice spellcaster for the time when such manipulation of the natural forces *might* mean life or death. Of course, while the practice was important, Aurim also simply *enjoyed* such fanciful creations. It was a challenge to him to see what he could design next.

He was just starting to expand the bouquet when a commotion from the stables made him dispel his creation. A roar from within hinted at one possible cause of the trouble. There were still some riding drakes and horses in the stables, and it was possible that one of the former was not taking kindly to being moved so that the stable workers could clean its pen. If it was a mother drake, then there was even more chance for disaster.

With Ssarekai and his men inside, Aurim doubted that the situation was very critical, but it behooved him to see if there was any way in which he could contribute to a speedier conclusion. He hurried to the stables, only belatedly recalling that he could have saved precious seconds by transporting himself, and cautiously entered.

"Massster Aurim! You should not be in here!"

Ssarekai himself pushed the warlock to one side just as a long, scaly tail whipped their direction. Aurim regained his balance and watched as two drakes and a short, bearded man, one of Ironshoe's helpers, struggled to keep a half-grown riding drake under some loose sort of control. The dragon men, one on each side of the beast, tugged at guiding ropes. The human stablehand, meanwhile, was attempting to use a pitchfork to prod the beast toward an open doorway just to the creature's right. Two other humans stood to the side, one of them binding a wound on the left arm of the other.

"What's wrong?"

"Nothing, my lord! Nothing!" Ssarekai bowed quickly. He and the other dragon men in the stable differed in some ways from the warriors most humans saw. The reptilian riding master and his helpers resembled, for the most part, their fiercer counterparts, but unlike the Dragon Kings and their warriors, these drakes were without crests. Instead, they appeared to be wearing round helms that partially covered the inhuman faces within. No hissing dragon's head adorned the top. Ssarekai and his kind were members of the servitor caste, a caste rarely seen, since most often servitors generally remained in or around the clan caverns.

The drake turned back to the struggling hands and hissed out a command that Aurim did not catch. The workers redoubled their efforts. Another pair of humans entered the stable. They raced to each side of the stubborn monster and joined the two drakes holding the guide ropes.

Slowly, the beast came back under control. Ssarekai hissed another command, this one evidently to someone beyond the doorway the men were trying to lead the riding drake through. There was an answering shout, then something outside and beyond Aurim's view caught the beast's attention and sent it scuttling almost gleefully through the desired entrance.

As the animal and its handlers vanished, Ssarekai hissed the drake equivalent of a sigh of relief. "I ssso much prefer horsssessss to sssuch ssstupid beasssts!"

It was strange hearing a drake speak so. "You like horses better than one of your own mounts?"

His companion smiled, revealing the predatory teeth. A forked tongue darted out and in. "People are alwaysss comparing horsesss to riding drakesss, but in my opinion, we should be comparing the ssstupid beasts like that one to your *mulesss*! Useful pack animalsss, but *ssso* stubborn! Horssses can be like that, but for the mossst part, they are quicker to learn and obey. I would choossse them over riding drakesss under almost every circumssstance."

"I seem to recall that Derek Ironshoe seems fascinated by the qualities of riding drakes," teased Aurim.

"Only asss animals of war! Massster Ironshoe wasss a cavalry sssoldier once."

By this point, it was clear that there was no need for the warlock's presence. Still, trying to give the appearance that he was as concerned as his parents were over the everyday running of the Manor grounds, Aurim asked, "How goes the cleaning, Master Ssarekai?"

The drake shrugged, a gesture more common to humans than to his own kind, but one he had picked up from his years working with Ironshoe. Ssarekai had been one of the first drakes sent to work for the Bedlams when they had been given custody of the Dragon Emperor's hatchlings. He, more than most drakes, had come to an understanding with the humans who lived here. There was no one who lived at the Manor who did not respect the reptilian stable master.

"We are, asss I sssuspected, behind in our tasssk. Master Ironshoe hasss a group ssstill working on the ssstables where the royal mountsss are kept." To Ssarekai, mounts used by the Bedlams were as royal as those utilized by Kyl or any of the Dragon Kings. It was debatable as to whom he was now more loyal. Aurim wondered whether the elder drake would depart with the others when Kyl finally left for the Tyber Mountains and his throne.

"Then, I probably shouldn't trouble you anymore. I just wanted to make sure that everything was all right."

Ssarekai nodded his head respectfully. "Your concern isss appreciated, Massster Aurim. Better to be sssafe, I always sssay."

"Father would certainly agree with that. Well, good luck to you." The warlock, his sense of duty satisfied, turned and started toward the doorway through which he had entered.

"And to you, my boy."

Aurim stiffened. There was a sudden twisting in his stomach, as if someone had thrust a blade through him and now sought to add further to the agony of that thrust. The golden-haired sorcerer remained still, trying to understand the reason for his horror. Something concerning Ssarekai? What? Ssarekai had said nothing out of the ordinary. Aurim turned around. The drake was making an inspection of one of the stalls and seemed to have already forgotten his recent visitor.

*Why do I feel like this?* His stomach continued to feel as if it were being twisted. A sense of dread crept over him, yet Aurim had no explanation for it. The scene before him was hardly conducive to fear. Ssarekai was the most trustworthy drake Aurim knew, more trustworthy than most humans. The warlock's only other choice seemed to be the stable, but since he had no part in the cleaning of it, for which he was thankful, Aurim could not see how the building could possibly unsettle his thoughts.

Perhaps sensing that he was not alone, Ssarekai looked up from his work. "Wasss there sssomething else, Massster Aurim?"

"No. Sorry." What could he say to the stable master? Aurim backed out of the building, unable to tear his eyes from it until he was well away. Even then, the feeling of unease continued to shake him. So occupied was he, in fact, that the youth did not notice the trio that stood quietly talking to one another at the edge of the garden until he was almost next to them.

A breathtaking maiden with long, dark hair and exotic, narrow eyes filled his vision. Her face was a dream, her lips full and inviting. The dress she wore was the color of roses and did nothing to hide the lush form beneath it. Had he not grown up with her, played with her as though she were a sister, Aurim might have been spellbound. As it was, he could only think again of the fortunate male who would someday be Ursa's choice. Peculiar as it seemed, however, that male would not necessarily care that much for her present appearance; he would likely prefer her in her *true* form.

Ursa was a female drake: sister, albeit from a different clutch of eggs, to both Kyl and Grath. She also bore the royal birth markings, which meant that while she could not be empress, the drakes not permitting such, the young female could be the mother of one. Ursa did not care about that, however. All she cared about was her best friend, her sister in all but the physical sense: Valea.

The two were together even now, but this time a third person was with them.

Benjin Traske looked up from what he had been doing and stared at him, stopping Aurim in his tracks with just that glance. Valea was partly turned to the scholar, as if the two had been in earnest conversation. All wore rather serious expressions, but whether those expressions had to do with whatever conversation he had interrupted or whether they concerned his own agitated countenance, the young warlock could not say. At the moment, that did not matter nearly as much to him as the reason for his own uneasiness. Flickering memories danced about in his mind, teasing him.

"Are you all right, Aurim?" Ursa asked, coming to his side.

"It's nothing." A face surfaced in his memory, but it was blurred and distorted.

Benjin Traske gently moved Valea aside. He walked over to Aurim and looked him in the eye. "You do not look well at all, lad."

"It's . . . night . . ." The warlock had no idea why he had mentioned nighttime, yet somehow it made sense. He tried to focus on both night and the face, trying to fit them together. "I thought I saw . . ."

"Look at me." Traske took him by the shoulders. The two matched gazes. The scholar studied Aurim carefully. "I do not see anything. Your eyes look clear. Your face is a bit pale, but nothing terrible."

The pressure on his mind faded. Aurim began to breathe easier. The memories slipped away, but they no longer seemed of any real importance. All that remained was a slight headache.

"Do you wish to lie down?"

He shook his head. "No, sir. It's nothing. Just a little headache."

The massive tutor released him. He still eyed the younger man closely. "Well, if it happens again, come to see me. A reoccurring problem is nothing

to be ignored. I should be able to find some way to deal with it. You understand me?"

"Yes, sir." It all seemed rather silly now. Aurim could not even recall what
had caused the headache, which was already receding.

"Do you want someone to walk with you?" Ursa asked.

He found that he was a little embarrassed by their concern. At least Valea
was not fawning over him. His sister remained behind the others, also concerned but only watching. Her mind appeared to be elsewhere, but at the moment Aurim had no interest in whatever it was his sister was thinking about. He
only knew that he still felt ashamed at the fuss he had just caused.

Aurim extricated himself from Ursa's hold. "I'm fine. I am. I didn't mean to
interrupt you."

"Not at all, lad."

"If you'll excuse me, then?" Executing a half-bow, the embarrassed youth
departed quickly, leaving the others to return to whatever conversation he had
disrupted.

*What was I doing?* he chided himself. *Now they'll think I can't run this place on my
own! Can't even put up with a small headache!*

Tramping across the Manor grounds, he turned toward the kitchens. Some
food and water would do the trick. He was probably just hungry. Aurim had
hardly eaten at all today. That was all it had probably been: a headache brought
on by a lack of food. Considering his normal eating habits, his body had likely
just not been used to so little for so long. *I'll feel fine after that! No more headaches!*

The throbbing had already all but ceased, and as for the peculiar memories . . . they were once more forgotten.

IN A PRIVATE conversation some minutes after the fact, the Green Dragon informed the Bedlams that he had been unprepared for the request Kyl had flung
before the rulers of Talak just prior to the supper's end. Neither the emperor-
to-be nor Grath had given any hint in previous conversations with him. It had
startled the Dragon King as much as it had Melicard.

It had startled Cabe equally as much, although he had been able to hide his
surprise better than most of the others. Only Darkhorse, who simply shook his
head, and Grath, the only one with whom Kyl *had*, perhaps, discussed his decision, had seemed fairly calm about the matter.

The heir to the dragon throne had requested the opportunity to perform
a special ceremony, one that he had claimed was long overdue. It was to be a
private but formal ceremony, with wreaths and a speech of apology to both the
city and its rulers. Kyl had claimed that he wanted to prove once and for all that
the sins of the father would *not* be ignored by the son.

What was most stunning about the request was that the dragon heir desired to have this special ceremony take place before the burial chamber of Melicard's *father*, Rennek.

At first the king had been dumbstruck. Then he had stopped just short of calling the notion something that certainly would have raised the threat of war between the two races. At last, he had looked to his queen for guidance. Erini had simply put one slim hand on his elfwood arm and nodded. That had settled it for Melicard. If Erini thought the idea had merit, the king could not argue. This was a situation where Cabe had known that Melicard would be unable to trust his own judgment. The warlock was rather surprised that the queen had so readily agreed to it, but he, like the king, trusted her intelligence.

That had been last night. By now, late in the morning, the entire castle, perhaps even most of the kingdom, would be astir with rumors. When exactly the ceremony was to take place was still undecided, but the master warlock hoped that it would be soon; if the event was delayed more than a few days, then Cabe feared that . . . well, to be truthful, he had *no* idea what might happen, just the feeling that something *would* happen.

"What could've possessed Kyl to make such a daring move?" he asked his wife as the two spellcasters walked the grounds of the palace. Unlike most visitors, the Bedlams did not require an escort. That did not mean they were not watched. Cabe could sense eyes on him: eyes, and weak, inexperienced probes. Melicard had himself one or two mages now, it seemed, but neither were of any high level of skill. The warlock knew that Gwendolyn had also noted them and found the probes almost as amusing as he did. With a simple spell, either Bedlam could have left the hidden mages following a false trail for the rest of the day. As guests, however, it would have been bad form. Melicard was only acting in the manner of all cautious rulers past and present. He was by no means either the most paranoid or the most troublesome.

"I am curious as to that myself," the Lady Bedlam finally responded. "That even Lord Green had known nothing about it bothers me a little. I understand that Kyl did not need to consult anyone, but such an act should have, I think, made him think about doing so. You saw Melicard's face."

"Every variation."

"Yes, well, we can thank Erini for his relative calm toward the end. Melicard's parents have always been a touchy subject. Rennek IV was not the best of rulers, evidently, but he had a soft place in his heart for his son."

"And too fragile a mind," added Cabe. Ahead of them, he heard the laughter of a child and the sound of the queen's voice.

"It *is* a clever suggestion," the crimson-tressed enchantress admitted. "Now that Melicard has gotten over his initial confusion, he should be able to see that himself. It allows Kyl to show his willingness to admit to the terrors committed in the name of his sire, while at the same time it enables the king to show his people that he is strong enough to have the respect of the new emperor of the drakes. That no one but we will witness it makes no difference. Word will get out and that will be sufficient."

"Providing it ever takes place."

She grimaced. "I think I will urge Erini to convince her husband that it should take place either tomorrow or the day after that. Most likely the day after; with the formal reception this evening, tomorrow would make everyone feel hurried for time."

Cabe looked at her, a wry smile spreading across his plain features. "Exactly who runs this kingdom? You? Erini? Lynnette, perhaps?"

Gwen had no chance to respond to his jest, for suddenly both of them became aware of the sound of soldiers running. The sound came from the same direction where they had both heard the queen and her daughter playing not a moment before.

No word passed between the two, but suddenly Gwen no longer stood at his side. Cabe hesitated only long enough to ready himself, then also vanished.

He materialized in the midst of spear points and sword tips. More than a dozen guards surrounded the scene, with yet another contingent arriving even as the warlock drank in his surroundings. Erini stood to one side, a small, delicate-looking girl holding her hand and two massive guards shielding them both from possible danger. Darkhorse stood near the center of the circle the soldiers had formed, but it was not the eternal at whom the weapons were pointed.

A drake cowered before the captain of the guard. Darkhorse was on the dragon man's other side, looking more curious than wary.

"Pleassse! I meant no—"

"Be silent!" The captain struck the drake across the false helm. Cabe noted the lack of crest; the prisoner was one of the servitors, not a warrior. That did not mean that the drake was not capable of killing, but it did make it unlikely. They were generally not very aggressive for their race, even in dragon form.

It seemed doubtful that *any* of the drakes would be so foolhardy as to attack one of the royal family, even as a dragon. True, any one of the draconian visitors had the potential to become one of the legendary leviathans, but in Talak that was more likely to mean death to the shapeshifter than to his prey. It was reasonable to assume that Melicard had planned for such circumstances; the king would never have allowed the drakes in otherwise. And prior to the departure of the caravan, Lord Green had made certain to remind his folk that even an accidental transformation meant punishment . . . possibly at the discretion of Melicard himself.

To most drakes, Melicard was a demon in human guise. Cabe had been confident from the start that none of the reptilian race would risk themselves so.

Which brought up the question as to what had happened *here.*

"Captain, I command you to stop that."

The guardsman looked at his queen, rather befuddled that she would give such an order. With evident reluctance, he lowered his hand. "But Your Majesty—"

"Stay here, Lynnette," the queen whispered to the slim, ivory-skinned child. The young princess, despite her appearance, was no fragile flower, but this was one time, Cabe saw, that she would obey her mother without question. Erini stepped past the two reluctant guards and confronted the captain. "I gave you a command."

Her words were spoken softly, but the soldier nonetheless paled. He saluted and stepped back.

The queen finally seemed to notice the Bedlams. "I am glad the two of you are here. Do you recognize this drake?"

Cabe thought he did, but Gwendolyn spoke before he had a chance to commit himself. "Osseuss, isn't it?"

"Y-yessss, my lady!"

"He was trying to sneak up on the queen and the princess!" snapped the captain of the guard.

The drake shook his head. "Nooo! No!"

"Lies!" The soldier made to strike the drake again, but a glance from Erini made him falter. "My men saw him creeping around the trees, Your Majesty! Creeping around the trees and watching you and the Princess Lynnette!"

"And *me!*" rumbled Darkhorse. "Come, come, Captain! Do you think one drake is any threat to *me?*"

Even under the chilling gaze of the shadow steed, the veteran warrior remained steadfast. "I was doing my duty!"

"And very well," soothed the queen. "I thank you for your concern, but I have my doubts as to the danger posed by this particular drake. Tell me, Osseuss; why did you come here?"

The dragon man glanced at the Lady Bedlam, who nodded to him and said, "Tell the truth."

Keeping one eye on the captain, Osseuss explained, "I wasss lossst. The landsss, they are ssso beautiful, ssso well-kept! I wandered, then realized that I had become turned around. I thought I knew the way back, Your Majesssty, but found myssself here insssstead! I grew fearful, knowing that I wasss where I wasss not meant to be, and when I sssaw you and your daughter, my heart pounded! I was certain that I had condemned myssself by not paying attention!"

"Why is that?"

"A *drake* near the bride of Melicard the Terrible? Only for the royal party isss that possible! For the ressst of usss, that is surely sssuicide!"

Judging from the guards' expressions, it was clear to Cabe that Osseuss was correct in that assumption. These men were ready to kill the servitor simply because he was what he was. To be fair, Osseuss *should* have known better, but if men could be foolhardy, then so could drakes. In some ways the races were too similar.

Queen Erini looked at the Bedlams. Gwen studied the cringing drake for a moment longer, then said, "I will vouch for him. His duties at the Manor concern the care of the gardens there. Osseuss has always been one of the most loving caretakers. I will definitely vouch for him."

"So will I," Cabe added in support. Unless Osseuss was a cunning mage comparable in power to the trio of spellcasters before him, his story was genuine. While neither Cabe nor his wife had delved into the drake's thoughts, it was simple enough to read the truth in the emotions radiating from the mind of the servitor. There was true fear there, fear mixed with confusion and self-recrimination.

The guardsman was still not convinced. "But *Your Majesty!* We can't just—"

"Are you questioning the word of our guests, Captain? If so, you will also be questioning mine, because I find I agree with them in this matter."

As if that was not enough in its own right to crush what protest there was left in the officer, Darkhorse added, "And if you question the word of my friends, then know you that you also question *my* word!"

Seeing that there would be no more interruptions, the queen did the unthinkable. She held out her hand to the prisoner. He stared at it for several seconds, trying to decide what she intended. When it was clear that Erini did not plan to withdraw the proffered hand, Osseuss reluctantly took it. He rose, then executed a perfect bow.

"Can you find your way back on your own now?"

The drake hesitated. His reptilian eyes continued to flicker between the queen and the captain. A forked tongue darted out and in as he nervously considered her question. "I . . . I am not sure."

"I would give you an escort, but I think that emotions run too high for that at the moment."

"*I* will return him to his companions."

Everyone looked at Darkhorse, whose attitude so far had been surprising. He had sided with a drake and now offered to see that same drake back to safety. It was almost amusing. Osseuss was at least as fearful of the eternal as he was of the guards.

"Are you certain you wish to do that, Darkhorse?"

The ebony stallion chuckled. "I thought I had just said so! Do you doubt *my* word, Your Majesty?"

"Never." The queen smiled. "Thank you, then."

"I am your servant!" Darkhorse trotted up to the still-anxious drake. The captain of the guard—and the rest of the guards, for that matter—retreated as the shadow steed neared the prisoner. "Come with me, dragon!"

Osseuss looked to his master and mistress for confirmation.

"Go with him," Cabe responded. "There's nothing to fear."

It was clear that the servitor could have argued that point, but he nonetheless obeyed the warlock. The circle of guards gave way for the duo, the nearest soldiers wisely deciding to lower their weapons as Darkhorse trotted by.

Erini watched the strange pair depart, then summoned the recalcitrant officer to her. "I want you to know that your loyalty is commendable, Captain. These next few days *will* be difficult for all of us. Caution is good, but we must never lose control."

There were many things that the guardsman probably wanted to say in response, but this was his queen and so he could only obey. The captain saluted her. "I understand, Your Majesty."

"You may resume your duties, then. I wish you the best of luck. This *will* be a taxing situation for you and your men, but I have every confidence in your abilities."

"Thank you, Your Majesty."

The captain organized his men and led them off in record time. Only four soldiers still remained, the personal guard of the queen herself.

"I thank you, Erini," Gwen said when the captain was gone.

"It was a mistake; I saw that, too. I was glad that you were there to verify it for me, however. My skill at sorcery will never be as great as either of yours."

"Yours is formidable enough. You have done us proud." The queen had been the Bedlams' first student and, so far, their most promising. The handful of spellcasters that had been brought to Penacles were, for the most part, folk who would never be able to do much more than light fires with a glance or lift small objects into the air. There were one or two who might go beyond that, but so far no one who had the potential to even remotely approach the power of either the witch or the warlock.

This did not mean that such did not exist. Cabe could count four whose powers were adequate at the very least. Three of those worked for King Lanith of Zuu. The other was a wanderer, a blond beauty who had used the name Tori and who had, at one point, attempted to seduce Cabe. Considering the way these four had turned out, the sorcerer wondered whether or not it was a good thing that so few others of any measurable might had appeared so far. The present crop of spellcasters was not by any stretch of the imagination a shining example of what a new age of sorcery might offer the world. Too many people already feared those like the Bedlams, who had done them no harm at all. If more like Lanith's lackeys appeared, the reputation of sorcery would only be tarnished further.

Queen Erini had blushed slightly at the compliment. "I thank you for your confidence in me, Gwendolyn." Her expression changed almost immediately. "But enough about that. I am glad that both of you are here. If you will excuse me for one moment. . . ." She turned back to her daughter and the remaining sentries. "I believe it is almost time for your lessons, is it not, Lynnette?"

The little princess made a very unladylike face, but under the queen's steady gaze she finally nodded. "Yes, Mother."

"I thought so. Then you had best be on your way—" Erini raised a hand as her daughter started to run off. "*Not* like that and *not* without some company. Also," she added in softer tones, "it would be nice if I could have a hug first."

Smiling, Lynnette rushed over to her mother, who leaned down and took the girl in her arms. They held one another tight, then Erini reluctantly allowed her daughter to slip away. Lynnette curtsied to the two mages, then returned to the guards. One pair followed the princess as she started back toward the palace.

Queen Erini sighed as she watched her only child depart. "It gets hard to watch them grow up so fast! I remember when she was but a baby!"

The Bedlams were quiet but sympathetic, understanding all too well the sensation the queen was experiencing.

"Enough of that!" The slim woman looked at her two old friends. "I am glad you happened along, because I have need to talk to you. Melicard has agreed to the ceremony taking place soon after the formal reception but has not set a specific day and time. Do you have any suggestions?"

Cabe looked at his wife, who smiled back at him. Turning her gaze back to the queen, the Lady Bedlam replied, "We were *just* discussing that very subject before we heard the soldiers!"

"And what did you decide?"

The warlock could not resist. "My wife the royal counselor thought that the day after tomorrow would be best. It would allow a day of calm for all of us after the excitement of tonight's reception."

Erini could not hold back her smile. "The royal counselor may be correct. I was thinking along the same lines. What time of day would the royal counselor suggest?"

"To be fair," began Gwendolyn, giving Cabe a piercing but playful stare, "I think the royal counselor's *husband* should contribute on *that* matter."

"And what do *you* say, royal counselor's husband?"

Unschooled in the eccentricities of proper royal behavior, Cabe had no idea what time of day would be appropriate for such a solemn ceremony. Thinking of his own preference, he hesitantly answered, "In the morning?"

Erini considered this for quite some time. Cabe hoped that he had not erred in some way. Better to face an angry Dragon King than try to muddle his way through the idiosyncrasies of the monarchy.

"Yes, the morning might work. I have always thought that there was something captivating about the first few hours of the day, something touching the soul."

The warlock relaxed.

"I will take your suggestions to my husband. If he finds them agreeable, then they will be presented to Lord Kyl and Lord Green." The queen hugged them both. "Thank you, both of you. I always know that I can depend upon your sage advice."

"We're glad to help in any way we can," Cabe returned. Gwen echoed his sentiments. Erini was a good friend.

"The day after tomorrow," repeated the slim monarch. "In the morning. Early, so that the wonder of a new day will touch us all . . . those of us who can *appreciate* morning, that is."

"How fare the preparations for the reception this evening?" asked the Lady Bedlam, changing the subject.

"Everything is moving swimmingly. I have been planning for this day since it was first suggested some time back. The food will be ready. The ballroom is being prepared even as we speak. All the arrangements are proceeding exactly as I hoped." Some of the queen's high spirits faded. "Now, if only the *guests* could be so obliging. Not everyone thinks that peace with drakes is a good thing."

Drakes eating and drinking alongside the cream of Talak's leadership. Cabe tried to hide his own anxiety from Erini. It was one thing to have a private supper between the two rulers, but the reception invited so many new and unpredictable elements into the situation.

"I'm sure that they'll—"

"*Erini!* Are you all right?" called a frantic voice.

They turned to see the king come rushing across the lawn. Behind him and having difficulty keeping pace with the distraught monarch were Baron Vergoth and Melicard's personal guard.

"It is all right, Melicard! I—" The queen had no chance to say more, for the tall form of her husband suddenly enveloped her.

"I just spoke with the guards protecting Lynnette! Curse those drakes! I'll have the whole bunch of them slaughtered, with that snake who would sit on the throne beheaded before the entire city!"

"*Melicard!*" Erini's eyes were wide with fear, but fear for her husband and her people, not for herself. "You will do no such *thing!* Think what that would mean! The rest of the Dragon Kings would see no choice but to fall upon Talak with their full combined might!"

"I do not care!"

"But it was a *mistake!* The drake did nothing! He was lost and happened to wander too near. The sentries saw him and mistook his presence for a threat, but he was only trying to find his way back to the others. If anyone was in danger, it was *him!* Just ask Cabe or Gwendolyn."

Melicard turned his unsettling gaze toward Cabe, who was forced to steel himself when the unseeing, elfwood orb fixed on him. "What is she saying?"

"The truth," the warlock responded. He did not allow the king any time to argue. "It was a servitor drake. They're more inclined to work than assassinate. This one was scared out of his wits. Your guards did their duty," he added, not wanting to sound too recriminating, "but in this case they had nothing to fear."

"Where is this . . . lizard?"

"Darkhorse led him back to the others. Both my wife and I will vouch for the drake, Melicard."

"As will I, husband." The queen forced the hesitant ruler to look at her again. "It was *nothing.* Perhaps the guards still worry because they are not used to even the presence of a drake in the city, but they were wrong if they told you that I was attacked."

The king stilled, but the tension had by no means left him. *Why did this have to happen now?* wondered Cabe.

Baron Vergoth dared speak. "Shall we locate this drake, my lord? Question him ourselves?"

Melicard stared at his bride. Erini gave him a look of defiance. "No, Baron. Not this time. It seems we were mistaken."

The aristocrat looked rather disappointed, but he nodded.

"Thank you," whispered Erini. She hugged her husband, then gave him a light kiss. "And thank you for your concern."

"I would give up all of Talak if it meant your safety."

"Let's hope it will never come to that, then, shall we? I think the people deserve better."

With some effort, the king turned to the Bedlams. "I thank you two for your assistance in this matter. I also apologize for any inconvenience that this may have caused you."

The sorcerer would have liked to have said something concerning the fact that the one who had suffered the most inconvenience was the drake Osseuss, but such a bald statement would not have sat well with the king. Instead, he replied, "I hope that this doesn't make Kyl more reluctant."

Beside him, Gwen gasped. For once, he had thought of the ramifications before she had.

Melicard, too, saw the possible consequences. "I will have a most sincere message relayed to the Lord Kyl. You also might inform him of my regrets, should you see him before the messenger does."

"As you wish." Cabe was too relieved about Melicard's acquiescence to point out that he was hardly at the beck and call of Talak's master. "I'm glad that everything is back to normal."

"*Nothing* will be back to normal until those drakes are gone," the lord of the mountain kingdom snapped. "Even after that happens, I doubt if we will ever be able to relax! For the sake of my family and my people, I hope that I am wrong, but the history of the drakes, at least during *my* lifetime, has been fraught with nothing but troubles."

"Hopefully," interjected the Lady Bedlam, "this visit will alter that."

"Yes . . ." Melicard squeezed his wife hard, but his eyes never left the mages. "I hope it will, but you would all be wise to remember what I said earlier: if I find any proof, *any at all*, of a threat to either my family or my kingdom, I will take the drakes, no matter what the cost, and execute each and every one of them . . . beginning, I think, with *Lord Kyl*." Melicard released Erini and began to turn toward Baron Vergoth and the guardsmen. "Now if you will excuse me, I have a reception to prepare for."

The king, trailed by his men, stalked away, leaving in his wake three silent, thoughtful figures.

# VIII

**THROUGHOUT THE DAY** and into the evening, various folk in the kingdom of Talak were greeted with an unsettling sight. Before them they would suddenly find the dread legend known as Darkhorse. The demon steed appeared in the alleys of the dankest parts of the city, the open fields of the surrounding countryside, and even among the silent ancestors of the king laid to rest in the royal necropolis. Those who stayed around long enough to observe the shadowy form might have noticed how the glittering, blue eyes of Darkhorse took in everything, as if the legendary creature was seeking something. Yet, whatever it was, Darkhorse did not appear to find it. Through the day and into the evening the shadow steed searched, reluctantly foregoing his quest only when light finally gave in to darkness.

There was, after all, a reception he had been requested to attend.

*IF THINGS ARE going so well, then why does it seem as if everyone in the room is about to burst from tension?*

Cabe sipped his drink and watched the proceedings. Kyl, flanked by Erini and Melicard, was being introduced to various members of the kingdom's aristocracy and civilian leadership. The king knew the importance of maintaining a balance between the two groups. In Talak, the divisions between the aristocracy and the upper-class merchants were less strict than they were in some kingdoms. Living under the continual shadow of the Dragon Emperors had a way of drawing people together. That, however, did not mean that the two groups did not constantly attempt to gain some advantage over one another.

Kyl was not a lone drake among humans, however. Next to the monarchs were both Grath and the Green Dragon. Grath followed every introduction with avid interest, while the Dragon King kept a wary eye on everyone. Farther back, an honor guard consisting of a dozen drake warriors, Faras and Ssgayn first and foremost among them, stood at attention, willing to take on the entire palace if need be. While outnumbered by the Talakian guardsmen, Cabe had no doubt that the drakes, if given the opportunity, would be able to wreak great carnage in defense of their lords.

As a sorcerer of renown, Cabe had not needed to dress for this occasion, but Gwendolyn had insisted on it. Therefore, the mage now wore a dark, dignified outfit akin to those once worn in the courts of Mito Pica. Cabe considered himself a survivor of that kingdom, his foster father having raised him in the wooded lands surrounding the city. The outfit consisted of dark blue pants and coat and a high-collared shirt of gray. Black, shin-length boots completed the conservative suit. In truth, the suit would have been considered conservative even in Mito Pica, for the sorcerer had decided to forego the more decorative aspects of his former kingdom's tastes. Even doing that, however, did not make the suit anything a proper mage should wear.

The Lady Bedlam, however, was by no means so reserved. She was clad in a dazzling gown of emerald and pink that had many of the elite of Talak looking a bit on the shabby side. Cabe could not think of another woman in the ballroom who was more beautiful, more resplendent, than his wife, an opinion he suspected was shared by many of the male merchants and aristocrats, for some of them seemed almost as attentive to her as they were to either their monarchs or the drake heir.

Yes, everything *seemed* to be progressing smoothly, but now and then Cabe would catch a frown or a surreptitious glare among those gathered. Just enough to keep him tense.

The last of the introductions were made. After a short conversation with the king and queen, Kyl turned to Lord Green and said something. The Dragon King shook his head, but Kyl was adamant. At last, the Green Dragon nodded.

Kyl signaled to Grath, and the two began to walk unprotected among the Talakians.

"I don't know whether he's amazingly brave or simply majestically foolhardy," said Gwendolyn as she rejoined Cabe. "We had best keep a careful eye on him."

"He does wield power of his own."

"Yes, but this *is* Talak."

His wife had a point. If ever there was a place where the people would be prepared against dragon tricks, it was the mountain kingdom. "What's he hoping to accomplish by doing this?"

She took a sip from her goblet. "That only Kyl and maybe Grath know. Kyl *says* that he wants the people to really know him, to understand that he should not be feared the way his father was."

"The Talakians don't fear him as much as they hate him." It was a sweeping statement, even Cabe would have been willing to admit that, but it held more than a grain of truth. The most evident hate was that of the older soldiers and aristocrats, the ones who could still recall the days before the last Dragon Emperor's death. Baron Vergoth could be numbered among those, although he was much more expert at hiding that hatred than many of his contemporaries. The warlock did not care for the way the baron's eyes followed the dragon heir. Had looks truly been able to kill, Kyl would have been dead now, a blade in his throat. Vergoth, fortunately, was too loyal to his king.

"Where is Darkhorse?" the Lady Bedlam asked suddenly.

"I don't know." Cabe could sense his presence somewhere in Talak, but could not fix on one location. Still, it seemed as if the eternal was suddenly making his way to—

There were shrieks from just beyond the king and queen. Both human and draconian sentries readied their weapons, prepared for the worst. Kyl, speaking softly to an elegant if somewhat plain-faced countess, turned slowly toward the direction of the cries.

The shadow steed had finally made an appearance.

That there was not more panic was due to the earlier presence of mind of the queen. Erini had very carefully warned her subjects of the coming of the legendary creature. Most of those gathered here had long been aware of her peculiar friendship with the creature from the Void, and while many of them were aghast at such a relationship, it was well-known that Darkhorse had saved the lives of both the king and queen.

Still, one could not blame anyone for becoming startled at the abrupt materialization of a huge, ebony stallion. Two women fainted and several more guests, both male and female, looked ready to join them. Darkhorse, as usual, ignored the effect his arrival had had. He trotted across the marble floor, his hooves making no sound and leaving no marks. When he finally stood before Melicard and Erini, the eternal dipped his head in both greeting and respect.

"My greetings to Your Majesties," he rumbled.

His respectful attitude toward their monarchs helped settle in part the nerves of the other guests. A few even eyed the eternal with satisfaction. The warlock sipped his drink again, thinking *they see Darkhorse as an ally of Talak, a weapon to use against the drakes.* He glanced at Kyl, who also seemed quite pleased that Darkhorse had come to the reception. The emperor-to-be was quietly studying the reactions of the Talakians. Grath whispered something in his ear that made Kyl smile and nod his head. *Is this what you wanted, then, Kyl? To make Talak feel that it has nothing to fear from the new Dragon Emperor because they've got allies such as Darkhorse to aid them if need be?*

If that was the case, then Kyl was even more devious than Cabe had imagined.

Things slowly returned to something resembling normal. It was almost humorous to watch some of the guests constantly look from the dragon heir to the eternal and then back again. This was likely the most unusual reception any of the Talakians had ever attended. It would make for tales to tell. As the warlock continued to observe, he saw that with Darkhorse's presence now an accepted thing, people were beginning to approach Kyl. The handsome drake was less of a shock compared to the eternal. Now he was simply exotic. True, his teeth were a bit sharp and he spoke with the characteristic sibilance of his kind, but the rest of his appearance made him worthy of any royal court.

He had already charmed most of the women he had talked to, but this time Kyl was careful not to aggravate the men who were with them. For the most part, the young drake was in his element and whenever it seemed he might falter, Grath was there to whisper in his ear or even add a rare word of his own to the conversation.

Yet, Cabe still did not feel confident about the night. Perhaps it was simply because this was Talak, hated enemy of the drakes. . . .

*You share my fears, then?* came a voice in his head.

He knew that it was Darkhorse, but it still gave him a start. Gwendolyn looked at him, but Cabe only smiled and made a comment about the wine.

If Darkhorse desired to talk to him alone, then he would respect the shadow steed's wishes . . . to a point. There was little the sorcerer hid from his wife.

*You may tell her what you wish when I am through. I certainly have nothing to hide from the Lady of the Amber,* remarked the great stallion. Darkhorse was one of the few who still called Gwendolyn by that title, but he was careful not to use it in her presence. For roughly two centuries, she had been kept sealed in a prison of amber, the legacy of Cabe's mad father, Azran. The Lady of the Amber was almost as great a legend as Darkhorse himself, but few knew that Gwendolyn Bedlam was the same woman.

*What do you want?*

Several yards away, Darkhorse continued to speak with Erini. It was astounding the way he could hold two conversations at the same time without ever becoming confused. *I have found something of interest . . . or perhaps I should say that I found nothing and find that of interest!*

Cabe held back a sigh, hoping against hope that this was not to be one of the eternal's murky explanations. There were times when the shadow steed could leave him more befuddled than informed. *What exactly are you talking about?*

*There is no trace, no sign, of the sort of sorcery such as what was used to bait the traps that almost snared me and did capture you!*

That did not surprise Cabe, and thus should not have surprised Darkhorse. *I haven't noticed anything and I doubt that there is anything to notice. Melicard knows better, Darkhorse! He wants peace, too. The days of genocide are over.* Cabe hoped they were. *You should have told me that you were looking for some sign of guilt. I could have told you that Melicard is innocent.* Erini *could have told you that!*

To the naked eye, there was still no hint that the eternal was doing anything other than conversing with the queen. Yet, in the sorcerer's mind, the shadow steed practically roared with impatience. *But that* is *what I mean! Of course you cannot sense any trace, but neither can I! Me! I should be able to find some trace; no one knows the Vraad . . . or especially* Shade *. . . as well as I, yet I find absolutely no evidence here!*

It *was* to be one of the stallion's murky explanations. *And that means?*

*Someone else is responsible.*

As worldly as the eternal was, he somehow still retained a childlike attitude in many things. Cabe *hmmphed,* but fortunately Gwen did not notice. *There are others who despise or fear the drakes. Zuu, for example.*

*No, it was not Zuu. I have been there.*

Cabe still had no idea as to how Darkhorse could be so certain about his findings, but he knew better than to argue that point. *Well, there can't be too many remnants of Shade's legacy, can there?*

*I do not know.* With that, the eternal broke the link.

*So that's what he's been doing,* the warlock mused. *Using his invitation to make a thorough check of this place.* Cabe was glad that Darkhorse had found nothing in Talak. It would have crippled the possibilities for peace if Melicard was discovered returning to his old ways. Not only that, but it would probably have also meant the end of his marriage to Erini. That bothered him almost as much as the threat of a return to war.

Cabe despised the intrigues of government. Sorcery was so much simpler, so much more straightforward, in comparison.

"What do you suppose is happening there?"

Gwen's question concerned a young noble who was speaking with Grath. They appeared to be having a somewhat heated discussion, at least where the human was concerned. While what Grath was saying was not audible, the drake's demeanor indicated reason and calm. Yet, each word seemed to incense the noble.

Stepping between his brother and the human, Kyl muttered something to the Talakian.

The noble replied.

Kyl, hissing loudly, started to swing a fist at the man.

"Trouble!" Gwendolyn breathed.

Before either of them could move, Grath took hold of his brother's arm and prevented the blow from landing. Unfortunately, the noble took the aborted assault as excuse to draw a ceremonial knife from his belt. Even from where he stood, Cabe could see that the blade was as well-honed as any normal knife.

"Jermaine!" Melicard called. "Stop!"

Both the king's men and Kyl's honor guard began moving toward the struggle. Neither Bedlam could get a good enough view of those at the center to dare a spell. It was possible that the wrong reaction would leave either the dragon heir or the noble open to attack. The death of either would shatter the peace, no matter what the original reason for the argument.

Jermaine, the noble, slashed at Kyl. Grath's hand blocked the attack, but not without incurring a jagged cut. One of the courtiers behind Jermaine grabbed the noble's other arm. Jermaine struggled free, then took a step toward his adversary.

The entire situation threatened to get out of hand . . . if that were any more possible. The two honor guards had already taken up positions around the combatants, old hatreds causing both of them to choose their own kind. A full-scale battle was brewing.

"I'm going to try to pick Kyl out of there!" Gwendolyn hissed. "I don't understand why the fool hasn't done so himself!" Although the warnings against using drake magic were supposed to apply to the emperor-to-be as well as his retinue, it was doubtful that Melicard would have held Kyl responsible for using his sorcery in self-defense. Still, perhaps the drake felt it was safer to fight by hand rather than risk the defenses of Talak.

Then, just as it seemed that everyone was converging on the battle, a blast of thunder shook the entire room. It was so intense that everyone froze, many perhaps thinking that an earthquake or siege had commenced.

"Children, children! Behave yourselves *now!*"

It was Darkhorse. His stentorian voice echoed throughout the room.

"Milady," he continued, now looking at the queen, "I regret to say that I may have cracked your floor down to the foundation! For that, I do apologize."

Queen Erini was barely able to hide a smile. She nodded to the shadow steed. "You are forgiven, I think."

"My gratitude for that." The ice-blue, pupilless orbs focused on the king. "Your Majesty, the situation is now in *your* hands."

Melicard reacted immediately. His expression unreadable, the lord of the mountain kingdom marched toward the struggle. Two courtiers held the noble named Jermaine by the arms. Kyl and the others watched in silence as the tall king stopped before them and stared.

"My Lord Kyl, I hope you will forgive this distasteful display. It should never have happened."

The dragon heir exhaled. The fire in his eyes faded. He eyed the noble, then his brother. Something passed between the two drakes. To the king, Kyl replied, "It isss underssstandable, Your Majesssty! Mossst regrettably underssstandable."

"I will have someone see to your brother's hand."

"Let *me.*" The queen stepped forward. There was a murmuring among the guests.

"The wound is slight," argued Grath. "There is no need."

"Nonsense!" Erini took the drake's hand. She inspected the wound, then cast a disappointed glance toward Jermaine. The noble had the good sense to look at least a bit ashamed.

It would have been simple for any spellcaster of reasonable strength to heal the flesh wound. Grath himself could have done so, given a little time, but Cabe understood what the queen was doing. Talak was responsible for the wound and so Talak, in the form of Queen Erini, would heal it.

Meanwhile, Melicard had turned on the young noble. "Have you anything to say, Jermaine? What was this all about?"

Jermaine's mouth moved, but no sound came out. One of the courtiers holding him cleared his own throat and quietly said, "If I may, Your Majesty; I think it was a misunderstanding."

Pulling his attention away from the queen's ministrations, which had already caused the wound to seal, Grath announced, "Yes, that was all." Curious eyes turned his way. "A very great misssunderstanding. We were discussing the future relationship of our two kingdoms—"

The king raised a hand, silencing the drake. "That will be sufficient. I know this lad and I know how he thinks." The disfigured monarch paused. "I know very *well* how he thinks. Baron Vergoth!"

The baron stepped out of the assembled throng. "Yes, my liege?"

"Will you see to our unruly guest here?" The king indicated the petulant Jermaine.

"One moment, Your Majesssty," interrupted Kyl. "What do you plan to do with him?"

The two lords confronted one another. In level tones, the king asked, "Did you have some particular punishment in mind, Lord Kyl?"

"I had *no* punishment in mind. I underssstand hisss way of thinking. There isss much reason behind it, consssidering the passsts of our two racesss. I would rather hope that you will take that in mind and treat him accordingly. Better to work to break down old hatredsss rather than reinforce them. The latter will only ssslow the peace we both desssire."

Melicard stared at the drake as if seeing a different person there. He visibly mulled over what Kyl had said. "I cannot very well reward him for shaming Talak, but I understand your point. Very well." Melicard turned to Jermaine. "You know what I could have done to you for endangering the kingdom?"

"Yes, my liege. I . . . apologize for everything. I would make some restitution."

"You will. I'll see to that. I will have you work to help make this peace real, lad. We cannot let it be said that Talak was incapable of changing when the chance was offered to it. We're not merely speaking of peace with the drakes, you fool, but also with the other human kingdoms. Who would trust us if you had more seriously injured—possibly even *killed*—one of those to whom I have granted protection under a banner of truce?"

"I had no intention of killing him, Your—"

"Which excuses nothing." Melicard folded his arms. "Baron Vergoth and some guards will escort you from this palace. Tomorrow afternoon, you will return here, at which time I will tell you how you will make amends for this. Is that clear?"

Jermaine went down on one knee, his eyes downcast. "Yes, my liege."

The king turned to Vergoth. "If you please, Baron?"

"Aye, Your Majesty."

The impetuous noble was led silently off. The other guests whispered among themselves. Cabe read a variety of emotions among them. There were many who felt that the king had been more than generous, considering the importance of the affair, but there were also several who revealed sympathy for Jermaine. The warlock made a mental note of the names and faces of the most conspicuous of the latter just in case.

Once more, King Melicard turned to his special guest. "I apologize again, Lord Kyl, for this disastrous incident. Despite what *anyone* might imagine, such behavior will not be tolerated. The next one who shows such colors will not benefit from your good will."

"I undersssstand and appreciate your wordsss, Your Majesty."

"He is healed, Melicard," Erini informed her husband just then. She held Grath's unblemished hand toward the king so that he could see for himself.

"Very good!" The king raised his arms to the assembled folk. "My friends! This incident is at an end! Please return to what you were doing! There is still food and drink!" Melicard nodded toward the emperor-to-be. "There is still a peace to plan."

Slowly, the guests spread out again. Kyl and Grath joined the king and queen, who were on their way to thank Darkhorse for his timely assistance. Gwendolyn looked at Cabe. He nodded his understanding. The crimson-tressed enchantress followed after the monarchs. Conversations sprouted up elsewhere. People began to relax, albeit not too much. The drake and Talakian sentries returned to their assigned positions, but not without last glances toward one another.

For all practical purposes, the reception returned to normal, though every conversation now tended to revolve around what had happened. Drinking also slowed as many became fearful that a drop too much would cause them to say the wrong word to the young drake lord.

"That was very fortunate, friend Cabe."

The warlock looked up into the half-concealed face of the Green Dragon. He had completely forgotten about the Dragon King. Now he wondered where the drake had been during the altercation. The emerald warrior had taken no part in the event, not even when the life of his lord had been in jeopardy.

"It could not have happened better than if we had planned it," the drake went on. "The moment Melicard stepped forward to put an end to it, I realized that it would be better if I remained behind. Let the king of Talak take responsibility. The significance of that would not be lost on the other guests . . . and how *true* that turns out to be! Yesss, things have moved to cement the ties between our two races!"

"I'm just glad that no one was hurt."

"Of course!" The Green Dragon looked slightly offended. "I would not have wanted that, either, but I had confidence in the outcome of the sssituation."

Cabe was glad that one of them had been so confident. There were times when, despite the years he had known him, the warlock found the Dragon King an enigma. The mistake, he suspected, was trying to see the drake's desires in terms of human ideals. There were similarities, but also significant differences. *Very* significant differences, at times.

The sorcerer took a sip from his goblet and let his eyes wander toward where Talak's rulers and the future Dragon Emperor were speaking with one another. Kyl had been raised among humans, but while he more resembled one of Cabe's kind than something akin to the Dragon King, he was still a drake . . . wasn't he?

Was he *neither*? Kyl and the others had been very young hatchlings when the mad Dragon Emperor had fallen, young enough to still be influenced and molded to other ways. Knowing that the only way for them to survive—and for his own race to continue as a power equal to the rising humans—the Green Dragon had taken it upon himself to create this unusual situation.

It had not been an easy task. There had been many humans and even some drakes who had threatened the young heirs over the years. The avian Seekers had actually even kidnapped them once in an attempt to use them as leverage against the Ice Dragon. Yet, despite all the dangers, despite those who still sought to end the possibility of a new Dragon Emperor, Kyl had grown to adulthood. However, no one, not even Cabe, was certain as to what the young drake would be like once he assumed the throne. How much of his personality was influenced by his guardians and how much was influenced by his race's history?

"The ceremony will top this visitation off grandly," the Dragon King was saying. "It wasss an excellent suggestion, would you not say, friend Cabe?"

Only half aware of the conversation, the ebony-haired mage nodded. "It was."

"It wasss Grath's idea, you know. I only dissscovered that this day."

"Grath's—" Cabe stirred, but before he could say anything more, the Green Dragon had turned from him.

"Excuse me, Massster Bedlam, but my emperor desiresss my presence."

"Grath's idea?" whispered the spellcaster. It made sense the more he thought it through. The ceremony had not seemed like the sort of notion Kyl would have come up with on his own. He was intelligent, there was no denying that, but such a personal display was not generally his way. Grath . . . now that was more reasonable.

He caught sight of the younger drake, ever near Kyl's side. Now and then, whenever the emperor-to-be looked hesitant, Grath would speak. In fact, Cabe now noted that Grath generally spoke *only* when necessary. He was like a shadow of his elder sibling.

*Two emperors.* The drakes would be gaining two emperors, not one. Taking another drink, the sorcerer was glad that at least *one* of them could be trusted.

The Dragonrealm needed such an emperor if it was to have peace.

**TWO DAYS LATER,** in the early hours of the day, the drake emperor-to-be journeyed to the necropolis in which were buried the kings and queens of Talak. He was accompanied by Cabe, Gwendolyn, Kyl, the Green Dragon, and, of course, the royal family. Darkhorse was not with them, having said that there were things to which he had to attend. A contingent of the royal guard had escorted the group to the tall, iron gates of the vast cemetery, but Melicard had ordered them to follow no further. The necropolis was a sacred place, a place of final peace. Here the king demanded that his ancestors and those others buried here received the quiet they deserved.

The day was as Erini had said it would be. A light mist lent a sense of tranquility to the morning, putting everyone into a contemplative state of mind. Even Kyl seemed changed. He was subdued, perhaps thinking about his own heritage. In some ways, his background was much like that of Melicard. Both their sires had been driven mad, then had died because of that madness.

Despite his differences with the young drake over the Bedlams' daughter, the warlock could not help but feel some sorrow for Kyl . . . and Grath, for that matter. He also felt relief that they did not hold him responsible for the Dragon Emperor's madness. After all, Cabe had only been defending himself.

They were led through the cemetery by the master groundsman, a surprisingly young if pale man with white hair. Cabe had expected an ancient cadaver clad in black, enveloping robes, but the groundsman, while indeed clad in dark, respectful clothing, would have belonged among the courtiers at the reception save for the short, eagle-headed staff he carried.

"He is new," Queen Erini whispered to the Bedlams, "but his family has held the post for the past two centuries. Roe knows and reveres this place as much as anyone could. His own family rests nearby, as is only just, considering the care they have given this place."

On the queen's other side, Princess Lynnette stared at the surrounding mausoleums and tombs with childlike fascination. She had been here many times before. Melicard had insisted that she come to know the history of her family the moment she was old enough to understand. Lynnette had little fear of the necropolis, which had surprised Cabe until the petite princess had told him that she could never be fearful of a place where so many members of her family watched over her.

The tomb of the kings and queens of Talak was actually a series of interconnected mausoleums that had gradually spread across much of the necropolis. Cabe had actually expected a massive ziggurat, but the low, flat structure before him was by no means inferior to the pyramid of the spellcaster's imagination. Elaborate gargoyles stood watch over the doorways, the latter of which were flanked by thick, marble pillars bearing the royal crest. Talak was unique in that its human rulers had risen more or less from one family line. The people of the mountain kingdom had been very loyal to their monarchs.

The master groundsman led them to the grand entrance of the structure, a more recent addition that enabled one, so the guide said, to find their way to any of the crypts, including the most ancient. As they approached, however, Cabe heard a slight rustling from all around them. He was suddenly alert, his powers already gathering for whatever stalked them.

A band of armed and hooded men appeared from within and around the entrance.

No magic that the warlock could detect had been used to camouflage them; these men were simply adept at concealing themselves. The warlock had never seen an armed force in a cemetery, at least not before now. They were not of the royal guard, for instead of the eggshell breast plates, these men wore chain mail under their cloaks. The sentries, a full dozen, resembled to Cabe avenging wraiths risen from the grave. They eyed the newcomers blankly, somehow radiating a sense of dread power. Cabe was surprised to sense a bit of power among them. So far, that power had not been used, but it was potent enough that he remained wary.

The master groundsman raised his staff. "Stand aside for King Melicard I, the Queen Erini, Princess Lynnette, and their most respected guests!"

The guards did not move despite the command, and it took the warlock little time to realize why. He doubted that drakes had ever sought entrance to the necropolis before, much less the royal crypts.

Roe waved his staff at the reluctant guardsmen. This time they obeyed, albeit casting distrustful glances toward the drakes in the party. The master groundsman waited until they had stepped aside, then turned to his charges.

"My liege, I must apologize for this behavior."

It was Kyl who replied, "Pleassse, King Melicard! Assure him that I undersssstand the hesssitation."

"Again, that is most gracious of you, Lord Kyl," Queen Erini said. She looked pointedly at Melicard, who nodded.

"Lead on, Roe," the king commanded, putting an end to the incident.

The groundsman led them up the steps and to the doors, which opened up as the party reached them. A pair of gray sentries stood at attention behind the doors. Cabe found the situation rather ironic. Melicard had left his soldiers at the gate in respect to the dead, at least so he had indicated, but the monarch had failed to mention that his ancestors had protectors of their own, protectors with sharp weapons and secret magic.

If the party had expected a dank, frightful tomb, they were disappointed. *It's almost as if we were walking through the libraries of Penacles!* was the warlock's first thought. The corridor connecting the various crypts was clean and, if not well lit, at least sufficiently illuminated. Cabe wondered if the rest of the necropolis was so well preserved.

"This way," announced the keeper, pausing to point to a corridor to the party's left. They followed him down the new hall, passing empty spaces in the walls that were obviously reserved for the future. Cabe shuddered and saw Gwendolyn do the same. Neither Erini nor her daughter seemed bothered by the reminders of their mortality, perhaps because they had come here so often that the crypts no longer held any anxiety for them.

The corridor was short and ended in a stairway leading into the earth. Roe began to descend, with Melicard close behind. The Green Dragon also had no qualms about the descent, but Kyl and Grath both froze. Then, the emperor-to-be stiffened and literally forced himself down the steps. Grath hesitated only a bit longer. The queen and her daughter followed after them.

Bringing up the rear allowed the two spellcasters to take a moment to ready themselves. The enchantress squeezed Cabe's hand, took a deep breath, and started down. Grimacing every step, he shadowed her, trying not to think about the sort of hole they were entering.

The remainder of the trip was thankfully short. The names and faces carved into the stone plaques became more recent until at last the party confronted the final resting places of Rennek IV and his wife, Queen Nara, who had died many years previous to her husband.

It should have been darker, for a single candle was all that was burning when they arrived, but the master groundsman's staff proved to be a surprise—the head glowed brighter the darker the path became. Thus it was that the illumination available to them was almost as great as if they stood out in the open air.

Before Kyl was permitted to begin, the king had a ceremony of his own. One day each week he journeyed to this place, often with his family beside him. A wreath already hung over each of the stylized images of his parents, wreaths fairly fresh, since Melicard had been here four days prior. Nonetheless, the king removed the wreaths by hand, then reached into a sack he had been carrying. From it the monarch of Talak brought forth new wreaths, which he then placed where the previous pair had hung. Melicard then stepped back and knelt before the two plaques.

He spoke, but was so quiet that no one else could hear what it was he was saying. Cabe did notice the queen silently mouthing words, tears running down both cheeks. She, at least, knew what her husband was saying.

After several minutes, the king rose. There was a hint of moisture on both cheeks, which disconcerted the warlock a little since the one eye was only supposed to be a carving. The magic of elfwood, however, was a mystery to even the most learned. There was argument as to the extent of its ability to mimic life. Over the years, Cabe had come to the opinion that elfwood did *more* than mimic.

Now at last it was Kyl's turn.

He signaled Grath, who carried a bag similar to the one the king had been holding. The younger drake reached into the bag and pulled out not a wreath, but rather two bundled packages about half the length of his forearms. Grath gently opened each bundle, revealing what at first appeared to be a pair of roses. He held out the roses to his brother, and as the dragon heir reached for them, they caught the light.

The roses glittered. The sight was breathtaking. Only now did those gathered realize that the scarlet flowers were not real, but rather *sculpted* from some magnificent crystal. In every detail did they match or, as impossible as it seemed, surpass their real counterparts. It was almost possible to believe that sniffing one of the sculpted roses would reveal a tantalizing fragrance.

No one spoke as the drake stepped forward and placed one rose before each of the two plaques.

Straightening, Kyl broke the silence. "May thesssse lasssst as a sssymbol of both regret and hope, King Rennek, Queen Nara. Long after the beauty of a true rossse would have faded, let the not ssso cold beauty of thessse pieces show my pain at what my kind hasss done to thiss kingdom. Let it alssso symbolize my promissse to the lords, both passst and presssent, of thiss mountain kingdom that the days of terror are now forever passst. I cannot remake all of what wasss lossst thanks to my sssire and hisss predecesssorsss, but I shall do what I can; that I ssswear in memory of all of you!"

There was more after that, much of it concerning regret to Rennek in particular for the atrocities of Kyrg and Toma, who in the name of their sire and emperor, had been willing to do most anything, no matter how vile. Kyrg had paid the penalty at the siege of Penacles and no one had seen Toma in years, but the memories of the terror the duo had spread remained vivid to those who had been involved, including Cabe. Kyl's words faded as the warlock pondered the evils of the drake dukes and their master. He knew that he would not rest easy until he was certain that Toma had followed his brother and his emperor to oblivion.

The young drake finished. It was an elegant and worthy speech, no matter what the true reasons behind it. The king was too intelligent a man to fall prey to pandering, but it was impossible for him not to be affected by something such as this. Erini had tears in her eyes.

Kyl turned to Melicard. "I hope I have acted with sssensitivity toward your esssteemed progenitorsss, my lord. If you find the rosesss not to your liking, I will replace them with sssomething elssse."

"The fire roses were . . . appropriate," replied the king. His voice shook a little. "I've not seen such beautiful work in years."

"The skill isss almossst lossst. A ssservitor in the Manor knew how to make them, but had not done ssso since coming there. When I was made aware of sssuch skill, I had him make thessse two with the original intention of them being given as farewell giftsss to your lovely queen, but that changed when I dissscovered I had no proper token to bring to thisss ceremony. I hope you will forgive me, Queen Erini."

"Of course I will. They shall have a place of honor down here, Lord Kyl," the queen said, her eyes still a bit moist. "I will see to it."

"I thank you. Perhapsss when I return to the Manor, I will be able to convince Osseussss to make another pair for you."

"Osseuss?" Erini glanced at Cabe and Gwendolyn. "A good thing then that we were able to prevent a terrible injustice. It would be a tragedy for the world to lose such an artisan!"

Cabe, who had never been aware of the servitor's talent and wondered how Kyl had come to know, had to agree. The roses had been the crowning touch to the drake's performance, a perfect complement to the carefully crafted, yet emotion-turning speech he had given. Even Grath and the Dragon King had been touched by it. Roe was staring at the dragon heir as if seeing him for the first time.

There was nothing more to be done here, but it was several seconds before Melicard appeared able to organize his thoughts. His gaze darting back to the roses, he commanded, "Have someone watch these closely, Roe. I want nothing to happen to them. I also want you to personally devise the best way to keep them safe here. They must *never* leave."

"Yes, my liege."

Again there was silence. At last, Erini seized control of the situation from her husband. "I think it's time we return to the palace. I have arranged for a midday meal in the gardens. I hope that will meet with your satisfaction, Lord Kyl?"

The drake bowed. "Mossst assuredly, Your Majesty."

"Good! Master Roe, if you would be so kind as to lead us back to the gate?"

"As you wish, my queen. Please follow me, everyone."

The master groundsman started down the corridor, Melicard and the others following. Gwen took Cabe's arm, both of them more than happy to be departing this place. They waited while Kyl, Grath, and the Green Dragon followed the royal family, then fell in place behind the drakes.

As the party wound its way toward the steps, the Dragon King suddenly looked back at the warlock. He said nothing and but a moment later returned his attention to the trek. With the only true light emanating from the staff that young Roe carried, it was a struggle to see the expression on the half-hidden face within the dragonhelm, but Cabe was almost certain that he had read in the eyes of the drake lord a deep sense of satisfaction at the outcome of this ceremony. Things, as the Dragon King had put it at the reception, could not have happened better than if they had planned it.

Strangely, the warlock could find no comfort in that thought.

# IX

*THEY'RE BACK!* VALEA'S heart rose as she heard the rattle of wagons and the voices raised in cheerful greeting. Ursa, sitting beside her, glimpsed the expression on her companion's face, but said nothing. Valea knew that the drake was aware of how her human friend felt about her brother. Ursa herself associated little with either male. Drakes were more divisive; females tended to associate with females and males with other males, save in matters of mating, of course. That was changing as living among humans affected the drakes here, but the change was a slow one that would need generations.

Ursa had never spoken against Valea's desires, which the young sorceress had decided meant that while she might not approve, the drake was also not going to interfere. That was probably for the best. The novice witch would have felt terrible if the friendship the two had developed over the years was destroyed by this.

She waited for Ursa to rise, but when the drake made no move to do so, Valea finally flung herself from her chair and rushed to the window. For the past few days, she had spent nearly all of her free time either in her chambers or in the gardens—anywhere that allowed her seclusion. Other than Ursa and the very understanding Benjin Traske, she found the company of others to be cloying, especially when that other was Aurim, who seemed to think that while he was in charge he was their father and mother combined. Around other folk she could not let her thoughts drift, could not dream of Kyl and the future she wanted.

Now she did not have to dream. Kyl was back . . . and in triumph, of course. Valea had expected no less from him. She peered out the window and watched as the caravan entered the Manor grounds.

*There* he was! Riding at the forefront. Father and Lord Green rode with him. Valea's mother and Grath close behind. Kyl was in high spirits. Everyone seemed to have a smile on their faces, although her father's was slight. Even Darkhorse was there, but the eternal's presence did not thrill her as much as it had when she had been younger. She still loved the shadow steed's company, but being what he was, he could never understand the emotions coursing through her. It was very likely that if she told him of her dreams, of her belief that Kyl might flout everything and make her his bride and queen, Darkhorse would act just like her parents. Everyone knew that he despised drakes.

"Do you see them?" asked Ursa, finally coming to the window.

"Yes! There they are!"

Her alluring companion followed Valea's gaze. "Things certainly seem to have gone well."

Ursa's perfect profile caused a brief twinge of jealousy in the young witch. She was aware how beautiful and exotic the drake seemed to males of both races. Then she consoled herself with the thought that to Kyl *she* was exotic. He was used to the magical splendor of female drakes and Ursa was, after all, his sister. Besides, was it not to Valea that Kyl paid the most attention? If he did not think her beautiful, then he would not have continually pressed for her favor.

Before he left for Penacles, Valea hoped to make the handsome drake admit his love.

"I want to go downstairs!"

"To be there to greet your parentsss?"

Her intention had been to be where Kyl could not fail to see her, but Ursa's pointed question struck home. Valea was not on very good terms with her mother and father. The long and very boring lecture her mother had given to her just before departing for Talak had only underscored that. Now would be the best time to start mending that relationship. She loved them both, and even though they were wrong to think so badly of Kyl and her, Valea did not want to lose them. It would be terrible enough when they discovered that their protests had gone for naught.

A horrible notion occurred to her as she and Ursa departed the room. What would happen if Kyl did *not* acknowledge her? What would she do *then*?

It was too monstrous to imagine. Besides, Scholar Traske had almost sworn an oath to her that Kyl returned her love. Somehow, their love would come to pass. Kyl would be able to make it so. After all, as Dragon Emperor, he would be wielding more power than any other single being. He would *make* everyone accept her as his love.

Valea did not question her extravagant dreams. To her, that was the way things would occur. To have the future follow any other path was unthinkable.

They were down the stairway and at the outer doors of the Manor before she even realized it. The short trip down the steps and across the grounds to where the rest of the Manor's inhabitants stood cheering passed even more quickly.

She chose a location ahead of the slow-moving caravan. A gap opened as people realized she was there. Valea halted as she reached the forefront, then tried to pretend that she had not run most of the way. Ursa joined her a moment later, looking just a little dismayed at the behavior of her friend. Valea ignored her completely, for Kyl was just riding into view.

He was talking with the Dragon King when suddenly his eyes swerved her direction. Valea fought down her emotions, not wanting to seem like a giddy little girl. The Dragon King followed Kyl's gaze, but what he thought was insignificant to her. She was only interested in the handsome figure riding at the forefront.

Kyl smiled at her. Valea vaguely noted a greeting from Grath.

The riders reined their mounts to a stop. Stable hands rushed to take control of the animals. Kyl and the others dismounted, including the young Lady Bedlam's parents. Steeling herself, Valea did not go directly to the drake, but rather greeted her mother and father first.

Of course, Aurim was already there. He had just finished hugging their father and was now doing the same with their mother. Valea was a little annoyed; trust her brother to be ready and waiting. She had wanted to be first, the better to impress upon them her desire to heal the rift that had spread between the three.

Father saw her first. He gave Valea a hesitant smile, which she returned. Truly, she hated arguing with them. It would have been so much easier if they could have gotten past their old prejudices and accepted her choice. Perhaps there was still time.

"Valea." The blue-robed mage hugged his daughter. Without a word being spoken, the rift was suddenly closed. Cabe Bedlam could not stay angry at his daughter. Her father was like that. He had always been the easier of the two to deal with, the most willing to bend. That was not to say that he was not stern with her at times, but it was generally easier to sway her father than her mother.

The enchantress was already with her, arms encircling her daughter. Valea returned the warm greeting, adding a smile nearly identical to that of her mother. Whereas Aurim and their father somewhat resembled brothers, Valea had long ago come to grips with the fact that she and her mother would forever seem more like two nearly identical sisters. It was, admittedly, a tiny bit annoying to think that a male, especially Kyl, might find the elder Lady Bedlam more attractive, but fortunately that did not seem to be the case with the drake. He had already proven which of the Bedlam women he preferred. Besides, everyone knew that her parents were inseparable.

"How have things been?" her mother asked.

"Well enough." There really was not more to say, but parents never seemed satisfied with such short responses. "I spent most of the time at my lessons or with Ursa." There was enough truth in that answer to make her feel as if she had not been lying. Telling her parents that she had spent the last few days thinking only of Kyl would have quickly reopened the chasm.

"Welcome back, my lady."

Valea had not realized that Ursa had followed her this far. She momentarily feared that her friend would betray her by expanding on the truth, but then Ursa simply repeated her greeting to Valea's sire. The Lord and Lady Bedlam returned the drake's welcome, which then seemed the end of the matter. The novice witch breathed a little easier.

Cabe Bedlam turned to talk to Aurim, no doubt wondering how her brother had fared in his role as lord of the manor. Valea desperately sought some reason to leave her mother. She wanted the chance to welcome Kyl back before he vanished to his rooms.

It was too late. Glancing in the drake's direction, she saw that he, Grath, and Lord Green were already starting to walk away, the heir's shadows, Faras and Ssgayn, close behind. Perhaps it would have been better after all to risk her folks' ire by greeting Kyl first. Now her one opportunity was lost.

Then, the heir to the dragon throne looked her way.

The smile was there again, the smile that was just for her. Kyl did not pause, but the smile and the look in his eyes told Valea that he *would* see her before long.

*Scholar Traske spoke true!* she thought, barely able to keep her pleasure hidden. Her mother, though, was talking to one of the servants about some household matter and therefore missed the brief struggle. Even had the Lady Bedlam noted the flush of pleasure spreading across her daughter's countenance, it was probable that she would have assumed that it had to do with her own return.

None of that truly mattered now. The novice sorceress had confirmation. Kyl truly *did* care for her.

"IF YOU DO not have need of me at thisss time, I would like to return to my kingdom immediately, my lord. There are duties I, too, must attend to."

Grath nudged Kyl, whose attention had been on Cabe Bedlam's fiery daughter. Pausing, the dragon heir gave the drake lord an understanding nod. "By all meansss, Lord Green! You of all here do not need to ssseek my permission!"

"It would be improper otherwise. Although the formalities must still be observed, you *are* my emperor. If there wasss any doubt, it was dispelled by your excellent behavior in Talak."

Kyl basked in the compliment. "Thank you for sssaying ssso. When shall we be graced with your company again, Lord Green?"

"I shall return before it isss time to depart for Penacles, be assured of that. Asss to the exact day, that I cannot say."

"There isss no need. Let me sssay before you go, that I am ever appreciative of your loyalty and guidance."

The Dragon King bowed. "I do what I must, Your Majesty."

Kyl and Grath watched as the Green Dragon departed, then continued on their way to their chambers, the two drake guards ever maintaining a respectful distance behind them. The heir turned to his brother. "Without Green'sss sssupport, none of thisss would have been possible, would you not sssay so, Grath?"

"It would have certainly been more difficult, but you would have overcome it, brother."

"With your aid, perhapsss. I mussst again commend you for the wordsss and gift you sssuggested for the ceremony. They were perfect! Hisss Majesty King Melicard wasss overcome! I will have hisss sssupport now!"

"I merely made recommendations, Kyl. It was your execution of them that made it work." Nevertheless, there was a smile on Grath's visage.

"What would I do without you at my sssside, my brother?" The dragon heir put a companionable arm around his brother's shoulders and smiled. "Talak wasss a sssuccess! Penaclesss will alssso be a triumph! With ssstrength from both drake and human elementsss, no one will quessstion my right to sssit upon my father'sss throne!"

"They would be foolish to do so now," commented Grath. His face hardened. "But sssome will. There are always a few."

"Asss long asss they are not ssstrong enough to caussse me any worry, Grath. You will sssee to that, will you not? I could trussst no one elssse ssso."

The younger drake nodded thoughtfully. "As you wish, Kyl. Asss you wish."

A formidable figure abruptly loomed before the drakes, but his presence brought slight smiles, not scowls, from Ssgayn and Faras. Grath immediately bowed in respect, and even Kyl could not resist a slight nod of his head. Benjin Traske had that effect on others, especially those who had been his pupils.

"I'm glad to see you back, lads," rumbled the scholar. "I would have greeted you and the Lord and Lady Bedlam sooner, but I was ensconced in my chambers and did not know that you were back until a servant informed me."

"There wasss no need, Ssscholar Trassske," Kyl returned. "But it isss indeed kind of you to come to usss now. I am sssorry that you could not be with usss in Talak. Your fine inssstruction made all the difference, I mussst sssay."

Traske chuckled. "You sound very much like the diplomatic monarch, Kyl, and I thank you. It pleases me to think that I might have had some small part in your success. A tutor always likes to see his pupils excel. When you have the opportunity, I would love to hear of your experiences."

The thought of impressing his former tutor was enticing, but Kyl was a bit weary from the long trip. Besides, there were other things he needed to prepare for, not the least of them being a chance encounter with Valea. Of course, Kyl never left chance encounters to chance; he and Grath made them happen. The handsome drake had a suspicion of where the Bedlams' daughter would be for the next hour or two, and he intended on stumbling on her at some point during that period.

As ever, it was Grath who stepped in to solve his dilemma. It was *always* Grath. Who else could it be? "I would be happy to relate our tale to you, Scholar Traske! It would give me the chance to ask you a few questions that I have about the mountain kingdom. I wasss amazed by it!" He waved his hands as he exclaimed the last. "Would that be satisfactory to you, Master Traske?"

"I would be delighted. You have time now?"

"I will make time. I've questions that cannot wait."

"You should first perhaps make certain that your brother has no need of you," Traske reminded Grath. "This is a crucial time for him. Your trip to Talak might be a thing of the past, but there is still Penacles to consider and the Dragon Kings afterward."

Grath had always been the scholar's most avid student. Kyl knew that the heavyset scholar enjoyed conversing with his former pupil. Grath also enjoyed the conversations, especially since Traske was a fount of information. Whenever there was a question that the younger drake could not answer—and those seemed to be becoming increasingly fewer—he would turn to the human who had taught them.

Had it been within his power, Kyl would have offered Benjin Traske a place in his empire, if only because between the human and his brother, he would have had the best counselors that any ruler could hope for.

Why *not* ask him at some point? The human had no plans once his role at the Manor was finished. His only pupils were Aurim and Valea, but Aurim was nearly finished with his lessons and Valea . . . well, perhaps that would be the final factor. Valea would need friends. There would be Ursa, but the witch would need more than one companion.

When Grath returned from this conversation with the human, Kyl would present the suggestion. His brother would know best whether they could trust Benjin Traske to be loyal to them when the time demanded it.

"By all meansss, he may go, Ssscholar Trassske! I have no need of him at thisss time. I have many things to attend to that will keep me busssy for the next few hoursss. If I have need of my brother, I know where to find him."

"My gratitude, Kyl." Benjin Traske bowed his farewell. Grath did the same, a barely perceptible nod following.

Left alone with Faras and Ssgayn, which was almost the same as being completely alone, Kyl contemplated his next move. He needed but a moment to refresh himself. It was true he was weary, but not weary enough to forget the importance of letting the exotic young witch know that he had not forgotten her. The glance he had been able to give her would keep her hoping, but it would be wise to follow with an actual meeting, even if it included her parents. All that was essential was to make her think that he had spent the entire visit to Talak thinking of her, which was, at least, half true. Valea was a prize he and Grath had worked long and hard to obtain, and Kyl knew that she was at last within his grasp.

She was both beautiful and a pleasure to be around, which only served to make each encounter that much easier for him, but those facts were secondary next to her greatest asset to the drake.

Valea was a Bedlam, a scion of the most powerful line of sorcerers. She was the daughter of Cabe Bedlam and the Lady of the Amber, an enchantress of vast might. The young witch had not yet displayed more than a fraction of the extraordinary power the line was known for, but everyone knew that the potential in her was possibly as great as it was in Aurim. If not, she could still pass the power of the Bedlam line on to her offspring.

*His* offspring. It *was* possible for the two races to interbreed, although how that could be was a question not even Grath was able to answer. Kyl knew that it was true only because his brother had come across evidence—evidence which Master Bedlam seemed to know about, too.

He realized that he had not moved from the spot where he had been standing when Grath and the scholar had left. Precious time was being wasted. Turning to his two shadows, he hissed, "Well? What are you two waiting for? Come!"

The two draconian warriors, looking properly chastised, hurried to keep pace as the dragon heir moved on. He would have to dismiss them before he located Valea. There was nothing romantic about two scowling lizards, which, in his opinion, was what the duo resembled. Kyl was quite pleased with his more human looks, mingled as they were with his draconian origins to create a unique, provocative appearance. Grath was the only one who resembled him at all, but even his brother's looks were more rough-hewn than his own.

She could not fail to want him. All that really stood in his way was her parents, but Grath had assured him that they would be no trouble whatsoever.

Kyl had been careful not to ask how his brother could be so certain. He simply had faith that loyal Grath would do what had to be done . . . whatever that might be.

THINGS WERE AT last calming down, and none too soon as far as Cabe Bedlam was concerned. The caravan was being dismantled and the Manor itself appeared in fine order. Aurim had only had control of the Manor for a short period of time, but the warlock was aware of how many things could go wrong in just one day. It was a wonder that the place was not more chaotic. Sometimes he thought that the ancient edifice itself watched over those who lived in it, much the way the Dragonrealm seemed to watch over its people. Yet, the mind of the Dragonrealm, assuming it had one, was a rather perverse one, for it seemed to take fondness in thrusting Cabe and his friends into one danger after another whereas the Manor simply seemed protective.

The Green Dragon had given his apologies and had departed only minutes after returning with the caravan. Cabe understood; the Dragon King had neglected his own realm for much too long already. Gwen and their offspring—it was growing impossible to call them *children*—were in the gardens talking about Talak, Darkhorse also adding a word here or there, but mostly just enjoying the companionship of his mortal friends. Aurim and Valea loved visiting the mountain kingdom, if only because the spectacle of the Tybers looming in the background was breathtaking. They also loved the strangeness of the city, having lived much of their lives in the relative calm of the Manor.

Cabe had left them in order to organize some notes Aurim had given him. One of the few peculiar things his son had reported to him was a sudden increase in the number of hauntings by the memories of the Manor. At first, Aurim had simply ignored them, but when three sightings had occurred in the same day, all suffered by the younger Bedlam himself, he had started to make a list. Almost all of the hauntings had occurred in the last three days, a record eleven. One had appeared as recently as last night. All but two had involved Aurim; the others had been seen by Valea.

Most of the visions were familiar ones. The archaic wedding ceremony. The Seeker landing on the terrace overlooking the gardens. A closed book with the symbol of a tree on it . . . which had always puzzled Cabe since it did not exist in the old library. A being who resembled a wolfman, probably of a race that had preceded not only the Dragon Kings but the Seekers and the Quel as well. All of these had been registered by the master warlock, some of them many times. But Aurim had experienced *three* first sightings as well, images that, especially in one particular case, his father would not have expected.

A Quel had stalked through the halls. Aurim had never seen one, but knew of them from his father's tales. The huge, armadillolike race existed only in the very southwest of the continent, their once mighty empire reduced to a few ruined, underground enclaves. Cabe had never known them to exist this far east, although it made sense to think that at one time their empire had covered much of the continent the way the drakes' or the Seekers' had.

The massive, armored figure had been swinging an ax at something, but what it was Aurim could not say. He only knew that the beastman had been frightened out of his wits, and the last image of the Quel had been that of the monstrosity falling on his back in terror.

Sometimes it was sobering to think of all that must have happened in this place. Cabe had little desire to know what had attacked the Quel as long as it no longer existed to threaten his own family.

The second image had been barely glimpsed, but in his scribbled notes Aurim had described what sounded to Cabe vaguely like a sword slicing through the air. What that was supposed to represent, the sorcerer did not know. It was different from other images in that his son had sworn that, being so nearby when it had materialized, he had actually *felt* a slight wind as the blade had moved. To Cabe's recollection, no other ghostly memory had ever proven even the slightest bit tactile.

Even that paled in comparison to the final new vision. It was the first of its kind that any of them had ever come across, and its existence shattered every theory that the master warlock or his wife had ever devised concerning the ghostly images.

Aurim had seen his *father.*

Cabe had joined the ghosts of the Manor.

The image was a very recent one. That, too, was unsettling. Aurim's description of the short scene had registered in the elder Bedlam's memory. It had taken place but a few days prior to their departure for Penacles. The occurrence had not been of any significant moment as far as he could see. It was merely Cabe using a knife to cut open a srevo, one of the lush fruits often found in the markets of Penacles and long a personal favorite of the sorcerer. Cabe was not one to use his power for something so simple as cutting up fruit. He considered such misuse both wasteful and criminal. That day, however, the black-haired mage wished that he had broken his cardinal rule.

Aurim's description of what had followed was exactly as Cabe recalled it, save that much of the surrounding scene was missing. The vision revealed Cabe holding the large, round fruit and making the first cut. Then, as he had readied one half for another attack with his knife, something had caught his attention, making him turn as he lowered the sharp blade. In real life, that something had been Benjin Traske, come to ask a question about the then forthcoming trip to Talak. The interruption itself had been minor, but the warlock, eyes turned away, had cut into his thumb.

He still remembered the pain. The wound had not been deep, but surprise had amplified his agony. Cabe had no qualms about using sorcery to repair even the most minor injuries, particularly those causing him torment, and had healed it almost immediately. By the evening of that same day, he had forgotten all about the incident.

For some reason, though, the Manor had not.

*And why is that?* he wondered. The spectral images had never made sense to him. Why would the ghost of such a trivial incident be created? What logic did the Manor follow? *Is there any logic? I keep assuming that there has to be, but who knows who built this place? They might've been mad, for all I know!*

The situation was certainly insane enough. Cabe slumped back in his chair, willing to admit that after all these years he was no closer to understanding the magical citadel than he had been the first time he had entered it. It reminded him of the fact that the structure would probably still be standing long after he and his children had become nothing more than . . . *memories?*

A movement behind him quickly dispersed all thought of the Manor's eccentric ways. Cabe pushed his chair back and turned, expecting one of his villagers. His eyes bulged as what should have been an impossible sight stood before him.

It was a drake warrior. His eyes searched the room with avid interest. He wore a cloak, and the dragon's head crest on his helm was one of the most extravagant that Cabe could recall. The drake's red eyes seemed to burn. His coloring was dull green mixed with touches of gold.

It was a drake warrior, one known to Cabe Bedlam.

It was Duke Toma.

Although to the warlock it seemed as if his reflexes had slowed almost to nothing, still he succeeded in gathering his power and striking at the deadly drake before Toma even seemed to notice him. A whirlwind formed around the reptilian invader, a funnel of dizzying speed that affected nothing else in the room, for its object was Toma and Toma only. At Cabe's silent command, the tornado seized the sinister drake and threw him to the ceiling.

That is, it was *supposed* to throw him to the ceiling.

Toma stepped through as if not even noticing the whirlwind. His eyes

still darted left and right, never seeming to focus on his foe. Cabe pointed
a finger at the draconian figure's armored chest. Sleek, black tendrils formed
around the deadly duke's upper torso, tendrils designed to pin the drake's
arms to his sides.

The tendrils tightened . . . and continued to tighten *through* Toma's body.

"What—" Daunted but not defeated, Cabe began to rise from his chair. At
the same time, Toma's piercing eyes turned his way . . . and continued past, at
last focusing on the wary sorcerer's desk.

Only then did Cabe Bedlam realize that, if he stared hard, he could just
barely make out the door *through* the chest of the drake.

*An illusion? I'm fighting an illusion?* He stumbled closer, still not positive that
this was not a trick. Toma seemed to walk toward him, although after a moment
Cabe decided the horrific duke was actually walking toward his desk. The warlock stepped to one side, studying the figure as it went past.

There was something familiar about the illusion. It was not a proper illusion,
for if it had been, he would not have been able to see through it. Toma was a
phantom, a ghost.

Ghost or not, the drake seemed very familiar with this chamber. He walked
quickly to the shelves that held Cabe's personal library, works that the warlock
himself had gathered over the years, as opposed to the ancient library elsewhere
in the Manor. As the specter searched the shelves, Cabe struggled to understand
the madness happening before him. This was either a very elaborate hoax, a
trick played by Aurim, perhaps, or . . .

Toma began to fade away. There was no warning. His form simply began to
grow murkier and murkier and his movements slowed until they came almost
to a halt.

It was the final confirmation. Everything about the ghostly drake screamed
only one possible answer.

The Duke Toma before him was nothing more than one of the Manor's
phantom memories . . . and that could only mean that the deadly drake had
paid a visit to the one place the warlock had believed was forever safe from him.

Toma in the Manor. It seemed impossible, but the proof was *there.* How,
though? How could the draconian renegade have made his way past the defenses of the ancient structure?

There was also the question of *when.* Perhaps it was an old memory from the
time when no one had actually lived in the Manor, a time when Gwendolyn had
been a frozen prisoner in Azran's amber cage and a trio of sinister female drakes
had usurped the fabled place. The original spells protecting it *had* begun to deteriorate. Darkhorse had been unable to enter, but Cabe had stepped through
without even really knowing what had happened. Of course, at the time, he had

been bedazzled by the temptresses' beauty, not realizing that he was to be their meal.

Could Toma have been here back then? It seemed a far more sensible conclusion, yet that reasoning held flaws, terrible flaws. The first and foremost of those was what the drake had been doing. Toma had walked to the desk, which was an addition of Cabe's. The chamber had originally been devoid of any trace of furniture or other contents. Also, the monstrous figure had been inspecting the shelves, his eyes lingering on particular tomes.

The shelves and their contents were *also* additions made by the warlock. Before that, the wall had been bare.

He could not deny it any longer. Duke Toma had been in the study chamber searching through the knowledge that his rival had gathered over the years. How long ago, though? It could still have been years—but if so, why had the drake never struck at them? If there was anyone Toma desired to see dead, it was Cabe and Gwen.

*Gwen . . . Valea and Aurim . . .* Suddenly the warlock grew fearful for his family. He had to know.

". . . as I've said before, Valea," his wife was remarking as he appeared in their midst. The trio paused in their conversation, eyes widening at the unexpected visitation.

"You're all . . . right!" Cabe gasped, relief bubbling over. In truth, he had expected to find them prisoners of the drake . . . or even worse.

Gwendolyn was on her feet instantly. She put her hands on his shoulders and looked him in the eye. "Cabe! What's wrong?"

Seeing them there, all concerned about his well-being, made his fears now seem laughable. Yet, Toma *had* invaded their sanctuary at some point in the past. That meant that there had been a threat to them . . . and, in fact, there might still be. The drake had never been one to pass up a golden opportunity.

He exhaled, forcing himself to relax. Only when he was certain of his control did the sorcerer permit himself to speak again. "Toma. It was *Toma.*"

*"Toma? Where?"* The emerald-clad enchantress warily scanned the grounds around them. Valea and Aurim looked worried but not panicked. Like their mother, they prepared themselves for the worst.

"Not here. Not now, Gwen. I don't know when he appeared, but at some point in the past, Toma somehow invaded my study."

"How do you know that?"

Cabe indicated Aurim. "When I went to the study with the notes Aurim had given me, the ones about the hauntings . . ."

"Your pet project."

He nodded. "I was just considering the last one, the image of myself. I felt a prickling . . . or something. All I know is that when I turned around, *Toma* was standing behind me, eyeing the room the way a dragon eyes fresh meat. After looking around, he stalked toward the desk and the shelves above it."

"And then?" No one seemed to be breathing. Anticipation had made slaves of his family.

"And then . . ." He shook his head. "And then I realized that the Toma I saw was another of the Manor's living memories!"

"A very timely one, if it was. You are certain that it was not an illusion? Not some trick?" It was clear that Gwen wanted that to be the case.

"No illusion . . . or rather, yes, it was, but only if you count the Manor's ghosts as such. This was one of those! I know the difference between them! Toma *has* been here before, Gwen. Not only that, but he had time to search this place thoroughly, I think."

The sorceress released him. Her hands, Cabe saw for the first time, were shaking. "It *has* to be an illusion! How could he have succeeded in passing the barriers? Only we can let anyone in or out!"

The warlock looked at his family. "I don't know."

"What should we do?" asked Valea. Duke Toma had always been something of a nightmare monster to her, like the creatures children thought lived under their beds. To find out now that the nightmare had invaded their very sanctuary . . .

The master warlock thought it out. "We have to search this place using our power. We have to carefully go over everything and every place. We—" He blinked. "Where's Darkhorse?"

The shadow steed had been with his family when last he had left them, and that had not been very long ago. Darkhorse was the only one other than his wife and offspring that Cabe would have trusted with all of this.

"He asked permission to depart only a few minutes ago." Gwen was perturbed. She, too, realized how useful the eternal's skills would have been for this deadly matter. "He was anxious, as if he had somewhere urgent to be. It was fairly sudden."

Was there a possible connection? Cabe was not certain. He hoped that Darkhorse would have informed him if there was some danger to them. The shadow steed was generally not that carefree with the lives of his friends. *Maybe it had something to do with the traps . . . and maybe there is a connection!* Darkhorse, however, had departed before the warlock's encounter with Toma's specter. "We'll have to do without him, then. He could be anywhere. The search will be our responsibility and ours alone."

"What are we looking for?" asked Valea.

He wished it was possible to leave her out of this, but Valea's power was needed. Even with the four of them working in concert, it would take the rest of the day to scour the Manor grounds. "Quite frankly, I don't know."

"We *have* to search, though," Gwendolyn impressed upon their daughter. "Toma was . . . *is* . . . a vicious, cunning creature, the epitome of every terrible tale ever spoken about the Dragon Kings! You know what we have told the two of you about him. Toma was so treacherous, so *dangerous*, that he became a renegade even among his own kind! He has never forgiven the fact that, had he received the birth markings Kyl was born with, *he* would have been Dragon Emperor."

The young witch's mouth opened and her face grew pale. "Do you think . . . do you think that he might try to hurt Kyl?"

Cabe disliked the intensity of her emotions. She had not only not forgotten her infatuation with the drake, but it seemed that somehow it had even *grown* in their brief absence. That, however, was a matter for another time. All that mattered now was discovering whether Toma had left behind a legacy of his visit.

It bothered him that the drake had been so bold as to wander the Manor as freely as the image seemed to indicate. Toma was arrogant, yes, but to go stomping around in his full glory? What was the drake plotting? Had it been madness that had made him so daring?

He also could not help but wonder why the Manor had happened to reveal the image to him at this particular time. Toma would be interested in the coronation; there was no doubt about that. Perhaps Kyl *was* in danger. *Immediate* danger.

*Or is he maybe in league with that demon? Should I confront him about it?* There was no proof, however, and it would have been unfair to condemn the young drake without such proof. If anything, Kyl was probably in danger. Still, until they knew otherwise, the affair would have to be handled with caution.

His wife had come to the same conclusion. "Kyl may be in danger. *All* of us may be in danger. This is Toma we are talking about." She paused, paying particular attention to Valea's reactions. Cabe knew that she, too, was thinking of their daughter's interest in the handsome heir. "Which means that we must keep this to ourselves for now."

"To ourselves?" Clearly, Valea did not like that.

"The more that know, the worse the danger. Toma may have some allies among the drakes here. I hate to think that way, but it could be true. The four of us need to do this on our own."

"I still don't know what we're looking for!"

"Neither do we," Cabe reminded her. "The only thing I can say is to look for anything out of the ordinary . . . as far as the Manor goes." He raised a hand in warning. "If you *do* notice anything, though, I want you—and that goes for both of you—to find *us*. Whatever Toma might have left behind would be very deadly. I have faith in your skills, but believe me when I say that even the Dragon Kings fear him."

"Do we start now?"

Cabe and Gwen considered their daughter's question. The enchantress finally nodded. "We do not seem to have any choice. It might be that there is nothing to fear, but I, for one, will not be able to relax until I know that we are safe."

After a moment, Valea nodded her agreement.

Throughout the conversation, Aurim had remained quiet. Cabe had paid scant attention to that fact until now, originally believing that his son had simply been mulling over the possible threat they faced. Now, however, he noticed the peculiar expression on the younger Bedlam's countenance, as if his son were trying to recall something of import. "Is something wrong, Aurim?"

The expression faded. Aurim briefly looked annoyed with himself, but then even that expression faded as determination took over. "Nothing, Father. I'm ready to begin whenever you like."

Cabe wanted to sigh, but held back. *He* most certainly was not ready. Nonetheless, they had no choice. He tried to sound confident as he began, "Then this is how we start. . . ."

# X

VALEA DOUBTED THAT Toma had bothered with the stables, but her father had insisted that she search them regardless of that doubt. In truth, she was certain that it was *because* Toma would not have come here that her parents had chosen her to be the one to investigate the stables. Her mother and father had chosen to search all of the more likely spots. Aurim, too, had been relegated to probing areas of the Manor grounds where the drake had most likely never set foot. On the one hand, the young enchantress appreciated her parents' protectiveness, but on the other hand, she also resented it. After all, she was a grown woman now, was she not?

Standing to one side of the nearest stable so as not to draw so much attention, Valea began her search. Tendrils of magic visible only to her own senses snaked over and around the building next to her. Unimpeded, they began to sink into the walls and ceiling, hunting. If there was anything unusual in the stable, she was confident that she would find it. Of course, since it was highly unlikely that there *was* anything to find, the novice sorceress found it impossible to become very excited about her work.

As she had expected, her initial search brought nothing significant to light. The horses used by the Bedlams were stabled here. It had seemed as likely a target for Toma as any of the other structures here, and the fact that she found no trace of the renegade's passing only served to strengthen her belief that this entire location was a waste of her efforts. Still, the witch knew that if she failed to search the stables thoroughly, it would be on her head if Toma *had* left something behind, something that might later endanger her family.

"Ssseeking a place of sssolitude, Valea?"

She gasped in surprise, then silently reprimanded herself for her reaction. Her probes faded as her concentration broke, but Valea hardly cared.

From behind the stable emerged Kyl. He had changed from his traveling clothes into a fresh outfit—a sleek, dark green piece that happened to be one of her favorites. The high collar and the lack of any lighter colors to contrast the darkness made the drake seem a man of deep mystery.

He had worn it for her; she was certain of that. It thrilled her to think that Kyl had gone to such trouble.

"I found myssself ressstive after I had cleaned up and ssso I decided to take a walk," Kyl continued, shortening the gap between them as he talked. "When I reached the ssstables, it occurred to me that a ride might be in order. Then, I caught a glimpssse of you and recalled that I had never properly greeted you after our arrival."

"There was no need." It was a struggle for her to sound calm. Inside, Valea was again a maelstrom of emotion.

"There *wasss* need, though. It wasss unforgivable."

Only an arm's length separated them now. The young witch waited for Kyl's strong arm to bridge that gap, and for a breath it seemed it would, but then the drake's hand continued beyond her to brace against the stable wall. It was not what she had hoped for, but the action still left the two of them so very close. All he had to do was lean forward a little.

"Talak wasss fasssscinating, Valea! Ssstrange and beautiful! You have ssseen it before, I know, but I wish you could have been there to sssee it with *me*."

She was beyond words.

Kyl seemed not to notice . . . or perhaps he only pretended. Valea could not say. "Sssuch splendor! Sssuch majesssty! King Melicard isss rightfully proud of hisss kingdom. He hasss a loyal following, a magnificent city, and mossst beauteous queen."

Jealousy pricked Valea. Erini *was* beautiful, a true fairy-tale princess. She also looked little older than Kyl. With Talak so close to the citadel of the Dragon Emperor, there was no doubt that the demands of his throne would bring the handsome drake and the queen of the mountain kingdom together fairly often.

She realized that she should say something. *Anything.* "She loves him very much, you know."

It was not what Valea had meant to say. She was certain that her cheeks were crimson now.

"She doesss, indeed." Somehow, the drake had lessened the distance between the two of them even more. Valea was struck by contending choices. One part of her was afraid and wanted to step back. The other part of her wanted the last remnant of the chasm closed. "It wasss ssstrange, though. Talking to her, being around her, I found myssself thinking of *you*, Valea."

Her reaction to this declaration infuriated the young Lady Bedlam. As if acting under some impulse of their own, her feet moved, propelling the maiden *backward* three or four steps until she was beyond the stable wall and out in the open.

To her vast relief, Kyl did not look repulsed. He followed her, albeit stopping at the corner of the building. The special smile that he reserved just for her was there. "I thought about you mossst of the time I wasss there, Valea. I like to think that you were alssso thinking about *me.*"

Even having heard all that she had, Valea could not believe her good fortune. "Then, it's true? It's as Benjin Traske said?"

Now Kyl looked puzzled. "Ssscholar Traske? What hasss he to do with thisss?"

Valea took a deep breath. This was it. He had all but said the word, his fear that she would reject him probably the reason he had not taken the last step. She would do it for him.

Slowly, hesitantly, Valea began, "Scholar Traske . . . he said that . . . he said . . ."

CABE PROBED THE library one more time. There was no trace of any hidden spell or physical trap. There was not even any sign that Toma had ever been in this room.

The warlock sighed. He had been carefully inspecting each room of the Manor, and although he was still not even half finished, much of the day had passed. So far the results of his thorough search had yielded nothing. Unfortunately, with Toma that did not mean that the drake had not been here. The duke was a master sorcerer who had often in the past surprised even those who had thought that they had known his limitations. His skills were far more versatile than those of the more traditional Dragon Kings. Toma dared to do things that no one else did, which made him the wildest of wild cards. He had more or less vanished after the terror of the Ice Dragon, but now and then rumors of his activities surfaced. However, so far as Cabe had been able to tell, the rumors had never proven to bear any truth.

Which, of course, did not mean that Toma had been idle all these years.

Cabe wondered how the others were doing. None of them had contacted him, but he tried not to be paranoid. If something *had* happened, he would have known.

The constant probing was making his head throb. Cursing under his breath, the warlock decided to get a breath of fresh air. He stepped out of the library, crossed the hall, and made his way to the nearest window. A minute or two of relaxation was all that the sorcerer needed. It was odd how small, fairly simple spells could often take more out of the caster than huge, earth-shaking ones.

Leaning out the window, Cabe surveyed his tiny kingdom. Somewhere, possibly even beneath his very feet, there might be a clue to whatever Toma had done while here. Studying the bookshelves had revealed nothing. Perhaps there was nothing to find, not even a trap of some sort, but the warlock could not risk that chance.

His eyes alighted on a crimson-tressed woman standing next to one of the stables. It could not be his wife, who searched the lower floors of the Manor, which meant that it had to be Valea. Cabe recalled that she was supposed to be searching the stables, but at the moment, she was simply standing there. Why?

He had his answer when Kyl stepped part of the way out from behind the stable wall.

The enraged sorcerer did not even wait. He was gone from the window and next to the stable in less than a breath.

"Valea."

At the sound of his voice, she froze. Whatever his daughter had been about to say died on her lips, probably a fortunate thing in his opinion. Even Kyl looked satisfactorily guilty for a change.

"Father, I—"

"I gave you a project to do, Valea. A very important project. Have you finished it?" Cabe tried his best not to let his anger show through, but even he was aware of the harshness tinging his words. Kyl's eyes flickered, but other than that there was no sign that the drake might have noticed. The warlock had no doubt that he had, however.

His daughter's expression told him the answer to his question even before she replied. "Not yet." Her cheeks were crimson. "I only paused for a moment . . . I . . . I'll get back to it now."

Curtseying to Kyl, the young witch rushed off. Cabe's anger drained away. He had embarrassed his daughter. Granted, the search was of the utmost importance at this time, but that was not why the warlock had come down here. He had come down here because his daughter had been alone with a . . . with a *creature* . . . that had designs on her.

It could have been handled differently, but when it came to his family, the master sorcerer could not always think straight. Now, he and Valea were at odds again—and his actions had most likely pushed her further toward the drake.

"There isss sssome major project underway, Massster Bedlam?" Kyl asked politely, his entire person radiating innocence.

"More of an exercise, Kyl." The warlock now wished that he had thought of some better excuse, but for most of those living at the Manor, calling the search an exercise would have been sufficient. Cabe had been too concerned with beginning the hunt to think about what Kyl or Grath, who understood the ways of sorcery, might conclude from the Bedlams' peculiar activity. *Two decades and I still think with the cunning of a serving boy!* It could not be helped, though. Kyl might suspect, but unless he was somehow in league with Toma, he would be able to do no more than guess.

"Ssso sssoon after our return? We have only just arrived!"

"I felt it was necessary, Kyl. Didn't Scholar Traske ever surprise you and the others with sudden tests or projects of his own?"

The drake verified his supposition with a grimace. "Massster Trassske had an amazing talent for the unexpected tesssst. Yesss, I sssee your point."

It was doubtful that Kyl actually did, but the warlock was happy to let it go at that. Kyl would think whatever he wanted to think. Once the search was ended, it likely would not matter very much. Whether any trace of Toma's passing was found or not, Cabe's family was now warned. Toma would not find entry into the Manor so simple the next time he tried.

*What did he want, though? That's what I would like to know!* The obvious motive concerned the very drake before him. Cabe realized that he would have to speak to the Green Dragon as soon as the Manor was considered safe again. The Dragon King would want to know what had happened. He might also be the best one to handle the delicate matter of questioning Kyl. For all he disliked the heir's manner, especially toward Valea, the warlock *was* concerned about the drake's well-being. Toma could offer the emperor-to-be nothing; therefore, the renegade sought to *take* from Kyl.

It was tempting to warn the young drake even after he had commanded Valea not to do so, but Cabe persevered. Best to wait for the Dragon King. The lord of Dagora would better know what to do about his nephew.

"I shall leave you to thisss, then," the dragon heir was saying. "I apologize if I interfered in sssome way. I happened by, sssaw Valea, and sssince I had not yet greeted her since our arrival, I thought it polite to do ssso now. Again, Massster Bedlam, my apologiesss."

"It's nothing, Kyl."

"That isss very kind of you to sssay. I shall trouble you no longer, then, Massster Bedlam." With that, the drake bowed and quickly departed.

Cabe watched him walk off, more certain than ever that he had just interrupted something important between his daughter and Kyl. He hoped that whatever it was had not gotten out of hand. *Only a few more weeks and he'll be far enough away that she can start to forget him.* It would be wise, he thought, to take Valea and Aurim to some of the more peaceful human kingdoms, such as Penacles or Gordag-Ai. Let them meet more people their own age. There were a few at the Manor, but unfortunately, here Aurim and Valea were considered the young lord and lady of the house. That was why the drakes had become their closest friends over the years; the others considered the two their masters as much as Cabe and his wife were.

Yes, it would be wise to do some visiting after Kyl assumed his throne. Penacles especially seemed a good choice.

That was still weeks away, however, and in the meantime, Cabe would have to continue to watch his daughter. It might have been easier on him if she had at least chosen Grath; the younger drake had always seemed kinder, more sensible. Less *deadly.* He was thankful that Aurim, at least, had not gotten involved in any romantic entanglements. At this point, the master warlock was not so certain that he could have handled yet one more situation.

Which reminded him that there was still a search to complete. Toma was, by far, the most immediate danger to everything. They had to make absolutely certain that neither he nor some legacy remained within the boundaries of the Manor. Cabe knew, however, that even if they found nothing, he would still be unable to relax. The mere presence of the renegade had shattered his sense of security. Not even his home was safe.

*Something will have to be done to put an end to your legacy of terror, Toma,* the sorcerer thought as he prepared to resume the hunt. *And if it would cost me my life to see that accomplished, I'd gladly give it if only it meant that you were never able to threaten my family again.*

He meant every word, he truly did, but Cabe hoped that it would not come to that.

Unfortunately, with Toma involved, there was a very good chance that it *would.*

**DARKHORSE MOVED SWIFTLY** through the forest, darting in and out among the trees with an ease no earthly steed would have been able to imitate. The shadow steed squeezed between trunks or overran fallen trees that would have daunted any true horse. Darkhorse barely noticed. He, like the Bedlams, was on a hunt, but in the eternal's case, there was a trail. It was slight, so *very* slight, but it was the first true clue that he had discovered.

Darkhorse had picked up the trace at the site of one of the spell traps. He had not thought to search for this particular type of trail, having been more consumed with the obvious scent. His adversary had been a clever one, using the traces of Shade's sorcerous mark to cover the true one. Now, however, the shadow steed knew what to look for . . . in part because he suspected who was responsible.

Oddly, though, the trail was now sending him in a direction he had not anticipated, toward a destination that had to be false. The ebony stallion rode on, though, determined to let nothing, including personal trusts, cloud his judgment.

*I should have come across him by now!* he thought. *There is no possible way that I could have passed him by!*

Nonetheless, the next several minutes revealed no sign of his mysterious quarry. The eternal finally paused and surveyed his surroundings. There was little that should have been able to evade his senses, but more and more Darkhorse wondered whether he had somehow missed what he had been searching for. The trail was fading before him. Had he been duped again?

It seemed so. Several more minutes of searching proved the futility of his hunt. The trap maker had covered his path all too well.

"So be it!" rumbled the eternal. "I will waste no more time on this!" Still, he could not help pondering his failure as he turned and renewed his run through the forest. Darkhorse did not like mysteries, or at least mysteries that he could not solve. Perhaps it was time to visit Penacles. The Gryphon was there, and although he no longer ruled the so-called City of Knowledge, still he had access to many sources of information there, including the fabled libraries underneath the very city itself. *Perhaps the lionbird can pluck some useful knowledge from the libraries' contrary contents!*

Whoever had created the libraries of Penacles had to have been a madman. All the great knowledge of sorcery was said to be found there, written down in one great tome or another. The difficulty lay not only in *locating* the proper volume, but making sense of the insane script within. The knowledge of the libraries usually came in the form of some peculiar riddle or nonsensical passage. Why that was, no one now knew. Still, if there was anyone who could solve those conundrums, it was the Gryphon.

Feeling much more pleased with his situation than he had felt but moments before, Darkhorse increased his pace. He made no sound as he ran and his hooves left no mark on the uneven ground. When it was his whim, he could do both, but for the most part Darkhorse preferred to move as a ghost. It would have been simpler to transport himself to Penacles, but the shadow steed loved to run. It seemed to clear his thinking. Besides, a few minutes more or less would not matter. Darkhorse was so swift that he could cross miles in seconds if he chose. He did not run so fast now, but even still it would take him little time to reach Penacles.

His path took him across the trail that the caravan had taken in order to reach Talak. Darkhorse vaguely recognized it, although he had not joined the party until farther north. At first, the eternal ignored it, set as he was on his destination, but then the presence of many inhuman minds made the powerful stallion come up short.

He wasted no time looking around. If they chose to, his new companions could keep themselves well hidden among the treetops. Instead, the shadow steed kicked at the ground, raising a cloud of dirt and loose vegetation, and roared, "Play no games with me, birds, or I will knock your roosts down one by one until this part of the forest is nothing more than a field!"

There was the rustling of leaves in the treetops—rustling that the light breeze around him could not have caused.

A man-sized creature burst through the foliage and alighted onto one of the larger, lower branches. He was shaped more or less like a human, but in every other way resembled a bird of prey. The newcomer snapped his beak once at the eternal, then cocked his head to the side so as better to see the huge stallion.

"What do you want, Seeker?" Darkhorse shifted so that he looked directly up at the avian. "A challenge? A threat?"

The Seeker pointed a taloned hand toward the southwest and squawked.

"Aaah, so very enlightening!" snorted the stallion. He kicked at the ground, digging huge ruts in the dirt. "And why is it I should go that way?"

An image of a tree in summer, its crown green and full, formed in his mind. Under the protective foliage, was an area of cool shadow. It seemed to be this that the avian desired to emphasize, but Darkhorse was puzzled by it. What did the base of a tree, a shaded area, at that, have to do with—

*Shaded? Shade?*

The Seeker's eyes informed him that he had correctly guessed the answer.

"A tree and *shadow.* How perfectly *obvious.*" He hated communicating with the bird folk for this very reason. With humans, the images were more direct. Cabe Bedlam would have seen an image of the blur-faced warlock himself. However, Darkhorse's mind was different from that of any other creature in this world. Using such clues was the only way the Seekers could communicate with him other than pointing. They had no written language, at least not one that anyone understood. The shadow steed was thankful that he had little congress with the creatures. Of course, much of that was due to the fact that the Seekers were, in general, more devious than helpful. If they wished to help him now, it was only because it served their desires, too.

Again the Seeker pointed southwest.

Was he trying to say that *Shade* was there? That seemed highly improbable. Even Darkhorse had come to the conclusion that the warlock was long dead . . . but then what did it mean?

Not Shade, then, but perhaps the one who had used the memory of the warlock as bait to catch the eternal?

It could be that this was also a trap, but the shadow steed's curiosity was piqued. Caution warred with that curiosity, with the latter at last triumphing. The eternal started off in the direction in which the avian had pointed. He shielded his thoughts, however, not wanting the Seekers to know just how little he trusted the bird folk. Should they have a snare prepared, they would find him more than ready for it.

The male who had pointed the way flew ahead several yards and alighted onto another branch. When Darkhorse was near, he again pointed.

"Are you to be my guide, then?"

The Seeker nodded, then fluttered off ahead once more.

So the trek continued. Much of the trail was straight, which raised his temptation to rush ahead without the avian. Darkhorse decided against that, however. The Seekers had planned long and hard, he supposed, so the least that he could do was not disappoint them . . . yet.

He could hear the fluttering of many wings above him. A full flock of the bird people were trailing after him. Darkhorse estimated that there could be no more than twenty, including his guide. That seemed a fair combat to him.

Once again, his guide located a new perch. Darkhorse sighed audibly, hoping that the bird man would understand that he was tiring of this chase. The avian again pointed, adding an annoyed squawk to emphasize the importance of the situation . . .

. . . and then the trees were full of warring Seekers.

The eternal stopped and quickly gazed skyward. Through the tangle of trees, he watched in amazement as a second band of the bird folk attacked those who had been shadowing him. Claws raked across chests. Beaks strong enough to crack bone tore flesh. Now and then, a small but potent spell was unleashed and some combatant would wither, burn, or simply fall to its death.

A savage squawk brought his attention back to his guide. Despite the chaos above, the Seeker was *insisting* that he proceed.

Darkhorse, however, had decided that he would not. Things had become a bit too confusing. Seekers *never* fought Seekers. It was unheard of. "I think, perhaps, my friend, that I will decline your guidance from here on!"

As he began to turn away, the avian leaped for him. Out of the corner of his eye, Darkhorse saw that the Seeker now held something in one taloned hand. The shadow steed doubted that he wanted it to come any closer than it already was.

The bird man was swift, but still too slow in comparison to his attempted prey. Darkhorse dodged the grasping claws. Under other circumstances, he would have stayed where he was and laughed as the Seeker was trapped within him. Many over the endless centuries had described the eternal as a living hole from which nothing that was pulled in ever again emerged. It was a very accurate description. Drakes, humans, beasts, Seekers . . . how many there had been Darkhorse could not say. He did not care. Those who sought to harm either him or his companions deserved no mercy. They would fall forever into the abyss that was the shadow steed, who was very aptly called a child of the empty, endless Void, the place in which he himself had been spawned.

This Seeker, though, was a danger as long as he was able to wield the mysterious object. Darkhorse knew that no creature would be so foolish as to attack him unless they believed that they could defeat him, and while stupidity was a trait among many races, the Seekers had always struck him as a little more intelligent. That meant that whatever his adversary held, it promised nothing but harm to the shadow steed.

Rising up again, the lone avian eyed him. It was clear that things were not going as the Seeker had originally intended. He glanced skyward, where his companions were clearly losing, then back down at the shadow steed. At last, with a squawk that somehow relayed frustration and anger, the bird man turned and began to fly back in the direction from which he and Darkhorse had come.

His flight was short. The limbs of the nearest trees bent in a manner no wind could have made them bend, suddenly blocking the swift avian's path. The Seeker, moving with the intention of quick escape, struck the heavy limbs head first. There was a cracking sound that had little to do with the branches themselves.

The limp form tumbled to the mossy ground, where it lay a twisted, still shape.

Darkhorse did not even wait for the Seeker's body to strike the ground. He started to back away, eyes scouring the visible world and senses formed in the Void searching those worlds beyond. It occurred to him that he could no longer hear the combatants above, surely not a good sign. Still, the eternal was not fearful. It had been too long since he had been faced with a proper challenge.

"Come, come!" he roared, still unable to locate the foe by either set of senses. "You wanted Darkhorse and so you shall *have* Darkhorse! *All* the Darkhorse you could ever want!" The eternal roared with mocking laughter.

He felt something pass his way, but the sensation was brief. Darkhorse glanced that way, then turned his head the opposite direction as he felt yet another presence on his other flank.

"Skittering like mice, are you? Perhaps I can shake you from your holes, then!" The shadow steed raised a hoof and brought it down hard on the forest floor.

There was a crash of thunder and the land around him shook as his hoof struck the earth. Birds flew off in panic while Darkhorse laughed, taunting his foes.

Then . . .

It had the stink of Vraadish sorcery, as great a stink as the eternal had ever known. The shadow steed drew in just a little, slightly disconcerted at the intensity of it. Vraadish sorcery was a legacy of another world, battered, maimed Nimth, the place from which the ancestors of humans had come after nearly destroying it with that very power. Yet Nimth was sealed off, the barrier between this world and that one stronger than ever. Darkhorse had been there when the way had been closed.

The eternal sought to back away from the foulness, but found he could not move. Gazing down, Darkhorse stared in astonishment at his hooves, which were several inches deep in what seemed to be *molten grass and earth.* The land still retained the form of the forest floor, but it moved like quicksilver. Stunned, the ebony stallion still had the wherewithal to attempt to free himself. With effort, he pulled first one hoof free, then another.

A gleaming tentacle snared one of his free limbs. Horrible, shocking pain coursed through his very being. The stallion's shape grew distorted as his control of it slipped. One leg grew too long. His head drooped as if melting. Ripples ran across his torso. Fighting the agony, Darkhorse regained control, but was unable to restore himself to his proper shape.

Another tentacle snaked around a second limb. This time, he saw what it was. It was not a beast of some sort, but rather a whip, a weapon. Darkhorse followed the length of the horrific weapon back to a slight shimmering in the air. Even as he watched, the shimmering coalesced into the form of a cloaked figure. The shadow steed's first startled thought was to imagine that Shade *had* returned from the dead, but then he realized that this was not the warlock but some human minion, for a quick glance the opposite way showed that an identical figure had materialized there.

There was something familiar about the trap, but it took the struggling Darkhorse a moment to recall what it was. *The whips! I know these whips!*

They were toys of the Vraad. Darkhorse knew them *very* well, for it was with whips like these that the ancient sorcerers had guided him. These whips and other foul toys.

Had it been only the eternal and the whips, Darkhorse was certain that he would have been able to triumph easily. The molten soil, however, slowed his counterattack by seizing his limbs again and again. Darkhorse gave up trying to

maintain his shape, deciding that he stood a better chance of success by returning to the amorphous form that had been his until the sorcerer Dru Zeree had
stumbled into the Void and discovered him.

Like melting wax, the huge stallion's form sagged and dripped toward the
ground. His head became almost indistinguishable from his body as the two
began to fuse together. His legs were twisted things with the consistency of
molasses. Only the two icy orbs that were his eyes remained as they were.

He was little more than a blob of darkness when it became clear to him
that even now the whips and the earth maintained their holds on him. Shock at
last became tinged with fear when Darkhorse also discovered that he was now
trapped in his present form. He could neither complete the transition to living
shadow nor return to his equine form no matter how hard he fought to do so.

As the eternal fought futilely to regain control of himself, a third cloaked
figure shimmered into being before him. Darkhorse saw the clawed hands of a
drake emerge. His attention then became fixed on a small object cradled in the
hands of the hooded dragon man. A box. An old—no, *ancient*—box with a pattern on the top that the shadow creature could not make out clearly from where
he was trapped.

It was not until the drake opened the lid that Darkhorse recalled this particular toy of the Vraad. For all he knew, it was the very same box which the
Vraad Barakas Tezerenee had turned on him.

Although he no longer had a mouth, still Darkhorse roared. He struggled
as he had not struggled since last he had seen such a box, since last the maw of
such a monster had been opened wide so that it could receive him.

His struggling went for naught. He felt the pull and knew that the link between himself and the box had been made. Despite the inevitable, however, the
eternal continued to fight. He could *not* go there again!

The box was stronger. A black stream, the essence of Darkhorse, flew toward
and into the devilish container. All the while the shadow creature roared, but
there was no longer any hope. Darkhorse continued to flow until all of him had
entered the Vraadish device.

The drake shut the lid, silencing his scream.

# XI

NO TRACE OF Duke Toma was found. The next several days passed without
incident, save that specters of the Manor continued to appear in burgeoning
numbers. Every member of the Bedlam family experienced at least one, with
Cabe taking the brunt of the ghostly assault. Not a day went by that he did

not witness two, sometimes *three*, manifestations. Most he was familiar with, but again there were the new ones. He himself experienced the unsettling sight of watching his image cut into his thumb.

The Toma image reappeared only once. It followed the same pattern as before, then vanished. No one observed the blade Aurim had described in his notes.

The journey to Penacles was mere days away now. The short span of time between the visits to the two human kingdoms had been intentional from the first, but now Cabe wished that he could have another week to prepare himself. Toma's mysterious invasion still bothered him. Worrying about the renegade drake and his continuing concern over the way Valea was acting around Kyl combined to make the sorcerer too weary even to think about the journey ahead.

Thus it was that when an emissary of Penacles arrived unexpectedly at the borders of the Manor grounds, Cabe Bedlam almost refused him entry. Only when he discovered who that emissary was did he agree to let him pass through the invisible barriers that protected his domain.

They met in the garden, the warlock immediately bowing in the presence of his old friend.

"I am no longer king, Cabe, so please stop that; it's rather embarrassing."

"Toos would be glad to turn the throne back over to you, Gryphon."

"Too true," the former monarch of Penacles returned. The Gryphon was, in his own way, as fascinating a being as Darkhorse. Manlike in his general form, he otherwise shared much in common with the Seekers, especially his countenance. The Gryphon, who had no other name, resembled the very creature of legend. His visage was that of a predatory bird, in this case a majestic eagle. Yet, the eyes were closer set, falling somewhere between bird and human. The lionbird, as he was nicknamed, also bore the aspects of the feline part of the creature he so resembled. His mane was thick and long and only at the bottom did it taper to feathers, although that sometimes changed depending on his mood. Underneath the cloak and loose clothing he wore, the Gryphon's form was more animallike than one first suspected. His legs were jointed like those of a cat, and on his back were tiny stubs, vestigial wings. The Gryphon's hands were more human than those of the Seekers, but his claws were as sharp as a cat's, at least on his remaining eight fingers.

Cabe eyed the maimed hand out of the corner of his eye. It was a legacy, a magical wound from the war that the Gryphon fought overseas. The war had gained for him a bride and their two children; yet it had taken away so much as well, stealing from him the eldest of those children, the warrior-child Demion.

All knew that the lionbird would have rather lost both hands or even his own life than his eldest child. As it was, he and the cat-woman Troia now doted on their second son.

"Your visit's a surprise, but a pleasant one, Gryphon. I have to admit, though, that I don't know why you're here."

One of the servants brought them drinks. The Gryphon thanked her for the goblet, then raised it to his mouth. As he did, his features blurred, becoming those of a handsome, somewhat older man with fine patrician features. The transformation startled the servant, who almost dropped the wine. She scurried off before the Gryphon could lower his drink and apologize. His features had already reverted to those of the eagle.

"I forget sometimes that there are so many outside of Penacles who are not used to me."

"I think it was just the suddenness of the change. Drakes change, too, but it takes them more time."

"Perhaps." The Gryphon paced the terrace as he thought. Like the predator he was, the former mercenary could not sit still when disturbed by something. He did, however, manage to pause when he spoke. "I'm chiefly here because Toos wants to hear how things went in Talak."

The warlock gave him a conspiratorial smile. "I'd think that Penacles would already know more than I could relate."

"He was especially interested in your personal observations," responded the lionbird, ignoring Cabe's comment about the spies that Penacles no doubt had spread throughout the mountain kingdom. Of course, Talak had its own spies in Penacles just as they likely had them in Gordag-Ai and Zuu. Spies were a favorite pastime of rulers.

"About the entire visit or something in particular?"

"Both, actually. Let us start with your view of the stay itself." The lionbird took another sip of his drink, again momentarily transforming his features.

"Gwendolyn should be here for this." The warlock looked around, but there was no sign of his wife. He projected a summoning, but the only response from her was that she would come when she was able. Cabe decided to leave it at that. The Lady Bedlam and the Gryphon were old comrades of a sort, both being survivors from the days of the Turning War, although they had not met then. If the enchantress chose not to be here, it was not because of any lack of love. The Gryphon and his wife were as dear to her as Erini.

"My visit must be necessarily short, Cabe. I understand if the Lady Bedlam cannot be here. She could never cause me affront."

The lionbird had always struck the warlock as the sort of monarch that he had hoped Kyl would become. Sadly, the young drake had chosen among his own kind for guidance, but fortunately he had at least chosen the Green Dragon as one of his mentors.

Cabe launched into a detailed description of the journey and their stay in Talak. Mention of the Seekers made the Gryphon's mane ruffle in concern, but the emissary asked no questions. The lionbird was visibly surprised at Kyl's handling of the untrusting Melicard, especially the request for the private ceremony acknowledging to the lords of Talak the travesties performed in the name of the Dragon Emperor.

Cabe was about to point out Grath's influence in most of those situations when he felt the presence of his wife's mind within his own.

*Cabe. I tried not to disturb the two of you, but would you please come to Aurim's chambers?*

*What's wrong?*

*I am really not certain.* She broke the link.

"Something is amiss, Cabe."

The warlock eyed his guest. "You know?"

"You grew slightly distant and your gaze drifted. I have studied sorcery for far too long not to recognize that you were communicating with someone, likely the Lady Gwendolyn. If she feels that something is important enough to create the need to summon you, then I can only assume it is nothing good."

Rising, the warlock could only marvel at the Gryphon's guesswork. "You assume right. I'll explain later, but for now, if you'll excuse me—"

"Nonsense!" The Gryphon also rose. "If there is something wrong, Cabe, I don't plan to sit by." He unsheathed the claws of one hand. With his regal bearing and his polite manner of speech, it was sometimes easy to forget that the figure before him could be every bit as savage as his namesake.

"All right, I won't argue. You could be right." The warlock took hold of the Gryphon's arm. "We're going to Aurim's chambers."

"Lead on."

The transfer was immediate. Cabe and the Gryphon looked around, searching for any sign of danger. The room, though, appeared completely normal, save for the pensive expression on the face of Gwendolyn Bedlam.

"Always a pleasure to see you, my lady," the Gryphon said, bowing as gracefully as was possible for him.

"I apologize for not greeting you, Gryphon." The emerald enchantress continued to look slightly anxious. Every few seconds, her eyes would turn from them to gaze at some random location in the chamber. "I'd planned to, but first I had wanted to talk to our son."

"*Aurim?*" Cabe noticed that their son was not in the room, but before worry could overwhelm him, his wife shook her head.

"He's all right, Cabe. I haven't summoned him, yet, but I do know where he is."

The warlock relaxed. "Then what's the danger?"

She put a hand to her chin and stared into space. "I am not absolutely certain if there even *is* any danger, but . . . but when I stepped inside, I noticed something that unnerved me." Gwen blinked, then spread her arms. "Tell me what *you* sense. Both of you, if you don't mind, Gryphon."

"Not at all."

Cabe cleared his thoughts and sent out a probe. At first, the room seemed no different. Aurim's presence was everywhere, which was to be expected in a place that he frequented so much. There were other, older traces, but they were so faint as to be inconsequential. Besides, the sorcerer recognized them. They could not be what his bride had wanted him to notice.

He briefly touched the presence of the Gryphon, vaguely noting the differences in their magical signatures. Since that, too, was quite obviously not what he was hunting for, Cabe moved on. He wondered again what exactly it was Gwen had noticed and contemplated asking her, if only to better aid his search.

Barely had the warlock thought that when he discovered the answer. It was an answer he could have done without.

The trace was barely noticeable. He had to concentrate hard to keep from losing the tenuous trail.

"What is it?" the Gryphon asked from beside him. His probe, too, had located the trace, but he did not recognize its origins.

"It feels as if . . . as if . . ." Cabe did not want to complete the sentence, as if that would make it not true.

"It tastes of Toma, does it not?" the enchantress demanded, arms folded tight. Like her husband, she also wished to deny it.

"*Toma?*" The former mercenary's voice went cold. "Toma? In the Manor?"

Hearing the hatred, Cabe quickly added, "Not now, but sometime in the past."

"But how?" demanded the Gryphon. "How could that murderous lizard have gained access to your domain?"

"We have no idea, Gryphon," the Lady Bedlam replied. She explained how they had come to know the startling truth. The lionbird listened in awe, and even Cabe felt chills as he relived seeing the renegade duke standing in the doorway of his study. Gwen went on to describe the careful search they had made of the Manor grounds, a search which had yielded nothing for all their hard work.

"But then how do you explain this?"

"The trace is very faint. I cannot explain why I noticed it, but I can see how it might have been missed before, especially since Aurim practices his spells in his room. You can feel his overwhelming presence here, can you not?"

The Gryphon nodded. The room was very much the young Bedlam's domain.

"What worries me is that this might not be the only evidence that we have missed."

Cabe had not thought of that. True, it was unlikely that he and Gwen had missed any such trace, but what about the areas that Valea and Aurim had been searching? He recalled where he had interrupted Kyl and his daughter. "We should probe the stables again . . . just in case."

"If I may be permitted, Cabe, perhaps I could do a search of my own."

"There's no need for you to—"

"Please. We have been through that before, haven't we?" The Gryphon turned to Gwendolyn. "What say you, my lady? Will you permit me to attempt a spell of my own? It promises a very thorough scrutiny of this place."

There was no hesitation on her part. "Do it. I want to be able to rest easy. I want to know."

The lionbird nodded. Without another word, he closed his eyes. Cabe could feel the stirring of power.

It was as if the Gryphon were everywhere at once. A force radiated from him, a force that spread throughout Aurim's chambers and continued on, unimpeded by any physical presence. It moved beyond the outer halls and the balcony, out beyond the very Manor itself.

The inhuman mage grunted. Next to him, the warlock sensed a renewed push that expanded the Gryphon's spell farther and farther beyond the Manor walls. The terrace was engulfed. The stables. The outer buildings, where most of those who served the Bedlams lived. Even the gardens were enveloped. The lionbird's claws unsheathed and sheathed as he worked to maintain his concentration. The spell did not require that much power, but it did require concentration if it was to be effective, especially since they were searching for what were likely very thin traces of the duke's former presence.

"The spell's reached the barriers," the Gryphon finally announced. "It can go no further without your permission."

"Let it go just beyond, if you will."

"A wise thought, Lady Gwendolyn." The inhuman sorcerer did just that. "My spell now covers the surrounding forest for almost fifty yards in every direction."

"Do you sense anything?" Cabe asked, fascinated.

"A moment." The Gryphon's voice grew distant. "This is a spell that works slowly, and by doing so more thoroughly searches. Let me . . ." He nodded to himself. "Yes, that does it. There are ancient traces of sorcery in this chamber, but they're so old that we need not worry about them. *Curious!* Did you two know that an aura surrounds this edifice? A very *strange* aura."

Both Bedlams knew of the aura of the Manor. It was, as the Gryphon had exclaimed, a very curious aura. Even Gwen, whose knowledge of such was far more complete than Cabe's own, had never experienced anything like it. However, they had long ago come to realize that whatever surrounded the Manor meant them no harm and had left it at that.

"I don't think Toma was in this room," the lionbird continued. "He reached in with his power. The trace comes from beyond, somewhere in that direction." He raised a taloned hand and pointed.

Following the Gryphon's direction, the warlock went to the balcony and peered outside. His eyes narrowed as he found himself looking down at the stables.

A figure stepped out of the nearest building, the one most directly in the path the Gryphon had indicated. Ssarekai. The drake seemed intent on heading toward the Manor, but then paused. After a moment's deliberation, Ssarekai turned his gaze upward. His eyes widened just a little as he met the stare of the sorcerer.

Cabe acknowledged him with a slight nod. Ssarekai dipped his head in what might have been an abortive bow and scurried on.

"Did you see anything?" Gwen called.

He turned back. "Just the stables. The stables and Ssarekai."

The Gryphon, meanwhile, had moved on. "I sense Aurim and another with some talent for sorcery. Not Valea; she's elsewhere. The drakes are everywhere." All drakes had inherent magic, although it varied greatly from one to another. "But no other telltale marks of the renegade save the trace in the study, of which we are already aware." He paused. "Yet . . ."

Both humans tensed.

"Nothing. I was wrong. Too hopeful, I suppose."

In one respect, Cabe found himself disappointed. Yet, if the Gryphon discovered nothing else, that did mean that the Manor was clean of all but this one trace of Toma's taint.

"There are some other odd sensations emanating from the Manor and the grounds, but they all seem to be a part of what makes this place what it is . . ."

A faint noise near the doorway caught the warlock's attention. He turned quietly, so as not to disturb the lionbird's work, and saw Benjin Traske. The massive scholar had one hand on the knife he always wore on his belt and the other on the arched doorway. He appeared startled at the presence of the Gryphon.

Cabe put a finger to his lips. Traske, recovered from his surprise, nodded once. He did not enter, but simply remained in the doorway.

"Some of your human servants have the natural potential for sorcery, did you know that? It's been suppressed."

"I shall have to look into that when we have more time," Gwen replied.

"I can let you know which ones at some point in the future." Slowly, the Gryphon turned. He did not stop turning until he had performed three-quarters of a circle. "I think . . . that's all. I find no other vestiges of his work. They might have dissipated beyond the spell's abilities, but at the very least that would mean you had nothing to fear from them. I can find no spells or traps anywhere."

The mood in the chamber lightened. Cabe noted that even Benjin Traske, who could not have understood what was being done here, relaxed.

Without warning, the Gryphon opened his eyes. The spell dissipated with astonishing speed and simplicity. "As near as I can tell, the Manor is safe. I cannot promise that the spell was perfect in its execution . . ."

"I am quite satisfied, Gryphon." A very relieved Gwendolyn moved to the lionbird's side. She put her arms around him and leaned forward to kiss him in gratitude. Cabe noticed that the former monarch managed to transform his monstrous features into the more handsome, human ones before the enchantress' lips touched his cheek. Even knowing that the sorceress loved him and that the lionbird loved his own mate, the warlock suffered a twinge of jealousy.

He extended his hand and gave the Gryphon his own thanks, adding, "It was fortunate that you arrived today. This will mean that we will be sleeping a lot easier again."

"You've done much for me in the past, both of you." The Gryphon, however, did look pleased. As he shook Cabe's hand, he finally noticed the figure in the doorway. "Benjin!"

The huge figure performed one of his miraculous bows. "Lord Gryphon."

"Will we be seeing you in Penacles when the heir comes? I would like to show you some improvements we've made with the school. I would like your opinion."

"I cannot say, my lord."

The lionbird's feathers and fur ruffled in growing annoyance at those around him. "Must I keep repeating myself? I am no longer king of Penacles! I have *no* title!"

"Only in your own mind," countered the Lady Bedlam. "You might have refused to take back the throne, but everyone, including Toos, agrees that what you did for the kingdom when you did rule there deserves respect. You *are* the special counsel to the regent, aren't you? That in itself infers some sort of title. I know that Troia wouldn't mind that."

He sighed. "I give in. There are those who believe that I am unusually stub-born, but Toos would still have me resume the throne even after all the time since my return to Penacles. Now *there* is stubbornness!" The Gryphon waved away what to him was a most distasteful subject. "You are not traveling with your former pupil to Penacles, Benjin?"

"That is for my lord and lady to decide."

The scholar gave no indication of his feelings one way or the other, but somehow his words made Cabe feel guilty for having left the man behind on the journey to visit Talak. Glancing at his wife, he saw that she, too, was having second thoughts.

"I think that something can be arranged, Scholar Traske," the enchantress finally conceded. "We'll talk later."

"Yes, Lady Bedlam." Benjin Traske's somber demeanor gave way to growing curiosity. "Lady Bedlam, what, if I may ask—"

"We'll talk about *that* later, too."

"As you desire." Bowing once more, the tutor departed.

"What was that you said about him coming with us to Penacles?" Cabe asked his wife. "I thought that he would be staying here just as he did when we journeyed to Talak."

"First, we really had no right to make him stay here last time. You and I both know that. Traske could have traveled with you if he so desired, but he chose not to rather than argue with us. Arguing is not his way. Second, he really should have the opportunity to see his work in Penacles . . . and I have decided that I shall stay home for all but the most essential days of the visitation."

The Gryphon did not take this news well. "Troia was hoping that you would come with the others. She does not feel as comfortable around the people of Penacles as she does around you, Gwendolyn."

Considering his mate's feline tendencies, Cabe did not find that at all sur-prising. The attention that she received as the former king's bride did not help the matter any. Troia was not used to being such a center of attention, and now that she had a small child to rear, it bothered her even more.

The Lady Bedlam smiled, thinking of the cat-woman, but still said, "I promise that I will see her when I do arrive, Gryphon. I remained behind when Cabe traveled to Penacles because I wanted to help the children prepare for being masters of the house, but on that score I no longer have any worry. You know what still bothers me, though. I'm sorry, but even the thoroughness of your spell can't completely shake the fear from me concerning Toma's invasion. I *need* to be here, can you understand that?"

Cabe certainly did. Had he been given any choice, he, too, would have re-mained behind. One of them, however, had to go to Penacles. Had his wife been the one forced to make the journey, she would have spent most of the time fearing for their home, their children, and all those whose lives depended upon them. Cabe himself would certainly worry, but knowing that the enchantress was watching over everyone would ease much of his fear.

The Gryphon also understood her concerns. "Then I will pass on that message to Troia."

"When time permits, I *will* come for a more extended visit; I promise her that."

"And she will hold you to that." The lionbird chuckled and clasped his taloned hands together. "Now, I regret to say, I must depart. There are some other tasks I must perform before I transport myself back to Penacles." The distinctive human/avian eyes widened. "Aaah! What a fool I am! Before I forget again, will the eternal be coming to the gathering? I know he joined you on your trek to Talak, Cabe. Will he also do so when you bring to us the Gold Dragon's heir?"

Thinking back, the sorcerer could not recall whether or not he had ever discussed Penacles in particular with Darkhorse. They had mostly talked about the mountain kingdom. Still, Darkhorse was always more welcome in the court of Toos the Regent than he was in that of Melicard. Cabe saw no reason why the shadow steed would not make the journey. "I would think that he would be there, but no promise was made."

The Gryphon laughed at that. "Then I shall warn Toos to be ready for him! The shadowy one, for all he is known in Penacles, still makes most of us jump! If he could only be taught to appear in a less dramatic fashion than is his wont, things would be so much quieter."

"If I see him, I'll be certain to pass on that suggestion." Having seen the reaction of the Talakian guests to Darkhorse, even after Melicard's warnings, Cabe had no desire to witness a repetition.

"Good! Then if the two of you might be willing to lead me to the edge of the barrier spells . . ."

"I could simply transport us there," reminded the warlock.

"I think that I can spare the two of you the extra few minutes . . . unless you fear my close proximity to your lady?"

"Not as much as you should fear the claws of *your* lady if she learns about that close proximity," Cabe countered.

"Yes, there is that."

"We would be delighted to walk with you, Gryphon." The scarlet-tressed sorceress took hold of the lionbird's arm.

With Cabe leading, they departed Aurim's chambers. More at ease, the trio's conversation turned to more pleasant things, such as the activities of the

Gryphon's second child or the school of magic. Cabe had hopes for the future of the school; while its initial students seemed destined to be minor spellcasters at best, the openness in which the school operated was making the people of Penacles more comfortable with the concept. None who showed any promise was refused a testing, and none who took the test could claim that they had not been treated fairly, whatever their place in society. That was another reason both Bedlams desired the chance to return more often to the City of Knowledge. It behooved them to do whatever was in their power to keep the school a place that folk everywhere would admire, not fear. It was not merely for their own sake; it was for the sake of their children and other mages to come.

The Gryphon was describing the practice sessions of a student whose impatience rivaled that of Aurim when the young warlock himself appeared in the hall. With him was Ursa, who seemed to be supporting the Bedlams' son.

The brief interlude of peace was immediately shattered as parental concern seized control. Stepping toward his son, Cabe asked, "Aurim, are you well?"

The younger Bedlam glanced up. Embarrassment colored his cheeks. "I slipped and struck my head, Father. It's nothing, really."

"Merely a large lump and a maddening headache," Ursa added with a wry smile. "I still don't know how he did it."

"I wish *I* knew, so that I wouldn't do it again!"

"Where did it happen?" Perhaps it was because of the discovery that they had made in Aurim's room, a discovery that Cabe was still debating about mentioning to his son, but the warlock needed to know.

"At the beginning of the maze. It was such a good day that I'd been practicing in there instead of here. I supposed I was still thinking about the spellcasting and just misstepped." The young warlock shook his head. "Everything pounds now!"

Cabe was disappointed. For reasons that were not yet clear even to him, he had almost expected that his son's accident had taken place in or around the stables.

"Then, there's no sense in you standing here," admonished Gwendolyn. "Ursa, if you would see him to his room, I will be back in a few minutes."

"Certainly, my lady. I will stay with him until you return."

Aurim did not like being treated so. "All I need to do is lie down, Mother. There's no reason to worry."

"I will be the judge of that. If you please, Ursa?"

The beauteous drake led the feebly protesting Aurim away, his mother's gaze remaining on the pair until they were well on their way.

"A fine boy," remarked the Gryphon, but his tone hinted that his thoughts were, in part, on another boy long dead.

"But very stubborn," insisted the Lady Bedlam.

"I, for one, am not surprised."

She took the comment for the compliment it was supposed to be. As they moved on, the enchantress added, "It is not the *worst* trait he could have."

"Not by far. Will you be bringing Aurim and Valea to Penacles when you make your extended visit?"

Cabe's wife considered that. "It might be a good idea. With Kyl, Grath, and Ursa gone, the Manor will certainly seem empty for the two of them."

"The Manor will seem empty to you, too, won't it? After all, many of those who live here will be leaving with them, won't they?"

"Many of the drakes will be leaving, and some of the humans, too, but some of those are returning to the domain of the Green Dragon, who originally brought them to the Manor. Actually, anyone, either human or drake, who desires to remain behind is welcome to do so. I have hopes that most will."

They had reached the staircase. The Gryphon glanced at Cabe, who had been silent for the past several moments. The warlock had been listening, but he had also been brooding over his earlier notion concerning the stables. He could not say why; after all, the Gryphon's search had yielded nothing, and if there was anyone other than Darkhorse whose power Cabe respected, it was the lionbird.

"I hope you and your entire family will dare to take some time to visit us after Kyl is ensconced on the throne of the Dragon Emperor, Cabe. Things should be much more peaceful by that time, and I think that Troia may not desire to travel much out of the city. Not, at least, for several months." There was a twinkle in the lionbird's arresting eyes as he saw comprehension slowly creep into his hosts' countenances. "I would say that Troia will be showing very soon."

"Another child? How wonderful!" The sorceress hugged the Gryphon.

Cabe, forgetting all else, reached forward and shook his old comrade's hand again. "Was that the true reason you came?"

"Oh, the others were good, too, but I decided to save the best news for last." The Gryphon tilted his head a bit. "I would be happy with a female this time, but another male would be loved just as much!"

"I'm amazed that you kept the truth hidden from us so long."

"I wanted to tell you when I first arrived, but I had sworn that I would save this news for last, it being the best possible news there could be!" He laughed. "I tell you, there is no reason that Toos could give me now that would make me take the throne back from him! I intend to enjoy the coming peace by watching all my children grow up while Troia and I make up for all the time the war kept us from truly enjoying one another."

"We shall have to visit you the moment after Kyl has ascended to the throne, no later than that!" exclaimed the Lady Bedlam. She and Cabe both knew what children meant to the Gryphon and Troia. For all his warlike past, the lionbird adored the young, but that fact had not been noticed until he had met his mate.

"Kyl . . ." The Gryphon squawked and shook his head. "I am more than happy to be free of the curses of monarchy, but if that's what he desires, may he rule long as long as he rules fair. I wish him the best of luck, of course." He shrugged, and when he spoke again, some of the joy created by the announcement of his forthcoming child gave way to consideration of another child's impending future. "But I hope that he may *never* have need of it."

# XII

UNLIKE THE CITY of Talak, Penacles, situated to the southeast of the Manor, was a place of tall towers, many of them topped with majestic, pointed spires. It was also a land of gardens, reminding those who had journeyed from the Manor of their home. The gardens were everywhere and ranged from small plots of earth in the center of the bazaar to huge, rolling landscapes toward the eastern part of the kingdom.

Cabe could hardly believe that this day had finally come. It seemed as if the past few days had dragged slowly by. Preparing for this second visit had been only a part of the problem. Cabe and Gwen had also had to cope with the nagging fear that they had missed some legacy of Toma's. There had also been the more realistic problem of Valea, who stared after Kyl at every opportunity. Somehow, Cabe had kept the two apart save on occasions when they were all together, but he knew that after Penacles something permanent would have to be done. Because of Kyl's rank, the warlock had forborne from directly confronting him on this issue, but no more. This was one situation that could not go on.

Penacles had known no overseeing Dragon King for well over a century, not since the Gryphon and Cabe's own grandfather, Nathan, had brought down the Dragon King Purple. The Gryphon had then ruled here until his long-hidden past had forced him on a journey across the seas and into the dark empire of the Aramites. While he fought to bring down the wolf raiders' regime, his most trusted aide, General Toos, also known as the Fox, had ruled in his place . . . and had proved quite an impressive monarch in his own right. Still, even after roughly two decades as lord of Penacles, fiery-haired Toos still insisted he was only holding the fort until his king came to his senses. Hence the tall, narrow ruler's nickname of Toos the Regent.

After Talak, Kyl did not seem as awestruck with Penacles, although that did not mean that the dragon heir was not fascinated. He drank in the wonders of the City of Knowledge. The dizzying heights of the many towers most impressed him, for Cabe noticed the young drake eye them again and again. Grath, too, was amazed. The Green Dragon and Benjin Traske, on the other hand, seemed oblivious to the beauty of the ancient kingdom. Of course, they had been to Penacles many times before.

Things were going well, but Cabe could not shake his uneasiness. He felt that he had a good reason, though; one of his party was missing.

Darkhorse had never promised that he would also accompany them to Penacles, and it may have been that the shadow steed felt it unnecessary since Toos was a much more reasonable ruler than tempestuous Melicard. Certainly, both the former and present monarchs of Penacles were on fair terms with the eternal. Kyl would not have impressed them by maneuvering Darkhorse into journeying with him to this place. The eternal would have understood that, too.

Still, Cabe had expected *some* word from the massive stallion. That this had happened virtually on top of their discovery of Toma's intrusion was likely why the warlock was so bothered. It was not as if Darkhorse had not disappeared without explanation before. The eternal was governed by no one save himself.

"Is that the palace?" Grath asked him, leaning close so as to be heard over the trumpets and the crowds.

Cabe shelved his thoughts and studied the structure looming ahead of them. "Yes, that's it."

He knew why Grath had asked him. The palace of the lords of Penacles was a sharp contrast to that of the kings of Talak and also, in fact, to the city of Penacles itself. With so much beauty everywhere else, it was surprising to first-time visitors to discover that the palace resembled nothing more than a great stone fortress. The walls were a drab, unadorned gray and the only entrance was a massive iron gate. Huge marble steps that seemed to go on forever led up to the palace. There were no decorative columns, no gardens, and no statuary save the lone marble figure of a gryphon in flight. The last had been a gift to the lionbird from some of the citizenry during his long and productive reign. Toos had left it where it was as one more reminder that he was *not* king.

The honor guard that had been provided for them led the caravan directly to the palace. As in Talak, they were met at the steps. Toos was there, accompanied by the Gryphon, four officers who were a part of the regent's personal staff, and a small honor guard. The former general had never taken a queen, although in the past year he had begun to court one or two women. Despite his resemblance to a man entering his latter years, the vulpine monarch had at least a good fifty years left of life. That was because mixed in with the graying red hair—red hair that had once made Cabe joke that Gwen and the regent might be very long lost cousins—was a streak of silver. Toos, like Cabe, was a mage, but in the former mercenary's case, the magic apparently manifested itself as an uncanny ability to outmaneuver his opponents, be it on the field of battle or in the intrigue-laden courts of Penacles. The only other sign that Toos was a man of magic was his age. A sorcerer could live to be three, and in some cases, four, centuries old. Toos was already well beyond the normal life span of a human.

"Welcome, Lord Kyl." The voice was strong and, while formal, still quite different from the practiced tones of the aristocracy. There was also a look in the regent's eye, a look that hinted of humor.

"Greetingsss to you, General Toosss," replied the young drake, executing a bow. The two then shook hands.

Cabe held back a smile. The heir, possibly with a little reminding from Grath, had remembered that Toos did not care to be called king or lord. The regent considered himself a soldier and so preferred to retain his rank.

"Your journey went well?" asked Toos.

"Quite well, thank you. I had forgotten what a wondrousss land Penaclesss wasss, or what a fassscinating place the city proper isss."

"You're not referring to the block of stone behind me, I hope," commented the regent with a foxlike smile.

Kyl was momentarily taken aback by the openness of Toos. The young drake had met the human on occasion over the years, but not for quite some time and most often for only a few minutes. Cabe had warned him about the general, reminding him that Toos had been a mercenary and warrior for far longer than he had been lord of a mighty kingdom. Even the warlock, who had known Toos since the days when the angular commander had led the defenders of a besieged Penacles against the invading dragon forces of the Dragon Emperor, could not always adjust to the man's mercurial style. As a soldier, Toos had constantly kept his adversaries off guard, the better to defeat them swift and sure. The style had suited him in his present role as well.

"The palace isss very—"

"Functional. The inside is not much of an improvement, although the grand ballroom and the royal court are decorative enough, I suppose. We'd best leave it at that." Again, there was the foxlike smile. "Now, Lord Kyl, if you will allow my staff to see to your people, we shall end this greeting and instead save our breaths for climbing these steps."

The drakes were not at first certain as to how to take the almost flippant manner of their host. The warlock smiled slightly. Toos *had* changed since their first introduction.

Grath whispered something to Kyl, who eyed the steps. The emperor-to-be nodded, then replied to the waiting Toos. "Yesss, the sssuggessstion hasss merit, General. *Much* merit."

Snapping his fingers, Toos sent two of his officers to deal with the caravan. Then, waiting for Kyl to step up beside him, the general led the way. Everyone soon saw the wisdom of the regent's words. The climb was exhausting, even to those who had been prepared for it. Progress slowed the higher they climbed, but at last the party reached the top of the steps.

Toos glared at the path they had just tread, grumbling, "That you can blame on one of your own, Lord Kyl. Someday, I must do something about it."

"I said that for years, Toos," retorted the Gryphon. "You would have to tear down everything here, though. That would be a massive undertaking."

"Each time I climb those steps, it becomes more and more tempting, I'll say that."

Cabe surveyed the others and found to his surprise that, other than the sentries, who would not think of showing their exhaustion, the only one who appeared unaffected by the climb was Benjin Traske. The warlock stared hard at the massive tutor and finally had to ask, "Are you well, Benjin?"

"I have always believed in maintaining both the mind *and* the body, Lord Bedlam."

"So I see now." He shook his head. With a minor spell, the sorcerer could have reinvigorated himself easily, but like Talak, Penacles had its special defenses. Some remained from the days when the Dragon King Purple had ruled, and others from the reign of the Gryphon, but there were also a vast number of new spells protecting the city, placed there at the regent's request.

Toos looked over his guests. "If we're all ready to continue, I've planned some food and entertainment. Lord Kyl, have you ever witnessed a living chess game before?"

The young drake's eyes were wide with curiosity. "I mussst sssay that I have certainly not." He glanced down at his brother, who shook his head in equal confusion.

"Then I think that you have a treat awaiting you. If you'll all follow me?"

PENACLES HAD BEEN at peace for years, their neighbor to the east, mistenshrouded Lochivar, having been quiet since the Gryphon had nearly dealt its master, the Black Dragon, a mortal blow. The darksome lord of the Grey Mists still lived and ruled, but it was said that he could barely speak and that his powers were waning.

That meant that Penacles had an army that trained and trained, but had no enemy to fight. While Toos looked forward to peace as much as most other folk did, he believed in maintaining a strong force. One never knew when times might change. Therefore, it had behooved him to find some way in which his men could keep their skills paramount.

War games had solved that problem, at least where his soldiers were concerned. Each month, various units would maneuver against one another in the nearby hills and valleys. Men who excelled in skill and ingenuity were rewarded. The soldiers also kept wary, for it *was* possible to be injured. Officers worked to see that such injuries happened as rarely as was possible, though.

Yes, Toos had solved the problem of keeping his men at their best, but he could hardly join them on the field, however much he would have wanted to do so. There was the risk that something might happen to him, either by accident or due to some assassin. No ruler who desired to survive dared believe that there was *not* an assassin lurking nearby. Simply because the Black Dragon had made no new assaults on the kingdom in years did not mean that he had withdrawn his spies.

From his long years as the Gryphon's second, the vulpine soldier had picked up a fondness for chess, especially its constant demand for reevaluating one's strategy. Simple chess had been sufficient for some time, but then, while visiting the magical libraries of Penacles with the Gryphon, the bored regent had commented on his need for something further.

"To my surprise," Toos said to his guests as he considered his next move, "the *gnome* spoke up."

The libraries of Penacles were a magical wonder dating back possibly beyond the present city. No one knew much about them save that they were larger than should have been physically possible, some corridors stretching for what seemed miles underground, yet apparently movable, and accessible only through a wondrous tapestry hidden in the palace.

The libraries also had a librarian . . . or perhaps many, although if the latter was the case, then all of them were identical in form. For as long as either Toos or the Gryphon could recall, they had always been served by a small, squat, completely hairless gnome wearing a robe much like that of a mage. All one had to do was tell the gnome what one was searching for and the odd little figure would locate it. Rarely, however, did the gnome offer words of advice.

Toos made his move and continued. "He suggested a field, a life-sized board, and living champions to do combat. I scoffed at the idea at first, but . . ." The general indicated the area just before them. "You see what I've done."

In what had once been a small arena where human slaves had fought for the personal amusement of the Dragon King, there was now a black-and-white pattern of squares, each approximately three feet by three feet. There were viewing boxes on each end of the board, providing seating for perhaps two dozen people apiece.

On the board, or sitting off to the sides, were soldiers clad in armor representing the various pieces in the game. These were the game's living chessmen . . . and women, too, since not only did each side need a queen, but female soldiers had been a part of the army of Penacles since the days of the Gryphon's reign.

Cabe took his mind off of the game to observe the lionbird himself, who was the general's opponent. The first time the warlock had been invited to witness the tournament, he had come fearing that the regent had finally fallen prey to his power and had become a decadent tyrant. However, after watching the game and learning the rules behind it, he had come to enjoy it himself.

The chessmen were volunteers. Over the years, it had become a bit of prestige to be a combatant in the chess tournament. Unlike the true board game, a chess piece was not removed simply because another piece had captured it. Instead, the two warriors had to duel, utilizing their skills while remaining within the two squares involved. Fighters were removed if they lost or if they attempted to truly wound their adversaries. It had become a matter of honor for most soldiers involved to win as cleanly as possible, as the best were often chosen for a place in the royal guard.

At the moment, Toos was in grave danger. His rook, his last line of defense against the Gryphon, had just fallen in combat against the other's knight. The rook, a man armed with a mace and shield, had been disarmed by the knight, an armored figure also using a shield, but instead of a mace had wielded a broadsword.

"I knew that would happen," the regent muttered. "Luck of the draw! He's current champion among the champions!"

The game ended three combats later. The rule involving checkmate particularly fascinated Cabe. First the player would have to assure that his opponent's king had no escape. That was the same as a normal game of chess. However, in the general's variation, the checking pieces then had to do battle with the beleaguered monarch. It was possible for the king to free himself from checkmate if he could eliminate every opponent involved, but he had to fight all of them; he could not move to safety after defeating the first adversary.

The drakes, especially Kyl and Grath, were eager to direct the game themselves. The Dragon King had already played on one or two of his previous visits, so he offered to stand aside and let brother go against brother. Toos repeated the differences in the rules from normal chess, then chose their pieces for them. Chessmen were always chosen by lottery, so that no player could ever come to trust too much in his warriors. It made for a more balanced game and, in fact, after the countless battles the Gryphon and Toos had played, the lionbird was up by only seven victories. Of course, if there were ever two opponents who knew how one another thought, it was the two former mercenaries.

While the regent guided Kyl and the Green Dragon, who had always had a fondness for the human game, coached Grath, the Gryphon made his way back to where Cabe and Benjin Traske sat watching the opening moves. As usual, Faras and Ssgayn took up a spot near the dragon heir, which made for some crowding as the general's own guards insisted on watching the drakes.

"They will be quite occupied with this game," the Gryphon commented as he joined the two humans. "This might be a good time to visit the libraries."

"For what reason?"

"I'm doing some research, trying to see if I finally understand some of the methods by which the libraries pass on information. I'm certain now that long ago something happened that distorted the original function of the place. I thought that I might save my next visit for when you were here. Do you wish to come?"

"I'd be a fool to say no." As the Manor was the warlock's pet project, so were the libraries the Gryphon's. Both researchers had achieved about the same amount of success so far . . . meaning very little. If the lionbird had finally made progress, Cabe wanted to see it for himself.

"Good!" The Gryphon paused, then eyed Traske. "Benjin, you've never been in the libraries before, have you?"

"No, my lord."

"You *haven't?*" That startled Cabe. "After all these years?"

"I blame Toos for that!" The former monarch of Penacles shook his head. "Toos has never trusted the libraries . . . and who can blame him? You and I were virtually the only ones he would allow to enter until fairly recently, warlock. The old fox rarely even visits them himself!"

Cabe had known the last, but not that Toos had been so restrictive. Surely, Benjin Traske, whose expertise had helped create the school of sorcery, deserved that much trust. Once again, he was reminded of the paranoia of the monarchy.

"Well, I think that it's time the scholar was given permission to visit them," the Gryphon commented with a glance toward the regent. "You may certainly join us, Benjin."

"Thank you, my lord." The calm veneer momentarily twisted into a look of extreme pleasure. Then, apparently remembering himself, Traske quickly reverted to his more stolid, scholarly expression.

As they rose to leave, Cabe could not resist quietly commenting to the Gryphon, "I thought that you no longer ruled this kingdom."

"You may consider me king emeritus for the time being."

"Perhaps you'd better hope that Toos will consider you that."

The Gryphon chuckled, an incongruous sight, considering his features. "My old comrade-in-arms would be happy to consider me king of *anything*, just so long as he can relinquish the throne to me!" He pretended to shudder at the thought. "Now, come! We really should give Benjin all the time we can in the libraries!"

They left the drakes and the general to their game. The Gryphon led his companions back into the palace and through its halls. As the visitors had noticed on their initial walk through the gray edifice, the inside of the palace was little better decorated than the outside. A few pieces of art, most recent and all of them reminiscent of war, dotted the halls here and there, but for the most part the palace interior looked as if the architects had left their project undone. Only when they passed the grand ballroom was there a radical change. Cabe glanced inside as they passed by and marveled at the bright, glittering array of crystal and gold decorations. After the rest of the building, the sight of the ballroom was almost jarring.

On and on they walked. Cabe began to wonder why the Gryphon had not chosen to transport them there. Most likely it was because the lionbird preferred physical activity and considered such use of magic frivolous. While this pattern of thought was much akin to the warlock's own way of thinking, this particular trek was one where he would have happily made an exception.

At last they came before a doorway beside which two huge, iron figures stood, roughly hewn warriors that, like the palace, seemed to have been abandoned before they had been completed. The Gryphon signaled his companions to halt. He continued on for several paces until he stood no more than two yards from the center of the doorway.

"Well? Will you let us pass?" the lionbird asked.

What happened next made Benjin Traske gasp and clutch the hilt of his blade, an action which, in retrospect, Cabe realized might have endangered all of them.

One of the iron figures slowly turned its head toward the waiting Gryphon. The other looked not at the lionbird, but rather at the two behind.

The warlock took hold of the scholar's arm and whispered, "Make no false moves, Benjin. If they perceive you as a threat, they might attack. You'd be surprised at how fast they can move!"

"Iron *golems*," the tutor muttered, still stunned. "I have heard of such, but only in old stories."

"Did the stories mention what they could do to those they were sent against?"

Traske did not release his blade, but he made no other move, which was perhaps the best that Cabe could hope for.

Oddly, the Gryphon was still waiting for the doors to be opened. The golems continued to stare at the trio, as if uncertain what to do.

"You *heard* me. The three of us will enter here; is that understood?"

Very slowly, the golem watching the former monarch returned to its original stance. As its head swiveled back, the creature rumbled, "You may enter."

"Thank you *very* much." The Gryphon waved the other two forward.

The doors suddenly swung open of their own accord. Beyond was a chamber that, like the ballroom, was a contrast to the stark simplicity of the regent's palace. That was because the chamber before them had once been the Gryphon's very room, his private sanctum in the days when he had ruled Penacles.

With careful steps, the three entered the chamber. Cabe noticed that the other golem continued to observe the Gryphon's two guests. He could not recall the last time that the iron monsters had taken such interest in him. Then he realized that it must be Traske in whom the metal man was interested, for the scholar had never been permitted entrance before.

Benjin Traske still clutched his knife hilt, but he had almost forgotten the golems. Now he was busy inspecting the room that they had entered, his eyes quickly fixing on one ornament in particular, a skillfully woven tapestry hanging on one of the walls.

"I still use this place on occasion, although for the most part my stays last only the day. Troia would never forgive me if I left her and Darot alone overnight. Since we live not that far from here, I cannot blame her. Mostly, I use this chamber when I'm researching the libraries."

The doors suddenly swung closed and as they did, they revealed two more of the metal colossi standing guard inside. Cabe had seen these two often enough, but for the first time that he could recall, they were watching the Gryphon's guests closely.

Leading them to the tapestry, the Gryphon explained its importance to the scholar. "This is the only way—the only way we know of—that one can gain entrance to the libraries."

"The detail is fantastic!" whispered Traske. "And it appears to be very ancient. I have never seen such a style before."

"We don't know *how* old it is, Benjin, but it may be from the first Dragon King. No one is certain."

Traske squinted. "But . . . this is present-day Penacles! That cannot be right!"

"The tapestry is quite magical. It always shows the kingdom as it presently is. We could watch a building being torn down, return to this chamber, and find that it's also vanished from the image."

"How does it help us journey to the libraries? I do not even see them."

"You have to know how to look for them, Benjin. Where the libraries are concerned, you won't see an actual building. Instead, there's usually a symbol of some sort. It varies now and then. Sometimes it's a book, other times it might simply be a cross or star. Knowing the tapestry as I do, I merely have to search for something that is out of place." The Gryphon studied the image. "And I think . . . that's certainly a strange choice!"

"What is it this time?" Cabe asked.

"See for yourself." Their host put his finger next to the mark, then shifted to the side so that the others could look at it.

Just under several buildings in what was the eastern edge of the city was the symbol. Cabe had never seen its like in all the times he had watched the Gryphon use the tapestry, and its very pattern disturbed him.

Benjin Traske peered at it. "A very stylized version of a dragon, is it not?"

"It is. That's not the symbol you find on each tome in the libraries, though. Looks very familiar."

"It should," whispered the warlock. "Kyrg and Toma both used it as one of their banners."

"I'd *forgotten* that! Of course!"

Cabe frowned, suddenly filled with tension. "I don't like that coincidence. This could mean that Toma somehow gained access to the libraries." Traske, who had finally been told of the drake's other intrusions, frowned at this. "He could be in there *now*."

The Gryphon nodded agreement, but added, "I can't see how he could have gotten into the libraries, but then he did get into the Manor. There may be danger in the libraries. Perhaps you should stay here after all, Benjin."

The scholar looked disappointed but understanding. "If you think I should."

"If nothing's wrong, then we'll immediately return for you. Now, if you could please step back ten paces?" He waited for Traske to obey. Then, placing his finger directly on the symbol, the Gryphon began to rub it. As he did, Cabe moved next to him.

The golems, the chamber, and Benjin Traske began to fade away. Only the tapestry remained the same. It was as if a great fog were building up, a fog that somehow did not affect the duo or the artifact.

The Gryphon continued to rub. Quickly the chamber and all in it vanished, only to be immediately replaced by the dim image of a corridor and countless shelves. Within seconds, the image became distinct. The last vestiges of blurriness faded away before a full minute had elapsed since the transfer had begun.

Cabe and his companion stared down both directions of the corridor. All the great books were in place and everything was as neat as was possible. Yet, once before a drake, the fatalistic Ice Dragon, had somehow obtained entrance to this magical place. The warlock wondered if that intrusion had at last been repeated.

"That's odd," commented the Gryphon.

"Seems quiet to me."

"Yes. Absolutely quiet. *Where* is the librarian?"

The hairless little gnome was nowhere to be seen. Always he, or perhaps another exactly like him, appeared to those arriving in the libraries. This time, however, it was as if the vast structure had just been abandoned.

"Maybe he was too far away for once." Even Cabe doubted his suggestion. The gnome should have been awaiting them.

The Gryphon continued to scan both ends of the corridor. "I think that perhaps we'd—"

Cabe glanced at his companion. The lionbird was staring past him at something far down the passage. The warlock turned and saw that the gnome had at last made an appearance.

The crooked little figure stood no higher than Cabe's waist. Somehow, despite his size, he had always impressed the mage as a creature not to be trifled with. The notion had always lingered despite the fact that the gnome had never made any hostile gesture toward any of them.

"I am afraid that the libraries must be closed to you for a time, former lord of Penacles."

"Closed? That's ridiculous! They've never been—"

The sudden silence filled Cabe Bedlam with fear for his companion. He tore his gaze from the gnome and looked at the Gryphon . . . but found *no one* beside him. Immediately, he turned his attention back to the ominous little figure. "What have you done with him?"

"He is back in the chamber, as you will be, too, Bedlam." The creature sighed. "Your family will insist on disrupting my existence for all eternity. I have never seen such a consistent streak for falling into trouble as your tree bears."

"What does that mean?" The gnome had known some of his ancestors? Cabe doubted somehow that the librarian was speaking of Azran or Nathan. He suddenly had the suspicion that this gnome was incredibly old.

"Your line will probably be the death of me yet . . . or rather *again.* By laws that I myself put into effect, fool that I was, I can tell you nothing more save that the face of your terror is before you often."

It was a warning as twisted in riddle as any other answer given by the tomes of the libraries. Cabe wanted to demand a better answer, but before he was able to say anything—

—he was back in the Gryphon's old chambers.

"Cabe!" The lionbird grabbed him by the arms as if to assure himself that the robed warlock was real. "What happened? Where were you?"

"Being told puzzles by the gnome. I do know one thing; not only has he existed for as long as the libraries, but he seems to have met a few of my ancestors over that time."

"Did he explain what he meant by that nonsense about the libraries being closed?"

"I *think* he did." Cabe repeated his short conversation with the crooked little figure. When he was finished, the Gryphon and Benjin Traske both looked as confused as he felt.

"It suggests something about Toma, I would think, but with so much else going on, there could be other meanings. How typical of the libraries."

"Whatever the meaning, he indicated that there would be no more information or aid. I gathered that he *couldn't*."

"We shall see." Returning to the tapestry, the Gryphon raised a clawed hand with the intention of rubbing the libraries' symbol and returning to the hidden edifice. However, midway to the ancient artifact, the lionbird halted his hand.

"What's wrong?"

"The symbol . . . it's *disappeared!*"

The warlock could scarcely believe that. Trailed by Benjin Traske, he joined the Gryphon in his search. The dragon symbol had not only disappeared, but there was no new symbol to replace it. Even if Cabe had somehow missed it, he knew that the sharp eyes of his companion would not have. The Gryphon knew every detail of the tapestry and every nuance of its function.

"I didn't think that was possible!" muttered the former monarch. "It *shouldn't* be! He has to obey! The libraries serve the lord of Penacles or whomever he permits access to it. The libraries know that Toos has given me leave!"

Cabe considered that. "Perhaps that's why we can't enter now. Perhaps the libraries are somehow serving Toos or you by doing this." He suddenly thought about the visions that had appeared in the Manor. Was it, too, trying to warn or protect those who lived within? "Is that a possibility?"

"A very peculiar possibility, but, yes, one that might be worth contemplating." Still bristling, the Gryphon glanced at the third member of their party. "I apologize, Benjin. This was hardly expected. Perhaps next time that you are here we will be able to make the journey."

"I am patient, my lord." Although his face was bland, the scholar's eyes again revealed his disappointment.

"Then let us return to the others and see how the game is progressing."

Despite his attempts to be cheerful, the Gryphon was clearly still upset about this development. Never had the libraries defied him so.

By the time they returned to the arena, the game was almost in its climax. Cabe and the others joined Toos, who stepped away for a moment to speak with them.

"It's Grath's turn. He's trying to find a way out of his predicament, but I think it'll be checkmate in a few moves. He was threatening to beat the young emperor-to-be, but then his luck turned. Made some bad moves. Misjudged his champions' opponents. There's no way the king can fight his way out if he's cornered, which he will be soon enough." He glanced back to make certain that Grath had not yet moved. "Lord Kyl will hardly need my help now."

"How well do they play?" asked the Gryphon.

"Early in the game, I would have said that Grath could have given either of us trouble, but now I'd have to say that both of them are good players who still have to learn. Lord Kyl looks to be the better of the two."

A warrior on the field moved. The general excused himself and returned to the game, but Kyl was already commanding his knight forward. Toos remained next to the dragon heir just long enough to discuss the move, then left the young drake to his own efforts.

"Not the move that I would've made, but it'll bring the battle to an end soon enough. The Gryphon informed me earlier that he might bring you to the libraries. Is that where you were? Did you enjoy them, Scholar Traske? I don't believe that you've ever been to them."

The Gryphon answered for them. "We were *forbidden* entrance, Toos. The gnome said that the libraries were closed to us!"

It was evident that the regent did not believe what he was hearing. "That's *preposterous!*"

"True, but it happened."

"Tell me everything."

They did. Toos listened in disbelief, shaking his head when they were finished.

"Madness!" he snarled. "I'm inclined to take this as a sign that we should cancel this entire affair, but that's out of the question. Perhaps it's so many drakes nearby. There's not been this many dragons in the land since the siege led by Kyrg."

The others had not considered that fact . . . or, at least, the warlock had not. He eyed the Gryphon who was nodding thoughtfully. "That, too, is a possibility, but I think that there's no doubt that Toma is somehow involved. Cabe's conversation with the librarian was a murky one at best, but I feel that that's what it concerned."

"Well, I think that I'll try to see if they'll let me enter, though I doubt it. In the meantime, you can rest assured that measures will be taken in this matter."

"We know that we can trust you to do that. Toma may try to get near to our young emperor-to-be, so perhaps you might want your people to keep a special watch on him."

"Oh, believe me; they are."

An exclamation of triumph informed them that the game was at an end. As expected, Kyl had emerged the victor. Grath waved his congratulations from where he sat. Behind the younger brother, the Dragon King put a consoling hand on Grath's shoulder.

"We should inform Lord Green," Cabe suggested.

Toos studied the drake lord. "Yes, I'd thought of that. I'll do so this evening, when we discuss the final details of this visit. You all know that there's the required reception so the aristocrats and merchants and such can feel impressive. I'd also planned a ride out to where two of our best units are having their field exercises, but it might be best to postpone that. I'll have to see what the lord of Dagora thinks about it."

Kyl chose to join them then, which ended the conversation. The young drake was elated with his victory. "Did you all sssee? What a fassscinating game! I shall have to devissse sssomething akin to it once I asssume the throne! What a marvelousss passstime!"

"I'm glad you enjoyed it so much," returned Toos, pretending that nothing was amiss. "There will be opportunity to play again, of course, but I'm sorry to say that for now matters of state must take my time. If you will excuse me, I think the Lord Gryphon will be happy to show you the armory. Penacles might be called the City of Knowledge, but we have amassed quite an interesting array of armaments, too."

Kyl's eyes were bright with eagerness. He had not yet calmed down after his victory. "Yesss! I would be delighted!"

"Excellent! There are also some last arrangements to be made for the events of the next few days, arrangements that will be passed on for your approval later this evening. I hope you'll find your time here well spent."

The regent bid them all farewell, including Grath and the Dragon King, who had just rejoined the party. Grath, too, looked exhausted from the game, but he seemed slightly less enthusiastic. Considering the outcome, Cabe did not think the younger drake's attitude at all surprising.

"An excellent game, Your Majesty," the Dragon King commented.

"Yesss, it wasss! Lord Green, when I am emperor, I would like your help in creating a version of thisss tournament for our own kind."

"I will be happy to be of ssservice, although I fear our warriors might be a little more inclined to blood than these humans were."

That did not seem to bother the heir at all. In fact, the warlock thought that he looked much too hopeful.

"If Your Majesty is ready to depart," the Gryphon interrupted, "the royal armory requires a short ride."

"Armory?" questioned the Dragon King.

"It isss sssupposssed to be fassscinating, Lord Green!"

The drake lord acknowledged Kyl's words. "You will certainly enjoy it, my liege, but I must request you permit me to stay behind. I mussst really see how things are progressing with the rest of our caravan. We want no incidents such as happened with the artisan Osseuss. I would like to make certain that everyone knows what they are and are not permitted to do."

Kyl was not about to miss the armory. He waved away the Dragon King. "Of course, you have my permission. You will report to me later?"

The Green Dragon's tone was neutral. "Of course, my emperor."

Once again, it amazed Cabe to see how willingly the Dragon King bent before the young heir. Green truly had to want this peace to work, for there could be no other reason for his willingness to suffer Kyl's bouts of lordliness. The warlock sincerely doubted that he could be so understanding.

The matter dismissed from his thoughts, the eager young heir turned back to the Gryphon. "We may depart whenever you wish, Lord Gryphon."

"Thank you." Kyl did not notice the slight touch of humor in the lionbird's tone, but it was all Cabe could do to keep from smiling. "Lord Green, if you'll join us for a short time, I will find you a proper escort to lead you to your chambers."

"That would be sssuitable, thank you." Even under present circumstances, any drake who walked alone in Penacles risked danger. Not as great a danger as in Talak, but enough that such a risk was not to be taken.

They had only just begun walking when Cabe felt someone touch him on the shoulder. He turned to find Grath behind him, which startled the sorcerer a bit, since the younger drake always seemed either at the side of his brother or next to the Dragon King.

"What is it, Grath?"

"Master Bedlam, is Darkhorse coming? I think Kyl was expecting him to be here. He will not disappoint us, will he?"

"I don't know. I haven't talked to him since we returned from Talak." Realizing that, the mage's earlier worries came back multiplied. It *had* been quite some time since he or anyone had seen the eternal. Had something happened?

The young drake's thoughts apparently mirrored his own. "Do you think he's all right?"

"He should be. Darkhorse has a tendency to turn up at the most unexpected times. He'll likely materialize in the midst of the reception, just like he did in Talak."

That brought a brief smile to Grath's handsome face, but then the smile slipped as he said, "I hope nothing's wrong."

The conversation ended there. Moments later, Grath drifted back to his brother's side.

Try as he might, the warlock could not stop thinking about the shadow steed. He was certain that Darkhorse had continued on with his investigations into the mysterious traps some unknown enemy had planted.

*Unknown enemy?* With all else he had been blamed for, could not such cunning, magical traps have been set by *Toma?* It made perfect sense to Cabe, although he was willing to admit that he was paranoid when it came to the renegade. Still, it would explain a lot.

Darkhorse in the claws of Toma. . . .

# XIII

THE HEADACHE HAD not gone away even after several days. Aurim calculated that by now his father was spending his second day in Penacles. His mother planned to leave tomorrow, but not if Aurim was not well. Aurim had insisted that the headache was nothing, which was something of a lie. However, the throbbing in his head was nothing compared to the thought of looking weak.

It was a peculiar headache. For the first day, it had seemed like any other, but after that, the throbbing had taken on a strange quality. It was as if something was trying to break free. Each day seemed to weaken whatever held that thing back.

For reasons he did not understand save perhaps that it might end the pain, Aurim felt as if he *wanted* the mysterious force to burst free.

Eyes open, he stared at the ceiling of his bedchamber. His mother had suggested that he take an afternoon nap, something that he had not done since he was five. There was no arguing with the Lady Gwendolyn Bedlam, however, and so Aurim had retreated to his room. To his surprise, he had actually slept. Unfortunately, when he woke it was to find that the headache was, if anything, worse than ever.

He rolled over and stared at the balcony. Aurim found himself drawn to it for what must have been the dozenth time since he had stirred but minutes before.

Groaning, Aurim rose. Whatever fascinated him about the balcony drove him almost as crazy as the headache did. *Maybe if I look outside, that'll make it stop!* He hoped so. Aurim was certain that he could overcome the headache, but not the headathe *and* this peculiar compulsion.

No great revelation came to him as he stepped out. Still, the breeze that touched his face calmed him a little. He leaned on the carved handrail and peered down. People, both human and drake, went about their businesses. Off in the distance, Aurim could make out his sister and Ursa. *Probably pining for Kyl!* he thought with a snort. Kyl was his friend, but Aurim doubted that any relationship between the drake and his sister was a wise thing. Try telling that to *her*, though.

The throbbing continued unabated. Trying to keep his mind from it, Aurim continued to study the areas below. Perhaps if he took a walk through the maze. That always soothed him. If his mother had no need for him, he would do that. The garden maze had been his own personal world when he had been tiny: a fantasy realm where he had sometimes fought heroic battles and other times simply sat and enjoyed the peacefulness.

He looked to his left. The stables, as usual, were fairly active. Some of the horses were being walked. Two figures were inspecting the hoof of a bay. One of them straightened, shaking his head. Ssarekai.

*Ssarekai.*

"Toma . . ." he whispered, not realizing what he had uttered until a moment later. When he became aware, Aurim's countenance paled. He did not remember everything, but he remembered something.

*Toma! That night I woke . . . the stables . . .*

"Ssarekai?"

He did not even recall transporting himself, but suddenly Aurim was standing before the drake. The bay whinnied and tried to shy away from him, but the stable hand who had been conversing with Ssarekai managed to maintain his hold.

"Master Aurim! You should never—"

"What *happened*, Ssarekai? What did he *do*?"

The drake looked at him as if the warlock had gone mad. Perhaps he had, but Aurim did not care. He only wanted some answers to the horrible memories suddenly filling his head. Without thinking, he reached for the servitor and pulled him close. Ssarekai did not struggle, perhaps recalling that as a mage of great potential, his young master could have as easily thrown him across the span of the Manor grounds.

"You were with him! Somewhere below my chambers! You were with Toma!"

He had never seen a drake blanch before, but Ssarekai managed to do just that. The drake shook his head and his tongue darted out and in. He was so frightened that his sibilance became even worse than Kyl's.

"Not sssso, Masssster Aurrrim! Not sssso! I would neverrr have anything to do with that rrrenegade, that monsssster!"

"I saw you! I also saw him——" *Saw him do what? Do something, but I can't recall what it was Toma did!*

"I know nothing; I sssswear that by the Drrragon of the Depthsssss!"

"Aurim!"

He ignored the call, his concern only for an answer to the scene replaying in his head. It was like reading the same page of a book over and over. He saw—— or rather had *sensed*—the two of them below. Ssarekai himself the warlock could not really recall noticing, but he *had* been there; Aurim knew that now. Ssarekai had stood in silence while something had happened to Toma, a spell that the renegade himself had cast.

"Aurim!" This time the voice would not be denied. A hand clamped onto his shoulder to emphasize that fact.

Abruptly aware of what he was doing, the young sorcerer released his grip on the drake. Ssarekai hissed in relief, then stepped back just enough to be out of reach. Everyone was staring at Aurim . . . including his mother.

She almost seemed ablaze. The enchantress took hold of her son by the arms and looked him straight in the eyes. Under that gaze, he could not turn away.

"Listen to me!" she demanded. "Do you know what you've been doing?"

Much of the fight left him. He had come close to using his power on a trusted retainer, on someone who was a friend. He had been about to unleash his power without any thought as to the consequences.

"Do you know now?"

Aurim nodded. Only then did it become possible for him to look away. In a voice much younger, he whispered, "I'm sorry."

"I'm not the one to apologize to."

He understood. Turning around, he faced the still wary Ssarekai. Two stable hands were half-supporting the drake. "I'm sorry, Ssarekai! I really am!"

His extended hand was at first greeted with a stare. Then, the drake slowly extended his own. The two clasped hands. Ssarekai even smiled.

Although everyone else had begun to relax, Aurim was still anxious. His mother must have noticed, for she again drew his attention to her.

"Now tell me what happened, Aurim. Think it over carefully and answer me as best as you can."

Taking a deep breath, Aurim related his tale, beginning with waking up and feeling the urge to go to the balcony. The emerald sorceress's eyes burned when he mentioned suddenly recalling the presences of Toma and, belatedly, Ssarekai.

What they had been doing, he could not remember. Aurim only knew that something had been happening to the renegade.

When his story was finished, Gwendolyn Bedlam turned to the unnerved Ssarekai, who had spent the last several seconds shaking his head in denial of his young master's condemning statements.

"You've been with us since the beginning, Ssarekai. I won't judge you without first hearing what you have to say."

"I am innocent of thissss, missssstressss!"

"Calm yourself." She touched him on the shoulder, touched him gently so that he could know that she was not going to harm him. "Tell me."

Hissing, the drake sputtered, "I remember nothing of the fantastic tale Massster Aurim related! I would *never* deal with the likesss of that monster Toma! Never!"

Gwen glanced at Aurim. "What night was this? Do you remember *that*?"

He tried hard to recall. The best he could give her was a period of time spread across four days.

Again, Gwen questioned the drake. "Do you recall anything about those nights?"

Ssarekai looked even more distressed. "Missssstressss, I generally sleep very sssssoundly at night. I recall nothing of thosssse nights!"

"Nothing?" Her hand slid an inch or two across his shoulder.

"Nothing."

"I know what I saw!" Aurim exclaimed. Now that he had remembered, it amazed him that he could have ever forgotten. How had it been possible, unless . . . unless Toma had cast some *spell* on him?

Toma in his mind. He recalled *that* now, too.

"His mind has been tampered with."

His initial thought was to believe that his mother was speaking of him. Only when he realized that she was looking at Ssarekai did Aurim understand.

"The spell is very subtle," the enchantress went on. "And unless we were looking for it, it would be almost impossible to notice. I'd wager you have something akin to it in your own mind, Aurim, but because of your power, the spell could not affect you as thoroughly as it did Ssarekai."

The drake should have been pleased to have verification that he was innocent of the young warlock's accusations, but discovering that the renegade had toyed with his mind had quickly destroyed that brief pleasure. Still, Ssarekai was not the type to let his fears rule him. "Can you remove it, Mistress Gwendolyn? I would remember whatever shameful thingsss the monsssster had me do ssso that we can begin tracking him down!"

She concentrated on him, seeming to stare into the drake's very soul.

However, after more than a minute of this, a minute which to Aurim felt as if it were an hour, the enchantress shook her head. "No, not now. He's somehow bound it to you. It will take more effort, more study. I think I would prefer that my husband or perhaps the Gryphon worked with me."

"What if I try, Mother?" asked the young warlock. They had always talked about his potential; why not let him prove himself here and now?

"I know what you're thinking, Aurim, and it's true you have the power, but this is a spell crafted by a black mage far more experienced than you. With time, you'll likely be able to do this without anyone's aid, but this is a predicament requiring long mastery of sorcery."

"I understand." He did, too. Duke Toma no doubt knew a thousand different ways to tangle his spell so that removing it would likely tear apart his victim's mind. Aurim did not wish to be responsible for Ssarekai's death.

It then occurred to him that the drake was not alone in his predicament.

"Mother, what about me?" His voice shook just a little. "I have the same spell on *me*."

Her voice was calm, but her expression hinted at her great concern. "I know, Aurim. I thought about that the moment I realized I could not remove the spell on Ssarekai. However, you should bear one thing in mind. Your ability to focus and use your power far exceeds that of Ssarekai. The fact that you recall anything—and I suspect you've been struggling to do so for days—proves that your own mind is fighting back. It could very well be that this is the beginning of the spell's unraveling. You could recall everything else that happened that night at any moment."

"The headache *has* lessened."

"As I thought it might have. We shall have to see what happens now. This is something that must be monitored carefully."

"Will you still be going to Penacles?"

"I don't know." She eyed both Aurim and Ssarekai. "There are different options, and all of them should be weighed first. I should contact your father, however. Although what I can tell him that won't simply add to his worries, I don't know. If you could only recall more . . . with so much going on in Penacles, I hate to add this. Worse yet, the formal reception is this evening, and once again I've promised to be there." Lady Bedlam uttered a mild curse, which still managed to startle a few of those who had gathered around them. "Cabe has the right of it: this land *does* seem to like nothing better than to complicate and endanger our lives!"

Aurim could only nod grimly. She would get no argument from him on that matter. As far as he was concerned, the Dragonrealm had chosen them to be players in some game. The moment one crisis seemed past, yet a new one would come to life. His father found it all very frustrating and had mentioned quite often that he hoped the peace would mean an end to that game.

Head still throbbing, Aurim's only question was what the land would *do* with its pieces when the game was over.

"SO THE DEVIL has been busy, has he?"

The Gryphon's words rang in Cabe's ears. After much deliberation, Gwen had contacted him and described what had happened to their son and Ssarekai. The warlock was, of course, concerned for the drake, but he could not help being more fearful for his son's life. Toma particularly hated anyone of the name Bedlam; unraveling the spell blocking Aurim's memories might kill him . . . and none too pleasantly, either.

His wife had wanted to bring both victims to Penacles, but then both of them realized that doing so would leave the Manor with no one to keep an eye on it. With Toma's whereabouts unknown, that might be as good as inviting him to wreak more havoc. Neither Cabe nor Gwen planned on leaving Valea in charge; she was not yet old enough or skilled enough to take on a drake as experienced as the renegade. The warlock was wondering whether even *he* was prepared for the drake duke.

"I wish Darkhorse was here," he muttered to the figure standing before him. The two of them had retired to the Gryphon's chambers as soon as the sorcerer became aware of Gwendolyn's mind touching his own.

The news had not been good. That Toma had dared to do what he had done to Aurim and Ssarekai disgusted Cabe. He was only thankful that the renegade had not done worse.

"I've got to go home, Gryphon! I've got to do what I can to help free my son of that spell. There's no telling *what* might happen otherwise!"

The lionbird nodded. "I understand completely, Cabe. You know that."

His statement made the anxious sorcerer feel a little guilty. The Gryphon had lost a son already; Aurim was still alive and healthy.

"We'll have to explain to Toos and the others. I'll also need to get word to Troia."

"You're coming, too?"

The human/avian eyes stared coldly at him. "Did you think I would abandon you on this? Whatever aid I can offer is yours. You should know that by now."

He had been hoping for his old friend's help, but it was good to be reassured. "I can't thank you enough."

They both rose. The Gryphon patted the warlock on the shoulder. "We've always been there for each other and for each other's family. There's no need for thanks. I owe you as much as you think you owe me."

Cabe differed on that, thinking of how the former monarch had shielded a young, confused man running from the hunting armies of the Dragon Emperor. From that moment on, he had considered himself forever in the lionbird's debt.

Their news was received with both dismay and shock. Benjin Traske insisted on returning with them, his deep concern for the mage's family touching Cabe's heart, but the warlock refused, knowing that the scholar was needed in Penacles more than ever. Without Cabe there, it would be up to Traske to aid the Green Dragon in watching over Kyl. Benjin Traske finally gave in, but only with great reluctance.

Toos, of course, approved of their departure. He leaned close and added, "Your children, warlock, are my children too, as are the Gryphon's. It would pain me dearly, son, if anything happened to any one of them."

The drakes, too, were adamant that Cabe return to the Manor. Kyl, like Benjin Traske, also wished to return in the hopes that he might be able to do something for the young warlock. The Green Dragon and Grath reluctantly convinced him to do otherwise, for which Cabe was grateful. He was surprised at the heir's shock at what had happened to Aurim; his son and the drake were evidently dearer friends than he had imagined. The sorcerer had been convinced that Kyl generally associated with Aurim in order to be near Valea, but the concern he read in the drake's visage told him otherwise. It made him just a little uncomfortable to realize that he might have misjudged Kyl, at least in part.

"Things will be fine here, Cabe," Toos concluded. The regent waved a dismissing hand at them. "Go! See to your son and Ssarekai. Good horseman for a drake, that one. He doesn't deserve Toma's games any more than Aurim does."

"We shall do what we can for both of them," replied the Gryphon. "As soon as we are able, one of us will return with news." He turned to Kyl. "Your Majesty . . ."

"Formality isss not necesssary now, Lord Gryphon. All I desssire isss that you do for my friend what you and Massster Bedlam can!"

The others nodded their agreement. Cabe laid a hand on the lionbird's arm. "Ready?"

"Of course."

THEY WERE ALL waiting in the largest of the Manor's underground chambers. The first time Cabe had been down here, many years before, he had expected to find dungeons. To his relief, most of the rooms evidently had been used for storage. There were traces of old magic, but the spells had either been fairly simple or had been cast so long ago that no danger remained. As for the largest chamber, the table and chairs he had discovered in it indicated that its last use had been as a council room or something akin.

Aurim and Ssarekai sat in chairs in the middle of the room. The table had been moved away, no doubt at Gwendolyn's request. The party looked up as Cabe and the Gryphon materialized.

"Was there any difficulty?" the enchantress asked her husband.

"None save that everyone wanted to give what aid they could."

"I'll be sure to thank them when I can." Her gaze shifted to the figure beside Cabe. "For now, I want to thank *you*, Gryphon, for coming."

"As I keep telling your mate, my lady, there is no need to thank me. We are family."

"I wish everyone would stop talking as if I were about to die," interjected an apprehensive Aurim.

"No one is going to die, Aurim," Gwen replied, walking over to the young man, "but you know that Toma's left something in your head. We can't help but feel a little anxious. I know it doesn't help to hear that. Just rest assured that there's nothing Toma's done that we can't untangle."

"I hope," Aurim muttered.

"Aurim!" Gwendolyn Bedlam stared down at her son.

The Gryphon raised his hands in an attempt to calm everyone. "Please! We should begin as soon as possible. Make no mistakes, this is going to take the rest of the day and likely tomorrow, too."

That made the young warlock grimace. "*That long?*"

"I'm afraid so. You won't have to sit there the entire time, though. First we have to see what's there. Then, we have to see how we can get rid of it."

"Let's do it, then," added Cabe as he joined the Gryphon.

"What about the reception?" asked his son. "Won't you miss that?"

"Toos will give our apologies." The Gryphon sighed. "Now, please, Aurim. You have to remain silent for this."

Next to Cabe, Gwendolyn whispered, "I wish Darkhorse was here! I think that with his peculiar brand of sorcery, he would stand a chance of unraveling this spell by himself."

The warlock nodded. He decided it was not the time to express his concerns about the eternal. Darkhorse had been missing far too long for his tastes.

"Let me look first," the Gryphon suggested. "Once I have an idea what is there, I will know better how to proceed." He met Aurim's nervous gaze and chuckled. "I should thank you, young warlock. You have no idea how bored I am at receptions. Before your mother contacted us, I had just resigned myself to looking forward to five or six hours of empty talk and stuffy faces. It really was kind of you to drag me away from such wonderful entertainment."

Aurim smiled, which Cabe suspected was the Gryphon's intention. His subject more relaxed now, the lionbird summoned his power. Although they could not see his probe, the others could sense the spell progressing.

Forced for the moment to wait, the warlock thought over his old comrade's words. More a creature of action than speech, the Gryphon despised affairs of state. But at the moment, Cabe would have preferred nothing more than fighting boredom at the royal reception in Penacles. At least that would have meant that his son, his entire family, was well.

His reverie was shattered by an intake of breath by the Gryphon. "Well, what do we have here?"

Everyone leaned forward. Anxiety spread once more across Aurim's pale countenance.

"What is it?" Cabe asked.

The Gryphon sighed, then looked at his companions. "This is going to take much longer than I had hoped." If it was possible for a creature with a beak to grimace, then the lionbird had done just that. "We seem to have run into a problem."

# XIV

GRATH OBSERVED THE reception from his usual place a bit behind his brother. Penacles he found more fascinating than Talak, possibly because Penacles was a kingdom built to honor knowledge, one of Grath's personal gods. The young drake prided himself on his mind. He had already discovered that the majority of adults, be they drake or human, were his inferiors in terms of intellect. Grath did not hold that against them, though. He was certain that he had been born with a superior brain. After all, had not his dam, his mother, once been a part of the clan Purple, the dragons that had ruled Penacles before the Gryphon? All knew that Lord Purple had been the guiding force in the Turning War, not Grath's sire, the emperor. Had he not died in mortal combat with Master Bedlam's grandfather, Grath was certain that the Dragon King would have eventually seized control from Gold, the emperor.

Hatchlings were not supposed to know their mothers. All were raised in a communal setting with the matriarch overseeing everything. Grath, being who he was, had had little trouble in tracing his background. It prided him to know that his mother had come from the most intelligent, the most cunning of the dragon clans. That did not mean that he did not appreciate his late sire. If not for Gold, Grath might have never been born. He owed the late Dragon Emperor for that, if nothing else.

Toos was introducing them to yet another functionary. Grath waited for Kyl to perform his peacock routine, then bowed when it was his own turn to exchange greetings. His brother was every inch what one expected from the heir to a throne and Grath took great pride in that, for he felt that he above all others was responsible. Kyl followed his instructions to the letter and performed as well as any trained dog. That he did not realize what was happening, Grath could forgive him. Kyl was intelligent, true, but hardly on the same level as his younger brother. At least he was intelligent enough to realize how quickly he would flounder without his brilliant, loyal counselor by his side.

*It's not who sits on the throne that rules,* Grath's mentor had told him. *It's the one who has his ear.* The truth of that was plain for him to see. Queen Erini truly ruled in Talak. Her husband could deny her nothing. Here in Penacles it was the same. Toos the Regent—a fairly knowledgeable human, he was willing to concede— ever listened to the counsel of the Gryphon.

Grath admired the Gryphon, who pretended he no longer ruled but in reality did. The young drake had once dreamed of being emperor himself, but now it made so much more sense to stand behind the throne. If things changed and it became necessary to step forward, the support would be there.

He had the best of all possible worlds awaiting him.

It would have been preferable if Master and Mistress Bedlam or the Lord Gryphon were also here. They were clever enough to appreciate his skill at handling his brother, even if they did not realize the extent of that handling. Grath had been warned to stay some distance from them, especially his soon-to-be former guardians, but this was one point on which he and his mentor differed. The Bedlams were his family, too, and he saw no difficulty in maintaining a balance between the two aspects of his life. Besides, was it not planned that Valea would join Kyl after he assumed the throne? Better to keep on good terms with her parents for when the time came to convince them of the inevitability of Valea's departure for the caverns of the Dragon Emperor.

That did not mean, of course, that he would not be willing to destroy them if it proved necessary for the success of his plans.

Something caught Grath's attention. He shifted his gaze from the attractive young human woman curtsying before his brother and discovered that Lord Green was trying to gain his attention.

Turning to Kyl, he whispered, "Lord Green desires my attendance."

His brother nodded his permission, never taking his eyes off the woman. Grath forced away a condescending smile as he left his brother. More so than him, Kyl had a fondness for human females. It had made planting the suggestion of seducing Valea that much easier. Kyl actually enjoyed her company, although that was not going to stop him from flirting with others. Grath was more dedicated; when her dashing emperor finally tired of her, Valea would find Grath waiting. She was everything he desired in a female: exotic beauty, a mind, personal strength, and, best of all, the power of a Bedlam.

The dragon king looked impatient by the time Grath joined him. He respected Lord Green very much, even if the elder drake seemed a bit too subservient to his brother. Yet, the Dragon King also found much time for him. How ironic it would be if the tall, hellish knight knew the truth. That was one problem that Grath had not yet solved. If the Dragon King discovered what the young drake was involved in, it would mean having to do something that Grath did not find appetizing.

*It won't happen, though. I have control now! I have become the kingmaker, the power behind the future of the entire Dragonrealm.*

"How isss he doing out there?"

"Perfect, of course." Grath thought that the Dragon King had become too nervous of late, as if anything could go wrong at this point. The meeting with Lord Blue, the Dragon Kings' chosen representative, was a foregone conclusion what with Grath to coach Kyl through it. Soon, Kyl would renounce his name and take on the mantle of Gold, Dragon Emperor.

"I do not like thisss." The Green Dragon was more sibilant than usual, a definite sign of excessive worry as far as Grath was concerned. "The Bedlams are gone and the Gryphon with them. The demon steed is also missing. Our defenses are weakened."

The Bedlams had sent word just prior to the reception that they would be unable to attend. The cunning spell attached to Aurim's memory had so far defeated their best efforts. Toma had planned well when he had devised that one. Grath could not help but admire the spell's obvious complexity. How many were there who could so cleverly befuddle his guardians?

"Things will be all right, my lord," he answered dutifully. "We are in Penacles, after all. There is no better guarded kingdom than this one save Talak, and yet there we faced much more resentment. Here, people already accept us . . . to a point, of course." Grath hoped to find reasons to make future excursions to the City of Knowledge before necessity demanded that it be returned to drake control. Since the latter would not take place for some time, he did not feel too concerned.

His eyes suddenly focused on a fantastic figure entering the reception. Here was one whom Kyl would find most appealing, he thought. *And so do I*, the young drake was forced to admit.

There was no one in the Dragonrealm like the Lady Troia, mate of the Gryphon. She had met him across the sea, at the beginning of the revolt against the Aramite Empire. She was lithe and graceful, yet still a predator, her tawny color in keeping with her feline appearance. When she smiled—a bit uncertainly, he thought—her slightly pointed teeth reminded him of a female drake. She also had talons that were supposed to be every bit as deadly as those of Grath's race.

If not for his desire for Valea, Grath would have been tempted to see what a flirtation with the cat-woman would have revealed. Likely his dismemberment, if what they said about her love for her mate was true. Still, he doubted that knowing that would stop his brother from trying. Kyl *had* to flirt. It was one trait of his that, while frequently useful, Grath was as yet unable to completely control.

"I would have thought that the Lady Troia would have remained home with her son sssince her mate hasss been called away," muttered the Green Dragon. "She should not be here."

"Why?"

"She isss also with child," responded the Dragon King, as if that answered everything. Grath tried to puzzle it out, failed, then decided that it was not worth his time.

"Perhaps she has a message from the Gryphon. Perhaps the Bedlams and he are preparing to return to Penacles."

Lord Green looked at him, but said nothing. Grath decided there and then that he would mention to Kyl that perhaps it would be an excellent notion to allow the Dragon King to return to his own domain. The drake had worked hard to bring them to this point, but it was clear that he needed some rest.

Without warning, the Dragon King started toward the Gryphon's mate. After a moment, Grath followed, in great part because he wanted to see Lady Troia up close.

The cat-woman noticed them coming and, unlike most of those attending, gave them an open smile. This did not surprise Grath, who was aware that one of the Gryphon's closest comrades during the war against the Aramite Empire had been the very scion of the Blue Dragon, a great drake warrior called Morgis. Through Morgis, Troia had perhaps become more used to the drake race than anyone else at the reception.

"It's . . . Lord Green . . . is that the way to say it? I always forget."

The Dragon King executed a slight bow. "That is one of the accepted forms of address."

"Would you prefer 'Your Majesty'?"

"With my emperor present, it does not strike me as proper. 'Lord Green' isss perfectly fine."

She looked him over. "If you were of a more bluish tint, I'd *swear* that you were Morgis."

"We do tend to look much alike to your kind."

Another very feline smile spread across her fascinating face. Grath realized he had not yet bowed and quickly did so. Seeing her hand near enough, he followed his impulse and took it in his own. To the Lady Troia's flattered amusement, he kissed it.

"Not *all* of you look the same. You've become a daring one, Grath. Do you stalk the same prey as your brother?"

It took him a moment to decipher her comment. When he had done so, the young drake smiled. "Kyl does well enough for both of us, my lady."

"I'm sure he does."

"What brings you to the reception?" the Dragon King asked without warning. "Are your mate and the Bedlams returning?"

Her smile changed to a frown. "I only wish. No, they're still hoping to solve the riddle. The Gryphon contacted me long enough to let me know that they would not be returning this evening. Cabe and Gwendolyn don't plan to cease their efforts until their son and the drake with him are free of this Duke Toma's spell." Her light, short fur began to bristle. "He sounds as foul a creature as the Senior Keeper D'Rak!"

Grath had no idea who this D'Rak had been save that by his name he had been an Aramite, a wolf raider. Lord Green, however, nodded his agreement. Grath made a mental note to ask the Dragon King about D'Rak and wolf raiders in general. Their empire might be in ruins, but a number of their ships still prowled the seas as pirates. Desperate men like that might be willing to bargain their services to a great power.

"I decided that with everyone else gone, it would be a good idea for me to be here. If there's trouble, I'll be around to lend a claw." She unsheathed a handful of deadly talons impressive even by drake standards.

"But you have children of your own to be concerned about," insisted Lord Green. "Both your son and the one within you."

The young drake could not detect any swelling. Of course the gown prevented a better examination.

Troia laughed, an enchanting, throaty sound. "Your concern is appreciated, Lord Green, but I come from a sturdy people. I fought in battle only days before our first child, Demion, was born. It was not by choice, but it gives you an idea of how resilient my folk are. The way I am *now* will by no means slow me, I can promise you that! There is almost a full month to go. As for our other son, I have good people watching him." She glanced past him at where the regent and Kyl were standing. "Would you excuse me, Lord Green? I want to ask a favor of Toos before I forget."

"Certainly, my lady."

They both bowed as the cat-woman moved on. Grath watched her walk with renewed appreciation for females, then recalled himself. It would not do to be so coarse among present company. What he did reflected as much on his brother as what Kyl himself did. Still, he was amazed that she could be so far along. What he could see did not in the least remind him of any of the pregnant human females he had seen.

His gaze drifted to Lord Green, who appeared rather preoccupied. The elder drake stared as the Lady Troia joined Kyl and Toos. For some reason, Grath doubted the Dragon King's interest centered around the cat-woman.

"Grath, have you ssseen your tutor lately?"

The question caught the young drake by surprise, but he quickly recovered. "Scholar Trassske is not one for receptions, my lord. He felt it would be best if he retired to his chambers. I believe he isss studying the progress of the school of sorcery. The Gryphon planned to take him to visit it the day after tomorrow."

"He may have changed his mind, but feels uncertain about arriving so late. Go and see whether that isss the case."

"But—"

"Do it, Grath." The Green Dragon walked toward Kyl and his companions, preventing any further protest the younger drake would have made.

Grath hissed quietly, incensed by the Green Dragon's tone and attitude. He was *not* a servitor to be talked to so. He was the brother of the new Dragon Emperor, not to mention that emperor's counselor. The Dragon King should be treating him with *deference*, not indifference.

Still, as much as it rankled him, Grath chose to obey. Lord Green had been good to him for the most part and was still a necessary ally. He would forgive the Dragon King his mistake this time, but if it happened again, Grath would remember for the future. *Patience and memory are important driving forces*, his mentor had said, *allowing one to survive for years until the time is ripe for vengeance.*

As usual, it all made perfect sense to him.

Lord Green wished him to find Benjin Traske. Very well, then, he would find Benjin Traske. It would give him the opportunity to ask a few questions that had arisen this evening.

The walk was a long one, and at other times he would have contemplated sending a messenger, but Grath knew that this once it would be better if he obeyed the command to the letter. He walked through the halls, unaccompanied but not alone. Toos had indicated that this night no escort would be necessary for the drakes, but that did not mean that security had been relaxed. Tonight, sentries lined the major corridors, the regent's precautions against

assassins and possibly wayward drakes. Grath admired their order and stead-
fastness as he walked. Too many drakes still underestimated their human counterparts, but he did not. Underestimating your opponents was the best way to
open yourself to utter defeat.

There were guards even in the corridor outside of the chambers that had
been set aside for Grath and the other visitors. Again, it was supposed to be for
their own safety, but he was certain that the regent had also ordered the soldiers
stationed here in the hopes that it would discourage his draconian guests from
wandering off to where they were not desired. The rooms he sought were far-
thest down the hallway. He walked past the remaining sentries, faced the door,
and softly rapped on it.

The door swung open without preamble. The face of the tutor appeared.
"What is it, Grath?"

Disconcerted, he still managed to reply, "I was sent here by Lord Green. He
thought that you might yet make an appearance. He insisted that I personally
go to you and ask if that might be so."

"The Dragon King insisted that you come for me?"

Grath nodded.

The massive figure stepped out into the hall. He was clad in the robes of a
scholar, making it appear as if he were just about to begin class. The nearest
guards glanced the tutor's direction, but when they saw who it was, they immediately resumed their statuelike stances.

"Did he say why he wanted to know?"

"No, Master Traske," replied the young drake after a quick look at the sentries. "He simply insisted I go, then walked over to where Kyl and the regent
were standing."

"Did he now? I'd not planned to be there, but if Lord Green is so interested,
it would behoove me to come."

That was somewhat of a relief to Grath, who was not certain how the
Dragon King would have reacted if he had returned alone. Eyeing the guards
once more, Grath asked, "Would you prefer that I wait out here while you prepare yourself?"

A brief smile spread across the bearded face. "Yes, that would be good of
you."

Benjin Traske slipped back inside. Grath took up a place just to the side of
the door and watched the guards. They did not even so much as twitch. These
were veterans, men who had fought in battle. The young drake hoped that no
reason would arise that would force him to fight one of them.

The door opened but a minute later. The scholar, slightly neater but overall
looking much the same as he had a moment before, stepped out into the hall

again. After making certain that the door was secure, he turned and began marching down the corridor.

Throughout most of the journey back, the large figure beside Grath said nothing. The drake attempted questions once or twice, but they were met with short, unenlightening responses. Grath gave up and concentrated his efforts on keeping up with the other. His companion was setting a swifter pace than he had expected, almost as if there was some urgent need to appear at the reception as soon as possible. He would have liked to have asked if there was some reason for the speed, but if one of the sentries overheard, it might make for some misdirected conclusions.

As they neared the ballroom, Grath noticed that the reception had grown much quieter during his absence. He wondered if perhaps something had occurred that had made Toos call an early end to the event. If so, it could not have been anything terrible, for the few voices that he did hear seemed as unconcerned as he would have expected.

"Is something the matter, boy?"

"No . . . nothing."

A soldier opened one of the doors for them. Grath nodded in the manner of a superior to a servant, but his cool demeanor was shattered by what he saw in the ballroom.

It would have perhaps been more appropriate to say what he did *not* see. More than half of the guests had vanished. Small groups clustered here and there, but the bulk of those who had come to meet the new Dragon Emperor were gone. As were, Grath realized in a quick, anxious survey of the ballroom, Toos, Lady Troia, the Green Dragon, and Kyl.

A heavy hand clutched his shoulder. "Where did they go, Grath?"

"I don't know! They were here when I left."

Traske looked around. His eyes alighted on a trio of elderly men wearing robes like his own. "Wait here a moment."

Grath was tired of being commanded by everyone, but he did as he was told. The scholar marched over to his counterparts and immediately questioned them, ignoring their annoyance over his rude interruption of their conversation. One of them made a reply that Grath could not hear, a reply which was then apparently supported by a nod of the head from another in the trio. Benjin Traske gave them a curt response, then returned to the waiting drake. His expression puzzled Grath; it looked as if his companion was suffering a number of conflicting emotions, none of them good.

"They are outside. The arena. Some tournament. I was not told *anything* about this."

"Tournament? You mean the chess game?"

"Yesss . . ." The huge man came to a decision. "Come, Grath. We do not want to be late."

"What are—"

Grath's question died abruptly as his companion glared at him. Clamping his mouth shut, he followed the other through the ballroom.

TOOS WATCHED THE game unfold with uneasiness in his heart. There was no reason for him to be anxious, not with the safeguards that he and the Gryphon had implemented for this visit, but simply having the drake heir out in the open like this, with not even a roof to protect his head, made the regent uncomfortable. The night sky was dark, there being no moon out. He kept imagining Seekers or some other airborne danger circling above, biding quietly until the proper time. A part of him knew that it was paranoia, but another part argued that there was a basis for his fears.

His entire *life* was a basis for those fears.

Kyl, with the subtle aid of Toos himself, was playing opposite Baron Andrean. Toos had confidence enough in Andrean to know that the aristocrat would do his best to see to it that his royal adversary looked good. As to whether the baron would actually allow the young drake to win, the regent could only guess. Baron Andrean was an intelligent man. He was capable of judging what results would best serve Penacles.

The dragon heir was actually doing fairly well against the much more experienced Andrean. Either that, or Andrean was much more skilled at manipulating the game than Toos had ever imagined. Both players were fairly even at this point. Andrean had a slight advantage, but it was one based more on the strength of his champions than numbers. Through sheer circumstance, the baron had drawn some of the best of the guardsmen who played as pieces. Fortunately, Kyl had a few masters of his own.

In point of fact, the young drake's knight was about to defeat Andrean's pawn. This particular combat had gone on for more than the normal two or three minutes. Since they were confined to a single square, duels by champions often ended when one player was forced beyond the boundaries. In this case, both men had succeeded in remaining in place. However, the knight had finally beaten down the defenses of the baron's pawn and had the man only inches from the back edge of the square.

A final blow ended the battle. Spectators applauded as the pawn stumbled backward, not only stepping out of bounds but also falling on his back. It was as clean a victory as any. Clean and without any bloodshed. Toos was aware that some of his guests would have liked to have seen blood, but that was not the point of the game. Anyone exhibiting more than a little fondness for what little blood was spilled was not invited back for quite some time. Most learned from that. To earn the regent's disfavor was something few desired.

Kyl was considering his next move. Toos leaned forward and whispered, "Beware Andrean's bishops. He likes to put them into play fairly quickly. Likely when he does, he'll go for your knight using both of them."

A slight nod was all he received in response from the young drake. Kyl already understood just how unorthodox the baron's playing was and appreciated his host's guidance. However, how the drake chose to counter the move was entirely up to the emperor-to-be himself.

With his part done for now, the tall, narrow regent studied the assembled guests. Still nothing out of the ordinary, but the same sense of uneasiness that had allowed him to survive decades of mercenary work insisted that something was amiss. Kyl glanced at the Green Dragon, who stood off to one side with the draconian sentries. The Dragon King had them spread out and ready for immediate action. There had been room enough for them behind the heir, but the Dragon King had insisted that they would be of more use out in the open, where they could better watch over the entire area. As it was, the two bodyguards who always accompanied Kyl stood behind both the heir and the regent. Toos, who was a good judge of warriors, thought they looked capable enough, if somewhat distant. *But then, they're drakes, aren't they, Toos? You know them only from across the battlefield, not from the same side.* It was strange to have drakes at his back, but the regent's own bodyguards also stood behind the master of Penacles and his guest. Toos had the utmost confidence in his own soldiers; they had ways of dealing quickly with treacherous drakes.

And Toos had a few tricks of his own.

A disturbance near the entrance caught his attention. He turned to see Grath and Benjin Traske. The scholar tried to hide it, but it was clear to the trained eye of the former mercenary that he was upset about something. Even if Traske's face and form had not indicated anxiety, Grath's own evident nervousness was enough to garner the regent's concern.

Time passed, the game went on, and still nothing happened. Toos wondered whether the danger was all in his mind, but whenever he looked around, he felt somehow vindicated in his beliefs. Grath, the Green Dragon, Traske . . . wherever he looked, the regent found faces whose concern matched his own. It was as if they were all waiting for something to happen, something that *should* have happened by this time.

Kyl hissed. The wary general shifted his gaze immediately to the heir, but the drake's reaction was at the loss of a valuable piece and not because of any danger. Kyl glanced his way. "If hisss championsss can defeat my king, I am lossst!"

Pulling his thoughts back to the game, Toos saw that his royal guest's summation was correct. Andrean had two men, a knight and a rook, in position. Another rook stood nearby. All the baron had to do was give the command, and that piece would put the drake's king into checkmate. Kyl's man would then have to fight each piece until he had either defeated all three or had fallen to one of them. Sizing the soldiers up, Toos was willing to give the heir's man one, maybe two combats, but fatigue would prevent him from salvaging the game for his player.

Kyl's king carried shield and mace and knew well the advantages and disadvantages of each. As Baron Andrean commanded his second rook forward, the champion readied himself. Under the rules that Toos had formulated, Andrean could choose any of the three with which to begin. Kyl's man had already positioned himself so as to face the knight. Toos nodded; it was the same opponent that he would have chosen. To the regent's amused surprise, however, Kyl's adversary chose instead to use his first rook, the least of his three champions. There were a few murmurs in the crowd, but most did not comprehend what Andrean was doing. The regent did, and the knowledge brought the shadow of a smile to his foxlike features. Andrean, very much the politician, was giving his opponent as much aid as he possibly could. The game was already his, but if Kyl's man could defeat at least one rival, then so much the better for the heir's showing. The closer the game appeared to be, the better the dragon heir would feel.

Weapons clanged as the rook took on the king. Champions were ofttimes given the option of choosing their own weapons, and so this was a battle of mace against scepter, the latter in reality simply a more elaborate mace. Both men struck hard at the shields, each hoping to knock the other's defense away or at least open a hole. People cheered, and not a few bets were placed on the outcome. As an old soldier, Toos had no qualms about betting as long as it was kept under certain limitations. Now and then he liked to make a bet himself. The years had given him a practiced eye when it came to the art of war.

The rook tried to get his mace under the king's shield in order to lift the latter away, but the drake's champion turned the trick against the younger soldier, pushing down with his full mass. The rook's grip loosened on the mace as the weapon was pulled down. Wasting no precious time, the king struck with his own weapon, almost getting around the other's shield. His opponent struggled to free his mace even as the king attacked again, but the elder champion would not permit that. Changing tactics, Kyl's man suddenly turned his assault from the rook's shield to the imprisoned mace, bringing his scepter down on it.

Several people gasped, thinking that the king intended to crush the hand
of his opponent, a move that Toos would have condemned. The general,
however, understood what the champion was doing. As the mace came
down, the rook, obviously stunned by what he thought was happening,
pulled his hand back as if bitten. The mace continued to come down, but
midway it suddenly shifted. Instead of striking where his adversary's hand
would have been, the king brought his scepter down on the upper shaft
of the other mace. Had the rook realized that his hand had never been
in danger, he could have used that moment to seize the wrist of Kyl's
champion and possibly balance out the odds. As it was, the rook was now
weaponless. The king knocked the loose mace far away and wasted no time
pressing his attack. The bout ended but seconds later, to the sounds of
great cheering.

Kyl was hissing, but Toos recognized his reaction as one of extreme pleasure. The heir had half-risen out of his chair, the better to view the battle.
As Andrean's knight stepped forward, the young drake rose more. A slight
frown escaped the regent; he hoped that the heir was not given to bloodlust
like some drakes. Toos looked around for Grath and discovered that neither
he nor the scholar had moved from the doorway. Unlike Kyl, the younger
drake still appeared more apprehensive than anything else. He was glad to see
that Kyl's brother, at least, was not given to bloodlust, but he also wondered
what worried Grath so. When the opportunity presented itself, the general
intended to talk to the lad about it. Perhaps doing so would clear up some
of his own mysterious anxieties.

"Thisss one will be much clossser!" remarked the dragon heir to his host.

Forcing himself back into the game, Toos agreed. "You must be prepared to
accept it if your champion loses, Lord Kyl. The knight's very skilled."

"I am prepared, General. I do not give up hope jussst yet, though. If I lossse,
I lossse; if victory isss sssalvaged, ssso much the better."

The statement pleased Toos, more because of the way it was said. Kyl's tone
indicated he meant every word. *Perhaps I've misjudged him. He might be more level-headed
than I thought.*

His attention was again diverted, this time by the Green Dragon, who
signaled to Grath and Benjin Traske to join him. The Dragon King had a
goblet in one hand, though, and when he shifted position, the better for
those he was signaling to see him, the hand with the goblet bumped against
one of his guards.

The goblet slipped from his hand, its contents spilling on the floor. The draconian soldiers nearest to him converged on the fallen cup.

Snapping his fingers, the regent summoned one of his own men. The man saluted and waited for orders. Toos pointed at the huddled figures. "Get someone over there now. His Lordship might need something to clean himself off with. Make certain not a spot remains and give the Dragon King whatever other aid he desires."

"Yes, sir."

Kyl, still standing, had not noticed what was happening. His own attention was fixed on the two combatants. Toos blinked. He could not even recall the beginning of the bout, but the drake's champion and Vergoth's man had obviously already been at it for several seconds. The skill of the knight was already telling, however, for Kyl's king was beginning to lose ground. The general scratched his long, narrow chin. He had expected better of the king, but that was the way of the game. The soldiers who took part did not play the same way twice. One time, they might seem unstoppable; other days, they might fall after only a few blows. It was part of what made his variation on the game of chess a much more interesting one in his opinion.

The sense of danger again pervaded his being. Yet, surveying the scene, Toos could find nothing amiss. Servants had not yet reached the Dragon King, who, surrounded by his own soldiers, was virtually invisible. Grath and the scholar were wending their way toward the lord of Dagora, but they appeared to be safe. What could—

As it had happened so many times in the past, he saw what was to be. No one, not even the Gryphon, truly understood the workings of the former mercenary's limited yet potent magic. Toos himself did not, for he had never met another in whom the power had so focused itself in one direction. Had he been asked to transport himself from one end of the arena to another, the regent would have been unable to comply. Had he been asked to levitate a sword, even that would have been beyond him. Yet, despite this seeming lack of skill, he had one of the most unusual gifts of sorcery, one that had saved his life time and time again.

He had heard of only one mage skilled in prophecy: Yalak of the Dragon Masters, who had once created a crystal egg that could show images of possible future events. Knowing prophecy had not prevented Yalak from being murdered by Azran Bedlam, however, which was why Toos had always been careful to cultivate his ability and had shared its full secrets with no one, not even the Gryphon. He had always felt guilty about that, but what was done was done.

The image came at its own chosen time, just like all the others. He had only time to gasp at its implications and marvel at the audacity of the one behind it before he became aware that the true event was *just* taking place.

It began with the striking of the two champions' weapons against one another. The mace of Kyl's king was knocked from the warrior's hand and, before the startled eyes of the many, flew almost unerringly toward the astounded heir. As it neared, however, it was clear to most that it would fall short. Kyl took a step back, but did not otherwise protect himself from the misshaped projectile.

Only Toos knew that the true threat was only now coming into play. Leaping toward the drake, he cried, "Get down!"

The former mercenary reached Kyl just as the draconian guards stirred to life. Perhaps they had not heard his cry, or perhaps they felt that it was their duty to protect their master, not his. Toos only knew that he had barely thrust the dragon heir to the floor when a massive, armored figure shoved him aside, causing the general to spin in a half circle.

Something hard and swift thudded against his back.

He thought at first that the mace had somehow managed to fly over the arena wall, but then a fierce pain wracked the general's chest and it was all he could do to keep from collapsing there and then. Grimacing, the regent forced open his eyes, which he could not recall closing, and peered down. To his surprise, Toos saw no sign of the wound that should have been there. Then, as his legs began to buckle, it occurred to him that the entry point had to have been from the back. The bolt, or whatever the assassin had used, had not quite pierced him all the way through.

The world spun around. Toos fell to his knees, which did nothing to alleviate the agony. Around him he knew that there was panic. Someone called out to him, but it was as if they were receding even as they spoke.

He knew he was dying. For once, his magic-wrought ability to outmaneuver his foes had worked against him. He *had* beaten the assassin, for Kyl must certainly still live, but it had *not* been the general's intention to make himself the new target.

*Sloppy,* Toos thought. *Been away from the field too long. Shouldn't have listened to those jackanapes! Next maneuver, I go out with the men . . . get myself back in shape. . . .*

Things grew hazy. Someone was in front of him. Toos tried to focus. The figure coalesced into that of the Gryphon, but that was nonsense, the regent knew. The Gryphon was with the Bedlams.

He chuckled, which caused him to shake as renewed pain coursed through him. Toos tried to speak to the imaginary Gryphon, but all that escaped his lips was blood. Putting one last great effort into his attempt at speech, he told the apparition, "It's . . . yours again . . ."

Toos closed his eyes, knowing that the meaning of his words would be clear. After so many years of trying, he had *finally* found a way to force his old commander to reassume the throne. It was the Gryphon who had made Penacles what it was. Toos had simply been its caretaker while the lionbird recovered from his great labors. Now, however, the regent's work was done. It was time to move on.

A sound caught his attention. Horns. He had little trouble recognizing the notes; it was the call to arms of his old company, the one in which he had first followed his commander.

Rising, Toos the Fox unsheathed his sword and went to join his old comrades in one last, glorious battle.

# XV

"THEY'VE KILLED HIM, Cabe...." The Gryphon snarled, his claws unsheathing and sheathing. His entire body quivered with unreleased fury. His mane bristled as the lionbird struggled to maintain his control. "They *killed* Toos!"

Cabe Bedlam stared in horror at the grisly tableau before him. The regent of Penacles lay face forward in the Gryphon's arms, a scarlet blossom of blood across his back. The bolt had penetrated so deeply that it had nearly burst through the rib cage, if the warlock was any judge. It was a wonder that the old mercenary had lived even the few moments he had. That he had done so had made the situation that much more tragic, for Toos had lived just long enough for the Gryphon to return, then had died almost in his former commander's arms.

When the Gryphon had looked up from his so-far futile attempts to free the minds of Aurim and Ssarekai and warned about danger in Penacles, his companions had been stunned. Cabe knew that his old friend kept some sort of link with both his mate and his former officer, but not even the warlock had known how strong or immediate those links were.

The lionbird had not even paused to explain. He had asked permission to leave, received it, and had vanished, leaving the Bedlams to recover their wits on their own. Naturally, Cabe and his wife had followed as quickly as they could, but even then it had been too late.

The arena was in chaos. Guests ran about in full panic and there were shouts of "Assassin!" from all corners. Toos was sprawled on the floor of one of the boxes used by the chess players. Kyl was gone, evidently spirited away by his two bodyguards. Around the fallen regent and his former commander stood a wary and fearful group of human soldiers.

Cabe had never seen the Gryphon this distraught. It was clear to the warlock that he would have to handle matters for the moment. "Which way did the bolt come from?"

One of the guards pointed upward and to his right. He added, "Our men already give chase, Master Warlock! We shall have them before the hour is ended!"

The mage was not so certain. "Have you discovered how they got so close?"

The sentries looked frustrated. The spokesman slowly replied, "No, Master Warlock. . . ."

"This . . . smells of . . . of magic," Gwen commented. Cabe glanced at her. There were tears streaming from her eyes, but there was also a hardening in her face. He knew that his own visage now held a similar cast.

He made a decision. Too much time had already passed. "You stay here with the Gryphon, I'll—"

Cabe was interrupted by a group of pale guardsmen. Two of them carried bundles. An officer, a captain by rank, gave the Gryphon a half-hearted salute, which the lionbird did not even notice. Cabe signaled the officer his way.

"You know who I am?"

"Yes, Master Bedlam!"

"You can tell me everything. Have you found them?"

This last caused the captain to grimace. "In a matter of speaking, my lord. . . ."

"*Please*, Captain . . ." begged one of the men. In one hand he carried a glove that appeared to be full of some substance. The Bedlams glanced at one another, then Cabe indicated that the officer should explain his words.

Swallowing, the captain indicated the bundles two of his men were carrying. "I think . . . uh . . . I think this is all that's left of them, Master Bedlam."

"What?" For the first time, the Gryphon acknowledged the presence of the newcomers. Still clutching the form of his old comrade, he glared at the captain and added, "What do you mean?"

"One of the men s-saw it, Your Majesty." The captain had the bundles brought forward. He also signaled the man holding the one glove to join them. "The assassin . . . he . . . he was . . . my lord . . . he was *crumbling!* Darion saw him and Darion doesn't lie, Your Majesty!"

"Aye! I'll swear to it, my lord!" added one of the guards laden with a bundle. The burly soldier looked around as if daring someone to contradict his words. "It's truth!"

"Explain in more detail," encouraged Gwendolyn Bedlam.

His arms filled, the guard called Darion used his chin to indicated his captain. "He said it all! I saw the man . . . it *was* a man, lordships—ugly and bearded. Looked like a northern type maybe. All I really saw was him look my way, then his eyes, they went wide, they did." The veteran hesitated, still unnerved by the sight. "Then . . . then, he just went to pieces, like he dried out and crumbled to *sand!*"

The captain took over. "Your Majesty, we brought all that was left of him. Some others found a second figure, but he . . . he was already dust."

The Gryphon looked up to his two comrades. "Could you . . . do you think you can verify . . . ?"

Gwendolyn nodded. Without a word, the two spellcasters took the bundles from the grateful warriors. The third man held out the filled glove toward Cabe.

"What's this?" the warlock asked.

"It's one . . . uh . . . it's one o' them, lordship."

Cabe almost snatched his hand back, but if the guards had forced themselves to bring back some of the remains, it behooved him to do what he could with it.

The enchantress inspected her bundle. "What about the weapon? Where is it?"

There was something stiff in Cabe's bundle. Gingerly, he opened up the cloth, which appeared to be some sort of glittering cape folded inside out, and discovered a crossbow. Oddly, there were no more bolts to go with it. "I've got it here."

"These will need a more thorough examination later," Lady Bedlam commented, her interest in discovering the truth for the moment overwhelming her sorrow, "but there is something we can do now."

Both of them were already at work. Those who had gathered around watched in wary curiosity. To the eye, all that the two did was pass a hand over each bundle, Cabe also repeating the process for the glove and its grotesque contents. He gasped as his fingers traced patterns over the glove. It was as the guard had said; this had once been human. He could tell no more about the unfortunate assassin save that whatever had killed him was no ordinary sorcery.

"This . . . is . . . *strange*," was all his wife could add at first.

From where he squatted, the Gryphon cocked his head. There was an unhealthy look in his avian visage, Cabe thought. "You said 'strange.' How so?"

"It reminds me of . . ." She looked at her husband for aid.

"We both know what it reminds us of." The warlock hesitated, but when he saw the further tensing of the Gryphon's body, he decided that a swift response was the better choice regardless of what results the truth might then bring. "It reminds both of us of Darkhorse. It bears his trace."

"Or something akin to him," interjected the enchantress. There had once been a time when Gwendolyn Bedlam would have been the first to call Darkhorse demon, but now she was his champion. He had saved the lives of all the Bedlams more than once.

"There is nothing we know of in all the Dragonrealm that is akin to Darkhorse." Yet it was clear that the lionbird did not think the eternal was responsible for the day's tragedy. He looked down at the still form in his arms and in a much gentler voice added, "But perhaps he, like old Toos, has become a pawn."

"He's still missing," whispered Cabe, his blood going cold. He had feared that the shadow steed had been captured by the one who had set the magical snares, and now it seemed that that fear was likely a thing of substance.

The Gryphon started to rise, but could not without leaving the body of Toos lying alone on the cold floor. Freeing one hand, he waved the nearest sentries over. "Take him gently. Bring him to his bedchamber and have the doctors clean him up as well as they can. I also want a pair of you to take these bundles and bring them to my rooms. They should be guarded until I have time to more thoroughly inspect them. I shall give you further orders when you return."

The ease with which leadership shifted from the murdered regent to the former king did not surprise Cabe Bedlam in the least. The Gryphon was legend and the regent had always made it quite clear that he would have gladly stepped aside at any time. There was also inherent in the lionbird's manner a natural sense of command, one which made others willing to follow him. He was, the warlock concluded, meant to be a leader, and now, despite his best attempts to forever discard such a role, it appeared as if the Gryphon once more had a kingdom to rule.

With great care, the guards slowly lifted the body of Toos from the floor. The Gryphon, rising, watched each and every movement. Under such a baleful gaze, the men dared not fail in maintaining their holds. No one desired to test the wrath of the distraught monarch.

Two of the men who had brought the remains of the assassins took both the bundles and the glove back. Cabe was not sorry to give up the gruesome objects. The Gryphon was welcome to do what he wished with them as long as it helped them discover who was responsible for the death of Toos.

When the guards and their terrible burden were out of sight, the Gryphon at last returned his attention to the mages. From the crowd still gathered emerged his mate, Troia. She moved past the Bedlams and enveloped her husband in her arms. The cat-woman was well aware of the place Toos had had in the Gryphon's life. The tall, cunning general had been family, a brother in spirit if not in blood.

Taking hold of his wife, the Gryphon looked at Cabe Bedlam. There was now a cold calm in his voice that did not bode well. "I want the one behind this, my friend. Was it . . . do you think it was *Talak*?"

"There's no proof one way or the other," Cabe quickly responded, the notion of a war between the two powerful kingdoms filling him with horror. "And I don't think that it was Melicard, Gryphon."

"I *know* it isn't," added Gwendolyn. "Erini would never forgive him, and he cares more about her love than he does his old vendetta."

"Then it seems to me," growled the lionbird, unsheathing his claws again, "that it must be *Zuu.* They would gain in a war in the east."

Cabe put a hand on his friend's free shoulder. "Before you do anything, you'd better make certain. We're *so* close, Gryphon! Toos would've advised caution; you know that."

At first, the angry monarch simply stared at the warlock with his unsettling avian gaze. Then, some of the anger faded. The Gryphon nodded. "You are correct, of course. There are others who would benefit by what happened today. It's . . . it's hard to recall that Toos was not even the target; it was Kyl, after all."

"Kyl!" gasped the enchantress. "We haven't even seen how *he* is!"

"Then go to him, friends. I've lost a dear comrade, true, but the young drake's faced death up close." The Gryphon looked around at the gathered guards and functionaries. "Besides, I think that there is enough here to keep me occupied . . . for a lifetime, even."

"Will the guards have taken Kyl back to his suite?"

"That would be most likely, yes." The lionbird sighed. "And good luck with him. I cannot say what effect this may have on the heir; we will have to watch him closely."

The warlock agreed. "Once we know a little more about how Kyl is faring, one of us will have to search for Darkhorse. More than ever I fear that he's in grave trouble."

"I think you are correct." With a shake of his head, the Gryphon added, "Why is the process of peace always so violent?"

Cabe had no answer. Instead, he simply wrapped his arm around his wife and asked, "Are you ready?"

"Yes."

Their surroundings altered. The scene of the regent's assassination became the extravagant chambers put aside for the visiting emperor-to-be. Several draconian guards leapt to action as the pair materialized, but the Green Dragon, standing to one side of the room, signaled for them to relax.

Kyl sat in a tall, cushioned chair next to his bed. At first he stared ahead, but upon the Bedlams' sudden arrival, he turned to the mages. His eyes gleamed with a combination of anger, confusion, and fear. Grath stood beside him. He looked at the two spell-casters with an unreadable expression.

"They tried to *kill* me!" the heir to the dragon throne abruptly spat. "They tried to have me *assssassssinated!*"

"Did they catch the assassins?" the Dragon King asked in a quieter, calmer voice.

"The assassins are dead. They either killed themselves or were killed by whoever sent them."

"Ssso no one claimsss to know, then. Convenient." Kyl looked to his brother, who only shrugged. The heir leaned back, his hands gripping the chair arms tight. "I want to go back to the Manor."

"There are still—" began the Green Dragon.

"I want to go back *now!*"

Under the circumstances, Cabe could not really blame him. Kyl had been confronted with the ugliest of all aspects of rule: the desire by someone to remove him from the throne even before he was allowed to sit on it. The only reason that they had not succeeded was due to the quick but unfortunate interference of Toos. "Kyl, I hope you don't think that Penacles was responsible for this—"

The handsome face twisted into a look of incredulity. "I think it pretty clear that it wasss not, or at leassst that it wasss nothing to do with the lamented regent, but the fact remainsss that I am not sssafe here!" Kyl's hands were shaking. He turned to the enchantress. "Missstresss Bedlam! Will you allow me entrance to the Manor?"

Gwendolyn met Cabe's gaze. "It might be for the best right now."

"Someone should stay at the Manor, anyway," he returned. "It might be that Darkhorse will still turn up—"

"Darkhorse?" asked the Green Dragon in a confused tone.

"He's missing. It may be that he's fallen prey to the same forces behind this assassination."

The Dragon King's only response to that was a low hiss and a nod.

"Will you take usss, then, my lady?" Kyl asked again, more plaintively. "Myssself, my brother, Faras and Ssgayn, and Lord Green?"

The Green Dragon straightened. "With your permission, my liege, I would like to conduct my own invessstigations into this terrible event. Between Massster Bedlam and myself, I think then that we shall have most probabilities covered."

Kyl was clearly on the edge of collapse. He waved a dismissing hand. "Then by all meansss, go. If you can find the fiendsss ressponsible for this disssassster, then so much the better . . . but I want them brought before me."

"Of course."

"If I may," said a voice from behind Cabe. "I would like to return to the Manor with the others. I can serve no true purpose here."

The Bedlams turned to find Benjin Traske standing next to a small wall table. He had been so still and quiet that the warlock had not even noted his presence, an unnerving thing to Cabe. Still, it was not as if he had been consciously searching for the man.

The emperor-to-be gave his former teacher a cursory glance. Kyl now seemed only half-aware of what was around him. "If you mussst. I don't care. I jussst want to go back *now*."

Traske bowed, then joined his two former students.

Cabe hugged his wife goodbye. As they pulled one another close, he whispered in her ear. "Keep a very good eye on Kyl and wish me luck. This could be more complicated than we imagined."

"What are you saying?" she whispered back. "Was Toma responsible for this, too?"

"I don't think he's any more responsible than Talak or Zuu is. I . . . I have some strange suspicions." Cabe released her without explaining further. She looked him in the eye, then finally accepted his enigmatic response. The Lady Bedlam knew that her husband would not long hide things from her. If Cabe did not want to tell her now, it was only because he did not have much to support those suspicions.

Stepping away from her husband, Gwendolyn Bedlam joined the two drakes and the scholar. She waited just long enough to assure herself that they were prepared, then, with one last glance at Cabe, vanished with her charges.

The remaining drakes looked to Lord Green for guidance. He seemed to consider their position, finally commanding, "Rejoin the rest of the caravan. Someone will be there to take command before long." Facing the warlock, he asked, "Friend Bedlam, do I have your permission to have sssomeone take charge of the caravan and return with it to the Manor?"

Cabe had not given that part of the situation any consideration, but he realized that they could not just abandon the drakes and humans in Penacles. "Yes, I think that would be fine."

"You have your orders, then," the Dragon King told the guards. "Be certain that you have a human essscort, however, and by all meansss, do not become involved in any altercation with our hosts here. Those who do and survive to tell about it will *not* be pleasssed that they did. I will guarantee that."

"Perhaps we had best escort them as far as the arena, Your Majesty," the warlock suggested. "With tensions the way they are at this moment, we don't dare let any of your people wander around without guides."

"Yes, that would be best."

As it turned out, their return to the arena was uneventful. The Gryphon was still there, as Cabe had rightly assumed. He was talking to two warriors clad as champions of the chess game. Brow furrowing, the curious sorcerer stepped up his pace.

Noticing the mage's return, the lionbird dismissed the two combatants. He acknowledged the Dragon King but focused his attention on Cabe. "I have been speaking with the two warriors who did battle when the assassination occurred. They told me one or two interesting things."

"What would those be?" the drake lord asked before Cabe could speak.

Looking at both of them, the lionbird replied, "During their battle, at the moment just prior to the attack, both had difficulties keeping their grips on their weapons. The man who wore the armor of king, especially, claimed his weapon seemed to have a life of its own. He reports that it fairly flew out of his grip and headed straight for where the heir and Toos stood."

"It fell several feet short, if I recall," commented the Green Dragon.

"Yes, it did. The timing is too good, however. At the very least, the flying weapon was a decoy, I believe, designed to draw the attention of the victim and those around him. No one would be watching. The assassins would then strike . . . and die. Someone invested much sorcery to make this work, but they underestimated poor old Toos." The Gryphon blinked. "How is the emperor-to-be doing?"

"He requested to be brought back to the Manor," Cabe replied, judiciously avoiding mentioning the manner in which Kyl had put the request.

"No longer trusting Penacles and its ability to protect him, eh? I cannot blame him. My Lord Green, Cabe, I'll tell you now that any agreements made between Toos and the drakes will be held to. I will see to that—" the lionbird sighed "—as the ruler of this realm."

"That isss good to hear."

The king of Penacles bristled, but it was not due to anything the Dragon King had said. "I will not let Toos die in vain. He wanted peace more than I did. I will do anything I have to to see that peace succeed." He closed, then reopened his eyes, visibly trying to keep himself calm. "But you desire something. How may I help?"

Cabe quickly described the situation, emphasizing his need to hunt down Darkhorse before any more time had passed. As much as he tried not to think about it, the fear that it was already too late to save the shadow steed nagged at him. The warlock was aware of how many times in the past he had underestimated Darkhorse, for in truth the eternal was more powerful than he, but knowing the shadow steed and how willing he was to go charging into the fray, Cabe could not help but worry that each time Darkhorse vanished would be the last any would see of him. Darkhorse had the capability of living forever—as long as he was not destroyed.

The Gryphon wasted no time once his friend had explained. He quickly summoned one of the general's aides and ordered him to lead the drakes to the caravan.

"I will go with them and arrange their departure," suggested the Dragon King. "When I am through, with your permission, I will depart for my own realm. It may very well be that through my own methods, we shall overcome Toma'sss plotting yet."

"You think that Toma did this?"

The drake's eyes burned red. "I do."

"I wouldn't have expected him to use such methods. He is more likely to move behind the scenes."

"Then, if it isss not him, I may also discover that." The Green Dragon bowed to both Cabe and the Gryphon, then joined the draconian soldiers. "Rest assured, I, too, want this peace to succeed."

As the drakes followed the aide, the monarch of Penacles rubbed his beak. "An odd farewell, but then, I've never completely understood drakes."

"I think that they have the same problem with us."

"Yesss. . . . Cabe, where will you search?"

The warlock kept his face neutral. It was too early to tell anyone of his suspicions. "I have a few places in mind. I knew where Darkhorse planned to be at certain times after he last departed the Manor. I'll check them first."

"He may be dead . . . like Toos."

"Then I'll find the one who did it."

The Gryphon's unsettling eyes seemed to twinkle. "You had best find him— or them—before I do if you hope to have anything left." He toyed with his talons, extending them to their full lengths. "I do not intend to hold back this time."

Recalling how hard it had been for the lionbird to "hold back" when he had been tracking the murderers of his firstborn son, Cabe shuddered. He hoped that it would not come to that. If the Gryphon lost control, there was no telling what he might do.

Evidently, the lord of Penacles was thinking much the same thing. He almost glared at the warlock, but managed to prevent himself. Instead, he simply turned a little away, his eyes shifting to nothing in particular, and said, "The sooner you leave, the more chance you have of saving him."

Cabe did not need another hint. He bowed to the former and present ruler of the City of Knowledge, then vanished.

VALEA WAS WITH Ursa and Aurim when her mother returned with Kyl and the others. The trio, along with a nervous Ssarekai, had finally abandoned the underground chamber, assuming that it might be some time before their parents returned. Aurim was the first to see the newcomers as they materialized in the front hall of the Manor.

"They're back!" he pointed out to the others. "But Father's not there and . . . and Kyl and Grath are!"

They hurried to meet the returning party, Valea with conflicting emotions. Fear stemming from the knowledge that *something* had happened in Penacles intertwined with relief that Kyl was safe. She started to greet him, but the expression on his handsome visage made her pause. It was both cruel and confused. Even Grath showed signs of anger, although he hid them much better than his brother. Scholar Traske revealed nothing.

"What is it? What happened in Penacles?" asked Aurim, his own problem not even a concern to him at this point. "Where's Father?"

"Your father is all right," Lady Bedlam replied quickly, so as to relieve some of her family's fears. "He searches for Darkhorse, who's missing." Her face grew more somber. "You should all know . . . Toos the Regent was killed during an assassination attempt on Kyl."

"Gods!" The young warlock shook his head.

Ssarekai swore an oath by the mythical Dragon of the Depths. Valea could scarcely believe what she was hearing. Her relief at finding Kyl safe gave way to her grief for the towering old soldier. He had been like the grandfather she had never had—and who would have wanted *Azran* anyway?—giving her presents and tolerating her questions about the war years.

In the midst of their grief, Kyl suddenly snapped, "If he had not died, it would have been *me*, inssstead!" He straightened his clothing and tried to look unruffled. "If you will excussse me, Lady Bedlam, I desssire greatly to return to my roomsss."

"I quite understand, Kyl."

The drake had not even waited for her response. Already turning, he snapped his fingers at Grath and his bodyguards. "Come with me!"

With the dragon heir in the lead, the drakes departed the still-stunned group. Valea found herself just a bit put out by Kyl's attitude, although, admittedly, he had been through much today.

"How do you feel, Aurim?" Benjin Traske asked suddenly. His question first struck the novice sorceress as incongruous to the situation at hand, but then she recalled that the massive tutor had been in Penacles. He would know more about the events that had taken place there than the progress, or lack thereof, of the Bedlams' attempts to free the minds of her brother and Ssarekai.

"The same," her brother remarked halfheartedly. It was clear the news about dear Toos was far more important to the young Bedlam.

"I see." Traske turned to Valea's mother. "My lady, perhaps it might be good if I left your company for now. This is a matter for you and your family, and I can perhaps be of better use to Lord Kyl. I do not doubt that he is going through a conflict of his own."

"I should go to him—" the enchantress began.

"You are suffering also, madam. Your family knew the regent better than I. I mourn his death, true, but not near as much as you. I think that you should explain things to the young here. I will do what I can for my former pupil."

"Thank you. In truth," responded Gwendolyn Bedlam, "he probably would listen to you more than he would either Cabe or myself."

An uncharacteristic smile spread across the scholar's bearded countenance. "It pleases me to hear you say so." He performed a bow. "My lady . . ."

Ursa suddenly looked anxious. "Scholar, may I go with you? He isss my brother."

He hesitated. "At this point, young lady, it might be better if you waited. Let me do what I can. Too many new voices might drive the emperor-to-be to further distress. He needs a guiding hand at the moment."

Valea thought she knew the true reason why Benjin Traske did not want Ursa along. Ursa did not really get along with Kyl. One of Kyl's greatest faults, subconscious or not, was that he saw the females of his race as inferior creatures. The courtesy he freely gave to Valea, the young drake only forcibly gave to his own sibling. It was a strange double standard that she would never understand. Valea had tried to question Kyl about it, but it was one subject he refused to discuss.

Her mother looked as if she wanted to speak in Ursa's defense, but Valea's friend acquiesced before she could do so. "You are right, of course, Scholar Trassske. Will you let me know how he is?"

"As you desire." The tutor bowed again, this time taking his leave immediately after. Valea wondered if other households were as abrupt as hers. Throughout her life it had always seemed as if people were in a hurry. Everyone was always rushing someplace.

She, too, wanted to be there when the scholar told Ursa how Kyl was faring. It was purely for selfish motives, she knew, but she was aware that the kind of tragedy he had faced could change him permanently. Valea feared that those changes would put them farther apart from one another.

Her mind returned to poor Toos. She felt guilty that she should be so concerned about Kyl when the regent had died saving his life. *I wonder how the Gryphon is taking it? They were good, good friends. . . .*

Lady Bedlam was doing her best to maintain control. She said, "Why don't we go to the drawing room? I think it would be wise to be as comfortable as possible while we talk. This situation is hardly over. We are going to have to be wary for some time."

They all understood what she was saying. Valea knew that where there had been one assassination attempt, there might be others.

The enchantress began to lead them away, then paused when she realized that there was still another member of the party. The drake Ssarekai had remained behind after the others had left. Valea liked him; he hardly seemed like a dragon at all. *How left out he must feel right now!*

"Ssarekai? You are welcome to join us, you know. Don't think that you aren't family after all these years. You've gone farther than many toward making cooperation between our races work."

The stable master had been staring down the hallway Benjin Traske, Kyl, and the drakes had used. With effort, he shifted his gaze to the sorceress. "I thank you deeply for thossse wordsss, my lady, but I have let too much time pass. There are dutiesss that I realize I must see to before it isss too late."

"Very well. We have not given up on the spells that bind you and Aurim. I want you to know that they are still priorities with us."

The drake shrugged. "I have had it this long; I think that if Master Aurim can wait, then so can I."

Valea's mother swore an oath, so upset was she. "There's always too much happening at the same time! These spells *should* be removed as quickly as possible!"

"They don't seem to be harming us, Mother. I can wait, too." Aurim's face was pale. "Besides . . . I need to hear what happened. I need to hear about Toos. How did Toma sneak assassins into Penacles? How does he find his way into everywhere?"

For some reason, this made their mother pause. At last the fire-tressed sorceress admitted, "Your father thinks it might have been someone else who plotted the assassination. He hopes to find out more. . . ." She hugged herself, obviously worried. "I pray that he doesn't find out more than he planned."

The others nodded, Valea making her own private wish concerning her father's safety . . . and the rescue of Darkhorse. At least, she thought, the assassins had failed in their goal; Kyl was alive and well.

She would have to see him at first opportunity. He would certainly not turn *her* away. As selfish as she knew it was for her to think so, Valea could not help wondering if perhaps this tragic event would be what finally brought them together. She would be good for him, especially now. Kyl would not have to fear for her; Valea had the power not only to protect herself but to further augment the heir's own magic. Between them, no assassin, however well armed, would stand the slightest chance of success.

*Not even Toma*, she decided.

GRATH HAD A great desire to slap his brother's face again and again until the idiot calmed down and thought properly once more, but he knew that such action would only see him dismissed from Kyl's side. That would ruin everything that had been planned.

The death of General Toos had been a tragic loss, both politically and emotionally, but Grath had long ago learned to put the worst aside, leaving his mind clear for thought. He would miss the regent, miss him much more than his mentor would, of course, but overall the human's death had been worth the price. After all, if not for Toos, Kyl would be dead and Grath would be forced to take his place. It was much too soon for that. Perhaps later, once it was clear that the power of the Dragon Emperor was secure.

Of course, first he had to free his brother from the shock and paranoia Kyl now suffered.

"They tried to kill me, Grath! Thossse misssserable humans! I should overrun them all when I am emperor! They cannot be trusssted, the furry ssscavengers . . . but . . ." Kyl's face twisted into an expression of extreme uncertainty. "The regent gave hisss *own* life to sssave mine! I would have been *murdered* but for him!"

Faras and Ssgayn exchanged glances that Grath noted out of the edge of his eye. They were beginning to question both their emperor-to-be's sanity and his bravery.

He put a brotherly hand on Kyl's shoulder. "Now isss not the time to think about all of this, Kyl. The best thing to do right now is rest. You *need* rest. In only a few days, the Blue Dragon, representing the other Dragon Kings as well, will arrive in the Dagora Forest. He will want to question you. This will be your moment."

To his astonishment, Kyl pushed him away. "I don't care about the drake lord! If they cannot accept me asss emperor already, then I will *make* them come to me on bent knee!" A frightening glint came into the drake's eyes. "Could it be that Blue or one of the other hesssitant onesss sssent thossse killers? They *do* all have their human agentsss, do they not, Grath?"

The last thing he wanted to encourage was a fear that the recalcitrant Dragon Kings might be trying to kill Kyl. True, it was a possibility that he had considered—only minutes before, in fact—but that was something that could be dealt with once Kyl and he gained the power of the Dragon Throne. The drake lords would be less inclined to attempt the assassination once his brother was officially their master.

Grath exhaled, trying to gather his thoughts together enough to give Kyl some sort of reassuring answer. The chaos in the arena had not been nearly so draining as trying to keep his brother in line. *And he is to be the emperor?*

He was still trying to decide what to do when there came a heavy knock upon the door. Faras stalked toward the door, weapon at the ready. Kyl, Grath was ashamed to see, actually drew back into his chair.

The guards tensed. Faras opened the door.

Relief washed over Grath as he saw who it was who had dared to join them.

Kyl looked up at the newcomer, still wary. "Ssscholar Trassske. You desssire something of me? I am rather busssy at the moment."

"So I see," remarked the tutor with obvious sarcasm. Grath knew that his brother had never heard the figure before him speak with such impudence. "Busy falling prey to your fears when you should be using them to strengthen you. A ruler must learn to control his weaknesses and make them work for him."

"I don't have time for your sss—"

Grath allowed himself a brief smile as Kyl broke off at the look on the massive figure's face. At last there was someone who could make his brother see sense . . . and who else was better suited?

Benjin Traske ceased glaring at the heir to the dragon throne just long enough to deal with Kyl's bodyguards. "Leave us."

To Kyl's astonishment—but not to Grath's—Faras and Ssgayn bowed and hastily retreated from the chamber.

The dragon heir rose, intending to command the two to return, but Traske stepped directly in front of him. Kyl, trying to back away, fell into the chair.

"Things are moving much too swiftly now, but we can compensate. The death of the regent, while unexpected, does nothing to change the fact that you *will* be emperor in only a very short time. You survived the assassination, and now it will be almost impossible for whoever was responsible to attempt something else. I will see to assuring that."

"You will see to that?"

"In whatever way is open to me, of course," Traske corrected. "What is more important is to consider the next step you must take on the road to the throne. If I may suggest—"

This made Kyl laugh harshly. "Teacher, you are a human I admire, I freely admit that. Your advice I would generally find good, but you could not posssssibly undersssstand what I am going through. You do not undersssstand the *challenges*, the myriad *pitfalls*, that I face in asssuming the throne of my kind."

"Perhaps I understand more than you imagine. . . ."

"You would have to live through it yoursssself. There isss no other way to undersssstand it ssso well."

Benjin Traske started to speak, then paused in consideration. At last, he simply said, "I can see that for now I am wasting my time here."

He was leaving. Grath could not believe that. Here was the one being able to drag Kyl back to his feet and he was leaving without having even tried. "Teacher—"

Benjin Traske shook his head. "No, Grath. I will waste no time here. I can see that Kyl needs time to let his thoughts cool." The huge figure loomed over the heir. "Then, Kyl, you and I will talk again. Much longer, this time."

The heir had already slipped deeper into his chair. "I have no desire to do so."

"You will." Traske's tone was such that Kyl could not help but straighten.

It was the voice that had kept both drakes highly attentive throughout their lessons. It was a voice that brooked no disagreement, one that Grath knew his brother had not yet learned to control completely and probably never would.

Benjin Traske turned to leave, the issue of Kyl's permission negligible under the circumstances, but then paused. He glanced first at Grath, then at Kyl, to whom he added, "You will be emperor. You will be strong. We will see to that."

The dragon heir glanced up. His gaze did not leave the figure of the scholar until Traske had closed the door behind him. Then, Kyl simply turned to stare at one of the walls. Grath remained where he was, silent as the night. When Faras and Ssgayn returned, he indicated silence, then pointed where he wanted them positioned. They obeyed him without a sound.

Kyl continued to stare at the wall, but from where Grath stood, it was possible for the younger drake to see the look on his elder brother's visage. Still brooding, but now Kyl was at least thinking. It was the first stage to recovery.

"Grath? What do you think of our esssteemed tutor?"

How to phrase it best? Grath hesitated, then responded, "He came here to see you made emperor, brother. He is not the kind to let years of work go for naught. When he says that you will be emperor, he means it."

"Ssso I felt." The dragon heir hissed. "I sssometimesss wish that Toma had sssucceeded our sssire after all. *He* would have brooked no threat from asssasssin or king, human or drake."

"There isss much to admire in Toma," Grath ventured. "He was loyal to our sire."

"Ssso I was thinking."

The young drake smiled at such a response, but only because his brother could not clearly see his face. Faras and Ssgayn could, but they were of no consequence; they knew their places.

"Perhaps, when you are emperor, you will be able to arrange to talk with him."

The notion made Kyl blink. "I could do that, couldn't I?"

"As emperor, who would stop you?"

"Who, indeed?"

Behind the emperor-to-be, Grath allowed himself another smile.

# XVI

CABE FROWNED AS the night aged. The evidence he had hoped to find had failed to turn up, but still the warlock could not abandon his suspicions. He *wanted* to, very dearly in fact, but some part of him forced the mage to push on.

Twice already he had contacted his wife and the Gryphon. There had not been much to report from either side. Thanks to a private conversation between Benjin Traske and Kyl, the heir had at least calmed down. He remained secluded in his chambers, however. Gwendolyn reported some lingering signs of his earlier nervousness, but it appeared that Kyl had his fear under control. There was nothing else to report from the Manor. Aurim and Ssarekai were still afflicted by the mysterious spell Toma had cast upon them, but so far it had not affected anything but their memories concerning the renegade.

The news from Penacles was little better. Order had been restored and most in the kingdom seemed perfectly satisfied with the return of their former monarch, but the lionbird had been forced to admit that the spells of searching that he had cast upon the remnants of the two assassins had revealed nothing new. He had, however, promised the warlock that he would keep the garments under guard until Cabe or Gwen had the opportunity to study them thoroughly.

In a wooded area near the northern edge of the Dagora Forest, Cabe sat on a high rock contemplating the lack of success on everyone's part. Even he had not had anything to report. It had been his decision to continue the search through the entire night if necessary, for, in his mind, each second he delayed meant more danger to Darkhorse. Fortunately, he could revitalize himself for a time through the simple use of sorcery. Cabe did not like substituting magical energy in the place of normal rest—it was a danger in the long run for *many* reasons—but he did it rarely enough that now would not cause him trouble. What *did* bother him was the possibility of finding his last clues as useless as the others. Then, the only choices left to him would be to confront the source of his suspicions, or forget the matter—and Darkhorse—forever.

He could never do the latter, but the former unnerved him almost as much.

Exhaling, the warlock floated off the rock and slowly descended to the ground, where he landed in a standing position. Cabe surveyed the area, seeing it well despite the darkness. For once, he had dared to adjust his eyes to better see at night. As much as Cabe disliked altering any portion of his form, especially something as sensitive as the eyes, the missing Darkhorse deserved at least *that* much effort. The warlock was willing to give his life, if that was what it took to save the ebony stallion.

*I should've sensed something! What am I missing?* What, indeed? Cabe had tried to follow Darkhorse's trace, but so far it had led him nowhere. It was as if his last few days had been erased from—

Then it at last came to him. He cursed himself for a fool. *I should've seen that before! And people think of me as a master sorcerer! I'm a* novice, *that's what I am! A wet-behind-the-ears, all-knowing, first-day novice!*

The traps set for Darkhorse had been designed in a variety of manners, but one consistent trait had been the creator's use of one bit of sorcery masking another. What better way, then, to cover the trail of the shadow steed by use of the same, or rather, *similar* technique?

Tensing, the spellcaster reached out and looked at the world anew. There were different levels of vision, and while Cabe made use of both the mundane and magical, he did not usually utilize all of the latter. He could not remember a time when he had been forced to reach beyond the most common of the magical dimensions. Cabe *had* viewed the world from every level, but only for practice. He had never had to truly make use of them until now.

In the first shifting, the land around him became fluid, but everything still held its basic shape. Trees and rocks wiggled like overfilled water sacks, yet did not burst when he touched them. The night sky was blue. Lines of force, the same forces that Cabe's body drew upon when he utilized sorcery, crisscrossed everywhere. Colors were askew, with green things now red and brown things now yellow.

Unfortunately, for this realm, everything was as it was meant to be. There were no variations that would have signaled the necessary aberration that Cabe was hunting.

He tried the next level beyond. Now, the night was green and everything, including himself, was pierced by a thousand tiny blue lines. The fact that all else was normal by human standards did nothing to keep him from becoming disconcerted by the strands. He was almost grateful to see that there was no evidence of the masking sorcery on this level.

His third attempt gave the warlock the ability to see the world as a land of glittering spheres. Each time something moved, be it by its own choice or simply the touch of the wind, the tiny spheres went flying hither and yonder. The landscape also glittered, making it appear that the trees, rocks, and all the rest had been formed out of volcanic glass. It was one of the most exotic and most beautiful of the magical planes, and Cabe made a note to himself to view it again when things calmed down.

There among the beauty he finally found the black trail. To his eyes, it appeared as a jagged scattering of black glass. In some places there lay only a single piece, but still there was enough to follow. Cabe reached out with his power, which in this level was represented by a gleaming blue stream, and linked himself to the trail.

It was childishly easy to follow it through a series of hops. Each time he materialized, the warlock expected to find some difficulty, some barrier, but there was none. Cabe began to fear some trap, but if there was one, it was so subtle that it escaped his careful monitoring.

On the twelfth hop, he came across the hooded figures. The suddenly still warlock did not know exactly where he was, although the region reminded him of somewhere near the ruins of Mito Pica, but *location* hardly mattered now. What did matter was that he had no doubt whatsoever he had found the ones he sought.

As he saw the world, the dismounted riders were mounds of black steel among the glass trees. The images disconcerted him until he shifted his vision back to night sight. Even then, however, the silent figures were ominous shapes. They wore cloaks identical to those of the assassins, huge things that only now and then revealed the race to which their wearers belonged.

They were men *and* drakes. Three of the former and two of the latter, all seated around a fire that was little more than embers and so gave some heat but hardly any betraying illumination. It was a surprising but not unbelievable sight, and whether it confirmed his suspicions, Cabe could not say.

Shielded by a pair of tall oaks, the silent mage surveyed the group. One of the humans seemed to be in charge. He muttered something to one of the drakes. In the drake's hands was a small box that, at first, the warlock's gaze passed over. Only when he belatedly sensed the strangeness of it did he probe the object. To his surprise, it resisted his best attempts to unveil its contents, but what he learned about the container made him shiver.

It was Vraad . . . or at the very least, based on Vraadish sorcery. It was by far not the first artifact he had been confronted with over the years. In the short time that the alien magic had thrived in this world, millennia before, it had certainly left its mark, the warlock thought. A *black* mark, in his opinion.

Suddenly, he had a horrible feeling he knew what the box contained.

"We wait, then," grunted the leader. "I can have a little more patience."

*Wait?* For who? For the assassins? That seemed peculiar, considering that the two had clearly been intended to die regardless of their success or failure. Was the leader then waiting for reinforcements, or was someone else planning to join them?

A quick but cautious search of the surrounding region revealed no other intruders. The warlock came to a decision; he would have to strike now lest he lose this one chance. Cabe had no doubt that he had found what he was searching for, and so in his eyes waiting only threatened to lessen his opportunity to take the foul container without a greater struggle.

He knew that there was magic about the riders, but could read nothing more. They might have enchanted daggers or be untrained but lethal mages. It might even be their cloaks alone, which he had already discerned had some spell interwoven in them.

Magic or not, it was time to act. Reaching out, the warlock sent tendrils of power toward each of the figures. With any luck, the battle would be over before any of the five noticed what was happening. A simple sleep spell, one that should be effective regardless of the sorcery he sensed. Surprise was ofttimes a more useful tool in magical combat than all the power of an archmage. Surprise mixed with caution, that is. There were many instantaneous spells that he could have unleashed, but Cabe wanted to take no chances. It was *his* way. If this failed, then he would be more direct, more instinctive in his attack.

He encountered no barriers, no protective spells. That made sense. Unless one was very skilled, protective spells tended to be noticeable. This was not a party that wished to be noticed, as the pitiful fire had already indicated.

Slowly, each tendril took its place. Cabe found himself sweating. He wanted to hurry the spell through, but was aware how such impatience had a tendency to backfire. There might still be some sorcerous shield in place that he had not noticed.

Still the hooded figures seemed unaware of what he was doing. The ease with which his plan progressed worried Cabe. Despite his vast power, he always expected the worst to happen. If he was wrong this time, so much the better, but until then . . .

Before he realized it, his spell was finally ready. When he chose to, each tendril would strike the head of the figure before it, unleashing the unstoppable command to sleep. He had drawn enough power into the making of the spell to down five times the number of riders before him. That, unless he had miscalculated horribly, would be sufficient to overcome each.

*So why are you waiting?* Having no good answer to the silent question, Cabe Bedlam unleashed his spell.

Two of the men and one of the drakes collapsed.

The human leader and the drake who held the box rose. Their hoods kept their faces all but obscured, but Cabe could read consternation in the dragon man's movements. The human, however, was furious.

An armored hand shot forward as the leader pointed directly at the warlock's hiding place. *"There! He's there!"*

Shifting his prize to one hand, the drake pointed a taloned finger.

One of the oaks burst, sending tiny spears of wood flying. The warlock folded himself into a ball as the deadly shower enveloped him, his robe making a seemingly insufficient shield against the storm of tiny but lethal spears.

"Give me the box!" growled the leader as the fearsome rain poured down. He pulled out a short sword. "Go and make certain that he's finished!"

The drake thrust the container into the human's hand and stalked toward the curled figure, his speed increasing the nearer he came. When he finally stood over Cabe, the drake raised one hand high in preparation of a new spell. The hand glowed with pent up power.

Cabe materialized behind the leader just as the huddled form exploded at the dragon man's touch.

The drake went flying backward, stunned. The warlock's simulacrum had not been created to kill; Cabe desired prisoners, not corpses.

He reached out for the leader even as the explosion rocked the immediate vicinity, yet somehow the hooded man sensed him coming. With astonishing dexterity, the leader swung the blade behind him, almost severing the warlock's hand from his arm. Cabe barely pulled back in time, yet still he managed to release his spell.

The outline of the hooded figure flared white, but the man was otherwise unchanged.

"Yes . . . I *am* protected against your little tricks, magic man, but are *you* protected against *mine*?"

Still clutching the box in his other hand, the armored leader advanced on Cabe. This close, the warlock's enhanced vision allowed him a better view of the armor beneath the robe. It was dented and worn, but there was no mistaking the familiar ebony armor. His foe was, or rather had been, a wolf raider.

Their empire was all but a memory, but that did not mean that the Aramites, the wolf raiders, were also. They still held pockets of the neighboring continent and their ships now prowled the seas as true pirates. Even in the Dragonrealm, half the world away, there were remnants. This one might even have been part of the large force that had attempted to build a new power-base on this continent. Those wolf raiders had been defeated, but more than a few had no doubt escaped the cataclysm that had befallen the army in the southwesternmost region of the Dragonrealm. Reports of survivors being captured in various places all over the continent had been verified. It was, therefore, not so surprising after all to find one here. Somehow the Aramites seemed to have a hand in almost every plot that touched the lives of Cabe and those he cared for.

However this one had come to be here, Cabe knew that he could not let him escape. The warlock backed away as the raider advanced, but that was not something he could continue for very long. In fact, he did not have to. The surprise of discovering what his adversary was had finally faded and now Cabe was prepared to finish the task at hand. The Aramite could not be allowed to escape with the box.

"I've not worked for so long to have you destroy everything!" snarled the wolf raider. Suddenly his sword's reach was longer than it should have been. Although the blade missed the sorcerer by a good arm's length, still there was suddenly a slash in Cabe's robe. The raider's sword had some limited magical ability. What *other* tricks did the man have hidden beneath his robe?

Enough was enough. If he could not affect his adversary directly, then Cabe was prepared to work *around* him.

The leader swung again, this time leaving not only a small rip in the sleeve of the warlock's garment but also a thin, red line across Cabe's lower arm that stung almost enough to make the warlock forget what he was doing.

However, as the Aramite pulled back his weapon for another vicious cut, a tree branch suddenly got in the way of his sword arm. Cursing, the hooded attacker pulled his arm around, but his swing was ruined. He sidestepped the tree, but then another branch caught him in the face.

"Dogs of war! What is—" The rest became unintelligible as yet another branch shifted, despite the direction of the wind, and struck him soundly in the unprotected throat.

Upturned roots caused his advance to falter. As he stumbled, the raider almost dropped the box, but at the last moment, he managed to retain his grip. That was his only success, however, for now he could not manage to lower his sword arm. Worse yet, the blade itself was now tangled in a mesh of smaller, intertwined branches above the raider's head.

Cabe allowed himself a slight smile at the sight of his handiwork. His adversary had blundered directly into it. In fact, it had almost been too easy. The warlock had never truly been in danger. It was an odd sensation, so easily defeating the threat. Cabe kept expecting some last-second trick by either the trapped leader or some henchman still in hiding, but inside he knew that no trick would be coming. Each passing second left the raider more and more hopelessly entangled. Already he could no longer move.

*One time I garner a quick and easy victory and I can't be satisfied with that!* He tried to shake the doubts away, but failed. Sighing, Cabe decided to simply ignore them. The doubts could not take away the fact that he had won.

Walking over to the imprisoned leader, Cabe reached out and pried the box from his helpless hand. "Thank you."

His prisoner said nothing.

Cabe looked close, utilizing his enhanced vision to study the one before him. He did not recognize the man, but he had the look of an officer. Aramite officers were, to his bitter recollection, deceitful monsters with sadistic streaks. One of them had killed the Gryphon's firstborn. That one was dead, but Cabe knew that the lionbird would find this one of almost as much interest.

"Tell me about this box, wolf raider." He held the offensive artifact up close to the Aramite's scowling face.

There was a peculiar look in what Cabe could see of that ugly visage. With a rough, humorless laugh, the leader replied, "You'll have to find out about it on your own, spellmonger. It'll be my last gift to you and yours."

It was too late by the time the warlock reacted.

With a gasp, the imprisoned raider began to shake. His entire form convulsed, so much so that he almost shook free of the binding branches. That was not the man's intention, though. Cabe tried to counter whatever spell was upon the raider, but the same defensive measure that had prevented him from directly attacking blocked these spells as well. What it did not block, however, was the thing killing his prisoner, which to Cabe meant that the source lay somewhere *within* the Aramite's body.

"Drazeree!" muttered the warlock, calling upon a legendary and possibly blood-related hero/god of the age of the Vraad. What Cabe witnessed now was worthy of the foul Vraad and possibly would have revolted even a few of them.

The guards had spoken of the assassins literally crumbling to ash. He could only assume that this was the same spell, for it seemed unlikely that anyone would devise two such similar horrors.

The Aramite grew ashen-faced. His clothing, with the exception of the cloak and the armor, appeared to crackle and break. The raider laughed, but the laugh quickly became a gurgle as first the man's teeth and tongue, then his entire *jaw*, fell away.

Without warning, the decomposing figure slipped free of the branches and slumped to the ground. A terrible mound of gray flakes formed around his diminishing body. Now, there emerged no sound from Cabe's hapless prisoner. The appalled spellcaster doubted that the man was still alive. The graying skin crumbled off of the raider's face, followed without pause by the skull and hair.

Cabe turned away, too sick to his stomach to watch the final moments. In little more than the blink of an eye, he had watched a living creature be reduced to dust.

By the time he had recovered enough to look again, all that remained of the leader was his cloak, partly tangled in the tree branches, empty bits of black armor . . . and an unsettling mound of dust. He forced himself to sift through the remains, but there was no sign of what had protected his adversary from his spells or what had finally killed the wolf raider. In fact, there was not much of anything. No clues. Nothing.

Then it was that Cabe Bedlam recalled the other hooded figures. His stomach recoiled, but he had no choice. He suspected what he would find, but that did not mean he did not have to look.

It proved to be as he had feared. Of the others, even the drake who had fallen for his trick, there remained nothing but bits of armor, metal objects, the mysterious cloaks, and foul piles of ash.

Had they willingly let this be done to them? He could hardly believe so, despite what the leader had said, and despite the words that had given credence to the notion that the Aramite had been responsible for this entire plot. He was aware that he was grasping at straws, but too many things had fallen into place easily while others had not.

The warlock studied the carved exterior of the box as if it could give him some of the answers he craved.

To his surprise, it gave the two most important answers of all. Both he desired, but one he would have preferred not to have known.

The box was what he had feared it would be. An artifact so ancient but still capable of the evil for which it had been created. Exhaling, the weary sorcerer cautiously touched the front. At least it had not been designed to confound. Opening it would be the easy part, possibly the *only* easy part from this point on.

Cabe turned the box so that it would open away from him. Then, taking a deep breath, he pressed the lock and lifted the lid back.

The scream shattered the night and almost caused the warlock to drop the box. A black cloud burst forth from the box, a black cloud darker than night.

"I am *free!* Free!" A mocking laugh followed, a laugh almost as horrifying in its own way as the shriek preceding it.

The black cloud sprouted long legs and a tail. A head, at first twisted and unidentifiable, grew from the front of the cloud, while at the same time the tail rose in the back.

Darkhorse coalesced before him, the shadow steed's hooves more than a yard from the earth below.

"I am free!" he roared. The eternal looked down and the ice-blue orbs that were his eyes widened at the small figure below and before him. "Cabe!"

"Darkhorse, I—" He had no chance to finish his statement, for the shadow steed was suddenly whirling about in the air, eyes seeking. "Where *are* they, Cabe? Where are those misbegotten vermin who have dared reintroduce me to my worst nightmare? I will draw them in and let *them* taste eternal emptiness! Where are they, Cabe?"

"They're dead."

At first the shadow steed did not believe him. He snorted and darted toward the nearest cloak, not yet realizing what it represented. Kicking it aside, the eternal studied with confusion the ash beneath. "What is this dust?"

The spellcaster closed the box and placed it in the folds of his robe. He would deal with the box in prompt order, but first he had to calm the maddened stallion. "That's all that's left of them, Darkhorse. I saw it happen to the leader."

"No! I *will* not be denied! I cannot be!"

He kicked at the cloak, then trotted to one of the other piles. Watching the huge form dart about in the darkness, Cabe was torn between letting things end here or voicing his beliefs. To him, the box was the deciding point between taking the struggle here at face value or seeing the wolf raider and his men as the pawns they might be. In the warlock's eyes, the Aramite and his henchmen had died so that someone else would remain anonymous.

Unfortunately for that someone, Cabe had not fallen for the ploy.

Suddenly the eternal loomed over him. "It's true, then? My captors are dust?"

"All of them." Cabe almost winced as he told the lie. "It wasn't a pretty way to go, Darkhorse. I think you can be satisfied that they've paid."

The shadow steed snorted. "I will *have* to be, I suppose." He cocked his head. "I wonder what they wanted of me. How long have I been a prisoner?"

It had not even occurred to the sorcerer that his friend knew nothing of the dire deeds that had transpired since his imprisonment. Cabe swallowed. "There's much you've missed, Darkhorse. Too much."

Some of Darkhorse's fury abated. "Your tone is not one I find I like, Cabe. What is it? What's happened?"

The tale spilled out of the warlock's mouth almost of its own volition. He described the foul spells that Toma had imprinted on the minds of his son and Ssarekai, then proceeded to tell of the tragedy that had befallen the kingdom of Penacles.

Darkhorse was still when Cabe at last finished. The icy eyes glowed with much less fury but more frustration.

"I am . . . sorry . . . about Toos. He was an interesting human, Cabe. Such an end was hardly fitting. So his assassins also are dead?"

"By the same manner as their leader. He was a wolf raider, probably an officer."

"Wolf raider. . . ." Darkhorse glowered as only he could. "Even without an empire, they still manage to meddle. This explains such a fanatical mission. Only an Aramite officer would see to it that neither he nor his men would survive if the plot failed. Good in one respect, for it means less to hunt down afterward. May the Lords of the Dead have no pity on their souls. It's over, then?"

Cabe could not prevent a sigh this time. He hoped that his companion would not read too much into it. The warlock was not certain that he could maintain the lie if pressed. "This is. There may be repercussions, though. Kyl was quite shook-up."

"So I would think." Darkhorse scuffed the soil, sending large chunks of earth flying. "I am still not certain about this matter, Cabe. I think someone else was behind this."

"You do?" He tried not to reveal his anxiety.

The eternal dipped his head in an equine nod. "I would not be surprised to find the talons of *Toma* sunk deeply into this travesty!"

Seizing the notion and turning it to his own use, Cabe agreed. "You may be right."

"We need to find that reptilian fiend and put an end to his misdeeds! I will not rest until that has happened!"

This time, the warlock had no difficulty agreeing. Even if the renegade drake had not been involved in Darkhorse's capture, which was still not a notion that Cabe could entirely dismiss, he had much else to answer for.

"We'll find him, Darkhorse. Somehow we will."

The nightmarish stallion again pawed at the ground. The spark in his eyes rekindled, becoming a blaze. Yet, his form noticeably wavered, as if he still did not have complete control over it. The pupilless eyes peered down at him. "Do you intend to return to the Manor now?"

Cabe gently touched the box in his robe. He hoped his own presence shielded the artifact from Darkhorse's senses. Despite the shadow steed's manner, it was clear that he was weak, which was the only reason that the warlock hoped he could keep the box concealed. Darkhorse would want to destroy the box and, in truth, Cabe would have been hard-pressed to prevent him from doing so without revealing just exactly why it was necessary to keep it in one piece. The mage himself was not exactly certain why; he simply felt that the sinister device would prove a damning bit of evidence when he faced the one responsible. "Yes. I want to look around here a little first, then I'll be returning to the Manor."

Again the shadow steed's form wavered. This time, when Darkhorse spoke, his voice was muffled, as if someone had in part succeeded in gagging him. Yet, his tone was still one of unbridled self-confidence. "Then I shall trust to your safety since all the villains are dead. In the meantime, there is a hunt that I must begin. *Toma* must needs be taught a proper lesson for this!" The eternal began to turn away. "If I find anything of significance, I shall come to the Manor; I promise you."

"Are you . . . are you certain that you'll be all right, Darkhorse?"

The ebony stallion swung his head and chuckled. "Of *course*, I will be! I *am* Darkhorse, am I not?"

Cabe could only smile and shake his head. No matter what dire straits the shadow steed faced, it seemed that there were some character traits forever ingrained in his rather eccentric personality. On the one hand, the sorcerer would not have wanted Darkhorse to change, but on the other hand, it likely would have been better for all concerned if the shadow steed *was* better able to restrain himself when it came to certain matters. Certainly, Cabe would sleep easier. Unfortunately, Cabe was aware that nothing but imprisonment or destruction would sway the injured stallion from his chosen path.

"Fare you well, Cabe, and my thanks. . . ." The massive equine began to trot . . . and was suddenly nowhere to be seen. Swifter than the wind was a phrase that failed to describe the eternal's speed.

*He doesn't realize*, the master mage thought as he stared where his companion had stood not a breath before. *Hopefully, it'll remain that way.*

Alone, Cabe finally turned and gave the dusty remains of the conspirators one last cursory glance. Already Cabe knew that there was nothing to be learned from these. Even the leader's empty armor and cloak left no secrets. After a minute or two of futile searching, the warlock turned his attention to the horses, but a thorough examination revealed that the saddlebags contained only some food, water, and a few other necessities for travel. The contents told him only one interesting thing; the sparsity of food meant that either the hooded figures had planned to locate supplies elsewhere, or they had not expected to ride much further after this. Cabe knew of nothing nearby. They could not hope to catch sufficient game in this area, either.

The evidence would have been circumstantial to most, but to the uneasy spellcaster, what he knew was sufficient to condemn. He dared not deal with the matter this night, though. *Best to return home and face this when I've rested. Maybe I'll still find another answer. Maybe.*

He remained long enough to send the horses through a blink hole, one of the large, magical portals a spellcaster could create, that would leave them in the royal stables of Penacles. One of the animals carried a note on its saddle, a missive from the warlock to the Gryphon explaining what had happened. As with the explanation to Darkhorse, it left some things unsaid.

Satisfied that the Gryphon would know best what to do with the dead assassins' things, Cabe prepared for home. A good night's sleep was what he would need, especially if he planned to go through with his accusations. He would need *all* the strength he could when it came time to reveal what he knew.

Even then, Cabe was not certain that he would be strong enough.

# XVII

DESPITE HIS DETERMINATION the night before, the new day found Cabe ensconced in his study, his mind a raging maelstrom of doubt and contradiction. He had been there since his return from tracking down the assassins. Neither Gwendolyn nor the children had been able to stir him from the emotion that bespelled him, and they had finally resigned themselves to allowing him to find his own way back.

Cabe could not explain to them, not without revealing what he felt should not be revealed. There had been enough tragedy and violence already; the knowledge . . . the suspicions . . . he entertained were enough to start a new war.

The damning box sat on the table before him, a dark thing both revealing and mysterious. No one knew it was here; he had cast a cloaking spell around it at first opportunity. Since no one here had known of the box in the first place, the few moments it had been unshielded had not mattered. Besides, there were so many other concerns already being dealt with that it was doubtful anyone else had had the time to even notice the brief existence of the foul artifact.

"What do I do about you?" Cabe muttered not for the first time. He prodded the box ever so slightly. "I should destroy you now, that's what I should do." Destroying it was not truly the answer, however. That would only leave the incident unresolved, possibly forever. The box was proof.

He knew that, but the warlock could still not bring himself to take it to its former owner. *This could set kingdom against kingdom . . . create civil wars. . . .* Cabe wondered if the one responsible for the box had foreseen that. Had they actually *wanted* that?

*Cabe?* The voice that suddenly echoed in his head made him grateful he had also taken the precaution of shielding part of his mind. Despite the fact that she was now linked to her husband, Lady Bedlam would *not* be aware of the thoughts running through his head. She, especially, could not be told just yet.

It was possibly the first time he had kept something of such importance hidden from her. Cabe struggled with the shame as he responded to her mental summons. *Yes?*

*At last!* came her response. *I was beginning to fear for you, you know! This isn't the first time I've tried to contact you.*

He grimaced. Cabe did not even know how long he had been sitting here, save that the small breakfast he had forced down no longer was enough to sustain him. At present, his stomach was sounding much like a volcano preparing to erupt. *I'm sorry.*

*Where are you?*

*In my study.*

The surprise was almost vocal. *Still? Darling—*

Before she could ask the question that he would again be forced to ignore, Cabe interjected, *What is it? You sound as if you have some news.*

*I do.* It was clear that she did not like her questions being shunted aside again, but knew better than to argue at this point. For that, the frustrated mage was happy. *This morning there was a missive from the Green Dragon.*

He straightened. "What does he want?" he asked out loud before recalling the link. Fortunately, asking the question was the same as framing it in his mind.

*The master of Irillian by the Sea is demanding to see Kyl sooner than we'd planned. In fact, the missive clearly indicates that we can expect him to leave his kingdom tomorrow or the day after.*

Of all the things that the missive might have contained, the meeting between Kyl and the Dragon Kings' chosen representative had been the only matter the warlock had *not* worried about. Yet, it should have not been so surprising. Of course the Dragon Kings would know almost instantly about the botched assassination; they would be justly concerned about the state of affairs at this point. This alteration in the schedule was as much to assess the change the attempt might have had on the heir's mental state as it was anything else. Cabe could not blame the drake lords, but he certainly wished that they had not reacted so. It meant one more terrible concern to add to the mountain already looming before him.

*Is the meeting place still the same or has he changed that, also?*

*That's what makes this even more important. The Blue Dragon is coming here.*

Cabe grunted. There really had been no reason to think that the Blue Dragon might have wanted to change the location of the meeting, but the warlock had wondered. Now he was being rewarded for the curiosity.

*There is no stopping the Blue Dragon. Therefore, Lord Green would like one of us to come see him. There are some details that he would like to go over; things we might have to do differently now that the Manor is the location. I think he might have some concern about Penacles and its stability, too. The Dragon Kings might be anxious about the Gryphon resuming control. That may be one reason that Blue will not wait. I know that doesn't quite make sense, but the message indicated such a fear.*

*Toos only died the other day,* the somber mage noted to his wife. *Does the entire continent already know?* There really was no reason to be concerned about the return of the lionbird to the throne of Penacles; the policies of the general and his former commander were of a like nature. If the Dragon Kings had not been overly fearful of the regent's rule, then the return of the Gryphon should not be bothering them that much. They could certainly not be thinking that the monarch of Penacles had war in mind. Cabe found the Green Dragon's fears questionable.

*Will you go or shall I, Cabe?*

He realized that he had drifted away from the silent conversation. The warlock tapped a finger on the arm of the chair. He knew what he wanted to say, and he also knew it was the coward's way. After some deliberation, Cabe finally sighed and replied, *I'll go.*

There was a still moment as she obviously waited for him to continue. When it evidently became clear that he had finished, the enchantress returned, *All right. I hope everything goes well.*

Her concern, her love, was quite genuine, as it always was, and knowing that only served to make him feel even more guilty for hiding what he knew from her. Not for the first time, he was amazed that she still loved him so after all these years.

*It'll be fine*, he promised.

*Please hurry back.*

"I won't stay any longer than need be," he promised out loud. A breath later, the link was broken. Left alone once more, Cabe at first resumed his pensive staring, but then guilt forced him to sit up. Guilt and the glimpse of some figure at the very edge of his vision. Using his body to shield the box from the newcomer, he quickly cast a spell that sent the artifact to one of the chests in which he stored objects. The chest was protected by other spells, so Cabe knew that the box would be secure there.

That left the intruder to deal with. The warlock finished turning around. "Who is—yes, scholar? Did you want something?"

It was indeed the form of Benjin Traske, but the huge man was acting in a peculiar manner. First, he did not respond to the mage's question. Second, the tutor appeared obsessed with the books just to the side and above where Cabe presently sat.

"Scholar Traske? I asked you a—"

Through the massive girth of the man the warlock could see the opposing wall.

The Benjin Traske before him was nothing more than one of the Manor's ghosts. Even as the realization sank in, the bearded figure, hand outstretched toward the shelf of tomes that Cabe kept in the study, ceased to be.

Knowing that the tutor had been in the study more than once in the past, Cabe's interest in the phantom dwindled somewhat. Out of habit, he located the notebook in which he kept track of all sightings and wrote down this latest addition to the parade of images. Cabe eyed the list, briefly wondering if he would ever discover the pattern or reasons for any of the ghostly intruders, then replaced the tome among the others. His gaze rested on some of the titles.

Aurim was still not free of Toma's spell. Cabe knew that he would not rest easy until that problem was also dealt with, but he had run out of ideas . . . of his own. It occurred to him now, though, that he had not consulted any of the books in his small collection here. Perhaps there was something he could quickly thumb through. It would but take a few minutes of his time to decide whether the books would be of any use. The Green Dragon could wait that long. Certainly Cabe could, if only for his son's sake, he told himself.

The master mage scanned the titles. To his disappointment, he knew almost immediately that he could eliminate virtually all of them. There was, however, one volume that he decided might offer some hint of what he sought. Cabe reached up, but as he took hold of the tome, the notebook, several volumes to the left, suddenly slipped and fell onto his desk. The book flipped open before him, revealing the page upon which he had just recorded his sighting of the Traske ghost.

Cabe took the book he was holding and set it aside. Then, with more care than he had apparently used the last time, the annoyed mage returned the notebook to the shelf, this time making certain that it would not slip again.

A quick glance through the book he had chosen revealed that it held no clue to a swift and safe manner by which to unbind the spell Toma had cast. In point of fact, it held *nothing* of use. Disgusted, the warlock rose from his chair and returned the tome to the shelf. As he pulled his hand away, Cabe happened to notice that the notebook was now a good third of the way over the edge. Quietly cursing himself for the carelessness with which he had undoubtedly returned the last book to the shelf, the warlock pushed the notebook back into place.

That took some doing. It was like trying to squeeze a watermelon into a wine goblet, but at last he managed to accomplish his task. *I'll have to transfer a few of these to the Manor library. This shelf is far too overladen.*

Giving up his quest for the time being, he turned from the shelf and mentally prepared himself for the journey to the Green Dragon's domain. It was not a meeting he looked forward to for many reasons, but Lord Blue's sudden decision made it necessary that alterations in the plan be made and made with swiftness. Gwendolyn had too much to contend with already; Cabe could not place this on her shoulders, too.

Steeling himself, the warlock pictured the lair of the lord of Dagora . . . and vanished.

HAD HE NOT been so engrossed in his thoughts, had he looked back even for a moment, Cabe Bedlam would have perhaps noticed one peculiar thing. The notebook that he had so carefully returned twice now was already slightly over the edge of the shelf . . . and *moving*.

"I HAVE BEEN thinking, Grath," announced Kyl. The heir to the dragon throne was visibly calmer than he had been previously—a good sign. For Kyl to fall to pieces this late in the game would have been tragic. Everything that had been planned depended upon his ascension to the throne. Grath had been ready to drag his brother to the throne if that was what it took to see the coronation done. After that, the younger drake would take his just due. That was fair enough, he thought. Grath deserved much for enabling things to have gone this far. Even his mentor had praised his efforts.

"What've you been thinking about, my brother?" He hoped that Kyl had not devised yet another insane plot for dealing with invisible assassins and the like. Kyl put on a devious front, but he lacked Grath's depth in cunning and subterfuge. Besides, the heir had a hidden ally who was working even now to prevent a reoccurrence of the travesty perpetrated in the regent's arena.

"Benjin Trassske."

"And what about our tutor?"

The two of them were in Kyl's chamber. Grath had been reading while his brother, becoming more daring since yesterday, had wandered to the balcony. Granted, the Manor was the one place where even Grath was certain nothing could happen, but the hours just after the assassination had left his elder brother in such a state that he had secluded himself in his bedchamber, not even deigning to eat his meals with the Bedlams, specifically Valea. The younger drake had been annoyed by such cowardice, for it had ruined a perfect opportunity to play on the beautiful witch's sympathies.

Kyl turned from the balcony, every inch the dazzling emperor-to-be he had been trained from birth to become. The improvement was remarkable and could easily be traced to the visit by the very person the heir now spoke of. "We have known Ssscholar Trassske for many yearsss, from the day he firssst came to educate us. How many yearsss isss that?" He waved aside the response that Grath was about to make. "I do not need the exact count. What I mean isss that throughout ssso long a period, the man hasss tutored usss well and guided usss as much asss any other. Hisss knowledge isss great and hisss ssskillsss many. Yesterday, I know that I sssaid he could not undersssstand all that I face, but today I sssee thingsss in a new light. Asss ever, he hasss been a steadying force." Kyl eyed his brother. "You ressspect him greatly, do you not?"

"More than you could ever know," replied Grath, suspecting where this was going but afraid to reveal his enthusiasm.

Unseen by the smiling Kyl, Faras and Ssgayn exchanged brief, unreadable glances.

"Asss I thought. My own admiration for him isss alssso very high. That isss why I think that I shall apologize to him for my earlier wordsss and asssk him quite sssincerely if he will join me after I become emperor and . . . and become a trusssted advisssor, sssecond to you, of course, brother."

Inside, Grath was fighting back the urge to cry out his triumph. The seed he had planted long ago had finally taken root: Kyl wanted his former tutor as a counselor. Keeping his voice properly restrained, Grath nodded his approval and replied, "I could not have made a better suggestion myself, Kyl."

"The only trouble may lie in whether he will accept." The heir paced back and forth, a habit that his brother secretly found very irritating. Kyl finally paused and looked again at Grath. "You have much influence with our dear teacher. Perhapsss if you presssented him with the offer, he might be more willing to agree. He isss human and a sssurvivor of Mito Pica, which definitely will be wallsss needing to be ssscaled—"

"No wall is too high for a dragon." It was an old drake saying, one which his mentor had taught him long ago. "I think that I can do it, Kyl. I think that he might be interested."

His brother's eyes drifted from his to fix upon the empty air. "It'sss almossst time, Grath. Only the confrontation with Lord Blue remainsss asss a ssstumbling block." A hint of nervousness tinged his words. "That will prove an interessting meeting."

"But one not to be fearful of." Grath put down the book he was reading and rose. He met Kyl's glare with a confident expression. "I am not insinuating that you are afraid, Kyl. Simply that you will so impress Lord Blue that none of the others will question him when he gives you his support. The rest will fall in line then, especially when they learn that the daughter of Cabe Bedlam follows you to Kivan Grath."

"Valea . . ." The look in the heir's emerald-gold countenance made it clear that the elder drake had completely forgotten about the enchantress he had been courting. "She may not come."

Grath walked over to his brother and straightened the narrow collar of Kyl's tunic. "You're wearing one of her favorite outfits. She finds you almost irresistible in it." He pretended as if an idea had just struck him rather than had been simmering since earlier in the morning. "You should look for her. Lead her to a place where the two of you can be alone. Now would be the best time to strike, to ask her to be *yours*."

Kyl looked uncomfortable. "She'll be expecting marriage. Asss emperor, I could only take one of our own kind asss a mate. You know that."

"Do you have to mention the word? A bonding is all you need talk about, Kyl, if you don't wish to lie. She *will* be bonded to you."

That brought a hiss of anger from the heir. "I would rather that she came *willingly*. I am not ssso loathsssome that I mussst ressort to a ssspell, am I?"

"Of course not, but we are rushed for time! When your position as emperor is more secure, then you can release her from the spell if you so wish." *By that time you will dare not, brother, and we both know it*, Grath silently added. Again, he knew that Kyl would tire of her as a female and see her only as a tool. The bond would allow her to keep her personality, but prevent her from disobeying her masters. Valea Bedlam would still need comfort . . . and giving that comfort would link her with Grath in a way that would grow stronger as the spell grew weaker. *You'll bring her with you for my interests alone, if nothing else. After all of this, I will have my rewards, too, and she will be my most prized!*

Slowly, the emperor-to-be agreed. "You are correct asss usssual, Grath. With you and Ssscholar Trassske to advissse me, I will make the throne of the Dragon Emperor once more the ultimate power in all the Dragonrealm!"

*It will certainly have the proper flair for the dramatic!* the younger drake decided, stepping away. "Speaking of our tutor, if I am to persuade him to join us, I must first talk to him. The sooner the better. You should do the same with Valea, Kyl."

"Yesss, you are correct, of course." As Grath started for the door, Kyl turned away from it. "But firssst, I should make certain that I am my very bessst. Then, she will not be able to help but be ssswept off her feet, asss the humansss sssay."

Grath held back a groan. There was, it had to be said, something for the way Kyl was behaving, but over the years he had grown weary of his brother's preening. Grath knew that he himself was considered quite fascinating to both human and drake females, but his role did not allow much time for making full use of his charms. It was Kyl who was supposed to be the mark of perfection.

*But, in the end, she'll be mine. That's what matters. I will have the sorceress and I will be the true lord of all the land!*

In only a matter of days. . . .

*ONLY A MATTER of days left and I still haven't talked to him,* Valea thought morosely as she walked the halls of the Manor. The ancient structure seemed so cold, so oppressive to her. She had not seen Kyl since he had retired to his chambers after the attempt on his life. Grath and Benjin Traske had both said that he was well, but clearly the botched assassination had had some effect. The young Lady Bedlam wanted dearly to go to Kyl and see if there was any comfort she could give him, but that would be throwing herself at him. She had her pride, after all.

That was *all* she would have if he left without speaking to her. While on one hand it was clearly ridiculous to think that he would remain in his rooms until his ascent to the throne, Valea could not help imagining that it might be so.

Ursa had been of little assistance in assuaging her fears, mostly because she had hardly been around. The female drake and Aurim were up to something in his room. Nothing romantic, of course. The two might as well have been brother and sister as far as Valea was concerned. They got along better at times than Valea and Aurim did. No, the young enchantress suspected that they were attempting to find the key to releasing her brother from the spell on his mind. Valea would have been worried if Aurim had tried to do this on his own, but with the more pragmatic and patient Ursa to guide him, it was possible that the two would succeed where even the Gryphon had so far failed.

Which still meant that she had no one to talk to about her situation. Mother was busy with some preparations and, as far as she knew, her father was still ensconced in his study, being moody over who knew what. She could not have talked to either of them, anyway, not about this.

Valea sighed and abstractedly created a flying ring of roses that she then made spin slowly around and around. She bored of the sight very quickly, however, and changed the flowers to paper birds, which fluttered about and danced in some sort of aerial ballet her subconscious had decided upon.

There was only one person that she could turn to, only one person who would understand: Benjin Traske. She had tried to avoid disturbing him, for he, too, had seemed pressed since returning from Penacles. Twice Valea had tried to talk to him, but both times he had seemed preoccupied with something else.

*I can only try. I have to talk to someone.*

She turned down a hallway that would take her toward the scholar's chambers, the paper birds vanishing in little puffs of smoke as the young Lady Bedlam's concerns turned to what she would say to her tutor. He might not even have time to speak with her, but Valea had to try. She was fairly *bursting*. She needed someone close to talk to, and Scholar Traske had already more than proven himself in that regard. Had he not been the one to tell Valea that Kyl loved her? Had she not discussed her quandary with him several times since then? If he could just give her a minute, it would at least make Valea feel a little better. Perhaps he would even have a solution.

It certainly could not hurt to ask.

There were times when the Manor seemed larger on the inside than it did from the outside, but Valea was fairly certain that the feeling was an illusion more than any magic inherent in the ancient edifice. There was no denying that the unknown builders had been great craftsmen. The enchantress did not even mind the long walk this time, for there were still things that she had to resolve with herself.

Along her path she met few others. Most of the people were outside, either working or enjoying the weather. The Manor itself was a surprisingly easy place to care for; it practically cared for itself. Valea had often thought that the true purpose of the many servants in the house was to give it some life. Granted, this had been her home since birth, but the Manor could seem very lonely when no one else was about.

She hated to think what it would be like if she was left behind after Kyl headed north to his throne.

Valea turned down yet another corridor and, because her mind was engrossed in her terrible problem, she did not at first see the figure at the other end of the hall. Only when she heard the sound of boots did she stir from her contemplations.

To her surprise and pleasure, it was Benjin Traske himself. The scholar had evidently not been in his room after all, but the direction in which he was heading indicated that he was likely on his way there now. The young woman wanted to call to him, but she had been raised not to do such mannerless things as shout across halls, so Valea had to content herself with increasing her pace and hoping that she might attract his attention before he entered his chambers.

Valea reached the intersecting corridor and followed after the scholar, but despite his immense girth, Benjin Traske was a swift man. Already he was nearly to the door of his chambers. She tried to hurry more, feeling somehow that to disturb him after he stepped inside was a greater inconvenience to the tutor. Benjin Traske had been so kind to her, she wanted to be as little trouble as possible to him.

Concentrating on reaching the scholar, Valea paid no attention to the side corridors and alcoves. There was no reason to do so. That was why when the draconian figure stepped out from around a corner she did not at first notice him. Only when he rushed silently toward Traske's unprotected back did she pay him any heed.

Only *then* did the enchantress see the curved blade rise.

Her reaction was instinctive, the memory of the regent's death and Kyl's near assassination still fresh. She raised a hand in the direction of the would-be killer and cried, "Nooo!"

The assassin hesitated, obviously surprised to have been discovered. Valea was never able to unleash her spell, however, for with reflexes surprising even for Benjin Traske, the heavyset scholar whirled around to protect himself. The two figures became tangled together. Uncertain as to the effectiveness of her spell, she dared not use it for fear that the tutor would also suffer. Hoping for a better opportunity, Valea rushed forward. If the two separated for even a moment, she wanted to be ready.

Traske and his attacker spun about. For the first time, Valea saw the countenance of the assassin—saw it and stumbled to a halt as she tried to make sense of what was happening.

It was *Ssarekai*. As difficult as it was for most humans to recognize individual drakes from a distance, she knew the stable master too well not to know it was him now. Dear sweet Ssarekai, who had helped train her to ride her first horse and, later, her first riding drake. Ssarekai, who listened to her stories and told fascinating ones of his own about the days of the Dragon Emperor. Servitor drakes saw much that their superiors did not realize.

Dear sweet Ssarekai was trying to murder Scholar Traske?

She remained where she was, caught up in her confusion. Valea could think of no reason for the drake's behavior at first, but then her chaotic thoughts happened to touch upon the spell that Toma had woven into the minds of both Ssarekai and her brother. Was this attack the result of that?

The two hissing combatants seemed not to recall her at all as they spun back and forth, the blade dangling between them. Ssarekai still held it, but Benjin Traske had his wrist and was trying to push the blade toward the face of his adversary.

"I know you again!" Ssarekai suddenly hissed. "I should have sssmelled your foul . . . foul ssscent and recognized it! You were alwaysss ssso certain of yourself!"

Traske did not reply, but his bearded face had taken on a most—*evil,* was the only word Valea could find that fit—look, and as he pressed his counterattack, he appeared almost inhuman. His eyes seemed to blaze. His lips curled back in what reminded her of the toothy reptilian "smile" of an angry drake.

She still did not know what to do. Somehow, the young sorceress could not bring herself to try to bring down the drake, no matter that he had tried to murder her teacher. There was something about the desperation in Ssarekai's voice and the increasingly dark visage of Benjin Traske that prevented her from doing what should have seemed obvious. Summoning aid did not even enter her mind, so ensnared was she in the situation. Two of those who had been a part of her life from the beginning were fighting to the death, and she could not decide which one to save.

The blade inched closer to the drake's half-concealed face. Ssarekai evidently saw the inevitability of its path, for suddenly he released the knife, sending it clattering to the floor. At the same time, Valea felt a tug on the powers from which all mages drew, a sign that a spell of great magnitude was being formed and executed in rapid order.

Ssarekai opened his mouth as if to scream, but no sound emerged. The drake froze in place and his entire form turned a mottled gray.

It was Benjin Traske who had released the spell, the novice sorceress realized: Benjin Traske, who was supposed to have barely enough ability to raise a *feather* a few inches from the ground.

It was Benjin Traske, a man who, still engrossed in crushing his opponent, was also beginning to melt.

More and more he looked less human. His mouth was open in a triumphant smile, but the teeth within were noticeably jagged even from where Valea stood. The scholar's skin had taken on a peculiar coloring, one that was faintly . . . *green?* He looked taller, thinner, and beneath his robes it seemed as if he might be wearing armor. Even the blade he always wore on his belt had changed, for now it gleamed as if it had become a source of light itself.

Benjin Traske was a drake.

He could be only one drake, but Valea tried to deny it. Tried and failed, for too many things were falling in place, many of them involving her.

The stern but understanding man who had taught her and the others over the years was in reality the most hated creature in the Dragonrealm. He was Duke Toma, the renegade.

He began to turn her way. His face and form were again solidifying into the one she was so familiar with, but it would be impossible for Valea to ever believe that what she had just witnessed had been some illusion.

Traske/Toma fixed his gaze on her. "Valea—"

She transported herself away without even thinking of where it would be best to go. The hallway before the tutor's chamber door became another corridor. At first, the enchantress was uncertain as to where she had chosen to flee, but slowly Valea recognized her location. She was near Kyl's room . . . only a few yards from his door, in fact.

It was impossible to move. The realization of what she had just witnessed was finally catching up to her. Valea stood where she was, gasping for air and shaking. Only now did guilt touch her; guilt for leaving poor brave Ssarekai to Toma. It mattered not that she could have done nothing, but the weary sorceress felt that she should have been able to do *something*.

Ssarekai must have recalled what it was the spell Toma had put on him had made him forget. That suppressed memory had probably concerned the horrible truth about Benjin Traske. Something had stirred the stable master's memory enough to break the spell. Why Ssarekai had chosen the path he had, a daring assassination attempt, she did not know, but it likely would have succeeded if Valea had not chosen to be there at that moment.

*I have to warn everyone.* Stirring, she tried to recall where her mother and father were. Father had been in his study. Perhaps he was still there. Valea tried to focus on the blue-robed figure. Father would make things right; he had always managed to overcome what she had often considered impossible odds. He would save them all from Toma.

Perhaps he would have, if he had been in his study. Valea called to her father, but sensed only that he had been in the Manor but recently, which helped her not in the least. Toma could only be moments behind her. Valea knew what sort of chance she stood against the renegade. Toma was a spellcaster on a par with her parents. Aurim, whose skill and power were greater than hers at the moment, had easily fallen victim to the drake.

She was almost ready to begin an attempt to contact her mother when the door to Kyl's chambers swung open. The scarlet-tressed woman paused as the tall, elegant figure of the heir stepped into the corridor.

"Valea?" Kyl's mouth broke into a dazzling smile, making Valea almost forget what was happening. "Thisss *isss* a pleasssant sssurprise, I mussst sssay! I wasss jussst—"

The sound of his voice stirred her to action. She seized him by the arms and cried, "Kyl! Toma's in the Manor! Toma, he's right behind—"

Confusion and dismay spread across the drake's exotic visage. He looked at her close. "What'sss that? What are you sssaying?"

Before she could answer, however, an armored drake stepped out of Kyl's chamber. Whether it was Faras or his counterpart Ssgayn, Valea could not at that moment have said. "My lord! We heard her ssspeak of Toma!"

"She sssays that—"

The guard did not wait for him to finish. He took hold of each of the two by an arm and began to steer them inside the room. "Bessst not to talk out here, my lord! What Toma cannot see he may not find! Hurry!"

Valea wanted to protest, but Ssgayn—she had recognized his voice at last—already had them through the doorway. As he led them through, Faras, standing nearby, closed the door and bolted it.

"We can't simply wait here!" the sorceress finally shouted. "Toma will come here before long!"

"I agree." Kyl hissed in obvious nervousness. "Toma! I was jussst ssspeaking of him, wasss I not?"

The two guards nodded solemnly.

Valea had no time for this. Again she took hold of Kyl. Another time, such close contact would have thrilled her, but now what mattered was their lives. "Listen, Kyl! I tried to contact my father, but I couldn't find him. I'll try my mother, but you have to know something first. He's *Benjin Traske*, Kyl! Benjin Traske!"

The heir apparently misunderstood her. "Toma hasss the ssscholar? Where? How?"

"No! Benjin Traske *is* Duke Toma! I discovered it by accident. He caught poor Ssarekai, who tried to kill him."

Kyl simply stood there, as if unable to accept what he was hearing. "Ssscholar Trasssske isss *Toma?*"

The two guards said nothing, but both had grown very tense. Valea could hardly blame them; how many times had they left their lord with the tutor, not realizing the truth? "I have to try my mother. Everyone is in danger! I think he dares not hide any longer, Kyl! He had to fight Ssarekai and he knows that I saw him!"

"No more talk, then, my enchantress! Do what mussst be done." He gave her an encouraging smile.

Strengthened by that, Valea put as much will as she had left to muster into the magical summons. She had no idea where her father must be, but her mother was usually in the same place at this time of day. If she failed to contact Lady Bedlam, Valea then planned on trying a scattered call, which, theoretically, would send her message to all parts of the Manor. Valea had trouble with that method, though, which was why she hoped that she was successful with her first attempt.

However, a peculiar thing happened when she tried to reach out and make contact with her mother. Valea felt the summons stretch forth from her mind, felt it building in strength, but when she tried to reach out beyond Kyl's chamber, it was as if she had run into a mental wall. She tried to push harder, but still could sense nothing beyond the room. Valea tried again, but the results were the same. Try as she might, she could not have contacted her mother even if the emerald enchantress had been standing on the other side of the door to Kyl's suite.

Toma knew where they were. It was the only answer.

"What isss wrong? Why are you shivering?"

Shivering? Valea had not even noticed that she was shivering, but under the circumstances, she did not think that she could be blamed for doing so. Quickly, Valea explained what had happened.

After she was done, Kyl glanced at his two guards, but their faces betrayed nothing. Valea simply assumed that they would follow whatever command he gave them. She had never been close to either Ssgayn or Faras, but then, they had never tried to be more than what they were. It was as if they had been born to be bodyguards all their lives.

"Perhapsss . . ." Kyl began. "Perhapsss if we pool our abilities, Valea. I have alwaysss thought that between the two of usss, we could accomplish mossst anything!" He gave her a brief smile. "But talk of that can wait. What do you think? If your power and mine were combined, we might be able to contact one of your parentsss or, if need be, even deal with the renegade."

This at last caused the two guards to move. It was clear that they did not relish the idea of Kyl fighting Toma.

"My lord—" Faras began.

"Sssilence! Well, Valea?"

Someone rapped on the door. A moment later, a familiar voice hissed, "Kyl! Let me in!"

Grath! Valea had completely forgotten about Kyl's brother. She had simply assumed that he was in one of the connecting rooms. If Grath had been elsewhere all this time, then he, too, had been in danger. In fact . . .

The heir hissed. "I sssent him to talk to Benjin Trassske! Thank the Dragon of the Depthsss that he isss safe! Open the door! Quickly now!"

Faras had almost unbolted the door when Valea called, "No! You can't!"

The drake paused, then looked to Kyl for guidance. "My lord, your brother isss in danger while he is out there. You know that your chambersss are alssso spelled against intrusion by sssorcery."

Kyl waved aside Valea's protests. "I know my own brother's voice . . . and his mind." He turned to face the door. "Grath! Did you ssspeak with Ssscholar Trassske asss I asked you?"

"No!" returned the voice. "I—Kyl, you would not believe what I have to tell you! Let me in!"

"Let him in," whispered the emperor-to-be to Faras. "But I want all of you ready. Even Toma would not think to take the four of usss on, now would he?" The last was obviously for Valea's benefit. She was certain that he was making a mistake, but there was nothing that she could do. Besides, it was cruel to let Grath remain out there. If he *was* alone, each second he was forced to wait left him vulnerable.

Faras unbolted the door and peeked around it. Ssgayn and Kyl stood ready, the guard with a sword and Kyl with a spell of some kind. Valea readied a crude but powerful spell of her own. If Grath was the puppet of Toma . . .

Slowly, Faras swung the door back just enough for a single person to slip through. Grath, or at least someone who looked exactly like him, did just that. Once the figure was through, the draconian guard immediately shut and re-bolted the door.

"There isss sssome reasssonable concern that you might not be who you look like, Grath." Kyl's tone was incredibly apologetic. "I hope you will forgive usss for having to determine the truth."

Grath stood still, his arms hanging at his sides. "I am me, but if you need to verify my honesty, please do so in whatever way you feel most suitable, Kyl."

Kyl looked at the guards. "Are you ready, jussst in cassse?"

The two nodded. Satisfied, the dragon heir stepped in front of the one who might be his brother. He carefully reached out and put one hand on Grath's shoulder.

Valea felt the power that passed between them. All those with even the most minor tendency for sorcery had a special magical signature, a particular touch, that other mages could sense if they knew how. For two with as strong a bond as the brothers, it was virtually impossible to fool either one of them with a false signature. Even Toma would be hard-pressed to mask his own magical pattern as that of Grath.

Kyl exhaled as he removed his hand. "You are Grath."

"Of course I am."

"We could not be certain. We could not trusssst that it wasss you, brother."

Grath eyed him, an enigmatic expression on his face. He glanced Valea's way very briefly, then returned his gaze to Kyl. "*Do* you trust me, Kyl?"

The heir was surprised by the question. "With my life!"

"And you should know that I want nothing more than to see you on the throne. That is why you must trust me now."

Valea did not care for Grath's tone. She took a step toward him, not quite certain as to why he was making her nervous. "What do you have in mind, Grath? Do you have some sort of plan in mind for dealing with Toma?"

He looked at her. "You have tried to contact your parents?"

"I couldn't find my father and something prevented me from contacting Mother." Grath's calm was annoying her. Did he not realize how dire a situation they faced?

Grath reached up and put a comforting hand on her shoulder. "That's what I wanted to know. Thank you."

She wanted to ask him what he meant by such an odd response, but then she noticed the buildup of power within him. Too late did she realize that she had yet *again* been betrayed. As she tried to pull free of his grip, a grip suddenly tight and painful, her body refused to follow her desires. Instead, Valea found herself unable to move, unable to even speak.

"What have you done to her?" snarled Kyl, realizing too late that his brother had cast a spell on the startled witch.

Grath looked beyond his brother. "Faras. Ssgayn."

She could still see, and so at the edge of her vision Valea was able to watch as Kyl's two trusted bodyguards seized hold of their emperor-to-be and kept him pinned by the arms no matter how much he struggled.

"We are sssorry to do thisss, Your Majesssty," Faras added with much anxiety.

Grath stood before his brother. "If you will calm down and listen, I can have them release you that much sooner. I am sorry about this, but you didn't look as if you were going to wait for me to explain. Will you please do that now, Kyl?"

"I ssseem to have little *choice* in the matter, *brother!*"

"Actually, you have much choice. Do you remember our conversation just a short while ago? How we talked about the throne and the troubles it has brought? We talked about Toma, didn't we?"

Grath's transformation dismayed the frozen Valea. She had always known him to be a studious, somewhat shy person. He had always walked in the shadow of his brother, although even she would have been willing to admit that

Kyl had always benefited from his advice. Now, however, Grath more resembled a smooth, cunning courtier, like some of those the young Lady Bedlam had met among the aristocracy of Penacles or Talak.

Kyl did not reply to his brother save to reluctantly nod.

"We've talked about Toma, our *brother*, before. You and I both know that he wasss loyal to our father and remained with him long after the other Dragon Kingsss had abandoned him. You know that he wasss there to rescue us from Lord Ice when we became caught between the machinations of the mad lord of the Northern Wastes and Master Bedlam. Among all the drakes, Kyl, you will have to admit that no one hasss been more loyal to the throne than he."

That was not quite the history that Valea had grown up knowing. It was close enough to the truth, however, to disguise itself as fact. Her father would have been able to relate the entire tale, but she doubted that anyone but she would have listened.

"I remember the Northern Wastes, I think," Kyl admitted with reluctance.

"Toma can never be emperor. You know that. I know that. *He* knows that. He has known that for years. Therefore, only one path was left open to him. Despite the need to hide, despite the enemies who have sought to kill him because he represents the might of the emperor, the duke has continued to work to see the day that a new, stronger leader will bring our kind back to the pre-eminence we once held."

Slowly, Grath stepped back to the bolted door. He reached for the bolt. "No one is more regretful than he that all his work had to be done under the guise of another. He had hoped to present himself to you after your crowning. His life would have been yours to take or end there. At least the goal he has sought for the last several years would then be secure."

Valea tried her best to break the spell that held her, but Grath had cast it too well. She doubted that even Aurim would have been able to escape.

Unbolting the door, the younger drake seized the handle. He looked so very apologetic to his brother that Valea wanted to spit in his face. "Kyl, I present to you one who isss not your enemy, has never *been* your enemy, but rather has been your most loyal servant . . . even moresso than I, I have to admit."

The drake swung open the door. Valea's heart sank as Benjin Traske entered.

"Ssscholar . . ." Kyl muttered, more awestruck, the sorceress was sad to see, than fearful.

"Not scholar, my lord," said the massive figure, and even as he strode forward, he resembled less and less the bearded tutor and more and more something terribly inhuman. Then the scholar began to melt. The heavy girth became a river of glowing liquid that faded as it poured away. Yet, while Benjin Traske grew thinner, he also grew taller still.

Traske's clothing also changed. Quickly the scholar's robe became armor, scaled armor that covered the teacher from head to toe. His hands twisted and the fingers lengthened, becoming much like those of either of the brothers.

Kyl gaped and Grath smiled as the face also became something different. The stern, bearded visage pulled in and the head reshaped itself, at last forming a partial shell. The shell defined itself into a helm within which the last vestiges of Benjin Traske reformed into the flat, incomplete features of a drake warrior. Yet, unlike most drake warriors, the helm of this one had as elaborate a dragon head crest as any of the drake lords themselves.

Crossing the little distance that still remained between the two of them, the immense drake warrior stopped, then knelt before the dragon heir. Within the false helm, the lipless mouth curved into a toothy smile.

"Your Majesssty," announced Grath as he shut the door and bolted it again. "It pleases me to presssent your mossst humble and *loyal* ssservant, *Duke Toma* of Kivan Grath."

# XVIII

CABE WOUND HIS way through the vast underground cavern of the Green Dragon, his escorts trying their best to keep pace with the hurrying warlock. Having known the Dragon King for as long as he had, Cabe could have transported himself directly to the main hall of the subterranean labyrinth without asking permission, but he had needed the time to think. Think and plan.

"This way," he muttered, turning down yet another corridor. The guards and guide stumbled after him. None of them thought to order him to slow down, for everyone who followed the master of the Dagora Forest knew of the warlock and how powerful he was said to be. He was also known to be a friend and ally of their lord. If there *had* been some question as to his motives, then they would have tried their best to either capture or kill him, but it would not have been something any of the guards would have looked forward to with eagerness. They were quite aware of their chances against the robed figure stalking ahead of them.

Only at the end of the corridor did Cabe at last pause. Here at last was the great central chamber that the Green Dragon utilized as his throne room and hall. Here the Dragon King met his guests.

Unlike the caverns of most of his counterparts, that of the Green Dragon was covered with lush plant life, most of it of the kind that should not have been able to thrive so far from the sun. Yet, thanks to the power and skill of the drake lord, vines, shrubs, and flowering plants made the chamber resemble more a forest than a cave. Over the past few years, the Dragon King had redesigned this hall, adding further to his vast collection of foliage.

In the midst of the underground grove and seated upon his throne was the armored form of the Dragon King himself. He was flanked on each side by the fiercest pair of guards that Cabe could recall ever having faced. As was typical of Lord Green, one of the guards was a drake, but the other was a human. It was debatable which was the more terrible of the two. The Green Dragon prided himself in carrying on the ways of his predecessors; here, humans and drakes were almost as equal as at the Manor. What made things different in Cabe's home, however, was that it was a human who ruled there, not a Dragon King. The experiment at the Manor represented the first time that drakes had ever coexisted peacefully with humans in a place where they did not dominate. The idea had been the Green Dragon's.

There was so much about his host that the warlock had always admired.

"Thank you for coming, Friend Cabe." The reptilian knight indicated a chair that had been set near his throne. The chair was set on a level with the Dragon King's own, which was supposed to indicate the drake's long-standing belief in the equality of the two races, but the mage had always noticed that both Lord Green and his throne stood *taller*. He had often wondered whether that was intentional, or whether the Dragon King had simply never noticed it.

"Thank you, but I prefer to stand." Behind him, his escorts vanished down one of the other tunnels.

The Green Dragon straightened a bit. "As you desire. You know the contents of the missive, then?"

"Gwendolyn informed me, yes. It's not surprising when you think about it. Not even the fact that Lord Blue is coming here. Of all the Dragon Kings, other than yourself, of course, he is the only one I would trust enough to allow entry, *temporary* entry in his case, into the Manor."

"Yesss, I trust him, too. The others are upsssset, Friend Cabe, although none of them would be able to give you the same reasons."

Cabe frowned. "Imagine what they would have been like if the assassins *had* succeeded in murdering Kyl. Thank goodness for Grath, if that should happen."

It appeared to take Lord Green time to translate what he was saying. "Yesss, we may be thankful that if some tragedy did seize the life of the heir, may the Dragon of the Depths prevent such, there would be Grath to step in and take hisss place."

"We've often commented to one another that he would make just as good, possibly *better*, an emperor as Kyl."

The Dragon King shifted position. "That we have, which is not to say that Kyl isss not already coming into his own. He will do sssplendidly, I am sure."

Cabe walked around the chair set aside for him. He stared the drake lord in the eye. The warlock heard the guards suddenly straighten but paid them little mind.

"*You* are the one who sent the assassins to murder Kyl. *You*, my Lord Green, tried to have your new emperor killed. We both know that, don't we?"

The guards readied their weapons and started for the warlock, but the armored tyrant raised a mailed hand. Both warriors paused, but the glares they gave Cabe Bedlam were dark and murderous.

"Friend Cabe, are you aware of the wordsss you jussst spoke? We have known each other since you firssst were forced to acknowledge your heritage. I consider you and yours not only close allies but close companionsss as well."

"Which doesn't change the fact that *you* tried to murder Kyl and ended up murdering *Toos*."

There was an edge to the Green Dragon's voice. "How could you sssay something like that?"

"You captured Darkhorse," the bitter sorcerer went on, ignoring both the questions of his host and the seething faces of the guards. "As good as tortured him by using that box. I think that you had confidence enough to handle everyone but Darkhorse . . . and you found a way to make use of his power, too. You forgot one thing, though. I know you as well as anyone does. We've discussed the history of the Vraad over and over. I've seen your collection, and I know from my own researches some of the tricks and toys that my unesteemed ancestors devised, especially when they realized that most of them were losing their vast powers." Cabe folded his arms. "There was also the band of assassins that I was supposed to think was part of an Aramite plot. Drakes and humans working together on this? Did you *want* to be discovered, my lord? Was that why you made it so obvious to me?"

He knew that he had really said little that could directly be tied to the Dragon King, that would have been considered proof by anyone, but to the warlock's sad surprise, the Green Dragon slumped back in his throne. He glanced back at the guards and commanded, "Leave usss, pleassse."

With obvious reluctance, the two obeyed.

When they were alone, the lord of Dagora finally spoke. "I do not know whether I desssired to be found out, Cabe Bedlam, or sssimply wasss so full of anxiety and horror at what I was doing that I did not take more care. Yesss, I *am* the one responsible for nearly assassinating Kyl and inssstead killing the brave and honorable regent of Penacles."

Try as he might, Cabe could no longer stay angry. Instead, disappointment was all he felt. Great disappointment. It was as if the world he had known had proven to be a falsehood. In some ways, it was even more terrible than when he

had been torn from his uninteresting existence as a server at an inn and thrust
into a world of sorcery and intrigue. He had learned so much from the Dragon
King, shared so much with him. There were few beings that the warlock felt
comfortable with; in the small circle of true friends he had thought he had, the
Dragon King had been one.

Yet, after what the drake lord had done . . .

"I did what I felt was necessary, warlock. Kyl was an arrogant, conceited
creature who threatened to repeat the mistakes of hisss sire. Grath, who the
powersss that be had brought to this world *after* his brother, wasss by far a more
level sssort. He would deal with the relations of both races fairly, evenly. Kyl
might suddenly be of the mind to reconquer the continent, plunging usss all
into a war none can afford. He might even be the great enemy of hisss own
kind, for I know that he still holdsss much bitterness toward sssome of the surviving kings for abandoning his predecessor. Kyl isss even the sort who might
find the renegade, Toma, more of an ally than a danger."

"I find *that* hard to believe."

The Green Dragon rose from his throne and looked down at the human.
Cabe did not flinch, much less back away. "*I* do not."

The warlock matched his counterpart's gaze. He was not pleased, however,
when the Dragon King finally looked away. Things should not have deteriorated
to such a point that the two had to attempt to stare one another down. "Kyl
had Grath to guide him."

"But our esteemed emperor-to-be doesss not have to *listen* to hisss brother.
Should Kyl grow furiousss at something Grath suggests, he has only to order his
brother from hisss sight. Then, the voices that whisper in his ears will become
those of my fellow kings' spiesss. Where would the Dragonrealm be then? No,
the only certain method by which the stability of the throne could be assured
was to remove Kyl and replace him with Grath."

"I don't agree." Cabe shook his head, still unable to completely believe that
the figure before him had created so much chaos and tragedy. "That also doesn't
condone what you did to Toos and Darkhorse—or the Gryphon. Toos was
a brother to the Gryphon, my Lord Green; you saw what the general's death
meant to him. He wants the one responsible. So does Darkhorse."

The inhuman knight started to turn away. "I did what I knew *had* to be—"

"*Don't turn from me!*" roared Cabe. Without meaning to, he almost unleashed a spell on the recalcitrant monarch. Cabe barely contained it in
time, and the power was such that his body glowed red for several seconds
afterward.

The Green Dragon stared at him, jaw hanging. The warlock calmed enough
to see that, for the first time, the Dragon King was truly afraid of him.

"I should tell them the truth, you know! Both Darkhorse and the Gryphon *deserve* to know. Do you realize the extent of Darkhorse's claustrophobia? He existed in a place without time or end. I know that the Vraad used a box very much like that to capture him! He's never told me everything, but I've never seen as much terror in his eyes as when he is reminded of that!"

"What did you do with the box?" interrupted the drake lord.

"I still have it. It damned you more than anything else; I could recognize your knowledge in it. No one else had access to such an artifact, and no one else would have understood it the way you do!" Again, the accusations were flimsy, but now that Cabe had had confirmation of his suspicions from the Green Dragon himself, the claims had weight. "There was so much. The spells that masked one magical trace with another. The cloaks of the assassins—men you callously assured would not live so that anyone questioning them would discover the truth. They died too easily, Lord Green. Even the Aramite. *More* futile deaths on your shoulders."

"I will take no blame for their deaths, Cabe Bedlam! They were condemned criminals, one and all. They would have been executed. I am not like Black, who would carelessly send his enchanted human legions against the walls of his enemies again and again until the mindless unfortunates either overran the foe or died to a man!"

The warlock, his face carefully neutral, shrugged. "I don't know *what* you're like anymore."

"I am as I have *always* been."

"That worries me even more, then. What will you decide next serves your needs? The deaths of me and my loved ones?"

The Dragon King hissed and his talons unsheathed. "Of course not!"

"How can I believe that anymore?"

For several seconds, the tall, armored tyrant stood there, eyes burning embers, claws at the ready. Then, the talons slowly sheathed and the fire in his eyes died. Lord Green returned to his throne and slumped back into it again. "There isss no promise that I could give you that you would believe, isss there?"

Cabe slumped, too. This had taken more out of him than the drake lord knew. "No. There isn't."

"Will you tell the others, then? Shall I prepare to receive the visitations of either the eternal or the lionbird?"

"It would mean only more chaos and tragedy, neither of which we can afford these days."

It was clear that his reply puzzled the Dragon King. "Are you saying that you will keep what you know a sssecret?"

Some of Cabe's anger returned. "Not because of the friendship we once had, but because if peace is to work in the land, nothing else can go wrong. I may not even tell Gwendolyn, although I probably will. I know that she'll think as I do, that we can't afford another war." He paused. "What she'll think of you, I couldn't say."

His host nodded slowly. "I understand what you sssay. I understand your view of thisss. You will do nothing else?"

"There's nothing I can do that wouldn't make the situation worse than it is. I'm more concerned now with seeing this coronation through to the end . . . with Kyl assuming his *rightful* place. When he's emperor, then we can judge his abilities. No sooner. Prejudgment is no one's right, however often we *all* fall prey to it."

Silence filled the chamber for several seconds. The Dragon King finally looked up into the eyes of the warlock and quietly asked, "Isss there more? I had assumed you would be gone the moment your piece had been sssaid."

Cabe took a deep breath and smoothed his robe. "We still have Lord Blue's change in plans to talk about. We still have to make all of this work. Are you prepared to accept things the way they are?"

"After Penaclesss, I swore that I would do nothing else to risssk this peace. I desire it as much as you, even if it meansss Kyl on the throne."

With a small flicker of power, the exhausted warlock brought the other chair to him. He also enlarged it slightly, this in order to allow him to look directly into the eyes of his host, not *up* at them. "Then we should begin. Tell me what I need to know about the Blue Dragon and what he might have planned for Kyl."

The Dragon King began to discuss his counterpart, but although the conversation became more comfortable as they went on, Cabe knew that his relationship with the drake lord would never be the same.

AURIM SAT CROSS-LEGGED on his bed while Ursa sat next to him. His fingertips were pressed against his temple and his eyes were shut tight. Although he could not see her, he knew that the drake watched him with concern. Neither of his parents knew what he was doing. That was fine with him; they had far too much on their minds already. He had relied on them and their friends far too long. It was time to prove that all the talk of potential meant something.

The young warlock intended to break Toma's spell on his own.

Not *completely* on his own. Ursa was assisting him, albeit with reluctance. Some of the paths he had tried required more manipulation than he could muster by himself. She was also there in case something *did* go wrong . . . which he had assured her several times would *not* happen.

His methods of search bordered on the unorthodox. Aurim had already observed his parents and the Gryphon going through most of the more normal paths, and not a few unusual ones they were familiar with, which left him only the ones he was taking. One of those methods, he was certain, had to be the key to unraveling the renegade's spell.

The past few minutes had left him encouraged in that respect. It was difficult to be certain, but Aurim almost felt as if the web Toma had spread over his mind had weakened a little more. It *felt* different.

"Are you all right, Aurim?"

"Yes." He dared not answer further. At the moment, the tiny magical probe he was guiding was slipping past one of the multiple safeguards Toma had planted. This was his first *major* triumph over the spell. The warlock felt the pressure in his head ease just a bit more as he removed the safeguard and weakened the spell further.

Images flashed in his mind. Ssarekai, a look of shock on his face that even the dim light of night illuminated all too well. A figure halfway between two forms, and although neither had been recognizable, he had known that one of them was Toma.

There was something more, but it remained just out of his mental reach.

"I've broken through," he whispered, glancing up briefly at Ursa. His throat felt astonishingly dry. "Just a little, but I've made more progress than they did the other day."

She clapped her hands together. "How *wonderful!*"

"It gets harder here, though. I think that I might need for you to—" Aurim was interrupted by a knock on the door. The sound shattered his concentration, which, in turn, shattered his probe. The warlock was frustrated, but at least he had forged further than anyone else. Once he dealt with the interruption, Aurim intended to try a stronger probe in an area near the location he had just freed. If the safeguard Toma had planted there also fell to him, Aurim suspected that he stood a good chance of completely dismantling the spell before it was time for dinner.

"I'll see who it is," offered Ursa.

Aurim was glad to let her. The moment he tried to rise, the room began to whirl.

The drake opened the door. "Yes? Scholar Traske!"

Aurim glanced toward the door to see the huge tutor waiting in the hallway. A shiver went down his spine as he met the eyes of the man.

*Now why*—he started to think, but then Benjin Traske spoke, interrupting Aurim's train of thought.

"My apologies. I expected to find you alone, Master Aurim."

"Ursa was just helping me with something." He hoped that the scholar would not ask what it was with which she had been assisting. Aurim was fairly certain that Traske would not have approved. Likely the tutor would have reprimanded him and then informed his parents.

"I see." Benjin Traske took a step closer. "May I enter?"

Ursa quickly darted aside. Aurim slid over to the edge of the bed, lowered his legs, and started to stand, but Traske raised a hand to stop him. "Sit, please. There's no need to stand, boy."

Ursa started to move for the open door. "I should leave you two alone. If you will excussse me, Scholar Traske, then I—"

"No, I think it's best at this point that *you* stay also. Yes, that would be for the best, indeed. Why don't you close the door and sit down next to Aurim. That will make everything much *easier* for me."

Puzzled, she nonetheless obeyed his suggestion, closing the door, then settling down beside the curious warlock.

It seemed to Aurim that Benjin Traske was apprehensive about something. There was just the slightest hesitation in his movements and his breathing was a bit fast. "Are you all right, Scholar Traske?"

"Sssome decisions had to be made at the proverbial spur of the moment, Master Aurim. They are not decisions that I am comfortable with, but there really is no other choice that I can see at this time."

"What do you mean?"

The tutor advanced so that he was within arm's reach of both of them. He looked down at the two with what Aurim believed almost fatherly concern. Why not? Benjin Traske had watched all of them grow up. Surely he must sometimes think of them as his own children?

Putting a hand on each of their shoulders, the tutor sighed, a sound that was almost a hiss. A slight smile peered out from within the beard. "I mean that I can take no chancesss."

Aurim felt the power swelling within Benjin Traske, but the comprehension was too late in coming. A thick malaise suddenly enveloped his mind. Somewhere distant, he heard Ursa gasp. Traske himself seemed to shift, becoming something else briefly, something that stirred memories.

The warlock *remembered*. It did him no good to do so, but nonetheless, he remembered. He remembered seeking out with his power and, through it, discovering something terrible happening. Ssarekai, his mind pleading, had been put under some spell. The other mind, that of the caster of the spell, had been two minds. On the surface, it had been Benjin Traske. Below, it had been a creature most vile.

Toma. Aurim had discovered that Benjin Traske was Toma.

He managed to rise to his feet, but that was all. Even that made the false Traske hiss in surprise. Then, however, the golden-haired warlock's strength gave out and he fell back onto the bed.

Consciousness fled.

**ALTHOUGH SHE HAD** no control over her movements, Valea found that she could still shed a tear. Her world was in tatters. Benjin Traske was—possibly had always been—Duke Toma, the deadly renegade. He had listened to her as she had revealed all her deepest secrets to him. He had betrayed the trust her entire family had placed in him. Now, evidently in part because of her, Traske/Toma was going to seize control of the Manor by making one last use of his false identity. The drake intended to use the face of Benjin Traske to get close enough to each member of the family, whereupon he would catch them unaware with his power.

She had no idea why he did not kill them all outright. She did not even have any idea as to why he had left her frozen like a statue in Kyl's room, her mind still very much functioning.

None of that completely explained the tears. Valea was well aware that much of the reason for her crying concerned Kyl. Kyl and his betrayal of her.

The other drakes remained in the room, awaiting Duke Toma's return. They were all highly anxious, especially the traitorous heir himself. Valea hoped that Kyl was feeling pain. She hoped all of the drakes, Grath, Faras, and Ssgayn included, were feeling pain and remorse, but most of all she hoped that Kyl did. The enchanted witch wanted him to feel so much pain that it would make his heart burst.

"Where isss he?" muttered Kyl as he paced.

"You know very well where he is," responded Grath, looking up from a book. The younger drake sat in one of the chairs, hands steepled, eyes keeping track of his brother's movements. "If the spell on Ssarekai has failed, then it stands that Aurim, too, is near recalling. That hasss to be the first thing that is dealt with and the duke must do that on his own. It would look too suspicious for all of us to go with him."

"I want them handled with care, that isss all." Kyl glanced rather guiltily at Valea. "They dessserve that much."

"I know that. Our brother only does what he has to do. They would kill him instantly if they knew he was here, Kyl. Do you think *that's* fair? Toma will fight to preserve his life, that is all. Look how long he has lived among us, yet never has he tried to harm anyone. *That* more than anything else, isss proof of his intentions."

*He's killed no one here because that would mean chancing discovery. It was enough just risking the spell on Aurim and Ssarekai. Toma wants Kyl to give him a place at his side, one where the Dragon Kings can't touch him!* She wondered how long Kyl's reign would last once the renegade had a secure power base again. With the confederacy of the dragon clan survivors to back him, the duke would have enough influence to perhaps alter the law that said he could not be emperor himself.

Despite her bitterness over Kyl and all else, Valea could not help but admire Duke Toma's incredible patience. All those years of masquerading so that he could be an influence on the life of the young emperor-to-be. He had helped mold Kyl—and Grath, too—had learned the innermost secrets about his greatest enemies, and prepared the way for his return to power.

She tried to speak, but, as before, Valea might as well have not even made the attempt. There was no movement whatsoever. She could see, blink, swallow, and breathe, but nothing more. The witch remembered the stories her mother and father had told her about her mother's imprisonment by her grandfather. Azran had left her sealed in amber for . . . what? One? Two centuries? At least Gwendolyn Bedlam had not entirely known what was happening around her. The few minutes that Valea had been helpless were already driving her close to the edge.

Concern for her family was what kept her going. She knew that Toma had no intention of letting any of the Bedlams live. Kyl and even Grath might believe otherwise, but she knew too much about the history of the renegade to think he would do otherwise. The Bedlams would always be a threat to him.

There was a quiet knock on the door. Faras, who stood nearest to the door, unbolted and opened it.

Aurim stepped through. Valea's spirits rose, then sank. Behind Aurim came Ursa, but behind her followed Toma, the renegade once more clad in the form of the tutor.

"You see," said the duke after the door had been closed. "As I promised, my lord, here are your friend and your sissster, both unharmed."

"Why did you bring them here?"

With no warning, Traske melted into Toma. The transformation continued to both fascinate and horrify Valea. "If anyone saw them after I had bespelled them, they would have realized something was amiss. I could not simply make them forget. As I said earlier, Your Majesty, things must now be resolved with ssswiftness." Toma looked properly upset, an expression Valea knew was as false as his words. "Thisss is hardly the way I wanted it. I would have preferred your transition to the throne to be peaceful. If you like, I will sssurrender myself to the Bedlams and take their brand of justice. If you think it will benefit your ascension, that isss."

*Accept his offer!* Valea wanted to shout. It was not that she believed that Toma would follow through on his promise, but rather that she wanted Kyl to understand the dark creature with whom he was dealing.

Kyl, however, shook his head. "No, I know what will happen. Jussst . . . jussst ussse care."

"That I will, my brother. I have promisssed that from the beginning, have I not, Grath?"

The younger drake looked at the heir. "That he has, Kyl. Toma has only worked to serve you for all the time I have known him."

"Now that I have the opportunity to prove myself to you persssonally, I dare not fail to live up to your ssstandards."

Kyl stepped away from the others and out of Valea's view. "What will you do with them?"

Indicating the emperor-to-be with his hands, the draconian knight returned, "As I sssaid earlier, it isss my hope to capture them all and, once that is accomplished, place the entire family under a more subtle, more thorough forgetfulness spell. Already, the children—and, regrettably, sister Ursa—are mine. As Benjin Traske, I should be able to approach both Lord and Lady Bedlam and take them without warning."

"And *kill* them? I'd imagine that you hate them dearly."

Again, Toma looked properly subdued. "My hatred hasss dwindled away over the years here, Your Majesty. I've seen them doing both good and ill. Now, I hold no grudges. I cannot say that I have come to love them; I simply understand them better. If they can be convinced to leave me be, then I shall leave *them* be."

"And if they won't?"

"I would rather not think about that unlessss it becomesss necessary to do so."

"There is no time to discuss this further," Grath interjected. "We must deal with Lord and Lady Bedlam asss soon as possible."

"There is a piece of news that I have not informed either of you about yet." As Toma spoke, he began to shift once again to the scholarly shape of Benjin Traske. This time, Valea clearly saw that the belt blade, the only item true to both Toma and Traske, glowed. She was fairly certain that it was what allowed the renegade to so well retain the form of the tutor. Drakes generally had two shapes. The first was the dragon form that they were born with, the latter was most often the reptilian knight, such as how Duke Toma looked when he was not being Traske. While the renegade was, by her parents' own admissions, more versatile, there were still limitations. The enchanted knife was apparently a way around those limitations.

"And that news is?" asked Kyl. His tone was so matter-of-fact, so calm now, that Valea wanted to scream. He was, in her opinion, worse than the rest of them, for Kyl, as heir to the emperor's throne, should have been strong enough to withstand Toma's ploys. Instead, he had accepted every word as easily as a sheep would have accepted a handful of grass. It made the imprisoned witch furious, which only served to fuel her frustration.

"The master warlock is not in the Manor nor is he on the Manor grounds. He has gone to speak to Lord Green. It seems that the monarch of Irillian will be here in only two, at most, three days."

Valea, unable at the moment to think of any drake save dear Ssarekai as trustworthy—and Ssarekai might be dead, although no one had told her so—did not see the visit as any buffer against the renegade's plans. Toma knew the Dragon Kings well. They would be easier to fool than her mother or father.

"Ssso sssoon? I'm not ready for him!" Kyl stepped back into her field of vision. The veneer of confidence had been stripped from his face. He was openly nervous.

"You will be. Grath and I shall see to it that Blue himself will become one of your most ardent supporters by interview's end."

"Have *we* failed you so far, Kyl?" asked Grath, almost mimicking Duke Toma.

"You know that *you* have not, Grath, however—"

"Much of what I did, what suggestions I made, originated from Toma, Kyl. He has guided you more than anyone else, both as Benjin Traske and as himself."

Traske/Toma moved toward the door. "We will have time to talk later. For now, I mussst locate and deal with the Lady of the Amber before her mate returns home." He bowed. "With your permission?"

"You may—" Kyl began, but then he glanced at Grath. "One moment. You should take Grath with you, perhapsss. The better to occupy Lady Gwendolyn's attention while you prepare to take her. What do you sssay?"

Valea saw the merit in the heir's plan, which made her hate him all the more. Grath found it of interest, also.

"An interesssting notion," returned the renegade, his smile more open. He was no doubt pleased by this sign of Kyl's cooperation in this foul venture.

*If I only had a few seconds of freedom!* She had already planned and replanned how she would have dealt with the drakes. As to whether or not her ideas would have succeeded, Valea did not care. Trapped, the mental images of Toma and the others, especially *Kyl*, at her mercy was the only thing she had to keep up her hopes.

"Interesting," Traske/Toma continued. "But unnecessary. I have thingsss worked out, Your Majesty. Besidesss, your safety isss as great a concern. The humans tried to assassinate you once; they may try again. Grath'sss place should always be by your side."

"Surely I am sssecure here."

The false scholar indicated himself. "Where I can enter, who can sssay what others might have followed?"

Kyl quieted instantly.

Traske/Toma bowed again. "Once more, with your permission, I shall now leave." His eyes darted from Kyl to Valea. The glance was only brief, but the hatred she felt in that look would have been enough to make her stumble away had the spell not prevented her from doing so. "Before thisss day isss done, Your Majesty, I promise you that the Manor will be secure." He returned his gaze to the heir. "Then, your future may begin in earnessst."

# XIX

CABE LEFT THE caverns of the Green Dragon feeling drained and still more confused. He did not know how to behave toward the Dragon King and was aware that he might possibly never resolve that problem. Eventually the warlock would also have to tell his wife. She would know that something was wrong.

He had left the matter of the Dragon King's relations with the Gryphon and Darkhorse in the claws of Lord Green himself. The only thing that Cabe had promised was that he would not permit war. Somehow, if the truth came to be known to either of the two, Cabe would have to see to it that they did not attempt to seek justice—or *vengeance*—against the master of the Dagora Forest. That would be only the beginning, for the drakes would see such an attack as an assault on their race. Even the more level-headed Blue Dragon would likely join the fray.

*Why is it that justice and right aren't always necessarily the same thing?* Cabe pondered as he exited the cavern mouth into the forest. *I can see why the Green Dragon did what he did and I can see why he should be punished for doing so. Yet, to punish him would create an even greater conflict and accomplish nothing good. Might as well punish the drake guards who, trying to rescue Kyl, pushed Toos into the path of the bolt.* No one intended to do the last. The drake bodyguards had only been performing their function. They had not known about the assassin with the bow until it was too late.

There was only one thing good about this situation. The Green Dragon was very remorseful about what he had caused to happen. He had known Toos well; Cabe knew that the Dragon King was already punishing himself for the assassination. Behind the false helm, the reptilian eyes stared too often into empty space.

*The only Dragon King who would feel remorse in the first place over something like this. It's almost ironic. If Black or the Storm Dragon had been behind this, they would have shrugged their shoulders in disappointment that more had not died.*

He took a moment to simply stand in the midst of the forest, drinking in the peacefulness of his surroundings. Cabe would have liked to have stayed longer, but Gwendolyn would be expecting him and there was much to do before the Blue Dragon's arrival. They might have as little as a day and a half before the drake lord showed up. Someone would have to see to Kyl so that he would be prepared when the time came. That might take some doing, Cabe thought, for the last he recalled, the heir had still been secreted in his chambers.

The warlock did not intend to argue about the Dragon King traveling to the Manor, even though it went against his earlier wishes. Under the circumstances, Lord Blue could hardly be blamed for wanting to come so quickly. Had it been any other drake lord, Cabe would have remained adamant in his refusal, but Blue he trusted, if only because of the Gryphon's friendship with the Dragon King's son, Morgis.

Knowing he could delay no longer, Cabe pictured the main hall of the Manor. With a sorcerer of his skill, thought was as good as action. Cabe's surroundings faded away to be replaced but a moment later by the very location he had just imagined. The warlock was pleased by the smooth transition. Sometimes, when his thoughts were as scattered as they felt now, his travel spell either took more time or left him more weary. On a rare occasion, he even ended up in a different location.

With his sorcery, he sought out his wife. Unlike the travel spell, this proved more troublesome, for, although he found her with little effort, she seemed not to notice him at first. At least, the sorceress did not *respond* immediately. Only when Cabe pressed for contact did the link establish itself.

*Gwen?*

*Cabe. You're back.*

Her thoughts did not reach him as intensely as they should have had. *Are you all right? You don't sound very strong.*

She took a second or two to respond. *There has just been so much to do, so many things to keep track of.*

*I understand.* Now was not the proper time to tell her the truth about the Green Dragon and the assassination. That suited the exhausted mage. He was very much tempted, in fact, to simply wait until Kyl was on the throne and he and Gwendolyn finally had some time for themselves again. *You're in the library?*

*Yes, I am.*

*I'll come to you, then.* He broke off contact with her. Cabe was almost ready to transport himself to the library when a terrible ache in his stomach reminded him that he had still not eaten. Not wanting to disturb his wife again, the warlock decided to make an unscheduled stop in the kitchen.

When he materialized in the kitchen but a second later, the familiar smells of herbs and spices almost overwhelmed him, so hungry had he become. Cabe looked around, intending to apologize for his entrance, but neither Mistress Belima nor any of her helpers were present. The kitchen was completely empty. There was not even anything baking or cooking at the moment, a truly rare occurrence. Mistress Belima *lived* in the kitchen. She had once informed the master warlock quite testily that cooking was how she relaxed. Considering the delicious meals that the woman organized, Cabe no longer even brought up the subject.

"Hello? Is anyone in here?"

His question was greeted with silence. Cabe studied the room again, but other than the fact that no one was here, there was nothing unusual to see. He finally shrugged it off and began searching for something to eat. It would have been easier to conjure up bread and fruit, but with Mistress Belima's kitchen, it paid better to search. One never knew what delight she had concocted and set aside.

Sure enough, besides the fresh bread that the woman always had ready, Cabe also found fresh oatmeal and raisin cookies, cheese, and a small bowl of some sort of vegetable mix. The warlock made himself a quick, makeshift meal, then bolted it down. He would have liked to have savored it more, but Gwendolyn would be wondering where he had gone. He located some milk to wash down the food and finally, because it was a rule no one dared break for fear of incurring Belima's wrath, cleaned up after himself. Cabe was just about to shift to the library when he noticed that he was no longer alone.

Aurim stood across the room from him. The younger Bedlam looked rather bleary-eyed, as if he had not had much sleep in the past few days. The sun-tressed warlock stood on unsteady legs, gripping one of the tables. He blinked two or three times at his father, but said nothing.

"Aurim!" Cabe rushed to his son's side. "Are you well?"

"Father, I . . ." He shook his head. "I don't remember what I was going to say. . . ." A sickly yet somehow triumphant grin crossed Aurim's countenance. "But I know that there's something else to rememb—remember. . . ."

The master sorcerer slipped an arm around his eldest. "You shouldn't even try to speak right now, Aurim. Let me take you back to your room."

He blinked again. "No . . . I have to tell you . . . the spell, I played with it. . . ."

*The spell? Toma's spell?* What had his son done to himself? "You shouldn't have worked on it on your own. I'd better bring you directly to your mother. She'll better understand what you've done. Hopefully, she'll also know what to do about it."

"Mother?"

"She's waiting for me in the library," Cabe explained, but his son no longer appeared to be listening. Aurim's brow was furrowed in an attempt at deep thought, although the attempt was already looking to be a failure. "You relax. Don't try to think about it. There'll be nothing to worry about."

"Yes, there *is*."

"Sssh! Hold tight."

Aurim obeyed without protest. Cabe cleared his thoughts and transported the two of them from the kitchen to the library.

The room was immaculate, as always. The Bedlams treated the collection—and books in general—with respect. Volumes were always carefully returned to their original locations. Pages were never bent; bookmarks were always used. A preservation spell kept the books from deteriorating, but Gwendolyn had laid down a rule that no unnecessary light enter the room, for sunlight still damaged books over time. Instead, carefully positioned reading chairs were spread throughout the library. Some caught the light from the one window allowed for circulation while all had candles nearby. However, most of the Bedlams, being spellcasters one and all, provided their own illumination in the form of tiny spheres that they conjured. The magical light did not harm the books and generally gave better illumination than either the candles or the narrow stretch of sunlight. In truth, the library had been well-kept before their coming, but Cabe and his wife had felt that they should not allow the Manor's ability to fend for itself cause them to become careless and slovenly.

He did not see Gwen at first, not until he turned halfway around and discovered her standing only a few feet from him. She looked mildly surprised at the sight of his companion.

"What's wrong with Aurim?" she asked quietly. The enchantress made no immediate move to aid Cabe with his burden.

"I think that he's been trying to free himself from Toma's spell. I think he's done something worse now." Cabe began helping Aurim to the nearest chair.

"He should be in his room, then."

"We can look him over just as easily here," the warlock returned, just slightly annoyed. He could not shake the sudden feeling that he had missed something. The enchantress spoke much too calmly, and the only times that Cabe could recall when she had spoken in such a way was when she had either been ill or angry with him. Glancing her way, he noticed no sign of sickness, but neither did she seem upset with him. Gwendolyn simply seemed . . . detached.

"I can't right now." She gave no explanation.

He started to straighten. "What do you mean you can't d——?"

"Is everything all right here?" asked a voice from the doorway of the library. Cabe looked up and saw Benjin Traske standing there. "I thought——" His eyes alighted on Aurim and his mouth shut. After a breath or two, he finally added, "Master Aurim . . . are you well?"

Cabe was about to answer for his son when Aurim quietly asked, "Father, will you help me to my room?"

The scholar stepped toward the Bedlams. "Allow me to do that, my Lord Bedlam. I am certain that you and the Lady Bedlam have much to do. Is that not correct, Lady Gwendolyn?"

"Yes, let Benjin help him, Cabe."

The warlock gaped at his bride. Could she not see how disoriented their son was? Benjin Traske, for all his offer of assistance, could hardly aid Aurim in this. The situation called for a knowledge and skill in sorcery. Traske barely had even a glimmer of ability.

From his chair, Aurim leaned toward his father. "Would *you* help me, please?"

That was enough for Cabe. The younger man was almost pleading. Aurim was probably afraid that he had caused more harm than good to himself, which was the way his father also felt. That Gwen could not see it astounded Cabe. Later, he would have a word with her, but for now, it was best that he brought Aurim back to his room and did what he could to help.

"Take my arm," he ordered his son. To Traske, he added, "I thank you for your concern, but I'll take care of this."

The massive tutor's face grew expressionless and he bowed. "As you wish, my Lord Bedlam. Then, if I may have but a word with your wife, I'm certain that she will be along shortly to help you."

"Of course," replied the enchantress.

Cabe had no more time to consider Gwendolyn's behavior. With Aurim holding on to him, albeit unsteadily, he simply turned to her and said, "Please hurry."

Her reply was a rather disinterested, "I will."

He was still frowning when Aurim's bedchamber took the place of the library. The tired mage helped his son to a sitting position on the edge of the bed. Aurim looked around as if he had lost something. Cabe scanned the room, but saw no object that might have been what the younger sorcerer was seeking.

"She . . . they . . ." Aurim let loose with an uncharacteristic snarl. "Just a little *more*! I only need a little more and then I'll have it!"

"Aurim, what *are* you talking about?" Cabe knelt by his son and tried to meet the latter's gaze. Aurim stared past him, however, a haunted look in the young man's eyes.

"*Benjin* . . . he's the key . . . Traske with a 'T' . . . that's how I remember it. 'T' also stands . . ."

"Son . . ."

The other waved him silent. "The spell didn't . . . didn't set right. Not this time. Traske with a 'T' . . ." Aurim suddenly looked up. A smile slowly grew. At last, he met his father's gaze. This time, the haunted look had been replaced by one of weary triumph. "Father! Benjin Traske—"

"How is he doing?"

Startled, they both looked up to see Gwendolyn standing by the door. Cabe had not noticed her materialize, and he was certain that neither had their son.

Aurim was pleased to see her. "Mother! I was just about to tell Father! I remember! I think he must have not known that I'd worked on destroying the original spell. When he tried to cast it again, he only turned it into something even *more* haphazard."

The warlock turned his back on his wife. Something that Aurim had just said had struck him almost dumb. "Aurim! Did you say that it was cast *again*?"

"Yes! Listen! He's been here all the time, laughing at us! Father, *Benjin Traske is Duke Toma!*"

He stared at his son, unable to make sense out of the pronouncement. Benjin Traske . . . *Toma*? "Aurim, you can't mean that, can you?"

His son grabbed him by the arms. "Father, we have to act! He's taken Ursa and I think he must have Valea!"

It was still inconceivable. "But we just left Traske at the library, Aurim!"

"I know, but it wasn't quite clear to me, then. I only knew that I had to get away from him! I—" Aurim looked past him to his mother. Cabe saw his eyes widen.

*If I may have but a word with your wife . . .*

"*Look out!*" shouted the young spellcaster. One arm thrust forward in a defensive maneuver as Cabe was suddenly thrown to the side.

The room was suddenly aglow with emerald green flame. Intense heat buffeted Cabe, but he knew that it should have been far worse. The spell should have killed him instantly, killed him and Aurim, too.

At the hands of Gwen.

Cabe rolled over just enough so that he could see what was happening. Before him, the doorframe outlining her, stood the scarlet-and-emerald enchantress. Her hands were outstretched, and even behind the magical shield that Aurim had managed to just barely create, the master warlock could sense the incredible river of power being thrust at them.

Gwendolyn's face was still indifferent, almost blank. How long had she been under Traske's . . . *Toma's* cursed spell? Not for very long, but definitely before the disguised renegade had entered the library. Traske had been surprised to see

Aurim there, too, which meant that he had thought that he had already dealt with Cabe's son.

The library had been a trap, one set to snare him in particular. Had Aurim not been with him, Cabe would have gone there alone to talk with his wife. Toma would have no doubt entered when he had anyway, thus giving the warlock too little time to realize what was wrong with his mate. Then, with Cabe unsuspecting, the renegade would have struck from both sides.

He would have made Gwen Cabe's murderer.

Cabe held his anger in check, realizing that the situation now required thought, not emotion. Aurim's shield was still holding, but he did not have the experience to keep pace with his mother. Fortunately, it appeared as if the witch did not have the full use of her senses, else she would have gotten around her son's defenses by now.

The warlock added his own power to the shield. Toma had expected the enchanted sorceress to catch both her son and her husband off guard. Under his spell, she was only a puppet, which meant that the knowledge and cunning of Lady Gwendolyn Bedlam was almost completely lost.

Engrossed as he was in trying to understand what had become of his wife, he barely sensed the black tentacles coming from behind him.

They darted toward him, but the warlock had already shifted position, materializing just a foot or two out of the way. The tentacles struck the floor, then immediately sought him again.

Evidently not *all* of her cunning was lost. The mage cast his own spell, severing the tentacles from their source. The magical extremities dropped to the floor and wiggled around once or twice before they dissipated.

"Father! How do we fight her? I *can't* hurt her!"

There lay the gist of their problem—and Toma's final ploy. Gwendolyn would continue trying to kill them unless they defeated her, but doing so might cause her injury, or worse, *death*. For the renegade, that would be as great a victory as it would be if she succeeded in her mission.

*I swear that you'll pay for all of this somehow, Toma!* It was so easy to swear oaths, though. Fulfilling them, however, was another matter, one which would first require a resolution to the situation at hand.

The ensorcelled Gwendolyn chose that moment to look at the ceiling. Cabe did not understand until the room began to shake.

"The ceiling! Aurim! You take care of it! I'll watch her!"

It was possible that a look of relief and gratitude crossed his son's countenance, but things were moving too swiftly to take the time to be certain. *At least he won't have to worry about harming his mother.*

Aurim also looked up. The shaking slowed, but did not cease. Out of the

corner of his eye, Cabe saw the younger warlock squeeze his fists tightly together in an attempt to force his will on the weakening ceiling.

The quake became imperceptible.

That left Cabe to deal with his wife. He dared not attempt a direct attack.
As desperate as his own predicament was, to harm her was out of the question.
Knowing that she would probably die at Toma's hand if he *did* sacrifice himself
did not make things easier.

Part of Gwen had to be in there. It was the only way by which the drake
could make some use of her skills. Otherwise, she would have been no more
than a statue. For Toma to twist her to his bidding, he would have had to keep
a flicker of her soul awake. All Cabe had to do was find something that would
shock her enough to weaken the spell holding her in thrall.

The deaths of her husband and son would do that, but faking such
a scene would require too much concentration. It would leave the shield
weakened, something that his bride, even in her present state, would be
unable to miss.

The true deaths of her husband and son *would* awaken her.

He needed something else, but it had to be something stunning or a fear or
even possibly—

*A fear?* Cabe knew of one. It was a fear so powerful that as hard as she had
tried in the past to hide it from him, he had noticed the tension, the shaking,
time after time.

It would have to be that. The warlock gritted his teeth and whispered to his
wife, "I'm sorry for this, Gwen. Another thing that Toma owes us for."

It was easy in one sense. All Cabe had to do was picture the enchantress as he
had first discovered her.

A golden glow materialized around the sorceress. She did not pay it any heed
at first, focused as she was by Toma's command on the process of trying to kill
her family. Then, as the glow condensed, took form, a slight look of uncertainty flashed across the otherwise emotionless face.

Beside him, Aurim tried to watch while maintaining his counterspell on the
ceiling.

Cabe continued to solidify the glow. It now had a rocky, translucent look
to it. He knew that what he was creating was an illusion, but he doubted that
Gwendolyn's mind in its present state would be able to make the distinction.

*The Lady of the Amber.* That was the name by which she had been known in legend. The story of her imprisonment by Azran had become folk legend. Azran
had worked his spell well and only Cabe had somehow managed to shatter it.
Perhaps it had been because he was of the mad mage's bloodline. Whatever the
reason, release her Cabe had. Yet, the memory of her imprisonment remained

rooted in her mind, haunting her dreams on occasion and filling her with a dread whenever she saw even a small piece of the substance. She feared being entombed again, and while that was not likely to happen, it was impossible to rid Gwendolyn of that dread. The amber prison had become a demon to her. It was why she insisted that no one, without exception, use the title in her presence.

Gwen's eyes abruptly rounded. Her face twisted from disinterest to outright horror.

She screamed as Cabe had never heard her scream.

Her spells died at the moment of her cry, much to Cabe's relief. Aurim, groaning, slumped onto the bed, but the warlock could see that his son was merely exhausted. This was the first time the younger Bedlam had been forced to use his power on such a level. Practice would make it easier.

Still his wife screamed, but Cabe could not stop now. She was not yet free of Toma's control. Only when her mind was completely her own could he dare cease his attack. The sorcerer only prayed that she did not lose her mind in the process of recovering it.

At last, the enchantress ceased screaming and dropped to her knees. She began to cry. Cabe heard his name and those of his children amidst her sobs. Immediately, he dismissed the illusion of the amber prison and rushed to her side.

"Gwendolyn!" Cabe put his arms around her.

The distraught woman gradually looked up. "Cabe?"

He held her close. "It's all right. The amber wasn't real. I had to do it to break you out of Toma's spell."

"Toma? I don't . . . I don't *think* I remember. . . ."

Of course she would not, the warlock realized. His wife had never actually seen Toma. "Gwen . . . Traske came to you, didn't he?"

It was clear that, as with Aurim, it was an effort for her to think. "Yes . . . he did. I don't recall what he . . . what he wanted to talk about, but . . ."

"Gwen . . . Traske *is* Toma. He may have always *been* Toma."

Cabe felt her body grow perfectly still. For a brief moment, he began to fear that she had slipped back into panic, but then she spoke. Her voice was steady but filled with growing hatred. "All this time we've cared for a *viper* in our midst? All this time he's walked among us, laughing inside?"

"I don't know if he's always been Traske, but he has been for some time, I think."

"Rheena!" The oath was one that the disheveled enchantress used rarely these days, which to Cabe revealed just how horrified his wife felt. "He would have made me kill . . . kill . . ."

Cabe silenced her. "He *didn't*. He failed."

"But not for my lack of trying. . . ."

He dared not let her collapse now. "You're not to blame! Toma's to blame!" Cabe made her look him in the eye. "He's still *here*, Gwendolyn. He's still here and he may have Valea."

"Valea!" The enchantress tried to rise, but her legs would not support her. Toma's spell and Cabe's illusion had combined to drain her completely, both emotionally and physically. "We . . . we have to save her!"

"You'll do nothing but rest here."

"I *can't* leave my daughter to that demon!" Straining, the weary sorceress tried to rise again. This time, she almost fell over.

Cabe helped her to the bed, where he put her down next to Aurim. His son sat up. Aurim's face was drawn.

"I'll go with you."

The master warlock shook his head. "No, you stay with your mother. This is something that requires gradual recovery and we can't leave her defenseless. *I'll* take care of Toma."

Aurim wanted to argue, but he knew better. He frowned, however. "Father, I think Toma must also have Ursa. She was in this room, helping me with the spell, when Tra—*Toma* came."

Another hostage. Another life to worry about. Toma, however, was not one to indiscriminately take hostages, which meant that he would hesitate before doing something to them. Cabe knew that at the very least the renegade had Valea in order to confound him, and Ursa had probably been taken because of her bloodline. Grath? He was the one that the warlock worried about most. Kyl was no doubt allied with Toma, but did the heir need his brother? Did he really care that much for Grath?

*Maybe it would've been better if your assassins* had *managed to kill him, Lord Green!* If Kyl *was* Toma's ally, then he would pay along with the renegade duke, emperor or not.

Although only a few minutes had elapsed since the beginning of his battle with his ensorcelled wife, Cabe knew that he had delayed too long already. Leaning over quickly, he kissed the worn enchantress and patted his son on the shoulder. "I have to go. I have to get Valea."

"You'll need help," insisted Gwen, trying to rise again.

Cabe briefly looked away, his gaze drifting to empty air. After a moment, he turned back to his family. "I'll get it. Don't worry. Toma *has* to be stopped."

"Good—" the witch began, but Cabe was already gone.

HE HAD NO doubt where they would be. Cabe Bedlam had been able to sense the renegade and the others all the time he had been in his son's chambers. Toma, Valea, Kyl, Grath, and at least three others occupied the chambers set aside for the heir, his brother, and their bodyguards.

The odds were very much against him; the warlock was aware of that. Yet Cabe was concerned only about Toma. The others would be more hindrance to themselves. Kyl was possibly a threat, if Cabe was correct in his assumption. Toma, however, would have his hands full keeping Valea, Ursa, and likely Grath under control. The drake duke would insist on doing so himself. Toma trusted no one enough, not even his supposed emperor.

He materialized just a few feet from the royal chambers. The spell that prevented magical intrusion was still in place, another reason why Toma would have chosen these rooms rather than his own. The drake had dared not place such a spell on his own suite, for someone would have noticed and questioned why a tutor needed such safeguards.

How best to do this? Toma was making Cabe come to him. Despite Cabe's intentions otherwise, the warlock was once more being played with by the renegade. Duke Toma had always excelled at manipulating others, but his game of the past several years had been his crowning achievement. Even now, he simply had to wait for his adversary to come to him.

*Well, I am coming to you, you damned lizard and, believe me, you will regret that!*

Cabe sent a probe toward the doorway, the obvious entrance into a place protected by sorcery, but he also sent out two more subtle probes to seek out the windows on the other side of Kyl's bedchamber. He doubted that either the door or the windows would do him any good, but it was always a wise idea to investigate.

The probes finally informed him of what he had already assumed. None of the obvious entrances were available to him. There were spells crisscrossing them, spells whose intentions were to assure his immediate death. He could not fight both Toma and the traps the renegade had laid, not at the same time. That was far too much for even Cabe, with all his power, to concentrate on.

It became clear to Cabe that he could either stay here and hope that Toma would tire of waiting—or try to fight his way through the drake's traps. Neither was a particularly attractive choice. He could not take long in deciding, either, for Valea's life lay in the balance. Kyl did not likely want her killed, but Toma might. Whatever master plan the renegade had hatched all those years ago, when he had first donned the mask of Benjin Traske, had been shattered, likely by Aurim's appearance in the library. Traske *had* seemed visibly startled. With Gwen having failed him, Toma now had to revise his moves.

Which did not mean that the drake had not already planned for this somehow.

He could not wait out Toma. Cabe *had* to assault the magically defended suite. He had to do it alone, too, for neither his wife nor Aurim were—

There was a sudden *tingling* in his mind. The tingling was followed by the intrusion of a familiar, albeit ever unique presence. *I am here, Cabe! Let me in!*

*Darkhorse! Enter freely! Come to the hall beyond Kyl's suite! Quickly!*

"What is it?" rumbled the eternal, suddenly beside him.

With the tension so great already, Cabe fairly jumped at the abrupt appearance of his old friend. He quickly scanned the shadow steed. Darkhorse did not look as powerful as he generally did. His presence was just a bit less imposing, as if not all of him was there. "Are you well enough? Can you help me?"

The eternal looked insulted. "*Can* I help you? I am Darkhorse, Cabe! I am your *friend!* To not help you, to do less than I am able . . ."

"Toma's in there."

That silenced the ebony stallion. The icy orbs that were his eyes narrowed. "*Is* he now?" Darkhorse started toward the door. "Then I think that we should *join* him . . . so that we may *tear* him apart!"

"Wait!" Cabe leapt in front of the eternal. "Listen! Toma is Benjin Traske. He used that identity to draw us to him. I think he has Valea and Grath in there, and I *know* that the doors, the windows . . . *everything* . . . are bespelled!"

"Bespelled against *you*, Cabe!" snorted the shadow steed. "I am Darkhorse! Move aside! I owe the renegade for much and I will see him pay now!"

Somehow, the hulking form of Darkhorse slipped around him. Cabe cursed, reminding himself for the thousandth time that what the eternal resembled was *not* what he was. It was too late by that time. Darkhorse was already at the doorway.

The massive black stallion rose on his hind legs and struck out with his hooves. The warlock felt a rush of sorcerous energy encompass the eternal. Cabe shielded himself, but nothing struck him. He heard Darkhorse laugh and knew then that his companion had absorbed the sorcery and was now mocking the one who had cast the spell.

"I am *coming* for you, bloody duke!" Darkhorse kicked the door again. It still stood, a testament to Toma's own skills, but Cabe estimated that one, perhaps two more kicks would shatter it. He readied himself to enter the fray the moment the way was clear.

It took only one more kick. The door splintered, bits flying this way and that. Again, spells were unleashed. The wary sorcerer was amazed at the preparation his adversary had made. Once more, however, all the preparation went for naught, for Darkhorse absorbed all the power with only a slight glow to show that he had noticed the attacks at all.

The eternal did not wait. He charged into the suite. Cabe prayed that the Manor would be able to withstand all the damage. It would not do to have the ancient edifice come down around them just as they were about to capture Toma.

*"What in the name of the Void?"* roared Darkhorse in absolute confusion.

Cabe, just entering, paused. He stared at what had so confounded the stallion, his heart sinking as he realized the latest ploy the duke had played on him.

Huddled together like frozen statues were Lady Belima and six of the household staff. They stared without seeing, but Cabe could at least tell that they were breathing.

"Look what hangs on their chests," Darkhorse muttered.

Stepping forward, a demoralized Cabe saw that each person wore a simple loop necklace from which hung an object. Mistress Belima, a graying, busy-looking woman, wore a small dagger. Another woman wore a ribbon that resembled one worn often by Valea. The warlock studied the other items, finally muttering, "Those are personal items. Something from Valea, something from Kyl . . . something from everyone in Toma's little group, including himself."

"We have been *tricked!*"

He nodded. Darkhorse had the right of it. Toma had played the warlock as a master bard played his harp. Kyl, Grath, Ursa, Valea—they were all gone. Frustrated, the warlock stalked through the suite. He knew that the renegade had departed, but desperation made him hope that perhaps he was wrong. This had to end here and now, not drag on and on and on . . .

In one of the side rooms, the warlock made a grisly discovery. Whereas Mistress Belima and the others were simply under an enchantment, this poor soul had been murdered most horribly. He forced himself to walk up to the figure, whose features were frozen in a scream, and touch it.

"*Gods,* Ssarekai . . ." he whispered. "You, too. . . ."

Perhaps this murder had been the beginning of the end of Toma's patient waiting. The drake servitor had not simply been frozen or made to forget again; he had been turned into *rock.* Solid rock. There was no bringing him back to life, not from this particular spell. The spark that had been the stable master's essence was gone.

General Toos, the real Benjin Traske—if he had ever existed—and now Ssarekai. More names to add to Toma's list. More things to condemn the duke, already many times condemned.

Cabe did not like to kill, but he knew that it was up to him to see to it that Toma caused no more deaths.

*Cabe?* came a weak voice in his head.

*Gwendolyn?*

It was clear that she was still in no shape to help him. *Is it . . . is she . . . what's happening?*

The warlock sighed and told her. She relayed nothing back to him as he quickly described what had happened, but Cabe could sense her growing despair.

When he was finished, she asked, *Valea? He still has Valea and we don't know where he is now?*

Cabe started to shake his head, recalled that his wife would not be able to see him do so, then suddenly paused before answering her.

Perhaps he *did* know where Toma had gone. Considering the renegade's past, considering his companions and his manner, it seemed to the warlock that there was only one place that the duke *could* go. Toma's arrogance would permit him to go no place else.

"I know where he has to be," he said out loud.

"Where is *that?*" asked Darkhorse, trotting into the room. The shadow steed's eyes narrowed thoughtfully as he noticed what remained of poor Ssarekai. The stable master, after getting over the typical drake's fear of the eternal, had pleased Darkhorse to no end with his constant compliments concerning the stallion's magnificent appearance.

In his head, the enchantress echoed the eternal's question.

Cabe's hands balled up into fists as he thought of the place. It was appropriate, for it had been, in a sense, the birthplace of Cabe Bedlam, master sorcerer. From there, the harbingers of fate, in the form of Dragon Kings, had gone out to seek an unsuspecting young man.

"We have to go to Kivan Grath."

# XX

ALTHOUGH THE WIND and cold could not touch him, Cabe Bedlam nonetheless felt a chill as he stood on a ledge high atop one of the smaller peaks of the Tyber Mountains. In the distance, Kivan Grath stood above all else. Somewhere within, the warlock knew, Toma and the others waited. The spells that now enshrouded the citadel of the Dragon Emperor made it impossible to locate those inside. They also made it impossible for Cabe and Darkhorse to simply materialize there.

"We are not alone," remarked Darkhorse. The shadow steed had insisted on joining him in this confrontation and, despite Cabe's awareness of the fact that the eternal was not entirely well, the warlock had been unable to turn down his offer.

Cabe nodded. Besides the creatures who inhabited the Tybers, he could sense two other forms in the direction of Kivan Grath. Two monstrous forms. *Dragons.*

"Are you ready?" he asked the eternal.

Darkhorse chuckled and kicked the edge of the ledge. A portion of it broke off and tumbled down to the valley below. "Of course!"

"Then let's see what Toma has waiting for us. You know what I want of you?"

The ice-blue orbs flashed. "I will watch for Valea; you may rest assured on that, Cabe. I will take her from this place and bring her safely back to the Manor. Grath, too?"

"Please. It's not his fault Kyl is allied with Toma."

"I wonder. The young drake is clever; I find it amazing that he could be so ignorant of his brother's doings."

Cabe tried to fix on the two hulking figures he could sense near the mouth of the Dragon Emperor's sanctum. They were most definitely keeping guard. He sighed. "Follow my lead."

"As you say."

With a thought, the warlock sent the two of them forward. They materialized only a short distance from the very mouth of the cavern, but still far enough so that its two immense guardians were not on top of them.

Even still, the sight of the two dragons *was* an impressive one.

Green they were, but mixed within was a trace of gold that made them glitter a little even in the cloud-enshrouded Tybers. Their wings, presently folded, looked to have a span at least equal to the length of their bodies. They were a pair of the largest dragons that Cabe could recall encountering, and he had encountered some of the greatest. Each drake guarded one side of the massive doorway. The warlock glanced between them and noticed that someone had repaired the entrance but recently.

"Come no farther, Master Bedlam!" rumbled the dragon on his left.

"Faras?" the warlock asked, slightly disoriented. The two leviathans were almost identical in appearance, but something in the first one's voice reminded him of the drake.

"You have not been given leave to enter," hissed the other.

"Ssgayn." Cabe nodded to each of them. He had never seen the two drakes in dragon form, not since they were hatchlings. In truth, it was almost as surprising that they could actually shift to such shapes, not having practiced it . . . or had they? "You know why I'm here."

Faras dipped his huge head. His teeth were jagged spikes as long as the human's arms. Ssgayn's were no less impressive. Even for dragons, these two were giants. "Duke Toma hasss given us strict ordersss."

"Duke Toma? Is he emperor now?"

The dragons snapped their heads back in discomfort. Faras hissed, "Duke Toma ssspeaks for the emperor!"

"Does he?" The warlock's eyes darted over the forms of the two dragons. He had seen almost all he needed to see. Faras and Ssgayn were not as comfortable in their present shapes as they would have liked. Their movements were slightly awkward, as if they understood the functions of their bodies but had not had enough practice. Still, knowing dragons as well as he did, Cabe did not doubt that they would be swift and deadly foes.

"So Toma speaks for Kyl now. Does Kyl know that?"

Ssgayn hissed. "You would be wissse not to mock, Master Bedlam."

"Let me through, Ssgayn. I want my daughter."

"We cannot. We have been charged to protect thisss entrance from all in-trudersss. We mussst obey."

They would, too. It saddened Cabe, because, knowing the two as he did, the warlock understood that Faras and Ssgayn truly saw this as their duty.

"I'll have to enter. I won't be kept from Valea."

The two dragons simultaneously raised their heads. Ssgayn opened wide his maw while Faras simply replied, "Then you mussst pass *usss* first, Massster Bed-lam!" The dragon lowered his eyes. "I *am* sssorry."

Cabe started to raise his hand toward Ssgayn when the green-and-gold levia-than called out, "Wait!"

The warlock paused, but did not lower his hand. "Why?"

Both guardians had distant looks in their eyes. Cabe Bedlam recognized that look; someone was speaking to them through their minds. He glanced at Dark-horse, who dipped his head in understanding. They would wait for the dragons to listen, but no longer.

Faras was still listening inwardly when Ssgayn finally returned his attention to the warlock. "Fortune sssmiles upon us all, Massster Bedlam." The massive dragon almost sounded relieved. "You have been granted entrance."

Without pause, the two guardians began to shift aside. Faras, too, had bro-ken contact with whoever had spoken to the two of them. He dipped his head in what might have been construed a draconian bow.

"This is a trick," rumbled Darkhorse softly. "They shall let us pass and then try to catch us from all sides."

Eyeing the dragons, Cabe scratched his chin. "I don't know. They *look* as if they're telling the truth," he whispered back.

"How would you *have* them look if they wanted you to believe their story?"

"Good point, but there's only one way to really find out whether they're lying or not, isn't there?"

"And if they are, we shall easily take them, won't we?" The eternal chuckled, which made the dragons, who had been unable to hear the conversation, tense.

The warlock and the shadow steed started forward, but then Faras, who more directly faced Darkhorse, hissed and shook his head. "Noooo . . . only *you*, Massster Bedlam! Only you. Ssso the emperor hasss *spoken.*"

"Through Duke Toma, no doubt," muttered Cabe.

"I will *not* accept this!" roared his companion. "We go together!"

The two dragons shifted nearer one another, effectively cutting off any glimpse of the entrance to the Dragon Emperor's sanctum. "That isss not permitted," added Faras.

Darkhorse looked ready to charge both scaled titans, but Cabe quickly put out a hand to halt him. "No, Darkhorse. If we fight, then we certainly endanger Valea. I'll go in alone."

"You cannot walk blindly into such an obvious trap!"

"But I *won't* be blind, will I?"

Ssgayn moved a stride closer, a great distance when one considered that he was a dragon. Darkhorse thought it *too* great, for he suddenly darted ahead of Cabe, becoming, in effect, a shield between the warlock and the leviathan.

The drake did not retreat, but he did pull his head back. "I only convey my liege'sss promissse that this will be a proper, peaceful audience." Ssgayn's reptilian eyes met the sorcerer's own. "Thisss my *emperor* ssswears!"

Whether or not he truly believed the guardian, the warlock had no true choice. Valea needed him. "Very well. I'll enter alone."

"Cabe! I—"

"You'll be near enough, Darkhorse," Cabe interjected, glancing at his companion. "If this *is* a ploy, do whatever you have to do."

Neither dragon looked comfortable with that notion, but they did not appear ready to back away. *I hope it doesn't come to that,* Cabe thought. *Darkhorse isn't as strong as he generally is and . . . and I've known Ssgayn and Faras so long.*

The ebony stallion settled down, albeit with reluctance. He glared at the two huge drakes. "Very well . . . but I shall be waiting for your summons, Cabe. Do not hesitate in the least, and rest assured that I *will* come to you . . . no matter what or who I must go through."

From the expressions on the draconian visages of Faras and Ssgayn, Cabe knew that Darkhorse would have to fight both of them if he did try to pass. The warlock shook his head as he started toward the guardians. If this was the path to peace, then perhaps the old days *were* better.

The two behemoths again moved aside, making a clear path for the warlock. Faras kept one eye on Cabe while Ssgayn studied the shadow steed carefully. The warlock paid no further attention to the guardians; his gaze was on the great bronze gate before him. It *had* been repaired recently, possibly by the Dragon Kings in preparation for the ascension. Toma would not have had the time or patience, not even if he had been willing to use sorcery. He could also not have replaced it during his long exile, for the other drake lords would have investigated immediately. That the gate had been repaired interested Cabe. It meant that at least someone had been fairly certain of Kyl's success, and since only the Dragon Kings ever came here, it *had* to have been one of them.

That was something he could think about later . . . always providing there *was* a later.

He was just about to reach forward and knock on the gate when it swung open to receive him.

There was no one within. Cabe stepped into the gloom of the cavern and looked around.

A figure suddenly stepped out of the darkness, a figure who the warlock knew quite well.

"Ursa!"

Her sorrowful smile told him that she was not under the sort of spell that Toma had cast upon Gwendolyn. Cabe was glad to see that, but at the same time, he felt worse because Ursa was clearly a slave. She was clad in fine emerald-and-gold raiment worthy of her status as drake dam of the royal line, yet being here was clearly not by her choice.

"If you will follow me, Master Bedlam, they are waiting for you."

She started to turn away, but he caught her arm. "Ursa, can you tell me if—"

"We have to go to them, Massster Bedlam," the beautiful drake insisted, turning anxious. "I cannot sssay anything."

"Toma?"

The look in her eyes was answer enough. Cabe quickly released his hold on her. With Ursa in the lead, they began the trek through the dark cavern entrance. Creatures fluttered about above them. The warlock heard something fairly large scuttle away.

"May we at least have some light?"

The words were no more off his tongue when a dim, golden sphere materialized before them. From Ursa's gasp, he gathered that she was not responsible. Toma was keeping a very keen eye on his old foe.

It was the longest short walk in which Cabe had ever partaken. He knew that the distance to the main cavern was but three or four minutes, yet time seemed to slow during the journey. It felt more like an hour. That might have been due to his own anxiety concerning Valea or, knowing Toma, it *might* have been a spell.

Certainly, his first glimpse of the main cavern when he and Ursa finally emerged seemed to be the product of a spell.

When last Cabe had left here, the throne room of the Dragon Emperor had been a fallen ruin. The huge stone effigies that lined the path to the throne had been in total disarray, with many of them tipped over and shattered. Vast portions of the ceiling had collapsed. While the massive stone throne itself had more or less survived, the steps of the dais it stood upon had been cracked and broken. All around, the Gold Dragon's treasures had been crushed.

Here, too, someone had tried and succeeded in repairing much of the damage. Now there were barely any signs that the destruction created in the process of bringing down the mad emperor had ever taken place. Only a few telltale cracks and some missing fragments gave any indication that the warlock's last visit had not been a delusion.

On the throne once occupied by his sire sat Kyl.

To his left stood Valea.

At the sight of his daughter, the mage started forward. Ursa shook her head and tried to grab hold of his sleeve, but Cabe moved too swiftly for her. He stalked toward the path and the effigies, his only concern being to get Valea safely away.

"*That* . . . will be far enough, warlock."

From behind the statues nearest to the dais stepped Toma. The renegade duke wore the form of the knight, but instead of his more normal green coloring, the drake was a resplendent gold and green. Cabe had seen him like this only once before, when Toma had invaded Talak and had captured both Gwendolyn and him.

A movement near Valea tore Cabe's gaze from the deadly drake. To the sorcerer's shock and amazement, he watched as Grath, materializing out of the shadows, seized hold of the young witch's arms. Kyl's brother bore an expression of interest in the proceedings, nothing more. Cabe did not even have to utilize his skills to know that Grath was no prisoner, no enchanted victim. He was a willing participant in Toma's madness.

It was all the mage could do to keep his fury under control.

"It isss cussstomary to kneel before the emperor," Toma announced.

"I am not a drake, as you know," returned Cabe. He gave the renegade a slight smile. "Besides, I recall the ascension being some days away still . . . if it still comes after what you've done."

At that, Kyl leaned forward. There was something in his manner that the warlock thought bespoke of built-up tension. The heir resembled a trap set much too tight, so that the slightest touch would set it off. Cabe thought it an interesting contrast to the attitude of the other two drakes. "What do you mean by that?"

"He meansss nothing by it, Your Majesty. He isss seeking to undermine you, to ssstir phantom fears in the hopess that you will be a less able monarch becaussse of them." Toma took a few steps upward as he spoke. Almost midway to the top, he turned to again study the human. "He hasss never desired a *strong* ruler for our race. That would be too much a danger to growing *human* control. That would be too much a danger to the power that he and hisss friends wield."

Cabe wanted to laugh, although the duke's words were anything but humorous. "I'm hardly *you*, Toma. I never asked for or desired *my* power the way that you covet not only yours but everyone else's. Neither I nor any of the others have tried to seize the entire land . . . unlike you."

"I did what I did in the name of my father, the *emperor*."

"And now you do it in the name of your brother?"

"Of course," replied the duke in all solemnity. "Ssserving the emperor hasss always been my duty . . . but perhapsss you cannot fathom sssuch thinking, warlock."

Cabe took a defiant step forward. Kyl leaned back in the throne, his eyes darting from the warlock to Toma and then back to Cabe again. Grath tightened his hold on Valea, who was clearly under some spell that did not allow her to move of her own accord. Cabe was, however, fairly certain that she could both hear and see him. "Oh, I can fathom such thinking, as you say, but not in regards to *you*, Toma. I know you. I remember. Perhaps you did have some loyalty to the Gold Dragon, but I wonder just how much of that has been transferred to the one who, because he bears the markings that you feel life cheated you of, sits on the throne that *would* have been yours, otherwise."

The duke hissed in anger, but said nothing. Cabe noted with interest how Kyl studied his supposed champion. It was not the type of look that he would have expected. The heir was not so pleased with Toma as the warlock had first imagined. *What else have I been mistaken about?*

"You have ssstill not anssswered my question, Massster Bedlam. What do you mean when you sssay that my ascension to the throne isss now in jeopardy?"

He had Kyl listening. That was more than Cabe could have hoped for under the circumstances. Toma clearly wanted to find some reason to prevent the warlock from answering, but to interrupt again would only serve to indicate the danger the duke felt Cabe's response represented.

"First, I must assume that it was not the duke's original intention to cause such chaos so close to the culmination of his plans. I must assume that he wanted you to be firmly ensconced on the throne . . . with Grath beside you acting as his mouth." The last was only a guess, but from the way Kyl's brother behaved, Cabe had to assume that he had spent most of his life misreading Grath. The younger drake was no innocent; he was definitely allied with Toma. The reasons behind that alliance would have been interesting to know, but now was hardly the time to pursue such questions.

Toma laughed, a harsh, raspy sound containing little humor. He turned partially toward the heir and pointed an accusing finger at the warlock. "You see how hisss mind works! You need to forget whatever supposed friendship he extended to you, my liege, and recall only hisss dissstaste for you whenever you were near hisss daughter." The renegade's eyes burned bright as he returned his attention to Cabe. "Hisss Majesty isss well aware of the circumstancesss that forced me to abandon a plan ssso well conceived and executed that I walked *among* you for years! An accidental encounter that could have been forgotten if not for your precocious ssson! No one would have had to come to harm or trouble. You would have all sssimply been made to forget. What your get did to my ssspell I do not know, but by meddling when he should not have, he forced me to defend my emperor."

Now it was the sorcerer's turn to laugh. " 'Defend my emperor'? Nothing would've happened to Kyl if you'd left. In another day, he would've simply met with Lord Blue and, I've no doubts about this, Kyl would have gained his support without trouble." Cabe's expression turned grim. "I wonder, too, how you planned to make us forget Ssarekai's death on top of matters, Toma. He remembered you, didn't he? Poor Ssarekai. Knowing him, he tried to stop you himself. You didn't have to kill him, especially not the way you did, but that's typical of you—"

"*Toma!*" hissed Kyl. "You told me that Ssssrekai wasss alive but bessspelled!"

The duke's taloned hands folded into fists. Cabe felt a mild tug on the powers around them. Toma was doing something, but it was too weak to be a spell of any danger. *What* then?

"An accident, my liege," replied the sinister drake. "I acted without thinking, for a knife wasss at my throat. I assure you, I did not want the ssstable master's death—"

"I've told you about Toma, Kyl," interrupted Cabe. "Others tend to die around him."

"I will have you *sssilent!*" roared Toma. This time, there was the definite buildup of power. Cabe quickly threw up a magical shield, all the while silently praying that he had not underestimated the intensity of the duke's assault.

The area surrounding the warlock flared bright orange.

"Toma! Ssstop! I forbid you!"

The renegade did cease his attack, but was otherwise paying little attention to Kyl. He descended to the last step, eyes wide with hatred and lipless mouth open to reveal the sharp, predatory teeth. Cabe strengthened his shield again, but Toma unleashed no new spell.

"Ssso much *planning* wasted after ssso much success! Dayss from my goal and *children* ruin everything! Ever hasss there been a Bedlam acting as a thorn in my hand! The cossst of the ssspell that allowed me to masquerade as the tutor left me without physical ssstrength for days and little ability to touch upon the powers for *monthsss.*" Here, Toma clasped a hand over the blade that Cabe recognized as the one Traske—*the drake*—had always worn. Now the sorcerer knew what it was and the knowledge made him curse himself for never noticing. Small wonder that Toma had been so weakened after endowing the blade with his spell. The complexity of such a design staggered Cabe. Toma would have to look, act, sound, and even *feel* like Benjin Traske, a human, at nearly all hours. He could never be certain that someone might need to speak to him in the middle of the night. More dangerous was the fact that, with so many others around him, the drake would have to be concerned over an accidental touch by a passerby. Yet, despite living among his enemies for so very long, Toma had been able to succeed with his masquerade. Cabe had shaken his hand on many occasions. He *should* have been able to note the difference. Worse, the warlock *should* have sensed the sorcery at work.

Something must have happened that night that Aurim had noticed Toma. Perhaps Toma had lost control of the knife. Aurim probably recalled now. If Cabe survived . . .

"Jussst a little *longer,*" Toma continued, oblivious to the intense interest Kyl now had in what he was saying. "Jussst a little longer and then he would have been emperor. I could have been introduced to him ssslowly, firssst as Benjin Trassske, his advisor, and then asss myssself."

Someone would have had to pave the way for that to happen. Cabe looked up at Grath, who was growing uncomfortable. That was why Toma needed Grath. Kyl had always looked to his brother for advice; if the younger drake recommended leniency, even a position of importance for the renegade, Cabe did not doubt for one moment that the new emperor would eventually grant the duke both.

How long after would Toma be all but emperor? Could Kyl not see what Toma's plans would ultimately mean?

Cabe was not quite certain how he hoped to end this situation, but he knew that much of it rested on Kyl now. The heir was obviously neither the steady ally nor the outright pawn the mage had expected him to be. If Kyl no longer supported Toma . . . "Kyl, the Dragon Kings will never accept Toma. Ask Blue what they think of him. You already know how Lord Green feels about him. When I spoke of the danger to your ascension, I was referring to this. If you support Toma—and have no doubts that even if I should remain silent, the Dragon Kings *will* discover what happened today at the Manor—they will reject *you.*" The warlock shrugged. "Some might not—I suspect that Toma has support from some quarter—but that will only mean a potential civil war among your kind. I can't allow that to happen. The fate of the drakes is tied to the fate of my kind as well."

Kyl brooded on this in silence, which Cabe took as a good sign and Toma, it appeared, took as the opposite. The drake turned toward his supposed emperor and, forcing himself to remain calm, again pointed at the warlock. "Subtle wordsss in their own way, my brother, but surely you sssee what lies *beneath* them?" At the heir's puzzled look, Toma quickly continued, "He says give in to the Dragon Kingsss in this and give in to the Dragon Kings in *that*. He tellsss you not to be a ssstrong emperor, but rather a weak *puppet* of theirs, fearful of offending them. Let them sssee you back down once and they will make you back down again and again! You will be an emperor in *name* only. A mockery to be paraded around whenever they have need to impressss the humansss. It will be Black, Ssstorm, and the others who will dictate and it will be *you* who obeysss!"

*As opposed to you giving him sage advice, Toma?* The trouble was, there *was* something to what the duke had said, just enough, in fact, to lend credence to his warning. It was clear that Kyl thought so, too, for his face took on a troubled expression, as if Toma had reminded him of something he had already feared.

The renegade drake saw that he had touched a nerve and pushed his advantage. "It wasss what they tried to do to our father, Kyl, but he persssevered . . . at leassst until they entirely abandoned him." Toma's tone grew sad. "They tried to overthrow him, but when that failed, they turned their backs on him in his hour of need. Left him to be driven *mad* by the very human before you! *That* isss the thing you mussst truly remember, my brother and my liege! The creature ressssponsible for the fall of our father, our emperor, ssstands before you now spouting *lies!*"

Kyl raised a hand, silencing everyone. He rose from the throne and peered down at both the duke and the warlock. The heir's expression was unreadable. He clasped his hands behind his back, then glanced at Grath, who had remained by Valea all this time. Cabe did not like the way the younger drake held his daughter so possessively. He was almost willing to swear that Grath was *obsessed* with her, which would be yet another thing he had failed to notice during the past several years. *What have I been doing all this time?* There were obviously *many* things he had failed to notice and realizing that now did not in any way assuage his guilt. Should this situation somehow be resolved, Cabe swore that he would be more careful . . . and more caring. How much of what Toma had accomplished might have been avoided if the warlock had not suffered from his own prejudices against drakes?

Kyl faced him again. "There isss much merit in what you sssay, Massster Bedlam, but at the sssame time, there isss much, even you will admit, to what the duke saysss. Asss emperor, I will have to make decisions on mattersss far more complex than even thisss. I mussst consider what ssserves bessst. I cannot be weak, but I cannot try to be too ssstrong, for that, alssso, hasss itsss dangers. I mussst learn to heed the advice of many," here the heir indicated Grath, Toma, and Cabe, "but make the final choice basssed on my own evaluation of the sssituation."

Triumph returned to Duke Toma's expression and Cabe could not blame him for reacting so. While Kyl's words impressed upon the warlock the fact that the drake would make a more able emperor than he had once supposed, the tone left little guesswork as to his decision regarding Toma.

"I will *not* bend to the Dragon Kingsss. With or without an official coronation, they mussst learn that *I* am emperor. They mussst accept *my* decisions. Lessst they think that I will have no sssupport without them, the duke hasss informed me that the legionsss of the drake confederation will act as my handsss. They are more than a match in number to any Dragon King's army."

At this revelation, Toma hissed in dismay. Cabe, on the other hand, found it interesting that Kyl would reveal such a secret. It was almost as if he was trying to warn the warlock.

The confederation. After the debacle with the Silver Dragon, survivors of those clans without a Dragon King had finally banded together, first slowly and then quicker and quicker as the benefits of an independent "clan" became clear. They held lands to the west and, if the rumors were true, kept on fairly good terms with the human kingdoms there. However, among the clans of their kind, they had no recognized status. The backing of the emperor, even an embattled one, would give them some recognition in the eyes of both the drake and human races.

No doubt Toma had presented it to their leaders in much that way.

Kyl looked at his brother, who appeared almost as upset as the renegade, then returned his gaze again to Cabe. He nodded slightly to the wary sorcerer. "I have made my decision. If you have no other reasssson for being here, then thisss audience isss at an end."

That suited Toma. Recovering from his consternation, he started to point at Ursa, no doubt to tell her that the warlock was to be escorted out *now*. Cabe, however, did not give him the chance to speak.

"You know that I can't leave yet, Kyl. Even if I grant you all that you say, I can't leave here without my daughter."

Grath held Valea's arm in an even tighter grip. Toma backed up a step. Kyl, oddly enough, did not seem put out by the demand.

"I once thought to make her mine," he began almost apologetically. "She doesss fasssscinate me, Massster Bedlam. I would have treated her like a queen."

"But not an empress. At the very least, Kyl, as emperor you would *have* to take one of your own kind to be your prime mate, the matriarch of the hatching chambers." Dragon Kings took several mates, mostly because many eggs were either sterile or were damaged before the young could hatch. Young drakes also often perished in their first several months.

"True." Kyl stared long at Valea. There *was* something more than fascination in his eyes. Cabe was unnerved by the notion of the heir actually *caring* for his daughter.

"Give me back my daughter, Kyl, and I promise you I won't interfere in whatever comes of your fight for the throne. Leave my family alone—make *him* leave my family alone—and we will remain distant."

Toma gave him a mocking look. "I find *that* a—"

"I agree to your termsss."

Duke and warlock stilled. Cabe could hardly believe his ears. Kyl was giving up one of his strongest cards so easily? Without Valea as his prisoner, his hold on the Bedlams was almost nothing. Under the same circumstances, Toma would have laughed in the warlock's face and threatened the young witch unless Cabe and the rest of his family agreed to obey the renegade.

The differences between Toma and Kyl were becoming more and more evident with each passing moment.

Grath would have none of his brother's promise. "Kyl, are you insssane? Give her up? I—you cannot do that! Think of what you are saying!"

Toma, too, was incensed. "Lisssten to your brother, Your Majesty! If you give up the female, what's to ssstop the mage from trying to bring you down next?"

"His *word*." Kyl, sounding a bit tired, gave Cabe a polite smile. "In all the yearsss I have known Massster Bedlam, he hasss rarely broken his word, and thossse times were not generally by choice. Thisss time, I know he will hold to his word, becaussse he truly does want peace. Ssso do I, Massster Bedlam. After all this, I mossst definitely do." He reached a hand in the direction of the ensorcelled woman. "She isss yoursss, with no ssstrings, no *tricksss*, involved. I ssswear this by both my sssire and the throne of the Dragon Emperor."

Cabe found that he believed him. It hardly seemed possible, but he could find nothing in the heir's manner to make him suspect a ploy of some sort. Kyl *wanted* to release Valea to him.

Unfortunately, the emperor-to-be's brother did not feel so. Still holding Valea by the arms, he turned with wild eyes to Toma. "He can't do that! It would ruin everything!"

Toma was seething, his breathing an audible hiss. Yet, he restrained himself where Grath could not. In a very quiet, overly calm voice, he told the young drake, "He isss our emperor, Grath. He may do asss he pleases. Release the female from the sssspell and let her go to her father."

Grath was aghast. He had clearly not expected such words from the duke. It was only with effort that Kyl's brother slowly released his grip on Valea. He did not step away, however, instead continuing to stand uncomfortably close while he began to unravel the spell he had cast on her.

For the first time since Cabe had followed the drakes to the cavern, his daughter was able to act of her own accord. He expected her to come running to him, but instead, she suddenly whirled on Grath, who resembled, of all things, a forlorn lover, and *slapped* the drake hard on the cheek.

"*That* is the least you deserve!" she snapped. Ignoring him from there on, Valea turned to Kyl. Unlike her tone when speaking to Grath, the young witch's manner was now cool yet polite. "Thank you for doing this, Your Majesty."

Kyl's expression shifted, indicating that he would have preferred a slap.

Moving a bit unsteadily, Valea made her way to the steps of the dais. She carefully avoided descending anywhere near Duke Toma. The drake clasped both hands behind his back in a manner reminiscent of Kyl's earlier stance, but in the renegade's case, it was evidently more to assure that she need not fear him trying to grab her.

As she neared the bottom, Valea's expression finally turned to joy. Cabe could not keep the happiness from his own face.

"Father!" Valea cried as she began to hurry across the remaining distance. At the edge of his vision, the warlock caught Kyl staring directly at him. His attention was pulled somewhat away from his returning daughter. Had he not known better, he would have sworn that the drake was trying to tell him something, but it could *not* be what Cabe thought it was.

Valea stretched out her arms to hug him. Forgetting Kyl for the moment, Cabe opened his own arms to receive her.

"No! You cannot!"

The horrified voice was Grath's, but he was not protesting his brother's decision again, rather something that Toma was doing.

Cabe cursed silently for forgetting the duke even for as long as the blink of an eye. As his gaze snapped back to the renegade, something flashed in his direction.

His first thought was *Toos!*, despite the differences between what had happened in Penacles and what was happening now. Cabe only knew that a knife—no, *the* knife—was hurtling toward his daughter. Everything around him slowed as the warlock threw Valea to the ground. He knew that his shield would not hold against the ensorcelled blade. Toma would not, of course, have forgotten the original use of the object that had controlled his shaping spell. A knife was made to be used. Trust Toma to ever remember that.

Cabe tried to transport them away, but for some reason, his spell failed. He had no time to consider the reason. Cabe Bedlam now fully expected the blade to strike him and knew that, at long last, Duke Toma would have his death. The drake would not have thrown the knife if he had not been certain of the results. Cabe threw himself onto Valea and closed his eyes, wondering just what form his death would take. From a blade magicked by Toma, it would not be a painless one.

Valea gasped as she struck the floor. Cabe's shoulder scraped against stone, but the pain was muted by the realization that he had suffered no other injury. No knife had sunk into his side.

Rolling onto his back, he discovered the sinister blade frozen in the air above him. From where it floated, the warlock estimated it would have struck him squarely in the back. The thought was an unsettling one even despite the knowledge that he had in some way escaped.

The reason for his survival stood gasping at the top of the dais. Grath, face covered in sweat, had one hand stretched toward the blade. From the look on his face, he was struggling with something. It slowly dawned on the warlock that Kyl's brother was still battling the magical knife.

Kyl, furious, had taken a step toward Toma. "Ssso *thisss* isss an example of your *loyalty!* Ssso thisss isss a sssign of your *complete* obedience!"

Toma said nothing, but abruptly glanced at the dark blade.

The knife spun around and flew toward the top of the dais.

Kyl gasped and raised a hand to protect himself, but too late he realized that he was *not* the intended target.

Grath stared round-eyed as the blade sank deep into his chest, too stunned by the swiftness of what had happened to scream.

"Interfering little fool!" growled the renegade.

Bright orange flame enveloped the younger drake. Grath was outlined but a moment as he started to fall . . . then the knife pulled away and flew back to the claws of Toma, leaving the unfortunate drake a sprawled form on the dais.

"You . . . *murdered* . . . Grath!" Kyl, his eyes darting from the corpse of his brother to the knife nestled in the renegade's hand, clenched his fists and took yet another wary step toward Toma. "I gave you sssanctuary! I *protected* you and thisss—"

Duke Toma gently wiped the blood from his blade. He eyed the heir and hissed. "No more *gamesss,* Your Majesty. Do you think that I do not know what you were planning? Have you forgotten how well I know all of you? I know how you think; I know how you plot. I saw your eyes when you ssspoke to the human. I read the truth in there." Toma toyed with the knife. "I know just how secure my place with you would have been once *she* was safe in the care of the warlock."

Cabe and Valea had risen, with the mage shielding his less-experienced daughter. Ursa joined them. Watching the duke, the warlock whispered, "Valea, get ready to transport the two of you away when I say to. We don't dare do it until Toma's fully occupied. Otherwise, he could easily pull you back."

She looked astounded. "I'm *not* leaving you, Father!"

"We don't have time to argue! He—"

"Hasss heard everything, Cabe Bedlam!" Duke Toma backed away from them all, the knife still at the ready. There was a strained look in his eyes and Cabe, who had already wondered about the renegade's instability, knew that Toma had nearly reached the brink. He could no longer tolerate the slightest interference with his dreams. Grath's death was proof of that, and now the duke had even turned on the one being who might have given him succor.

"Ssso much work for nothing . . ." muttered Toma. "So many *yearsss* wasted on raising an *unfit* hatchling for what should have been mine in the first place. I had my doubtsss time and time again, but the promissse was still there."

Kyl worked to keep his own temper in check again. "Toma, if you sssurrender now, I will give you a jussst judgment."

"A 'just judgment'? With my *lissst* of crimes? I think not."

It was now or never. Cabe leaned toward his daughter and whispered. "Leave! Now!"

She hesitated for a moment, but knew he was correct to send Ursa and her away. It was fast coming to the point where Toma would talk no more, and that left little other choice but battle. Valea was aware that she especially would be more hindrance against the drake than help. At least she could go for aid.

The only trouble was . . . she did *not* disappear. Neither did Ursa.

Toma ignored Kyl for the moment and smiled at the two humans from within his false helm. "Did you think I had not consssidered thisss eventuality? I am *Toma!* I led my father's forces. *I* planned his campaigns! How sssimple, then, to consider the possibility that a wavering, would-be ruler would waver the wrong direction or that my foes might come to this very sssanctum! How simple, alssso, to plan ahead, come here, and leave a few sssurprises. You will not be leaving."

*Darkhorse!* Cabe called in his mind. *Darkhorse! I need you!*

His silent cry could not go beyond the cavern walls.

"You are alone. Cut off," Toma informed him needlessly.

"What do you hope to gain by this? You've lost everything already, Toma! Kyl's offered you a fair judgment. It's the best you can do now."

"Not quite." The renegade held up the knife. At first it appeared that he was going to throw it, but then Toma did a strange thing. He took the dark blade by the grip and replaced it in his belt. "There will be a terrible battle in here, yesss. Alas, only one will sssurvive. Toma will have killed the daughter of Cabe Bedlam, but the warlock and his arch foe will die together in a blaze of power that will leave few remains. Caught up in that sorcerous conflagration will also be the perhapsss not ssso trustworthy heir to the throne and the female called Ursa. Only one will sssurvive, a young lad who hasss alwaysss been more of a favorite to some of the Dragon Kingsss than his own brother."

"What are you babbling about?" hissed Kyl. "What sssort of fanciful ssstory isss that? You have—"

The dragon heir swallowed the rest of his words as a horrific transformation took place. Toma melted, growing smaller. The massive dragonhelm crest shriveled to nothing and the helm itself pulled away. A handsome, almost *human* face took the place of the broad, flat visage of Toma.

Moments later, where the drake duke had been, *Grath* now stood. In every way, in every movement, Cabe would have sworn that it was Kyl's brother and not the renegade.

"Did I do well, Master Bedlam?" asked Toma in Grath's voice. An uncharacteristic sneer crossed the golden-green features. "I contemplated a masquerade like this in the beginning, but there were many reasonsss why the other path wasss better." Toma/Grath tilted his head to one side and gave the others an innocent look. "Still, I think that I can easily fool those great drake lords. I have done so before. I'm sure that Lords Green or Blue will even give me sssanctuary when I tell them that I do not trusst my safety at the Manor. For obvious reasssons, of course."

The knife gave him the power to create such a thorough masquerade. Cabe knew now that there *had* been a Benjin Traske at one time and that Toma had killed him as he had killed so many before. His present plan had merit, too, for none of the Dragon Kings, not even the Green Dragon, knew Grath well enough to see the difference. Toma had probably studied everyone of importance living in the Manor, all the better to know his enemies. The warlock was certain that, given the opportunity, Toma's new form *would* fool the drakes. How the duke planned to rule through illusion for possibly the next few centuries, Cabe did not know. What he *did* know, however, was that if there was one creature capable of succeeding in such madness, it was Toma.

There was still one question, though. . . .

As if reading his mind, which for Toma might be possible, the false Grath added, "And surely you mussst be wondering how I plan to make all of thisss work."

Toma blinked once. It was, to Cabe's eyes, a very deliberate blink. Cabe felt a mild tug of the surrounding powers and recalled when the duke had earlier done the same thing.

*A signal. He's summoned someone . . . someone inside!*

A peculiar, almost mournful howl echoed through the chamber from within the deeper parts of the cavern system. By the echo, whatever had made the cry was not far. A second wail indicated that it was drawing nearer at an incredible pace.

"What in the name of the Dragon of the Depthsss *isss* that?" whispered Kyl, so stunned he had temporarily forgotten his rage.

Toma/Grath smiled. It was a smile that told Cabe he should recognize the sound.

The warlock did. It was a cry that he had not heard since a day years ago when he and Gwendolyn had fought a frenzied Gold Dragon. It was the call of a monstrosity, a thing that should not have survived its time in the hatcheries of the drakes but somehow had. Only through a combined effort had it been defeated last time, to go fleeing deep into the vast underground system. Cabe had hoped that it had died there.

A misshapen form lumbered out of the tunnels and into the throne room of the Dragon Emperor. It caught sight of the warlock, and there and then Cabe knew that, as he had remembered it, so had the beast remembered *him.*

The monster started toward him, jaws wide.

# XXI

DARKHORSE PACED, AND as he did, he eyed the two great dragons guarding the entrance into Kivan Grath. They returned his gaze with steady ones of their own. He knew that this pair would not be stared down, however much that would have been preferable to the other choice. If it came to battle, the eternal was certain that he would be victorious, but any combat would leave him even weaker than he was now. Darkhorse had not yet had the time to recover from his imprisonment; whatever his captors had done with him while he had been a victim of the box had sapped much of his strength.

He did not want to endanger his friends. Better he remain here and do nothing than become a detriment during a possible duel with foul Toma.

What made the situation more worrisome was the silence that greeted Darkhorse every time he attempted to reach Cabe. He was aware that the sanctum of the Dragon Emperor likely had spells that kept whatever was said within a secret, but both dragons had received commands from someone inside. That meant that it *was* possible to forge a link with Cabe. Certainly, his human friend had intended to send him word of the conditions of Toma's captives. The warlock knew how much Darkhorse cared for his children; there *should* have been some word. He was certain of it.

Had there already been a battle? Had Cabe been prevented from summoning him?

Darkhorse ceased his pacing and turned to confront the two mammoth guardians. The dragons studied him with wary eyes.

He tried to look his most impressive. "I must know what is happening in there."

Their responses were the same. Both dragons hissed and readied their claws. The eternal felt each guardian draw power in possible preparation of a magical assault.

Darkhorse gouged a ravine in the rocky soil beneath him. His pupilless eyes glittered. "Yes, I did not *think* you would like that statement."

"You will have to passs *usss* to gain entrance, demon sssteed!" snarled the one Cabe had identified as Faras.

Sighing, the shadow steed started toward them at a trot. He tried to ignore the vast reservoirs of power the two behemoths were gathering. Between the two of them, they did have sufficient ability to end his existence. He told himself that he would just have to learn to ignore that particularly unsavory fact. Otherwise, thinking about it might be the death of him. "I still have hope that you *might* reconsider the necessity of that. . . ."

"*HALT!*"

At the sound of Duke Toma's voice, the monstrosity paused. It looked, absurd as the image was, like a puppy that had just been forbidden its favorite chewing bone. As he was to have been that bone, Cabe appreciated the reprieve, but the warlock also knew very well that the drake had not protected him out of any sudden change of heart.

Duke Toma, again resembling himself, looked from the creature to his adversary. "I think he *remembers* you, Master Bedlam!"

"Father!" whispered a horrified Valea. "What *is* that?"

"Misfit . . ." muttered Ursa, breaking her silence. "Freak of nature . . . they usually don't live this long. . . ."

It only remotely resembled a dragon. The thing was several times taller than a human, but that was in part because it stood on two legs instead of four. The tail that dragged for several yards behind was all that allowed it to balance. Even still, the monster teetered at times, in great part because its head was far too large for its body. Strange follicles almost resembling whiskers hung down from above its maw. Two spindly, almost useless arms waved back and forth in agitation.

It should have been dead. It should have died of starvation or *something* after Cabe and Gwen had forced it into the depths of the immense cavern system. *Trust* my *luck that not only did it survive, but* Toma *found it first!*

The renegade was laughing, no doubt in part because of the expression that had crossed the warlock's countenance when the beast had first started toward him.

"Yesss, I think you recognize each other. He isss more than a dumb beassst like a riding drake, human. He is very much like usss, a thinking—to a point, that is—creature. Doubt not that he recalls what you did to him and the one who gave him care and purposesss. Doubt not that he remembers well when you took his provider from him."

At the comment, the thing howled. Everyone but Toma was forced to put their hands to their ears until the monster ceased.

The duke silenced his pet with a glare. Had he not known what the creature was capable of, the mage would have felt more sympathetic toward its plight. It craved guidance. It needed *someone* to command it. Unfortunately, that someone had first been the Gold Dragon and now was the renegade.

"How did you find it?" Cabe asked Toma, not so much because he wanted to know but because he was desperately trying to think of some way to defeat the monster before it literally destroyed him with a glance.

To his relief, Toma was willing to explain. After so many years of silently coordinating his various plots, it was not surprising that the renegade might desire to boast of his success to his enemies. "After the death of my sssire in the Northern Wastes, I returned to this cavern. Although I dared not leave signs of my stay in the upper system, I was still able to spend quite some time here recuperating and thinking." There was a distant look in Toma's eye. "I know the cavernsss of Kivan Grath better than anyone. I explored their depths asss no one before me or sssince. There are few sssecrets here that I am not privy to." He pointed at the waiting monstrosity. "Who do you think firssst noted the potential and informed the emperor asss to the possibilitiesss? I am *always* look-ing ahead, plotting for every circumssstance . . . but then, you know that now, don't you?"

Kyl moved a step, but Toma's pet turned and eyed him, causing the young drake to grow still once more. The monster seemed a bit confused by Kyl, Cabe noted. Why that was, he did not know, but it was something definitely worth considering . . . provided that Toma gave him the time to do so.

The duke gave Kyl a mocking smile. "It would be ill-advisssed to move much, *Your Majesty*. Asssk Master Bedlam. He knows what this creature can do. A magical marvel! A fire-breathing dragon in reverssse! Let him fix his bale-ful eye on you long enough, and suddenly the world will feel like an *inferno*. It will be asss if all the heat of the world isss building up within you and there is nothing you can do to douse those fires. All thisss will happen in but the blink of an eye, too.

"You will burst into flamesss and be consumed from within. A truly novel death, at the very leassst. Our sssire found him to be a very useful tool, much to the *permanent* regrets of the traitorousss kings Bronze and Iron."

Everyone knew that something had happened to the two Dragon Kings who had sought to usurp control from their counterpart, Gold. What the emperor had done had been a mystery. The only thing that most knew was that there had been little left of either drake lord. The deaths had, for a time, quelled any further notion of rebellion by the surviving monarchs.

"Massster Bedlam!" whispered Ursa in as quiet a voice as possible. "I remember that thing . . . I sssaw it once; heard our sire talk about it. The . . . the creature was blindly obedient to the emperor!"

*Blindly obedient?* To the Dragon Emperor? A plan, admittedly thin in substance, came to the warlock. At the very least, it would throw Duke Toma's plans into chaos . . . hopefully *all* of them, this time.

"The emperor must've taken good care of it for it to have survived at all. It must've been very loyal to him."

Toma was visibly amused by the continuing conversation. He was clearly prolonging it only to give his foes desperate hope. In the drake's eyes, he held all the cards.

Cabe hoped that did not prove to be true.

"Only my sssire had greater control over him than I did . . . and now, only *I* am his massster!"

The monster's attention strayed to Toma while the renegade spoke, but then the head slowly swung toward Kyl again. It was not simply the young drake who seemed to interest him, though, but also Kyl's proximity to the throne.

"But if Gold—if the Dragon Emperor were here," persisted Cabe, "it might not even look at you."

Toma now only looked annoyed at his comments. Cabe dared not look at Kyl, for fear that the renegade would realize what he was attempting to do. The drake duke folded his arms and stared at the warlock. "I think that this missserable attempt to drag out the last few momentsss of your lives has come to an end, human." He had eyes for no one other than Cabe. "I think that it isss time to end our long and colorful association, don't you?"

The renegade turned to the monstrous creature, who seemed to shiver in anticipation.

"Stop!" roared a commanding voice that echoed throughout the caverns. "I, your *emperor*, command it!"

Even Toma could not help but turn.

Cabe thanked the Dragon of the Depths and whatever else might be watching out for Kyl and the others. The heir had picked up on what the warlock had been hinting at . . . picked up on it and taken it further than Cabe could have believed possible.

Kyl no longer stood near the throne. Instead, impossible as it was to believe, there loomed before them a dragon as had not been seen in years. To Cabe, it was as if time itself had stepped backward, resurrecting for all to see the glory of the Dragon Emperors in the form of the drake lord Gold.

He had confronted the emperor only in the final moments, when that glory had been, in great part, tarnished by madness. Kyl, on the other hand, was a sleek, gleaming leviathan, the epitome of glory and command.

For several seconds, even Toma was speechless. He gaped at the dazzling sight, then recalled himself. Hissing loudly, the duke whirled to his pet beast and pointed at the sun-drenched form atop the dais. *"Slay him!"*

In response, the monster emitted a mournful howl. Duke Toma stepped back as if slapped. The creature took a few tentative steps toward Kyl, then paused to glance at the renegade.

*It remembers the Dragon Emperor as its guardian!* It did not matter that this was not the same dragon. Kyl was similar enough in form that even Cabe had had to look twice to see the differences. Toma's pet had evidently sensed the kinship from the beginning. Moreover, to it, the throne represented the emperor, the one who had given it a place. The beast was understandably torn in its loyalties. Kyl had solidified that impression by taking on the form of his sire.

The heir had done something more than simply copy the appearance of his father. Cabe doubted that Kyl had ever so completely changed form before. What everyone saw now was the form that the drake, had he not been influenced by human presence, would have certainly worn when he had reached adulthood. What stood before them was truly Kyl, *emperor* of the drake race.

It was a realization that did not sit well with Toma.

"What are you waiting for, you misssguided monstrosssity? That isss not the one who gave you purpose! That isss an enemy of hisss in disguise! *I* am the only one you can trussst here!"

The beast wavered, again unleashing its mournful howl.

"How horrible!" whispered Valea. Cabe glanced at her, thinking that she meant the misshapen drake, but his daughter's eyes were fixed on Kyl. It occurred to him then that Valea had never considered the heir's other form. Not truthfully. She had no doubt realized that as one of the drake race Kyl had another form, but imagining it and *seeing* it were two entirely different things. Kyl was a handsome dragon, but he was still a *dragon* and not the exotic young man the witch had grown up knowing. It mattered not that she had seen Ursa change, either. Ursa was not Kyl.

"You will obey *me*," roared the heir to Toma's pet. "Obey me and I will protect you."

That was all the monster evidently needed to hear, for it started to trot toward the dais much the way a small, lost animal that has finally found its mother might have.

No one betrayed Duke Toma. Grath had learned that, much to his misfortune. The renegade evidently intended Kyl to learn that, too, for the warlock barely had time to act as he saw Toma pull the deadly blade from his belt and stretch his arm back in order to throw it at the heir, who was preoccupied with guiding the monster to him.

As quick as Cabe was, Ursa was even quicker. She leapt toward the turned Toma, already shifting her form. Yet, if the female drake had hoped to catch the renegade off guard, she had not counted on Toma's propensity for survival. Somehow, the drake always had some response ready, even if circumstances warranted it to be a swift one.

Toma barely succeeded in maintaining a hold on his blade. There was, much to Cabe's relief, no time for the duke to turn the knife directly on the attacking drake, but he was still able to bring down the hard handle on the side of her head. As she had not yet completely altered her form, her head lacked the scaly armor and thick skull of a dragon. More importantly, the spark that flew off when blade met skull was clear proof that the dark knife was ensorcelled on many levels.

Ursa struck the floor already unconscious. All vestiges of her change dwindled away, leaving her in the human form she had always so much preferred.

"Ssstupid, *ussseless* female!" sneered Toma.

Unable to act before without possibly harming the brave drake, Cabe attacked the moment Ursa was out of his line of sight. The spell was not an intricate one; the warlock's only intention was to permanently part Toma from his blade. The weapon was the key to much of the renegade's work, including, Cabe suspected, the spell that surrounded the cavern.

Near the dais, Toma's monster had turned back at the sounds of struggle. Now the creature wanted to join its former master, but repeated commands by Kyl were so far keeping it in check. It continued to howl, frustrated by the two conflicting loyalties.

Cabe did not strike at the blade itself, suspecting that among the powers that Toma had imbued it with was some sort of shield. Grath had been able to hold it a short time, but that was because he had simply been trying to halt its flight, not affect the weapon itself. Instead of the blade, the warlock chose to strike at the renegade. Granted, Toma was probably also protected, but what Cabe planned was not exactly a direct attack.

Without warning, the duke's hand opened wide. The drake's expression was indication enough that he had not *wanted* to open his hand, especially as that meant he no longer had a grip on the knife. Toma tried to seize the falling weapon with his other hand, but it was too late.

The blade struck the cavern floor point first and bounced a foot or two away. Cabe noted no change in the conditions around them, despite Duke Toma having no direct control of his toy. Of course, he had not had any such control when Grath had attempted *his* spell. *The blade's tied to him. It has to be destroyed to be stopped.*

That was something easier said than done, especially with the renegade now turning his attention to his old adversary. The drake stretched forth one hand toward the knife while the other he balled into a fist and pointed in Cabe's direction.

As the knife rose from the floor, the warlock felt his shield buckle under an unseen but incredible force all around him. Cabe strengthened the shield, but doing so drew his concentration from seizing the blade. He watched with frustration as it neared Toma's open hand.

Then *another* hand thrust upward from the floor and snared the knife by the handle. Ursa, not so unconscious as Duke Toma had supposed, reversed the blade so that it pointed toward its master. At the same time, she tried to plunge the weapon into the belly of Toma.

There was no doubt that it would have sunk deep, armor or no, but the renegade drake was swifter than Ursa had evidently hoped. Although taken unaware by her sudden revival, Toma recovered quickly. This close, he did not have time to protect himself with a spell, not against such a powerful device as his own magical blade, but he could still move. Toma's hand came down on the female drake's own, forcing the blade lower and to the side. Ursa gasped in obvious pain as the duke squeezed.

The knife missed his stomach, but Ursa was evidently stronger than he had supposed. Stronger *and* swifter.

A hissing cry burst from the renegade as his own dagger plunged almost halfway into his thigh. Armorlike skin failed to slow the sorcerous weapon.

Pulling away, the knife still in his thigh, Duke Toma cursed. The knife and the wound glowed a peculiar green. Fueled by his pain, he struck Ursa as she tried to rise and finish what she had begun. It was quite clear from the angle at which the female drake fell that this time there would be no trick.

From the dais, the dragon Kyl turned to the monster and roared, "Kill him!"

The creature remained where it was, looking confused and almost panic-stricken. It could no more destroy Toma than it could the one it believed was the previous emperor. Distraught, the beast looked up to the ceiling and renewed its howling.

The ceiling shook. A rain of tiny and not-so-tiny fragments buffeted everyone. Even Toma paused in his pain to cover himself as one particularly large chunk of rock fell within a few feet of him.

Cabe tried for what seemed the thousandth time to focus on Toma, but again something prevented him from unleashing a new spell. The something this time proved to be Kyl, who, realizing that there would be no victory through his new pet, charged toward the wounded renegade.

Toma looked up to see several tons of dragon converging on him. He did not seem panicked, however, but rather *furious*. Foregoing the removal of the enchanted blade, which still glowed, the duke faced his awesome foe and clenched his fists. Kyl was already almost upon him, frustrating the warlock's attempt. Only a powerful spell could take down Toma, but such a powerful spell would likely include the heir as well. *So much power and I stand around like a dithering fool!*

There was, however, one thing he could do. That was pull Ursa away from the vicinity of Toma and Kyl. With a glance, he raised the still form of the female drake and brought it swiftly toward himself. At the same time, he whispered, "Valea! Take hold of Ursa the moment she's near enough. Bring her to the gateway. You have to find some way to open it and summon Darkhorse."

"But Father, that will leave you alone!"

"Do as I say! Quickly!" Although the tasks he had given her were of great importance, there was a part of the warlock that admittedly desired Valea to be out of harm's way. Even if she failed to open the gates or contact the eternal, the simple fact that Valea was no longer in here would allow Cabe to fully concentrate on Toma. It was his daughter more than anything else that made it almost impossible for Cabe to completely commit himself to battle.

Even as she took hold of the floating form of her friend with her own sorcery, Cabe's attention returned to the battle before him. Kyl had reached Toma . . . almost. The majestic golden drake stood above the tinier figure of the renegade, one massive paw attempting to squash Toma. Unfortunately, some unseen barrier prevented Kyl from closing the last two or three feet above the duke's helmed head. The emperor-to-be roared and attempted to smash through the shield, but the result of his attack was a shriek of pain as the barrier proved even stronger than his full draconian might.

Kyl raised his paw to try again . . . and was enveloped in a ball of lightning.

Above the combined din created by both the crackle of the lightning and the roar of agony unleashed by the dragon, the voice of Duke Toma hissed, "Impudent little fool! *You* challenge *me*? You dare think yoursssself a match for me becaussse you wear that color? Becaussse you wear a few sssuperficial markings that in no way determine your power or your cunning?"

Still holding the dragon at bay, Duke Toma reached down and seized the blade in his leg. With obvious strain, he plucked out the deadly toy. The renegade wobbled a little, but did not fall.

There was at last distance enough between the two dragons for Cabe to utilize his master spell. He stared directly at the knife and concentrated.

The knife flared white but was in no other way changed. In fact, the only other result of his attack was that Toma now turned to him. "And *you*, human! That you could *ever* think yourself my equal! That I have tolerated you for ssso long isss to laugh!"

Kyl took the brief moment of inattention to attempt a new and more daring assault, this time in the form of an attack on the ground around Toma's feet. The golden dragon tore at the earth, obviously trying to undermine the renegade's footing.

Pointing the blade toward Kyl, Toma muttered something under his breath.

Blue lightning turned the emperor-to-be into an azure inferno. Cabe watched in horror and stupefaction as Toma's spell raised Kyl's overwhelming form several feet above the ground and tossed him toward the far side of the vast cavern.

The huge, gleaming form crashed into the hard, rock surface of the chamber wall. Kyl's shocked roar became, for a brief moment, an immense grunt of surprise and pain. The grunt was followed by another crash and then silence, as the dragon crumpled to the floor. As with Ursa, Kyl suddenly reverted to his more human form, a transformation that did little to improve his battered look. Unlike his sister, however, it was clear that the heir was not playing at unconsciousness.

The monster started toward Kyl. Toma called to it, but the beast paid him no mind. With its oversized head, the beast nudged the heir's still body. When Kyl did not move, it squatted next to him and began once more its mournful howling.

"Your plans are crumbling, Toma," taunted Cabe, a spell at the ready. He wanted the drake just a little farther away from the direction of the entrance. Valea had finally slipped past with Ursa's floating body, but if the duke realized what was happening, he stood a good chance of taking the two women before the warlock would be able to stop him. "Just like they always do."

"If there hasss been any fault in my planssss," hissed the renegade, forgetting all else save the robed figure, "it isss because I have been naive enough to trusssst the competence of *others*. In the end, I musssst always rely on *myself*."

"Yourself?" Cabe took a step back and away from the entrance. To his relief, Toma matched his steps, unconsciously moving farther from where Valea had fled. "It was *your* incompetence that destroyed your plans. It was *your* incompetence that forced you to abandon the Manor mere days before your plot would have seen fruition."

Reptilian eyes blazed within the false helm. Toma was finding it difficult to restrain himself. "That was the fault of trusssting *children* and bumbling fools!"

"Maybe, but who was it who was *truly* to blame for bringing down the Dragon Emperor in the first place? Who was it whose *ambition* pushed Gold to make the decisions he did?" The warlock straightened and stared Toma in the eye without blinking. "Who was it who secretly urged the kings Brown and Black to hunt down one lone human boy and kill him because of what his grandfather had been? If not for *you*, I might not be here to stop you now and, perhaps more important to you, Toma, Gold might never have fallen."

"I will have your *tongue*, human!"

Cabe had drawn the power that he needed. There was but one more thing that he wanted to say, one more fact he wanted Toma to know, whatever the outcome. "You've always desired to be the shaper of the Dragonrealm, Toma, but have you ever considered that you already *are*? You've done more to make the land what it is today than almost anyone else. You brought down the Dragon Emperor, put the drake lords into disarray, and helped make humans and drakes equal." Cabe Bedlam bowed humbly before the renegade, but his tone, he hoped, held just the proper level of ridicule. "For that, you deserve the thanks of all of us, especially *me*."

"You arrogant little vermin!" Toma raised the knife toward Cabe. "You . . . *human!* I will have you ssstuffed and mounted! I will have you made the centerpiece of a collection of thossse who fell before my glory!"

The sinister dagger blazed.

Cabe released his counterspell just as Toma committed himself.

The warlock was buffeted by an incredible wave of sorcerous energy. He stumbled back and fell to one knee, but then the pressure eased, becoming less and less with each passing breath.

Toma did not understand at first, so caught up was he in the intended destruction of the mage. He did not comprehend until the blade began to shimmer in an odd fashion, alternating between a glow as bright as the sun and a blackness as dark as the night.

"What are you—" was all the renegade managed. Then, Duke Toma hissed in pain.

The dagger dropped from his hand. The palm of his hand was black and blistered.

The knife struck the cavern floor, but this time it did not bounce. In fact, it struck more with a *splatter*, for the blade was already half-melted.

"Nooo!" Reaching down with his good hand, the renegade attempted to retrieve what was left. He was too late. All that remained was the lower half of the handle, and that melted even as Toma tried to pick it up. The duke snarled and rubbed his fingers.

Around Cabe, it suddenly felt as if a vast barrier had been lifted . . . which, in truth, had happened. Against the power of the blade, Cabe's options had been limited. Toma had worked his magics all too well in creating the knife. Not only had it helped the drake defeat Kyl, but it also still shielded Darkhorse from the knowledge of what had transpired in the cavern.

Cabe could have wasted his own strength fighting against the shielded walls, the knife, and Toma himself, but there could have been only one outcome to such an unbalanced struggle. Therefore, the sorcerer had instead concentrated on the blade and one of the weaknesses its very function forced upon it.

Only one power was certainly equal to the task of defeating Toma's plaything. That was the power of the blade itself. It was a trick he had made good use of several times in the past. Cabe's spell had not been an attack on the knife nor had it been a simple shield against the weapon's might. What the warlock had instead cast was a conduit of sorts, a magical path that would turn the power of the blade to another purpose. Cabe had refocused the deadly force of the knife against the invisible barrier that cut off all communication between those in the cavern and those in the outside world.

The blade had worked against itself, feeding more and more of its power into the attack on Cabe, which was then turned on the barrier that it projected. In order to strengthen that barrier from the sudden attack, the magical dagger had been forced to further drain itself. Yet, it could not do so for long because Toma's will continued to force more power into his battle against the apparently impervious shield of his warlock rival.

The result had been too much for Toma's toy to handle.

He did not wait for the renegade to recover, attacking while the duke still clutched his injured hands. Crimson loops formed around Toma's legs and torso and attempted to bind his arms together. However, the drake proved to be less disoriented than Cabe had hoped, for suddenly a green aura formed, an aura that proceeded to melt away the loops covering each arm. The aura spread over Duke Toma's body, dissolving the loops as it touched them. Only when the last of the loops faded to nothing did the green glow dwindle away.

"You *continue* to pessster me like a flea biting at my flesh!" Toma held his hands palms forward so that Cabe could see them. A haze formed briefly over each palm. As it passed, the burns healed, until there was no sign of the injuries. The renegade hissed again, his forked tongue darting out once. "But that isss *all* you are, Cabe Bedlam! A flea! A *flea!*"

Duke Toma's shape twisted. His form was quicksilver, fluid and changing. He began to expand, as if filling with air. Hands arched, becoming taloned paws. Arms and legs bent at angles that should have broken them. From the renegade's back tremendous wings sprouted and with them a tail. The savage, leering dragon's head crest began to sink down and merge with the half-hidden countenance behind the false helm. In but the blink of an eye, Toma grew to several times his original size and continued to expand.

He was not as huge a beast as either Kyl, Faras, or Ssgayn, but Toma the dragon was possibly the most ferocious drake that Cabe had ever encountered. The jaws opened wide as the transformed duke roared, revealing an impossible number of long, sharp teeth. The forest green and sun gold form was lithe and swift in appearance. Toma's eyes burned with such hatred that the warlock half-expected to drop dead simply from the rage he saw in them.

The dragon rose on his hind legs, obscuring all sight of the dais and the throne. He hissed again, the long, snakelike tongue darting about like a frenzied whip.

"It isss time you learned, flea, what a dragon is *truly* capable of!" Toma inhaled . . . then exhaled an inferno.

Flames licked the area all around Cabe. His robe burned and the heat seared his flesh. He held in check the scream he wanted to release, instead turning the pain into power. His shield strengthened, cutting off both the flame and the heat. A simpler spell doused the fires on his clothing. The burns he healed just enough to ignore. It would take all his will and ability to fight back. A little pain would have to be endured.

Toma inhaled again. Cabe chose the respite to attack in turn, severing a number of the largest and sharpest of the stalactites from the ceiling. The rain of missiles came down on Toma just as he was about to unleash a second firestorm. The barrage caught the dragon by surprise. One stalactite pierced a wing, while several others battered the outraged leviathan's head.

Cabe's success was short-lived. A barrier formed around Toma, a barrier that seemed adept at deflecting the stone missiles. Cabe brought a hand up and turned the swarm aside. The deadly rain pummeled the restored effigies and created a second massive shower of rock that further reduced the area to the wreckage it had been after the warlock's previous battle here, the one with Toma's sire, Gold.

The dragon laughed and a malevolent smile crossed the reptilian features. "Flea bitesss! Nothing but flea bitesss! I shall scorch you, rend you, and crush you, human! Then I shall take your precious *daughter*! Perhapsss I shall make her one of my dams! Humansss and drakesss *are* capable of procreating, you know. I have . . . ssseen it. Then, I shall take your son and your lovely bride—*all* of your companionsss—and, one by one, teach them the meaning of ssslow death! I should be able to keep mysssself amusssed with them for *months* at a time!" Toma laughed again, loosening a few more stalactites that fell harmlessly around him. "And, knife or not, as *Grath,* I shall look on, properly mournful but unable to end the terror!"

He would do it, too. Everything that Toma had just promised, even without the baleful dagger to aid him, he would do. Cabe knew that, and a cold, ever so cold, fear overwhelmed him. Yet, instead of being left numb and paralyzed, the fear stirred within him a rage, a need to react and overcome that very fear.

His voice was surprisingly calm as he started toward the malignant drake. "You won't be doing anything to anybody, Toma. I can't allow that. I can't let you leave to cause more horror. It has to end here."

Toma laughed again and, raising one huge, taloned paw, caused a storm to form above and around the tiny figure that dared to defy him. Wind and rain rocked Cabe, while thunder deafened him and lightning sought to strike him down.

Gritting his teeth, the warlock somehow found the wherewithal to continue forward. Fueled by his fatalistic determination, Cabe's shield spell held against the onslaught of the magical storm. Toma roared and increased its fury, but still his foe advanced.

Within only yards of the leviathan, Cabe at last attacked. He raised his hands before his chest, and from between them there suddenly formed a sphere of blinding blue light. The sphere grew to twice the size of a man's head, then flew forward as if shot from a catapult.

Wings stretching, the dragon snorted his disdain and nodded almost minutely at the oncoming projectile. A second sphere, this one a dark, decaying green, formed instantly and flew to meet its blue counterpart.

The two balls of light collided.

Toma had already forgotten Cabe's sphere, assuming that his counterspell had eradicated it. His gaze had already returned to Cabe when the dragon became aware that, instead of dissipating the moment it had touched its emerald counterpart, the blue sphere had exploded into a thousand fragments. A thousand fragments that continued on toward their intended target with no loss of velocity.

Skilled as he was, it took the dragon little effort to strengthen his shield, but Cabe's spell was stronger in intensity than anything Toma had yet faced. Most of the glittering fragments faded as they met the magical wall, but several burst through.

Toma howled in pain as dozens of tiny, fiery avengers assailed him. Several scored hits on his torso while a few lucky ones burned through the membranes of one wing. The dragon staggered back, knocking over yet more of the ancient statues and coming to a halt only when the floor gave way to the steps of the dais. Cabe raised his arms toward Toma to give his attack better focus, ignoring, as he had so many times in the past, the agony caused by an old wound suffered facing the Aramites. None of his pain mattered now; it was secondary to keeping the dragon at bay.

The battle had at last drawn the attention of the monster, although it still made no attempt to leave Kyl's side. Toma noticed its attention and, pointing a claw at Cabe, roared, "Kill him now! Kill him before he leavesss you once more without anyone! Kill him before he leavesss you *alone* again!"

*No!* Cabe swore as he heard the creature's howl take on a new, deadlier tone. A furtive glance informed him that Toma had at last managed to stir the beast from its stupor. Rising, the monstrosity began to lumber toward the warlock, who was quite aware that even at his best he could not possibly take on both the wily dragon and the baleful monster. All the creature had to do was fix his gaze on Cabe long enough . . .

He was caught between the two of them. Worse, with Cabe forced to spread his attention between the dragon and the monster, Toma was also recovering from his terrible onslaught. There would be no hope whatsoever if the weary mage allowed that to happen, but he could foresee no way to prevent it.

*I've failed.* . . . Toma would find some way to escape the caverns and eventually Grath, possibly even Kyl, would return to claim the throne. No one would realize that it was Toma making use of some new devious spell.

A second howl nearly deafened him. With an awkward leap, Toma's pet covered much of the remaining distance between them. It could have easily dealt with him before this, but Cabe guessed that it was debating between using its inherent magic to destroy him or simply seizing the human morsel in its mouth and swallowing him whole.

"Kill him!" hissed Toma once again. Still weak from his wounds, which this time he did not instantly heal, the renegade appeared to be satisfied with keeping his adversary occupied enough so that Cabe could not deal with the other threat until it was too late.

The beast paused. It howled again, but moved no closer. Its horrible eyes focused on the haggard mage.

A curtain of absolute darkness covered the warlock. At first he thought that this was the prelude to death, but then the curtain moved, and for the first time since the beginning of the struggle, Cabe's hopes rose high.

"I have seen some ugly drakes in my time," boomed a welcome voice, "but you, my misbegotten friend, are positively the most repulsive thing I have *ever* come across!"

"Darkhorse!" gasped the thankful warlock. Destroying the blade had worked better than he had hoped. Valea must have made her way through the gate once the spell surrounding the cavern had been broken and warned the shadow steed of what was happening.

Whether it was due to the eternal's derisive comment or simply because of Darkhorse's sudden presence, the creature forgot the warlock and fixed his deadly gaze on the ebony figure confronting him.

Cabe remembered that Darkhorse knew nothing of the beast's frightful abilities. "Don't stand still!"

It was too late. The horror stared and howled. The warlock could not recall whether it was the stare or the cry or a combination of both that caused the victim to burn from within. Whatever the cause, it was too late to help his companion. The eternal had arrived in time to do nothing but die.

Yet, even after the creature had long stopped howling, even after it had blinked in confusion more than once, Darkhorse still stood.

*A child of the Void.* That was how legends had often described the eternal. He was not like any creature in the world, simply because he was *not* from this or any other world.

The power of Toma's pet was useless against the black stallion. Perhaps there was no inherent heat within Darkhorse upon which the monster could work its horrible spell.

Even Toma briefly forgot about his part in the battle as he and Cabe stared at the stunning tableau.

"Well?" mocked Darkhorse. "Was *that* supposed to mean something?"

Outraged, the monstrosity howled and charged the eternal.

"No!" Toma snarled. "Ssstop!"

His words went unheeded. The creature leapt as it came within range of its motionless prey. Not once did it hesitate to perhaps wonder why the massive horse did not try to flee or fight. It was too furious, too filled with a bloodlust. A victim had survived its power; that could not be allowed.

Jaws opened and talons flashed as the beast fell upon Darkhorse . . . and continued to fall *into* his would-be prey. There were those who would have described the eternal as a living hole, a dark abyss with no bottom. Darkhorse was that and so much more. He was and was not the very emptiness in which he had been spawned.

The howl of anger became a cry of fear. Darkhorse's form grew distorted from effort; as Cabe had suspected, his companion had not yet completely recovered from his captivity. The stallion persevered, however. It was a strange sight—it was *always* a strange sight—to behold. Despite the fact that the beast had stood far, far taller than Darkhorse, the monster's entire form was dragged into the body of the shadow steed. Smaller and smaller the shadow steed's adversary became, until at last it vanished within. The howling ceased but a moment after.

Despite all the times he had seen Darkhorse do this to his enemies, Cabe could not help but feel unsettled.

There was something different about this particular instance, however, for Darkhorse made no immediate move to take on Toma. He did not move at all, but rather stood where he was. His body literally rippled, but it did not collapse as it had done once in the past.

With effort, the shadow steed finally turned to face the renegade. The dragon eyed him warily.

"You . . . have attacked my . . . friends . . . monster! You made me a prisoner . . . and tortured me. For that . . . I will make you pay."

It was clear that the comments concerning Darkhorse's imprisonment only puzzled Toma, but the stallion paid that no regard. He started toward the renegade at a somewhat irregular pace.

This Toma noticed and a calculating look crossed his draconian features. "Come to me then, old nag, and show me what you can do!"

His form still shifting, the shadow steed prepared to attack.

Cabe gestured. A wall of energy appeared between Darkhorse and Toma. The shadow steed turned in confusion. "Cabe! What do you do?"

The warlock took a deep breath. His fear and rage had not been quelled, and now that he had committed himself to his present course, the two emotions began to burn with renewed force. "Take care of Kyl, Darkhorse. Forget Toma. He belongs to *me*."

"What care have I for that traitorous young—"

Cabe cut him off. "Kyl helped us, Darkhorse. Grath was the traitor. Now do as I say and take Kyl from here. He needs the aid of a healer badly. If you don't hurry, I'm afraid he might die."

"But—"

"Take care of Valea and Ursa, too . . . please." He had been about to say *especially if I fail*, but Cabe did not even want to acknowledge that likely possibility. "Now."

Toma absorbed the exchange with something approaching amusement. "Have I given permission for thisss, human? Do you think that I will jussst let him depart with the heir?"

The warlock was grim-faced. "Yes."

"You are mistaken, then."

The dragon raised a paw toward Darkhorse, who, obeying Cabe, had backed toward Kyl. Dust began to rise around the shadow steed, dust that somehow clung to the eternal's form.

*"Let him be."*

The force of Cabe's blast threw the great dragon against the steps of the dais. Toma thundered in new pain, his spell dissipating as he lost control. Smoke rose from his form. There was now a gaping hole in the already injured wing.

Darkhorse paused. "Cabe, if you and—"

"Do what I said, Darkhorse." The mage dared not reveal just how weakened he already was. Each new assault drained him, but he could not relent. Toma was his. Toma had *made* himself Cabe's. He would take the dragon whatever the cost. Whether that was the right thing or the wrong thing to do, the warlock did not care. Toma was *his*.

"You *insolent* mortal!" raged the wounded leviathan. "Who do you think you *are*?"

The exhausted sorcerer pulled himself up to his full height and quietly responded, "I am *Cabe Bedlam*."

His next assault forced Toma partway up the dais. The renegade drake roared. Once again Cabe was awash in a storm of flame, but this time the heat and pain were barely noticeable. He pushed his way through the inferno until Toma could maintain it no longer.

The dragon was breathing heavily when the warlock again looked him in the face. For the first time, there was uncertainty in Toma's eyes.

Cabe took the opportunity to look Darkhorse's way. He was relieved to see that the stallion had obeyed him, for both Darkhorse and Kyl were no longer there. One weight lifted from his heart. Whatever happened here, the others were safe. Kyl and the others would spread the truth about Toma if Cabe failed.

"We're all alone now," he informed the renegade.

"A pity. Then no one will be able to die with you."

"You'll do."

The huge head suddenly dropped toward Cabe. The warlock belatedly noted that he had never estimated the length of Toma's neck. The world above Cabe became the wide maw of a slavering dragon.

Toma's jaws snapped shut on the place where his rival had been, but the sorcerer had been able to dive aside at the last moment despite the dragon's swiftness. The dragon tried once, twice, three times more. Cabe rolled over, bouncing again and again against the rock floor. He was bruised from head to toe, but at least he was alive to fight.

The knowledge did not much encourage him.

"Ceassse hopping and bouncing, flea! You only prolong what mussst be!"

"You . . . have a . . . point there," Cabe gasped. It was now or never. If he allowed this battle to go on, Toma would defeat him through sheer stamina. The warlock could hardly keep up his present pace much longer.

Again, the human struck, choosing force over subtlety. Toma recast his shield, but while it held, the dragon was still driven to the top of the dais. Toma tried to exhale another river of flame, but only a gust of heat greeted his efforts.

Cabe pushed on, knowing that he had to be relentless. A second bolt and then a third pushed Toma nearly to the throne. The mage ascended the steps, pausing only two or three from the top.

Toma straightened, unsteady but hardly defeated.

"What does it take to put you *down*, warlock?"

Cabe wanted to ask him the same question, but chose to save the energy for the combat. He attacked again, and this time the dragon's shield failed him.

Toma nearly fell upon the throne. His entire form crackled with the power that his adversary had unleashed on him. The dragon righted himself, but now he twitched from pain. His breathing was irregular.

"You *cannot* defeat me! I am *Toma!*"

Again, a taloned paw rose.

The steps around and beneath Cabe Bedlam sizzled. Bolts of blue lightning rose from the rock and assailed the warlock. They were not like ordinary lightning, for each one that assailed him remained attached like a parasite, drawing his power away and nearly forcing him to his knees.

"You are *mine*, warlock!" Toma the dragon roared his delight.

*Gwendolyn, Valea, Aurim, Darkhorse, the Gryphon . . .* all the faces formed before Cabe. They and others looked to him, called to him. Whether it was true or not, the warlock again felt that if he gave in to Toma, he would open the way for all their deaths at the renegade's claw.

The warlock fought the lightning, even managing another step up. Toma's cries of triumph faded as he eyed with disbelief the continued existence of his tiny bane.

Cabe drew everything he had into one last effort, aware that by doing so he might kill himself where Toma had so far failed. He met, for what he hoped was the last time, the eyes of the renegade. Cabe tried to imagine the faces of all those close to him whom Toma had already killed. Even Grath, despite the young drake's secret allegiance. Grath *had* saved Cabe and Valea from the duke's black blade.

"From the beginning," he called to the sinister behemoth, "you've desired that it be *you* and you alone who sat on the throne as Dragon Emperor."

"It *should* have been mine! I was the most *worthy!* I, *Toma!*"

Cabe ignored the outburst. "I can't make you emperor, Toma, but the least I can do . . . is give you the *throne.*"

The attack that Cabe had prepared was fueled as much by his own life force as it was by the sorcerous power at his command. He reached forward with his right hand and pointed at where he knew the dragon's heart to be. So ensnared was he by his own spell that he no longer even noticed Toma's own withered assault.

His last view before his bolt hit Toma in the chest was the dragon's absolute refusal to accept what was happening.

Toma's shield was nothing to Cabe's spell. Neither was the thick, tough, scaled hide of the deadly leviathan. The bolt burned through all, piercing the dragon completely through and not dissipating until it struck the wall far behind him.

The dragon stiffened, transfixed by the lethal assault. Toma's massive form shivered as Cabe continued to pour his life into the effort.

*"Fall, damn you!"* he cried, unconsciously mimicking Toma from but a few moments before. *"Why don't you fall?"*

Toma did.

With a last, pain-wracked roar, the renegade dragon fell back upon the very object he had so long desired to control. Toma's huge body was too much for the throne, and as he fell upon it, the throne crumbled under his weight. The drake's head swung back in a horrible arc and smashed against the rock wall to one side of the dais. A burst of fire shot briefly ceilingward as Toma exhaled.

Cabe did not move. He could not believe that, after all this time, Toma was defeated. Surely, the warlock thought, there must be some last trick.

There was none. Even as he watched, the dragon twitched feebly once or twice. The head slowly came round so that Toma could see Cabe, but the renegade's eyes were already clouding. Even still, Toma attempted one last sneer.

It was the expression that would remain frozen on his face as he died.

Cabe Bedlam crumpled on the steps, the knowledge that Toma was dead finally giving him release. He struggled to remain conscious, but the effort of his victory had drained him too much. His eyes closed. He forced them open again, only to find an anxious Gwen peering down at him, a vision which made no sense since not only was his wife not here but he would have had to have been lying on his back to see her so. Clearly, the haggard mage thought not so clearly, he had worn himself so thoroughly that he was suffering delusions.

Then the delusion told him to go back to sleep and Cabe, knowing that he could fight the darkness no longer, finally gave in.

# XXII

"ARE YOU FEELING better?" asked Gwendolyn.

Cabe lowered his cup and peered at his wife from the bed. She looked concerned, as she had since he had first been carried back to the Manor from Kivan Grath, but she also looked preoccupied with something else.

"Better than yesterday. Better than the two weeks I don't remember."

His last, fairly clear memory before waking in his bed but two days ago had been of his wife leaning over him, fear dominating her expression. It had not been a delusion, as he had thought, but rather a brief awakening just after Darkhorse had brought him to the Manor. The shadow steed had returned to the cavern the moment that he had assured the safety of Kyl, Valea, and Ursa.

The eternal had joyfully greeted his human friend yesterday, ecstatic to discover that the warlock had finally recovered. No one knew exactly what had happened to Cabe, only that he had hung between life and death for two weeks, then abruptly recovered almost completely.

Darkhorse had described the surprise with which he had viewed the cavern upon his return. He had expected a battle of epic proportions still raging, only to find the dragon Toma dead on the dais, maw still curved in what seemed a cruel smile, and Cabe sprawled on the steps. At first, the shadow steed had feared that his friend had died alongside the devilish drake, but then he had noted the thin thread of life remaining.

"Praise be that it was not yet time for you to journey down the Final Path!" the stallion had rumbled yesterday. Darkhorse, too, had recovered. He had re-covered so much, in fact, that he had made the rare transformation and given himself a pair of long, tentaclelike arms with which to hug the weary mage.

Everyone had come to give Cabe their best and express their pleasure at his survival . . . everyone except one young drake. Even Ursa had come, although when Cabe had pressed her about Kyl, the female drake had quickly excused herself.

No one would even tell him what had happened to the meeting with the Blue Dragon. It had, of course, not taken place due to Kyl's own injuries. The heir, however, had suffered much less than Cabe and had recovered some days ago.

After Kyl's heroism in the cavern, Cabe had not wanted to think ill of the emperor-to-be, but again doubts crept into his mind. Kyl *had* looked willing to join forces with Toma when it had seemed the renegade would win.

*Toma.* The Manor had been trying to warn them in its own way about the truth concerning Toma and Traske. The warlock knew that now. He wondered if the other images had any such meaning. He also wondered just how sentient the Manor was. More than Cabe had ever imagined? It would bear looking into once things calmed down.

"Do you want anything to eat?" asked Gwendolyn, stirring her husband from his thoughts.

"No, Mistress Belima's lunch should do fine for the next few days." The cook had been so gratified by the mage's recovery that she had made him a bit of just about every specialty she knew. Of course, with Mistress Belima, that was almost everything. Cabe's lunch could have easily served the army of Penacles. Despite all he had eaten—and his days of sleep had made him ravenous—he had hardly even made a dent in the vast meal. Gwen had used her power on Cabe, but that had only allowed him to survive. He looked forward to digging further into the pile of food later, but now he could only dream of eating.

"Then, do you think you can handle another visitor?"

"Another one? The Gryphon's been here despite now officially being re-crowned monarch of Penacles. Troia couldn't make it because of the nearing birth and the somewhat abbreviated coronation ceremony. Erini and Lynnette paid a visit yesterday . . . at the same time Darkhorse showed up, of course." It had not been surprising to find the trio depart at the same time. This way, Erini could visit with all of her friends without Melicard becoming disgruntled at the shadow steed's presence. Melicard could never seem to make up his mind about Darkhorse. At least the king had sent his own regards. "I think that everyone in the Manor has been here, including Master Ironshoe several times to thank me for, as he put it, 'putting down that mad riding drake once and for all for poor old Ssarekai.'"

"I'm sorry you missed Ssarekai's funeral." Despite the drake having been petrified by Toma, everyone had agreed that it would only be polite to his memory to bury Ssarekai as soon as possible.

"I'll visit his grave later. He deserves so much more than the end Toma gave him." *Who does that leave?* the warlock pondered. *Could it be . . . the Green Dragon?*

"Shall I tell him to come back?" The enchantress grew more concerned.

Cabe realized that she thought he was growing weary again. "No. Who is it?"

She stepped toward the door, giving him only a cautious look. "I think I'll just let him introduce himself."

The sorceress quickly departed through the doorway. Cabe heard her whispering to someone, but could not hear what was being said. Heavy footfalls announced the coming of the visitor.

"I am glad to sssee you better, Massster Bedlam."

It was Kyl, but Kyl as Cabe had never seen him. The young drake was clad in resplendent dress armor that glittered like the noonday sun. A dragonhelm, a *real* dragonhelm, lay crooked in his arm.

Cabe straightened. "Congratulations, Your Majesty. I would gather that the meeting with Lord Blue went well and that he's thrown his support behind you."

"Only just thisss morning."

That made the warlock's eyes widen. "This morning?"

Kyl looked him straight in the eye. "I informed the massster of Irillian when I first woke after the battle that I would not even consssider a meeting until I knew that you were going to recover." The heir looked embarrassed. "I have been here every day for asss long asss the Lady Bedlam would permit, awaiting your return to usss. Each day, I thanked you for all you've done."

That stirred a vague memory. Kyl, kneeling by him. Kyl's voice, apologetic and promising to make amends.

"She will vouch for the truth of my words, Massster Bedlam."

"I don't doubt you. You have *my* best wishes, also, Kyl. I've evidently been wrong about you."

"Not entirely." The emperor-to-be hissed. "Pleassse alssso relay my apologiesss to Valea. She will not ssspeak to me and I can hardly blame her. I *did* intend to ussse her asss a pawn, and for that I shall never be able to forgive mysssself. She deservesss ssso much better."

"I'll talk to her."

"That isss all I asssk."

Cabe was silent for a time, then quietly said, "Kyl, I'm sorry about Grath."

The heir shrugged and took his helm in both hands. His countenance was neutral, but his eyes bespoke his misery. "I cannot sssay that Grath—or I— were innocents caught up by Toma's sssubtle teaching, but . . . thank you."

"What will happen to Faras and Ssgayn?"

The drake placed the helm on his head. Even clad so, he resembled more a legendary human king than the emperor of the drake race. "They chossse in the end to ssserve their emperor, not the beguiling renegade. Their greatest crime isss a narrow view of loyalty. They will be punished, but if they remain repentant, I will find a place for them."

Cabe had been relieved to discover that the two guardian dragons had not joined the lengthy list of those who had fallen because of Toma's obsession. They had decided in the end to stand aside and let Darkhorse pass when it became apparent that not all was as it had seemed in the cavern. "Good."

"I mussst go now. There are preparationsss to be made. Lord Blue isss waiting to essscort me to Irillian, where the final sssteps before the coronation can take place will be made. There isss alssso the matter of cleaning up the throne chamber again. The largessst refussse has been taken away and burned, but damage still remains. Also, a petition from the lord of this new drake confederacy demands my eventual attention."

So much for the grand designs of Toma. Still, something else Kyl had just said . . . "Lord *Blue?*"

Kyl walked to the doorway before answering. When he did respond, there was a note of question in his voice. "Lord Green hasss requesssted that his brother in Irillian take over the matter. He expressesss hisss apologiesss, but sssays that he believesss Blue will be better able to handle the event. Perhapsss when you are fully recovered, you could ssspeak with the lord of Dagora and find out what ailsss him."

"Perhaps."

Kyl bowed, indicating his intention to depart. "May I expect you to be at my ascension?"

"The Dragon Kings might not care for that."

"They will endure it if it isss what their emperor desiresss. I promissse you that."

"Then, we'll be there."

The heir unleashed an uncharacteristically childlike smile. "Thank you."

He departed, leaving Cabe temporarily alone. The warlock stared out the window of his bedchamber, thinking that the coronation would certainly be interesting at the very least.

"I asked Aurim to see Kyl and the Blue Dragon out of the Manor. I thought you'd like some company."

Cabe looked at the doorway to discover his wife had returned. Gwendolyn came to the bedside and sat down next to him. The two kissed. "Thank you. How is Aurim? Has there been any aftereffect?"

"Still nothing. I think he's safe. Once he succeeded in remembering, the spell apparently dissipated completely. Both the Gryphon and I have checked carefully for the past two weeks. Nothing remains."

"So no last vestige of Toma to haunt us." The drake and his evil *were* dead. Cabe sighed in relief for the first time. It had still been difficult to accept that the duke would trouble them no more.

"Hard to believe that it's finally all over," she whispered. "Peace has a chance . . . and through *Kyl* of all drakes."

"Peace has a chance," he agreed, "but it's hardly all over. There's a lot to do. The Dragon Kings will accept Kyl as emperor, but that doesn't mean they'll cease plotting. Then there's Zuu and the new generation of mages growing up. This confederacy of drakes . . . they were allies of Toma. There's a hundred other things that I can think of that will delay peace long past even *our* lifetimes."

She gave him a playful frown. "You are without a doubt the most pessimistic optimist I have ever met. Let's at least enjoy what we've achieved so far, all right?"

Cabe took her in his arms and kissed her again. He *did* feel more hopeful, despite his own words. Perhaps the path was still fraught with rocks and pitfalls, but there was definite hope . . . and who could ask for anything more than that?

The Dragonrealm at peace . . . it was finally possible.

# PAST DANCE

*Memories can be subject to change . . .*

# I

THE SHADOWS DANCED.

They danced to a noteless melody, a silent symphony. The shadows danced at the staircase, in utter darkness, repeating the same steps over and over, a brief display caught in time.

And then they disappeared.

# II

VALEA LIVED WITH ghosts.

That was what her brother, Aurim, said of her, anyway. She spent most of her time studying them, dreaming of them, wondering what they had been in life.

The images were not truly ghosts, not in the classical sense. Ghosts existed in the Dragonrealm, just as surely did shapechangers, elves, and sorceresses such as herself. No, the visions that would pop up at unexpected moments throughout her home were, in fact, memories.

The memories of the Manor.

She swept back long, flowing red hair from her face as she leaned over the book kept by her father, the wizard Cabe Bedlam. For years he had inscribed in the leather-bound journal the images he and others had seen throughout the towering structure, a building not only of marble, but, to one side, carved into the very trunk of an even more imposing tree. The Manor had existed by one name or another for longer than even the Dragon Kings, and during that time had been the focal point of many lives and events, not all of them involving the young race of humanity.

Valea not only shared her father's passion concerning uncovering the history of their home, she had made it her obsession. Her mother worried about the hours she spent in the library, fretted that her twenty-year-old daughter had become reclusive. Valea did not go with them when they visited Lord Gryphon in Penacles nor did she deign to go along when the family went on diplomatic missions to mountainous Talak, domain of disfigured Melicard and his beautiful queen, Erini. Ever the Bedlams' daughter stayed behind, concerned that she might miss a single apparition.

"Missstresss?" called a tentative female voice.

At the library's door stood a dark, almost sultry woman with narrow, exotic eyes and an almost elven appearance that made Valea's own pale, rounded face seem very unremarkable to the sorceress. Setera's plain but neat black dress perfectly outlined her curves. Even clad in a much more elegant gown of emerald green, Valea felt frumpy and plain.

Only when Setera opened her mouth did the servant reveal that, despite the image, she was anything but an elf. Her teeth were sharp, predatory, and her tongue was forked. Yet, despite this sinister aspect, she treated Valea with the utmost respect, even falling down on one knee.

"Rise up, Setera. You know my father will have no one bend to us, not man nor drake."

"It isss the cussstom of the emperor . . ."

An involuntary twinge of regret coursed through Valea at mention of the drake's former lord. The dragon people were very formal, that despite that their young emperor had once been Cabe Bedlam's student. Valea's father had tried to train Kyl to be a fair, open-minded ruler, but even he had not been able to weed out some of the race's ingrained manners.

"But you're not serving the emperor now. You're in the household of my father."

Setera rose, the glittering eyes that beguiled many of the human servitors watching her mistress close. Every time Valea stared into them, she felt plain, even ugly, that despite the fact that once Kyl had looked at her with favor. Of course, then he had also considered the ramifications of having at his side a bride whose lineage included some of the most powerful wizards ever.

Stirring herself from bitter memories, Valea asked, "What do you want?"

"Warnok claimsss to have been confronted by a vision." Setera made the announcement with a shiver. For all their warlike ways, the drakes who worked at the Manor were unsettled by its spectral images. "You wished to be told of thessse thingsss."

"Did he?" All thought of Kyl and her own foolishness faded as she seized hold of this news. "Did he recognize it? Where was it? Show me!"

The dark-haired female led Valea through the tall marble halls, heading toward that part of the Manor where stone melded perfectly with living wood.

The smooth, light gray walls gave way to rich, brown grain as if the two had always been one. Even the floor transformed.

Ahead, staring over his armored shoulder as if expecting ghosts at every turn, the drake servitor Warnok awaited them. Like Setera, he was a recent arrival from the mountain domain of the Dragon Emperor, a gift, so Kyl said to Valea's father, to show that the ties between drake lord and human wizard remained strong. That they might also spy for their lord was a given assumption on the part of all the Bedlams.

If Setera looked more than human, Warnok was far less. Unlike the emperor, whose fair face and form entranced women as much as Setera's did men, Warnok resembled most other male drakes. Almost seven feet tall, he stood armored from head to toe in green scale mail tinted gold, the latter the sign of his clan. His hands were gauntleted and any features were all but hidden in an enclosed helm. From deep within the helm, red, reptilian eyes stared forth and like Setera, from the slit of the barely-seen mouth a sharp, forked tongue darted past fanged teeth.

The image of an armored knight was simply illusion. Everything that Valea saw was a part of the drake, his very skin. This was as close as most older males could come to looking human, although the youngest generation seemed to be producing more like Kyl now.

For a fearsome figure—and one who was in actuality a dragon—Warnok continued to look around anxiously. When Valea called to him, he started.

"Missstresss," the armored servant gasped, bowing his head slightly.

"You saw it?" she began without preamble, gaze darting here and there in hopes of a repeat performance. "What was it? Did it speak? Was there more than one image? Was it on the staircase? Down the central hall?"

Long ago, Valea had given standing orders to each and every human or drake servant to study in detail the spectral visions that confronted them, ignorant ever of the fact that most people did not share her intense interest in such supernatural sights. Warnok, eyes slits and mouth becoming more and more of a straight line, withered under her inquisition.

"Only sssaw it for a moment," he hissed nervously, reacting not at all like a giant, scaled warrior. "Near the winding ssstairsss." The drake pointed at one of the many serpentine staircases filling the Manor.

Valea eagerly studied it, but saw nothing. A bit disappointed, she asked again, "What was it?"

"A figure in a hooded robe . . . a monk, I think, missstresss. Hisss face wasss turned from me and he only ssstood there for a moment before vanishing."

*A hooded monk . . .* The image struck no chord with her, but her father might have written it down in his book. She would have to look. The drake's revelation both interested and disappointed her; Valea wondered what the monk's part in the history of the Manor might pertain to, but at the same time she had hoped for some more arresting image, something like the dying Seeker her brother had once seen sprawled on the front steps of the building.

Questioning Warnok further garnered no new information. Undeterred, Valea headed back to the library in order to search through the listings for any mention of the monk.

"And where are you off to?" asked a musical voice.

Valea's mother, the Lady of the Amber, stood near the back entrance of the Manor. She wore emerald green riding clothes that accentuated her already-flawless figure. Her face was a perfect oval, with two gleaming green eyes, full round mouth, and a petite nose framed under a full head of hair both richer red and longer than Valea's own. Like her daughter, a streak of silver cut through the luxurious hair, the sign of wizards, warlocks, and sorceresses.

More than once Valea had been told that she was an almost perfect copy of her mother and it was the "almost" that to the younger Bedlam seemed a statement of her deficiencies. Certainly her face was not flawless, not with a mouth too big and a nose that tipped upward. Nor were her eyes so vivid nor her hair so striking. To Valea, "watered-down" would have been a better choice of words. That her mother was fifty years old at least—not counting a century or two captive in an amber prison thanks to Valea's own grandfather—could be attributed to the lengthy life spans of mages, but it did not help the daughter's self-image.

"I was off to the library."

The beautiful face broke into a frown. "Again? Really Valea, you need to be out more. Since Ursa left, you've become far too closeted. It isn't healthy." Gwendolyn Bedlam was herself an active person. Between those times when she and her husband were called upon to deal with some crisis, she found one interest after another to keep her busy.

Ursa was Kyl's sibling and had left with him when he had become emperor. She had been Valea's dearest friend. That, however, had not been the true reason why she had secluded herself and both knew it. "I'm fine, Mother. If you'll excuse me—"

But Lady Bedlam would not. "Valea. What Kyl attempted to do—"

"Kyl did nothing. I was the fool."

"A drake and a human can be friends, but never more."

Valea gave her mother an incredulous look. "Have you told Aurim that?"

"Your father and I will deal with Aurim."

"You'd better deal with him fast . . . or did you really think he went visiting Penacles again?"

Gwen Bedlam's expression left no doubt that her daughter had struck true with her barb. Valea felt some guilt as she turned from her mother, but in some aspects she also felt some justice. Her parents could not understand how she had felt about Kyl any more than they could her brother's feelings toward Yssa . . . who as the child of drake and woman was proof of the falsehood of Lady Bedlam's statements.

Valea heard her mother turn about as the latter no doubt went to investigate Aurim's latest perfidy. Lady Bedlam would have as much success in changing her son's mind as she had with redirecting her daughter's course . . . none.

More determined than ever, Valea headed on to the library and the journal . . . and the safety and security of the Manor's fleshless memories.

# III

THE MONK HAD never been listed before and that alone refueled her interest some, but what Valea found more fascinating was a pattern she had finally noticed. The staircase was the site of more than one encounter; in fact, through the years at least six different specters had been seen on or near it. Valea suspected that, as with many of the apparitions, they also materialized when no one was there to see them. Why her father had never noticed this, the young sorceress could not say, but clearly the area was one requiring more intense study.

And that was why she now sat hunched to the side, hidden from the staircase, watching the darkened area while the rest of the Manor slept. With both the grounds and the building surrounded by an invisible barrier that let no one in without the permission of the Bedlams, sentries were not needed. Besides, even if anyone managed to penetrate the shield—as the dread drake Toma once had—there were other spells in place that would alert the inhabitants.

Satisfied that no one would disturb her watch, Valea waited. She had purposely dressed in her favored light green sleeping gown just in case by a rare chance someone would rise from their slumber. This near the kitchens, she would have the perfect excuse. Her brother had made it a regular habit to wander down at night and take back a small snack. Why not her as well?

One hour passed, then two and three. Valea's confidence eroded and her clever plan now seemed absolutely absurd. In addition, lack of sleep began to take its toll. Despite her determination, her vigilance finally slipped. Yawning, Valea tied her hair back, then decided to lean against the wall just for a moment—

A slight creak from near the top of the staircase woke her. Silently cursing herself for her lapse, she drew back, hoping that whoever descended would be so bleary-eyed that they would save her a confrontation. With her mother now away in search of Aurim, the odds were decidedly in her favor, but still . . .

The creaking drew nearer . . . yet in the dark Valea could not make out anyone. She squinted, not daring to risk a spell that might alert whoever stood upon the stairs. It was quite possible her father had returned unannounced from his mission northwest, but somehow she doubted it.

Now it sounded as if the newcomer should be at the very bottom, but the staircase remained devoid of any user. It suddenly occurred to Valea that there existed one simple reason why.

The monk had not returned, but another ghost had come.

A thrilling chill ran down her spine. The creaking was suddenly replaced by a gentle tap on the floor, giving Valea the mental image of a light-footed person, perhaps a woman.

No one had recorded any such encounter, adding yet another to the staircase's collection. Valea stepped from her hiding place, trying to focus on the exact spot where the figure would be standing. More and more she had the sensation that it was a woman, a young woman.

A muffled cry nearly made her back away. Only at the last did Valea realize it was another sound from her ghost.

And then . . . a blue haze formed, a hunched figure.

A dying woman. An elf in blue, her face turned to the floor, blood pooling from somewhere around her stomach.

Valea acted instinctively, reaching out to help one who could no longer be helped. Her fingers, instead of touching cloth, sank into the vision.

"ARE YOU ILL, cousin?"

His face was narrow, but handsome, handsome much the way Kyl's was. He was tall, silver-haired but youthful, unless one stared at the eyes. The oak-brown eyes had seen much, perhaps too much, yet even they managed some gentleness as they looked down the slim, almost pointed nose at her.

*Cousin?*

That an elf called Valea cousin did not confuse her so much as his presence . . . and that did not confuse her so much as the fact that they both danced and danced, he in his regal, silver-blue jacket and slacks and she in a bright blue gown that spread like a bell at the waist. One hand of hers the elf held high, the other touched lightly the left side of his torso just above the belt. Likewise his own hand touched her torso, but in a proper yet affectionate manner.

Music played, a windswept sound like none Valea had ever heard. She had little experience with elves, although supposedly their blood and hers had ties . . .

*Blood!* She recalled the dying figure.

As she faltered, he caught her, his expression one of mild concern. Valea felt certain her face had grown crimson, but she could do nothing to stop it.

"Stop," the figure calmly ordered, but not to her. At his command, the music ceased.

As their dance finished, Valea realized that she stood near the staircase . . . and on the exact spot where the ghost had formed.

"My apologies, Galani. Sometimes when I lead, I forget to think about my partner." He said the last almost ruefully, as if the words held more meaning.

"No—" she managed. "No—apologies, Arak!"

"But, yes! Here you visit your cousin, and what does he do but throw you around like a leaf in the wind!" Arak frowned at himself. "Perhaps the others were wise to suggest you avoid this journey."

Valea did not know what to reply, but it seemed her lips did. "What the elders think is their own concern, cousin. They spend too much time worrying about nothing!"

"Such as my mad suggestions about our people staking their own claim in this world at last? Such as the elves no longer being passive in a world ruled in turn by such as the Garoot, the Quel, the Seekers, and now the Dragon Kings?"

"Our people have thrived under one master race after another, Arak. Though they have already ruled for several hundred years, we will survive the drakes, too. Certainly better than those beastly humans that seem to be sprouting up every-where." Valea listened with fascination at the words she—or rather Galani—spoke. The confidence of the speaker was undermined by the sorceress's own knowledge of the lengthy reign of the Dragon Kings and how humans, not elves, would begin supplanting the drakes.

Arak nodded—somewhat hesitantly, Valea thought—then led her toward what the sorceress knew to be the entrance to the back of the estate.

Outside, the fanciful topiary animals she already knew greeted them, as did the high, vast hedge maze in which Valea and her brother had cheerfully lost themselves as children. Instead of night, the bright sun illuminated everything. Yet, where Valea's world was one bustling with the activity of the human/drake settlement that dealt with the Manor's expansive lands, Arak's domain seemed one of emptiness, loneliness. The two of them looked to be the only inhabit-ants and Galani clearly had come as a guest.

"Why are we out here?" her mouth asked.

"I thought you'd feel more at home out among the foliage." Again, the male elf spoke with some hesitation in his voice.

The ties between the two clearly ran deeper than blood, that Valea could sense. She knew that among the elves cousins did marry, but for some reason any hope of that happening between Arak and Galani had long faded.

Her body shivered. "It is very pretty, but . . . there is something different about the plants here . . . something not natural."

"This place has been touched by magic in more than one way since its creation, cousin. You simply feel that."

Valea abruptly found herself staring up into the elf's eyes. She could imagine losing herself in them—until Kyl's visage briefly overlapped Arak's.

Valea pulled away. Valea . . . not Galani.

"What is it, cousin? Do I now disgust you the way I disgust the elders?" The handsome face twisted into something not so handsome.

The sorceress could say nothing, too stunned at having interacted. Fortunately, Galani answered. "Never that, Arak! I only fear that you underestimate the pressures you put upon yourself—" The eyes surveyed the grounds and the tall marble and wood facade of the Manor. The statue of a soaring Seeker, one of the avian humanoids Valea knew of even in her own time, stood perched on one edge of the sloped roof. "—and this place . . . this place is not good for an elf's mind. I feel that."

"Rubbish. This is why our people remain nothing more than incidental influences in the land! Beware of the unknown! Beware of change! Beware of outsiders—"

"Surely not all outsiders, my friend . . ." came a voice that, despite its calm, quiet tone, still made every fiber of Galani's and Valea's mutual body grow taut.

Arak reacted with anything but uncertainty, He spun around to face the Manor, a look of pleasure on his face. "You are back! How timely! Perhaps between the two of us we can talk some sense into my cousin. I told you of her imminent arrival, did I not?"

"You did."

Through Galani's eyes, Valea stared at the newcomer who had so brazenly appeared out of nowhere as if he, not the elf, was master of this domain. Valea tried to speak, but her host's own startlement kept both frozen.

Not at all sensing his cousin's mood, Arak reached out an arm toward the newcomer. "Cousin, permit me to introduce the most ardent supporter of my efforts, a fellow exile whose aid in my work has been invaluable! Galani, this is—"

The figure, a tall man in leather boots and wearing flowing—almost living—robes of black, reached forth a gloved hand to take Valea's own. He interrupted Arak's own introduction, saying, "Call me Tylan . . . this time."

Through Galani, Valea stared and stared at the imposing form, stared mostly at the face . . . or where the face should have been. Beneath a voluminous hood, she caught a glimpse of brown hair and a streak of silver. However, beneath that, the face remained just out of focus. No matter now hard her host or she tried, it never quite defined itself. Eyes could be made out and a mouth and nose, but seen as if in a fog or through water.

And the gasp that escaped belonged to Valea, for she, if not Galani, knew whom she confronted. The name burst forth, with its uttering the sorceress's entire world turning into a blur worse than that beneath the hood.

*"Shade!"*

# IV

"MISSSTRESSS VALEA! MISSSTRESSS, pleassse!"

Valea blinked, realizing her eyes had closed. She moved her head, only to feel a hard surface beneath. Above her, a blinding light coalesced, becoming a candle in a brass holder in the hand of a very distressed Setera.

The drake put the candle holder down, then knelt beside her mistress. Valea looked around, saw that she lay at the foot of the staircase and that the first hints of daylight had just begun to creep in through the windows.

"Are you well?" hissed Setera. She touched the sorceress's hand. "Missstress! You are cold!"

That was not a great surprise to Valea, considering that she had been lying on the floor all night in only her gown. She rose quickly, then regretted her swiftness when her legs nearly buckled.

Setera kept her from slipping. This close, the drake's much hotter, more rapid breathing quickly warmed Valea up.

"What—what are you doing here?" Valea asked her.

"I heard a noissse . . . a gasssp! And sssome word or name!"

*Shade* . . . She remembered calling out his name, but that had been in the dream.

Recollection of what she had experienced suddenly made all else insignificant. Valea had done something her father had never managed, to reach into one of the memories of the Manor and experience a part of its reason for existing. The elves Arak and Galani and their dealings with the warlock Shade . . . small wonder that the ancient edifice would have such an encounter burned into its core.

Gently shaking off Setera's concern, Valea hurried to her bedroom. Her mind raced over and over the scene and the final instant. She knew of Shade, of course, even though she had never to her memory met him. When last he had appeared, it had been when then-Princess Erini had been on her way to marry

Melicard I of Talak. The hooded spellcaster had nearly brought that situation
to ruin, but in the end had not only aided the new queen with her fledgling
magical skills, but had also prevented Talak from being overrun by one of the
Dragon Kings. At the time, it had been assumed that it had finally cost him his
life . . . but then Shade had died many, many times before.

Her father believed Shade to be as old as, if not older than, the drake race,
which had itself seemingly come out of nowhere far in the past. Cabe Bedlam
suspected that Shade was the last of the human race's precursors, the legendary
and sinister Vraad. Refugees from another world, if his research was correct,
they had colonized briefly what was now the Dragonrealm . . . and then vanished as a civilization.

If Shade was an example of the might of Vraad sorcery, he was also an
example of their arrogance and self-destructive natures. From the stories her
father had told her, Shade had early on attempted some mad immortality spell,
a spell driven on by a more than normal fear of death. He had succeeded in a
horrific fashion, much to his dismay. Shade *could* die, but each time he did, he
instantly resurrected far away . . . and returned not at all the same man he had
been prior.

Each incarnation of the warlock emerged with a splinter personality, one
that sought final domination of Shade's body. Worse, those personalities swung
from light to darkness depending on the previous one. Her own parents had
faced Shade as friend and foe and only the intercession of Darkhorse, the phan-
tasmic creature from the Void and a loyal friend of the Bedlams, had prevented
Cabe's death.

Entering her chambers, Valea went to a basin and washed water over her face.
The cool liquid brought her senses nearer to normalcy. She had seen Shade, yes,
but only a memory of him. This Tylan, this variation of the faceless warlock,
was as dead as the elves.

But what was the secret behind the ghosts she had encountered and the
memory she had lived through? For that matter, how had Valea actually made
contact with the vision? She had wanted to comfort the dying figure—a foolish
notion in retrospect—but that alone should not have enabled her to experience
Galani's past. Never in her father's records had there been any comment on such
an experience.

But never had there been recorded a vision that included the appearance of
Shade.

With her mother abruptly departed, Valea could not immediately look into
the episode, as she first hoped. Running the Manor demanded her attention.
There were overseers, of course, but they still had to have approval on certain
matters. There was also correspondence to receive, for her parents kept in touch

with friends and allies throughout the continent. One scroll spoke of bustling activity in those lands in the northwest held by the drake confederation, a loose-knit realm populated by the survivors of several clans whose masters had perished. An unmarked drake named Sssaleese commanded them, but his hold was said to be precarious at this time.

Valea put the scroll aside. Her father investigated other rumors near that vicinity. Had he been alone, she would have worried more, but Darkhorse carried him and together they were a team unbeatable.

The day passed much too swiftly and by the end of it Valea found herself worn out. She was rarely left in charge by herself, her brother generally taking that role when their parents were away. There had scarce been a moment when thoughts of her encounter had not been on her mind, but the duties of the Manor had prevented the sorceress from ever thinking them through. Only when she sat down to eat her supper in her room, her view from the terrace the sweeping, green lands protected by the barrier, did Valea finally begin sorting through matters.

It had taken only the touch of her fingers for her to enter the memory. Logic dictated that she should be able to do the same next time. The only question remained when that next time might be. The ghosts of the Manor did not necessarily come at her beck and call. It might be days, months, or even years before she had such luck again.

And yet . . . that night found Valea once more ensconced near the staircase, this time her garments warmer and her determination a hundredfold stronger.

Every creak of the building, every whisper of the wind, sent her sitting up straight, certain that the apparitions had returned. Each time, though, Valea faced only disappointment. The hours of darkness moved on in quick order, morning rapidly approaching.

Bleary-eyed, she abandoned her post just before the first gray light of predawn. That the visions might materialize during the daytime Valea had already taken into account, but she had felt certain that her best chance would be at night. Her assumptions now shattered, the young sorceress pushed back her unkempt hair and retired to her quarters for a few hours respite. The Manor could run itself for awhile.

Unbidden came images of Kyl, his exotic, inhuman features twisted into mirth. What a sight she would have been to him now, so disheveled. Biting her lower lip in bitterness, Valea threw herself onto the plush, down bed and buried herself in one of the pillows. Perhaps when she woke she would be able to make some sense of her foolishness . . . *all* her foolishness. Even the ghosts had let her down. Even they—

The hand slapped her harshly across the face. Stunned, Valea could do nothing but stand where she was and try to understand what had just happened.

"I warned you about saying such things again! If you must repeat their prattle over and over, cousin, you might as well just go back to the forest where you belong!"

Her cheek still screaming from pain, Valea watched Arak stalk away, the elf in a mood so foul he looked ready to kill. Valea—or rather Galani—shivered uncontrollably, something for which the young enchantress could not blame her. Then, tears pouring, the female elf turned and ran through the marble and wood halls, past a dark, empty ballroom and along corridors lit only by dying torches. If the Manor reflected its inhabitants, it certainly now reflected the mood of Galani's cousin.

Out of the Manor and into the moonlit garden they ran. Valea stared at the looming maze, now seeming to call to her. Her elven host heeded that call, darting in among the high hedges without any care.

Valea felt each scratch as Galani ran relentlessly through the dark passages. The elf's eyesight was better than her own, but even Galani's eyes revealed little more than hulking shadows and twisting limbs.

Finally running out of breath, the sorceress's host collapsed onto the soft ground near a bench. Valea gasped along with her, finding it impossible to tell who was more exhausted. The tears continued to rain down.

Caught up in Galani's distress, Valea could not tell how long they lay there. The crying might have gone on, but a pair of hands suddenly took hold of the elf's arms, guiding her up gently.

Gloved hands.

Even in such dark, it was impossible not to recognize the ethereal figure.

"You're injured," commented Shade almost blandly. "Your cousin had no such right."

Curiously, the fear that Valea had sensed in Galani earlier had vanished. The enchantress sensed some lengthy passage of time since her last visitation, but how much, she could not say. Now the elf looked at the murky form as if having found her champion. Galani's changing mood affected Valea's own. For all the evil he had performed, Shade had also done much good. He was as revered as he was reviled. If the present scene was any indication, Tylan was an agent of light . . . and someone who had already touched Galani's heart.

"Tylan . . ." murmured the elf. "It's been so long."

"I had . . . matters to attend to."

With a suddenness that caught both Shade and Valea unaware, Galani buried her face in the voluminous robes of the warlock. Shade hesitated for a moment, then put his arms around her as one might do for a child.

"What is he *becoming?*" she begged of the hooded figure. "What is his work with that—that thing he brought back from the Legar Peninsula—doing to him?"

She remained silent for a time, then answered, "You mean the Wyr Stone? It is a dangerous artifact. I warned him of that when he first asked me of it. It all but destroyed the Garoot. He plays with powerful forces . . . but the rewards will benefit all elves if he succeeds."

"At the cost of his own life? Our people have no desire to rule the land! They are satisfied with their privacy!"

He carefully pushed her from him. The blurred face fascinated Valea as much as it did the elf. A light seemed to radiate from it, allowing one to see the vague details, but never the complete picture. To Valea's mind, Shade had once been a pleasant-looking male. Not so perfect as Kyl, but better still in other ways.

*And what sort of thoughts are those?* she suddenly asked herself. Bad enough she had suffered such an infatuation for the future Dragon Emperor . . . now Valea entertained notions concerning an unstable, unpredictable warlock who had more than once nearly destroyed the entire continent.

But Galani entertained similar notions. Before Shade could speak, a slim, golden-clad arm reached up to his murky visage. Perfectly-formed fingers stroked his cheek.

Shade pulled away, but not immediately. "You know the news I brought your cousin. The Dragon Kings have declared among themselves that the elves must be brought to destruction. They distrust your magic. You're the strongest race other than them at the moment—"

"But what of your people? The humans? Surely they—"

A harsh laugh escaped the warlock. "My people? Galani, the Dragon Kings are much more my people than the humans are!"

Valea did not understand his comment and certainly her host did not. The sorceress wished that she could do more than observe, but this was after all a memory, a playing of events long past. She could no more truly interact with it than she could with the characters in a book. The last time had clearly been a fluke.

"The Wyr Stone . . ." Galani's voice went cold. "How I wish he had never found that abomination!"

"But it is the key to your people's salvation. You may trust me on that."

Again emotions that reminded Valea too much of her feelings toward Kyl surfaced. Galani took one of the gloved hands in her own. "I trust you, Tylan. At times I trust you more than I do my cousin these day." She suddenly took his other hand. "Dance with me."

"*Dance* with you?" Shade blurted, the legendary warlock clearly as dumbfounded as he had possibly ever been. Valea shared his astonishment. One did not ask someone like Shade to dance.

"I miss the life I had before I chose to come here. I miss the times I had with Arak, who is now an utter stranger to me. Yes, please. Dance with me," Galani begged, nodding once. As she did, the wind suddenly came to life . . . and with it also came a gentle music, the music of the stars and moon, of peace and love.

The elf drew Shade forward, not permitting him escape. She guided him around, showing him how the music flowed. The robes fluttered, but they seemed to do so in time with the notes.

Galani and the warlock danced . . . and so Valea danced with Shade also.

She had danced with Kyl, but somehow those times paled with this. Kyl danced like a drake, moving with perfect but martial steps. The tall figure before her danced differently, his movements not only following the music, but adding to it a hint of something else. Shade danced as one more than well-versed in the art; he danced as someone who loved life to its fullest.

If Galani's cheeks grew crimson, Valea thought that surely it was because of her, not the elf. Something in Shade now touched her, drew her to him as she had never been drawn to anyone. She looked into the hood, saw a bit of the vague features, and desired truly this time to see the face that should be there.

She raised a hand to his cheek. She, *Valea*, not Galani.

But at that moment, two silent forms leapt over the hedge to their right.

Shade threw Valea/Galani to the opposing side just before the figures overwhelmed him. Valea had a glimpse of an armored fighter wielding not a sword or ax, but rather a staff with a curved, open end that glowed faintly.

With a hiss, the first attacker slapped the curved end onto the back of the warlock's hooded neck. Shade howled when the peculiar weapon touched him, then dropped to the floor.

Without thinking, Valea cast a spell. A burst of light illuminated the intruders—savage, fork-tongued drake warriors with a faint purple tint to their otherwise dusky green forms. Startled by the intense glare, the one wielding the magical weapon dropped it—just before the sorceress's second spell threw him into the foliage.

The other drake charged at her, a short sword drawn. He leapt with a speed Valea had never witnessed in drakes wearing a humanoid form. She wondered why the pair just did not transform into dragons or at least cast spells, then forgot such questions as she defended herself.

In her eyes, lines of force suddenly crisscrossed over every part of the visible world. As she had been trained by her parents, Valea drew from the nearest, touched upon the natural magic and pulled it within herself.

The drake swung at her, crimson orbs glowing malevolently within the false dragonhelm.

Pure magical force threw him into the air, threw him beyond the maze, and even beyond the grounds of the Manor. Unwilling to slay, Valea sent him far away, so far he would be no trouble for months to come. It would take him that long simply to reach his own master . . . who would not be so gentle after such an abysmal failure.

As the spell waned, a garbled, horrific sound made the sorceress turn back to the first drake. To her horror, she saw him struggling futilely to free himself from a hedge that seemed determined to devour his armored form. A gauntleted hand tore uselessly at the enshrouding limbs of the tall plant while the other stretched forth in desperate plea to the figure nearest.

But Shade did nothing as the hedge inexorably pulled its victim within.

Valea charged forward, but the warlock blocked her with his arm. The drake let out one last hiss . . . then the hedge enveloped him, leaving no trace.

"The master of the Libraries delved well and deep for this treachery," Shade uttered.

At first, Valea did not know what to make of his words, for why her parents' friend the Lord Gryphon would send drakes to attack the Manor was beyond her . . . but then she recalled that the leonine ruler of Penacles, City of Knowledge, did not yet even exist. The sorceress also recalled the colorings she had seen when the light had been strongest, a faint purple tint to the green scale.

Purple . . . the color of the Dragon Kings who had ruled Penacles until the Turning War, two hundred years prior to Valea's birth.

Shade waved one hand at the hedge that had devoured the drake. The foliage shimmered briefly, then resumed its normal appearance.

"But how—" Valea stammered. "It's impossible! How can they pass through the barrier?"

The shadowed visage turned to her. "It is said that any answer can be found in the books of Penacle's magical libraries . . . if one knows how to phrase the question." He leaned forward, a specter that suddenly blanketed the night. "You are well versed in power, Galani. My gratitude." He took her hand. "One would say your power rivals even that of Arak. I am surprised. You have said your powers were minute."

Only then did Valea realize what she had done. *She* controlled the elf's body again. *She* had made the decisions, defended them both.

*She* had altered the memory.

Or had she? Perhaps her actions had just been akin to those that Galani would have chosen. Surely it was not possible for her to—

"What is it? What happened out here? Galani! Where are you?"

Shade's hood lifted. "We are here, Arak!"

A green glow rose from elsewhere in the maze and the hedges before them abruptly separated. Hand up, Galani's cousin stalked toward them, eyes surveying everything in search of a foe.

"What happened? I heard shouts and felt spellwork!" He seized Valea, practically tearing her from the warlock's grip. "Cousin! Are you all right?"

"She is well . . . and quite capable, I might add." Shade pointed at the ground, where the peculiar weapon used by the one drake still lay. "A possession rod. Designed to make its captive pliable through pain. I believe it was meant for you, not me. Lord Purple planned well, but did not take in account my resilience."

The elf was aghast. "Penacles? There were drakes here? Within the barrier?"

"You know that of all the Dragon Kings he has the wherewithal to find a way inside. Fortunately, some sacrifices had to be made. Neither drake could shapeshift or else we would have been overwhelmed by dragons. The two could not cast spells, either, I believe. They must have seen your cousin run out to the hedge and assumed when I joined her that I must be you."

"'Ran out to the hedge' . . ." Arak stared down at Valea, who chose to say nothing. A look of contrition spread over the male elf's countenance. "Galani, I am so very sorry. If I—"

"They must be after the Wyr Stone," Shade interjected.

All thought of apology vanished from Arak. "You think so?"

"What other reason?"

"Then . . . my decision is made for me. Their tyranny must come to an end."

Valea desperately wanted to ask what the Wyr Stone was and what it would do to the Dragon Kings, but suddenly her head pounded horribly. She swayed and would have fallen if not for Arak suddenly catching her.

"Galani! Galani! Gal—"

"Mistress Valea! My lady! Please awaken!"

Moaning, Valea opened her eyes. A rounded, elderly woman in brown, one of the human servants, leaned over her. The woman's face was flushed and she had obviously been trying for some time to awaken her mistress.

"Cora . . . what's . . . what's wrong?"

"Mistress Valea! 'Tis nearly dinner! You've slept all night and all day!" Cora felt the younger woman's forehead. "And you're cold to the touch! Do you feel ill?"

Her head throbbed and Valea felt hungry, but otherwise she seemed all right. She told Cora so.

With an expression worthy of Lady Bedlam, the senior household servant shook her head. "Well you'll still stay in that bed while I get someone to bring you some good broth. If you can down that, we'll see about hardier food. Wouldn't do for your parents to come home to find you on death's door, would it?"

Knowing better than to argue, Valea lay back on the pillow, watching as Cora fussed about for a moment before departing to find her mistress some healthy food. The young sorceress marveled for a moment that she with all her trained and natural skills still had to rely on someone without a single iota of ability when it came to magic.

Thinking of magic drew her back to her dream . . . or whatever it had been. Cora had said that she had slept through most of the day! What sort of dream would cause that? It was surely no coincidence that it had concerned the very characters out of the Manor's ghostly memory.

She bolted upright in bed. Had she somehow become tied to that memory? But why . . . and how?

And what would happen when she next went to sleep?

# V

THE NIGHT STRETCHED long. Too long, as far as Valea was concerned. Candle in hand, she strode through the high halls of her home, passing without gazing at wall tapestries collected by her mother or vases and other decorative gifts given to both her parents over the years. As the foremost wizards of the lands, the Bedlams had as many friends as they did enemies and among the former were some of those most influential. A three-foot tall rearing steed made of onyx and reminiscent of Darkhorse stood atop a pedestal to her right, a recent present from the ruler of Zuu, Belfour. The people of Zuu had an obsession for horses and their sculptors could fashion the most marvelous, intricate statues of the equines, but even this, a favorite of Valea's, did not distract her.

She did not want to go to sleep. Having done so all day should have aided her in that regard, but there had been no rest in that slumber. The dream had sapped her of her strength as if she had actually expended herself physically. Valea still wanted to investigate the events behind the apparitions and the dream, but on her own terms.

Once more she stopped in the library, this time to research what history of the Manor her father had chronicled. Valea already knew that there would be no mention of an elf called Arak nor of his cousin Galani. What she did seek, however, was any mention of an artifact called the Wyr Stone. Clearly it was of great significance, if both Arak and Shade had believed it useful against the Dragon Kings.

For the next hour, she thumbed through the first journal, finding reference to other past inhabitants but not to the object in question. Discarding that tome, the crimson-tressed sorceress seized a volume related to the Dragon Masters, a band of wizards and other spellcasters of whom her great-grandfather, Nathan, had been one of the foremost . . . as had been her mother. Gwendolyn Bedlam had put down with quill all that she could recall of her days as part of the group that had attempted to oust the drakes from rule . . . even her love for her husband's grandfather.

The story made for fascinating reading and Valea had pored over it more than once in the past, but now she hunted a specific section. Somewhere there had been made mention of the artifacts that the Masters had sought for their grand purpose and Valea wondered if perhaps one of them might be the one she hunted.

The candle sank into a waxy puddle as she perused page after page, finding nothing. One passage briefly seized her attention, for it spoke of a possession rod, but little more could Valea discern from it.

She rubbed her eyes, squinting more and more as the candle became less useful. Her father had raised her to use magic judiciously, not for every whim or minor physical activity, but Valea realized that soon she would be attempting to read in utter darkness. Raising her hand, she cast a minor light spell, one that surely her father would have seen as a very miserly use of her abilities—

A face stared back at her from the other side of the desk.

"No!" Startled, Valea pushed the chair back . . . and fell with it. She caught herself at the very end, preventing a possible broken neck but promising many bruises.

Rolling away from the chair, Valea amplified the light spell, filling the library with almost blinding illumination. Ceiling-high shelves filled with book after book, scroll upon scroll—all carefully collected by not only the Bedlams but some of their predecessors—revealed themselves to her, but of her intruder there was no trace.

Rising, Valea hurried to the doorway, but saw no sign. She frowned, recalling what she could of the face—and her mouth dropped.

*Arak.*

Yet, there had been something else about him, some details about his elven visage that had only partly registered. He had not been as she had seen him initially—tall, handsome, foreboding. What had changed?

She turned back toward the desk—and this time gasped as Arak once more glared at her.

Now Valea saw with horror what was different about him. He still retained elven features, but they had also become something different, something *reptilian.*

Arak moved, but he did not walk toward her. Rather he stared past her, his mouth working as if speaking to another in the room. Then the elf, his garments misshapen as if his body was not entirely normal any more, darted toward the far wall . . . and through the very shelves.

At the same time, feminine sobbing echoed through the corridors outside.

Valea stood momentarily torn between investigating the apparition in the library or pursuing the ghostly sounds beyond. When Arak did not reappear, she finally abandoned the chamber and hurried down the halls, wondering why no one else came in response to the anguished cries.

Not at all to her surprise, the sobbing led her back to the staircase.

Once more the elven figure bent down and once more blood pooled beneath. This time, Valea did not reach out, hoping that by holding back she would see the vision do more.

It did. Rather than finally crumple to the floor, it rose. In one hand something glittered despite no other light, a dagger fine and silver whose end was drenched crimson.

The female elf—surely Galani—shifted back toward the staircase.

Valea stared at her own face.

No . . . not exactly her own. Much akin to hers, save that the features were better defined, far more graceful. Valea's face without imperfection.

Yet another gasp escaped the sorceress at this revelation . . . and suddenly the spectral figure looked *her* way.

*"I had to do it, didn't I?"* Galani asked her.

The elf's wound finally proved too much. She doubled over, the dagger dropping from her failing grip. Valea reached forward, but her arms caught no body, for Galani's ghost vanished even as death claimed it not for the first time.

Shivering, the younger Bedlam gazed unblinking at the site where the elf had been. No blood, no Galani, no—

The silver dagger still lay on the floor.

No blood covered the tip now. Biting her lip, Valea approached the weapon, waiting every moment for it to vanish. When it did not, she cautiously pushed at it with her slipper.

With a slight scraping sound, the dagger slid a few inches away.

The sorceress hesitated, peering around. No one had as yet come in response to all the noise and that bothered her. This entire scene had been played out for her and her alone and now the weapon that had evidently ended Galani's life lay tantalizingly nearby. All she had to do was pick it up. Surely then with some spell she could divine some of its secrets.

But with her fingers only inches from the silver artifact, Valea paused. By taking the dagger, she also risked falling prey again to the ghostly apparitions.

The Manor played some sort of macabre game, one that went well beyond her interest in the phantoms inhabiting her home.

Valea pulled back.

The dagger *flew* from the floor, thrusting itself hilt first into her hand—

HER FACE STARED back at her.

No, not Valea's face, but rather Galani's. Valea sat at a high, gold-framed mirror, an emerald brush, not a dagger, clutched in her hand. The brush dropped from her grip as she studied the elven features closer. Still strikingly similar to her own, they had undergone some changes. The beauty was now not quite perfect, for there were dark circles under the eyes, which held much, much sadness. There was also a small scar on the left edge of the chin, a recent scar.

Valea recalled Arak's moods and grew angry. If he had done this—

An intense rumble of thunder suddenly made her forget all about the male elf's transgressions. The entire building shook as the rumbling continued. A bolt of lightning flashed outside, almost seeming to strike just beyond the walls.

The invisible barrier was supposed to protect the area even from the elements, but already two drake assassins had entered. Valea wondered if perhaps the Dragon King was also responsible for the storm.

Again thunder rocked the Manor. A crystalline vase toppled from a fireplace mantle and across the room an exquisite tapestry of what might have been the elves' forest homeland slipped free, landing in an inelegant heap.

Although Valea had control of Galani's body, unbidden from her mouth came her cousin's name. "Arak!"

Not certain where she headed but feeling that somehow Galani would guide her, the sorceress ran from the room, hurrying down the corridor leading to the staircase. The sense of urgency rose with each second. Something had gone terribly wrong; both she and her host knew that. Whatever Arak desired, it was not what he would reap.

To Valea's consternation, her path took her not to the grounds, as she had expected, but rather toward what would be the library in her parents' day. Even now, the room was much as it should have been; the same shelves greeted her along with sleek, well-crafted mahogany table and four matching chairs, the latter leather-padded and all the furniture under the same centuries-long preserving spell as the rest of the Manor.

Letting Galani's memories continue to guide her, the sorceress reached one of the bookcases near the rear. Her right hand went up, passing along three black tomes, then touching a crimson one two shelves below.

"It is here," the elf murmured. "I know it was here he touched."

Suddenly, the entire bookcase vanished, revealing a passage descending below, a passage carved into the mighty tree that made up this half of the Manor.

A passage none of the Bedlams had ever uncovered.

Muttering echoed from deep below. Valea recognized spellwork, but not of a type akin to her own.

The narrow passage wound around and around like some parody of the staircase. Valea constantly collided with the walls, which looked to have been formed from the tree's very roots. For a time, the steps seemed without end, but then at last the bottom appeared, opening up into a much wider corridor lit by small, glowing spheres of blue.

The muttering grew louder but still remained incomprehensible. An unsettling gray light radiated from a chamber ahead, devouring the blue illumination without mercy.

Planting herself against the nearest root wall, Valea peered around the edge. Acutely sensitive to magic, she had to steel herself before looking, so wild, so manic were the powers in play.

Before her stood Arak . . . and before him, the *Wyr Stone*.

It was not what she had expected. Valea had imagined some massive, glittering emerald or ruby. Perhaps even a pure white, transparent crystal. Certainly not this.

The Wyr Stone was just that . . . a stone. It was no larger than Arak's fist and was only vaguely round in form. It might have been found in any quarry or canyon. At a first glance, the sorceress would not have even paid it any mind—if not for its coloring.

One second it was brown, then gold, then red, then a myriad display of other colors. Never did it cease shifting. There were brief periods when more than one color displayed itself and sometimes impressive patterns played over the artifact. Several of the colors Valea could not even put a name to. The Wyr Stone constantly changed, the pace increasing with each phrase spoken by the elf.

And as the Wyr Stone changed, so, too, did Arak.

He looked taller, more gaunt, and his hair had begun to gray, although perhaps that was a trick of the peculiar light emanating from the stone. More dramatic, however, was his visage, which had *elongated* and grown scaly. His nose had nearly vanished. Valea could not see his eyes, but felt certain that they had also been altered.

The elf raised his hands . . . and in them the sorceress could see a dagger identical to the one the ghost of Galani had wielded.

As she watched, Arak took the dagger in his right hand, then stretched forth his left, revealing the wrist. Already the elf's limbs looked misshapen, his fingers curled and clawed, his arms twisted at odd angles. Undisturbed by his transformation, Arak held the blade over his wrist, then drove the weapon deep.

Stifling a gasp, Valea watched in horror and wonder as he held the bleeding limb over the Wyr Stone. Droplets of blood dripped from what should have been a terrible wound, spilling onto the artifact while Arak calmly waited.

She expected some force to burst free from the stone, but instead, it seemed to draw from around it. A sense of vertigo touched the sorceress and Valea suddenly realized that the stone was absorbing the magic around it. She drew back, fearful.

"Kaladi Dracos!" shouted Arak at the wall beyond. "Kivak Dracos!"

The vertigo lessened. Now the vampiric powers of the stone had been focused elsewhere, made to draw only from one specific source.

And recalling what Galani's cousin had preached, Valea could guess what source that was.

The Dragon Kings.

The Wyr Stone now soaked in his blood, Arak pulled free the blade. As he did he turned just enough for her to see his face.

The eyes were crimson, pupilless . . . and more inhuman than any drake.

It was Valea, not Galani, who stumbled back with a slight scraping noise. It proved enough to attract the attention of Arak. He turned toward the passage, arm leaving a shower of crimson in its wake.

She fled, certain that even in control of the elf's body her skills were no match for the elf. Trying to be silent, Valea rushed up the passage, praying that Arak had not noticed her. Could this be the moment of Galani's death that she had witnessed? But in the image, the elf had worn blue, not the gold she wore now.

The entrance to the library beckoned. Breathing heavily, Valea pushed to the top. As she did, a noise below caught her attention. Certain that Arak followed right behind her, the sorceress glanced over her shoulder. To her relief, Valea saw nothing—

She collided with a solid form.

Hands seized her by the shoulders. A struggle ensued until Valea heard Shade's calm voice whisper, "Quiet. If we depart now, he'll not know you were here, Galani."

Grateful for his presence, Valea let the faceless warlock lead her quickly away. Behind them, the opening had vanished, once more simply a bookcase.

Shade started to guide her to the elf's chambers, but Valea did not want to go there. She feared that Arak would still come up there looking for her and whether or not it was Galani's body that perished, the sorceress feared that this time it would be *she* who died.

"Take me away from here," Valea demanded of the warlock.

"The gardens—" he began.

"No! Far from here! Somewhere he won't be able to find me!"

"Galani—"

She clung to him, stared into the murky eyes. "Please!"

From the direction of the library, they heard footsteps. Shade glanced past her, then suddenly wrapped his shroudlike cloak about her, completely engulfing his companion.

A sense of displacement akin to that she had felt when first pulled into the ghostly memory overwhelmed Valea, but this time she did not wake up. Instead, her feet came down hard on some rocky surface. Shade caught her, then immediately after removed the dark veil from her eyes. A cold rush of wind made her shiver and her eyes widened to saucers as they took in the view around her.

The two of them stood atop a narrow mountain ledge overlooking an endless chain of ominous peaks.

Having visited Talak many times in the past, Valea readily recognized the Tyber Mountains.

"Your cousin won't find us here," Shade solemnly promised.

Perhaps he would not, but certainly others would. The Tyber Mountains— the vast, jagged peak called Kivan Grath, especially—were the domain of the most powerful of the Dragon Kings. Here, the Gold Dragon, emperor of his kind, ruled the entire continent. This would be no young, human-raised novice like Kyl; this would be a monster, an inhuman beast who would snap up two interlopers without a second thought.

"I come here many a time," her companion suddenly remarked. Shade stared at the stunning view. "The cool air refreshes the mind."

The dying light still enabled Valea to see far too much. She tightened her hold on the warlock, finding comfort in his stolid presence. Shade no longer tensed at her touch.

Not *her* touch, the sorceress reminded herself. It was Galani who was fascinated with Shade, *not* her. Valea only felt what the elf experienced.

She could not blame Galani, of course. Weeks, even months, must have passed from the first memory to this latest one, and there had only been Shade to be of comfort to the elf. Arak's mad work—and even now Valea was not certain if he could truly do what he desired—had taken its toll, turning a once-loved cousin into a monster akin to those he sought to destroy.

In the distance, something fluttered among the mountains. At first, it looked like a man-sized dragon, but then Valea made out limbs almost human save that the knees were reversed. It was also of a dusky gray color and had a face like a bird of prey. Had it stood next to her, it would have towered over her than Shade.

He felt her renewed tension. Following her gaze, Shade eyed the distant figure. "The Seeker will not try anything. His kind has learned not to where I am concerned."

As if to prove that, the avian suddenly swerved gracefully away from their lofty position. The wide, beautiful wings beat faster and faster, quickly sending the Seeker out of sight.

"I want to leave," Valea whispered.

"First, tell me what you saw."

She looked at him. "Arak has become a monster."

He cocked his head to one side much as Lord Gryphon, who shared with the Seekers an avian look, did when concentrating. "A monster?"

The words came tumbling out as Valea described what she had seen. The renewed memory caused her to shiver again. Perhaps misunderstanding the cause of her action, Shade wrapped both his arm and cloak tighter around her. The sorceress fought back the great temptation to bury her head in his shoulder as she finished her tale.

"His transformation is temporary, Galani," A touch of concern tinted his words. "But he's gone beyond what I suggested. The Wyr Stone is powerful, seductive. I warned him of its tendency to magnify one's desire beyond what one truly wishes! When they tried to save themselves in the end, it only quickened the changing, made them worse than what they might have been—"

"Who?"

"Friends. Loved ones. Fools." He would not let her press further. "It should have remained lost. I should have never told him about it."

"Sh—Tylan. What is he trying to do with the Wyr Stone? I know he's trying to destroy the Dragon Kings, but how? What will it do to them?"

For a brief second, she saw an expression, one that hinted of gratitude. "You always call me Tylan. Your cousin calls me Shade, just as all others do. The names I pick are always remembered, but in the end everyone calls me Shade. I strive to be more than the dark legend, to once again be the man, even if always a slightly different man." A gloved hand rose and caressed her cheek ever so slightly, then withdrew as if having presumed too much. The gratitude vanished from the warlock's voice as he finally answered her question. "Arak is an elf. Your people do not seek to destroy. Such an act is anathema to them. However, your cousin has found a way around that, so to speak. You cannot destroy what does not exist."

"What do you mean?"

In answer, he extended one arm toward the vast tableau before them. "Imagine if you could make it so that these mountains had never been. Imagine if you could cause them to revert to their state before the violence of the world thrust them up toward the sky. So will Arak do to the Dragon Kings, if he is successful. A much smaller scale than transforming a mountain chain, but difficult nonetheless."

Valea frowned, trying to make sense of what he said. "Do you mean that somehow he will unmake the drake lords and their people? They will cease to be?"

"In a sense. The Wyr Stone is the antithesis of this land. Some say it was a part of the essence of the Void, that great emptiness beyond our realm. When it was sought by the others in the past, they saw in it a way to reverse what the land did to them. It will take the magic around us, turn it inside out—so to speak—and make of the drakes what they would have been had not this cursed world played its own game."

He spoke of the Dragonrealm as if it was a living thing, a notion her own father had pushed from time to time. If she understood Shade, somehow the land itself had transformed other creatures into the drakes, creating their race. The Wyr Stone would undo this, a phenomenal concept.

No Dragon Kings. Instead, there would be a world of elves and humans— and whatever harmless race Arak would make the drakes become. Surely not so bad a thing. On the surface, Arak's arduous efforts looked to be worth any cost. How often had Valea heard her father or Lord Gryphon or especially King Melicard speak of a world where the Dragon Kings had never caused so much calamity?

"It's—it's incredible!"

"Incredible and dangerous . . . and from what you describe to me, perhaps beyond your cousin's reach. Clearly the Wyr Stone is overwhelming him in the process and he is only halfway to his goal."

"Halfway?" From what the sorceress had seen, the elf had looked very near his goal, too near.

The blurred face seemed even more so now. "Did you imagine erasing an entire race from the world a simple task? Why do you think those who originally used the Wyr Stone failed? When Arak told me he had found it, I was at first astounded, but your cousin is an elf of exceptional ability. When he claimed to understand why those before him had failed to control it, I made the mistake of believing him. I see now how terrible a mistake that is. He must be stopped before he destroys himself—and possibly much around him."

It did not matter any more that all this had apparently taken place long,

long ago. Valea only knew that something catastrophic was happening and that Galani's cousin might not only bring down the Dragon Kings, but possibly himself and much of the rest of the land in the process.

"What can we do?"

Shade paused, then, with even greater hesitation than earlier, answered, "To save your cousin, Galani—and perhaps much, much more—you must put a dagger through his heart."

# VI

GASPING, VALEA AWOKE, her body covered in sweat.

The warlock's last words echoed through her head. *you must put a dagger through his heart . . .*

So horrified was she by what Shade had said that at first her surroundings did not register with her. Only gradually did Valea realize that she no longer stood by the staircase. Instead, she lay fully-clothed atop her bed as if having gone to take a nap. Night still reigned, hopefully the same night.

As she moved her left hand, something slid from her grasp.

Despite a lack of much light, the silver dagger glistened.

Rolling off the plush bed, Valea glared at the horrid object. Galani's ghostly plea came back to haunt her. *I had to do it, didn't I?*

Now she felt she understood better what the ghostly image had represented. The elf had evidently done just what Shade had suggested—but something must have gone wrong.

More cautious than ever, Valea reached for the treacherous blade, but this time, instead of leaping to her fingers, the dagger faded . . . as if a dream.

Frustrated beyond belief, the young sorceress vented her anger at the walls around her. "What is it you *want?*" she demanded of the Manor. "What are you trying to show me?"

But the walls remained maddeningly silent, not that Valea had truly expected them to answer in such a fashion.

Footsteps hurried up to her door. The disheveled woman turned, at first expecting a new ghost to rear its ugly head, but instead Setera and two human servants stood nervously at the entrance, obviously drawn by her loud appeal.

"I'm all right!" she snapped. Taking a deep breath, Valea added more calmly, "It was just a nightmare. I'm sorry if I startled anyone."

The humans left immediately, but Setera took a moment longer, clearly a bit more suspicious over her mistress's actions. When the drake, too, had finally departed, Valea again glared at the bed and the walls. Something had to be done.

There was no reason why this horrific game had to continue. Valea had learned her lesson, had learned not to delve too close in the past of the Manor; what more did the magical edifice and its ghosts want of her?

IT WAS POSSIBLE for Valea to contact her parents through the means of spells, but she dared not disturb either of them now. That left her only one person with whom she could speak who might have some knowledge.

Seated on a bench in the center of the vast maze, the same location where Galani and Shade had been attacked, Valea concentrated. Drawing from the lines of force crisscrossing even her, the sorceress molded together her spell.

A light-blue sphere formed before her . . . and within it fire briefly reigned. Muttering, Valea envisioned the one she sought.

In the midst of the floating sphere, a fearsome avian head suddenly thrust forth.

*"Valea Bedlam . . . and to what do I owe this intrusion in my thoughts?"*

The young human swallowed as the predatory visage cocked to one side. "Forgive me, Lord Gryphon, I had some questions with which I had to turn to you."

The master of Penacles, the City of Knowledge, blinked once. His magnificent white and gold plumage transformed to golden brown fur near the base of his neck. Valea could just barely make out a regal red cloak and, below that, brown robes of state. The Gryphon was a creature both man and myth and one of the closest friends the Bedlams had. He could, if he wished, take on a human form, but that he did most for his mate, the feline woman Troia.

*"I have a few minutes I may spare for you, Valea. What is it you wish to know?"*

"Have you ever studied the ghosts of the Manor?"

*"Aah, your pet passion. No, I prefer my interests more earthbound."* Despite being a magical creature, the Gryphon had spent much of his two-plus centuries as a mercenary until fate had thrust him into the role of king.

"Did you ever hear of an elf named Arak? Was he ever famous for anything?"

*"Again, I must answer no. The elves are secretive. Did you wish me to consult the libraries for mention of him?"*

"No . . . definitely no." Valea could not send the ruler of Penacles searching for the name of a likely obscure figure in history. Clearly Arak's spell had somehow gone awry or the world she knew would have been very different. That left her only one question. "What, if anything, can you tell me about the Wyr Stone?"

The avian eye ceased blinking. Although it was only an illusion of the spell, Valea saw the Gryphon lean closer. *"Say the name again . . ."*

"The Wyr Stone."

*"The Wyr Stone . . ."* He tasted the words, mulled them over, so much so that Valea's hopes rose.

And were dashed again. *"I thought . . . but no. I'm wrong."*

"You don't know it, then?"

He read her disappointment. *"I was reminded of a tale or two I heard long, long ago, when I was still only a soldier. Nothing much, mind you. I cannot even recall the specifics . . . but I will do a little research."*

Research could only mean the libraries. "My lord, please don't bother! I'm sorry I interrupted your day at all! Please just forget! It was only a foolish—"

*"My interest is piqued, Valea Bedlam . . . and it might not take me so very long as you think. The libraries and I are beginning to understand one another . . . to a point."*

He would not be dissuaded. With reluctance, Valea accepted his offer. Inside, her hope rose slightly again. The Gryphon might find nothing, but then again he might find *something*. Anything that could aid her in solving this mystery and freeing herself from the dreams was welcome.

With greetings to both families passed back and forth, Valea broke the spell. Perhaps she had gained something, but that she could hardly wait and see. She had to take a hand in the situation.

**THE MANOR LIBRARY** looked as innocuous as ever. Ignoring everything else, Valea went directly to the library, to the very bookcase she, as Galani, had used to open the way to the passage below.

Trouble was, the tomes now set in the shelves were different and despite her diligent effort, the sorceress could make none of them do as the crimson one in the dream had.

Leaning against the bookcase, she knocked, but the wall sounded as solid as any.

Spellwork was, under most conditions, forbidden in the library itself, but Valea had reached the limits of her patience. Stepping back, she gave the bookcase a reproving look, then cast.

"You'll reveal me the truth if I have to tear a hole in you!" the sorceress growled. She did not really want to do that, of course. Instead, Valea acted as her father had taught her, reaching out with her mind to see the magic that might be playing around the case. If a spell hid the passage from her, she would find and unravel it.

But to her surprise, even her most cunning work revealed only a solid wall.

An investigation of the other walls of the library gave her the same results. Unless she had been very careless somewhere in her casting, there existed no passage. Yet, in the dream, it had been right before—

*In the dream . . .*

Valea had assumed that what she had dreamed had been an exact re-creation of events. Had she been wrong? Had the dream been all or at least part fiction? It had felt so true, though.

She could hardly argue with the obvious, however. The bookcase and the wall behind it were as solid as they looked. To eradicate any lingering doubt about that, Valea set both hands against the case and pushed with all her might, not just once, not just twice, but *three* times.

On the third time . . . she fell through.

A firm, even floor, not a death-dealing set of stone steps, welcomed her tumbling body. Valea crashed hard, every bone jarred.

And as she struggled to regain both her senses and the use of her body, a voice, Shade's voice, whispered calmly, *"It is time to strike, Galani."*

In her hand she once more held the dagger.

# VII

HIS GLOVED HANDS gently helped her to her feet. Valea saw that she was now in the maze again, lying on the bench where she had cast the spell contacting Lord Gryphon. The moon rose full overhead.

In its light, Valea saw that she wore a gown of blue.

Shade was even more a specter now than before, but Valea felt Galani draw strength from his presence and so, in turn, did she. It was hard to tell where her own emotions separated from those of the elf. For all the stories of evil she had heard about the warlock, Valea had also heard the tales of sacrifice and heroics. She had long sympathized with his curse, his inability to have one true identity.

The hood obscured his murky visage completely as he bent down to peer at her. "Are you up to it, Galani? I know what I ask of you. Rest assured, though, that he will be grateful in the end."

"By me stabbing him? In the heart?" The elf's voice was on the edge of hysteria. "Tell me again, Tylan! Tell me again that when this blade goes through . . . I won't simply be killing him!"

He put a comforting arm around her. "With the twin of this dagger—so foolishly provided by me—your cousin bound himself by blood to the forces inherent in the Wyr Stone. Heart and soul. You saw a part of that, remember? By striking true, you will unbind him. He will live, you have my word on that."

How could Galani not believe him? Certainly Valea did.

"Tylan," Galani whispered into his chest. "Will you dance with me?"

Valea and Shade shared confusion. *"Dance* with you? Now?"

"It will calm my nerves . . . make me ready."

The hood considered. "Arak will be quite some time with his casting. Very well, if it'll better prepare you, then come, my lady . . . let us dance once again."

He took the elf's hand and as he did, the wind shifted, playing a soft, drifting tune more felt than heard. Shade slowly turned his partner in a circle. Valea was quickly caught up in the dance. In her mind, *she* now danced with the warlock, felt the vibrancy, the heat of his body as they spun around and around. The maze vanished, only the moonlit sky accompanying the pair.

Only after several breathtaking turns did the sorceress realize that they truly danced on *air*, not earth, but that only added to the moment. Valea stared into what should have been Shade's eyes and felt certain that they stared back. Again, she imagined what the eyes, the brow, the nose, and mouth actually looked like . . . and suddenly what it would be like to kiss the last.

Valea never wanted it to end, but then she felt the ground beneath her feet and a cool—nay, *cold*—breeze at her cheek. The music had ceased.

"If you wish to save him, Galani . . . it must be now."

"Can you not do it?" Valea's mouth asked.

"You know that is beyond me. I cannot myself touch nor wield the Wyr Stone nor even stand near it. I've told you that. It must be you. Remember also that after you have used the dagger, you must touch it against the artifact and do as I've taught you."

His last comment stirred the sorceress's curiosity. What sort of spellwork did the elf have to perform? Was it not enough that she had to drive a blade into her beloved cousin's heart before Arak understood what was happening?

"I will be with you in spirit," Shade murmured. "You know that."

And to Valea's astonishment and thrill, his lips grazed her own briefly.

Then he was gone, his tall, black form literally becoming part of the night.

She felt Galani pull herself together. So now would come the culmination of these events. Perhaps after this Valea would understand. Perhaps after this the dreams would end.

The elf brought her through the garden, through the the back doors, and straight to the library. For Galani, the bookcase gave way as it always did. Down they went, as silent as the night. Valea marveled at the stealth with which her host moved, but still wondered if it would suffice.

But an army could have likely walked in on Arak and he would not have noticed. The silver-haired elf hunched over the Wyr Stone, eyes hollow and drawn from his efforts. He did not look so monstrous as when Valea had seen him last, but still the effects of manipulating the power of the sinister artifact were quite visible.

Galani had secreted the dagger in her gown, but now she began to remove it. Curiously, the silent action seemed to be the one thing her cousin noticed, either that or he had simply chosen that moment to look up.

"You! What are you doing here, cousin?" Arak grated. "You should not be here!"

The ferocity in his voice made Valea want to flee, but Galani stepped forward, outwardly cool, inwardly in a panic.

"I came because I was worried about you. You've hardly slept, hardly eaten in weeks. For almost a month, we've hardly spoken." The female elf stepped nearer. "You only take what barely sustains you. Surely that cannot be good for your work."

"As I have said to you many times over the past three months, you could go home any time. You'll be safe there . . . safe and blind to the world once again."

"I could never leave you like this, Arak! You know that! For the thousandth time, give up whatever madness you attempt!"

"Give up?" The unkempt figure waved a hand toward the Wyr Stone, which flared as if in response to him. "When my work is nearly complete?"

"Is it?" Galani's hand kept near the hidden dagger. Valea watched through her eyes in morbid fascination and horror as Arak's fearsome visage loomed close. "Are you certain?"

He laughed darkly. "You're just like him! Small wonder he's caught your fancy, cousin! He was certain I would fail, too! He said the binding spells keeping anyone from utilizing the full force of the Wyr Stone would be too strong, that I, only a poor elf and not a last sad vestige of a Vraad sorcerer like him, could never understand them, much less know how to remove them . . ." Arak grinned. "He threw down the gauntlet in challenge with those words! I told him all along that I could do it and so I nearly have! Even he was impressed when I told him that by tonight I would be able to manipulate the stone in whatever fashion I desire . . ."

"And will you use it on the Dragon Kings?"

"Of course!"

As if that settled matters for Galani, she suddenly drew the dagger. Valea screamed in her mind, trying to hold off an outcome she knew inevitable.

Galani's hand hesitated.

Arak snarled and seized her wrist, twisting it. The dagger fell to the floor. Pain coursed through both Valea and her host. Galani was forced to one knee.

"It *was* you who spied upon me that night! I had scarce believed my own suspicions!" he roared, twisting her arm further. "I tried to deny it . . . that those old fools would send my own cousin as their assassin!"

Through the haze of pain, Valea listened to his accusation with astonishment.

Arak actually thought Galani had all this time intended to kill him? Had the Wyr Stone driven him beyond the edge of sanity?

"I was right! It was not fear of change from which the elders suffered but fear that I would control those changes! They, of course, would be so much wiser masters of the stone's abilities, but they decided to leave it to me, the shameful renegade, to make their prize available to them!"

"I do not—you are wrong!"

He opened wide his free hand and the dagger flew into his grip. "This proves I am correct."

"I am trying to save you!"

The tip of the blade came within a hair's breadth of her throat. In a flat voice, Arak whispered, "I do not know which is more pathetic, your lies or simply you."

The Wyr Stone flared—and Arak sent Galani/Valea flying across the chamber. The sorceress tried to seize control as she had before, but could not stop the elf's flight. Galani struck the wall, her breath knocked out of her, then tumbled to the floor.

Tossing the dagger aside, Arak stepped toward his injured cousin. "So ironic. I, who respect the sanctity of life, am accused of plotting genocide while the supposedly pious elders turn one I once loved into a willing murderer!" His hands glowed crimson. "I'm sorry I have to do this, Galani . . ." Arak stood over her, entire body now ablaze with power, expression puzzling. He looked regretful and a bit uncertain.

Valea rubbed her head, trying to clear it—and then realized that at last *she* had control again. Her own thoughts now a confused mix with Galani's, Valea eyed the dagger.

The blade shot up off the floor, a swift missile heading for Arak's back. However, at the last moment, it swerved around, came at the elf from the front.

Just as he noticed its presence, the blade sank into his chest.

"Galani—" Arak stumbled away from her, horrified eyes on the hilt, which glowed a bright silver. He reached for it, but his fingers did not seem to work. "I wasn't going to hurt—"

Shade had said that the dagger would not slay Galani's cousin, but the silver-haired elf certainly acted as if he had been struck a mortal blow. He staggered to the side, fell against one rock wall, and slumped there. His eyes bulged and his breath came in quick, labored gasps.

"G-Galani . . ."

Still in control, Valea forced herself up, then stumbled to her victim. She herself would have let him be, but her host's emotions and memories tore at her. All the good, all the love, that the two elves had shared over their lives became part of Valea's life, too.

She had to pull the blade free. From what Shade had said, perhaps removing the weapon would enable Arak to recover.

But just before Valea could touch the hilt, a shadow fell over both her and the stricken elf.

No . . . not a shadow . . . a shade.

The warlock plucked the weapon from Arak's chest and the wound instantly sealed. The elf shrank in on himself, becoming smaller, more real. The sense of tremendous power that he had wielded vanished utterly. Arak looked older, much older than an elf should be.

"Well struck, Galani," the murky figure next to Valea commented clinically. "I sensed it happened and came as soon as I could."

Something struck Valea as wrong, but she could not put her finger on exactly what. She looked at the hooded man. "Will he—will he be all right?"

"He will live for so long as I need him, yes."

A warning went off in the sorceress's head. She suddenly had no desire to be near the warlock.

Stretching a hand toward her, Shade froze Valea in place. "And you, dear Galani, I want near also."

"Tylan—"

With a slow shake of his head, the black-clad figure chuckled and said, "Call me Zaros . . . this time."

Valea wanted to recoil . . . at some point since Galani had first met the warlock . . . Shade had died and been resurrected again.

And if he had been friend to the elves before, surely now he would be their most terrible enemy.

"How . . . when?"

He shrugged, as if the matter of his death was no significant event. "The Seekers. You recall how the one turned and fled when sighting me? That was because his kind had caught me unaware not long ago. They thought that they could destroy me . . . and so they did. Not the first time that the avians have done so . . . but they seem to keep forgetting that I come back . . . and when I did . . ." Almost it seemed a smile formed on the blurred countenance. "I made certain that this particular flock would not be able to repeat its mistake."

All the while Shade spoke, he ran one gloved hand over the dagger, drawing momentary patterns of magic. Beyond him, Valea noticed that the Wyr Stone began to change in concert with his efforts.

Then it occurred to her that the warlock should not be able to be so near the artifact at all.

"What an utter fool my previous self was. Here the key to preserving himself lay open to him and his honor would not let him take it." Shade paused dramatically, almost as if waiting for either Valea or the still-slumped Arak to make a comment. When neither did, he extended a hand toward the Wyr Stone. "They were too late to save themselves, my cousins were. The land—the damned, cursed land!—had already begun their transformation! By the time they wielded the Wyr Stone, saving themselves from being *adapted* to this realm was beyond even their skills."

Darkhorse, who had over the centuries battled beside or against more Shades than anyone, had told her and Aurim often of the varying degrees of madness with which each incarnation had been infected. She did not recall any with the name of Zaros, but then there had been so many, many Shades over the centuries that even Darkhorse could not keep them all straight in his memory. However many there had been, though, this one was the only Shade that mattered to Valea. So far, there had been no hint of her being able to escape this horrid dream or ghost or whatever it might be and that made her fear that if Galani perished, so would she. Even though these events had happened far in the past, where magic was concerned the distinctions of time were often as blurred as the warlock's visage.

With Galani's personality apparently dormant, Valea had to stall Shade while she tried to find some avenue of escape. An obvious question came to mind, one she suspected the bragging Zaros would be happy to answer. Fortunately, he had only frozen her legs and arms, not her mouth. "How is it you can manipulate the stone? You said you couldn't even get near it!"

"The dagger, of course . . . and your dear cousin." At mention of Arak, Shade leaned down to pat the male elf companionably on the shoulder. Eyes closed, Arak groaned. Although his wound was no longer visible, he seemed unable to otherwise recover. "This dagger and the one he used are twins, as I mentioned. You saw him use the other on himself without fear. They were designed to tie a sorcerer to the stone, mingle his life force with the forces within the artifact, thus enabling Arak to use it as he would his own arm."

"You gave him the first dagger . . ."

"No . . . Tylan did or else this would have been so much easier, dear Galani." The warlock stepped toward the Wyr Stone, his body, if not his face, revealing his great anticipation. "The dagger must first be tied to the user . . . and that is part of what you saw. Then the dagger ties the user to the stone." He held up his own blade. "This dagger, soaked now in his blood, is tied to me . . ."

Now Valea understood. He was working through Arak. The male elf was being used as both a shield and conduit for the warlock, letting Shade do what he could not before.

"Noble Tylan believed in your cousin's cause. He believed ridding this realm in one way or another of the Dragon Kings would earn him redemption. He gave Arak the first blade without binding it to him first, which forced me to other measures . . . but, fortunately, I had you, who could step where I could not. The binding had to be done with the Wyr Stone active and I could certainly not come near enough to do it myself."

Something else suddenly made sense to her. "Those cousins who wielded the stone didn't want you to be able to use its power, did they?"

"You are constantly amazing me now, dear Galani. Here you first struck me as even more of a fool than your cousin. You were certainly a more-than-willing tool. Yes . . . Vraad can be very unforgiving and he had already caused them much grief."

There seemed no rhyme or reason to how he referred to himself, sometimes speaking as one entity, sometimes referring to other incarnations, even his original self, like separate people. Valea entertained no illusions about trying to talk sense to this variation.

"Will you destroy the Dragon Kings now?"

Shade raised the dagger over the Wyr Stone. "I could care less about my former brothers and their barbaric offspring. Let the Dragon Kings rule a thousand thousand years. I require only one gift from the Wyr Stone—to end our curse here and now!"

And, in the process, make himself the ultimate incarnation of Shade.

"Now be a good little elf and stay there, mouth shut." A gesture from the warlock clamped Valea's jaw tight.

Whether or not this was all an illusion, a memory, or a terrible nightmare, the sorceress knew what threat an unencumbered and evil Shade would be to the Dragonrealm. Incarnations past had caused kingdoms to fall to ruin, thousands to die, and lands to be upturned.

But what could she do?

Arak, moaned. Valea wished she could do something for him. Arak would have known what to do, but she could hardly ask him now—

Something glinted near his waist.

The first dagger.

Her initial hope faded quickly. Shade had frozen her in place, kept her even from speaking. What good would the dagger do? Her elven powers were hardly comparable to—

No! She was not an elf! Her father was Cabe Bedlam, her mother the Lady of The Amber! The thoughts were *Galani's*, not hers.

She was a Bedlam. This was something well within her abilities.

Valea struggled against Shade's spell, knowing it had been cast to control the much less powerful elf.

It fragmented easily under her will.

What she intended to do, the sorceress could not say, but she felt certain that seizing the first dagger had to be part of it. She sped across the chamber, diving toward Arak.

Caught up in his own spellcasting, the hooded warlock did not immediately notice her escape. When he did, he shouted something in an unknown language, then turned to deal with her.

Bending down, Valea took the dagger.

In a replay of a few short minutes before, Arak's hand seized her wrist.

Eyes full of blood, the male elf gasped, "S-sever the tie, c-cousin . . ."

And to Valea's shock and dismay, her hand twisted of its own accord, freeing the wrist from Arak's grip, then turning and now *plunging* the second blade into his chest.

Her rebellious hand removed the dagger as quickly as it had thrust it in. Curiously, instead of dying at last, Arak immediately looked healthier. His breathing normalized and his skin grew less pale. His eyes opened wide and clear—at which point he shouted, "Galani! Look out!"

Valea or Galani—it was now impossible to separate the two souls—spun around to defend the still-recuperating elf.

Shards of pain ripped through her stomach as the warlock's magical assault caught her only half-shielded.

"You little wretch! I—" Shade abruptly screamed, his agony echoed throughout the chamber. At the same time, the Wyr Stone transformed, becoming as black as an abyss.

The warlock's body grew distorted, twisted, as if his bones had jellied.

With another mournful cry, he wrapped his cloak around him and vanished.

Arak tried to rise, but could not yet do so. Even filled with pain, Valea was determined to pursue Shade and so, she felt, was Galani. The sorceress eyed the Wyr Stone, the core of the situation . . .

The teleportation spell she cast moments later did not take her far, yet it nearly sent her blacking out from renewed agony. She put her hand to her waist and found more blood.

As her gaze rose again, she also found Shade.

His own flight had not taken him far. He lay sprawled halfway up the very staircase where Valea had begun her excursion into the Manor's memories. His body was still stretched slightly long, but reverted more normal with each of his ragged breaths.

"I am r-renewed, Galani. You may call me Erynar . . . th-this time."

"No," she returned grimly, stumbling toward him with the dagger pressed against her side. "You're not dead . . . not yet."

Pushing himself up, Shade pointed at her. His gloved fingers distorted, becoming black tentacles seeking her throat and chest.

Valea countered, creating a barrier of flame that sent his fingers swiftly withdrawing, the tips aglow. The warlock stumbled up several more steps before managing to recover.

He actually laughed. "Galani! How v-vicious you've become—and how p-powerful! The Wyr Stone can be very seductive, can it not?"

"I wouldn't know."

"But you had better be using the stone, dear Galani," the murky face mocked. "For if not, that large wound will soon be the finish of you."

It was already the finish of Galani, but the elf was as determined as Valea to end this. Both moved in concert in one body and Valea realized that Galani fully understood who and what resided within her.

She stretched out one delicate and quite empty hand—a hand covered in blood—toward the warlock. "Come dance with us one last time, Shade."

"*Us?* Have you become like me, then?" He laughed again and from the confines of his voluminous cloak a ferocious wind struck at his adversary.

The sorceress dismissed it as readily as the tentacles.

"You *do* wield the Wyr Stone!"

Valea shook her head. "She does. I don't." The bloody hand opened again. "Come dance with us."

A tremendous force tugged at the warlock, dragging him back down the steps. He struggled, but even his legendary power only slowed his descent.

Two souls inhabited the female elf's body, but it was Galani who had chosen to bind herself to the Wyr Stone. She lacked the knowledge and practice Valea had, but with the artifact, she had no such worry any more.

Separate, either would have been no match for the hooded madman. Together, he had no hope.

But in his madness, Shade did see that last. With a roar, he took advantage of the force pushing him toward his foe by suddenly leaping at her. Galani momentarily lost her resolve, but Valea strengthened her just as Shade reached them.

By rights, he should have sent all of them flying backward, but the sorceress's added might made it seem as if the warlock had struck a stone wall instead. Galani's/Valea's bloody hand gripped his gloved one tight, pulling him close. Momentum made them twirl around and around several times. Finally, the dagger came up, thrust this time in the back so that there would be no hope of Shade reaching it physically.

He screamed, his blurred visage revealing a huge darkness where the mouth had to be. He twisted and turned in their grip but could not free himself.

Around and around they spun, the shadowy figure now engulfed by the Wyr Stone's power fed through by the dagger. Galani it had been who had slumped over the cursed artifact, drenching it with her blood and making the dagger her key to its might. Valea now in a sense stepped back, watching warily from within her host in case something went awry.

But Shade continued to scream and once more his form distorted. His arms, legs, torso—even his head stretched and turned. An aura that constantly shifted color and pattern surrounded him, ate away at his very existence.

And for a brief moment . . . Valea *did* see the true face of Shade.

It was and was not what she had expected. A young face, not much older than her own, but with hints here and there of so many, many years of torment. It was an aristocratic face and not unhandsome. Dark hair hung over much of the forehead and framed narrow crystalline eyes, a brooding, pained brow, angular cheeks and jaw, and slightly curved nose.

Then the face returned to a blur and, with a last, agonized howl, Shade *melted* in her grip.

He melted like wax tossed into a hot furnace, literally dripping to the floor. There, what had once been a man quickly dissipated into smoke, spreading randomly throughout the corridors of the Manor and vanishing beyond.

Yet as the last vestiges of Shade dwindled away, Valea could not help immediately thinking *somewhere else he is being reborn this very minute.*

But she could not concern herself with that, for suddenly she felt herself slipping away. No. Galani was dying. She had bound herself to the Wyr Stone, but not to the extent of her cousin. To use its might even to save herself had seemed an abomination to the elf. The sinister stone had repelled her; she had only sought it to destroy Shade.

"F-fear not. I will not let it happen to you," the lips said to the sorceress.

Vertigo overcame Valea . . . and the next second, she found herself floating like a *ghost* in front of Galani.

The elf gazed at her, smiled weakly. "You look—you look like me. All those—those times—I wondered if you—if you were a ghost from the past. A lost s-soul." She coughed up blood. "Now I—I know—I w-was the ghost . . . but seeing you—I wonder if I am to be r-reborn just like him," she added, referring to Shade. The smile faltered. "Perhaps he and I—he and you—might meet and become as I once h-hoped . . ."

Valea knew that Galani would hear her if she spoke, but still the crimson-tressed figure said nothing. She did not want to tell the elf that Shade was dead in her time, never to return.

"Galani!"

Arak, completely healed, raced toward the staircase. Such was his concern that he did not really register Valea's phantasmal figure and so ran right *through* her to reach his beloved cousin.

"Arak," she gasped. "I had to do it, didn't I?"

Galani slumped forward, the dagger dropping.

Valea's world turned black.

# VIII

SHE WOKE IN her bed without any notion as to how she had gotten there. Rising quickly, Valea went to the window to get some idea of how far the day had progressed. By the sun's position she knew that nearly all of it had been spent.

Setera and the others who attended her again fretted over her peculiar behavior, but Valea shrugged off their concern and assured them that she would soon be better. Her *illness* had passed. Now that she had witnessed—even taken part in—the climactic moment, Valea felt certain that the dreams would end. Still, it irked her that some questions remained.

And that drew her back to the staircase.

The spot where Galani had died remained burned in her memory, as did the destruction of Shade. Making certain that no one watched, Valea retraced their movements, reliving each moment until the point where Arak had come too late to save his cousin. What she hoped to accomplish, she could not say, but it seemed the only thing to do.

From the library, she heard a peculiar, creaking sound.

Valea rushed to the room, certain that now the way had opened for her. She stepped through the entrance—and saw only the bookcases standing as they had all her life.

Dejected, the weary sorceress touched the one in question, already knowing that it would not move.

Suddenly, the strange groaning started anew. At first Valea thought that the book case did *open*, but then she saw that it was only a shadow of the case, a ghost. Before her stood not only the physical piece, but also, turned to the side like a door ajar, a phantom image with different books, different tomes, lining each shelf.

Valea reached forward—and her hand sank into the wall.

Without hesitation, she stepped through . . . into solid stone.

She walked through it, retracing the ancient path down. The entire underground system had been filled, leaving not one iota of empty space. Oddly, Valea had no fear; some inner sense soothed her, assured her that the way was safe.

At the bottom, in the chamber where Arak had kept the Wyr Stone, she found Galani.

The elf was perfectly preserved. Her arms had been placed over her midsection and her blue gown had been straightened. Care had been taken to clean and dress the area of her terrible wound. She looked calm, almost wistful. Again, the resemblance between them struck Valea.

Galani lay floating in the midst of all the stone, encased forever by Arak, no doubt. There seemed no sign of the male elf and Valea wondered what had happened to both him and the Wyr Stone.

Then the sudden knowledge came to her that she now walked *within* the latter.

It was and was not as the sorceress had known it. The Wyr Stone had been altered beyond recognition both in appearance and substance, yet still she felt its presence, knew it now for the artifact that had been at the center of the tragedy. More than that now, Valea realized that it was the *stone* that had led her through all this, was responsible for her particular ghosts.

Perhaps all the ghostly memories of the Manor.

As Valea thought the last, she immediately pictured Arak setting his cousin here. One last time he bound himself to the Wyr Stone in order to create this crypt. Valea could hear the elf as he touched the artifact, hear Arak's last, single-word command before his permanent departure.

*"Remember . . ."*

And so the stone . . . and through it, the Manor . . . did. But because of the immense power of the Wyr Stone, not just the memories of Galani were saved, but so many, many others after also. And with the peculiar properties of the artifact, even *older* memories were suddenly resurrected, adding further to the ancient edifice's growing legion of ghosts.

Valea blinked, realizing that she had envisioned all this too clearly for it simply to be her imagination. She had just been told what Arak had done . . . and she knew that she had been told by Galani.

Forever bound to the Wyr Stone, forever bound to the Manor because of it, Galani was now a part of each as much as they were a part of her. Her physical shell remained, but she had become, in a sense, much, much more.

Which explained perhaps further why Valea, who had been born in this place, so resembled her.

She felt a sudden urge to depart and wisely followed it. Almost in the blink of an eye the youngest Bedlam stood once again before a very real, very solid bookcase. Recovering her equilibrium, Valea touched the wall, but this time found it as solid as the stone it was. It did not surprise her that she somehow knew that never again would she journey below or that those particular ghosts had vanished forever.

A DAY LATER, Lord Gryphon contacted her through a spell. The proud, avian head peered at her from within her mind.

*"I hope I find you well, Valea Bedlam."*

"Yes, my lord . . . and you?"

*"Good enough. Some matters I won't trouble you with."* He cocked his head to the side. *"I fear, though, I have only disappointment for you."*

She had been at her desk, still writing down all of which she had been a part. The journal was a personal one and would not be seen by her father unless she deemed it necessary. "Disappointment?"

*"I find no mention of an Arak, as I suspected. I'm sorry."*

"I did not expect you to. My thanks, though."

He was not finished. *"Then there is the Wyr Stone."*

Her attention was absolute. "Yes?"

*"Nothing but a myth. I thought I recalled mention of it. I looked in my old journals from my mercenary years . . ."* He shrugged. *"We old campaigners like to look back at the wars fondly . . . once they're long over. Anyway, the subject of the stone came up once, but I had it verified by the best of sources that it was futile to go searching for it since it did not even exist."*

Valea barely held back a tired smile. "The best of sources? You're sure?"

*"It was your great-grandfather, Nathan . . . and he had queried Shade himself on the subject."*

For a moment, the sorceress was speechless. Quickly recovering, she thanked the lionbird for his diligence, then bid him farewell.

*Shade himself.*

It had remained a mystery to her why she had been the one who had been able to touch the Manor's memories after so many attempts by her father and others. Now she thought she knew. Perhaps Galani had reached out to her other self, her *reborn* self. Perhaps she had been trying to send a message, a warning. Perhaps another stirring presence had awakened her.

Darkhorse . . . Queen Erini . . . they had seen him perish. Everyone was certain that Shade was finally at peace.

Valea looked up to the walls, whispering, "He isn't dead, is he? He's been resurrected again, hasn't he?"

The walls did not reply . . . and that in itself told her the answer.

Closing the journal, the sorceress stared out her window at the lands of the Manor. Somewhere far beyond, Shade moved about again. The question remained, however, *which* Shade? His last incarnation had been a chaotic one, both evil and good combined. He had even seemed to regain some of his true self at the end, so Darkhorse had said.

A face came unbidden to her, but not Kyl's. This was a more human face. The face behind the legend, behind the curse.

"I will find him, Galani," Valea whispered. "And I will do whatever must be done."

And if that meant killing him again to finally give him peace, she knew that she would do even that.

It was time for *all* the ghosts to be laid to rest.

# STORM LORD

*Madness is a matter of perspective*

# I

THE WIND HOWLED like a hundred hungry wolves. The rain poured down in such torrents that it seemed the world's oceans sought to drown the land. Crisp crackles of lightning flashed from the sky, some of them darting precariously near to where he rode. His brown steed struggled to maintain its footing as it raced over the slippery hills constantly rising ahead, but he paid no attention. All that mattered was the rendezvous.

The chill night air forced him to bundle his long, gray travel cloak over his head. He could have used magic to protect him from the elements, but that would have risked discovery. In this benighted realm, absolute power rested in the hands of a ruler gone mad.

And there was nothing more dangerous than an insane Dragon King.

The hood barely covered his chiseled chin, his high cheek bones, clipped nose, and brooding, brilliantly blue eyes. Other than the eyes, which he had altered to fit another's tastes, his facial features were those with which he had been born. He had inherited most of his looks from his beautiful mother, but his reckless traits and skill with magic were more those of his father, the bravest, most powerful wizard he knew. With his golden hair—pure save for the wide, silver streak that marked him as a wizard—he looked like a prince out of a fairy tale, his pale shirt, forest green pants, and knee-high leather boots adding to that valiant image.

His mount stumbled, momentarily throwing him off-balance. He reacted instinctively, using just a touch of power to right himself before the wet saddle could make him fall. A whispered curse escaped him immediately after; even such a spell dared too much.

Then he forgot the risk he had just taken, for, at that moment, through the downpour he saw his destination. The old hut lay nearly obscured by the thickly wooded hillside. The tendrils from the huge willows draped over the crooked, black structure like grasping fingers seeking to crush what remained.

The dilapidated structure looked like the last place where anyone would dare to meet, especially in the midst of such violent weather.

And that was just as the two of them had planned.

He brought the horse to a natural alcove in the hill. Another, darker mount whose reins had already been bound to an outcropping within snorted as they approached. The rider whispered soothing words to the second beast, then tied the reins of his own steed to the same outcropping.

The hut quaked as he cautiously pushed open the creaking, rotting door. The darkness within did not disturb him, for he knew the danger of any illumination being noticed here.

Lightning crashed, revealing briefly the lack of any ornamentation or furniture in the old structure. He had long concluded that it had served only as a way station for messengers or perhaps an old guard outpost. When the occupants had abandoned it, they had taken with them everything of value.

Another bolt filled the lone room with white light—and in the far corner, he saw her waiting for him.

"Aurim . . ." The voice was low, melodious, and sent his heart racing.

Her features were slightly elfin, but overall more full, more human. Her long, flowing hair was nearly as golden as his own. The deep brown riding outfit she wore—blouse, shin-length skirt, and tapering boots—accented her curvaceous figure perfectly. Over her shoulders the young woman wore a green travel cloak similar to Aurim's own.

Despite the darkness, he could readily make out her eyes. They seemed to flare with life whenever she reacted to something—yet they were not always the same. Sometimes they were bright emerald, other times gold. On a rare occasion, Aurim had seen them become as bloodred and inhuman as those of a reptilian Dragon King.

Not a surprise, truly, considering that she was the daughter of one.

"Yssa . . ."

They fell into one another's arms with a passion built up by the two weeks since last they had dared sneak out of their respective domains. He was the son of the most prominent line of wizards, the Bedlams, and both his father, Cabe, and his mother, Gwen, had saved the Dragonrealm more than once from threats within and without. Yssa, on the other hand, was the half-human daughter of the Green Dragon, the Master of the Dagora Forest, and one-time ally of the Bedlams. But something had come between the wizards and the Dragon King and now the Bedlams treated both the father and the daughter with mistrust.

Which made Aurim's and Yssa's growing love for one another a terrible trial for both.

"Did you have trouble slipping out?" she asked.

"No, Father was away with Darkhorse and Mother had her own obligations. They think I'm visiting elsewhere, anyway. What about you?"

Yssa looked down. "My sire's illness makes his heir more watchful . . ." The Dragon King had become weakened in the eyes of his kind, especially his son, Yssa's half-sibling and a full drake.

"I'm sorry . . ." Aurim had, for a time, been part of that invading force, his will controlled by the malignant demon Yureel, the true power behind Zuu's monarch, the Horse King. He still felt some responsibility for the terrible wounds Yssa's father had suffered even though he had not had been directly at fault.

"All will work out . . . even for us . . ."

They held one another close, forgetting for the moment the terrible complications in their lives. Now, the world consisted only of the two of them.

Outside the storm raged, shaking not only the hut, but the hills surrounding it. The black clouds shook and twisted as if alive. Thunder boomed and lightning flashed over and over again. The rain poured down with more malevolence, threatening to wash away everything. Yet, ensconced in the hut, their minds only on one another, Aurim and Yssa paid scant attention to the violent storm.

But had they looked out at it, they might have found much to interest them—for if either had stared at the furious clouds, looked deep into the tempest itself, they would have noticed that the storm *stared back* at them.

# II

*HOW COULD HE be so foolish?* she asked herself again as she rode along the narrow ridge. Above her, a clear, starlit night greeted her, but just ahead she could already hear the boom of thunder, the crackle of lightning.

The border of Wenslis lay only an hour's ride away.

She reined the mare to a halt, staring in the direction of the other kingdom. That a storm raged over Wenslis despite the open heavens here did not surprise her in the least. Foul weather often swept over Wenslis, for was it not a symbol of the absolute hold its master had on the land?

Dragon Kings forsook the names they bore when they took up rule of their realms. Whatever title he had gone by long ago, this one was now known as the Storm Dragon. He wielded primal forces that shook even the neighboring lands at times. But wielding such godlike powers had eventually brought this reptilian monarch to the brink of madness and beyond. Now, he truly imagined himself a deity, if only of his own drenched kingdom.

Lady Gwendolyn Bedlam pursed her lips. A cascade of fiery hair accented by a deep streak of silver tumbled down both her back and her chest. Her emerald eyes gleamed dangerously at the thought of what might happen to her son. In truth, she looked no older than Aurim, her firstborn, a gift of her powerful wizardry.

The form-fitting riding outfit matched perfectly her eyes. The enchantress sniffed the air, her upturned nose sensing more than smells. Gwen could feel the powerful forces at work, but among them she noted something else, something only she and perhaps her husband had the skill to detect.

Aurim had ridden this way. His distinctive magical trail continued on to the northeast. She frowned again. There was no mistaking that he had entered Wenslis.

With growing anxiety, Gwen urged her horse on. Yssa was to blame for this. The Green Dragon's daughter had seduced her son as she had tried to once do to Cabe. How long it had been going on, she did not know. Only an argument with Aurim's sister, Valea, had caused the truth to come out. In an attempt to avert some of the fury directed toward her, Valea had pointed out her brother's own transgression.

Gwen had ridden off that same day.

Only a few hours out, she had used divination to seek his path . . . and then had made an even more horrible discovery. Against all common sense, he and the half-drake had apparently chosen an area just inside the border of Wenslis for their clandestine meetings. She understood the illogical logic of the lovers; who would seek them in such a foreboding land? Yet, to place their lives in such jeopardy made no sense at all . . .

*If only I can find them before the Dragon King notices their presence! That vixen! This is her doing . . .*

Trying to calm her heated thoughts, she concentrated on Aurim only. Yssa could handle her own affairs. The Green Dragon had been one of Gwen's early mentors, but he had betrayed her trust and it seemed the daughter followed the parent's trait.

"Focus!" Gwen hissed at herself. Aurim. She had to think only of Aurim.

Still the night sky directly above stood as cloudless as possible, yet just ahead the storm raged. Gwen drew her travel cloak tighter as she neared the border.

The moment she crossed the invisible line separating Penacles from Wenslis, the full fury of the tempest fell upon her. Her horse whinnied in shock, then stumbled. Gwen twisted the reins, regained control. The mare quieted.

Ahead of her, the enchantress made out the dark shadows of trees and other vegetation. It amazed her that anything could grow here, but Wenslis had more vegetation than she had ever imagined. As she passed the first trees, she identified them as willows, not a surprise in such a wet landscape. Still, plants were one thing; people were another. How did the humans and others serving the Dragon King survive the almost perpetual rain?

Aurim's trail suddenly grew more faint, more difficult to track. It was not that it had faded, but rather that the storm itself contained so much raw magic that it disrupted her higher senses. The crimson-tressed spellcaster gazed up at the turbulent sky, suddenly feeling as if she was being watched. A flash of lightning briefly illuminated the clouds, but nothing more.

Trying to shake away her uncertainties, she leaned forward and urged the horse to better speed. Perhaps eager to finish this madness and return to a more calm realm, the mare obeyed with gusto. Gwen breathed easier as she raced along. She still detected some hint of Aurim and so long as even a trace remained, she felt certain that she would find him.

Through the swampy forest Gwen rode. The lightning created monstrous displays—huge grasping tentacles and fingers, creatures with heads full of snakes. They were all merely the twisted forms of Wenslis's trees, but even knowing that, the enchantress could not help stiffening each time a new outline formed.

Then a bolt struck the willow just to her right. The explosion turned bright the entire vicinity and set the tree on fire. Gwen's horse veered away from the danger.

And in that instant, situated between two more distant trees, she saw a cloaked and hooded form watching her.

Before Gwen could refocus on the spot, the last vestiges of lightning faded. Even the fire from the willow proved insufficient to illuminate the area she desired.

Reining the mare to a halt, Gwen turned back to where the figure had stood.

Another bolt struck the tree nearest her.

Now the mare panicked. It was all Gwen could do to keep from falling off. Although wary of possible detection, she cast a minor spell to calm the animal.

But before she could complete it, branches enveloped her from every direction. They entangled her arms, blinded her, even snared her legs. The mare, now free of her control, pulled away, leaving Gwen caught like a fly in a web of wood and leaves.

She tried to concentrate enough to free herself, but the branches spun her around, turned her upside down. The leaves in her face made it almost impossible to even breathe.

An imposing presence touched her thoughts. It said nothing, but the sheer power behind it made her certain that it could only be one being.

The Storm Lord had discovered her intrusion.

Lightning flared again. Through a few narrow gaps in her tightening prison, Gwen caught a glimpse of several figures moving through the raging weather. They looked human in form, but wearing outlandish armor with broad, curved shoulders like tiny, overturned boats and helmets with wide, sloping brims. Pale faces peered out from under the helmets, the eyes all focused on the struggling enchantress.

One raised what looked like a pear with a flower on the end to her face. The figure squeezed the object and a puff of scented air struck Gwen full.

She did not even notice when she blacked out.

HE WATCHED WITH clinical interest as the soldiers removed their unconscious captive from the willows with remarkable gentleness. He could have saved her then, but he had not decided whether he wanted to or not. Still, she presented not only a marvelous coincidence, but an interesting diversion to keep him from having to contemplate other, more difficult matters.

He pulled his dark cloak tight around him and as he did, his entire body seemed to fold into it, growing thinner and thinner in the blink of an eye—until he was gone.

# III

THEY WERE NO longer alone.

Yssa obviously sensed him tense, for she suddenly asked, "What is it? What's wrong?"

"Someone—something's approaching."

The half-drake female pulled out of his arms, her gaze toward the ceiling. "I don't feel—no—I do now . . ."

Despite her own legacy, her powers were not always as great as Aurim's. He had first noticed the newcomers several seconds ago, but his mind had initially refused to accept such a dire intrusion into his time with her. Fortunately, common sense had finally prevailed over passion.

But was it been soon enough?

"They could be my father's warriors," she suggested.

Her tone, however, matched his own thoughts. "Not here. They'd never be allowed this far into Wenslis."

Neither had to say more, for they knew that those moving in on the hut could be the servants of only one other.

Aurim left Yssa in the middle of the room. Stepping to the rotting door, he peered through a wide crack.

With the aid of the lightning, he saw them. More than half a dozen shapes, all wearing odd, broad-rimmed armor and helmets. The human soldiers of Wenslis. The slaves of the Storm Dragon.

"They're surrounding us," he told her.

"He wouldn't dare harm either of us," Yssa insisted. "Even he isn't that mad."

"We're about to find out."

Aurim sensed the spell just before it struck. He raised the transparent, blue shield around his love and himself just before the bolts decimated the hut.

Fragments of wood flew everywhere, many raining down on the two figures protected by Aurim's magic. Smoke rose from the ashes despite the heavy rain. A few broken pieces thrust up from the stone base, but they were all that remained to mark where once the abandoned structure had stood.

Despite the destruction, the attack had actually not been very threatening to the pair. Aurim had had plenty of warning. He wondered why the Storm Dragon had not assaulted them with more ferocity.

As the last refuse settled to the ground, the armored warriors charged. Guttural shouts did battle with the thunder. Thick, curved blades swung back and forth.

The shield abruptly failed as another force struck Aurim's mind. He roared with pain, then, using the mental tricks his parents had taught him, refocused his will and thrust the intruder out.

Still, the damage had been done. He had no time to raise a second shield, the first of the soldiers upon him.

Yssa reached forward, palm extended. She struck the foremost figure full in the face. There was a slight green flash where the Dragon King's daughter touched the soldier—and then her foe went spiraling backward into the trees.

Drawing his left hand across the empty air, Aurim created a blazing sword with which he met the next two attackers. Sparks flew as the soldiers' blades touched his own. The flaming sword cut through both weapons cleanly, sending the top halves dropping to the wet ground.

One foe retreated, but the other lunged with what remained of his sword. Aurim easily parried the awkward strike, then, gritting his teeth, he slashed at the other's forearm.

He cut through the armor and the bone with ease. The soldier howled and fell to his knees.

"Get to the horses!" he snapped at Yssa.

"I won't leave you!"

Before the wizard could argue further with her, he was again struck by a spell focused at his thoughts. The world spun and Aurim nearly tumbled over. Only with the greatest effort did he manage to again push back the magical assault.

With the blade, Aurim quickly drew a fiery barrier that briefly held the soldiers of Wenslis at bay. He scanned the vicinity and saw what had to be the source of the two inner assaults. Behind the foot soldiers, the unmistakable figure of a drake warrior could be seen directing the enemy's efforts. A high crest that in better visibility would have resembled a perfect reproduction of a dragon's head perched atop the helm. Despite the rain, Aurim could make out the glowing crimson orbs and he imagined the flat, almost noseless face with the lipless mouth filled with teeth and a tongue forked. What appeared scaled armor covered the drake's body, but it, like the helm and all else, were purely illusion.

Every bit of armor, every little trace of reptilian flesh within the helmet—was the skin of the creature. The drake was a mimic of sorts, creating the image of a humanoid warrior when, in fact, he was a *dragon.*

Why the drakes so often preferred such forms, Aurim could only guess. His father had come up with the fantastic notion that the Dragon Kings' forebears had not been dragons at all, but rather *humans* who had somehow been transformed and had forgotten their past. Now, if that theory held merit, the drakes were slowly reverting to what they had once been . . . which meant their eventual demise as a separate race.

It certainly explained why they could breed with his kind, but Aurim could not imagine how such a monstrous transformation could have originally taken place.

The drake hissed something to the charging warriors. Aurim chose the moment to alter his sword into a long, burning lance, which he threw at the distracted creature.

The point of the magical lance tore through the armored hide of the drake, piercing him in the chest. The creature struggled for a moment, his arms waving furiously. Then, he fell against a tree and slid to the ground. Its work done, the lance dissipated.

"Now's our chance!" Aurim muttered to Yssa. As the soldiers milled about in sudden confusion, he and his companion hurried to their mounts. The horses whinnied anxiously.

But as the wizard reached for the reins of Yssa's horse, a figure dropped upon him. The two tumbled to the ground. A fearsome, bearded face glared fanatically at Aurim.

Yssa started toward the pair, but two more soldiers dropped down behind her. With a sudden, inhuman hiss, she slashed at one with her nails. They might have had little effect against the armor, but as her hand neared, the fingers stretched, grew crooked, and the nails became long, tapering claws like those of a huge lizard—or dragon.

The claws tore through the breast plate, through the flesh beneath. The soldier cried out and fell.

But in dealing so with the first, Yssa left herself open to the second for a few precious moments. However, instead of a sword or some other weapon, he held up to her face a small object with what appeared a flower on the end.

A puff of air blanketed her face—

Aurim saw her drop and his mind filled with fear and rage. Without thinking, he sent powerful, raw energy through his hands, energy that engulfed the warrior atop him. The armored figure shrieked as the blinding, red aura enveloped him . . . then the cry cut off as both the aura and its victim abruptly ceased to be.

Rising, Aurim turned on the soldiers trying to drag Yssa away. However, a horrific gale suddenly threw him back against the trees and only his instinct for survival enabled the wizard to create a cushioning force before he hit. Even still, Aurim struck with such force that he cracked one trunk and completely jarred his senses.

He slid to the muddy soil. Aurim blinked, expecting to find himself surrounded by the fighters. Instead, though, he discovered that they had all begun to retreat.

As he rose unsteadily to his feet, Aurim felt a terrible surge of power all around him. He looked up at the dark sky, saw eyes in the clouds staring at him.

Red, reptilian eyes.

And then the earth exploded as what seemed a thousand bolts of lightning struck where Aurim stood.

# IV

GWEN AWOKE NOT in chains, but the enchantress was no less imprisoned. The soft, silver cushions filling the high, white oak bed upon which she lay went on to the glistening, ivory walls—or rather, *wall*, since her chamber appeared perfectly round. The bed, perfectly matched to leave no space between itself and the wall, adjusted to her movements with such efficiency and care that she almost thought it alive.

There was no door, no window. The ceiling rose to a point some ten feet above. The illumination radiated from the wall itself, but Gwen could detect no magic in it.

At the far end of the bed, a square, gleaming tray held two bowls—one filled with fresh fruit, the other, well-cooked meats—and a glass flask of some red wine. Gwen felt the rumbling in her stomach and the dryness in her mouth. Despite her predicament, she climbed over the pillows and partook of the offered meal. Both the tray and bowls were of pure platinum and finely crafted. The flask and the small cup accompanying it had been molded from flawless crystal, not glass as she had first supposed.

As she ate, the enchantress inspected herself. Not so much as one scratch marred her pale skin and her garments looked as if they had just been cleansed. There was no trace whatsoever of the storm's wrath on her. In fact, the only thing she noticed wrong at all was that her travel cloak had been taken.

Pushing away the tray, Gwen leaned toward the wall, touching it gingerly. To her surprise, she found it not only incredibly smooth, but neither hot nor cold. In fact, the temperature of the chamber seemed just perfect to her and she suspected that to be no coincidence.

*What is he up to?* Gwen had expected much worse in the captivity of the Storm Dragon. Thus far, she had suffered more on diplomatic journeys to some of the obscure kingdoms. The pillows and sheets had a silken touch; the fare, the enchantress had to admit, would have done even Penacles or Talak well.

Running her hand along the wall, Gwen searched for some hidden doorway or window. She reached out with her higher senses, seeking to understand the nature of her prison. Where had her captor placed her? In the depths of his mountainous retreat? Amidst a raging volcano?

She let out an uncharacteristic gasp as the blank wall suddenly became a wide, distorted face that wrapped completely around her.

Atop the helm that covered much of the face, one of the most fearsome dragon heads she had ever seen peered down at her. It was flanked by massive, curved wings stretched as if in flight and under those wings clouds had been set. Both helm and crest were a deep gray with a combination of silver and blue hints.

The lower jaw of the dragon extended down to the nose guard. The helmet's rounded eye holes revealed within two miniature red suns that burned hotter when they met the enchantress's startled gaze.

"Our Lady of the Amber . . ." thundered the Storm Lord, using one of Gwen's older titles. The narrow slit of a mouth opened wide in what apparently was a smile. The jagged teeth and flickering, serpentine tongue did nothing to accentuate that smile. "You are most welcome here with us."

He spoke flawlessly, none of the oft-present sibilance of his kind noticeable. He also spoke as if to an honored guest, not one whom he had seized by terrible force.

But then, the actions of those who were mad were never predictable.

"Why am I here? I meant no threat to you, Dragon King! I had, by necessity, to travel along the edge of your domain, but surely you could sense there was no malice in my actions!"

The huge face shifted around, disconcerting her. The Storm Dragon chuckled harshly, then replied, "No, Our Lady, there was no malice in your actions! We simply saw the opportunity we had long desired to welcome you to our company . . ."

Gwen did not quite know what to make of his words, but that hardly mattered. "There is a peace between us—if not an easy one—my lord. If you'll let me be on my way, it shall remain peace."

"But you have only just graced us with your presence, wonderful Lady of the Amber! We would know you better first . . ." A hint of a frown escaped. "The meal was not to your liking? It was drawn from your memories . . ."

She stirred. Gwen had not even noticed that. Small wonder that she had enjoyed it so. In fact, the enchantress now recalled the wine being a rare vintage from Gordag-Ai.

"Were they not conjured to your satisfaction, Our Lady?" he asked, his dark visage giving more hint of menace.

"They were excellent," Gwen replied quickly.

"And your bed? You slept well?"

Again she answered with swiftness so as not to allow his anger to rise. "A more perfect sleep I couldn't have had."

The inhuman mouth twisted into a smile again. "We are so pleased by that."

*He always speaks of himself in the plural . . . his insanity grows . . .* That meant that everything she said the enchantress had to consider before the words left her mouth.

"Lord of Storms, I would be more than happy to visit officially, if that's what you would truly desire, but I fear that other matters press most urgently at this time—"

"You speak of your son," he interjected casually.

Gwen bit back her concern. That he knew of Aurim should not have surprised her. "Yes, my son. He may have errantly entered your domain and I wanted to make certain that you did not mistake said error for anything but what it was."

The great head bowed once. "You may be assured, Lady of the Amber, that we understand exactly what it was."

His words gave her some slight hope. "I can promise you that he'll not make the same mistake again. When we leave—"

"But you are in error yourself, Our Lady, for your time to depart is not yet now."

"But my son—"

A huge, gauntleted hand cut across the massive head as the Storm Dragon dismissed her protest without concern. "Enchantress, he is dead. We need no longer concern ourselves with his trespass."

She gaped. He could have told her nothing more horrible—and in so uncaring a voice.

Seemingly unmindful of her horror, the dread master of Wenslis continued, "Let us instead concern ourselves with a more pleasant subject now . . . your probable role as our glorious *consort*."

Gwen could barely comprehend his words, her mind still torn by the declaration that Aurim had been killed. Rage and confusion overwhelmed her. She rose atop the bed and tried to summon the power needed to shatter both the wall and the monstrous, arrogant face.

But nothing happened. She could sense no source of power upon which to draw. It was as if in this place magic did not exist.

"We have searched for those most worthy and found all lacking," he went on, oblivious to her fury. "No drake dam wields the might we deemed appropriate for one who would be the mate of a god. But fate offered us another choice, a far better one. We need not seek merely among our own kind, but among those where a proper companion for our august personage already existed."

The enchantress could not believe, could not imagine, that she heard right. The same monster that had so indifferently announced her son's death—at his hands, no doubt—believed she would become his mate? In the face of all else, the idea was so absurd that Gwen almost laughed.

"You will be our consort, our mate! You shall bear us offspring like no others, Lady of the Amber," the horrific visage declared, mouth wide and upturned. "And with you at our side, at last we shall began to spread our glory over the rest of this benighted world . . ."

"I would never—"

He vanished before she could finish, leaving in his place not the ivory wall, but something that left the enchantress frozen in shock. Perhaps the Storm Lord thought to impress upon his chosen bride the depths of his might. He certainly left the protests Gwen had been about to utter unspoken. She stood there, staring in horror, realizing that at every turn her captor stripped her of more and more hope.

Aurim was dead . . . and she . . . she now saw where her cell lay. Not in the depths of a live volcano, as Gwen had supposed, but the very opposite.

The storm raged around her, savage bolts crashing much too near. Black clouds collided violently and thick, pounding rain coursed earthward.

Coursed to a world far, far below.

The cell floated by itself amidst the clouds, amidst the terror of the unnatural storm. Pressing her face against the now invisible wall, Gwen barely made out the hazy form of a huge mountain peak flanked by two smaller but no less sinister siblings.

The lair of the Storm Lord.

AURIM LAY SURROUNDED by darkness and the odd feeling that the world had been turned upside down. He tried to push himself up, but a crushing weight kept him pinned in place.

"Shall I help him?" asked a quiet voice.

"Why?" asked a second one that sounded identical to the first.

"It might be amusing. It might be something to do."

What Aurim took for the second voice mockingly replied, "So would letting him die horribly."

"Yes, but that would take too long and I don't have the patience."

"Neither do I."

As the wizard tried to make sense of the conversation, something suddenly grabbed his ankles.

Aurim rose feet first into the air, a layer of earth falling away from his face and chest. A huge rock tumbled to the side, the crushing weight he had felt.

Belatedly he realized that a faint blue glow surrounded him. At first the blond wizard thought that his rescuer had created it, but then a hazy memory stirred. The blue glow was his own work, the last vestige of the shield spell he had cast just as the Dragon King's storm had plunged him into chaos. Aurim vaguely recalled being tossed over the landscape, landing here and there and everywhere as one bolt after another had ripped apart wherever he landed. An entire hill had collapsed upon him, all but smothering its intended victim. Only the strength of his own spell had spared him from the Storm Lord's wrath.

But had Aurim survived all that simply to still be captured by the scaly ruler of Wenslis?

Whatever held his ankles shook him so violently that he had to cry out.

"You see? He's still very much alive."

"That can be rectified."

"Wh—" Aurim choked. He spat out moist, congealed dirt from his throat. "Who's there? Who are you?"

"We were trying to decide that," answered what might have been either the first or second voice; the wizard could not say which. They sounded absolutely the same, down to each inflection.

Twins?

Then he realized what the last voice had said. They were trying to decide who they were?

"It's a matter of choice, you see. The decision to turn one direction or another. A name would be simple, then. Until that happens, though, the indecision splits us terribly."

But Aurim no longer listened to the babbling. Given the chance to breathe—even if he did so dangling upside down in the dark—the wizard now recalled a matter far more important to him than his own dire situation.

Yssa . . .

He tried to struggle free. "Where is she? What did you do with her?"

Suddenly he found himself falling. Aurim acted as best he could to strengthen his dying spell. Despite that, he still hit the ground with a harsh thud. Every bone in his body shook and vertigo nearly made the hapless spellcaster pass out.

And where a moment before he had only been able see a few feet around him, now Aurim's surroundings blazed with light. He had to blink rapidly several times before his eyes adjusted and even then he was not at first certain at exactly what he stared.

It resembled nothing more than an empty cloak and hood set by someone to loom over him. There was the outline of shoulders, yes, but Aurim could see nothing within the low-hanging hood or the rest of the earth-sweeping garment. Yet, something lurked within, that his higher senses could tell, but whether it was human or otherwise was still an enigma.

Then, from the shadowy depths of the hood came the voice he had heard so many times. "The armored ones took the female."

"The Storm Dragon's warriors have her?" Aurim vaguely recalled something of the struggle and how one soldier had used a curious device to render his love unconscious.

"If the armored ones are the the warriors of this Storm Dragon then they're logically the ones who took her," the hood remarked somewhat impatiently.

"He seems to lack much in the way of sense. Perhaps he was better buried head down in the earth."

Aurim's eyes widened. The second voice had also come from within the hood.

The shrouded head shifted as if looking to the right side. "Being a little addled in the head can be forgiven under the circumstances. . . ."

Now it turned to the left. "A little . . . not a lot."

"We've our own quandaries, remember."

"Compared to ours, his are moot. Dispose of him."

As he watched the hood switch back and forth, Aurim's concern magnified a hundred times. He had been rescued by some demented creature with an obvious skill for magic. Despite his own respectable abilities—which Aurim felt gradually capable of using again—he knew that he had to be wary.

"Forgive me," the wizard dared say. "And thank you for coming to my aid."

The hood shifted right. "See? He has manners."

To the left. "He has fear . . . and that is a good thing, too."

From the ground, Aurim finally gazed up at what lay beyond his macabre companion—and received yet a further shock.

The storm still blew. Lightning flashed; rain fell in torrents. Aurim had noticed none of this earlier because of more than simply his slow recovery from the horrendous attack. No, the reason he had paid scant attention to the elements had been because *nothing* had touched either him or the hooded form. Even the sounds of the storm had failed to reach the wizard's ears. They stood completely cut off from the rest of the world by an invisible force that no doubt could be blamed on the mysterious figure with the dual voices.

And that spoke of a spellcaster of *tremendous* skill.

"I—thank you for rescuing me." He repeated. Determined not to remain in so vulnerable a position, Aurim struggled to his feet. "But I must be on my way. I must find Yssa . . . wherever they've taken her."

"We know where she's been taken," the hood responded to the right. "Should we show him?"

To the left . . . with a shrug of indifference. "As you wish . . . this time."

The hooded figure raised its head and, looking straight at Aurim, quietly said, "We will lead you . . . if you dare come with."

But Aurim did not answer at first, staring at what little he could see at last of the face. What there was visible filled him with an anxiety that eclipsed all else. Now he understood just how powerful this other was . . . and how at any moment that power might be wielded against him.

What could be seen was but a blur. Try as he might, Aurim could not bring the hooded visage at all into focus. He knew why, *yes*, he knew why. His parents still spoke of the faceless warlock, the hooded sorcerer—friend and foe together in one deathless, resurrecting form.

"You—you're dead . . ."

The hood shifted left and right, then settled in the center again. His macabre companion finally nodded. "Yes . . . yes, I suppose we are."

Aurim had been rescued by Shade.

# V

GWEN BATTERED AT the invisible wall, knowing already that her efforts did her no good. Besides, even if she did break through, could she save herself from plummeting to her death? She only assumed that her powers would be restored to her once she escaped. What if the Storm Dragon's spell affected her personally? She would shatter herself on the landscape below without ever knowing if his words concerning Aurim were true or not.

The enchantress could not let herself believe that her son was dead. Surely the Dragon King simply sought to break her will. Perhaps in his madness he likely thought that she would then be more susceptible to his influence. Having been, for a time, the student of another drake lord, Gwen understood much of their cunning ways.

But what if he spoke the truth? It would not be above him to so callously kill one of those she loved, then expect her to accept the truth with ease. Gwen swore, trying to make sense of it all.

She could expect no aid from either her husband or Darkhorse. They were far west and although she should still have been able to link to Cabe, he had not responded to her mental entreaties. The Storm Lord had made certain that his "guest" remained entirely alone.

"There must be something . . . someone . . ." Gwen muttered, resting her head against the wall.

A flicker of movement caught her attention. She looked up, but saw nothing.

Assuming it only a manifestation of her distraught mind, the fiery-haired sorceress lowered her head once more.

A huge, winged form darted up from below her prison.

Gwen immediately pulled back, instinctively fearful that it would brush aside her cell without notice and send her plunging to her death. Instead, however, the gray leviathan flew carefully past the enchantress. As it rose further up, she saw that it carried in its massive forepaws an object about the size of her prison.

She blinked. Actually, it was *exactly* like her prison.

Pressing against the wall, Gwen watched as the dragon, surely one of the Storm Lord's own, circled the region twice before settling on an area far east of her. The beast hovered amidst the storm, then held out the other prison. The second cell had the same ivory appearance as hers had originally had, preventing Gwen from seeing who lay trapped within.

The huge dragon struggled to maintain its position, its master clearly making no effort to ease the storm for its sake. Gwen found that odd. After a few more moments of battle against the storm, the huge beast abruptly released the opaque prison.

It dropped a bone-jarring hundred feet or so, then stopped in mid-air. Gwen gave silent thanks that she had not been awake when her own had been so set. She wondered who the Storm Lord now set high in the sky. Someone of value to him, that was obvious.

Her heart skipped. Could it be—could it be *Aurim*?

But no, that was too foolish. Why would her captor tell her that her son was dead, then put him in a prison within view of her own? Someone else had to be held captive there . . .

Then, her expression took on a bitter cast.

Could it be that the other cell held Yssa?

Fury filled the enchantress as she thought of the half-drake woman who had beguiled Aurim and led him to this terrible place. Gwen battered at the wall again, wishing that she could at least confront Yssa. Because of her this had all happened . . .

The dragon circled the other prison, inspecting it. Apparently satisfied that it would remain in place, the leviathan turned then to gaze Gwen's way.

She almost expected it to fly to her, but it seemed that the storm was too much for even the Dragon King's servant. The beast dipped its massive head, then dove out of sight.

For some time, Gwen watched the other prison, waiting to see if it, too, would grow transparent. If Yssa did lay within, had the Storm Lord dragged her here so that she, too, could become his consort? It would not have entirely surprised the enchantress, considering her captor.

Nothing happened and at last Gwen sat back. In truth, as angry as she was against the Green Dragon's daughter, she also sympathized with her present situation. She wished such a fate no more on Yssa than she did on herself. If Gwen could have rescued the other woman, she would have, but all that was simply a flight of fancy. The enchantress could not save herself, much less Aurim's love.

The storm continued to churn. Several times, the other prison completely vanished as some thick, black cloud came between them. Gwen watched it, trying to see if at least she could discover some weakness in her own cell by what the other did.

But nothing came to mind. When next the other prison vanished among the storm clouds again, an exasperated Gwen fell back on the plush bed and stared up in frustration.

Only then did she see that someone stared back at her from above.

It was not the eyes of the Dragon King among the clouds, though, but rather something far more astounding. On the upper edge of the prison, sat a cloaked and hooded form who peered down at her in what seemed curiosity. "Seemed" was as best as Gwen could tell, for there was no sign of the face save a hint of chin. He—she knew it to be a "he"—sat atop the floating prison entirely oblivious to either the raging storm or the tremendous heights. Not a hint of wind tousled his hood, not a drop of rain moistened his flowing cloak.

Gwen could only gape and wonder if her nightmare had just grown worse, for she knew that figure, even if his face was hidden—and perhaps more so *because* it was.

"Shade . . ." she whispered. "It can't be . . ."

He was dead. Darkhorse had seen him die. Queen Erini of Talak had vouched for that death, too.

But then, Shade had died hundreds of times before.

No one knew for certain his origins, although Cabe believed him one of the Vraad sorcerers, the legendary progenitors of the humans living today. Whether true or not, what *was* known was that, somewhere deep in the past, he had attempted to make himself immortal. But the spell had gone horribly awry and Shade had instead been cursed with an endless series of lives, each blossoming full-grown whenever the previous was slain.

Had that been all there was to it, Gwen would have had no fear. However, Shade's self-inflicted curse was more complex, more devious. His face forever an incomplete blur, he came back from the dead the opposite in soul what he had been in his previous incarnation. The Shade who had been ally against the old Dragon Emperor had become a sinister villain seeking to suck dry the power wielded by Cabe through the crystal magic of the earth-burrowing Quel. Those two personae, each with their own chosen names, had been only the latest of an unbroken string of good and evil, good and evil. Over the centuries, Shade had both helped wreak havoc and build peace. To every race of the Dragonrealm, the name Shade was both revered and cursed, honored and feared.

He seemed to at last take notice of her interest in him. The hooded form stood up as if on a tranquil, even plain. Shade stamped his booted foot once— and suddenly sank through the wall of Gwen's prison.

She moved cautiously, trying not to stir whatever personality drove him now. It should have picked a name by this time, as they all did. Would it be like Simon, who had sacrificed himself in battle against Azran Bedlam's avian Seekers—or more like Madrac, the one who had hunted her husband?

Folding his legs, he hovered a few feet above her. Even close, Gwen could not make out the face within. She caught glimpses of a dark-haired man almost youthful, but never enough to be certain.

"Do I know you?" Shade suddenly asked.

His question so astounded her that the enchantress momentarily forgot her imprisonment. The personae always recalled their past friends and foes, yet another horrific part of the curse. Shade had often slaughtered those who had befriended him in previous incarnations . . . a fact that would sicken him only when again he returned to the side of light.

"I am—I am Gwendolyn Bedlam, Shade. Of course you know me." She would not cower.

"Shade . . ." He cocked his head to the side. "Yes . . . I remember that." The hood straightened. "Thank you," Shade added politely.

"What—what do you want?"

"I don't know yet. I haven't decided which direction to go. I've spent quite some time thinking it over, but I still couldn't choose." He hovered lower, stopping just inches above the bed. His visage remained murky, unreadable. "I might still be sitting there still if you hadn't come along."

Gwen tried to keep her tone calm. So far the warlock had done nothing harmful. He sounded more confused than anything. Perhaps she could guide him, then utilize his powers to escape this unsettling prison. "And why was my appearance so important?"

"I really don't know. I suppose from what you said that it's because I knew you once."

"We could discuss this at length, if you like. If you could take me from here to somewhere more—"

"But he wants you here," the hooded form interrupted. "Should I remove you from him? I haven't decided that, either."

There was no telling just how long before the Storm Dragon might check on her. Shade represented Gwen's only hope of escape. She had to convince him that they were better off solving his problems elsewhere.

She sat up and smoothed her hair. The enchantress did not do the latter in an attempt to infatuate Shade, but because it allowed her a moment to think.

"I know you better than most, Shade. I've made a long study of your—your situation. I can help you, but this is hardly the place. We need somewhere quieter." When her companion said nothing, she added, "He could come back at any moment and, if he does, he'll make certain that you won't ever be able to speak with me again."

A black-gloved hand went to the out-of-focus chin. "There is something in what you say."

"We should leave immediately—"

The words had not even finished leaving her mouth when, without warning, Shade reached out and seized her wrist. He stood, both feet firmly planted on the cushions, and looked out at the storm.

"I can sense him," the warlock said. "His thoughts are near, but not on you . . ." He pointed at the other cell. "Or there, even. They seem scattered, almost as if he sleeps . . ."

Gwen paid no attention to his babbling, her concern suddenly focused on the second prison. Yssa. Gwen had entirely forgotten about the half-drake. No matter what she thought of Yssa's involvement with Aurim, she could not leave the younger woman to the Storm Lord's insanity.

"Shade . . . we need to take her with us, too."

"Does she know me, too?"

It was doubtful that the Green Dragon's daughter had ever met Shade, but Gwen replied, "Not quite so much, but, yes, she should definitely be included."

He nodded decisively. "Then, we'll go get her now."

Without warning, Shade walked through the wall.

And Gwen, despite her sudden reservations, had no choice but to follow.

Immediately the howling wind and torrents of rain sought to bowl her over. Thunder threatened her eardrums and the lightning, so close, almost blinded her.

But Shade, ever the creature of fantastic actions, waved his hand and around them the elements all but stilled. He then guided her along as if they both walked on a quiet woodland path instead of thin air. The savage wind barely moved his hood.

As he led her toward the second prison, Gwen marveled at the depths of his power. She had known Shade to be in many ways stronger than any other spell-caster, but never had she imagined this.

Gwen tried not to think about what would happen if he released his grip on her. The enchantress doubted that she could maintain her concentration long enough to save herself, especially with the storm buffeting her.

Shade did not pause until they stood before the opaque wall. He cocked his head as if listening, then told Gwen, "His thoughts still drift. We may enter."

That said, the warlock touched the wall with his other gloved hand. His fingers sank through. Shade immediately stepped inside, taking Gwen along.

From within came a gasp. Yssa pressed against the opposing end, staring at the two newcomers open-mouthed.

Her eyes swept over Shade, then turned to the one that she knew. Her cheeks reddened. "My Lady Bedlam . . ."

The rage that Gwen had held in check suddenly threatened to boil over. She satisfied herself with a glare at the Green Dragon's half-human daughter, then replied, "You'll be coming with us, Yssa."

Standing, the half-drake woman glanced at Shade again. The hooded figure held out his hand. After a moment's hesitation, she took it.

"I hope you know much about me," Shade remarked casually.

Yssa frowned. "I don't under—"

"This isn't the time or place to begin our discussion," Gwen quickly interrupted. "Shade, if you please?"

As Yssa gaped at this new revelation, the cloaked warlock led the pair through the wall.

But the storm was not the only thing to greet the escaping trio.

Through the black clouds burst a monstrous form. The dragon soared toward them, its huge maw open. It roared, a harsh sound that cut through the thunder. Crimson orbs glared at the tiny figures and the dragon stretched forth its massive claws.

Undaunted, Shade walked toward it.

Both Gwen and Yssa struggled to pull him back, the notion of meeting a dragon in such a manner hardly sane, but the warlock dragged them forward with no effort whatsoever.

Gwen searched inside herself for her link to the forces from which she drew her magic. This time she felt it, but only as a faint sensation. Hardly enough to sufficiently cast a spell, especially one effective against the oncoming behemoth.

The gray dragon roared again. The huge maw opened wide, revealing sharp teeth nearly as tall as its intended victims. Its wings seemed to envelop the sky as it neared. It was one of the largest dragons that the enchantress had seen in her entire life.

As it closed, Shade suddenly released his grip on both women.

Gwen screamed as loudly as Yssa—screams that faltered when neither plummeted earthward. The two drifted helplessly in the storm, Shade's remarkable power keeping both of them alive even while he focused on the savage leviathan.

The hooded figure stretched his arms to the side as if seeking to embrace the winged giant. The dragon slowed, apparently suddenly wary of this tiny creature floating in the sky who showed no proper fear in his moment of death.

Shade brought his gloved hands together.

A crack of thunder dwarfing any so far heard shook the heavens. Gwen and Yssa put their hands to their ears in a futile attempt to block out the overwhelming sound.

As if struck by a solid blow, the dragon tumbled backward over and over. It roared in confusion and sought desperately to right itself. Only when it had tumbled far into the distance did it finally begin to recover.

"Did you see that?" Yssa called, as astounded as Gwen by the warlock's might. "I'd heard that he knew all manner of spells, but—"

The rest of her comment ended in a startled scream. Gwen had no opportunity to react, for, at the same time, a terrible force pressed against her body and she was flung high into the storm. A cry as desperate as that by Yssa poured from her mouth.

The second dragon flew the two stunned women far from the scene of the astounding battle. Gasping for air, suddenly soaked by the horrendous storm, Gwen watched in horror as the first beast soared toward Shade. At the same time, the dark clouds above and around the hooded figure rumbled ominously.

With a heart-stumbling roar, the storm unleashed a relentless barrage of lightning bolts at Shade. The dragon approaching him let loose with a fearsome spray of fire . . .

But the beast carrying Gwen and Yssa veered away from the struggle, leaving the question of Shade's fate hanging. The enchantress could not imagine that he could survive such an attack. But if Shade had died, did that mean that he would even now be resurrected elsewhere? If so, would he be in the same confused state of mind?

The leviathan suddenly began descending. Gwen forgot all about the warlock as she saw them approach a familiar trio of peaks.

With one swift turn to the east, the dragon headed toward a huge cave mouth carved out of the top of the middle peak. Atop one of the other mountains, another dragon roared at the newcomer, who responded in kind.

The beast who carried them folded its wings as it entered the cave. Gwen felt every bone in her body jostle as they touched the rock floor.

Time and hundreds of dragons had worn this area almost smooth. No stalactites or stalagmites decorated the interior, those long ago cracked free by the huge inhabitants.

As it slowed, the dragon shoved the two ahead. The enchantress immediately whirled on the beast and, to her credit, Yssa did the same. Unfortunately, before they could do anything, a voice behind them said, "It would be unwissse to anger the Great One further, femalesss . . ."

Behind them, a drake servitor stood waiting. He resembled one of the scaled warriors in every manner save that his helm was all but undecorated. He had no huge crest, only a thin, barely noticeable ridge going back. Even without it, however, he stood almost seven feet tall.

"I am Ssssurak. You will come with me."

To emphasize his command, a pair of strong hands pushed both forward. Glancing over her shoulders, Gwen discovered the dragon gone. In its place stood an even more towering drake warrior, his savage crest the exact image of the head of the dragon who had brought them here.

"Move . . ." he ordered, eyes flaring red.

Ssssurak waved one hand over the palm of the other. A small, blue pyramid about the size of an acorn materialized in the palm. A faint light emanated from it.

"I will lead," the servitor declared.

With Ssssurak ahead and the warrior behind, the four entered a darkened passage at the deep end of the cave. No sooner had the servitor stepped inside, then the light from the pyramid immediately increased, filling the area with blue-tinted illumination.

A slight sound from Yssa made Gwen glance the other's way. The half-drake had a determined look in her eye and her expression tensed even as the enchantress watched.

With a flickering frown, Gwen tried to warn her not to try anything. The power of the Dragon King prevailed here. Gwen could feel her abilities being muted by his spellwork. Did Yssa think that she could fare any better?

Evidently she did, for in the next second the Green Dragon's daughter threw herself back into the unsuspecting guard. Physically, he should have been no more affected than if a gnat had collided with him, but an orange aura flared to life as Yssa struck the giant and both of them went flying.

The drake hit one of the walls, bounced off of it, then rammed into the other. The collisions were hardly chance; Gwen sensed Yssa's hand in each harsh crash.

Behind the enchantress, Ssssurak hissed. He closed his hand tight, which would have plunged the passage into darkness save for Yssa's aura. Gwen turned on the servitor, but somehow despite his close proximity, he had become invisible to her.

Yssa seized Gwen by the hand. "Hurry!"

Gwen did not argue. Despite her own handicap, Yssa's skills seemed entirely untouched. The enchantress belatedly thought of the younger woman's origins. Perhaps both Gwen and the Dragon King had underestimated what a cross between human and drake might be capable. Still, it seemed odd that the Storm Lord would not take that consideration in mind.

They ran back along the corridor, racing down the dark passage toward freedom. However, it took Gwen only a few seconds to realize that they should be far, far closer to the exit than they were. Ssssurak had barely led them into it before Yssa had acted.

"Wait!" she called. "Yssa! We're being led!"

Her companion stumbled to a halt, but by then it was already too late. A blinding light assailed them from both directions. Gwen and Yssa threw themselves against one another for protection.

And as the light died, the voice that Gwen had dreaded to hear echoed loud.

"Welcome, welcome, my chosen . . ."

The corridor vanished. Gwen and Yssa now stood in the center of a looming cavern with walls of black onyx. Within the onyx, the primal fury of the storm played itself out over and over. The result was a violent, constantly shifting light that forced both to shield their eyes in order to focus on the massive figure seated above them.

Gwen had confronted several of the Dragon Kings over her life, had even seen the old Emperor at his height, but the Storm Lord dwarfed them all. Standing, he would have been eight, nine feet high, not even including the wide, menacing crest that surely added another three feet.

He smiled, revealing his sharp, reptilian teeth, and indicated with one broad finger that they should come closer.

The two women suddenly discovered themselves within only a few yards of the high stone dais upon which the gray marble throne had been set. With only that single gesture, the drake lord had transported them from one end of the chamber to the other.

"Yes, we have chosen well . . ." He leaned back, red, forked tongue flickering. "All that remains now is to see which one of you will succeed in slaying the other . . ."

# VI

AS A CHILD, Aurim had enjoyed being frightened. He had constantly encouraged his father, the Lord Gryphon, and even Darkhorse, to tell him stories that would fill him with delightful fear. He always knew that there were happy endings to the stories, but that made the images of nasty Dragon Kings, cunning Seekers, and brutish Quel no less spine-tingling.

But nothing had stirred him so much as tales involving the enigmatic warlock, Shade.

Yet, Shade was supposed to be dead. His father said so, Lord Gryphon said so, and even Darkhorse had finally, after years, reluctantly agreed. Still, the hooded sorcerer with the murky face whose curse constantly sent him swinging from good to evil and back again had become for Aurim a symbol of the unknown, the unexpected.

Now the unknown stared him in the face . . . so to speak.

Shade slowly and calmly led him through the rain-drenched landscape, moving as if Yssa would be just over the hill and not, as the golden-haired wizard suspected, miles away. The hooded figure appeared to be looking for something, but just what that something was he had so far not said to either Aurim or his other self.

This Shade was far different from the one in the stories. He did not appear either good or evil, but trapped somewhere in the middle for the time being. Aurim did not like traveling with him, but if he could find Yssa, that was all that mattered.

"We were dead," rambled Shade not for the first time. "So dead. Peacefully dead." He shifted his head to the left. "And we were quite furious when we no longer were."

Aurim noted the rising bitterness in the tone, the first emotion he had heard from his dire companion. He wisely kept silent, knowing that Shade would continue on.

The hood turned right. "I remember . . . I remember her name was Sharissa . . ."

To the left. "No . . . her name was Galani . . ."

To the center. "And she thought she could help me . . ."

He grew silent for a time, now and then inspecting various bits of the land around them. Aurim pondered the names, but they meant nothing to him. His sister and father had a better knowledge of the history of the Dragonrealm; perhaps they would have made more sense of the ramblings.

Shade paused without warning, nearly causing Aurim, who hunkered low in his cloak since he dared not cast a spell, to collide with him. The hooded sorcerer leaned down. "Aaah . . . Here it is . . ."

He pulled up what at first Aurim thought a peculiar white stone. Only when the gloved hand thrust it closer did he realize that it was more.

A bone fragment.

"I knew it had to be near . . ."

A shift to the right. "Of course it would be near! We're the reason it's here in the first place!"

Shade leaned over again, digging into the wet soil with gloves that got neither moist nor muddy. Within seconds, he had removed another, larger object from the earth.

A skull.

Overcoming his initial dismay, Aurim studied the skull. The jaw bone was missing, but enough remained identifiable. What he had at first taken for a small dragon was, in fact, something quite the opposite. Instead of the broad, toothed muzzle of a reptilian creature, this had a squat, almost noseless appearance that reminded the young wizard in some ways of a rodent whose muzzle had been crushed.

Shade set the mud-covered cranium on the ground, then drew with his finger a circle around it. A faint, sickly green aura arose from the circle, swiftly enveloping the skull.

"They will be warned, but it doesn't matter," the warlock commented.

Aurim paid scant attention to the cryptic statement, his gaze fixed on the astonishing display before him. As the aura covered the skull, the latter began to rise from the ground. However, no longer did it lack a lower jaw. Instead, a new one composed entirely of the green glow filled the empty space. As the skull continued to rise, other magical bones rapidly replaced those missing, building the entire macabre structure a piece at a time.

The creature, whatever it was, had surely been grotesque in life if this unearthly skeleton was any indication. It towered over the pair and would have stood even taller if not for the fact that it seemed designed to lean forward at almost a right angle. The legs bent as if the creature had to constantly run or else fall. Odd bones that Aurim eventually recognized as forming wings stretched forth from the sides, ending in horrific, clawed appendages capable of grasping or tearing a victim apart. Had someone taken the worst from a human and bat, it surely would have resembled something akin to how this horror had looked when flesh had covered it.

When the skeleton was complete, the undead creature bent low and opened its mouth as if to make some sound, but only the wind whistling through its naked bones reached Aurim's ears.

"The Necri will take us where we need to go."

"Necri?" The word sounded vaguely familiar, like something out of the old journals his father kept.

"It served the Lords of the Dead," Shade remarked offhandedly. His head shifted to the right. "And once sought to serve us to our cousins . . ."

*The Lords of the Dead. . . .* What had his desire to see Yssa tossed both her and Aurim into? He recognized *that* name, of course. Some saw the Lords of the Dead as the gods of the underworld, but they were both more and less than that. Darkhorse explained them as ageless necromancers seeking dominion over the world of the living by commanding the plane of the dead. However, they were not immortal. They could be destroyed, if only at great cost.

It did not surprise Aurim that Shade and they had crossed paths, even battled against one another, for surely he was a prize they desired to add to their macabre collection.

But—had the warlock just said that he and they were . . . *cousins?*

Shade gestured to the glowing skeleton. The Necri flapped its empty wings, ascending into the air. It fluttered around the pair once, then came down behind them.

Long, splayed feet with huge, savage claws cautiously seized the two around the waist and drew them up.

They flew high into the dark heavens, the fleshless creature somehow able to carry both with ease despite a lack of any muscle or membrane in its wings. The monstrous feet kept Aurim and Shade almost completely vertical, making the flight only somewhat harrowing.

As unnerving as both the journey and those who accompanied him made the wizard, Aurim reminded himself that they brought him closer to Yssa. In the end, she was all that mattered. It had been by his entreaties that she had agreed to cross the border into Wenslis. What a fool he had been to think that even they could keep their clandestine meetings hidden from the Dragon King. His parents had always warned him that the Storm Lord watched *everything* that went on in his realm.

That thought made Aurim frown. If so, then the drake should have even known about Shade's presence . . . which made it curious that he had evidently done nothing about the warlock.

But then, could even a Dragon King plan for *Shade?*

"AND WHY WOULD we slay one another, especially for you?" Gwen asked defiantly. She had reached her limits. Even despite the Dragon King's obviously threatening presence, the enchantress could not believe his audacity.

"Because we wish it so," the reptilian figure boomed. "Because the consort of so glorious a being as us must be the most powerful, most capable." The Storm Lord steepled his fingers. "And because if you do not, we will make you fight, anyway."

Yssa eyed him contemptuously. "I will never fight for the right to be yours."

The arms of the Dragon King's throne suddenly broke free, seizing the Storm Lord in a suffocating grip. The back of the throne stretched high, then folded over as if to swallow the master of Wenslis.

A black aura immediately surrounded the drake. Without the slightest effort, the Storm Lord rose, the arms pinning him cracking to pieces. The back of the throne instantly solidified, then retracted to its original state.

Gwen frowned, but not only because of the failure of Yssa's spell. When the aura had formed around the Storm Lord, the enchantress had sensed a peculiar—and yet somehow familiar—style of sorcery, one she had never noticed used by any previous Dragon King.

"You prove yourself worthy," the Storm Lord told the Green Dragon's daughter as if nothing had happened. "It is time to begin."

He raised his hands palm up and lightning crackled between them. Twin bolts shot forth, striking both women in the head. Gwen expected pain, but instead a frightening numbness took over her body—and once again she sensed something different about this Dragon King's spellwork.

Suddenly she found herself against her will turning toward Yssa—who already faced her. The half-drake's expression was emotionless save for her eyes, which radiated an intense apprehension that matched Gwen's own.

The enchantress's body moved. Gwen felt the summoning of power even though she herself had attempted no such thing. Across from her, Yssa radiated raw magical energy, but her eyes still held the same anxiety.

"Memory will serve," the Storm Dragon informed the two unwilling combatants. He almost seemed distracted, as if he had other, more significant matters to which to attend. "Memory will guide. Your bodies will recall what they must, when they must. They will determine your fates."

Gwen's hands suddenly clapped together.

From them came a swarm of black, buzzing insects that immediately encircled Yssa. They bit into her flesh, tore the skin free.

But despite the ordeal, Yssa quickly countered. A fearsome wind tossed the swarm about, then fiercely slapped them against one wall of the immense cavern. As the dead insects dropped in clusters, the same wind tore free a part of that wall and sent it hurtling at the enchantress.

Gwen's left hand made a cutting motion. As if tossed into some vast invisible grinder, the huge chunk of stone vaporized bit by bit as it neared her. In seconds, all that remained was a sizable pile of dust.

But Gwen leaned forward and, borrowing from Yssa, pursed her lips and blew. The dust poured over the younger spellcaster, choking her.

*This must stop! I'm sure to kill her!* Yssa might have her own astonishing skills, but Gwen had the experience of two centuries, in which time she had been trained by both the Green Dragon and Nathan Bedlam, Aurim's great-grandfather, and done battle alongside the Dragon Masters. Yssa had not lived long enough to experience all she had and that, in the end, would surely be the deciding factor.

She fought against the Storm Lord's will, refusing to become his tool of death. Gwen felt his control over her slip ever so slightly. The spell her body had been about to cast dissipated before it could harm Yssa. The enchantress managed a slight smile of triumph—

But in battling the Dragon King, she left herself open to the other sorceress. A chilling cold swept over Gwen. Her movements slowed to a halt and even the blood in her veins felt as if it had begun to freeze. She opened her mouth to scream—and it remained caught in that agonizing position.

Yssa blinked as if waking, then dropped to her knees in exhaustion.

Eyes wide, she stared into Gwen's own. Unable to move, the cold sapping her will further, Gwen could say nothing to assuage the horrendous guilt she read in the other's gaze. Yssa had only done what she had because the Storm Dragon had forced her to, but it made the outcome no less monstrous. With each passing second it proved more of a strain for Gwen to remain conscious. She was well aware, though, of what would happen when the cold finally took her. There would be no waking, no life. Yssa's spell would turn her literally to ice.

"How interesting," remarked the Storm Lord, approaching Gwen. "An unexpected outcome. We thought surely that the Lady of the Amber would prevail . . ." He touched Gwen on the chin, the arm. "Interesting."

Even despite her mental struggles, the enchantress could not help meeting his fiery gaze—and in that moment she had the odd sense that she stared at someone other than the Storm Lord.

But the Dragon King turned away before she could discover more. At his unspoken command, Yssa rose and went to his side. Yssa took his arm in her own, holding him as one would hold the arm of a mate.

Her eyes continued to radiate horror over what she had accomplished.

The Dragon King stared again at Gwen. "Now we shall see what the bait draws . . ."

And with that peculiar comment, he led Yssa away, leaving the enchantress standing helpless, her thoughts growing hazier . . . and her death growing nearer.

# VII

THREE PEAKS STOOD shrouded in the stormy sky. Aurim did not have to ask if he and Shade closed in on their destination, for he easily sensed the dark power emanating from the jagged mountains. If this was not the stronghold of the Dragon King, he could not imagine another.

"Down," the hooded figure quietly commanded. The skeleton immediately began its descent, flapping its useless wings as if they actually held air.

"Is it safe to land so near the lair?" objected Aurim.

"It's where we have to go."

For Shade, this settled everything. For his anxious companion, however, such a frontal assault presaged disaster.

And, seconds later, it seemed Aurim's fears proved well-grounded. From atop one of the two peaks flanking the largest, a huge, gray dragon took to the sky. It required little imagination to figure out exactly where the behemoth headed.

As the dragon approached, Aurim readied a spell. Yet, before he could cast it, the hooded warlock waved his hand in a circular motion.

Without hesitation, the dragon suddenly veered upward, passing by the two without noticing them. The behemoth continued on, disappearing into the black clouds.

"Be prepared," Shade told him calmly, as if the threat that they had just faced had not existed. "We land in moments."

With astonishing grace considering its fleshless condition, the Necri skeleton delicately deposited them feet first on the rocky ground. The moment it had done so, the batlike creature collapsed into a cluttered pile, the magically created bones vanishing even as they dropped. The skull rolled a few feet away, then clattered to a halt. The eye holes seemed to stare resentfully at the pair.

"Come," Shade urged a still-staring Aurim.

A flash of lightning illuminated the area as they came within sight of the lair. The dragon might have left, but that did not mean that the way was unguarded. Along the side of the mountain, armed sentinels watched from various points. Most wore the broad-rimmed armor of Wenslis, but Aurim noted a few drake warriors among them, no doubt the commanders. Drakes were not so numerous as humans and so Dragon Kings often had to make use of the very race that they distrusted most.

But Shade continued on as if entirely unconcerned about the guards. Aurim had no choice but to follow and hope that his disconcerting associate knew what he did.

Two human soldiers thrust out their spears in what at first appeared warning to the newcomers. Yet, as Aurim watched, the guards separated, their gazes sweeping warily over the vicinity and not once fixing on the duo. One guard came within arm's reach of the wizard, his bearded, scarred face as brutal as that of a drake. The wide brim of his helmet kept most of the rain from his eyes, but still he did not notice the blond figure so near.

Without a word, Shade and Aurim walked past the soldiers, ascending the path to the lair.

The way up was both the longest and shortest trek that Aurim Bedlam had ever taken. Each step he expected either a horde of guards, a dragon, or, worst of all, the Storm Lord, to fall upon them. Yet, at the same time, he moved with impatience, knowing that within he would find Yssa.

At the mouth of the cave system, Shade for the first time paused.

"He is within," the hood announced with a turn to the left.

"Of course," he replied to himself with a look to the right.

Aurim prepared himself. He, too, could sense the overwhelming force that was the Dragon King. If he had to face the Storm Lord to rescue Yssa, then so be it. His father had confronted the dread Toma, a far worse dragon than any, and had emerged victorious. Aurim was well aware that, if he kept his focus, his abilities had the potential to dwarf even those of his father. With Shade beside him, surely even this Dragon King would fall.

They continued past unsuspecting guards and even the grotesque, bestial lesser drakes, cousins of the dragons whom the latter used as mounts when in their warrior forms. The lesser drakes sniffed the air as they passed, but even the beasts did not truly realize their presence.

Deeper and deeper into the cavern system they went. The protection spell that Shade had surrounded them with had enabled them to see despite the storm and now it worked against the darkness of the lair. Aurim's confidence grew as they walked. No threat had so far reared its ugly head. Perhaps with the warlock so near, even the Dragon King would not notice them.

Then, without warning, they stepped into what could only be the Storm Lord's sanctum. The chamber was the largest and well-adapted for the movements of a full-grown dragon. The walls were of a peculiar onyx within which miniature storms raged. At the far end, a huge dais consisting of three great steps led up to a magnificently carved if oddly damaged throne.

Then Aurim sensed another presence, one whose nearness so startled him that he quickly looked around the vast chamber. To the side he eventually noticed what at first he took for a statue . . . until he saw who it resembled.

"Mother?" For the moment, all thought of Yssa fell to the wayside as Aurim rushed toward the figure. Surely he was overreacting; surely there was a good reason why the Storm Lord would have a statue of his mother here.

But as he approached, the wizard more and more sensed her so-familiar presence. He could have mistaken it no more than he could have his own.

"By the Manor!" Aurim gasped, putting a hand to her cheek and discovering only then that it was made of ice . . . rapidly melting ice.

And as it melted, so, too, would his mother.

She still lived, that much the wizard could feel, but for how long, he could not say. Aurim immediately began delving into the spellwork, seeking a way of unbinding it quickly. The casting had been done in a manner not at all like he had been taught and yet it had a familiar feel. Almost it reminded him of—of *Yssa?*

He tried not to think about why she would do such a horrific thing to his mother, whom he knew Yssa respected greatly and wished would come to accept their pairing. Instead, Aurim continued to search for the point of focus, the place where he could make the entire spell unravel.

So caught up was he in his task that he at first did not notice that someone watched him from another shadowed corner of the cavern. Only when the stare finally burned into him did Aurim gaze up to discover a figure literally perched on the wall.

A figure that was none other than *Shade*.

Aurim quickly glanced over his shoulder . . . and saw his companion just turning to look at him.

The hooded immediately shifted, tipping to the right as the warlock clearly looked *past* the young wizard . . . and at *himself.*

There were *two* Shades?

"We expected you," said the one who had accompanied Aurim. "We felt you."

"I sensed you in turn," remarked the figure on the wall with the same bland tone. The hood shifted so as to eye Aurim again. "She's mine."

"And he's ours . . ." said the wizard's Shade. "He knows us. He can make us whole, make us the original . . ."

"She could do the same for me," the other replied. "But I got curious as to what it would be like to feel her emotions as her life melted away."

Aurim's expression darkened. "That's monstrous!"

"Is it? I suppose it is . . ." The Shade on the wall rubbed his indistinct chin in thought, then nodded almost eagerly. "Yes! You're right! Monstrous! I've chosen, then!"

"Not fair!" snarled Aurim's Shade without warning. With a tilt of his head to the right, he added, "Not fair at all! We want to be the original!"

"But I'm ahead in the game! I've chosen the path! All I need is a name now . . ."

As fearful as he was about losing his mother, Aurim could not help but listen to the rantings of the pair, especially the one on the wall. He knew enough about the legend of the warlock to understand what it meant if this one chose a name.

It mean that the second Shade also knew whether he followed darkness or light.

"I have it . . ." The Shade on the wall spread his cloak wide. He literally stood on the onyx as if it were the floor. With a voice full of triumph and glee, he declared, "Call me Valac . . . this time . . ."

And without warning, without reason—but with only the flick of a finger—he created a ring of flame around Aurim's mother.

With a cry, the wizard fell back. Smoke rose from his garments and his right hand stung. He saw a covering of moisture form over his mother and droplets of water fell to the floor.

"No!" Powered by his emotions, a fierce wind blew over the fire, dousing it completely. Aurim seized his mother before her slippery figure could topple over. He looked up at the Shade on the wall, prepared to deflect whatever barbaric attack this newly evil figure next cast.

But there stood another between them. The first Shade faced himself, the two reminding Aurim in some way like a pair of children bickering over who was most favored.

"We want your name! Give it to us!"

"No! It's mine!" retorted the one above. "I'm whole now . . . I'm Shade!"

"No! We are! We deserve it! We make our choice . . . we'll help them! Be their friends!"

"You've no name, though! I've a name! I'm Valac!"

Time was running out for Aurim's mother, but he dared not focus on her. He watched his own Shade, who seemed to hesitate each time the other shouted his new name.

His name . . .

Aurim ran through his memory, picked the first name that came to mind. "I've got a better name for you!"

His Shade looked back at him. "A name? A better one?"

"Nathan."

"Nathan . . ." For just a moment, the face almost—but not quite—came into focus as the hooded figure tasted Aurim's choice. "Nathan . . ."

"You know the name. You know the strength of it."

"We—I—remember Nathan . . ." Shade seemed to swell. He faced his other self, who now retreated back somewhat under the sudden change in his counterpart. "Call me Nathan," he told the one on the wall. "This time . . ."

Well aware that the original Shade had known his great-grandfather, had even fought alongside him against the Dragon Kings during the Turning War, Aurim had gifted his Shade with the use of that name. He had counted on the hooded warlock to recall what Nathan had stood for and take that to heart.

Where one Shade had chosen evil, he hoped the latter would stay securely with good.

"No!" roared Valac. "I'm Shade! I'm the original! I chose first!"

Nathan stepped toward him. "I chose better . . . and I will protect my friends!"

Raw energy swirled around both cloaked forms. Aurim pulled his mother away from the pair. He delved back into the spell keeping her frozen and, perhaps because he now no longer had to concern himself with the Shades' argument, found the key.

His own spell acted instantaneously. His mother's body heated up and the layer of ice surrounding her melted in one quick rush that left a puddle on the stone floor. Gwen gasped and slumped in his arms, her hair clinging to her head.

She coughed twice, then managed to look up at him. "A-Aurim . . ."

"Easy, Mother! It's all right . . ."

"No . . . Aurim . . . Yssa—"

He steeled himself. "I don't know why she did this to you, but—"

"No!" Gwen shook her head. "Listen! The Storm Dragon is responsible! She couldn't help herself!"

As relieved as Aurim was to hear that, he could not concern himself with it now. Despite her attempts to look stronger, Aurim could tell that she could barely stand, much less cast a spell. It would be up to him to lead them from this place.

Then . . . then he could come back for Yssa.

But his mother seemed to read his thoughts. "Forget me, Aurim! I'll be fine! Go after Yssa! She's with him . . . and . . . and Aurim . . . there's something wrong . . . he's hiding a secret, I think . . ."

Aurim swallowed, barely hearing the rest of what Gwen had said. The Storm Lord had Yssa. Aurim stood there, torn between two courses of action. His mother needed him—but so, clearly, did the woman he loved.

Just then, a fearsome burst of golden energy sent Aurim and his mother rolling away. The two Shades had finally attacked one another. They stood outlined within that terrible burst, neither seeming at all affected by the awesome forces unleashed.

"What's happening?" Gwen managed, at last staring at the identical figures. "There are—there are *two* of him!"

"I don't know . . . hasn't this happened?"

"Never! There's only ever been one Shade . . . and that's been more than enough . . ."

Whatever the cause for the creation of the two Shades, they clearly had an utter hatred of one another. They tore free pieces of the cavern and tossed them at will at each other. They summoned energy and transformed it into monstrous mouths or slashing blades flying through the air. They cast one vile attack after another, unleashing power that would have slain any other creature a hundred times over.

But not once did either manage so much as a scratch.

Their power was so equal, their minds so identical, that they knew how to defend against each assault before it could cause any harm. The duel took on an almost comic aspect as each fruitlessly sought to slay the other to prove that they were the one and original Shade.

The chamber shook with each successive attack. Aurim wondered how the Dragon King could have possibly not noticed what was happening within his very citadel—and then realized that he surely had.

Which meant that they were all in much, much more danger than they had imagined.

"Mother, do you think that you can cast any sort of spell to shield yourself from danger?"

"I faced the Dragon Kings with your great-grandfather, Aurim. He showed me many tricks. I'll be fine. You go after her . . . but be careful!"

Aurim nodded. "He has to have been watching us. He must be letting everything play out."

"I know, Aurim. I've been trying to sense him, but he's kept himself shielded. Be wary, he's very cunning . . . and . . . and I can't explain it, but there's definitely something different about him, almost as if he's—" she shook her head. "Never mind. Just be careful."

"Don't worry, Mother. You just take care of yourself. I'll hurry."

"Stay linked to me this time, my son."

"As you wish." Aurim stepped away from her. Gwendolyn Bedlam drew a circle over her head. As she did, an emerald shield formed there. The enchantress pointed down with her finger and the shield followed, draping her from head to toe. Once the shield touched the floor, Gwen nodded to her son.

Aurim concentrated. The Dragon King might have shielded his presence, but had he done so for one that the wizard knew almost as good as his own family—and in some ways better?

*Yssa . . . where are you?*

At first Aurim felt nothing, but then, at the very edge of perception, he noticed a familiar trace. He clung to that trace, focusing his mind on it with all his will.

And then Aurim transported himself to its source. As he materialized, he immediately sensed the inhuman presence of the Dragon King in the shadows behind him. Without hesitation, the wizard cast a potent spell and hurtled it toward the direction he had noted the menace.

"No, Aurim, no!" called a feminine voice near him.

A tremendous force struck him hard. The wizard flew across the darkened chamber, smashing against what could only be one of the rocky walls. Tumbling to the floor, he rolled back to where he had first materialized, his entire body numb from pain.

Soft hands immediately touched his head, his face, and he heard Yssa speaking, but the words did not penetrate.

Yet, the voice of another had no difficulty piercing the fog.

"Welcome, Bedlam. I am pleased you prove yourself predictable. I am pleased that *all* of you have have acted so predictably."

It was not the voice he had expected. Forcing his head up, Aurim looked past Yssa to where a fiery light now illuminated the other end of the chamber.

The dragon dwarfed even those that Aurim had seen outside. A huge crest of jagged scale coursed down from his forehead to the tip of his tail. He was of an iridescent gray and silver and his unblinking eyes glowed a bright red, like the setting sun. Teeth taller than the wizard filled a maw capable of devouring a score of Aurims with a single snap.

A dark blue aura crackled around the Storm Lord and even from where he stood the blond spellcaster could sense the powerful forces emanating out from the Dragon King. Every bit of the tempest that covered Wenslis originated from the awesome power of its master.

A pedestal as high as the wizard's waist stood before the leviathan. Upon it, a black onyx crystal as large as Aurim's throbbing head glowed. In it, he could just make out the two Shades in mortal combat.

Aurim glanced from the crystal back to the Dragon King. He stared defiantly into the drake's eyes—and only then did he realize that they not only did not stare back, but they seemed empty, unfocused. The Storm Lord appeared utterly lost within himself, almost as if he were in a trance or even dreaming.

"He sleeps," said the voice that had welcomed him. "I give him his dreams of godhood and he sleeps and savors it while I deal with my own destiny."

Then Aurim noticed at last the smaller figure standing to the left of the gargantuan dragon, a figure whose mere presence answered much but created a host of new questions as well.

A third *Shade* . . .

# VIII

AS HER SON vanished, Gwen tried desperately to concentrate on the situation. Something was indeed terribly wrong. There was no reason that the Storm Lord would let this struggle go on in his own sanctum unless it served his purpose.

But what?

Something about the Dragon King himself still bothered her. Gwen had faced many of his kind, but now and then this drake lord spoke and acted different. Once in awhile, he sounded less a Dragon King and more—more human?

Gwen's eyes widened and her troubled gaze returned to the twin figures and their powerful if so far fruitless battle. The enchantress studied them, thought about what they represented—and suddenly a question that held the potential to answer everything reared its monstrous head.

How many more Shades *were* there?

"CALL ME MORDRYN . . . this time," the third Shade said with a cursory bow.

Aurim watched the hooded form with narrowed eyes. He sensed a difference in this variation. This Shade was more confident, more complete. He had known for quite some time what course he followed and what name he chose for himself.

"How long?" the wizard asked, gaze flickering to the dragon. The Storm Dragon's mouth curled up slightly at the end, as if he enjoyed his dream. "How long have you been here?"

"Since my . . . death," the murky figure replied. A hint of bitterness suddenly tinged his words. "I thought I had finally passed beyond, finally had rest . . . but instead I had only come *home.*" He stretched forth his arms to take in the entire chamber. "This is where it all went awry . . . this is where I tried for the last time to make the spell right . . . and instead the foul land cursed me for my defiance."

"But Darkhorse saw you die! Saw you dissipate—"

Shade lowered his arms. The hooded face somehow managed to radiate frustration. "And I regenerated here, weak, utterly confused . . . and discovered that my fate had only worsened."

Contrary to what he had hoped, the curse had not been lifted. Instead, it had been altered in a manner most diabolical. Where once there had been one Shade who fought for his identity, who fought to become truly human, truly one being—there were now several, all scattered far from one another.

The warlock touched the onyx crystal almost reverently. "This is how the lord of Wenslis wields such power. It draws from the earth, sun, and moons. It feeds him constantly—but now it also feeds me." He caressed the stone, then glanced back at the dreaming Dragon King. "I was sliced to so many shadows . . . *all* of whom were without purpose, without focus . . . but when *I* discovered his secret, I discovered it also the way to become whole again . . ." The warlock laughed, a harsh sound. "I took it from him so easily! The Storm Lord! So distracted by his visions of grandeur, of omnipotence, that he fell prey to a simple spell any apprentice could have cast! I caught him slumbering, dreaming of his perfection . . . and I simply made that dream go on and on and on . . ."

To fool the Dragon King's subjects afterward had been no trouble whatsoever. Drake or human, they feared their master and knew his reclusive ways. "A mere illusion," Shade added, briefly flickering to the form of his spellbound host. "A conjurer's trick."

"But why take us, then?" Aurim asked standing straight. "Why bring us into this?"

Despite the fact that what little he could see of Shade's face was a blur, the wizard thought he noticed the hooded figure scowl. "Even in dreaming, the Storm Lord is strong. He is still the storm over this realm and as it, he sensed you . . . first you pair, then your mother, come to find you. For the first time, it almost woke him . . . but I acted fast enough, playing into his dream and deepening his trance further to make certain that it would not happen again. I let all his desires play out." He nodded toward Yssa. "Even his absurd interest in finding a mate befitting his 'godliness'."

"And the other Shades? Why did one come to us, another to my mother? How does that work in your plans?"

"Pure coincidence. Nothing more. A fortuitous bit of luck, that is all."

But Shade said it so quickly that Aurim suspected otherwise. His other selves had been drawn to the outsiders, but for what reason, clearly even the warlock did not know. That gave the wizard hope, for it showed that this Shade did not entirely command the situation. It might yet be possible to free them from his grasp.

The onyx crystal suddenly flared. Shade leaned over it, his body radiating anticipation. "Yes!"

Aurim could not help but also look into it . . . and what he saw filled him with apprehension. The duel finally had a victor. Even as they watched, one of the other Shades shrieked. He staggered forward and as he did, his legs, his arms—everything—*crumbled* as if made of loose sand. The hapless figure spilled across the ground, leaving nothing but a pile of dust to mark his passing.

The second Shade dropped down on one knee, clearly exhausted by his effort. Whether he was Nathan or Valac, Aurim could not say. The pair had moved about so much that it was impossible to even guess.

But who had triumphed did not long matter. Taking advantage of the winner's exhaustion, the third Shade touched the top of the crystal—and suddenly his counterpart within twisted, turned. With a cry, he became as clay, folded together over and over until at last nothing, absolutely nothing, remained.

Aurim blanched. Yssa clung to him, her fingers digging painfully into the wizard's arm.

Shade stretched his arms back. He shimmered, seemed to momentarily swell—then suddenly reverted back to what he had been.

"They are returned to me," he uttered. "They are part of me again . . ."

Seizing the moment, Aurim took advantage of the distraction, casting a spell with which he intended to slay the warlock. Even if Shade's curse resurrected him again, he would surely be much less of a threat than now.

"No, Aurim!" Yssa shook him hard, shattering his concentration. "Didn't you notice before? You attack him and the attack comes back at you! Think!"

Aurim gasped for breath as the effort to disperse the energy he had summoned overwhelmed him. He remembered the horrific force that had struck him—the same spell he had been casting then. The wizard had nearly slain himself.

Shade laughed. "The work of the Storm Lord, I will admit, young Aurim. A so-clever god, wouldn't you say? But too clever for himself, in the end." The warlock touched the crystal and Aurim felt a sudden heat wash over him. "And that will end any other spells from you whatsoever." He turned toward a passage to his left. In the voice that passed for the Storm Lord's, he commanded, "Come!"

From the corridor rushed in several drake warriors, the servitor Ssssurak at their head.

"My lord," he murmured, bowing low to Shade. "Forgive us! We waited for your summons—"

"We are not interested in your excuses," the warlock replied. None of the drakes appeared to notice the gargantuan form to their side. In their eyes and ears, Shade was the Storm Dragon. "Secure them. I will deal with both at my leisure."

"Yes, my lord."

Aurim thought of telling the drakes that they were being manipulated, but he knew that they would never believe him. As the towering warriors surrounded them, the wizard prepared to fight them with his hands. He knew that once they were bound, they would have no hope of escape.

Ssssurak hissed in derision as Aurim prepared his futile stand. Shade, attention fixed on the onyx crystal, paid the spellcaster no mind. He seemed to be searching for something within.

The foremost warrior reached for Aurim. The wizard raised his fist.

And then a voice in Aurim's head said, *Do nothing.*

# IX

THEY WERE DEAD and their deaths verified to Gwen her suspicions. The victor had no sooner triumphed then he, in turn, had been horribly slain. True, it could have been the work of the Storm Lord, but the enchantress was instead certain that Shade had died at the hands of none other than himself.

And moments later, she had had her worst fears verified by her link to Aurim. Gwen had heard everything he had heard, felt every anxiety. They had all been fooled by this other version of the warlock, who clearly had chosen the path of darkness to follow.

Now Aurim and Yssa were prisoners and Gwen, despite the opportunity to catch her breath, hardly had the might to take on the shadowy warlock.

But she had to.

Summoning her strength, she rose. The spell used to protect her from the battle faded away. Gwen steeled herself, then tried to concentrate on her son.

Her legs gave out. She toppled over.

Hands caught her. A voice in her ears whispered, "I have you. Tell your son to do nothing."

"But—"

"Do nothing, I said . . . if you want him to live."

She did as she was bade, relaying the short message. When she had done so, the enchantress looked up at her rescuer.

"Now," said Shade, his murky features possibly smiling slightly. "What would make the Storm Lord so angry that he would wake up?"

THE FEARSOME TEMPEST spread across the entire continent, drowning the Dragonrealm. It spread west, across the Seas of Andramacus, and east, reaching the former empire of the Aramites.

And all of it was the Storm Dragon, power incarnate, a living god.

Lightning struck a thousand times in a thousand places. The puny mortal creatures inhabiting the lands scurried in fear or knelt down in prayer to him. Even the other Dragon Kings bent their massive heads low, stretched forth their necks . . . all to prove their loyalty.

The world belonged to him and rightly so. His magnificence spread over the heavens. He *was* the world . . .

But something suddenly disturbed his pleasure. It started as a tiny nagging sound in his ears, a buzzing like a fly. Gradually it became a voice, a taunting voice.

*The Storm Lord! So distracted by his visions of grandeur, of omnipotence, that he fell prey to a simple spell any apprentice could have cast! I caught him slumbering, dreaming of his perfection . . . and I simply made that dream go on and on and on . . .*

What feeble creature dared speak so about he who moved the skies at will? In the blink of an eye, the Storm Dragon searched the world over, but failed to find the blasphemer.

*A so-clever god, wouldn't you say? But too clever for himself, in the end.*

Someone mocked him and he could not find the culprit. The Storm Dragon flew into a rage. Hurricanes swept over Irillian by the Sea, inundating the realm of the Blue Dragon. Floodwaters poured into the bowl-shaped region housing the kingdom of Zuu, sweeping away its inhabitants. Lightning ripped into Penacles, City of Knowledge, turning the kingdom of the Gryphon into one huge fire . . .

But all this brought the Dragon King no closer to discovering the heretic.

Determined to find him, the behemoth drew within him his power. Raging tempests all over the Dragonrealm dissipated instantly. The Storm Lord focused all his omnipotent will on the one task; he *would* find the knave.

Oddly, the more he withdrew into himself, the more it seemed that the cause of his fury lay in his own mind. He almost shook off the absurd notion, but again the voice taunted him.

*See how he sleeps? A puppet with his own puppet world, playing the game I desire . . .*

Fueled yet again by the sacrilegious words, the Dragon King confronted some barrier in his own thoughts. Whoever spoke out against their god thought to shield themselves from his wrath! With a silent roar, the Storm Lord threw his full ferocity at the invisible barrier within—

And woke up.

He no longer hovered over the world, as much a part of the heavens as the clouds or sun. Instead, he lay cramped in the back of one of his personal chambers and the worse part of it was that other, lesser creatures invaded the sanctity of his domain. The Storm Lord had every intention of punishing all of them for their audacity—until he heard again the voice he had already grown to hate.

"You may take them away, now." It belonged to a tiny, cloth-covered figure that stirred some vague memory. The Dragon King did not bother to delve into that memory, for his entire mind suddenly fixated on the fact that, not only was this the one who mocked him, but now that very same creature pretended to *be* him.

No greater offense could there be in the history of the world.

The Storm Lord let out a roar of outrage—

**THE DRAGON KING'S** fury rocked the entire cavern complex, sending bits of the ceiling dropping on those below. Yssa pulled Aurim back as one large piece struck the floor just where the wizard had been standing.

The drakes stumbled away, startled more by the monstrous, unexpected roar than the collapsing ceiling. Ssssurak looked around in open panic—and was the first to see the awakening behemoth.

"M-my lord?" he blurted, looking from the Storm Dragon to Shade and back again.

"Blasphemy!" roared the scaly tyrant, ignoring his confused servants. All that existed for him was the one who had dared the unthinkable. "You will be punished for this sacrilege, mortal!"

The onyx stone crackled with energy. A monstrous wind assailed not only Shade, but everyone near him. Huge drake warriors flew against the walls. Ssssurak clutched at Aurim, but the wind took him before he could grab hold. He struck the rock face with a harsh crack, then tumbled to the ground.

Aurim expected both him and Yssa to be tossed after the drakes, but an emerald shield surrounded them, reducing the Storm Lord's fury to a slight breeze. He looked in surprise at Yssa, whose face was filled with strain. The wizard realized that, despite the warlock's spell, her mixed heritage had enabled her to do what Aurim could not.

Despite the Storm Lord's horrific assault, Shade stood untouched. The warlock's cloak did not even ruffle in the wind.

Behind Shade, the onyx crystal flared again—and the cavern walls around the dragon melted, pouring over the leviathan like hot lava. It covered him with such swiftness that even the immense creature could not stop it.

A drake warrior who had managed to regain his footing charged the warlock from the side. With an indifferent wave of his left hand, Shade sent a burst of crimson energy toward the attacker that struck the drake full in the chest—and burnt him to ash.

With a roar, the Dragon King shook off the steaming, hardening earth. He opened his mouth and flames scorched the area where Shade stood.

But again, the attack did not even singe the warlock's garments.

Shade drew from the crystal once more, sending a ring of fiery blades toward his adversary. The Storm Lord countered with a cloudless rain that washed the ring into oblivion.

And each time one of them cast a spell, the crystal flared more intensely.

Aurim eyed the stone. Even without the aid of magic, he could sense how the strain of both combatants actively drawing from it had begun to take a toll. The artifact could not much longer stand such abuse. At some point, the essential structure of the crystal would degrade.

When that happened, nothing would protect any of those still in the cave.

"Can you teleport us?" he asked Yssa.

She shook her head, unable to speak due to the continued effort of protecting them. The flames, the deadly rain . . . each attack spilled over on the pair. Aurim understood that if she tried to cast another spell, it would mean dropping their only defense.

Then a voice filled his head, a voice using the link with his mother—but that was not his mother's.

*You must be ready when the artifact fails. We will guide you.*

He glanced at the hooded figure battling the Dragon King.

The voice had been Shade's.

The crystal abruptly flared a deep crimson. Aurim felt the first hints of fragmentation. The stone had nearly reached its limits.

Caught up in their duel, neither Shade nor the Storm Lord seemed to notice or care. Scorch marks covered the Dragon King and the warlock's cloak had been reduced to tatters, but otherwise they had done little to one another.

"Give in to the inevitable, mortal creature!" roared the Storm Dragon. "And we shall grant you a merciful death!"

The warlock said nothing, but when he cast his next spell, the aura surrounding the artifact turned nearly as black as the crystal itself.

The crystal cracked.

*It is time!* said the unsettling voice in Aurim's head.

Hoping he was not being played for a fool, Aurim cast his spell. He felt the presence of both his mother and the one who had spoken last.

The artifact ruptured.

A titanic force washed over the wizard. He heard Yssa scream. From far away came the roar of a dragon—a dragon in agony.

And suddenly . . . silence reigned.

An anxious gasp stirred Aurim back to reality. He discovered that he lay face down in a muddy field. As the wizard pushed himself up, a pair of hands took hold.

Aurim looked up hopefully, but it was not Yssa. Instead, his mother's concerned, tearful face filled his view.

"Are you all right?" she gasped.

"I think . . . I think I am." As he straightened, Aurim desperately looked around. "Yssa—"

"There, my son."

The Green Dragon's daughter lay face up a few yards away. Aurim stumbled over to her, kneeling by her side. With relief, he saw that she breathed steadily.

Only then did he acknowledge his surroundings. The forest of willows, the swampy earth . . . "Wenslis?"

"Yes, far to the south. We cannot even see the mountains from here."

He paid no mind to that, more interested in something he had just noticed about their immediate surroundings. "The storm . . . it's *stopped*. It's not even raining."

It *always* rained in the Storm Lord's domain.

Gwen nodded. "Yes . . . it ceased almost immediately the moment we appeared here." She frowned. "It might mean something . . . and then again it might not. It's too soon to know. They both could be dead. They both could be alive. Whatever the case, only time will tell, for you and I are certainly not going back there."

Even the clouds had begun to evaporate. Aurim gaped up at a sun rarely seen in this region.

Yssa stirred. Her eyes opened and she saw him. She reached up and kissed Aurim gratefully, only afterward noticing Gwen's presence.

"Lady Bedlam, I—"

Pursing her lips slightly, Gwen said, "It's all right. We'll speak later. The important thing is that we're safe. I doubt any of the Storm Lord's minions are concerned about us at the moment."

"Thank you for saving us," the younger woman said.

"I?" The enchantress shook her head. "I did very little."

"Was it him, Mother?" Aurim asked as he helped his love to her feet. "Shade?"

Yssa frowned. "*Another* one?"

"No," Gwen responded. "Not another one." She gazed north, in the direction of the Storm Lord's stronghold. "The original one . . . I think."

Aurim looked around. "Where is he? What happened to him?"

She continued staring north. "He vanished after he dragged me here. You appeared on your own a moment later, as he promised. I think . . . I think he's gone back there."

"To the lair? For what?"

"I don't know, Aurim. I have this feeling that he knew everything that would happen, that he might have even planned all of this. Frankly, I'm too tired to care. Shade chose to save us . . . this time."

"And next time?"

"Forget that for now, Aurim. Can you teleport us home?" She nodded toward Yssa, her eyes softening a bit. "*All* of us, I mean?"

He checked. "I think I can."

"Then please do so at once. I need to speak to your father and the Gryphon. They have to know what happened in Wenslis." Her expression grew grim again. "*Everything* that happened in Wenslis."

Aurim nodded. The wizard took his mother in one hand, his beloved in the other and, with a last glance at the dour realm of the Storm Lord, concentrated . . .

HE FOUND THE body exactly where he knew it would be. Reaching down, he dragged it out of the earth. Even in death, the face remained blurred, indistinct.

Shade eyed his dead self, then laid one gloved hand across the face.

The hand glowed gold. The aura spread over the face, the head, then the entire body of the dead Shade. Quickly the aura enveloped the corpse, absorbed it . . . and fed it back to the figure leaning over.

When the last of his twin had been consumed, leaving no trace whatsoever, the warlock straightened. Turning, he surveyed the huge rock collapse caused by the explosion of the crystal. With a wave of his hand, Shade sent tons of rock and the corpses of dead drake warriors flying away, digging through the carnage until he came upon the one he sought.

The Storm Lord lay motionless, but alive. His entire body had been seared by the powerful blast, but, thanks to his great power, the dragon would survive.

One eye opened. It slowly focused on the figure before it. Hatred began to burn in the eye as recognition took place—

"Time to sleep again," Shade whispered.

The eye struggled . . . then closed. The dragon's breathing grew calm. The inner edges of the huge maw curled slightly upward.

Shade drew his cloak around him. "Now I am whole," he said to himself. "Now I can do what must be done."

And with that, he disappeared.

THE TEMPEST COVERED the world. Wherever the Storm Lord focused his will, lightning struck and fierce winds blew. Rain poured and thunder crashed. No place was safe from his godly wrath and the people knew that. From Dragon Kings to Seekers to ground-dwelling Quel to elves to humans—all fell to their knees before his glory.

And from the heavens, the Storm Lord looked down and smiled to himself. All was as it should be. All was perfection.

Just as he had always dreamed it would one day be.

# THE STILL LANDS

*Beware Death's shade . . .*

# I

SILENCE FILLED THE gray land, but despite that, the young, cloaked woman sensed that she was far from alone. At a glance, the murky, shadowy place only gave hints of dour hills and macabre trees with empty, clutching branches, but whenever she neared any of those landmarks, they seemed to fade away like dreams at waking. Peering over her shoulder, she would see a different background than the one she had walked and yet, if she tried to go back even a step, everything in the direction that she had originally been walking would also change.

Again, the hooded traveler sensed others around her. She focused her mind and what she saw in that brief moment caused her to utter a gasp that sounded like thunder in this still place.

Gray figures, countless grey figures, milled around her, moving with no purpose that she could see. They were young, old, human, drake, elven—even an armored Quel briefly made an appearance. All had the same hollow look.

And just like that, they were gone again—or rather, she could no longer focus on them.

Shaken, she paused to sip from the thinning water sack at her waist. The water had taken on a brackish taste since her arrival, no surprise to her. The young sorceress forced herself to swallow it, then took a bite of a biscuit that, like the water, now had all the consistency and flavor of clay.

As she retied the sack, she could not help but again look herself over. Her once-emerald travel outfit had, here, become a dull, faded green and the brown leather boots looked a dead black. Her skin, already pale, resembled that of a corpse and even her cascading rich, red hair had a coloring more akin to dried blood. Only the streak of silver running down the right remained as bright as ever. Everything else about her was a shadow of what it had been before her coming here, but while it disquieted her, it no longer surprised.

What would one expect in the realm of the dead?

She should not have come here alone. Her father and mother would have been horrified beyond belief that she had attempted this and they were not ones to shirk from danger. Cabe and Gwendolyn Bedlam were the most renowned of spellcasters, the former from a legendary line that had produced both heroes and villains. The two had become instrumental in transforming the collective lands called the Dragonrealm into a continent all but free of the once-sweeping tyranny of the drake lords. Humans now dominated, for good or ill, in most places. Her parents had faced dragons, warlocks, the avian Seekers, demons, and the incessant evil of the wolf raiders without hesitation, but here was one place that they and any sensible being avoided.

But Valea had set herself upon a mission from which she felt no obstacle could deter her. From the dead, a figure had emerged again in the Dragonrealm and the crimson-tressed young woman was certain that she had been marked as the one who had to deal with him. It had begun with dreams and ghosts haunting her own ancient home, a collection of events that tied her to that resurrected danger as none other.

Only she, Valea felt, could confront the warlock, Shade.

He had lived a thousand lifetimes, his curse alternating him between good and evil. He existed somewhere between reality and imagination, his hooded features ever blurred, indistinct. Shade had been friend and enemy to all, with each 'death' shifting from one end of the spectrum to the other. Valea found him a tragic figure, but she steeled herself with the knowledge that if he had returned, surely that meant danger to those she loved. Whatever sympathy the young sorceress felt—and whatever other emotions had arisen since her ghostly encounter with his past—they had to be kept in check. She had to stop whatever it was he intended.

That it had led to this place had stunned her, but Valea had persevered. She had fought her way to the realm of the Lords of the Dead and now she would cross their domain following Shade's trail no matter what impediment rose before her.

But so far, Valea had come across nothing. The unearthly realm was filled with phantoms all but invisible to her and a landscape that, despite its changing shape and murkiness, had held no dire threats. She sensed that Shade had been this way, but that was all.

A buzzing in her ears made her swat at it. With some frustration, Valea kept her hand in check. Now and then the buzzing arose and when she had listened close once, she had heard the voices of the shadows, the whisperings of lives long past. They were, like everything around her, a disturbing distraction, but nothing to concern the spellcaster.

The buzzing, however, suddenly increased in intensity. The whisperers sounded upset, fearful. They almost seemed to be warning each other . . . or even her.

Something fluttered among the dead trees ahead of her, moving so swiftly out of sight that Valea could not be certain that she had actually seen anything.

The buzzing grew more insistent. Now it became words that she could make out with some ease.

Coming . . . coming . . . coming . . . they said over and over.

A form flew overhead.

Valea reacted immediately, casting a spell upward. A flash of light illuminated both her and her surroundings and she heard a monstrous shriek.

Something with batlike wings darted from her view. She spun in the direction it had gone, trying as best she could to make out its shape.

Instead, a tall structure that Valea knew she had not passed earlier perched atop a high, jagged hill overlooking her location.

It was a castle or, being this place, perhaps the ghost of one. Certainly it was no place that welcomed the weary traveler. Like monstrous claws, five towers rose above the outer wall, each one topped by sharp, toothy battlements. Flanked on each corner by four of the towers and using the fifth as its centerpiece, a broad, rounded building made up the bulk of the castle. Further details, Valea could not make out. In fact, there was little else of descriptive value where the castle was concerned. No banners flew from its heights and she could not make out any gates. The battlements were empty of movement.

And yet . . . Valea took a step forward, squinting. Was there a light of sorts in the main building? Something hinting of red flickered there.

Every nerve in her body taut, the sorceress reached out with her senses and sought the evidence she needed. Almost immediately, Valea received the answer she had expected.

Shade was there. She knew his magical signature as well as she knew her own. Since that fateful journey into the memories of the Manor, her home, Valea had come to recognize the traces of his spellwork. She suspected it was because the two of them shared a link that went beyond that one experience. Deep beneath the Manor, Valea had discovered the tomb of an elven maiden, Galani. She had been perfectly preserved, almost as if time itself had frozen. This was the same Galani who had been part of a ghostly vision seen more than once in the huge house above. This was the same Galani who had, in life, been cousin to the sorcerer Arak.

Arak had been friend to Shade.

Galani had fallen for the tragic figure, but, as was his curse, Shade had died without her knowing of it. When he had risen again, his mind twisted, he had used Arak and Galani to further his own evil goals. Only Galani's sacrifice had saved her cousin and the Dragonrealm from the darker side of Shade. She had killed the warlock again before herself dying. Arak had sealed her body under the Manor and it had been Shade's reappearance now that had stirred some part of the dead elf's spirit to contact the only one who could understand and accept her message, her warning.

Valea, it seemed, was the reincarnation of the elf. With but a few subtle differences due to their respective races, the two had been identical of features and form.

Yes, it had to be Valea who finally put an end to the curse of Shade. Whatever his good aspects, the evil could not be allowed to return. Valea felt certain that she held the key, although whether that key would lead to her success, she could not say in the least.

The enchantress reached into her blouse, pulling out a chain she wore around her neck. At the end, an unprepossessing, brutally chiseled stone hung. It was barely the size of her smallest fingernail, but Valea treated it as if she carried the weight of the world.

"Let us hope this works . . ." she whispered to it. "Let us hope I've planned right, Galani . . ."

Then, undaunted by her tremendous doubts, Valea replaced the stone against her bosom and started for the castle. The whispering continued, the same word repeating over and over. The young spellcaster ignored the whispering, already wary of her surroundings. The winged thing that had almost fallen upon her had finally reminded Valea just what unnatural realm she walked. Every step meant danger. This was, after all, the kingdom of the Lords of the Dead.

And she doubted that they would long suffer a living soul in their midst.

HE PEERED OUT the window as he did every moment of his existence. It was both his only salvation and his greatest torture. Out there, he sensed the countless shadows flittering about, existing only because the masters of the realm desired them to do so. The scene was always the same . . . the grayness, the lifelessness . . . the eternity.

And then something so extraordinary that it made him leap to his feet appeared in the distance, a shock of life and color such as he could only dredge up from his most ancient memories. It moved with purpose, moved with an animation so foreign to the still lands surrounding the castle. Pushing his hood back slightly, he pressed his face against the bars, trying to make out more detail. It was as if he had been given a glimpse of paradise, so wondrous was this unexpected vision.

But as the figure neared and he made out exactly what it was, his expression grew both dumbfounded and fearful . . . the latter not for himself. He shook his head, blinked, and stared again, disbelieving the sight. His tormentors had finally begun the new, sadistic game that they had promised . . .

"Sharissa . . ." he murmured. "Sharissa . . ."

# II

THE MOST DISASTROUS trait running through his family, Cabe Bedlam decided, had to be its members' tendency to thrust themselves into dangers despite common sense. He had done so far too often. So had Gwendolyn, his wife, and their son, Aurim, who insisted on wooing the daughter of one who had betrayed the parents.

But now his daughter had outdone them all, literally stepping into a nightmare without apparently any sane regard for herself. She had gone where even Cabe in his wildest dreams would not have dared, a place that made even Darkhorse wary.

"She has come this way," bellowed the huge, ebony stallion despite their silent, ominous surroundings. "There is no doubt about it."

Cabe eyed the ruins of the castle through which they now journeyed. Under the hood of his gray travel cloak was a face that would have seemed more appropriate on a farmer or blacksmith. His broad, clean features and unassuming eyes hid power of which few could even dream. Average of build and clad in simple deep blue pants and shirt and high leather boots, he would not have garnered a second glance by most if not for the wide streak of silver in his otherwise plain, dark hair. That silver marked him as a spellcaster and one of skill. Cabe was a wizard from a long line of wizards that included the famous and the nefarious. His grandfather, Nathan, had been the leader of the Dragon Masters, mages who had sought to free the lands from the rule of the Dragon Kings. His father, Azran, had been a black knave who had betrayed Nathan and the rest for his own sinister designs.

And now Cabe and Darkhorse had entered what remained of his dire stronghold in the midst of the volcanic lands of the Red Dragon.

Memories of his captivity in his father's sanctum made the vein in Cabe's neck throb. The castle had been brought down during a battle between the previous drake lord and Azran, with the former losing both the battle and his life. Azran, however, had gone mad in the process, the evil power of his creation, the sword curiously and ominously called *The Nameless*, usurping his mind. Cabe's father was long dead and *The Nameless* had vanished down a bottomless crevice in a cavern, but the legacy of his father remained strong in the wreckage left behind.

Generations of dark sorcery and ties to otherworldly forces had left what still stood of the castle a place even drakes shunned.

"She should've never come to this place," the human murmured not for the first time. "Valea knew the stories."

"But stories are just that to the young, who have not experienced the true terror," replied the blue-orbed steed. That Darkhorse spoke was not the most astonishing thing about Cabe's companion, for he was not a horse at all. The huge stallion had chosen his form centuries prior when first coming to the Dragonrealm from the empty dimension called only the *Void*. He was a creature of pure magic able to transform at will or become insubstantial if necessary. Darkhorse had a fondness for his present shape, though, and rarely altered his appearance. He had befriended many humans over the centuries, but was feared by many, many more.

Cabe kept in check the remark that came to his lips in response to his companion's words. While Darkhorse sounded as venerable as a creature that, if not slain, could live forever should, he had himself a childlike habit of running into trouble headfirst.

Jagged pieces of stone still stood here and there, testament to the gargantuan size of Azran's citadel. In truth, much of the edifice had fallen quickly because it had been held together by the sorcerer's own magic. That any of it still stood amazed Cabe.

A skeleton half-buried in rubble caught his attention. The ribs were almost human, but the skull was quite avian, like that of a man-sized bird. The Seekers, the ancient predecessors of the Dragon Kings, had been forced to serve Azran and many had perished fighting the forces of the Red Dragon. This was not the first set of bones the pair had come across. The landscape surrounding the ruins still offered glimpses of the scores of creatures from both sides who had died fighting for two megalomaniacs. Cabe had even briefly caught sight of the gargantuan, telltale skull of the Dragon King himself, left half-buried by dust and molten earth by his successor.

"Turn west," he suddenly told Darkhorse. Valea's magical trace, albeit much faded, led that way. Other than her mother, Cabe was probably the only one who could have still sensed the remnants of his daughter's passing. Unless they worked hard to mask it, spellcasters often left a trail of sorts, a hint of their distinctive magical signature. Fortunately, Valea had not decided to hide hers, likely because she knew that one or both of her parents would surely follow.

And why not? When Gwen had summoned him back, her mental call filled with anxiety, he had known that the news would be dire. His wife had refrained from telling him just what it was about, fearing the slight chance that some other spellcaster might be able to eavesdrop. The Dragon Kings were always monitoring their enemies, awaiting the chance to regain some of their lost power.

But what the enchantress had told her husband had stunned him beyond belief.

*Shade had risen from the dead again.*

It should not have been. Darkhorse had witnessed what should have been the warlock's final, absolute demise. Cabe and everyone else believed it so, especially after the most doubtful of them, the black stallion himself, had spent years fruitlessly searching for some sign that Shade had once again been resurrected. Eventually, even Darkhorse had admitted that the warlock was surely no more.

And now . . . and now they knew that they had been wrong.

Terrible enough were the events that Gwen had relayed upon his return concerning her encounter with not only the Storm Dragon, but a *number* of variations of Shade. But worse was his wife's discovery of the note left by Valea announcing that she, too, had uncovered evidence of the enigmatic figure's return. For reasons her parents could not fathom, Valea had left every indication that she believed that only she could put an end to the curse of Shade.

With the vast knowledge and power available to them, the Bedlams had quickly followed her path—and found, to their dismay, that their daughter had journeyed to her grandfather's citadel. Gwen and Aurim had wanted to go with then, but Cabe insisted that only he and Darkhorse make the trip. Someone had to remain behind in case the worst happened . . . and nothing could be worse than finding out that Valea had crossed into the otherworldly realm of the Lords of the Dead.

Both he and Darkhorse knew where to find the entrance to the infernal realm. It had been buried under tons of debris, but someone—not Valea from what Cabe sensed—had cleared it again.

The smell of decay and rotting flesh invaded his nostrils. Even Darkhorse snorted with distaste. The pit bubbled and oozed. What exactly the greenish gray muck was, Cabe neither knew nor wanted to know. In his mind, he could hear the calls and cries of the dead and a few of those voices were familiar to him. When last he had stood in this place, Cabe had even sensed Azran seeking him out, but, fortunately, that malignant spirit seemed not about.

Darkhorse had tried to explain to him that the realm into which Valea had traveled was not truly the afterlife, that the Lords of the Dead were nothing more than monstrous necromancers who managed to steal slices of dying souls. Their domain was a mockery of death. Even the spirit of Cabe's father had only been a reflection of the true Azran.

On one level, the wizard understood and accepted the explanation. On a more base level, though, Cabe recalled what he had sensed when Azran's evil had invaded his mind. Mere reflections of the dead the inhabitants of the foul realm might be, but they had varying strength, depending upon their wills.

But his daughter, however foolishly, had dared enter and so Cabe would, too, even if he had to face the combined might of the ageless spellcasters.

And according to Darkhorse, they very likely would.

"But why here?" he asked. "Why to this place of all places?" This was the last spot that they would have expected any search for Shade to end. If there were those who hated the warlock more than anyone, it was the Lords of the Dead.

"They are his kin, his blood," Darkhorse muttered in a surprisingly subdued manner for his boisterous self. "They are, in fact, his cousins . . ."

Such a statement sounded so ludicrous when speaking of either Shade or the legendary necromancers and yet it also made terrible sense. It somewhat explained the power that both the hooded figure and the dread lords wielded.

Of the same blood . . . and willing to spill one another's gladly. Cabe understood that all too well.

"How do we enter?"

The stallion prodded the muck with one hoof, snorting again. "We dive in, of course."

"I was afraid you'd say just that."

"The entrance is not guarded, Cabe."

The wizard nodded. "Either they want us to come in or someone's forcibly removed the gate keeper." The macabre creature, a grotesque compilation of countless dead beasts, had served its masters since time immemorial. To find it absent boded ill. "I suppose it doesn't matter."

Darkhorse nodded. "Shall I, then?"

Gritting his teeth and holding tight to his mount, Cabe nodded. "Do it."

Without hesitation, the magical steed leapt up over the huge, bubbling mass—then dropped like a stone into it.

Cabe held his breath, expecting a massive wave to engulf both of them. Instead, the pit seemed to part and he and Darkhorse suddenly plummeted through a gray emptiness. Voices assailed the wizard, the words of centuries of the dead repeating endlessly the stories of their lives. Shadowy forms appeared in the corner of his eye, but when Cabe sought to focus on them, they were no longer there.

Their descent slowed, then halted. The two drifted in a hazy limbo.

Then, without warning . . . a dour landscape formed around them.

It was muted, silent. Cabe felt a slight chill, but not the kind one experienced from moist or cold weather. Rather, it resembled the unsettling sensation that had touched him when first entering the ruins. Here was a place of the dead, but dead who were not completely at rest.

"Where do you think she headed?" Only Darkhorse had any inkling of what existed in this realm where even color seemed to die.

In fact, even the ice-blue orbs of the stallion looked faded. Darkhorse peered around warily, then replied, "There is a castle . . . so he told me once. If you can still follow her trail, I suspect it will lead there."

Shutting his eyes, Cabe concentrated on Valea. Her trace was fainter, almost invisible, but he managed to get just enough of a grasp on it to point ahead. "Go that way."

The shadow steed trotted along. Both remained wary of their surroundings. The Lords of the Dead had to be watching, plotting. No one entered their domain without their knowledge.

Which meant that they had long ago noted Valea.

Time was an immaterial concept here, but still it seemed as if every step took an hour. The bleak sameness of the landscape added to that effect. Cabe quickly felt his impatience growing and sensed Darkhorse reacting much the same. It was dangerous, though, to fall victim to the emotion; even the smallest distraction could leave them open to an attack.

"I like this not," the stallion finally remarked. "They know we are here. They would not wish us here. Why do they not make some challenge?"

The wizard opened his mouth to answer, but another responded before him.

"Because they await me."

Darkhorse reared and Cabe's left hand flared with a ready spell.

But the hooded figure with the blurred face took their reactions in stride, simply repeating his words.

"Because they await me," Shade said without the slightest care. "Because my cousins have been waiting for me to take the bait."

THE ELEVEN STOOD in the pattern of the pentagram, each knowing his place, each maintaining the power that made them masters of their realm. Ten stood so as to form the design with the final one, the focus, directly in the center. Through him was all cast, through him was all sensed.

"He is coming . . ." rasped the focus. "He is here . . ."

"At last," murmured another voice, nearly identical to his own. Others repeated the response, they also sounding almost like copies of the first. For so long they had worked in sync with one another until they were as if of one mind.

They, the Lords of the Dead.

The chamber in which they stood was devoid of any trappings. No tapestries, no banners, no weaponry. Only an arched, open window out of which none of them ever looked gave the room any life . . . that and the thick, bronze door upon which the insignia of a dragon could just be made out at eye level.

The light that futilely illuminated the chamber originated from a crystal buried just below the lead necromancer's booted feet. The faint glow was misleading; the crystal was anything but weak. It was the only new addition to their sanctum since its creation . . . and had been set there specifically because of one being. One hated being. It gathered and amplified their work, fed more wholly the magic they cast into the one who would wield it.

The figure in the center raised a black, gauntleted hand. In his eyes, the arm within the mail was as thick and sturdy as it had always been. He did not see that the armor and glove hung loose and rusted and that what glimpses of the form within could be seen were dry of flesh and bony. "His ka is strong. He is much himself . . ."

One at the high point of the pentagram stirred. Like the others, he wore a partially concealing helm with the stylized image of a dragon atop it. The black armor and dark cloak in which he was also clad hung as loose as that of the leader. The cloak was tattered and unlike the first figure he wore no boots—and had no feet or lower legs to speak of. They had long ago rotted away, just as had various bits of the rest of the necromancers.

But in the eyes of all, they were still the same eleven who had, long ago, discovered this path and by unanimous vote had forever changed themselves. They were strong of sinew, determined of eye, the blood of the dragon, the blood of Clan Tezerenee.

They were Vraad, the race of sorcerers who were the predecessors of more than just the humans of the Dragonrealm.

"But he is not completely himself, is he, Ephraim? All depends upon that, doesn't it?"

Ephraim shifted one foot from near the crystal, a slight movement with vast overtones. The other necromancer also moved, his reaction one more submissive.

"We are one in this as we are in all else, are we not, Zorane? You question my work, my search?"

"No one questions," interjected another from Ephraim's right. "We are all anxious for victory. We are anxious to bring our dear cousin under rein."

"And he shall be. Gerrod will know his place . . . and ours."

The silence that followed his words indicated the acquiescence of the others. Since the beginning, Ephraim had been the planner, the instigator. All actions flowed through him. It was the way of things. It was as natural as breathing—which all of them had ceased doing centuries ago.

"The players are arranged. He is expecting us to react and she is expecting to find a tragic hero. We should not disappoint them."

Ephraim raised his arms high. As one, the other Lords of the Dead bowed their heads and concentrated . . .

# III

THE CASTLE HAD no entrance, at least none that Valea could find. She had skirted around it as much as possible, avoiding only the area where the land dropped off into an endless void. Valea had peered down into the haze, seeking some bottom, but none could she find. It was as if the realm of the dead ceased at this point.

Returning to where she had first reached the looming structure, the enchantress mulled over her situation. She had belatedly cast a shield around her that she hoped would blind the Lords to her location, but knew that such ancient sorcerers would eventually overcome it. That meant that Valea had to hurry.

Why had Shade come to this place? Was he now in league with the macabre necromancers? It seemed so unlikely. Even despite his shifts from light to dark, there was no record of him ever having allied with the Lords. It seemed that the depths of their hatred for one another likely ran very, very deep.

Was he a prisoner, then? That made more sense. Valea wondered if that was what the elf maiden's spirit had sought to tell her, that Shade was not a threat himself, but was in danger.

If the warlock *was* a prisoner, that presented potential disaster. It might be possible for the Lords of the Dead to finally turn him to their cause through some wicked spell. If that happened, Valea could not imagine the fate the Dragonrealm would soon after suffer.

She wished that Galani could have told her more, that somehow the spirit could have made clear what it was Valea faced and what was expected of her. If only—

An image flickered in and out of existence before her very eyes. The vision was so very brief, but Valea could never have mistaken the face peering back at hers—for it had, in many ways, *been* her own.

"Galani?" the red-haired young woman whispered.

Again, a flickering image, but this time posed differently. It was *not* Galani, for the hair was long, lush, and cascaded down past the waist. Even more startling, it was a brilliant silver-blue, so radiant in contrast to the starkness of the land. The face was more human, too, although the eyes were an arresting aquamarine and *crystalline* in design.

Crystalline . . . her father's journals spoke of people with crystalline eyes.

The Vraad.

Gasping, Valea instinctively backed a step away. Then the realization that this ghost wore her own face made her move forward again. Was there a link to this phantasm akin to the one with Galani?

Again her doppelganger appeared and this time the one hand pointed upward and to the east where a dagger-shaped rock twice as tall as Valea stood.

Biting her lower lip, the spellcaster followed. The phantom materialized every few yards, always anxiously pointing at the rock.

When at last Valea reached it, that changed. Suddenly the ethereal woman formed inside the very rock, reaching out to her earthly twin with beckoning arms. She seemed to want Valea to walk into solid stone, something which, while easy for a ghost, was not so simple for a living being.

But when Valea touched the rock, her hand sank through. She quickly withdrew her hand, then touched the rock once more. When her fingers again sank deep, she felt around. Part of the rock was illusion. An arched opening slightly taller than her lay hidden right before the spellcaster.

Valea stepped through.

She had a brief moment of vertigo . . . then stood in a dank, stone corridor lit only by some vague, sourceless gray illumination. A fine dust covered the floors and the walls and the corridor seemed to go on forever.

The ghost formed briefly again, pointing down the direction Valea faced. The enchantress headed along the hall, eyes and other senses ready.

But nothing barred her path. She continued on down the corridor, passing door after wooden door. The first few she tried, only to find them tightly locked and sturdy despite their rotting appearance. Her spectral companion continued to urge her on and Valea finally abandoned all attempts to check the rooms.

The dust thickened as she made her way deeper into the castle and that bothered the spellcaster. If this area was in use, why were there no footsteps? It was as if nothing lived here. Surely, though, at least the Lords of the Dead walked the castle . . .

Then Valea realized that she might be presumptuous to expect that the necromancers were at all mortal any more.

A slight sound suddenly made her freeze. Valea backed against one of the doors.

The sound reminded her of something being dragged. In such a place, in such a realm, the possibilities of what that meant twisted her stomach.

The noise grew louder, nearer. Valea raised one hand, ready to fight with a spell. The source of the sound had to be almost upon her, but still she could see nothing. Her hand clenched in anticipation and worry—

And just like that, the sound receded past her.

She glanced after it, refusing to believe that it could be possible. The sound continued on, growing fainter and fainter until it ceased to be audible. The dust on the floor remained undisturbed save where Valea's own prints were.

As she looked back the way she had been heading, the enchantress again saw her unsettling doppelganger. The figure pointed on, her face all urgency.

Again biting her lip, Valea followed the specter. The corridor finally came to an end several yards later at a narrow, winding stairway leading up. The stone passage had no rails, but Valea leaned against one wall as she ascended.

And at the top of the stairs, an iron door confronted her. The symbol of the dragon had been cast upon it and even through the dust Valea could see its malevolent eyes peering back. The style reminded her of the Dragon Kings and she wondered if there was some connection.

The ghost stood before the door, imploring her to enter. She vanished as her mortal counterpart neared. Valea touched the ringed handle, but it would not budge. There was no keyhole.

Concentrating, Valea let her higher senses show her what her eyes could not see. Draped over the door was a series of spells that kept the path sealed. The enchantress probed one and found it easily yielding to her power. After testing another and finding that as readily undone, Valea could come to only one conclusion. The peculiar earmarks of the spells indicated that they served one very specific purpose. They had been designed to work against a particular magical signature and one that she had come to know so very well.

Shade's.

So he was here and he *was* a prisoner of the Lords. That was what Galani had tried to impart to her and what this other phantom, this other incarnation of herself, had also sought to say. A peculiar sense of relief touched Valea. She had come fully expecting to confront and vanquish the legendary warlock in order to prevent his evil from ever erupting again. Yet, a good part of her had battled against that notion. Valea could not deny that she felt something for Shade. It was not merely some residue of the time that she had spent bound together with Galani. It went far deeper. To Valea, it was as if her soul, in whatever form it existed throughout time, had always been intertwined with his. Had she lived other lives that had crossed the warlock's path? Surely the second ghost indicated that.

Valea shook her head, clearing her thoughts of any foolish romantic feelings. Her brother would have mocked her and her parents would have looked down at her in pity. She risked more than her life coming here and to let her be distracted by such prattle endangered her further.

Still, she had come here to find Shade and she had done so. All that barred her from confronting him were some simple spells.

With an inherent skill that only a Bedlam could wield, Valea quickly and efficiently removed the remaining spells. There were no hints of alarms among them, which surprised her until she recalled just where she was. The confidence of the Lords in their own dread domain could hardly be surprising. Their only mistake had been not knowing that Valea would have unearthly help to guide her to this point.

As the last spell dissipated, the anxious enchantress tugged on the ring.

The door swung open with an utter silence that both relieved and astounded her. She quickly stepped inside.

The familiar gray cloak completely draped his back, making him look more like a monk than the fearsome figure he was. His face was to the barred and magically sealed window, the only feature of the small chamber. A long, stone bench enabled him to sit there. It was the only piece of furniture in sight. If Shade slept, then he did so on the floor and wrapped in his own garments. Her sympathy for the imprisoned spellcaster grew, but Valea kept it in check, aware that Shade might still prove a danger.

Still facing the window, he slowly rose. At the same time, the ghost, her arms at her side, formed before Valea. She faced not the enchantress, however, but rather Shade. Valea did not move, instead staring straight through the transparent figure.

And as he finished turning toward her, the enchantress came at last face-to-face with the one to whom she had been led.

Valea gaped—for there was indeed a *face* where there should have been none.

The aristocratic features were more handsome than those of her father, with the nose slightly aquiline. Dark hair hung loosely down over the forehead and the chin was narrow. It was a youthful yet ancient countenance, outwardly little older in appearance than hers. The eyes, however, were what made the true difference. They were, like the ghost's, crystalline, albeit of a deeper shade than the female's.

Vraad.

An expression of intense sorrow colored the startling face. In a voice that Valea knew all too well, the hooded figure muttered, "Sharissa . . . I am so very sorry."

And the door behind Valea abruptly shut tight.

# IV

"SHADE," CABE REMARKED with much more calm than he truly felt. "How long have you been waiting for us?"

"All my existence," the warlock responded with utter nonchalance.

"I saw you die!" roared Darkhorse, taking none of the situation as cautiously as Cabe. "You ceased to be! Even you were certain of that!"

"And so I was . . ."

The sudden shift in Shade's tone to deep bitterness silenced the shadow steed. The warlock slowly strode toward his old comrades and enemies. Even when he stood directly in front of Cabe and Darkhorse and peered up at them from under his hood, his features remained indistinct.

"Gwen told us of her encounter with you . . . and your other selves," said the wizard. "She also told us what you said to her."

"A shortened story, I promise, young Cabe. Perhaps one day we can discuss it in more detail . . ."

The wizard shifted uneasily. "You still haven't told us what we should call you."

Shade chuckled darkly. He performed a sweeping bow and answered, "You may call me . . . *Shade*."

"Nothing else? Not Simon, not Rork, not Joab, nor any of the countless other names you've had over the centuries?"

"No . . . that part of the game is at an end. I tire of this facade or that. Call me Shade, for I am, always have, and always will be, it seems . . . the shadow of a true man."

Darkhorse snorted. "And will you now tell us that we no longer need fear if you are friend or foe? Is that a facade also past?"

The slim form pulled the cloak tight around him, making him look even more an appropriate denizen of this plane. "No, my eternal friend, that is not. But for now . . . there is little to fear."

"He says in this of all places!" rumbled the ebony stallion.

"We may bicker until the sun shines over this dismal landscape or we may accept what is," Shade returned without the slightest impatience. "Ephraim has spent much time planning this and we would not wish to disappoint him."

Cabe frowned. "Ephraim?"

"It would be him. He was always the guide through which the others worked."

This brought a mocking laugh from Darkhorse. "The Lords have fought us before, Shade, and regretted it!"

"True, but they learn." The warlock suddenly tilted his hooded head skyward. "And *he* always has a twofold purpose to any plot—"

The sound of heavy flapping suddenly filled Cabe's ears. "What is that?"

Shade turned to face something just becoming visible in the sky before them. "Their welcome."

At first it seemed a huge black cloud flowing swiftly toward them. Then the cloud broke into a giant swarm of winged creatures that grew as they neared. What Cabe at first mistook for fiends the size of cats became so massive that he knew that they would tower over him by the time they reached the trio.

Their wings were wide, leathery, and part of their arms. Savage talons thrust out from each of the fingers, deadly blades they no doubt knew well how to use. The nearer they got, the more the wizard saw that they resembled pale, hairless bats wearing the forms of men, but bent over as if constantly running. Feet wider and longer than Cabe's ended in nails that made the other talons seem but tiny pins. Their eyes were red and monstrous and needlelike teeth filled their screeching mouths.

"Necri," Shade declared them. "It would be good not to let them bite you. They carry poison."

The teeth would also rip apart any flesh upon which they clamped, but Cabe saw no reason to mention that obvious fact. He made a fist, then concentrated.

Darkhorse's head twisted around completely, an impossible thing for a true steed. "Cabe! It would be better if I fought unhindered, yes?"

Without a word, the wizard slid off the back of his mount. Darkhorse let out a thundering roar and galloped toward the oncoming mass.

"His impetuousness will be the end of him someday . . . I suppose," Shade commented. The warlock held open one side of his massive cloak. Something leapt from its dark confines, moving so swiftly that Cabe could not make out exactly what it was. He thought he saw a beak and head like those of a gryphon, but the body was more lupine. It darted after Darkhorse, quickly catching up to him.

"I trust Master Zeree will not mind this borrowing of imagination," the warlock said cryptically.

Cabe did not bother to ask what he meant, for the Necri were then upon them. The wizard thrust his fist at the main mass and a huge, booming explosion scattered the batlike fiends. Several dropped to the earth, where they lay unmoving.

Shade spun in a circle once, twice—and on the third time a whirlwind formed that caught those circling just above the warlock and tossed them together like leaves. The Necri collided, bones breaking. The whirlwind cut into the swarm, dragging off more of the monsters as it went.

Several of the creatures dropped upon Darkhorse, who stood below the mass as if petrified. The first of the Necri made the mistake of seeking to slash the stallion with their clawed feet—and were drawn into the eternal's black form. They literally fell into him, plummeting to that unnamed place within.

Seeing their brethren vanish so, the next nearest Necri fluttered skyward again. However, the blur that had leapt forth from Shade's cloak suddenly jumped up, landing atop one beast and ripping out the back of its neck before the Necri even knew what happened. As the corpse dropped, the beaked familiar abandoned its victim, landing atop another and repeating the process. Cabe, who caught a glimpse of its work, noted that it did not seem able to fly, but, given any surface from which to start, could leap wherever it chose.

A massive shadow engulfed the wizard. Breath that smelled of the grave almost made him vomit. The horrific visage of a Necri filled his gaze, the teeth snapping at his throat.

Something white and sharp thrust through the Necri's chest, halting bare inches from Cabe's own. The Necri collapsed in a heap, nearly taking its would-be target to the ground with it.

Shade stood behind the monstrosity, the bone-white blade of a tiny dagger retracting. He gave Cabe no time to nod his gratitude, having to turn to slash at another attacker coming at him from the opposite direction.

Lightning crackled from the wizard's fingertips, striking in rapid succession five Necri, including one seeking to swoop down on Shade from behind.

But for every one of the winged demons they slew, there seemed half a dozen more. Sweating, Cabe caused the earth around them to rise up and bombard the swarm. The effort proved harder than he had imagined, though. Casting spells in this realm proved far more difficult than in the Dragonrealm. There, he knew how to touch and use the lines of power crisscrossing all elements of the world. Here, they were less apparent and weaker.

Another Necri landed a few yards from Cabe. Bent over like a runner, it charged him. The wizard gestured and three silver rings dropped over the beast, snaring its legs and wings. The Necri tumbled over, struggling futilely to escape.

Shade, meanwhile, thrust the tiny blade back into his cloak and removed instead what at first seemed black lightning. The fiery shape coalesced into a jagged sword that flared darkly. The first Necri to come at him left with its head flying from its body, the latter gliding some distance before crashing into the earth. Two more were rewarded with gaping chasms in their chests, from which spurted the foul, greenish fluid which was their blood. Shade handled the blade like an expert warrior. He moved with calculated swiftness, slicing wings here, cutting off grasping hands there.

Two more of the leathery fiends dropped upon Cabe. He pointed at the nearest, the spell already cast—

Both Necri disappeared.

Certain that it was some sort of trick, the wizard looked quickly around.

*All* of the Necri had vanished. Even the dead and the one Cabe had secured. The only traces of the monsters were a few tracks and some blood stains. Otherwise, it was as if they had never been.

The beaked wolf dropped to the ground just before Shade. The warlock opened the side of his cloak and it leaped into the shadows within, vanishing as readily as their foes.

As Darkhorse returned to them, Shade dismissed the unsettling blade to the other side of his cloak.

"You used that with skill," Cabe commented as the murky face of the warlock turned toward him.

"A family tradition," the warlock returned somewhat dourly.

Cabe raised an eyebrow at this further revelation. He had learned more about Shade's familial past and understood less than he ever had since first meeting the hooded spellcaster.

"We have vanquished the demons!" roared Darkhorse. "Let the Lords beware!"

"We held our own. What do you say, Shade?"

"Our strength was tested. They know our mettle."

He seemed poised to say more. "But that wasn't all?"

"Ephraim would have more in mind, yes. We shall just have to wait and see."

"And in the meantime?"

One gloved hand gestured in the direction that they had been heading before the attack. "We continue on."

Darkhorse snorted, but said nothing. His torso indented on the side, making footholds for Cabe. The wizard mounted and the gaps filled again. The shadow steed did not offer a ride to Shade nor did the warlock look at all inclined to ask.

Something had been bothering Cabe and he finally had to ask, "You watched her arrive. You saw Valea when she first came here."

The warlock no longer looked his way. "I did not see your daughter, but I sensed her."

"You should've done something to send her back!" Cabe felt his rage suddenly build. If Shade had let her continue on, it was because it suited his purpose. In that, he appeared no better than the Lords of the Dead.

The warlock wrapped his cloak about himself. "There was nothing I could do at the time. I could have no more stopped her than I could have this confrontation, Cabe Bedlam. It has been decreed. It is as it must be."

And with that said, Shade started off.

"SO MANY NECRI dead," muttered one of the Lords.

"There are always more Necri," pointed out another.

From his place at the center, Ephraim said, "They served their purpose. Our cousin and the others think we have taken their measure, which, in part, we have. They are not aware of what we also did." His fiery eyes stared down at the crystal. "And now their doom is set. Soon, we shall have not only our cousin at our beck and call, but the eternal and the wizard as well." Ephraim surveyed his comrades. "And then, at last, we shall stretch our influence to the realm of the living . . ."

# V

VALEA WHIRLED AS the door slammed behind her. She could sense no magic in the action, yet clearly some spell had come into play. However, before she could study it, the hooded figure said again, "Sharissa . . . You should've known better . . ."

Turning back, Valea saw the ghost vanish. She and the prisoner stared at one another as if both had sprouted second heads.

His eyes narrowed. "You are not she . . . but you are."

"She?"

"My Sharissa—no—she was never *my* Sharissa." He looked down in shame. "For her entire life, she never knew that desire."

From what Valea had seen of the ghost, she doubted that this Sharissa had been so ignorant of the man's interest. He had held some place in her heart, if not the one for which he had hoped.

She took a step toward him. "Who are you?"

"The fool of fools, the coward of cowards, the sorrow of my father's grand existence . . . Gerrod, by name, Tezerenee by birth, my unfortunate lady."

The last meant something to her. It was a name out of one of her father's journals, from his study of the Vraad. She could not recall what it was that had been written about them, though. "Why are you a prisoner?"

"Because my cousins are malicious and obsessive." Gerrod's features twisted into distaste. "And quite gruesome." He forced the expression away. "But come! I've been remiss! So seldom do I get a visitor other than them! In fact—never!" He indicated the bench. "Please. Sit. I'd offer you something, but—but I've nothing."

"I've no intention of staying here," Valea informed him. "The two of us are leaving."

She looked at the door, concentrating. For a brief moment, it trembled.

Then, nothing.

"You fail to understand, my lady," Gerrod said, coming up next to her. "They expected you to come."

"How do you know that?"

He looked at her in open surprise. "Why, Ephraim told me so."

"And who is—"

"I am Ephraim," came a voice from behind them.

Valea let out a gasp of surprise, then turned. Another gasp escaped her, this one of horror.

The figure stood a head taller than Gerrod and was clad from head to toe in black armor with the symbol of the dragon emblazoned on his breast plate. A thick, dark cloak hung over his shoulders and draped his back nearly to the floor. His helmet was topped with a savage dragon head crest.

But her horror came not from the sinister garments themselves, but rather their monstrous condition—and, worse, that of the wearer himself.

She took a step back as her eyes fixed on the rusting metal, the gaps where bone barely covered by dry skin could be seen. Within the helm itself the enchantress could make out part of the leering, fleshless mouth and the two gaps where the nose must have once been.

And the eyes . . . they still had the appearance of crystal, but within them flared a crimson light, an evil force that in itself stirred revulsion.

"Ephraim," Gerrod remarked almost casually.

"Gerrod . . ." the ghoul rasped. "You see? I brought her for you . . . as promised."

"You know that she is not who you pretend her to be."

"But she is," the Lord raised one gauntleted hand, his bony wrist just visible enough to shake Valea further. "Or are you blind?"

"I know what she looks like and what lurks within her . . . but she is still not her."

The Lord stepped toward Valea. Instinctively the enchantress raised her hand in defense.

A guttural chuckle escaped the ghoulish necromancer. "In this place you have no power."

Despite his words, Valea attempted to cast her spell. Nothing happened. She could faintly sense and see the lines of force crisscrossing the chamber, but they were, as so much else in these still lands, ghosts of what they had been.

Ephraim reached up and, with the arrogance of one supremely in command, took hold of Valea's face by the chin. He turned it for Gerrod to see. "Look beyond the face, which already tells the tale, and read into the eyes what you seek."

Gerrod's crystalline orbs reluctantly stared into her own frightened ones. Some of Valea's fear dwindled as she felt the sadness and shame of the hooded figure as he intruded in her very soul.

But as Gerrod invaded her, he, in turn, revealed something of himself. It was not intentional, merely a fact of his existence. Valea sensed it just as she had earlier sensed Shade's magical signature.

Which was, in fact, also *Gerrod's*.

The knowledge so startled her that she managed to pull free of Ephraim's grip. Gerrod, in turn, pulled away from the enchantress, again looking ashamed.

Ephraim, of course, laughed.

"What did you do?" asked Gerrod angrily.

"While you learned of her, she learned of you."

The prisoner scowled. "Ever you had more than one reason for doing anything!"

Valea eyed him. Shade's magical signature. She knew of no manner by which anyone could so duplicate it . . .

Gerrod was *Shade*?

Before Valea could delve further into the matter, the necromancer continued, "Well, my friend? You are convinced?"

"Whether I'm convinced doesn't matter, Ephraim."

The macabre figure tilted his horrific head, the lipless mouth ever in its eternal, mocking smile. "But it does, for it means you will do as I have requested. You *will*, won't you . . . dear cousin?"

"At least leave her out of this!"

"But like you, she is key." Ephraim leaned toward the enchantress again. "And in one manner or another, she will serve the purpose. You, Gerrod, have only to tell us how."

She looked from the ghoul to the prisoner and found the latter no more comforting. Gerrod wrestled with his decision, upon which her life clearly depended.

His shoulders slumped. "Very well . . . it'll be as you planned."

"Excellent!" Ephraim chuckled. "Then soon, very soon, Sharissa will be yours . . . and you will once more have hands with which you can finally hold her."

Despite her growing horror, the last statement made Valea frown. "What does he mean by that?"

The Lord evinced actual surprise at this question. "Dear cousin, have you been so hesitant? I would have expected you to try to welcome her with open arms—even though you do not have any!"

"Ephraim—"

"Take his hand, my lady . . . now."

His tone brooked no objection and Valea saw no reason to hesitate. She stretched a tentative hand toward Gerrod's. He started to pull back, then, with further resignation in his expression, reached to meet her fingers.

Valea's hand slipped *through* his.

Like all else in this realm, Gerrod, too, was a phantasm.

The hooded prisoner snatched back his hand, burying it in his cloak. Ephraim nodded triumphantly.

"Soon it will be different, though, cousin. Soon, that which is rightfully yours will be returned to you. Gerrod Tezerenee will live again . . . and Shade will truly be a shadow of the past . . ."


THE LANDSCAPE GRADUALLY took on a terrible monotony. Cabe grew more and more frustrated. He could sense that the trail continued on ahead of them, but something told the wizard that they should have reached Valea by now. The Lords of the Dead intended something, but what it was he could not fathom. Cabe did not like having to wait to react; it kept the party on the defensive, which lessened their chances.

"We need to do something!" he finally demanded. "We need to take this matter in hand and turn it to our choice, not theirs!"

"I have been attempting to do just that," Shade returned. "I have been seeking out that which would, I think, most distress our opponents."

"And?"

Puzzlement crept into the warlock's voice. "And he is not among the many shadows here. A most curious thing."

"Who is 'he'?" muttered Darkhorse.

"Barakas Tezerenee."

Darkhorse reared, nearly spilling Cabe. "That arrogant beast! Even his ghost I will not suffer to exist!"

The blurred face may have frowned. "Since I find no trace of his specter, then that becomes a moot point."

Regaining his balance, Cabe growled, "You thought some ghost would be of aid against the Lords of the Dead?"

"This is one they would have well feared and with good reason. My father brooked no betrayal." Before Cabe could say anything, Shade added, "and perhaps that is why he is not among their captures. Perhaps he is one shadow they wanted nothing of."

"Which leaves us where, Shade?"

"In a more complicated situation than I'd intended, but not in the impossible one you suppose. Like Ephraim, I can play more than one card."

The wizard felt his ire increasing. "This is no game, Shade! My daughter is somewhere in this realm and probably already at their mercy!"

"Do not underestimate your daughter," the hooded form murmured. "I've already made that mistake."

"What do you—"

But Darkhorse cut him off, warning, "The landscape is moving!"

The other two looked. Sure enough, the still lands were no longer still. They rippled and twisted and elements transformed. Hills became valleys and claw-like trees turned into macabre rock formations. The perpetual haze thickened and in it Cabe detected movement.

"Now what?" he snapped.

Shade only replied, "Stay close together. Do not become separated. In that they hope to achieve victory—"

The ground beneath them rocked. Darkhorse whinnied. Cabe slipped backward. He caught a glimpse of Shade tumbling to his knees, then the earth swallowed the warlock.

*Stay close together*, Shade had warned, but that proved impossible to do. Cabe managed to cast a spell protecting him from his fall, but as he landed the quicksilver landscape washed him away from Darkhorse.

With a roar, Darkhorse took to the sky. But as his hooves left the ground, the latter reached up and snared them. The eternal let his limbs stretch as thin as needles, but still he could not escape the grasping earth.

Another hill rose between Cabe and Darkhorse, cutting off the latter from the wizard's sight. The landscape, churning violently, sent him flowing farther and farther from his companions.

Concentrating as best he could, Cabe muttered. Immediately, a golden sphere surrounded him. It froze him in position despite the attempts of the earth to move him elsewhere.

He managed to catch his breath. Around him, Cabe could see only haze and ground. In the distance, he sensed Darkhorse and Shade, but which direction they were, Cabe could not say with utter certainty.

Then darkness loomed over him. He looked up, saw a wave of earth come crashing down on him. The sphere would never hold against its intensity.

Going down on one knee, the wizard thrust both hands up, his index and little fingers pointed at the oncoming avalanche.

The blue force that burst from his fingertips shattered his own shield, but Cabe cared not. The powerful, primal force continued up, striking the dropping earth with all the force that the wizard could muster.

The results were devastating. The gray sky filled with dust and bits of rock. Cabe covered his face with his own hood, then attempted to recast his sphere spell. However, the effort that he had used to shatter the attacking earth had drained him too much. Without a strong and proper source of energy from which to draw, the best he could muster was a weak travesty of the original.

Cabe folded himself into a ball, well aware that even if he survived the downpour, he would likely suffer terrible injury.

But after the first few pellets of dirt . . . the deluge ceased.

He did not stir at first, fearing some trick. Yet, when after several tense breaths he was still not struck down, Cabe finally gazed up.

Empty, gray sky greeted his dumbfounded eyes.

Slowly, cautiously, the spellcaster rose. The land beneath his feet had stilled once more. Cabe took a tentative step, but nothing happened.

The wizard dared exhale.

And that was when the voice said, "The necessary brute force, but hardly the proper dignity for my progeny . . ."

A fear that had lain dormant in Cabe for so very long burst to life. Gone were all the years of training, fighting, and learning. Suddenly he was again the young server from the inn who had been cast into a conflict that was his only because of his bloodline.

It took all his nerve to muster the strength to turn, to face the cause of his fear, the eternal fixation of his nightmares.

The black of the other's outfit—more like a uniform than anything else—was complemented by the navy blue band around his collar and his wrists. The red emblem of a dragon impaled upon a sword decorated the chest. Boots, hip-length in front, and gloves completed his clothing.

But if the garments were not proof enough of just what evil stood before Cabe, he had only to look at that face, that damnable face, to verify his worst horror. It too much resembled his own, but was older, darker of eyes, and the mouth continually wore a contemptuous smirk. Worse, the short beard and close-cut hair bore that impossible yet familiar half-and-half look, black on one side, silver on the other.

"Do close that chasm of a mouth, my boy," the bearded figure sneered. "Unless you'd like to say hello to your papa?"

*Azran . . .*

# VI

"Cabe! Cabe!" Darkhorse trod without fear over the landscape. As swiftly as it had begun, the shifting of the earth had ended. The eternal immediately understood that he had been intentionally separated from the others. The Lords of the Dead no doubt feared his power and why not? He had more than once put them in their places, although he had never fought them beyond proving a point.

The huge stallion tried once more to leap into the air. He managed only a foot or so before the ground seized his limbs. So, they desired him earthbound. Darkhorse laughed loudly, certain that the necromancers would hear. If they thought him weakened by that, then they were sorely mistaken.

But what could be their intention? Likely they hoped to deal with Cabe and even Shade first, then concentrate on him. This trap was likely only to keep him busy until that time—

A malevolent giggle echoed through his mind.

Darkhorse twisted his neck at an impossible angle. "Who is that? Who is there?"

Again came the giggle, a sound that more and more reminded the eternal of the one thing he had ever truly dreaded.

But that was impossible. That one was dead, dead, dead.

He turned about, trying to make out anything in the thickening haze.

"Aah, dear, dear Darkhorse! I've missed you so very, very, very much! How could you stay away so long?"

A tiny, black spot formed in the mist. The shadow steed snorted, then retreated. The spot drifted toward him, growing and coalescing. It swelled to the size of a pumpkin, then began taking on a different shape. Arms and legs thrust out and the general form shrank to a doll-sized figure with no features.

No features save two ice-blue orbs that suddenly opened in the darkness that covered what should have been its face.

The giggle echoed louder in Darkhorse's head. He reared, kicking at the ebony puppet even though it was too far to hit.

"You are no more!" he roared. "You have ceased to be! You are dead, *Yureel!*"

"What is death to us, my brother, who are immortal, who are without beginning or end?" Yureel floated closer. "But wait! You *do* have a beginning! I did create you, didn't I?"

"And from that moment on, we ceased to have any connection to one another! I abhor everything you are, Yureel! You torture and wreak bloodshed, manipulate the minds of others simply for your own amusement!"

The puppet spun upside down, giggling. "But whatever purpose do the ephemerals serve, hmm?"

"Their lives may be fleeting compared to ours, but they earn them far more than we ever have!" Darkhorse's eyes narrowed. "And you have already forfeited what foul existence you had!"

He reared again, clashing his front hooves together. Lightning crackled, striking out at Yureel.

But the bolts faded just before the malevolent puppet. "Shame, shame, shame, brother! It seems I must punish you . . ."

And as he spoke, Yureel swelled further in size. He grew as large as Darkhorse, then larger yet. As he grew, his form defined further, his outer shell becoming that of a monstrous knight with a horned helmet. One hand twisted, stretched, transforming into a huge spiked mace with twin heads.

"Come, embrace me, my brother!" the giant boomed. He brought the mace down hard. Thunder roared as the weapon cracked the ground, creating a chasm into which Darkhorse nearly fell.

The ebony stallion leapt over the gap, but just as before, the ground grabbed at his limbs. This time, however, Darkhorse reacted quicker. His legs shot into his body. As he landed, his torso shivered like a sack of water, softening the collision with the earth.

Immediately, eight spiderlike appendages burst free. Darkhorse raised himself up, stretching until he stood as tall as Yureel. The shadow steed's muzzle distorted, growing wider and toothier. Little of Darkhorse now resembled the animal from which he had named himself.

"You have no soul and therefore cannot be here, Yureel! Whatever you are, you are not what you appear!"

Even as he finished his declaration, Darkhorse charged. His head sharpened to a needle point, which he plunged into the knight's chest.

Yureel ripped in half, his upper torso flying over his adversary. The lower portion melted, turning into a huge, black puddle.

The mace came crashing down on Darkhorse, fiery sparks shooting up where it hit. Darkhorse roared in agony and lost hold of his shape. He flowed over what had been Yureel and the puddle sought to meld with him.

Another giggle escaped the monstrous warrior. Yureel's upper half spun about, then grew a new pair of legs. "Come, come, my brother . . . let our quarrel be no more! Let us be of one mind . . . and body . . ."

As Yureel combined with him, Darkhorse felt the horrific presence of his counterpart. Despite the stallion's denial, this *was* Yureel—or at least a part of him. There was something else, something magically created that enhanced what was actually Yureel—and surely had to be the work of the Lords of the Dead.

"You will be me and I will be me again . . ." whispered Yureel's mocking voice. "I will step forth from this boring place of shadows and again play with your favored world! I will write an epic of blood that will encompass all!"

And he swallowed Darkhorse.

**THEY HAD BEEN** separated, just as Shade had expected. He had thought that perhaps it could be avoided, but his cousins had planned better. Still, he felt secure that he could overcome whatever they had in mind for him.

It would involve the daughter. Ephraim surely had seen in her the truth long ago. Once, perhaps, twice, maybe, but never so often. Cabe Bedlam did not realize the secret his daughter held, perhaps unknowingly.

*How many times have you been reborn, Sharissa? I knew you as Galani and twice others, but there likely were more. Now you are Valea Bedlam, your soul combined once again with the bloodline from which you first sprouted . . .*

That was hardly the necromancers' work. They dealt in death and undeath, not life and reincarnation. No, this was most likely the intention of that which Shade feared more than any other, which had sent him on his path of immortal madness.

*But you will not have me . . .* he told that invisible foe. *Twisted though my soul has become, you will* never *have me!*

Did the Lords know that they unwittingly did another's bidding? Surely not. Not even Ephraim could foresee that. Only Shade recognized his ultimate foe, the same one he had battled since the son of Barakas Tezerenee. It was that foe, the warlock suspected, who had turned awry Shade's spell, the one that would have made death for him but a word. It was that foe who had sought his destruction, but who had failed. Shade had lived, albeit cursedly so.

And now his ageless adversary sought his life again through the necromancers. The irony was not lost on him.

Shade had no doubt that Cabe Bedlam and Darkhorse faced evils of their own, but to turn back to help them would only serve the purpose of Ephraim and the others.

The haze closed about him, forcing the warlock to choose his steps carefully. He sensed the ever-present spirits, but they were nothing to him. The one he had feared most was not among their invisible horde.

But no sooner had he thought that, when he noticed the outline of someone walking toward him. Instinctively, thousands of years of hardening slipped away. The booming voice and arrogant tone echoed through his memories and Shade almost cringed.

Yet, when the silhouetted figure spoke, the voice was one more calm, more concerned—and not that of Barakas Tezerenee.

"I hoped I would find you here," the ghost said.

If Shade's blurred features could have evinced surprise, they surely would have now. "Master . . . Zeree . . ."

"Ever the formal one," the bearded figure replied with a sad smile. He stood nearly seven feet tall and his narrow features were handsome in their way. He had a hawklike appearance that was complemented by the thin, groomed beard that matched the brown that was the color of most of his flowing hair. To one side of the ghost's head, a streak of silver darted back, but, unlike the Bedlams', it was an affectation, not a sign that he was a spellcaster. This one had lived before that had become the mark of the mage. "I would permit you to call me Dru, Gerrod."

"I will not call you that out of respect, Master Zeree . . . and you will not call me who I no longer am."

"Ever the stubborn one, too, as I recall." The specter stepped closer. The hazy landscape could be seen through his faded gray robe.

"They have sent you," growled the faceless warlock, unable to completely hide his anxiety. "What malignant purpose do *you* serve for them?"

The ghost of Dru Zeree smiled sadly again. "None, G—friend. Ephraim and the others know nothing of my presence here. If they did, they would be quite shocked."

"As they are the lords, masters, and creators of this infernal pocket world, I find that hard to believe even from your ethereal lips, Master Zeree."

"Your threat awaits you in the castle. I come as one who knew you and felt your fear—"

"I fear nothing and no one!"

Dru chuckled, an unearthly sound even to the jaded warlock. "Your father would beg to differ." His tone darkened. "They will be here quickly. You must listen to me. The death you fear is your victory . . . that, and *her*."

"Her?" Shade waved him away. "You can't possibly mean who I think, Master Zeree . . ."

"I always knew how you felt, as did Sharissa." The ghost shook his head.

"Your cause was not so hopeless as you think. You were just . . . at the crossroads at the wrong time."

"How eloquently put . . . and how useless to me now. If that's all you've to say, then begone with you!"

Dru Zeree's crystalline eyes narrowed. "Ever the stubborn one. Despite that, she'll try to do what she can for you . . ." He suddenly peered into the mist. "They're near."

Glancing in the direction his ethereal companion had looked, the hooded warlock saw nothing. "Who are—"

But the phantom of his past had vanished.

And almost immediately, Shade sensed the approaching figures. Five of them, a good Vraad number. They were spread all along the path behind, moving unafraid of his notice. They *wanted* him to know that they were there, the better to force his hand.

The Lords of the Dead were on the hunt.

Shade started away. He was not weak in their domain, but certainly weaker than he liked. They had planned long for this moment, perhaps even centuries, and it did not behoove him to wait to confront them, not yet.

As he picked up his pace, he probed with his mind his pursuers. Images flashed in his head of each. He saw the monstrous, armored warriors, the ancient symbol of their clan still visible upon their rusting breast plates. They marched toward him whether or not they still had flesh and bone with which to carry themselves. Some merely drifted along, bits of human ivory dangling limply across the ground. Most had no flesh upon their half-hidden faces, but all had fiery orbs that represented what truly remained of them after so long. They were a macabre, ghoulish parade, completely unaware that no life existed in their decaying shells. They were more ghosts than the slivers of souls that they collected.

But they were powerful, powerful ghosts.

He dared probe deeper, identifying each and recalling well when they had been of the same blood. Hirac and Ghan, the brothers. They strode near one another, the former with one leg, the latter, both arms gone and his jaw hanging loose. Delio, the giant among the necromancers. Nearly eight feet tall and almost intact. A few bits of flesh still hung to his emaciated form. Xarakee, the closest in bloodline to Shade, almost a half brother, if ancient rumors held truth. He was little more than a rib cage and a head.

And Zorane. Ephraim's shadow. Also lacking legs, although he, like the rest, moved as if fully bodied. Shade recalled Zorane and his immaculate beard, his fastidious attitude when it came to himself. The warlock envisioned the five as they saw themselves, proud sorcerers of Clan Tezerenee and members of the

Vraad race. Once stout of chest and perfect of face and form, their egos would not let them see the truth.

A fearsome, chill gale exploded, nearly sending the warlock tumbling. Shade dug in his boots, but still he was pushed back in the direction the necromancers desired him to go.

They would expect him to resist. He focused on Ghan, opening the earth beneath the latter. Ghan stumbled, seeking to retain his footing, and, as Shade had expected, Hirac moved to aid him.

The warlock reached into his cloak and pulled out a tiny, winged figurine honed from marble. He whispered to it and it disappeared.

In his thoughts, it reappeared before the distracted Hirac. Now the size of a man and screeching loud, the huge marble eagle pounced on the necromancer.

But no sooner had his golem attacked Hirac then the gale became a full storm, pummeling Shade relentlessly. It shoved him along the Lords' route. The warlock leaned against it, but allowed the magical tempest to do its work.

He felt Zorane's satisfaction at this apparent victory. Ephraim might have been more suspicious, but Zorane took matters more at face value. Shade was being forced toward the castle; therefore, all was as it should be.

*Keep assuming so, cousin,* the hooded figure thought as he pretended to lose track of a spell he had been about to cast.

With an almost contemptuous thrust of his hand, Hirac turned the marble eagle into so much dust. Ghan, meanwhile, levitated over the chasm. Emboldened, the necromancers regrouped and solidified their efforts against Shade. They had him on the run, so they believed, and he did nothing to dissuade them of that notion.

And as the storm forced him up and over a ridge, the hair on the warlock's neck bristled. Holding his cloak tight around him, Shade looked in the direction in which the Lords of the Dead sought to force him.

There, perched on the next hill, the immense stone sanctum balefully greeted his gaze.

"So," he muttered in half satisfaction, half anxious anticipation. "It's almost about to begin."

# VII

GERROD STARED AT the floor in shame. Valea turned away from him, preferring even the dismal landscape outside the window. Ephraim had left them to their own devices, stating that Gerrod would know when it was time for his part in their plot.

"You're him," she finally stated.

"He's me," Gerrod corrected. "A casting of me, that is. That which you call Shade is incomplete, has been incomplete since the day that damned spell was cast."

"But he's alive and you—" The enchantress broke off, suddenly feeling cruel in her choice of words.

"It's the land's jest," he replied bitterly. "Its foul humor is surpassed only by its audacity! It must conform all to its desire and when it finds something it can't conform, it seeks to break that thing until it can be made useful."

She looked back at him. "Such as you?"

"I defied it. I denied it. When my people became in flesh the monsters that they had been in mind, I turned to its own magic to force back my transformation, else perhaps there would have been one more lineage of dragons . . ."

His words did not make complete sense, but Valea understood the gist of them. "You fear the Dragonrealm itself? You fear the land?"

He reached with the instinctive intention of taking her by the arm, but then came to his senses. The ghost instead pointed at the world beyond the window. "That is a mere reflection of the true reality, one of hundreds of pocket worlds, bubble realms, that the first race created. Even we Vraad had no name for them. They were powerful beyond belief and when they realized that they were dying, they created from themselves the seeds for countless successors, each set so that only one group would live." He grimaced. "But while a few survived centuries, none flourished. Most races lived out their spans in their pocket worlds, never advancing enough to enter the true one."

The Vraad had made the leap, although more by accident than promise. Having ruined their own realm, they found a path to the original, arriving just as the avian Seekers began to fall into savagery after their war with their own predecessors, the Quel. The Vraad began filling in the niche, but by seeking to remake their new home as they had their old—which would have eventually resulted in a second catastrophe.

But the land, Gerrod had discovered, had a mind of its own. "I believe that the last of the originators became a part of their world so that they could watch and manipulate whoever came after. Those that fit, they left virtually untouched. Those that did not . . . they altered as their *whims* dictated."

For the Vraad, it meant extinction as a race. Some fled, falling prey to other forces, but many, especially the powerful, militaristic Tezerenee, transformed. From dragons they had created bodies to house their ka, their spirits, and these had been their method by which they had fled from their world to this one. Now, as if mocking their efforts, the land twisted them, shaped them into the very beasts that they had used. The Tezerenee would rule the realm as they had desired, but as horrors without any memory of their previous might.

They became the first of the Dragon Kings.

Despite herself, Valea listened in fascination. Her father had made some conjectures as to the origins of the drake lords, who had appeared quickly and as if out of nowhere, but even he had not quite made this connection as far as she knew.

"And you?" the enchantress asked.

"Spell after spell I used to keep me as I was. I feared even dying, certain that doing so would only surrender me to the land. Then, I thought at last I had the ultimate spell, one that would give me immortality and make me impervious to whatever the land desired—but in my eagerness, I failed to consider its interference in that spell."

His miscast attempt had resulted in a disaster which had destroyed a mountain and its surroundings for miles in every direction. Gerrod had felt as if ripped in twain. He had blacked out, then awoke in what seemed an endless haze. There he had drifted for what he likened to an eternity.

"Until that point when *they* claimed me."

They brought him before them, told him that he had died—and yet had not. They then revealed to him that part of his being that remained alive and how it sought to complete itself time and time again. He watched as his shadow self—who in mockery all too close to the truth had named itself *Shade*—wreaked carnage in one lifetime and then sought to pay restitution in the next. For a time, the Lords of the Dead let him watch the fruitless struggle of Shade as he attempted over and over—either when good or evil—to make himself whole. That, however, could never be, for he unwittingly lacked the one component that would have made it possible.

His true self.

"Shade, the Shade you know, can never be redeemed. He is not a whole creature, not even a true being . . . and so he is ever doomed to failure."

Valea wanted to deny that. Her own father and, especially, Darkhorse had regaled her with tales of Shade's sacrifices when he had been of better nature. Even if that had not been enough, she had experienced Galani's memories and knew what the elf had read within the warlock. The passion, the love, that the elf maiden had carried for Shade could not have been directed at a thing not wholly real. Gerrod had to be wrong . . .

But then . . . who would know better than him?

"What—what exactly do they want you to do?"

For a ghost, he gave a very real grunt. "I must merely reclaim what is mine. I *am* the true self. I have always been. When we touch, my will shall engulf his. He has no choice in the matter. Everything will be set to rights. He is but a body devoid of a true soul. I am the true soul and I will at last have my body again."

"And all the lives that he has led, for good or ill?"

Gerrod turned from her. "Forgotten. Known only to legends and history. I want nothing of them, for they're no part of me."

It all sounded too much like a slaying to Valea. Shade *was* a separate life from Gerrod, of that she felt certain. He had committed evil, yes, but had done so much good. More to the point, he had loved and no mere shell could do that. What Galani had exhibited had been returned.

"It's abominable! You can't do it!"

"I *must* do it," he replied without looking. "For Sharissa—"

She suddenly felt filled with a contempt for him, despite his predicament. "I've gleaned enough to understand your desire there! You lost her once, I'm thinking, and I doubt this path will guide you any better! Besides, what use is regaining your life when she's still dead?"

The ghost wavered, becoming translucent for the first time. Valea thought he intended to vanish, then recalled that he could not. "She will live again . . ."

His words struck her hard, for she immediately understood their meaning. "You're talking about me."

"You are her already. You simply don't remember any more. When Sharissa enters you, she will dominate. You will cease and she will walk the earth once more."

He sounded so horribly certain that Valea could not help but believe him. "And you want this . . ."

Gerrod said nothing.

After a drawn-out silence, the enchantress shook her head. "I won't just stand here waiting for it to happen."

"It's all already in play. Ephraim's planned long for this. You are here. Shade is out there. Even your father and the black beast he travels with have been taken into account. Ephraim was quite willing to talk of his work and its inevitable success."

"My father is out there? And Darkhorse, too?"

"Yes."

Valea smiled. "Then the Lords are doomed to defeat!"

Her confident statement was met by a look of pity. "They're not alone out there, my lady. You forget whose domain this is. As I await Shade, others await them."

"Who?"

"For the one called Darkhorse, that which created him. For your father . . . your grandfather . . ." Gerrod ignored her astounded and suddenly fearful expression. "And as I and Sharissa have been promised, Azran Bedlam and the thing called Yureel have been offered their lives . . ."

"COME, COME, HAVE you nothing to say to your dear father?"

"Several things come to mind," Cabe retorted, his hands balling into fists. "I doubt you'd want to hear them."

The silver-and-black-haired figure smiled malevolently. "A pity I was never given the opportunity to raise you properly! Respect is the first lesson you would've been taught."

"Respect?" blurted the younger spellcaster. "From the man who slew his brother, killed his wife—my mother—and betrayed his own father and humanity's chance to escape the Dragon Kings?"

Azran's own expression hardened. "I was betrayed first! My due was not given to me!"

"I thank the day Grandfather managed to steal me away . . ."

"He's probably about here somewhere," Cabe's father sneered. "Should there be anything left of you when I take your body, perhaps the pair of you can have a long, long philosophical discussion . . ."

Azran's arms stretched forth, twisting far beyond what should have been their limits. His act caught Cabe by surprise, who, despite knowing that his father was a ghost, had still placed upon Azran the limitations of flesh and bone.

As the foul phantasm's elongated fingers touched him, Cabe felt a chill in his heart and a growing sense that he was being smothered. Azran's horrific face filled his eyes and he felt his father intruding in his mind. The fingers probed deep and Cabe's soul seemed to rip, as if a piece of it had been torn away.

*You are the flesh of my flesh, my son . . . it's only proper you give something back to your father . . .*

But Cabe had no intention of granting Azran anything. He had not come to the dread realm without considering that he might face its ghosts. He also had his past encounter with Azran's grasping spirit to serve him and, aware of the Lords' perverse nature, had assumed that he might confront his father at some point.

Cabe's hand slipped into a pouch at his belt. Azran sensed what he planned and tried to freeze the wizard in place by burrowing deeper into his soul. With a cry, Cabe fought the pain and clutched tight the object he had been seeking.

He tore it from the pouch and held it toward the ghost of his father. Azran's face distorted, becoming a thing of rotting flesh and monstrous evil.

"Now is that any way to treat your father?" the ghoul mocked.

Cabe held out his hand. The object, a tiny box of rich, quicksilver wood—elfwood—opened.

A tremendous wind sucked in Azran's ghost. The dead sorcerer howled as he fought in vain to escape it. He tightened his hold on Cabe's soul—almost taking his son with him—but the wizard managed to keep his position.

And then—just like that—Azran Bedlam disappeared into the box. The lid shut tight and the crack flared golden as Cabe's creation sealed itself.

"It's exactly the way to treat you," Cabe muttered to the magical container. He had fashioned it after artifacts left behind by the Vraad, one of which had been used in the past to trap Darkhorse.

He had not expected Azran to fall so readily, but had no complaints that it had turned out that way. Still, the box would not hold even his father's spirit for very long and so Cabe had to hurry. He had no idea what had happened to Darkhorse and while he feared for the eternal, Cabe knew that he had to go after the one who mattered most to him . . . Valea.

Silently asking Darkhorse's forgiveness even though he knew that the shadow steed would have urged him to the same course, the wizard eyed the box. It vanished immediately, cast out by Cabe to some random part of the necromancers' realm. He did not want to risk carrying Azran's sinister spirit with him, the dead sorcerer's will so strong it might influence Cabe's mind even when trapped.

As he looked up from his task, the wizard stared. The haze had thinned again with Azran's defeat and in the distance stood the only structure he had so far seen. That it was a castle only verified what he already knew. The Lords of the Dead were not far—which meant that neither was Valea.

Cabe started walking again.

# VIII

DARKHORSE FELT YUREEL invade his essence. The fear that had existed for a thousand mortal lives swelled. He had thought himself rid of such horrors when he and the others had trapped his twin, and Yureel, rather than be cast out forever into the Void, had destroyed himself. Darkhorse had never told his friends how much of a relief that had truly been for him.

Now it appeared he would yet be devoured . . .

But how could this be? As Darkhorse had proclaimed, Yureel had no soul, not in the sense that it was utilized by mortals. The pair were creatures of pure energy, pure magic. They no more had souls than did rocks.

The Lords of the Dead had, therefore, not taken the same thing from Yureel that they had from others. The only way by which Yureel could be here was if the necromancers had recovered some fragment of his essence that had not been destroyed . . .

And that knowledge fueled Darkhorse's resolve. Whole, Yureel might have been too much for him. but if much of what battled the stallion was a construct of the Lords, then the opposite was true.

He steeled himself and fought Yureel's invasion to a standstill. As the two struggled, Darkhorse secretly probed, seeking the key to the truth.

There! In the midst of the blob that was his foe, he found the only true bit of Yureel. It pulsated like a sinister black heart, malevolence radiating from it.

"Aaargh!" Even as he located the true Yureel, it attacked, literally devouring part of him. The loss was minuscule, but served as a vicious reminder of what could happen.

A brilliant sunburst surrounded Darkhorse as he defended himself. It burned away the false bits of his twin, forcing what was left to quickly withdraw into itself. Darkhorse, however, did not relent. He next burned away the haze surrounding them, shedding light for perhaps the first time on this one part of the necromancers' dire realm.

Yureel suddenly exploded.

Caught by surprise, Darkhorse lost control of his spell. As it faded, he was inundated by a downpour of what had once been his adversary. Black splotches struck him everywhere, burning him even when the eternal sought to make himself incorporeal.

But at last, Darkhorse shook off the last desperate attack. The blotches moved swiftly around the landscape, gradually gathering together. Restoring himself to his full stallion form, Darkhorse leapt from spot to spot, stomping on each blotch and eradicating it. The bits of Yureel began scurrying here and there in an attempt to confuse him, but the shadow steed hunted them down wherever he saw them.

Then he sensed what appeared to be the remaining part of his twin. The inky form, blacker yet than all the others, sought to seep into the cold earth, but Darkhorse's hoof crashed down before it, cutting off escape. With almost pitiful movements, Yureel attempted to race under his foe.

With a harsh laugh, Darkhorse created another limb right above where he knew the splotch would go.

The hoof came down, stamping out the last of Yureel. Blue lightning briefly crackled as the last bit burned away.

Darkhorse looked around quickly. He neither saw nor detected any other traces. Still, if anything had managed to slip by, it surely amounted to nothing. Unless the Lords of the Dead deigned to be generous and give Yureel a second opportunity—which was highly doubtful considering the latter's abysmal failure—then any bit of Darkhorse's twin still remaining was doomed to forever be only a glimmer crawling uselessly over the empty land.

Satisfied, the shadow steed considered his next move. Whatever else happened, Cabe would head toward the castle in order to find Valea. That was what Darkhorse expected of him. The children of his friend were almost as dear to the eternal as they were to Cabe and Gwen. Darkhorse would have willingly sacrificed himself for any of the humans' sakes.

So the castle was his next destination . . . yet, where *was* it?

Probing the haze, he discovered not the lair of the necromancers, but rather a more welcome thing. A very familiar, comfortable presence.

*Cabe?*

*Darkhorse?* returned the wizard. *Where?*

The stallion strengthened the link between them. *I know where you are,* he told Cabe. *Wait and I shall be with you . . .*

Picturing the human in his mind, Darkhorse concentrated.

The next moment, he stood right before the wizard.

"Praise be that you're all right!" Cabe said, smiling in relief.

"Their trap was clever, but not clever enough!"

"You, too? Darkhorse, Azran's ghost confronted me."

"Indeed?" The shadow steed recalled all too well Azran Bedlam and shivered. "And I was faced by a Yureel still intent upon devouring me."

The wizard frowned. "Yureel? But how could he be here?"

"The Lords no doubt salvaged some small bit of him after our last struggle. I sent that final piece of refuse to oblivion."

Cabe could scarce believe it. "Azran *and* Yureel . . ."

"Yes, we were both quite fortunate!"

"A bit too fortunate," muttered the human, not explaining. "It doesn't matter. You and I are together and the castle's just ahead."

Gazing up, Darkhorse saw the grim sanctum. "Indeed! We shouldn't let our hosts await us any longer, then, friend Cabe!"

"No, we shouldn't." The wizard mounted. His tone matched well their surroundings. "And if I find they've harmed her in any way, not a thousand Azrans and Yureels combined will keep me from making them *pay.*"

The eternal snorted ferociously, echoing his companion's sentiments, then the two started off toward the castle . . .

EPHRAIM MATERIALIZED IN the midst of the pattern, taking his rightful place. The five who had not gone with Zorane and the others looked to him for their next move.

"The Bedlam and the eternal?"

"The wizard readily sealed his father in a box much like our old 'catchers.' The eternal proved that his twin was now but a shadow of him," reported one sorcerer, his jaw bone completely missing and his ribs showing through his rusted armor.

"They failed miserably," mocked another in similar condition.

Ephraim nodded. "Then everything goes as I predicted." To the others—and even himself—his lips curled back in a triumphant smile. The sight would have been no less macabre than the eternal, fleshless grin he actually wore. "Now it is time for the female."

# IX

THEY WOULD BE coming soon. Whether the ghoul called Ephraim or one of the other nightmarish Lords, Valea could not say. Likely Ephraim, as he seemed the most animated of them. Whichever the case, though, the enchantress intended to be ready.

"Gerrod . . . you said to Ephraim that he ever had more than one intention whenever he did something, is that right?"

"What you see on the surface is never all there is, not where he is concerned. He looks to all details, never wastes what may be of value."

Valea nodded. Everything about Ephraim's plan seemed to focus on the removal of Shade as a threat, but what after? The Lords of the Dead had always desired to expand their dread might beyond their realm, to make the land of the living theirs as well. Yet, surely they expected resistance, especially from her own family, unless—

Unless the Bedlams were *removed* as an obstacle first.

It all began to fall into place. This was more than a final confrontation between the warlock and the Lords. They had expected all along that one or both of her parents would follow her trail, most likely her father. Darkhorse, his constant comrade, would also come. The two most powerful forces of magic in all the Dragonrealm in one place. Between them, they were certainly more of a threat to the necromancers than even Shade. The Lords would have to destroy them if they hoped to conquer the living world.

Or *would* they? *Ephraim never wastes what may be of value.*

Surely Cabe Bedlam and Darkhorse would be more valuable if they could be *turned.*

She stifled a gasp. If they turned her father and Darkhorse, they could use them to take down her mother, the Lord Gryphon, and Queen Erini—the most powerful mages. The Dragon Kings, already much weakened, would fall one by one. The deathly, still lands of the necromancers' realm would spread across the continent . . . and perhaps beyond.

But they could never have expected Valea to journey here. Her decision had been but a recent one. Only when the spirit of the elf, Galani, had spoken to her in her dream—

The *spirit* of Galani . . .

Had the entire situation in the Manor been the creation of the Lords? Surely not. The tale had been too real, too true. She had felt Galani's presence and the elf had, in turn, acknowledged hers.

But perhaps Ephraim had given the matter a nudge. It sounded very much like him.

And at that moment, the chill voice of the necromancer filled her ears. "You shall come with me, daughter of the Bedlam, willingly or not."

Gerrod gasped, ever seeming so real, so alive, despite his being a ghost.

She looked up into the fleshless, ghoulish visage, steeling herself as she met the Lord's inhuman, fiery gaze. "What could I do to stop you?"

"Pragmatic. Like death itself, this is a fate you must accept." To Gerrod, the necromancer said, "He is here."

The ghost dipped his head. "I know. I've felt him."

"You know when he will be weakest."

"Yes, Ephraim."

The necromancer laughed. "Come, Gerrod! You act as if you don't want to live again!" He suddenly clutched Valea by the back of the neck and thrust her face toward that of hooded specter. "Remember . . ."

Gerrod growled at his tormentor. "Have no fear, Ephraim. I'll do what I must."

The other nodded. "Then it is time to finish this."

Valea's surroundings instantly changed. Instead of the tiny cell, she and Ephraim now stood in a dark and foreboding chamber upon whose floor had been etched a huge pentagram. Within *its* interior had been inscribed countless runes. The enchantress sensed the immense forces in play the moment she appeared.

"We are ready," Ephraim announced.

Five figures even more grotesque than he stood at the points of the pentagram. As one, they bowed their helmed skulls in concentration. A moment later, their numbers doubled as other Lords took up secondary places within the main pattern.

Valea tried not to shudder. Around her stood *all* the necromancers, all the Lords of the Dead. Even despite their monstrous conditions, she was aware that the group wielded tremendous power.

"Kadaria. You have the slivers?"

"Here," said a voice whose femininity startled the enchantress further. So thoroughly decayed were the Lords that she had not even realized that one—no—*two* of them were women. Now she saw that hints of long hair, once possibly silver, hung limply under the edges of the helmet.

The female necromancer tossed forth two tiny spheres of glittering black. They paused in the air just before Ephraim and his captive.

"Bring forth the Bedlam and his pet . . ." the lead spellcaster commanded.

The other ten kept their heads low.

And to Valea's horror, her *father* and Darkhorse both materialized within the pentagram.

Cabe Bedlam had time only to utter, "What—?" before his eyes suddenly glazed over. Darkhorse reared in fury, but Ephraim touched one of the two spheres and the eternal, too, stilled.

Tearing herself from the Lord's grip, Valea went to her father. "What've you done to him?"

"He and the creature are now ours. They thought they kept their foes from possessing their bodies, but that was not the point to the attacks. Our pawns took what we wanted, small slivers of the wizard's soul and a bit of the demon's essence. Enough to garner us control over them . . ."

So she had been correct in that assumption. They *had* wanted the might of her family for their vile plans.

"Through them," Ephraim continued. "We shall take your mother, your sibling, the lionbird, and the rest. They shall all be made to serve us in bringing the perfection of our rule to the realm of the living."

"No longer will there be a line between life and death," added one of the newer arrivals.

"Now, girl," the lead necromancer uttered, reaching out to Valea. "It is your turn. Shade is coming . . . and you must be made ready."

As one, the other Lords began chanting, their words in some language that Valea had never heard. The entire pattern suddenly flared bright, the runes burning like fire.

The enchantress felt a sense of vertigo—then discovered herself once again before Ephraim. However, they were no longer alone, for a third figure now hovered next to the prisoner.

The ghost of Sharissa.

"Twins born out of sync," murmured Ephraim. "Such perfect reincarnation! Such uniqueness! It is almost as if time itself seeks to guarantee our victory over our cousin and mastery over the living lands!"

"Get on with it," rumbled the male who had last spoken. "This must be done!"

"It will be, Zorane! It will be because I have planned it so!"

Ephraim spread his hands to encompass both captives. Valea found that she could no longer move save to breathe. The tiny stone she wore rose and fell as she did, ever touching her skin.

The necromancer slowly brought his hands toward each other . . . and as he did, Valea felt another presence begin to melt into her body.

Sharissa's spirit filled her . . .

# X

SHADE SENSED THE powerful forces emanating from the castle.

"So," he whispered. "They've begun."

He started up toward the wall, not at all daunted by the lack of any door. When the warlock desired to enter, he would enter.

Suddenly, something launched from the battlements. Shade did not have to look close to know that they were a pair of Necri.

"I've had quite enough of your kind." He pointed at the first, which immediately exploded in flames. The Necri's shriek cut off as the fire swiftly burned it to ash.

The other creature started to pull up, but its doom had already been set in motion. Shade gave a twist of his wrist and the batlike demon crumpled together, every bone crushed magically. The warlock continued on his trek even as the mangled remnants collided with the ground nearby.

Coming to the wall, he tested the spells surrounding it. None were beyond him. In fact, most were quite infantile compared to what the warlock had expected. His cousins might as well have created a vast, open gateway for him to walk through. Clearly they desired his presence inside and Shade saw no reason to disappoint them.

He folded his voluminous cloak about him and disappeared.

VALEA FELT THE female Vraad's presence begin to overwhelm her own. It was not that Sharissa *wanted* to do this; on the contrary, the ghost's sadness was evident even as she began to take over.

If Valea hoped to survive at all, she had to pray that her will remained strong enough.

*Galani* . . . the enchantress called.

She sensed the stone stir. When she had decided that she must pursue Shade, put an end to his curse, the enchantress had returned to the place where she had discovered the entrance to the elf's tomb. She could no longer gain admittance, but that had not been what she had wanted. All that Valea had desired was a

tiny piece of that which surrounded Galani—the Wyr Stone. She had hoped
to use its intricate properties to transform things in order to craft a spell to
imprison Shade, then change him from the cursed warlock to a harmless and
quite mortal being.

To her surprise, though, not only had the piece chipped free with barely any
effort—but upon touching it, Valea had sensed the presence of her former incarnation. Galani intended to be with her on this quest, doing what she could.

No, Ephraim might have somehow stirred the matter up, but the elf's desire
to help had been very real. Now, Valea needed that help in a different way than
she had intended.

There were suddenly three minds within her head. Valea felt Sharissa's confusion. The latter's invasion faltered as she confronted two wills, not one.

"Hold!" Ephraim immediately shouted. "Something is wrong!" He strode
up to Valea, waving one hand across her form. Immediately it halted where the
stone hung.

The necromancer hissed and tore at her garment, revealing the source of his
frustration. Valea could do nothing as he seized the piece and pulled it free.

But as he did, a sense of total displacement enveloped her. A tremendous
force pulled her from her own body and into an eternal whiteness. Valea looked
around, found nothing. She put a hand to her face . . .

And discovered she had neither fingers nor face to touch.

Somehow . . . somehow *her* spirit had become ensnared in the Wyr Stone.

GERROD WAITED. HE knew that Shade would come to him. Like a fly drawn
to honey, the other piece of him could not stay away from that for which it had
ever searched.

Gerrod stood in the courtyard, where Ephraim had told him to make the
encounter. The ghost waited, head down, knowing that the meeting was imminent.

He sensed Shade before he heard him.

"So . . . there you are."

The specter looked up. He felt no fear, no anxiety, when he stared into that
blur that was all the visage that Shade could ever have. No, Gerrod only felt
sadness . . . and not just for the two parts of him. He felt sadness for what was
taking place and what the Lords would do when they had what they wanted.

But he had no choice but to obey if he wanted to live.

"I admit . . . I was startled when I knew that it would be you," Shade went
on. "I expected more from you."

"You know me as well as yourself," Gerrod chided. "You know what I want."

"And I'm supposed to give it to you?"

"You've no choice." The ghost stamped the floor. As with his cell, it reacted to him as if he was as solid as the figure before him.

The crash of his boot echoed in their otherwise silent surroundings. Immediately, a huge pattern covering the entire courtyard flashed bright crimson.

Shade sought to react, but it was already too late. He had no hope of leaving now. He could barely even move. His arms, his legs, everything acted in slow motion. Gerrod had a twang of guilt, seeing how his shell struggled in the face of the inevitable. Almost he could imagine the torment on the unseen countenance.

"You shouldn't battle so," the ghost said, closing on him. "I'll be giving you peace. You could've never had what you wanted . . ."

"Neither . . . can . . . you . . ."

"I'll *live*."

The warlock struggled futilely. "At what . . . cost? As . . . Ephraim's p-puppet? What . . . what is life . . . when the Lords . . . take over . . . the living?"

Gerrod drew back in bitterness. "Be silent! What would you know about life? A shell seeking to be real? You were doomed from the start because you weren't even our true self!" He beat his chest twice. "I am Gerrod Tezerenee! You are nothing but a walking mockery of my existence! When I've taken over, I will be whole again!"

"And the Lords . . . will have . . . won. And the . . . Land . . . will have won . . ."

"What do you mean?"

The murky features almost came into focus. "The Lords' rule . . . will be short . . . in the scheme of things. In the end . . . the Land . . . will do with them . . . as it has . . . the Seekers . . . the Quel . . . and others. Only this time . . . the humans . . . the hope . . . will go with them . . ."

"You're stalling," Gerrod decided. He started toward the warlock again. "Stalling the inevitable."

"And when you . . . are me . . . the Land . . . will have its greatest . . . triumph," Shade went on despite his approaching doom. "Gerrod Tezerenee. Not Shade. You will live . . . you will change . . . the Land will finally alter you as it did our people . . ."

"No . . . I will live! I will be me! I will have all I wanted!"

"All you wanted?" The warlock's head dipped low as his battle against the spell failed. "Any care . . . Sharissa had for one lowly . . . Gerrod Tezerenee . . . will die as surely as she."

"Sharissa will live, too!" the ghost declared, his hand almost upon the captive's chest. They both knew what would happen when he touched the warlock. "She will *live*! I give her the greatest gift—"

"As Ephraim's. Cursing life . . . cursing you." Shade shrugged, then leaned forward. "Do what you must. I look forward to missing the world you will help shape."

With a frustrated roar, Gerrod thrust his hand into Shade's ribs. It sank in without hesitation. The warlock roared in agony. The ghost pressed forward.

And as he did, he sensed the tumultuous emotions and thoughts racing through Shade's mind—his mind.

Gerrod gasped, almost pulled his hand back in horror. He had never expected to find such a rich trove of sensations—of life—within.

Then his eyes hardened. "No . . . I *will* do it!"

He entered the screaming captive.

# XI

"THE WYR STONE . . ." Ephraim's ghoulish countenance darkened. "Or, rather, a pathetic fragment of it . . . the Zeree cunning has not been watered down either by endless generations or incarnations . . ."

"Has it disrupted our work?" asked Zorane anxiously.

"A hesitation, nothing more." The lead necromancer thrust the chain through his rotting belt. "It will be remedied—"

"Ephraim . . ." the imprisoned female suddenly uttered. "This is madness."

The Lord performed a mock bow. "My Lady Sharissa . . . so good of you to join us . . . in the flesh."

"I am the only one here in any sort of flesh," the voice from Valea Bedlam's body snapped back. "If you could see what your obsession's made of all of you . . ."

"Spoken like the daughter of the self-righteous Master Zeree," smirked Zorane. "Ever the voice of temperance among those with no need to be . . ."

"And the result of not listening was the devastation of Nimth."

"But leaving Nimth brought us to power undreamed," returned Ephraim. "Enabled us to become *gods.*"

"Demons, perhaps, but never gods . . ."

The towering necromancer waved away her comments. "This conversation is superfluous. You are bound to our will. You will do as we demand. Now there is only one other we await." Ephraim looked to his right. "And he comes now."

As one, the other sorcerers looked to the far end of the chamber, where what seemed black light flashed briefly.

In its wake, a bent, hooded form unfolded the voluminous cloak that surrounded him.

"Our dear cousin, Gerrod. How appropriate a moment. Come. Let the two of you gaze upon one another alive again. Look upon one another's sweet faces . . ."

"Yes, Ephraim." But as he straightened, he revealed that he had no face upon which *any* of them could look.

Zorane shifted out of position. "That's not possible! Gerrod taking over should—"

Sharissa's pleased laughter erupted from Valea's mouth.

"Gerrod Tezerenee loved you, my lady," Shade murmured.

The captive's expression became sad but proud. "I know."

The warlock struck.

A shimmering, red field surrounded the Lords of the Dead, a protective spell cast at the last moment by them. Yet, the chamber still shook violently and several of the necromancers teetered from their chosen places. The field flickered on and off and on again.

But in the end, it held.

"Whether he took you or you took him does not matter!" hissed Ephraim. "You will find us more than before! You will bow to us this time and fulfill the role we have arranged for you, cousin!"

The Lords of the Dead stared at Shade . . . and with them stared Cabe, Darkhorse, and Sharissa.

The warlock drew his cloak around him.

From the walls, from the floors, erupted monstrous, winged fiends of yellow energy. They immediately clawed at Shade, ravaging his garments, ripping through the protected cloak. Some scored cuts on his arms and torso, but he never once cried out.

He opened his palm and a wind scattered to pieces the nearest. Shade spun about and the wind followed, whipping across his tormentors and decimating them.

But no sooner had he deflected the first horrendous assault when a new and more horrific sight surrounded him. They were ghosts, pained spirits—and all were victims of his past darkness. Worse . . . they had all been friends, close friends, whom he had betrayed.

"They haunt you every waking moment . . . and you *never* sleep, do you, cousin?" mocked Ephraim. "Now see their true sorrow, their true anguish . . . and know that it is all your doing!"

Although his hood lay in tatters from the first assault, nothing of Shade's head or face could yet be made out with any definition. His voice, though, spoke well of the emotions boiling within. "No! They are not my doing! I would never have willingly done such evil!"

"But you did, time and time over! You would happily do so again! Your own miscast spell ensures that!"

They crowded around Shade, pressed him close. "No! It's the Land that ensured it! The Land that twisted my work!"

Several of the necromancers laughed.

Xarakee bellowed, "Are you still on that? 'The land is alive! The land is out to change us into monsters!' Ha!"

"As it did the rest! You know how the drakes came to be! Their kings were my brothers!"

"Those were fools who used the dragon-based golems," Ghan returned. "The inherent traits of the flesh and blood taken from the beasts simply demanded their natural design! It was poor sorcery, not some malevolent plot by a thinking world!"

"If the land was such a horrific foe," Ephraim concluded, "we would not be as we are . . . masters of it, not its pawns . . ."

Despite the horrible memories surrounding him, Shade straightened. He no longer stared at the ghosts around him, only the eleven figures standing so confidently. "No? Perhaps you should see yourselves as others do, then, *cousin!* Perhaps you should see the truth!"

Grunting from agony and effort, he cast.

It flared like a silver beacon, spreading across the chamber. Its presence was so tremendous that the ghosts haunting the warlock fled from what it revealed to them. Shade ignored them, although the pain of their faces remained with him. He only cared that he make the Lords of the Dead see.

See *themselves.*

It was a mirror like no other. Perfect in reflecting in brilliance what the dank, still lands and the minds of the necromancers sought to hide. The chamber where the Lords worked their foul deeds was not the glittering, elegant room that they imagined. Instead it was a crumbling, dust-enshrouded tomb barely lit, with unimaginable shapes rotting in the corners or dangling from the cracked ceiling.

But none of that registered for long upon the necromancers—for they now stared at their individual forms. Each saw only him or herself in that mirror, saw revealed by Shade the truth.

"No . . ." gasped Zorane. "That can't be—that can't be—"

"'Tis a trick!" shouted Delio. He broke from his position with the intention of charging the mirror and smashing it, but the moment he saw his reflection move in turn, he froze again.

"My—my face!" Kadaria cried. "Serkadian Manee! My face!"

"This is your glory?" countered Shade. "This is your godhood? The Land has made of you the greatest jest of all! There is nothing deader in your realm than you yourselves!"

"Not possible . . ." Zorane insisted weakly. "Not possible . . ."

But among them, there was one untouched by the revelation. Ephraim gestured—and the mirror exploded.

"It changes *nothing!* My plan will go on!"

The warlock might have frowned. "You . . . knew."

"I know *everything!* I am—"

A shape fell upon him and two hands clasped tight against the sides of his helmet. A bright flash from each enveloped the necromancer's head.

Ephraim cried out—first in agony, then in anger. He swung with one gauntleted hand at his attacker, sending the figure flying across the massive chamber.

Valea's body crashed hard against the ancient stone.

"Sharissa!" Shade involuntarily called.

"As dead to you as we are," Ephraim said with loathing. He raised his hand into a fist and the other necromancers suddenly straightened as if they were puppets whose strings had been tightened. "But not nearly so dead as you'll be . . . *cousin.*"

But instead of Shade, it was again the lead sorcerer who was attacked, this time nearly crushed to the floor by a powerful, invisible force.

"If my daughter is dead," Cabe Bedlam uttered, "she'll be a far luckier person than you when I'm done."

Among the other Lords, chaos broke out as Darkhorse reared and kicked at them in rapid succession. Thunder cracked and each necromancer fought hard against tiny but furious showers of glowing spheres.

Rising, Ephraim rubbed his fleshless chin. "Focus! Regain focus and the wizard and the beast will be ours again!"

But while some of the Lords did attempt to obey, others moved awkwardly, even listlessly. The revelation wrought by Shade had left them dumbfounded. They could not accept their deaths, but neither could they deny the truth.

The wizard closed with him. "We'll never be yours, whether in life or in death!"

Fire covered Ephraim, a fire hotter than any natural one. It was pure white, so intense was its heat. The necromancer battled against it, but Cabe's fury fueled it as nothing else could.

THE EMPTINESS WITHIN which Valea's spirit drifted became stifling. She did not need to breathe, but the heat threatened to burn her to nothing. She struggled to find a way out, but there was none.

Desperately, she called out, seeking the only one she thought might hear her. *Galani! Galani!*

But instead, a far different presence touched her own.

*You are . . . Valea . . .*

With each passing moment, the heat grew more intense. The enchantress knew that she would not last much longer. *Please! The stone! It's—*

But the other presence had already vanished.


THERE HAD BEEN few beings that Cabe had ever truly wanted dead. The lead necromancer had joined that select band and the wizard knew that in a few more moments the monstrous sorcerer would see the afterlife as it truly was. Nothing would stop Cabe from avenging Valea.

Nothing, that is, save the hard blast of pure force that tossed him several yards to the side.

The flames instantly faded. Ephraim stumbled back, recovering.

Shade hovered over him. He grabbed at the necromancer's waist.

At which point, a black hoof capable of shattering walls nearly crushed the warlock into the floor.

"Traitor or friend, friend or traitor, one can nevermore tell with you, Shade!" rumbled Darkhorse. "A base attack on one who was ever your comrade!"

"You're being a fool!" gasped the ragged figure.

"I am being observant!"

Shade managed to shield himself enough to turn. "Then be—be observant of the pattern! The Lords are—are regrouping!"

"Eh?" Sure enough, six of the necromancers had pulled themselves together enough to reform part of the pattern. Two others looked near to joining them.

"I can save Cabe Bedlam's daughter, but they must be stopped! Look! In the center! That crystal!"

"What of it?"

"Smash it! Go now!"

The eternal laughed. "And turn my back on you?"

Shade lifted his blurred face toward his oldest companion. "Darkhorse . . . would I ever desire the Lords of the Dead to triumph?"

Darkhorse started. The ice blue orbs glittered. "No . . . good or ill, you never wanted that."

"Then, please . . . go!"

With a laugh, the black stallion whirled about. Letting out a gasp, Shade stumbled away from the still-stunned Ephraim.

In the hand pressed against his chest dangled the chain from which swung the piece of the Wyr Stone.


THE BODY LAY motionless. The chest did not rise and fall. A chill coursed through Shade like none he had ever experienced.

No . . . he had. When another who was the same as this one had died. Died because of him.

Just as Valea Bedlam had.

She looked so much like Sharissa, like the elf maiden Galani, like the witch Tyrnene . . . like so many others. Yet, she also was in herself distinct.

For reasons he could not explain to himself, Shade hesitated, lost in the spectacle of her face. He finally reached a hand to her cheek.

Her eyes abruptly opened. A slight, sad smile crossed her lips. Even though her chest still did not rise, her throat did not move, from her mouth came a single word.

*"Forgiven . . ."*

The warlock pulled back, stunned. Valea Bedlam's eyes closed again and her body went limp.

"No!" He brought the stone to her chest, placing it gently there. Shade knew no words would do what he sought, but trusted that the stone would do what it should.

The bit of the Wyr Stone, a thing he had once coveted more than love, briefly glowed.

At that moment, Ephraim's voice echoed throughout the chamber. "The pattern is still set! Focus your wills through me!"

Shade rose, knowing that if the Lords of the Dead had organized themselves, then all could yet be lost. Where was Darkhorse?

There! The shadow steed sought to reach the crystal, but the necromancers had already steeled themselves enough to keep him at bay. Cabe Bedlam aided his good friend, but although with time they might have won, such a precious commodity was not theirs.

He saw Ephraim come alive with the power the others fed him. All the lead necromancer needed was a moment more.

Shade glanced down at the figure by his feet. Her chest now rose and sank and he caught the gentle movement of her breath at her mouth. The warlock sensed the life rushing within her, a life so very young and yet, as he well understood, so very old—like his own.

Without hesitation, he turned and charged the Lords.

Caught up in their battle against the wizard and the eternal, they did not at first focus on the new threat. Zorane was the first to notice his approach, by which point Shade had reached the edge of the pattern.

"There! Stop him!"

Leaping, Shade collided with the necromancer. A monstrous shock went through him as he touched the ghoulish figure. Shade bit back a scream. Zorane clutched at him, but the warlock struck him a solid blow. The fleshless figure wobbled back, somehow maintaining his place, but now unable to grab at his foe.

Pushing past the Lord, Shade summoned all the strength he had and plunged toward the crystal.

Off to the side, he heard Ephraim cry out to Cabe and Darkhorse, "You will be ours! Your world will be ours!"

And then Shade fell upon centerpiece of the necromancers' work, pouring every bit of power he could against it.

The pain, when the crystal exploded, was mercifully brief.

# XII

THE HEAT CEASED abruptly, giving Valea respite. She sensed something else happening, but knew not what.

Then, an incredible urge to drift forward filled her. She did not fight it, the sensation feeling so right. Like a siren's call, it pulled her on.

As she neared what she felt her goal, Valea noted other presences, as familiar to her as her own family—and yet even more so. She sensed Galani among them. The elf's spirit comforted her. With the others surrounding her, the enchantress completed the last bit of her journey—and realized that she entered her own body.

But even there she was not alone. She felt the elf maiden and others stay around her, guide her.

And they were *all* her.

But there was one that did not join, instead receding. That one most of all Valea wanted to stay, but such was not to be. The enchantress felt a caress where her cheek should have been . . . and then the other departed.

Sharissa was gone.

"CABE! BEWARE!" DARKHORSE immediately enveloped the wizard, possibly the only thing that saved his human friend.

Cabe had only a moment to acknowledge the vision of a very battered Shade falling upon the crystal. Then, the faceless warlock vanished in a searing explosion of energy.

The entrails of the explosion spread throughout the pattern, catching each of the necromancers in turn. They screamed.

But if their suffering was terrible, it compared little to that which filled Ephraim. Set to accept the power offered him by his compatriots, the lead sorcerer now became the ultimate vessel in which the unleashed forces of the pattern spilled.

The ghoulish figure swelled, his armor groaning. His skeletal form burned bright from within. His fleshless jaw swung wide as he cried out the loudest and most agonized.

Ephraim vanished, still wailing. A thin trail of ash was all that marked his memory.

The castle, long held together by the will of the Lords of the Dead, began to crumble. On one side, the ceiling collapsed. The remaining sections groaned ominously.

Still caught, the rest of the Lords continued to scream. The floor containing the pattern began to buckle as it, too, lost cohesion.

"We must flee!" Darkhorse roared.

"Valea! I'll not leave her body here!"

The eternal snorted. "As if *I* would!"

Now resembling more of a spherical ant than a stallion, Darkhorse maneuvered toward Valea. As they neared, Cabe's eyes widened.

"She's breathing! Darkhorse! She's breathing!"

"And if we would have her continue to do so, we must get her and you out of this abysmal realm swiftly! It seems to be folding in on itself!"

Sure enough, not just the castle but the entire world seemed to be coming apart. The Lords had held their kingdom together and now that they could not, it was decaying rapidly.

Darkhorse scooped up Valea, placing her inside him as he had earlier Cabe. Then, with a prodigious leap, he soared through one falling wall and out into the open.

Beyond the castle, the landscape was still eerily silent. However, Cabe had the odd sensation that there was movement everywhere and all of it fleeing the direction of the Lords' sanctum.

"They are free!" the eternal rumbled. "The shadows held by the Lords are free!"

And as he said it, they suddenly saw thousands of flittering shapes moving off. Humans, elves, Quel, Seekers, and others undetermined appeared and vanished like flickering dreams. All headed with grateful purpose for some destination far from the collapsing center of the realm.

A screech caused Cabe some fear. Two Necri descended from the grey sky. However, they did not dive in to attack, but rather collided with the ground. As they struck, their bodies scattered like dust. They, too, had been held together by the necromancers' incredible minds.

"I am going to try to teleport us to the gateway!" the stallion rumbled. "With the Lords in disarray, I should be able to do it!"

Cabe looked back, where a tower from the castle had begun to collapse inward. "Hurry!"

Darkhorse shimmered—and their surroundings altered. Ahead of them, a sliver of blackness appeared. The gateway from this side.

"Hold her tight!"

He need not have said anything to his friend. Cabe would have held on to Valea even at the cost of his own life if it would somehow save her.

The shadow steed leapt at the tear, which suddenly began to fade . . .

**VALEA SCREAMED.**

"Hush," said a feminine voice. "You're all right, daughter."

"Mother?" She looked up to see not just Gwendolyn Bedlam, the elder enchantress a much more glamorous and beautiful version—so Valea thought—of herself, but her father and brother, too. The three stood over her, quite concerned. Valea lay in her plush, down bed back in the Manor. Outside, sunlight shone and birds sang merrily, all as if nothing had ever happened.

"Three days of sleep, that's the only aftereffect I sense," Gwen continued, pushing back some of her luxurious, fiery hair. Valea's mother gazed to the side. "Aurim, see if there's any sign of Darkhorse returning yet. He said he would be back by now."

The golden-haired youth, only a few years older than Valea, nodded. "Yes, mother." He eyed his sibling. "I'm glad you're safe."

Valea blinked. Generally when she and Aurim spoke, they argued. This time, however, he had looked so very serious she began to wonder just how close to death she had seemed.

Aurim suddenly vanished, a slight twinkle of stars in his wake. Possibly stronger even than his father, he had, of late, become something of a show-off. Valea found the familiarity of that situation comforting.

Then she remembered the Lords.

Her father must have read her expression. "Their realm was collapsing. Shade—Shade sacrificed himself to destroy their pattern. The chaos incinerated the lead necromancer—"

"Ephraim!" she gasped.

"Ephraim," Cabe corrected himself. "As to the others, the last I saw, their castle, their world, was crumbling, and they were caught by their own magic. They may be no more, but I'm not counting on it."

"Whatever the case," Gwen interjected, "they are nothing to fear, at least for the moment."

"No."

But Valea no longer thought of them. She recalled her father's other words. "Shade—he sacrificed himself?"

"Without hesitation."

That made no sense. "But Gerrod—the—the ghost of the original Shade—he was supposed to take over and use the body for the Lords' purposes. They had him under their control."

"Somehow, Shade overcame him, I suppose. It's what saved us."

No. Valea understood enough to know that only by Gerrod's own decision could Shade have withstood the possession. Gerrod had decided that his manic desire to live had been outweighed by what he would cause to happen afterward.

But it had not been that alone. Some part of her, some part that was and was not Valea, suddenly reminded her of Gerrod's love of Sharissa. Sharissa would have despised what Gerrod would have become. In the end, the ghost had likely come to that conclusion, too. He had instead given Shade the opportunity to undo the necromancers' evil and help the spirit of the woman he had loved.

"You said—" Tears wanted to flow freely from her eyes, but Valea fought them back. Tears for both aspects of one man. There was an emptiness in her heart at the sacrifices and the thought that he might be no more. "You said . . . he's dead?"

The grim expressions on both her parents's countenances grew. Her mother pursed her lips and quietly said, "This is *Shade* of whom we speak."

So he very likely was *not* dead . . . but they feared what he might have become.

"Darkhorse is already searching," Cabe added, growing more determined in his tone. "I've alerted the Gryphon and King Melicard of Talak. They have the resources to watch also."

Gwendolyn Bedlam nodded. "From what I've gathered, he could be more terrifying than ever, my love. He is more whole now. The Lords may have unleashed a threat that would make theirs comical by comparison."

"We won't let him. Shade will be hunted down no matter what."

The elder Bedlams continued to discuss the possible danger. Valea listened to them, but she did not feel the fear that they did. Instead, her heart seemed to leap to life.

He was *alive*.

Her parents, the others, they recalled the past all too well. But so did Valea. She recalled the past even better than them, she believed. In her memory were not only the events of Galani's life, but a hundred and more others—all her reborn again and again, in some ways just like the warlock. More important, Valea also remembered what she had learned in the castle and that, most of all, gave her hope.

*I've got to find him before they do,* she thought. *If I do . . . if I do . . . he may have a chance yet. He might become mortal again. This time he has a chance . . .*

Her face a mask, she listened to her parents talk . . . and began planning.

HE SAT UPON the winter peak, high above altitudes where most creatures could breathe. The winds whipped at his hooded form, but could not in the least dislodge him. Far, far below and some distance south, the young Dragon Emperor struggled to hold together his people. Farther on, near the base of those mountains, an aging king and his beautiful witch of a queen hoped that the dire news that they had received would not mean a return of fear to their realm. Much more south than that, where the lionbird ruled, the anxious monarch worried that his newborn son might be a target.

They all feared him. He could taste their fear. Shade looked to the horizon, looked to where the length and breadth of the Dragonrealm lay and sensed fear of him in every direction.

He had died saving them—saving her. They all knew what that meant. He had reformed, fully grown and garmented as his curse ever demanded, in the hot, fiery lands of the Hell Plains. His mind had been addled for a time—as always—but gradually cleared enough so that he could recall what had happened. He remembered his surprise at the ghost's decision to give itself to him, not take over as planned by the Lords. He remembered memories of his far past filling him and feeling more whole than in all his monstrous existence. He remembered the choices he had made and the results, good or ill, of each.

And as his mind organized itself, he came to that point, as he always had, when either the light or the darkness seized him, directed his newest mockery of a life.

But this time . . . this time *nothing* happened.

This time, he felt no different than when he had looked into the eyes that had been Sharissa's, Galani's, and all the others—but had especially belonged to a young, arresting enchantress who was the daughter of those most likely to now seek his destruction.

He had not transformed. He had not fallen to the side of darkness as the curse demanded. His face, which he had gazed at in a river, was still but a blur, yet Shade felt the same within as he had when he had chosen to sacrifice himself for his companions—and especially *her.*

The warlock sat upon the mountain, knowing he would have to flee from Darkhorse's probing spells soon, pondering this astounding turn of events.

Pondering and, for the first time in a thousand false lifetimes, *hoping.*

# ABOUT THE AUTHOR

**RICHARD A. KNAAK** is the *New York Times* and *USA Today* bestselling author of *The Legend of Huma, WoW: Stormrage,* and more than forty other novels and numerous short stories, including works in such series as Warcraft, Diablo, Dragonlance, Age of Conan, and his own Dragonrealm. He has scripted a number of Warcraft manga with Tokyopop, such as the top-selling Sunwell trilogy, and has also written background material for games. His works have been published worldwide in many languages.

In addition to this third volume in the *Legends of the Dragonrealm* series, his most recent releases include *Wolfheart*—the latest in the bestselling World of Warcraft series, the graphic novel series *Rune Keepers*—and *Dragon Mound*—the first in his Knight in Shadow trilogy. He is presently at work on several other projects, among them *Wake of the Wyrm*—the sequel to *Dragon Mound*—and, most significant to the series you have been reading, *The Tower of the Phoenix*—a brand-new Dragonrealm novel featuring the tragic sorcerer Shade.

Currently splitting his time between Chicago and Arkansas, he can be reached through his website: www.richardaknaak.com. While he is unable to respond to every e-mail, he does read them. Join his mailing list for e-announcements of upcoming releases and appearances. He is also on Facebook and Twitter.